AF093763

In the background on the cover of this book is the image of Jaroslav Hašek's letter of resignation from the Czechoslovak Corps in Russia:

To the Branch of the Czechoslovak National Council

I hereby let it be known, that I do not agree with the policy of the Branch of the Czechoslovak National Council and with the departure of our Corps to France.

Therefore I declare, that I am leaving the Czechoslovak Corps until such time, that both within it and the whole leadership of the National Council, a new direction prevails.

I request, that this decision of mine be noted. I will even now continue to work for a revolution in Austria and the liberation of our nation.

Jaroslav Hašek, in own hand

The Fateful Adventures of
THE GOOD SOLDIER
ŠVEJK [sh-vake]
During the World War

Book Two

presents
still as a samizdat

The Centennial Edition
of The "Chicago Version" English rendition of

Jaroslav Hašek's

The Fateful Adventures of The Good Soldier

During the World War

Book Two

Visit our websites
zenny.com
SvejkCentral.com
for additional information and enjoyment of the
Good Soldier Švejk

ISBN: 979-8-9943084-2-4

v. 1/6/2026

Dedication

To **Antonín Bukovjan**, *1890 - †1964

Farmhand

Infantry man, 25th Reserve Regiment, Austro-Hungarian Army

Wounded

Captured: September 17, 1915, Rovno, Volhynian Governorate, Russian Empire (currently Rivne, Ukraine), imprisoned in a POW camp

Private, 8. Rifle Regiment, Czechoslovak Legions in Russia,

Enlisted: September 1, 1917

End of service: March 30, 1918

This translation is based on ***Osudy dobrého vojáka Švejka za světové války***, edited by Jaroslava Myslivečková (**Praha: Odeon, 1968**). For certain readings, I consulted the Book One and Book Two manuscript transcripts (Book(s) Three & Four not yet transcribed) by Jaroslav Šerák (svejkmuseum.cz), which contain at least two lines inadvertently omitted and several typographical errors. Where variant readings or uncertainties arose, I confirmed the correct text by reference to high-resolution manuscript scans provided by Jomar Hønsi. The translation does not rely on the manuscript transcript alone for any passage where significant textual doubt or error is possible.

Table of Contents

Introduction to Book Two of the Centennial English Edition

WARNING! If you haven't read Book One, stop right here. Acquire Book One and read it first.

As Švejk himself explained, defending one of his many small disasters: *"Never in my life have I laughed so hard at something because I have, in my life, read already many books, but never have I started reading something beginning with the second volume."*

He was right. So once again: Stop. Go and read Book One first.

For the rest of you — well done. For being early birds, you had no choice (Book Two didn't exist yet). Either way, you already know all you need: it's all in Book One's text of STEP INTO THE WORLD OF ŠVEJK, PREFACE, ACKNOWLEDGMENTS, EDITORIAL NOTES, COMPARATIVE NOTES ON METHODOLOGY, FRANTIŠEK JOSEF AND THE GRAMMAR OF CZECH SUBJECTHOOD IN HAŠEK'S OPENING LINE, INTRODUCTION TO THE CENTENNIAL ENGLISH EDITION, the ENDNOTES, ABOUT THE AUTHOR — and, most importantly, in Jaroslav Hašek's own text, written for all posterity to ponder, and pass on.

Book Two

AT THE FRONT

1

ŠVEJK'S MISHAPS ON THE TRAIN

In a second class compartment of the Prague — České Budějovice[2] express there were three of them, Senior Lieutenant Lukáš, across from whom was sitting an older gentleman, totally bald, and Švejk, who was standing modestly by the door to the passageway and was just getting ready to hear the full measure of a new rolling wave of peals of thunder by Senior Lieutenant Lukáš, who, disregarding the presence of the bald-headed civilian, had been roaring into Švejk's soul along the whole length of the railway line, which they have traversed thus far, that he's a God's cattle beast and the like.

The matter was nothing more than a trifle, the number of pieces of luggage, which Švejk was looking after.

"They stole a suitcase from us," was the Senior Lieutenant admonishing Švejk; "that's easy enough to say, you churl!"

"I dutifully report, Senior *Lieutenant*, Sir," voiced softly Švejk, "they really stole it. At railroad stations[3] there are always hanging around a lot of such cons and the way I imagine it is, that with one of them **undoubtedly** your suitcase struck a chord and this man **undoubtedly** utilized the fact, that I walked away from the luggage, in order to report to you, that regarding our luggage everything is alright. He could steal that suitcase of ours exactly only at such an opportune moment. For a moment like that they watch out for. Two years ago at the Northwest Railway Station[4] they stole a baby carriage from one lady even with the little girl laid in baby duvets and they were so magnanimous, that they turned the little girl in at the district police station in our street, that they found her abandoned in a carriage passageway. Then the newspaper made the pitiful lady out to be a ravens' mother[5]"

And Švejk vehemently declared: "At railroad stations they have always been stealing and will continue to steal. It cannot be otherwise."

"I am convinced, Švejk," took his turn at speaking the Senior Lieutenant, "that you will end up in a miserably bad way one day. I still don't know, whether you're just making yourself out to be an ox or whether you were already born an ox. What was in that suitcase?"

"Altogether nothing, *Senior Lieutenant*, Sir," answered Švejk, not letting his eyes off the bald skull of the civilian sitting opposite the Senior Lieutenant, who, as it seemed, was showing absolutely no interest in the whole matter and was reading the *New Free Press*[6], "in the whole suitcase there was only the bedroom mirror and an iron coat hanger from the hallway, so that we actually suffered no loss, because both the mirror and the hanger belonged to our mister landlord."

Seeing the horrible gesture by the Senior Lieutenant, Švejk continued in a kind voice: "I dutifully report, *Senior Lieutenant*, Sir, that of the fact, that the suitcase would be stolen, I knew nothing beforehand, and as for the mirror and the coat hanger, I informed our mister landlord, that we would return them to him, when we come back from the war. In the enemy countries there are a lot of mirrors and coat hangers, so that even in this case we and our mister landlord can't suffer any loss. As soon as we conquer some city…"

"Shut your mouth, Švejk," with a frightening voice jumped into it the Senior Lieutenant, "I'll turn you one of these days over to the field court martial. Deliberate carefully, whether you aren't the most ordinary-as-dust numskull of a guy in the world. Another man, even if he were to live a thousand years, would not commit as many stupidities as you have during these several weeks. I hope, that you have also noticed that?"

"I dutifully report, that I, *Senior Lieutenant*, Sir, have been noticing it. I have, as the saying goes, a developed observational talent, when it's already late and something unpleasant happens. Bad luck sticks to me like sap, just as it does to some guy Nechleba from Nekázanka, who used to come to the Bitches' Grove pub[7] there. He always wanted to do good and starting Saturday to lead a new life, and always the next day he would say: 'So let me tell you, pals, toward the morning I was noticing, that I was on a plank bunk.' And it always afflicted him, when he put it in his head, that he'd go home while he was alright, and in the end it became clear, that he knocked down some fence somewhere or unhitched a cabman's horse or wanted to clean his pipe with a feather from the cock's tail on the hat of some police patrolman. He was all quite desperate from it and what he felt the most regret about was, that the bad luck dragged and stuck through whole generations. His grandpa once took to the road tramping …"

"Leave me in peace, Švejk, keep your expositions to yourself."

"I dutifully report, *Senior Lieutenant*, Sir, that all this here, that I'm saying, is the holiest of the holy truths. His grandpa took to the road tramping…"

"Švejk," said the Senior Lieutenant as he got upset, "one more time I'm ordering you, not to be telling me any yarns, I don't want to hear anything. When we arrive at Budějovice, then I'll settle it with you. Do you know, Švejk, that I'll have you locked up?"

"I dutifully report, *Senior Lieutenant*, Sir, that I don't know that," softly said Švejk, "you haven't mentioned it yet."

The Senior Lieutenant's teeth involuntarily chattered a bit, he let out a sigh, pulled from his overcoat a copy of Bohemie[8] and was reading the news about grand victories, the activity of the German submarine E in the Mediterranean Sea[9], and when he got to the news item about a new German invention for blowing cities up into the air with the aid of special bombs pitched from flying machines, which explode three times in succession, he was disturbed by the voice of Švejk, who was addressing the bald-headed gentleman:

"Allow me, yergrace, aren't you kind enough to be Mister Purkrábek, a representative of the Slavie[10] Bank?"

When the bald-headed gentleman failed to respond, Švejk told the Senior Lieutenant:

"I dutifully report, *Senior Lieutenant*, Sir, that I've read once in the paper, that a normal human should have on his head on average sixty to seventy thousand strands of hair and that black hair tends to be thinner, as can be observed in numerous cases."

And he continued mercilessly on: "Then once there was also a med student in the coffeehouse At the Špíreks'[11] saying, that the hair falling out is caused by a disturbance of the soul during the mother's six week postpartum period."

And now something horrible happened. The bald-headed gentleman jumped up to face Švejk, screaming at him: "*Get out, you swine*," kicked him out into the passageway and having returned to the compartment he prepared a small surprise for the Senior Lieutenant by introducing himself to him.

It was a slight mistake. The bald-headed individual was not mister Purkrábek, a representative of the Slavie Bank, but merely Major General von Schwarzburg. The Major General in civilian clothes was just then conducting an inspection trip making rounds of the garrisons and was on the way to surprise Budějovice.

He was the most terrifying inspecting general, who has ever been born, and should he find something out of order, he conducted only the following conversation with the commanding officers of the garrisons:

"Do you have a revolver?" "I do." "Gooot! In your place I would certainly know, what to do with it, because what I see here, that is not a garrison, but a herd of swine."

And indeed following his inspection trip here and there somebody would always shoot himself dead, which Major General von Schwarzburg commented on with a satisfying sense of vindication: "That's the way it's supposed to be! There's a soldier!"

It appeared, that he didn't like it, when after his inspection there remained anybody at all alive. He had a mania for always transferring an officer to the most unpleasant places. The littlest thing was sufficient, and the officer was already saying goodbye to his command and was on a journey to the Montenegrin[12] border or to some drunk, desperate garrison in a filthy corner of Galicia.

"Mister Senior Lieutenant," he said, "where did you attend a cadet school[13]?"

"In Prague."

"So you did attend a cadet school and yet don't even know, that an officer is responsible for his subordinate. That is nice. Secondly you talk with your servant as if with some intimate friend of yours. You allow him to speak, even though he wasn't asked to answer. That is even nicer. Thirdly you allow him to be insulting your superiors. And that is the most beautiful, I will see to it there are consequences to it all. What is your name mister Senior Lieutenant?"

"Lukáš."

"And which regiment do you serve with?"

"I had been…"

"Thank you, as to where you had been, there is no talk about that, I want to know, where you are now."

"With the 91st Infantry Regiment, Major General, Sir. They have transferred me…"

"They have transferred you? They have done a very good thing. It will do you good to have a look as soon as possible with the 91st Infantry Regiment at some battleground."

"That has already been decided, Major General, Sir."

The Major General was now giving a lecture on how he has been noticing the past few years, that officers talk to their subordinates in a familiar tone, and that he sees in that a danger of spreading some sort of democratic tenets. A soldier has to be kept in a state of horror, he has to be shaking in fright facing his superior, be afraid of him.

The officers have to keep the men at a ten-step distance from their body and not allow them to think on their own or even to think at all, that this has been the tragic error of the last few years. It used to be that the rank-and-file were afraid of the officers as of fire, but nowadays…"

The Major General hopelessly waved his hand: "Nowadays most officers pamper the soldiers. That is what I wanted to say."

The Major General took again his newspaper and dove deep into reading. Senior Lieutenant Lukáš walked out pale into the passageway, to settle the score with Švejk.

He found him standing at a window with so blissful and satisfied countenance, which can be worn only by a month-old babe, that has had its drink, sucked its fill and now is gone in sleepy-bye.

The Senior Lieutenant stopped, motioned to Švejk and pointed to an empty compartment. He entered after Švejk and closed the door.

"Švejk," he said ceremonially, "finally the moment has come, when you'll get a couple of slaps across the face, the likes of which the world hasn't seen. Why is it that you attacked the bald gentleman? Do you know, that he is Major General von Schwarzburg?"

"I dutifully report, *Senior Lieutenant*, Sir," sounded up Švejk, wearing the countenance of a martyr, "that I have never in my life had the slightest intention to offend anybody and that I have no idea or notion at all of some mister major general. He really is the complete likeness of mister Purkrábek, the representative of the Slavie Bank. He used to come to our pub and once, when at the table he'd fallen asleep, some benefactor then wrote on his bald head with an indelible pencil: 'We are taking the liberty hereby in accordance with the attached premium schedule IIIc to deferentially offer to you saving up a dowry and furnishing for your children through a life insurance policy!' It goes without saying, that all had left, and I alone remained there with him, and so because always I have bad luck, so he then, when he woke up and looked into the mirror, got upset and thought, that who did it to him was I, and he wanted to give me also a couple of slaps across the face."

The little word "also" slipped in such a touchingly soft and reproaching manner from Švejk's lips, that the Senior Lieutenant's hand slid back down.

But Švejk continued: "On account of such a small mistake the man didn't have to be upsetting himself, he's really supposed to have sixty to seventy thousand strands of hair, as it was in that article about all that, which a normal man should have. It has never in my life occurred to me, that there exists some bald-headed mister major general. That is, as the saying goes, a tragic mistake, which can happen to anybody, when one makes some remark and another right away latches onto it. Once years ago Hývl the tailor was telling us, how he rode from a place, where he was tailoring in Styria[14], to Prague by the way of Leoben[15] and had with him a ham which he bought in Maribor[16]. As he was riding so on the train, he thought, that he was the only Czech among the passengers, and when near Saint Moritz[17] he began slicing pieces off that whole ham, the man, who was sitting across from him, started throwing these love-struck glances at the ham and saliva started oozing from his trap. When Hývl the tailor saw it, he was saying to himself aloud: 'Wouldn't you want to feed on it, you miserable guy.' And in Czech the mister answered him: 'You know it goes without saying, that I would, if you gave me some.' So they devoured the ham together, before they arrived in Budějovice. That mister's name was Vojtěch Rous."

Senior Lieutenant Lukáš glanced at Švejk and left the compartment. When he was sitting in his seat again, there emerged after a while in the doorway the sincere face of Švejk:

"I dutifully report, *Senior Lieutenant*, Sir, that in five minutes we're in Tábor[18]. The train stops there for five minutes. Won't you command me to order something to eat? Years ago here they used to have a very good…"

The Senior Lieutenant jumped up furiously and in the passageway he told Švejk:

"One more time I am putting you on notice, that the less you show your face, the happier I am. I'd like it the best, if I wouldn't see you at all, and rest assured, that I will take care that it be so. Don't even show up in my field of vision. Disappear from my eyes' reach, you cattle beast, you stupid idiot."

"As ordered, *Senior Lieutenant*, Sir."

Švejk saluted, snapped an about face and walked to the end of the passageway, where he sat down in the corner on the conductor's seat and started weaving a web of conversation with some railway attendant:

"May I please, I beg you, ask you something?"

The railway attendant, not showing any apparent desire to converse, slightly and apathetically nodded.

"There used to come to see me," began to unwind his tongue Švejk, "a good man, some Hofmann, and he always claimed, that these alarm signals never have any effect, that the short and the good of it is it doesn't work, when one pulls on this handle. I, truth be told, have never taken any interest in such a thing, but since I have already noticed this here alarm apparatus, then I would like to know, where I stand, if by chance I would ever need it."

Švejk stood up and along with the railway attendant stepped up to the "In Case of Danger" brake alarm.

The railway attendant judged it to be his duty to explain to Švejk, what made up the essence of the whole mechanism of the alarm apparatus: "He told you correctly, that one has to pull this handle, but he lied to you, that it doesn't work. Always will the train stop, because it's connected through all the train cars with the locomotive. The emergency brake must work."

Both of them had at that time their hands on the grip of the lever handle and it certainly is a mystery, how it happened, that they pulled it out and the train stopped.

They could also not in any way agree, who actually did it and sent the alarm signal.

Švejk insisted, that it couldn't have been he, that he didn't do it, that he's no street punk.

"I myself marvel," he was saying good-naturedly to the conductor, "why the train so suddenly stopped. It is rolling, and all of a sudden it's standing. I regret it more than you do."

Some serious gentleman rose to the defense of the railway attendant and claimed, that he had heard, as the soldier was the first one to start a conversation about the alarm signals.

In contrast Švejk kept saying something about his honesty, that he has no interest in delaying the train, because he is riding to war.

"Mister stationmaster will explain it to you," decided the conductor, "it will cost you twenty crowns."

In the meantime one could see, how the passengers are crawling out of and standing by the cars, the chief conductor is whistling, some lady is running horrified with a travel suitcase across the rails into the fields.

"It really is worth twenty crowns," congenially said Švejk, maintaining absolute calm, "it's still too cheap. Once, when the Emperor was visiting in Žižkov[19], some Franta Šnor stopped his carriage by getting on his knees in front of the lord Emperor in the roadway. Then the police inspector of that precinct told this mister Šnor weeping, that he should not have done it in his precinct, that he should have done it one street over, which already belongs under the authority of the Police Chief Kraus, that there he should have been showing his respect. Then that mister Šnor they locked up."

Švejk took a look around, just when the chief conductor augmented the circle of the listening onlookers.

"So it's about time we got going again," said Švejk, "there's nothing nice about it, when a train gets to be delayed. If it were in peacetime, then Godspeed, but when there's a war, then everybody's supposed to know, that on every train there are riding military persons, major generals, *senior lieutenants*, *orderlies*. Each such delay is a touchy thing. Napoleon at Waterloo was late by five minutes and he was screwed, he and the whole of his glory…"

At that moment finished clawing his way through the listening crowd Senior Lieutenant Lukáš. He was terrifyingly pale and could not manage to get anything out of his mouth but: "Švejk!"

Švejk saluted and let himself be heard: "I dutifully report, *Senior Lieutenant*, Sir, that they've shifted the blame to me, that I have stopped the train. The railway sure carries utterly peculiar emergency brake seals in its inventory. One better not even get near them, otherwise he could get in trouble and they could want twenty crowns from him, as they want them from me."

The chief conductor was already outside, gave the signal, and the train got rolling again.

The onlookers went to take their places in the compartments and Senior Lieutenant Lukáš did not say as much as a word anymore and went to take his seat as well.

There remained only the train conductor with Švejk and the railway attendant. The train conductor pulled out the logbook and was putting together a report on the whole case. The railway attendant was looking with hostility at Švejk, who calmly inquired: "Have you been already a long time with the railway?"

Because the railway attendant was not answering, Švejk declared, that he knew some Mlíček, František by first name, from Uhříněves[20] near Prague, who also at one time pulled down on such an emergency brake alarm and spooked so, that he lost his speech for two weeks and he regained it again, when he came to Vaněk the gardener in Hostivař[18] for a visit and he got into a brawl there and they broke a blackjack in two when they whacked him. "That happened," added Švejk, "in the year 1912 in May."

The railway attendant opened a restroom door and locked himself inside.

There remained the conductor with Švejk and was trying to sweet-talk him out of twenty crowns in fine, emphasizing, that otherwise he'd have to bring him in Tábor to the station[22] master.

"Alright," said Švejk, "I like to talk with educated people and it'll please me a lot, when I get to see the Tábor station master."

Švejk pulled from his blouse a pipe, lit it up, and, releasing the pungent smoke of the military ration tobacco, he continued: "Years ago in Svitava[23] the station master was mister Wagner. He was as tough as a butcher on his subordinates and he was cruel to them, wherever he could, and the most he persecuted some switch operator Jungwirt, until that wretch out of desperation, went to drown himself in a river. Before he did it however, he wrote a letter to the station master, that he would haunt him at night. And I'm not lying to you. He did it. There is sitting at night the dear mister station master by the telegraph apparatus, the little bells start ringing and the station master receives a telegram: 'How is it going, you shameless rube? Jungwirt.' A whole week it lasted and the station master started sending down all the lines official telegrams like this as an answer to the specter: 'Forgive me for it, Jungwirt.' And that night the apparatus punches out this sort of an answer: 'Hang yourself on the signal pole by the bridge. Jungwirt'. And the mister station master obliged him. Then on account of it they locked up a telegraph operator from the station one stop before Svitava. There you see, that there are things between the heaven and Earth, of which we don't even have a notion."

The train pulled into the Tábor station and Švejk, before under the escort of the conductor he got off the train, announced, as is proper, to Senior Lieutenant Lukáš: "I dutifully report, *Senior Lieutenant*, Sir, that they're taking me to the station master."

Senior Lieutenant Lukáš didn't answer. He was overcome by total apathy toward everything. A thought flashed through his mind, that the best thing is not to give a damn about anything. Just as about Švejk, so about the bald-headed Major General sitting across from him. To sit calmly, get off the train in Budějovice, muster at the garrison, and ride to the battlefront with some march company. Once at the front, let himself as the case may be get killed and be rid of the miserable world, in which roams such a miscreant, as Švejk is.

When the train had moved, Senior Lieutenant Lukáš took a look out of the window and standing on the platform he saw Švejk, immersed in a serious conversation with the station master. Švejk was surrounded by a crowd of people, among whom one could see also several in railway uniforms.

Senior Lieutenant Lukáš gave a sigh. It was not a sigh of regret. His heart felt light with relief, that Švejk remained on the platform. Even the bald Major General did not seem such an irritating monster.

*

The train had already been long chugging toward České Budějovice, but at the railroad station platform the number of people around Švejk was not getting smaller.

Švejk was speaking of his innocence and convinced the crowd to the point, that one lady expressed herself this way: “Again they’re hectoring a soldier boy here.”

The crowd accepted this opinion and one gentleman turned to the station master with the declaration, that he will pay on behalf of Švejk the twenty crown fine. He is convinced, that the soldier didn’t do it.

“Look at him,” he said, inferring from that most innocent expression on the face of Švejk who, turning to the crowd, was declaring: “I am, folks, innocent.”

Then there appeared the state police sergeant and brought out from the midst of the crowd one citizen, arrested him and was taking him away with the words: “You’ll be held accountable for that, I’ll show you what it’s worth to be inciting people saying, that if that’s the way soldiers are dealt with, that nobody can demand of them for Austria to win it.”

The hapless citizen could not manage anything but a sincere claim, that he’s after all the master butcher from near the Old Gate[24] and that he didn’t mean it like that.

In the meantime the good man believing in the innocence of Švejk paid the fine in his stead at the office and took Švejk with him to a third-class restaurant[25], where he treated him to a beer, and having found out, that all his IDs and even the military fare card for the railway were with Senior Lieutenant Lukáš, he magnanimously gave him a tenner for the fare card and further expenses.

When he was leaving, he told Švejk in confidence: “So, soldier boy, I’m telling you take it from me, if you end up in Russia a prisoner of war, then pass on my greetings to brewmaster Zeman in

Zdolbunov[26]. After all you've got it written down, what my name is. Just be smart, so that you won't be at the front for long."

"Have no fear about that," said Švejk, "it is always interesting, to see some foreign lands for free."

Švejk remained alone sitting at the table, and while he was quietly drinking up the tenner from the high-minded benefactor, the people on the platform, who weren't present during Švejk's conversation with the station master and saw only from a distance the crowd of people, were passing along to one another, that they caught some spy, who was taking photographs of the railroad station, which however was being controverted by one woman insisting, that it was not a matter of a spy, but that she'd heard, how a dragoon slashed up an officer by the ladies' restroom, because that officer was creeping in there after his girl-friend, who was seeing off that dragoon.

These adventurous speculations, characteristic of the nervousness of wartime, were brought to an abrupt end by the State Police, who were clearing the platform. And Švejk kept on quietly drinking, reminiscing tenderly about his Senior Lieutenant. Say, what is that one going to do, when he arrives in České Budějovice and going through the whole train doesn't find his servant.

Before the arrival of the passenger train the third-class restaurant got filled with both soldiers and civilians. Prevailing there were soldiers from various regiments, formations and of the most varied nationalities, whom the windstorm of the war had blown into Tábor military hospitals, who were now departing again into the field for new injuries, maiming, pains, and were taking off to earn a simple wooden cross above their graves, on which there would still years later in the sad plains of eastern Galicia flail in the wind and the rain a sun-bleached Austrian military cap with a rusted frankie pin on it, upon which from time to time would land to perch a sad, grown old raven, reminiscing about the fat-filled feasts of years ago, when there used to be set for him an endless table of human tasty corpses and horse carcasses, when just under such a cap, that he's sitting on, there would be the most tasty beakful — human eyes.

One of those candidates for suffering, released after surgery from a military hospital, wearing a dirty uniform with traces of blood and mud, took a seat next to Švejk. He was somehow sort of stunted, emaciated, sad. He laid his small package on the table, pulled out a broken coin-purse and was counting over his money.

Then he looked at Švejk and asked: "Magyarul?"

"I am, my friend, a Czech," answered Švejk, "wanna have a drink?"

"Nem tudom, barátom."

"That doesn't matter, my friend," goaded him Švejk, putting his full stein in front of the sad soldier, "just take a proper draft."

He got it, had a drink, thanked: "Köszönöm szivesen," and kept on examining the contents of his coin-purse and in the end he gave a sigh.

Švejk realized, that the Hungarian would like to have a beer and that he didn't have enough money, therefore he ordered one beer to be brought for him, after which the Hungarian thanked again and started telling Švejk something with the help of gestures, pointing to his arm with a hole shot through it, while he spoke up in the international language: "Pif, paf, poots!"

Švejk was nodding in sympathy and the stunted convalescent passed additional information onto Švejk, lowering his left hand to a foot or two above the floor and then raising three fingers, that he has three small children.

"Nincs ham, nincs ham," he continued, wanting to say, that they have at home nothing to eat, and he dried his eyes, from which had sprung up tears, with the dirty sleeve of his military overcoat, in which could be seen the hole made by the bullet, that flew into his body for the Hungarian king.

It was nothing queer, that given such entertainment Švejk slowly came to having almost nothing left of that tenner and that he was slowly, but surely cutting himself off from České Budějovice, losing with each stein, to which he was treating himself and the Hungarian convalescent, the chance to purchase a military fare card.

Another train to Budějovice passed through the station again and Švejk was still sitting at the table and was listening, as the Hungarian kept repeating his: "Pif, paf, poots! Három gyermek, nincs ham, éljen!"

The last he would say, when clanking the steins with him.

"Just drink up, Hungarian boy," would answer Švejk, "tank up, you and yours would never feast us like this…"

At the next table some soldier said, that when they arrived at Szeged[27] with the 28th Regiment, the Hungarians were pointing at them and showing their hands raised up high.

It was the holy truth, but this soldier apparently felt offended by that, which then became a common occurrence among all Czech soldiers and which in the end the Hungarians were doing themselves, when they ceased to like the brawl in the interest of the *Hungarian* king.

Then that soldier also took a seat at their table and was relaying, how they had at Szeged rocked the Hungarians on their heels and how they had threshed them out of several pubs. At the same time he appreciatively praised, that the Hungarians also know how to brawl and that he had gotten one knife stab in his back, so that they had to send him to the rear to heal.

But that now, when he returns, the captain of his battalion will apparently have him locked up, because he had no time left to reciprocate the Hungarian for that stab, as would be decent and proper, so he'd get something out of it too, and the honor of the whole Regiment be preserved.

"*Your documents*, yoorr tohcumehnts?" was how nicely started with Švejk the commanding officer of the military roving patrol, a quartermaster, accompanied by four soldiers with bayonets, "I to see, seetink, *not going*, seetink, treenk, keep treenk, *orderly*!"

"Don't have them, miláčku[28]," answered Švejk, "mister *Senior Lieutenant* Lukáš, Regiment No. 91, took them with him and I stayed here at the railroad station."

"*What's that word* milatschek?" the quartermaster turned to one of his troops, an old Land Defense soldier, who according to all apparent indications did everything to embarrass his quartermaster deliberately, because he said calmly:

"Miláček, *that is like Quartermaster, Sir.*"

The Quartermaster kept the conversation with Švejk going:

"Tohcumehnts eetch zohljer, vizout tohcumehnts lohck up *the licebag of a orderly like a rabid dog at the railroad station military command.*"

They were taking Švejk to the railroad station military command, where at the guard house there were sitting troops, looking just the same as the old Land Defense soldier, who knew how to translate so nicely the word "miláček" into German for his natural enemy, the quartermastering overlords.

The guard house had been decorated with lithographs, which at that time the Ministry of Military Affairs had them distributing to all offices, through which soldiers would pass, as well as to schools and even military barracks.

The good soldier Švejk was greeted by a picture depicting, according to the caption, how Corporal František Hammel and Sergeants Paulhart and Bachmayer[29] from the I&R[30] 21st Riflemen Regiment[31] are encouraging the troops to persevere. On the other side was hanging a picture with the caption: "Corporal Jan Danko[32] from the 5th Regiment of the *Hungarian Land Defense* Hussars[33] will search out the position of the enemy artillery battery."

To the right a little lower was hanging a poster "Rare models of manly courage."

By such posters, the text messages of which, with fictitious rare models, composed in the offices of the Ministry of Military Affairs various German journalists drafted for the war, wanted that old asinine Austrian monarchy fill with enthusiasm the soldiers, who never read it, and when they would send such rare models of manly courage to them at the front bound as paperbacks, they rolled cigarettes out of them with pipe tobacco or utilize them even more appropriately, so that it would correspond to both the price and the spirit of the compiled rare models of courage.

While the Quartermaster went to chase down some officer, Švejk read what was on the poster:

TRANSPORT DRIVER JOSEF BONG[34]

The soldiers of the Medical Corps were transporting the seriously wounded to the wagons, standing by in a hidden hollow. As soon as it was full, they drove it to the medical aid station. The Russians, having discovered these wagons, started hurling shells at them. The horse of transport driver Josef Bong of the I&R 3rd Train Squadron[35] was killed by a fragment of a shell. Bong lamented: "Poor white steed of mine, you are done for!" At that moment he himself was hit by a piece of a shell. In spite of it he unhitched his horse and pulled a team of three horses behind a safe cover. Thereupon he returned for the harness of his slain horse. The Russians kept on shooting. "Just go on shooting, you damn madmen, the harness I will here not leave!" and he continued taking the harness off the horse, mumbling for himself those words. At last he was done and dragged himself and the harness back to the wagon. Here his fate was to hear out the full measure of peals of thunder of abuse by the medical corpsmen for his long absence. "I didn't want to leave the harness there, it's almost new. It would be a waste, I thought. We don't have a surplus of such things," apologetically said the intrepid soldier, driving away to the medical aid station, where only then he reported as having been wounded. His captain decorated later his chest with the silver medal for bravery.

When Švejk finished reading and the Quartermaster hadn't come back yet, he told the Land Defense soldiers at the guard house: "This is a very beautiful example of manly courage. That's how and why in our army there'll be nothing but new harnesses for horses, but when I was in Prague, I read in the *Prague Official Newspaper* then about an even prettier case of some One-Year Volunteer Dr. Josef Vojna[36]. He was in Galicia with the 7th Field Riflemen Battalion[37], and when it came down to bayonet skirmishes, he got a bullet in the head, and when they were carrying him to the medical aid station, he hollered at them, that on account of such a scratch he wouldn't let himself be bandaged. And again he wanted immediately to be on the attack with his platoon, but a shell lopped off his ankle. Again they wanted to carry him away, but he started hobbling with the aid of a cane to the battle line and with the cane he was defending himself against the enemy, and flying there arrived a new shell and ripped off the hand, in which he held the cane. He passed the cane into the other hand, yelled, that he would not forgive them for it, and God knows how he would have ended up, if a shrapnel a moment later hadn't definitely kill him. Maybe, if in the end after all they didn't finish him off, he would have also gotten a silver medal for bravery. When it severed his head, then, as it was rolling, it still yelled out: 'To faithful duty always rush, though all around against death's breath you brush!"

"The whole lot they'll write in those newspapers," said one of the troops, "but an editor like that would in an hour go bonkers from it."

The Land Defense soldier spat: "Where I'm from, in Čáslav[38], there was an editor from Vienna, a German. He served as an *ensign.* With us he didn't want to even try to speak Czech, but when they assigned him to a marchy[39], where they were all only Czechs, immediately he knew how to speak Czech."

In the doorway emerged the quartermaster, he was looking angry and let them have it:

"*When a man* to be *gone for three minutes, then he doesn't hear anything other than* in Cech, Cechs."

Walking out of there, apparently on the way to the restaurant, he told the Land Defense Sergeant, while pointing at Švejk, to bring that lousy hoodlum immediately to the Lieutenant, when that one comes.

"It figures the *Lieutenant* is again talking to the telegraph girl at the station," said after his departure the Sergeant, "he's been creeping after her for over two weeks and he's always tremendously rabid, when he comes from the telegraph office, and says about her: "*She's nothing but a whore, she won't sleep with me.*"

Even this time he was in such a rabid mood, because when after a while he came, one could hear him banging some books all over on the desk.

"No way around it, boy, go to him you must," the Sergeant addressed Švejk in a condolatory manner, "through his hands have already passed so many people, both old and young soldiers."

And already he was leading Švejk to the office, where behind the desk with papers scattered on it was sitting a young lieutenant, having on his face an immeasurably rabid expression.

When he saw Švejk with the Sergeant, he uttered with much promise: "Aha!" After which could be heard the report of the Sergeant: "I dutifully report, *Lieutenant*, Sir, that the man was found at the railroad station with no documents."

The Lieutenant nodded, as if he wanted to express, that he had already anticipated years ago, that indeed on this day and at this hour they would find Švejk at the railroad station with no documents, because whoever looked at Švejk at this moment, had to have such an impression, that it is absolutely impossible for a man with such a visage and figure to have any documents on him. Švejk at that moment appeared, as if he had fallen from the sky from some other planet and now is looking with naive awe at the new world, where they are demanding of him such previously unknown to him stupidity, as are some documents.

The Lieutenant deliberated a while, looking at Švejk, what he should tell him and what he should ask him.

At last he asked: "What were you doing at the railroad station?"

"I dutifully report, *Lieutenant*, Sir, that I was waiting for a train to České Budějovice, so that I could get to my 91st Regiment, where I am an *orderly* with mister *Senior Lieutenant* Lukáš, whom I was forced to abandon, having been detained and taken on account of a fine to the station master, because I was suspected, that I stopped the express train, in which we were riding, with the help of the safety and emergency brake."

"What the hell are you talking about," yelled out the Lieutenant, "tell it to me in some coherent way, briefly and don't babble any bullshit."

"I dutifully report, *Lieutenant*, Sir, that right from the moment, when *Senior Lieutenant* Lukáš and I were boarding that express, which was supposed to take us and transport us as fast as possible to our 91st I&R Infantry Regiment, we've been having bad luck as thick as sap. First our suitcase was lost, then again, just to make sure, some mister major general, totally bald..."

"*God in heaven*," sighed the Lieutenant.

"I dutifully report, *Lieutenant*, Sir, that it's needed, that it be coming out of me like being pulled out of a shaggy blanket, so that an overview of the whole event be available, as always used to say the now late shoemaker Petrlík, when ordering his boy, before he'd start belting him, to take off his pants."

And while the Lieutenant was steaming, Švejk continued further:

"So I had somehow not struck the fancy of the bald-headed Major General and I was sent outside to the passageway by mister *Senior Lieutenant* Lukáš, whose *orderly* I am. In the passageway I was then accused, that I had done that, which I was already telling you about. By the time that thing was taken care of, I had remained alone on the platform. The train was gone, mister *Senior Lieutenant* with the suitcases, including all of his own, my documents also gone, and I was left here gaping like an orphan without the documents."

Švejk looked so movingly gently at the Lieutenant, that it was now totally clear to him, that it is the complete truth, what he is hearing from this guy, giving such an impression of a congenital idiot.

The Lieutenant now enumerated for Švejk all the trains, which had left after the express for Budějovice, and put the question to him, why he missed those trains.

"I dutifully report, *Lieutenant*, Sir," answered Švejk, smiling good-naturedly, "that I, while waiting for the very next train, was beset by the mishap of sitting at a table drinking one beer after another."

"Such an ox I've never seen," thought the Lieutenant, "he'll admit everything. How many I have already had here, and each one kept denying, and this one calmly says: 'I've missed all the trains, because I was drinking one beer after another.'"

These musings he summarized in one sentence, with which he

turned to Švejk: "You, man, are a degenerate. Do you know, what it is, when it's said of someone, that he is a degenerate?"

"Where I'm from at the corner of Bojiště and Kateřinská[40] streets, I dutifully report, *Lieutenant*, Sir, there was also one degenerate man. His father was a Polish[41] count and the mother was a midwife. He used to sweep the streets and in the gin mills he wouldn't let them address him any other way than 'mister Count, Sir'."

The Lieutenant judged it good to somehow at last end it all, therefore he emphatically said: "So I'm telling you, you moron, you toe-jam hoof, that you will go to the cashier, buy yourself a fare card and ride to Budějovice. If I see you here again, I'll give you hell fitting a deserter. *Fall out!*"

Because Švejk didn't move and kept his hand on the bill of his cap, the Lieutenant hollered: "*Get out,* haven't you heard *fall out?* Sergeant Palánek, take this idiotic guy to the cashier and buy him a fare card to České Budějovice!"

Sergeant Palánek in a while showed up again at the office. Through the door, which was open a crack, was poking from behind Palánek the good-natured face of Švejk.

"What is it now?"

"I dutifully report, *Lieutenant*, Sir," mysteriously whispered Sergeant Palánek, "he doesn't have the money for the railway ride and I don't either. They don't want to give him a free ride, because he doesn't like have the military documents, that he's on the way to the Regiment."

The Lieutenant didn't make them wait long to see him come up with a Solomonic solution[42] to the difficult issue.

"Then let him walk," he decided, "let them lock him up at the Regiment, because he was late; who around here needs to bother with him."

"Nothing doing, buddy," said Sergeant Palánek to Švejk, when he stepped out of the office, "you have to go, my boy, on foot to Budějovice. We have over at the guard house a loaf of commissary bread, so we'll give it to you for the road."

And in half an hour, when they had filled Švejk up with black coffee and given him aside from the commissary bread a packet of military tobacco for the road on the way to the Regiment, Švejk stepped out from Tábor in the dark night, through which resounded his singing.

He was singing an old military song:

> When we drew to Jaromeř,
> let anybody believe or not …

And a demon knows how it happened, that the good soldier Švejk instead of south toward Budějovice kept going straight to the west.

He walked through the snow of the road, in the frost, covered in his military overcoat, like the last one of Napoleon's guard returning from the expedition to Moscow, with the only difference, that he was singing merrily:

> I've gone on a stroll
> into a green grove.

And in the snow-covered forests in the silence of the night the echo was reverberating, until in the villages round about the dogs started barking.

When he got tired of singing, Švejk sat down on a pile of gravel, lit up his pipe and having rested he went on, toward new adventures, the budějovická[43] anabasis[44].

2

ŠVEJK'S BUDĚJOVICKÁ ANABASIS

The ancient warrior Xenophon[45] trudged through the whole of Asia Minor[46] and he'd been God knows where else without a map. Old Goths also used to make their expeditions without topographical knowledge. To keep on marching forward, that's what is called an anabasis. To be scratching one's way through unknown lands. To be surrounded by the enemies, who are lying in wait for the earliest opportunity to wring your neck. When somebody has a good head on him, like Xenophon or all the robbing tribes had, which came to Europe God-knows-where-from around the Caspian Sea[47] or the Sea of Azov[48], he does genuine wonders on the march.

There someplace in the north by the Gallic Sea[49], all the way to where Caesar's[50] Roman legions also managed to get to without a map, they once said to themselves, that they would return again and march by a different route, in order to enjoy it even more, to Rome. And they got there too. Since that time it is said apparently, that all roads lead to Rome[51].

By the same token all roads also lead to České Budějovice. Of which was convinced to the full extent the good soldier Švejk, when instead of the Budějovice landscape he beheld the villages of the Milevsko region.

Nevertheless he kept walking ceaselessly on, because no good soldier can be bothered by such as Milevsko, to prevent him from arriving at České Budějovice in the end one day.

And so Švejk emerged west of Milevsko[52] in Květov[53], by which time he had already gone through all the military songs, which he knew about marching of soldiers, so that he had to start again, when approaching Květov, with the song:

> As we were marching,
> all the girls were weeping…

Some old grandma, who was returning from the church, struck up on the way from Květov to Vráž[54], which is still in the same western direction, a conversation with Švejk by a Christian greeting: "Good noon, soldier boy, where are you heading for?"

"Well I'm going, dear mother, to Budějovice to join the

regiment," answered Švejk, "going to that war."

"But then *they*[55] are going the wrong way, soldier boy," said the spooked grandma, "then *they* will never get there following this direction through Vráž; if *they* were to keep going straight, then *they* will come upon Klatovy[56]."

"I think," said Švejk with resignation, "that even from Klatovy can one get to Budějovice. It is, truth be told, quite a stroll, when one is in a hurry on the way to his regiment, in order not to have, on top of everything in return for his good faith effort to be at the spot on time, any unpleasant difficulties."

"Where I'm from there was also one such naughty boy. That one was supposed to go to Plzeň, to join the *Land Defense*[57], some one Toníček Mašků," sighed the grandma, "he's related to my niece, and he left. And in a week the State policemen were already looking for him, that he didn't arrive at his regiment. And another week later he showed up at our place in civilian clothes, that they let him go home on leave. So the mayor went to the State Police, and they picked him up off that leave of his. He's already written from the front, that he's injured, that he's missing a leg."

The grandma threw a long commiserating look at Švejk: "Over there, soldier boy, in that grove *they* wait, I will bring *them* a nice potato soup from our place, it'll warm you up. That cottage of ours is visible from here, just beyond the little grove, a bit to the right. *They* can't go through that Vráž village of ours, the State policemen there are as sharp-eyed as falcons. Then *they* take off from the little grove in the direction of Malčín[58]. From there *they* take a wide berth, soldier boy, around Čížová[59]. There the State policemen are as merciless as slaughterhouse butchers and they catch deserteers[60]. *They* go straight through the forest in the direction of Sedlec[61] near Horažďovice[62]. There is a very nice State policeman there, he lets everyone pass through the village. Do *they* have any papers on you?"

"I don't, dear mother!"

"Then *they* don't go there either, *they* better go to Radomyšl[63], but *they* try to get there toward evening, that's when all the State policemen are at the pub. There *they* will find, in the Dolejší street[64] behind the little Florian[65] this little house, painted blue at the bottom, and *they* ask there for master Melichárek. That's my brother. That I'm sending him greetings, and he'll be the one to show *them,* which way to walk to that Budějovice."

In the little grove Švejk had waited for the granny for more than half an hour, and when he warmed up with the potato soup, which the poor old woman brought in a pot wrapped in a pillow, so it wouldn't get cold, she pulled out of a scarf a slice of bread and a piece of bacon, tucked it all into Švejk's pockets, made a sign of the cross on his forehead and said, that she had two grandsons there.

After which she still thoroughly repeated for him which villages he was to go through, which ones he was to avoid. In the end she pulled out of the large pocket of her jacket one crown for him, to buy himself in Malčín booze for the road, because to Radomyšl the mile is long.

From Čížová went Švejk according to granny's advice in the direction of Radomyšl to the east, and he thought to himself, that he has to get to Budějovice from any one of the four corners of the world, regardless of which one it'd be.

From Malčín he was accompanied by an old accordion player, whom Švejk found in the pub there, when he was buying the booze for the long mile to Radomyšl.

The accordion player considered Švejk to be a deserter and advised him to come with him to Horažd'ovice, that he has a married daughter there, whose husband was also a deserteer. The accordion player had obviously tanked up over his limit in Malčín.

"She's had her husband hidden in the cowshed for two months already," he said leaning on Švejk to change his mind, "she'll hide you there too and the two of you will be there till the end of the war. And since there will be two of you, you won't be sad and lonely."

After Švejk politely declined, he got terribly upset and took off into the fields on the left, threatening Švejk, that he's on the way to turn him in at the State Police station in Čížová.

In Radomyšl Švejk found toward the evening on Dolejší Street, past the little Florian, master Melichárek. When he relayed the greeting from his sister in Vráž, it had no effect on the master.

He kept wanting papers from Švejk. He was some sort of prejudiced man, because he constantly kept saying something about rascals, ruffians and thieves, of whom a strong host was roaming the Písek district[66].

"They run away from the military and skip the war, don't want to serve in there, and so they roam all around here, and where they can, they steal," he said emphatically to Švejk's face, "each one of them looks as if he couldn't count to five. — Yeah, well yeah, people get upset the most on account of hearing the truth," he added, when

Švejk was getting up from the bench, "if such a man had a clear conscience, then he'd be sitting and let his papers be examined. But when he doesn't have them..."

"Then Godspeed, dear grandpa."

"Right, Godspeed and next time *they* find somebody dumber."

When Švejk stepped out into the darkness, the old geezer still kept grumbling for quite a while: "Says he's going to Budějovice to his regiment. From Tábor. And while he does, the rascal, he goes first to Horažďovice and only then to Písek[67]. C'mon, he's doing a trip around the world."

Švejk walked again nearly the whole night, only somewhere near Putim[68] he found a huge rick of straw in the field. He removed some of the straw and heard a voice quite nearby: "From which regiment? Where you're floating to?"

"From the 91st, to Budějovice."

"Why should you be?"

"I got my *Senior Lieutenant* there."

One could hear that not just one was laughing nearby, but three of them were. When the laughter died down, Švejk asked what regiment they were from. He found out, that two were from the 35th[69] and one was with the artillery, also of Budějovice[70].

That the Thirty-fivers ran away a month ago to avoid the march-gang and that the artilleryman has been since the mobilization on the road. He's a local from Putim, that the rick belongs to him. That at night he always sleeps in the rick. Yesterday he found the others in the forest, so he took them in, in his rick of straw.

They all had a hope, that the war must in a month or two come to an end. They had the impression that the Russians were already on the other side of Budapest[71] and in Moravia. That was the general rumor in Putim. Toward the morning, still before the daybreak, the dragoon's lady of the house will bring breakfast. The Thirty-fivers will then go to Strakonice[72], because one of them has an aunt there and she in turn has in the mountains on the other side of Sušice[73] some acquaintance, who has a lumber yard, and that there they will be well hidden.

"And you, from the one-and-ninetieth Regiment, if you want," they invited Švejk, "you can also come with us. Shit on your *Senior Lieutenant*."

"It's not that easy," answered Švejk and sank in, burrowed deep into the rick.

When in the morning he woke up, they all were gone already and somebody, apparently the dragoon, had put at his feet a piece of bread for the road.

Švejk went through the woods and at Štěkno[74] he met a wanderer, an old guy, who welcomed him like an old friend by a swig of booze.

"Don't go around dressed in this," he advised Švejk, "that military uniform could one day cost you big time. Now there are a lot of State policemen everywhere and to go begging dressed in that you can't. The State policemen of course aren't after us as they used be, now they're looking only for you guys. — Only you they're looking for," he repeated with such persuasiveness, that Švejk set his mind, that he'll better not be telling him anything about the 91st Regiment. Let the man take him for such as he thinks he is. Why spoil the good old man's illusions.

"And where are you heading?" asked the wanderer after a while, when both of them lit up their pipes and slowly detoured around the village.

"To Budějovice."

"Forchristhelord," the wanderer spooked, "there they'll pick you up in a minute. You won't even warm yourself up. You've got to have your civvies all ragged, you've got to be walking about and act like you're a crippie. But have no fear at all, now we're gonna go to Strakonice, Volyň[75], Dub[76], and there'd have to be a demon in it, if we don't chase down some civvies. Over by Strakonice there are still such very stupid and honest people, that they will still in quite a few places leave the door opened at night and during the day they don't lock up at all. They go now in winter over to the neighbor somewhere to chat, and you have civvies right away. What do you need? Shoes you have, so just something to throw on to cover yourself. The military overcoat is old?"

"Old."

"Then you keep that. That's what they wear in the countryside. You need pants and a coat. Once we have the civvies, then we'll sell the pants and the coat to the Jew Herrman[77] in Vodňany[78]. He buys any government issue and then he sells it in the villages. — Today we'll go to Strakonice," he was unfolding his plan further. "Four hours from here there's an old sheepfold of the Schwarzenbergs[79]. There is a shepherd there whom I know, also an old geezer already, there we'll stay overnight and in the morning we'll march in the direction of Strakonice, to spook and scoop somewhere in the vicinity the civvies."

In the sheep pen Švejk found a pleasant grandpa, who remembered how his grandpa in turn used to tell him about the French wars. He was about twenty years older than the old wanderer and therefore he addressed him as he did Švejk: my boy.

"So you see, my boys," he was narrating, when they were sitting around an oven, in which were cooking potatoes in their skins, "back then my grandpa also deserteered like that soldier of yours. And they caught him in Vodňany and they kicked his ass so, that tatters were flying off of it. And he could still talk of having had luck. Jareš's son from Ražice on the other side of Protivín[80], grandpa of the old Jareš, the pond warden, got powder and lead in Písek for having deserted. And before they ended up shooting him at the Písek's ramparts, he ran through a gauntlet of soldiers and received six hundred blows by canes, so that death came as a relief and salvation for him. — And when did you run away?" he turned his cried out eyes to Švejk.

"After the mobilization, as they were taking us to the garrison," answered Švejk, understanding that a uniform must not betray the old shepherd's trust.

"Did you climb over the wall?" asked the shepherd with curiosity, remembering apparently, how his grandpa was retelling, how he also got to climb over the wall of the garrison.

"There was no other way, grandpa."

"And was the watch detail strong and did it shoot?"

"Yes, grandpa."

"And where are you heading now?"

"Forget it, he's cracked up," the wanderer answered in Švejk's stead, "he wants to get to Budějovice by hook or crook. You know, a young man, without sense, he is rushing to his annihilation on his own. I have to give him a little schooling. Some civvies we will manage to spook up and from then on, everything will go alright. Until spring we'll have managed to get by somehow and then we'll go to work for a farmer somewhere. This year there'll be a great shortage of people, hunger, and they say, that this year they'll be pressing all wanderers into field work. So I think, it is then better to go voluntarily. There will be too few people. They will have been clubbed to extermination."

"So you think," asked the shepherd, "that it won't end this year? And you are, my boy, right! There have already been long wars. The

Napolionic[81] one, then, as they used to talk about them, the Swedish wars[82], the Seven Year wars. And people deserved those wars. After all, the Lord God could not watch anymore, how one and all got haughty. By then even mutton wouldn't be good enough for them to lift past their beard, they didn't want, my boys, to feed on it anymore. At other times they used to come here in a procession, asking me to sell them some ram on the sly, but the last few years they would only want to feed on nothing but pork, poultry, everything greased with butter or lard. So the Lord God got angry with them for that false pride of theirs and they will come to again, when they're cooking orache weeds for themselves, as they used to during the Napolionic war. Look, even the overlords of ours were so spoiled rotten that they couldn't decide on the next, even more rotten thing to do. The old lord Duke Schwarzenberg, he used to ride in such a coach, and the young dukey snot-nose reeks of nothing but automobile. Just wait, that's also why one day the Lord God will rub his snout in that gasoline."

The water over the potatoes cooking in the oven was already bubbling and after a short pause the old shepherd prophetically stated: "And he, our lord Emperor, will not win that war. There's no enthusiasm for the war, because he, as our mister teacher from Strakonice says, did not let himself be crowned[83]. Let him smear now, as the saying goes, honey around the piehole of anybody he wants to lure. When you have, you old hoodlum, promised, that you would let yourself be crowned, then you should have kept your word."

"Could be," mentioned the wanderer, "that now he'll somehow do it."

"Everybody will tell him to stuff it now, my boy," said the irritated shepherd, "you should be there when the neighbors gather down below in Skočice[84]. Everyone has somebody there, in that war, and you would see how they talk. That after this war supposedly there'll be freedom, there'll be no sprawling farms of the lords, no emperors and that the estates of the dukes will be taken away. And already on account of one such talk the State policemen have dragged away some guy Kořínek, that he's like inciting. Yeah, who has the rights nowadays are the State policemen."

"They used to have them even before," sounded up the wanderer, "I remember, that in Kladno the State Police Captain there used to be some mister Rotter. Imagine, he all of a sudden started breeding these, as they call them, police dogs with the wolves' disposition, since they manage to sniff everything out when they have been trained. And the Captain in Kladno had an assfull of those canine apprentices of his. He had a special little house for them, where the dogs lived like counts. And he put it in his mind all of a sudden, that he would conduct experiments with the dogs on us, the poor wanderers. So he gave an order, for the State Police in the whole Kladno region to be diligently collecting wanderers and supplying them directly into his hands. So this one time I am trekking from Lány[85] and I'm zooming through pretty deep in the forest, but to no avail, I never reached the ranger's house I aimed for, they had already had me and were taking me to the Captain. And you can't, folks, even fathom and consider what I suffered at the Captain's on account of those dogs. First he let them all sniff me all over, then I had to climb up a ladder, and once I was on top, then they let one such monster loose and after me, and he, the beast, carried me off the ladder to the ground, there he kneeled on top of me and was growling and baring its teeth in my face. Then they led the monster away, and to me they said to hide somewhere, that I could go anywhere I wanted to. I took off toward the Kačák[86] valley into the forests, into a ravine, and in half an hour two German Shepherds were already by my side, knocked me over, and while one was holding me by the neck, the other ran to Kladno and in one hour Captain Rotter himself came to me with the State policemen, called the dog and gave me a five-crown coin and a permit, allowing me to beg in the Kladno region for two whole days. But as for me, forget it, I ran, as if they had set my head on fire, to the Beroun region and I never showed myself in the Kladno region ever again. That region was being avoided by all the wanderers, because this mister Captain was conducting his experiments on all of them. He really just loved those dogs to bits. They used to talk at the State Police stations, how when he would come on an inspection, then wherever he'd see a German Shepard, that he didn't even bother to inspect anything, and out of the sheer joy of it he'd booze it up with the officer of the watch all day."

And while the shepherd was straining the potatoes and pouring sheep buttermilk into a bowl, the wanderer kept sharing more of his memories of the State Police justice: "In Lipnice[87] there used to be one state police sergeant down below the castle[88]. He lived right at the State Police station and I, the good old guy, was always, wherever I was, under the impression, that the State Police station had to be after all somewhere in a conspicuous spot, like a town square or something similar, and not somewhere on a tucked away little side street. So I'm combing the edges of the town and I'm not looking at the signs. I'm taking it from one building to another, until in this little one I come to the second floor, open the door and announce myself: 'I humbly beg your pardon, a poor wanderer.' Oh, lordy! My legs turned to wood on me; 't was the State Police station. Rifles by the wall, the crucifix on the desk, official papers on the top of the cabinet, the lord Emperor is looking right at me of all people from above the desk. And before I could blabber out anything, the *Station Chief*[89] sprang to me and slapped me so hard in that doorway, that I flew down the wooden stairs all the way to the bottom and didn't stop until I was in Kejžlice[90]. That is State Police justice."

They started eating their food and soon went to sleep in the warm sitting room, laid out on benches.

In the night Švejk quietly dressed and walked out. In the east the moon was rising and in its waking light was Švejk stepping east, repeating to himself: "C'mon, it's impossible for me not to get to that Budějovice city."

Because to the right, as he descended and emerged from the forests, could be seen some town, Švejk took a little more northerly turn, then to the south, where again some town could be seen. (It was Vodňany.) He avoided it nimbly on a path through the meadows and the morning sun welcomed him on the snowed over sloping hillsides above Protivín.

"Ever forward," the good soldier Švejk told himself, "duty is calling. To Budějovice I must get."

And by an unfortunate accident, instead of turning to the south of Protivín, in the direction of Budějovice, Švejk's steps took an aim at the north, in the direction of Písek.

Toward noon Švejk caught a sight of some village up ahead. Descending from a small plateau, Švejk thought to himself: "It can't go on like this anymore, I will ask, which way does one go to that Budějovice city."

And entering the village he was very much surprised having beheld the village designation posted on a pole by the first cottage: The Town of Putim.

"Forchristhelord," sighed Švejk, "so I'm again in Putim, where I slept in the rick of straw."

But by then he wasn't surprised by anything anymore, when beyond the little pond from the little house painted white, on which hung the hen (which in some places they called the dear little Austrian eagle), stepped out a State policeman, like a spider guarding his web.

The State policeman went directly to Švejk and said no more than: "Where to?"

"To Budějovice, to my regiment."

The State policeman gave a sarcastic smile: "C'mon, you're just coming from the direction of Budějovice. You have that Budějovice city of yours behind you," and he pulled Švejk into the State Police station.

The Putim State Police Station Chief was known in the whole surrounding area for acting with great tact and cleverly at the same time. He never berated the detainees or arrestees, but would subject them to such a cross-examination that even an innocent would confess.

The two State policemen at the station had changed their ways to conform to his and the cross-examination always took place to the smiles of the whole State Police staff.

"Criminology always depends on smarts and kindness," the State Police Station Chief would always tell his subordinates, "to be screaming at somebody, that won't get you anywhere. Delinquents and suspects must be approached gently, but at the same time one has to see to it, that they drown in a torrent of questions."

"It so nice to welcome you, soldier," said the State Police Station Chief, "have a nice seat, regardless, you must have gotten tired on the way, and tell us, where you are going."

Švejk repeated, that he was walking to České Budějovice to his regiment.

"Then you have taken the wrong road," said the State Police Station Chief with a smile, "since you're coming from the direction of České Budějovice. Of which I can convince you. Above you there is hanging a map of Bohemia[91]. So take a look, soldier. To the south of us there is Protivín. To the south of Protivín there is Hluboká and south of there is České Budějovice. So you see, that you are not going to Budějovice, but coming from Budějovice."

The Station Chief looked kindly at Švejk, who said calmly and with dignity: "And yet I'm going to Budějovice." It was more than Galileo's "And yet it moves!" Because that one must have said it apparently very furiously.

"You know, soldier," the Station Chief kept speaking to Švejk with the same kindness, "I'll talk you out of it, and you yourself will in the end come to the opinion, that each denial only makes confessing harder!"

"You're absolutely right," said Švejk, "each denial makes confessing harder and vice-versa."

"So you see, that on your own, soldier, you too will come to it. Have the good heart to answer me, where did you set out from, when you were going to that Budějovice city of yours. I'm purposely saying 'of yours' because apparently there must be some other Budějovice, which is located somewhere to the north of Putim and so far has not been plotted on any map."

"I set out from Tábor."

"And what were you doing in Tábor?"

"I was waiting for the train to Budějovice."

"Why didn't you go by train to Budějovice?"

"Because I didn't have a fare card for the rail."

"And why didn't they give you, as a soldier, a military fare card free of charge?"

"Because I had no documents on me."

"Here it is," said triumphantly the State Police Station Chief to one of the state policemen, "he's not as stupid, as he's making himself out to be, he's beginning to tangle up the story pretty well."

The Station Chief started over, as if he hadn't heard the last answer regarding the documents:

"You've then set out from Tábor. Where were you going then?"

"To České Budějovice."

The expression on the Station Chief's face gained in sternness a bit and his gaze landed on the map.

"Can you show us on the map, which way you went through to that Budějovice city?"

"I don't remember all the places and I remember only that I've been here in Putim once before."

The whole staff of the State Police station was looking at one another quizzically and the Station Chief continued: "In Tábor you were then at the railroad station. Do you have anything on you? Take it out."

When they frisked Švejk thoroughly and found nothing aside from a pipe and matches, the Station Chief asked of Švejk: "Tell me, why is there nothing at all, but absolutely nothing that you have on you?"

"Because I don't need anything."

"Oh, my God," sighed the Station Chief, "you're really troublesome! You said that you've been to Putim once before. What were you doing here back then?"

"I was passing Putim on the way to Budějovice."

"Then you see, how mistaken you are. You yourself are saying, that you were going to Budějovice, and now, as we have surely convinced you, you're coming from the direction of Budějovice."

"Apparently I must have made some sort of a circle."

The Station Chief again exchanged meaningful look with the whole station staff. "Those circles of yours, it looks to me that you are loitering around here. Did you stay long in Tábor at the railroad station?"

"Until the departure of the last train to Budějovice."

"And what were you doing there?"

"Talking with soldiers."

A new very significant glance cast by the Station Chief at the staff.

"And what were you for example talking about and what were you asking them?"

"I was asking them, which regiment they were from and where they were going."

"Excellent! And were you not asking them how many troops are for example in a regiment and how it is structured?"

"I wasn't asking that, because I've known that long since by heart."

"You are then perfectly informed of the structure of our forces?"

"Of course, mister Station Chief."

The Station Chief threw in the last trump, triumphantly throwing glances at his State policemen:

"Can you speak Russian?"

"I can't."

The Station Chief beckoned to the Watch Sergeant and when they both walked out into the next room, the Station Chief proclaimed with the enthusiasm of his total victory and certitude, wringing his hands: "Did you hear that? He can't speak Russian! A guy anointed with all the potions of deceit! He admitted all, until the most important thing he didn't admit. Tomorrow we'll be hauling him to Písek, to the district boss. Criminology depends on smarts and kindness. *They* saw, how I drowned him in a torrent of questions. Who would have thought it of him. He looks so stupid and so dumb, but it is just such people you have to approach cunningly. Now sit him some place and I'll go to write up an interrogation report about it."

And right away, from midday until toward the evening, was the State Police Station Chief, wearing a lovely smile, composing the interrogation report, in every sentence of which appeared the words suspected of espionage.

To the State Police Station Chief Flanderka, the longer he was writing in that curious bureaucratic German, the clearer the situation was becoming, and when he finished: "*So I dutifully report that the enemy officer will be sent this day to the District State Police Command in Písek*," he flashed a smile over his grand work and called out to the State Police Watch Sergeant. "Have *they* given that enemy officer something to eat?"

"By your direction, Station Chief, Sir, we provide food only for those, who are arraigned and interrogated by twelve o'clock."

"This is a big exception," said solemnly the Station Chief, "he is some higher ranking officer, somebody from the staff. You know that the Russians are not going to send a mere *Sergeant* here to spy. *They* send somebody to At the Little Tomcat's pub for some lunch for him. If they have nothing left, have them cook something. Then have them boil some tea with rum and have them send it all here. *They* don't tell them who it is for. *They* don't even mention whom we have here. That is a military secret. And what is he doing now?"

"He asked for a little tobacco, is sitting in the watch room and looks as content as if he were sitting at home. 'You have it nice and warm in here,' says he, 'and isn't your stove leaking smoke? I like it in here by you very much. And should your stove be leaking smoke, then have the chimney rodded. But only past noon, but never when the sun is standing above the chimney.'"

"That is really cunning of him," said in a voice full of enthusiasm the Station Chief, "he's acting like it had nothing to do with him. And yet he knows, that he'll be shot. Such a man we must esteem, even though he's our enemy. Such a man goes to certain death. I don't know, whether we could do that. Perhaps we'd waver, let up a bit. But he keeps on sitting calmly and says: 'You have it nice and warm in here,' says he, 'and your stove isn't leaking smoke.' That, mister Watch Sergeant, is a matter of character. That requires nerves of steel in a man like that, self-denial, toughness and enthusiasm. If there were enthusiasm like that in Austria… but let's better leave that alone. Even we have zealots. Did you read in the *National Politics* about this *Senior Lieutenant* Berger of the artillery who climbed a tall fir tree and set up there for himself on a branch an *observation point*? How our boys retreated and he could not get down anymore, otherwise he'd fall into captivity. So he waited, until our boys would chase the enemy back again, and whole two weeks it took, before he lived to see that. A whole two weeks he was up in the tree, and so he wouldn't die of hunger, he gnawed the whole top clean and was living on twigs and needles. And when our boys came, he was so weakened, that he couldn't keep hanging on up in the tree, he fell down and got himself killed. After he died he was decorated with the golden meritorious medal for valor."

And the Station Chief seriously added: "That is self-sacrifice, mister Watch Sergeant, that is heroism. — See, how we've started chatting away nicely again, *they* run now to order that lunch and send him for the time being over to me."

The Watch Sergeant brought Švejk in, and the Station Chief beckoned to him in a friendly manner to sit down, and started to inquire of him at first whether he had parents.

"I don't."

To the Station Chief it immediately occurred, that it is better that way, at least nobody would be mourning for the unfortunate. He bore his sight at the same time into Švejk's good-natured face and tapped him suddenly in a fit of congeniality on the shoulder, leaned toward him and asked him in a fatherly tone:

"Well, and how do you like it here in Bohemia?"

"I like it everywhere in Bohemia," answered Švejk, "on my journey I've found everywhere very good people."

The Station Chief nodded in agreement: "Our folk is very good and pleasant. A theft and a rumble here and there, that does not even count in the balance. I've been here already fifteen years, and when I calculate it, it comes to about three quarters of a murder per year."

"You mean an imperfect murder?" asked Švejk.

"No, that is not what I had in mind. In fifteen years we've investigated only eleven murders. Five of them were committed during a robbery and the remaining six, the ordinary sort, which aren't worth much."

The Station Chief paused and switched back again to his interrogation method: "And what did you want to do in Budějovice?"

"To join the service with the 91st Regiment."

The Station Chief asked Švejk to go again to the guard room, and quickly, so he wouldn't forget, added to his written report for the District State Police Command in Písek: "Having perfect command of the Czech language, he wanted to try and join the 91st Regiment in České Budějovice."

The Station Chief joyfully wrung his hands, rejoicing over the richness of the collected material and the exact results of his interrogation method. He remembered his predecessor, Station Chief Bürger, who would not speak with the detainee at all, would not ask him anything and send him immediately to the district court with a short report: "According to the statement from the Watch Sergeant he was detained for vagrancy and begging." Is that supposed to be an interrogation?

And the Station Chief looking at the pages of his report flashed a smile of vindication and pulled out of his desk the secret circular from the State Police Provincial Command in Prague marked with the customary 'Strictly Confidential' and read it one more time:

"All State Police stations are under strict orders to monitor with immeasurably increased alertness all persons passing through the district. The redeployment of our troops in eastern Galicia has brought about, that some Russian military detachments, having crossed the Carpathians, have assumed positions in the interior of our Empire, whereby the front has been shifted deeper toward the west of the Monarchy. This new situation has allowed Russian spies, given the mobility of the front, deeper penetration into the territory of our Monarchy, especially into Silesia[92] and Moravia, from where according to confidential reports a large number of Russian intelligence operatives have set out for Bohemia. It has been determined, that among them there are many Russian Czechs, educated at the Russian military staff colleges who, having perfect mastery of the Czech language, appear to be especially dangerous spies, since they can and certainly will conduct among the Czech populace a highly treasonous propaganda. The Land Headquarters therefore orders the apprehension and detention of all suspects and above all increased vigilance in those areas, where in the vicinity there are garrisons, military centers and stations with military transport trains passing through. The detained are to be subjected to an immediate search and transported to the next higher authority."

The State Police Station Chief Flanderka again flashed a smile of contentment and deposited the secret circular, "Sekretreservaten", among the others in the folder labeled "Secret Directives".

There were many of them prepared by the Ministry of the Interior[93] in cooperation with the Ministry of the Land Defense, to which the State Police was subordinate.

At the Land Headquarters of the State Police in Prague they could not copy and send them out fast enough.

There was:

The directive on controlling the views of the local population.

The guide for how to monitor in conversations with the local population, what influence the news from the battlefield has on its views.

A questionnaire about how the local population behaves regarding the publicly tendered war loans and collections.

A questionnaire about the mood among the drafted and those, who are to be drafted.

A questionnaire about the mood among the members of the local self-governing bodies and the intellectuals.

A directive on determining without delay, to which political parties the local population belongs, and how strong the individual parties are.

A directive on controlling the activities of the leaders of local political parties and determining the level of loyalty of certain political parties, represented among the local population.

A questionnaire about which newspapers, magazines and brochures get delivered within the State Police station's district.

An instruction regarding determining, whom the persons suspected of disloyalty are in contact with, and how their disloyalty manifests itself.

An instruction regarding how to recruit among the local population paid finks and informers.

An instruction for the paid informers from among the local population, registered at the State Police station as being in its service.

Every day was bringing new instructions, guides, questionnaires, and directives. Inundated by the mass of innovations from the Austrian Ministry of the Interior, the Station Chief Flanderka had a huge backlog of items and answered the questionnaires in a stereotypical manner, that on his beat everything was in order and the loyalty among the local population was of grade Ia.

The Austrian Ministry of the Interior devised the following grades of loyalty and steadfastness toward the Monarchy: Ia, Ib, Ic—IIa, IIb, IIc—IIIa, IIIb, IIIc—IVa, IVb, IVc. The last Roman numeral four in connection with the letter 'a' meant a perpetrator of high treason and the rope, with the letter 'b' internment, and with 'c' the order to monitor and lock up.

In the desk of the State Police Station Chief there were to be found all kinds of forms and records. The Government wanted to know of each citizen, how it was thought of by him.

The Station Chief Flanderka many times threw up his hands in desperation over the forms, which mercilessly kept coming and adding up with each mail delivery. As soon as he saw the familiar envelopes with the stamp "Postage free — official business" his heart always thumped a few times and at night, thinking everything over, he would arrive at the conviction, that he wouldn't live to see the end of the war, and that the Land Headquarters of the State Police would rob him of the last pinch of his sanity and that he would not be able to enjoy the victory of Austrian arms, because he would have either one extra screw, or one screw missing in his head. And the District State Police Command bombarded him daily with inquiries, why has not been answered the questionnaire issued under the number $\frac{72345}{721a/f}d$, how has the instruction issued under the number $\frac{88992}{822gfch}z$ been disposed of, and what are the practical results of the guide under the number $\frac{123456}{1292b/r}V$, etc.

The most of his worries were caused by the instruction, on how to recruit among the local populace paid finks and informants, in the end, because he figured it impossible, that it could be somebody from the area where The Marshes[+45] began and where the folk were such stubborn knuckleheads, he came across the idea to take into service the village herdsman, whom they addressed as "Joey, jump!" He was a cretin, who always jumped in response to this call. One of those poor, by nature and men neglected characters, a cripple, who for a few gold coins a year and some food grazed the village cattle.

Him he had called in and told: "Do you know, Joey, who old Procházka[94] is?"

"Maa."

"Don't bleat, and remember, that's what they call the lord Emperor. Do you know who the lord Emperor is?"

"Dat ish da Lawd Empeyor."

"Good, Joey. So remember, that when you hear somebody say, when you go for lunches from house to house, that the Emperor is a cattle beast or something like that, come to me right away and report it to me. You will get a dime, and when you hear somebody saying, that we won't win this thing, then you'll go again, understand, and come to me and say, who said it, and you'll get a dime again. If I hear however, that you are keeping something from me, then you'll be in a bad trouble. I'll pick you up and take you to Písek. And now jump!" When he jumped, he gave him two dimes and in a mood of contentment wrote a report to the District State Police Command, that he had already recruited an informer.

The next day the parish priest came to him and secretively let him know, that this morning outside the village he ran into the village herdsman Joey Jump[95] and that Joey was telling him: "Gentle Sir. The *Watch Sergeant* was saying yesterday, that da Lawd Empeyor is a cattle beast and that we won't win the thing. Maa. Hop!"

After a rather long explanation and a discussion with the parish priest the Station Chief Flanderka had them arrest the village herdsman, who was later at Hradčany[96] sentenced to twelve years for high treason. The prosecution proved his dangerous and highly treasonous intrigues, inciting, offending the Majesty and yet several other crimes and misdemeanors.

Joey Jump behaved in the court as if in the pasture, tending cattle, or among neighbors. To all questions he responded by bleating like a goat and after the sentence was declared he blurted out "Maa, hop!" and jumped. He received the disciplinary punishment of a hard bunk in the solitary and three fasts for it.

From that time on the State Police Station Chief had no informer and had to content himself with that he made one up, having reported a fictitious name, and thereby increasing his income by fifty crowns a month, which he would spend drinking in the At the Little Tomcat's pub. By the tenth stein he'd be getting a fit of diligence and the beer was turning bitter in his mouth and he always heard the same sentence from the neighbors: “Today is our Station Chief kind of sad, as if he were not in his usual mood.” Then he would be leaving for home and after his departure somebody would always say: “Our guys have gotten the shit beaten out of them somewhere in Serbia again since *Station Chief* is so reticent.”

And at home the Station Chief would again fill out at least one questionnaire: “Mood among the populace: Ia.”

Those were often long, dreamless nights for mister Station Chief. He was constantly expecting an inspection, an investigation. In the night he dreamt of the rope, of how they’re leading him to the gallows, and yet for the last time the Minister of the Land Defense[97] himself under the gallows was asking him: “*Station Chief, where is the answer to the circular No* $\frac{1789678}{23792}$ *X.Y.Z?*”

Only now! Throughout the whole State Police station, as if from all its corners the old gamekeepers’ slogan “Good hunting!” were resounding. And the State Police Station Chief Flanderka had no doubt, that the District Commander would tap his shoulder and say: “*I congratulate you mister Station Chief.*”

The State Police Station Chief was painting for himself in his mind even other magically delightful and illusory pictures, which arose in some fold of his bureaucratic brain. Decorations, fast advancement to a higher rank, appreciation of his criminological abilities, opening a career path for him.

He called the Watch Sergeant and asked him: “Have *they* gotten the lunch?”

“They brought smoked butt with sauerkraut and dumplings for him, there was no more soup. He finished the tea and wants one more cup.”

“He shall have it!” magnanimously consented the Station Master, “when he’s done drinking the tea, then *they* bring him to me.”

“How’s it going? Did you enjoy the food?” asked the Station Master, when half an hour later the Watch Sergeant brought Švejk, satiated and contented as always.

“It was still passable, mister *Station Chief*, only there should have been a tad more sauerkraut. But that can’t be helped, I know that *they* were not prepared for it. The smoked meat was very well smoked, it must had been home-made smoked meat from a home-raised pig. The tea with rum did me good too."

The State Police Station Chief looked at Švejk and began: "Is it true, that in Russia they drink a lot of tea? Do they also have rum there?"

"There is rum all over the world, mister *Station Chief.*"

"Just don't be wiggling out of it," the Station Chief thought to himself, "you should have watched earlier, what you're saying." And he asked, tilting his head toward Švejk in confidence: "Are there pretty girls in Russia?"

"There are pretty girls all over the world, mister *Station Chief.*"

"There, you son of a gun," thought the State Police Station Chief to himself once again, "you would now like to get out of it somehow." And the Station Chief charged with his forty-two pounder:

"What did you want to do at the 91st Regiment?"

"I wanted to go to the front with it."

The Station Chief contentedly aimed a long look at Švejk and remarked: "That is correct. That is the best way to get to Russia. — Really very well thought out," beamed the Station Chief, seeing what effect his words were having on Švejk.

He could, however, read from Švejk's demeanor nothing else, than absolute calm.

"This man won't even as much as move an eyelash," was what horrified the Station Chief in his mind, "that is their military training. Were I in his situation and somebody were to say that to me, my knees would start to shake...— In the morning we will drive you to Písek," he uttered as if in passing, "have you ever been to Písek?"

"In the year 1910 on Imperial maneuvers."

Following this answer was the Station Chief's smile even more pleasant and triumphant. He felt in his soul, that using his system of questioning, he outdid himself.

"Did you go through the whole maneuvers?"

"Of course, mister *Station Chief*, as an infantryman." And again, as calmly as before, Švejk was looking at the Station Chief, who was fidgeting with joy and could not hold himself back anymore from entering it quickly in the report. He called the Watch Sergeant to take Švejk away, and added to his report: "His plan was this: Having snuck into the ranks of the 91st Regiment, he wanted immediately to volunteer for the front and at the nearest opportunity to get to Russia, as he had noticed, that the return journey, given the vigilance of the authorities, was otherwise impossible. The expectation that he would prosper excellently with the 91st Regiment, is altogether understandable since, according to his confession, he admitted after a rather long cross-examination, that already in the year 1910 he had gone through the entire Imperial maneuvers in the vicinity of Písek as an infantryman. One can see from this, that he is very capable in his area of expertise. I would like to point out also, that the compiled charges are a result of my system of cross-examination."

In the doorway appeared the Watch Sergeant: "*Station Chief*, Sir, he wants to go to the bathroom."

"*Attach bayonet!*" decided the Station Chief, "actually no, bring him here."

"You want to go to the bathroom?" kindly said the Station Chief, "isn't there something else behind it?" And he bore his eyes into Švejk's face.

"There's really only number two in it Station Chief, Sir," answered Švejk.

"As long as there's nothing else in it," repeated the Station Chief meaningfully, snapping on his service revolver, "I will go with you."

"That is a very good revolver," he said to Švejk on the way, "for seven rounds, and it shoots accurately."

Before they stepped out into the yard, however, he called the Watch Sergeant and mysteriously said to him: "*They* go with the bayonet *attached* and once he's inside stand *themselves* in the rear of the bathroom, so he doesn't dig himself out through the dung pit."

The bathroom was a small, ordinary little wooden house, standing desperately in the middle of the yard over a pit full of dung water running off the nearby pile of manure.

It was already an old veteran in which whole generations have been performing their bodily needs. Now it was Švejk sitting here, holding the door closed by a piece of twine in one hand, while through the little window in the back the Watch Sergeant was looking at his rump, lest he dig himself out.

And the hawkish eyes of the State Police Station Chief were riveted to the door and the Station Chief was thinking over, in which of his legs he should shoot him, if he wanted to attempt an escape.

But the door opened undisturbedly and out stepped contented Švejk, addressing a remark to the Station Chief:

"Wasn't I in there too long? Haven't I held you up, perhaps?"

"Oh no, certainly not," retorted the Station Chief, having thought in his mind: "What gentle, well-mannered people they are. He knows, what's awaiting him, but all honor to him. Until the last moment he is well-mannered. Would one of our guys manage that in his place?"

In the guard room the Station Chief kept on sitting next to Švejk on the bunk of the empty bed of State policeman Rampa, who was on duty until morning, making rounds of the villages, and who at that time was sitting undisturbed in At the Black Horse in Protivín and was playing mariáš[98] with the master shoemakers, telling them during the breaks, that Austria has to win this thing.

The Station Chief lit up his pipe, gave Švejk to stuff his, the Watch Sergeant stoked another load into the stove and the State Police station was transformed into the most pleasant little place on the globe, into a placid nook, a warm nest during the onset of winter dusk, when people sit down to swap stories in cozy darkness before they turn on the lights.

However, they all were quiet. The Station Chief was following a certain line of thought and in the end expressed himself, turning to the Watch Sergeant: "According to my opinion it is not right to hang spies. A man, who sacrifices himself for his duty, for his, let's say, homeland, should be finished off in an honorable manner, with powder and lead, what do you think, mister Watch Sergeant?"

"Definitely just shoot him and not hang," agreed the Watch Sergeant, "let's say they would send us too and tell us: 'You have to search out how many machine guns the Russians have in their *machine gun detachment.*' So then we would put on a disguise and go. And for that they should hang me like some robbing killer?"

The Watch Sergeant got so upset, that he stood up and yelled out: "I demand, that I be shot and buried with military honors."

"There's a catch in it," chimed in Švejk, "if a man is smart, they will never prove him guilty of anything."

"Yes they will," expressed himself emphatically the Station Chief, "if they too are equally smart and have **their method**. You'll see it for yourself yet. — You'll see," he repeated in an already mild tone, adding a friendly smile to it, "here in our midst nobody succeeds with evasions, right, mister Watch Sergeant?"

The Watch Sergeant nodded in agreement and mentioned, that with some people their cause is lost before it begins, that not even the mask of absolute calm will help, that the calmer somebody looks, the more it proves him guilty.

"*They've* had my schooling, mister Watch Sergeant," stated proudly the Station Chief, "calm, that's just a soap bubble, artificial calm is the corpus delicti." And interrupting the exposition of his theory, he turned to the Watch Sergeant: "What should we have for dinner today?"

"You won't go to the pub today, Station Chief, Sir?"

With this question arose to face the Station Chief a new tough problem, which it was necessary to decipher immediately.

What if, making use of his nocturnal absence, that one were to flee. It's true the Watch Sergeant is a reliable man, careful, but he's already had two itinerant bums run away on him. Factually the way it happened was, that once in wintertime he did not want to be dragging with them in the snow all the way to Písek, so in the fields by Ražice he let them go and shot a round into the air pro forma.

"We'll send our hag to fetch the dinner and she'll shuttle with a pitcher getting the beer," is how the Station Chief deciphered the tough problem, "let the hag stretch herself jogging a bit."

And Pejzlerka the hag, who was their cleaning woman and gofer, sure did stretch herself jogging.

After dinner the route between the State Police station and the At the Little Tomcat's pub got no rest. Unusually numerous footprints of the heavy, large shoes of Pejzlerka the hag on that communications line were a testimony to the fact, that the Station Chief was compensating himself with full measure for his absence At the Little Tomcat's.

And when at last Pejzlerka the hag showed up at the tap room with the message, that the Station Chief respectfully sends regards and wants them to send him a bottle of kontušovka[99], the pub owner's curiosity burst through.

"Whom do they have there?", answered Pejzlerka the hag, "some suspicious individual. Just before I left, they both were holding him around his neck and the Station Chief was caressing his head and was telling him: 'You Slavic boy of mine, as precious as gold, you itsy bitsy spy of mine!"

And then, when it was long past midnight, the Watch Sergeant was sleeping, snoring hard, laid out across his bunk, in full uniform.

Across from him was sitting the Station Chief with the remnant of the kontušovka at the bottom of the bottle, he was holding Švejk around his neck, tears were running down his suntanned cheeks, his whiskers were stuck together with kontušovka and he was just babbling: "Say that in Russia they don't have such good kontušovka, say it so I can go to sleep with my mind at ease. Admit it like a man."

"They don't."

The Station Chief rolled over onto Švejk.

"You've made me glad, you confessed. That's the way it's supposed to be at a cross-examination. If I'm guilty, why keep denying it."

He stood up, and teetering with the empty bottle into his room, he was mumbling: "Had he not gotten on the w-wrong ppaaath, then everything could have turned out d-differently."

Before he collapsed in uniform onto his bed, he pulled out of the desk his report and attempted to augment it by this material: *"I have to add that Russian Kontuszówka on the basis of Article 56..."* He made an inkblot, licked it off, and smiling stupidly, he collapsed onto the bed and fell asleep like a log.

Toward the morning started the State Police Watch Sergeant, lying on the bed by the opposite wall, such snoring accompanied by whistling in the nose, that it woke Švejk up. He got up, shook the Watch Sergeant, and went back to lie down. By that time the roosters began to crow, and when the sun rose, then came Pejzlerka the hag, who also had to sleep off the nocturnal shuttle run, to start the fire in the stove, and here she found the door open and all submerged in a deep sleep. The kerosene lamp in the guard room was still spewing soot. Pejzlerka the hag raised alarm and pulled the Watch Sergeant and Švejk out of the bed. To the Watch Sergeant she said: "*They* should be ashamed to sleep with clothes on, like God's dumb cattle," and Švejk she admonished to at least button up his fly, when he sees a broad.

In the end she energetically suggested to the still half asleep Watch Sergeant, that he go and wake up the Station Chief, that it was not in proper order when people drooled into the pillow until so late.

"*They* sure fell into fine hands," growled the hag at Švejk, when the Watch Sergeant was waking up the Station Chief, "One's a worse boozer than the other. They'd booze away the nose between their eyes. Me they owe for service three years running already, and when I remind them, the Station Chief always says: 'Be *they* quiet hag, or else I'll have *them* locked up, we know that your son is a poacher and goes gathering firewood at the lord's manor grounds.' And so they've been vexing me coming up on a fourth year already." The hag sighed deeply and kept growling: "Watch out for *themselves* especially around the Station Chief, he's so ingratiating, while actually he is a vermin of the first order. Busting and locking up whomever he can."

The Station Chief would be woken up with great difficulty. The Watch Sergeant had a hard time convincing him, that it was already morning.

At last he managed to peek through the slits of his half-closed eyes, was rubbing them and vaguely started remembering yesterday. All of a sudden a horrible thought came to his mind, which, looking uncertainly at the Watch Sergeant, he expressed as: "So he's run away on us?"

"But of course not, he is an honest man."

The Watch Sergeant started pacing around the room, looked out of the window, returned again, tore a piece off the newspaper on the table and was rolling a little paper ball between his fingers. It was obvious, that he wanted to say something.

The Station Chief was watching him uncertainly and finally, wanting to gain full assurance of what he knew only by his intuition, he said: "I will, mister Watch Sergeant, help *them*. I must have been raising hell again and really carrying on yesterday?"

"If you only knew, Station Chief, Sir, all the things you'd hope you didn't say, and the kind of talk you'd hope you didn't carry on with him."

Leaning over toward the ear of the Station Chief he was whispering: "That we all Czechs and Russians are of one Slavic blood; that Nikolai Nikolayevich[100] will be in Přerov[101] next week, that Austria won't manage to hold on, so when he is being interrogated further, he should keep on denying all and driveling, in order to hold out until the time, when the Cossacks would liberate him at last, that it's got to crack and come down crashing any time soon, that it would be like during the Hussite[102] wars, that the farmers armed with flails would march on against Vienna, that the lord Emperor is a sick old geezer and will kick the bucket in no time, that the Emperor Wilhelm is an animal, that you will be sending him money in prison to make it a little better for him and still more such pronouncements…"

The Watch Sergeant stepped away from the Station Chief: "All of that I remember well, because at the beginning I was buzzed only a little. Then I got myself blasted too and I know of nothing after that."

The Station Chief looked at the Watch Sergeant.

"And I, for a change, remember," he proclaimed, "that *they* were saying, that we'd come up short against Russia, and *they* were screaming in front of that hag of ours 'Long Live Russia!'"

The Watch Sergeant started nervously pacing the room.

"*They* were screaming it like a raging bull," said the Station Chief, "then *they* collapsed across the bed and started to snore."

The Watch Sergeant stopped by the window, and drumming on it, proclaimed: "You too, Station Chief, Sir, weren't watching your mouth in front of that hag of ours and I remember, that you told her: 'Hey t*hey*, remember hag, that each emperor and king looks only after his pocket, and that is why he wages a war, even if he's such an old geezer as the old Procházka, whom they can't even let off the shitcan, so he wouldn't mess up for them the whole Schönbrunn[103].'"

"Is that what I am supposed to had been saying?"

"Yes, Station Chief, Sir, this is what you were saying, before you went out to the yard to throw up, and there's something else you were screaming: 'Hey *they*, stick a finger down my throat, hag!'"

"*They* expressed *themselves* nicely too," interrupted him the Station Chief, "Just where did *they* get such a silly idea, that Nikolai Nikolayevich will become the Czech king?"

"That I don't remember," sounded up timidly the Watch Sergeant.

"No wonder *they* don't remember it. *They* were like a soaked bale, had little piggy eyes, and when *they* wanted to go out, then instead of going to the doorway *they* were climbing onto the stove."

They both fell silent, until the long silence was interrupted by the Station Chief. "I have always said, that alcohol is annihilation. *They* can't hold much and yet still drink it. What if that guy of ours escaped from *them*? How would we account for it? God, what a splitting headache I have. — I say, mister Watch Sergeant," continued the Station Chief, "that precisely because he did not run away, the thing is totally clear, what a dangerous and conniving man he is. When they're interrogating him over there, he'll say, that the door was open all night long, that we were drunk, and that he could have escaped a thousand times, if he had felt being guilty. It's a lucky break, that such a man isn't trusted, and when we, being under the oath of office, say that it is a fib and a bold-faced lie from that man, then even Lord God won't help him and he's got one extra article of the law hanging round his neck. In his case however it doesn't make any difference. — If only my head didn't hurt so much."

Silence. In a while the Station Chief spoke up: "*They* call our hag in here."

"*They* listen up, hag," said the Station Chief to Pejzlerka, sternly boring his eyes into her face, "*they* go and chase down a crucifix on a pedestal somewhere and bring it here."

In response to Pejzlerka's quizzical look, the Station Chief hollered: "*They* better look to it, that *they* go and be back already."

The Station Chief pulled out of the little table two candles, which bore traces of sealing wax, from when he would seal official files, and when Pejzlerka at last hobbled in with a crucifix, the Station Chief stood the cross between both candles on the edge of the desk, lit up the candles and solemnly said: "*They* take a seat, hag."

The petrified Pejzlerka dropped into the sofa and bug-eyed took a look at the Station Chief, the candles, and the crucifix too. She was gripped by fear, and as she had her hands on the apron, one could see, that they were shaking along with her knees.

The Station Chief passed solemnly by her, and having stopped in front of her for the second time, he spoke up ceremoniously: "Last night you were a witness to a great event, hag. Could be, that your numskull brain doesn't comprehend it. That soldier, he is an intelligence officer, a spy, you hag."

"Jesusmaria," gave out a scream Pejzlerka, "Virgin Mary of Skočice[104]!"

"Silence, hag! In order to get anything out of him, we had to be saying all kinds of things. *They* heard, didn't *they*, what strange things we were saying?"

"That, if you please, I did," sounded up with a quivering voice Pejzlerka.

"But all the talk, hag, was only leading to one thing, to have him confess, to have him trust us. So we managed that. We dragged everything out of him. We bagged him."

The Station Chief interrupted his speech for a moment, in order to trim the wicks on the candles, and then continued solemnly, looking sternly at Pejzlerka: "You, hag, were present there and you are privy to the whole secret. This secret is official. You cannot even mention it to anybody. Not even on your deathbed, otherwise they may not even bury you at the cemetery."

"Jesusmariajoseph," lamented Pejzlerka, "why is it that I, unfortunate, ever stepped in here."

"Don't holler, hag, stand up, approach the crucifix, put two fingers of your right hand up. You will swear. Say after me."

Pejzlerka staggered over to the desk lamenting incessantly: "Virgin Mary of Skočice, why is it that I ever stepped in here."

And from the crucifix was looking at her the tormented face of Christ, the candles were spewing soot and all appeared to Pejzlerka as something horrifyingly unearthly. She was losing her bearings in it altogether and her knees were knocking, hands shaking.

She raised two fingers up high and the State Police Station Chief emphatically and ceremoniously recited for her to repeat: "I swear to God Almighty, and even you, mister Station Chief, that about that, which I heard and saw here, I will not mention to anybody not even one word of it until I die, even if I should be perhaps asked by Him. To that end help me Lord God.

"Now hag, kiss yet the crucifix" ordered the Station Chief, when Pejzlerka took the oath amid tremendously heart wrenching sobbing and crossed herself piously.

"So, and now again *they* carry the crucifix away to where *they* borrowed it from, and *they* say, that I needed it for an interrogation!"

The crushed Pejzlerka tiptoed with the crucifix out of the room and one could see through the window, that she was constantly looking back from the road at the State Police station, as if she wanted to verify for herself, that it wasn't just a dream, but that only a moment ago she had lived through something horrible in her life.

The Station Chief was in the meantime rewriting his report, which during the night he kept augmenting by inkblots, which he would smear licking them off right along with the handwriting, as if on the paper there were marmalade.

By now he had totally reworked it and he remembered, that he had not asked about one thing. So he had Švejk called in and asked him: "Do you know how to take photographs?"

"I do."

"And why don't you carry a camera on you?"

"Because I don't have any," was the sound of the sincere and clear answer.

"And if you had it, then you'd be taking pictures?" inquired the Station Chief.

"If, therein lies the error's whiff," simplemindedly retorted Švejk and placidly withstood the quizzical expression on the face of the Station Chief, whose head just started hurting again, so that he could not think up any other question than this one: "Is it hard to photograph a railroad station?"

"Easier than something else," answered Švejk, "because it's not moving and the railroad station keeps standing in one place and one doesn't have to be telling it, to put on a pleasant countenance."

The Station Chief was then able to add to his report: *"Regarding the Report # 2172, I report…"*

And Station Chief began to elaborate: "Among other things during my cross-examination he stated, that he knows how to photograph, and at that likes railroad stations the best. A photography apparatus was not found on him, that is to say, but an assumption exists that he is hiding it somewhere, and the reason why he does not carry it on him is, to turn the attention away from himself, to which points the evidence of his own confession, that he would be taking pictures, if he had the apparatus on his person."

The Station Chief, having a heavy head as a consequence of yesterday, was getting more and more entangled in his report on photographing and kept writing on: "The one certain thing is, that according to his own confession only the fact, that he does not have the apparatus of photography on him, prevented his taking photographs of the railroad station buildings and places of strategic importance in general, and it is indisputable, that he would have done so, had he the said photography apparatus, which he had hidden, on his person. It is only the circumstance of the photography apparatus not being on hand, to which one can give thanks, that there were found on his person no photographs."

"That's enough," said the Station Chief and signed his name.

The Station Chief was completely satisfied with the fruit of his labor and read it to the Watch Sergeant with great pride.

"That turned out well," he said to the Watch Sergeant, "now *they* see, that's how *reports* are to be written. There has to be everything in it. Interrogation, dear mister, that's not something just that simple, and the main thing is to compile it nicely into the *report*, so that the higher-ups stare at it like a dazed deer. *They* bring that guy of ours here, so that we make an end of it with him. — So now the Watch Sergeant will escort you," he pronounced solemnly in the direction of Švejk, "to Písek, to *District State Police Command*. According to regulations you're supposed to be handcuffed. However, because I think you are a decent man, we won't put those little cuff irons on you. I am convinced, that even on the road you won't be attempting an escape."

The Station Chief, obviously moved by the sight of the good-souled face of Švejk's, added: "And don't be remembering me with any hard feelings. *They* take him, mister Watch Sergeant, here *they* have the *report*."

"Then the Lord God be with you," said Švejk softly, "I thank *them*, mister *Station Chief*, for everything *they* have done for me, and when there is an opportunity, then I will write to *them*, and should I happen to have a trip round here still another time, then I'll stop by to see *them*."

Švejk walked out unto the road with the Watch Sergeant, and whoever passed them, as they were immersed in a friendly conversation, would consider them to be old acquaintances who happened to be on the same journey to town, let's say to church.

"I would have never thought," was Švejk telling, "that such a journey to Budějovice is associated with such difficulties. It seems to me to be like that case of the butcher Chaura from Kobylisy[105]. On one occasion at night he ended up by the Palacký[106] Memorial statue at Moráň[107] and kept walking round it all the way till morning, because it seemed to him that the wall had no end. He was totally desperate from it, toward the morning he couldn't take it anymore, so he started screaming "Patrol!", and when the cops came running over, he was asking them then, which way does one get to Kobylisy, that he'd been walking along some wall five hours and that there was still no end to it. So they brought him along with them, and in isolation he busted everything up for them."

The Watch Sergeant reacted to it by not saying even one word and was thinking to himself: "What's the nonsense you're telling me. Again you're beginning to tell me some fairy-tale about Budějovice.

They were passing a pond and Švejk asked the Watch Sergeant with interest, whether there were a lot of fish poachers in the vicinity.

"Here it's all poachers," answered the Watch Sergeant, "they wanted to throw the previous Station Chief in the water. The fishpond warden shoots bristles in their butts from his pond ward cottage, but that does not make any difference. They wear a chunk of sheet metal in their pants."

The Watch Sergeant started talking about progress, how people figure everything out and how one cheats the other, and he unfolded a new theory, that this war is a great fortune for mankind, because in the troubles of warfare, besides the kind people there will also be the rabble and rascals being bumped off.

"As it is there are too many people in the world," he declared deliberately, "one is already pressing cheek to jowl with the other and mankind has multiplied to the point it's a horror."

They came near a roadside inn.

"The wind is blowing damn hard right through the clothes today," said the Watch Sergeant, "I think, that a shot can't do us harm. Don't tell anybody anything, that I'm escorting you to Písek. That's a State secret."

In front of the Watch Sergeant's mind's eye spun, as if dancing, an instruction by the central authorities regarding suspicious and conspicuous people and regarding the duty of each State Police Station: "Exclude those from contact with the local population and uncompromisingly see to it, that there don't occur during transport to the next higher authorities unnecessary conversations in the environs."

"It mustn't come out, what you're all about," spoke up again the Watch Sergeant, "It's nobody's business, what you've done. Panic must not be spread. — Panic is in these times of war a nasty thing," he continued, "something is said and already it goes like an avalanche through the whole surroundings. Do you understand?"

"Then I won't be spreading panic," said Švejk and also behaved accordingly, because when the pubkeeper struck up a conversation with them, Švejk kept emphasizing: "The brother here says, that at one o'clock we'll be in Písek."

"And so your mister brother is on leave?", asked the nosey pubkeeper of the Watch Sergeant, who not even batting an eye had the nerve to answer: "Today it ends for him already!"

"We got him good," he declared smiling at Švejk, when the pubkeeper stepped away somewhere, "just no panic. It's wartime."

When before entering the roadside inn the Watch Sergeant had declared, that he thought a shot could not do any harm, he was being an optimist, because he forgot about quantity, and when he had drunk twelve of them, he declared absolutely decisively, that until three o'clock is the State Police District Station Commander at lunch, that it would be in vain to arrive there earlier, and besides a heavy snowfall is starting. If they are to be in Písek by four hours after midday, there's time aplenty. Till six o'clock there's enough time. By then they'll be going in the dark, as today's weather shows. It makes no difference whatsoever, going now or only later. Písek can't run away.

"Let's be glad, that we're sitting in where it's warm," was his decisive word, "there in the trenches in such blustery conditions they suffer more than we do by the stove."

A big, old, ceramic tile-covered stove was radiating heat and the Watch Sergeant found out, that the external heat can be supplemented advantageously by the internal kind, with the assistance of various kinds of booze both sweet and powerful, as they say in Galicia.

The pubkeeper of this secluded place had eight varieties of them, was bored and drinking to the sound of the wailing wind, which was whistling around each corner of the house.

The Watch Sergeant constantly kept challenging the pubkeeper to keep pace with him, accusing him, that he's drinking too little, which was an obvious injustice, because that man was already barely standing on his feet and constantly wanted to play ferbl[108] and insisted, that at night he had heard artillery fire in the East, after which the Watch Sergeant would hiccup: "Just no panic please. That's why there are in-instructions."

And he started an explication, that an instruction is a compilation of the most immediate regulations. While at it, he revealed several secret circulars.

The pubkeeper did not comprehend anything anymore, he only managed a declaration, that the war would not be won by instructions.

It was already dark, when the Watch Sergeant decided, that now he and Švejk would take off on the journey to Písek. In the heavy snowfall one could not see a step ahead and the Watch Sergeant kept saying: "Keep going straight to where your nose is pointing, all the way to Písek."

When he had said it for the third time, his voice did not sound coming from the road anymore, but from somewhere below, whereto he slid down the slope on the snow. Helping himself with the rifle, laboriously he clawed his way up again onto the road. Švejk heard his muffled laugh: "A slide." A while later however once again one could not hear him anymore, because he slid off the slope anew, having hollered so, that he drowned out the wind: "I will fall, a panic!"

The Watch Sergeant was transformed into a diligent ant, which, when it falls from somewhere, is again tenaciously climbing up.

Five times repeated the Watch Sergeant his airborne field trip down the slope, and when he was again by Švejk, he said helplessly and desperately: "I could very well lose you."

"*They* have no fear, mister Watch Sergeant," said Švejk, "we'll do best to tie ourselves to one another. That way we cannot lose each other. Do *they* have the little cuff irons with you?

"Every State policeman must always carry little cuff irons with him," said the Watch Sergeant emphatically, stumbling round Švejk, "that is our daily bread."

"So then we'll button ourselves together," Švejk prodded, "*they* just try it."

By a masterful move the Watch Sergeant attached the little cuff irons to Švejk and the other end to the wrist of his own right hand and now they were tied together like twins. Stumbling down the road they could not part from one another and the Watch Sergeant dragged Švejk over little piles of stones, and when he fell, he yanked Švejk down along with him. At the same time the little cuff irons were cutting into their hands, until at last the Watch Sergeant declared, that it couldn't go on like this, that he had to remove them again. After a long and futile exertion to rid both himself and Švejk of the little cuff irons the Watch Sergeant sighed: "We are united for ever and ever."

"Amen," added Švejk and they continued on the difficult journey.

The Watch Sergeant was overcome by total depression, and when after horrible suffering they made it late at night to Písek and arrived at the State Police Station, there, on the steps, the totally crushed Watch Sergeant addressed Švejk: "Now it'll be horrible. We can't part from one another."

And it really was horrible, when the Sergeant sent for the Station Commander, Captain König.

The Captain's first words were: "Exhale at me."

"Now I understand," said the Captain, having determined the undeniable nature of the situation with his smart, experienced sense of smell, "rum, kontušovka, demon gin, rowan brandy, nutty liqueur, cherry brandy and a vanilla. — Mister sergeant," he turned to his subordinate, "here you see an example, how a state policeman is not supposed to look. To carry on like this is such an infraction, that it will be a subject of deliberations of a military court. To tie oneself to the delinquent with little cuff irons. To come drunk, totally *blasted.* To crawl in here like an animal. Take it off for them."

"What is it?" he turned to the Watch Sergeant, who was saluting backward with the free hand.

"I dutifully report, Captain, Sir, that I'm bringing *a report.*"

"*A report* about you will go to the court," tersely said the Captain, "mister sergeant, *they* lock up both men, then in the morning *they* bring them to interrogation, and as for *the report* from Putim, *they* study it thoroughly and send it to my apartment."

The Písek State Police Station Captain was a man very officious, thorough in persecuting subordinates, remarkable in bureaucratic matters.

At the State Police Stations in his district they could never say that the storm had passed and flown away. It kept coming back with each written communication signed by the Captain, who was all day taking care of various admonitions, reprimands and warnings to the whole district.

Since the outbreak of the war, there hung over the State Police Stations in Písek district heavy black clouds of gloom.

It was a genuinely spooky atmosphere. Lightning bolts of bureaucratism were thundering and striking State Police Station Chiefs, Watch Sergeants, rank-and-file, and civilian attendants. For each silly thing a disciplinary investigation.

"If we want to win the war," he would say during his inspections at the State Police Stations, "an 'a' must be an 'a', a 'b' — 'b', everywhere there has to be a dot over the 'i'."

He felt surrounded by treason and developed a sharp sense, that each State Police cop in the district had some sins to his account stemming from the war, that everybody had left behind in these serious times a trace of some negligence committed while on the job.

And from above they bombarded him with written communications, in which the Ministry of Land Defense was pointing out, that from the Písek district, according to the reports of the Ministry of Military Affairs, they were crossing over to the enemy.

And they were after him to search for loyalty in the district. It looked spooky. Women from the vicinity would see their men off to army service, and he knew, that those men are certainly promising their wives, that they would not let themselves get killed for the lord Emperor.

The Black-and-Yellow horizons began to be cast over by the clouds of revolution. In Serbia, in the Carpathians regiments were crossing over to the enemy. The 28th Regiment, the 11th Regiment. In the latter one soldiers from the Písek region and district. In that sultry atmosphere of an imminent mutiny, there arrived recruits from Vodňany with carnations made of starched black gauze. Rolling through the Písek railroad station were soldiers from the direction of Prague and they were throwing back the cigarettes and chocolate, which were being handed to them into the pig cars by the Písek society ladies.

Then followed one march battalion and several Písek Jews were hollering "*Hail, down with the Serbs!*" and got a few of such nice slaps, that for a week they couldn't show themselves on the street.

And while these episodes were happening, which were clearly showing, that when they play the "Save for Us, Lord God, Our Emperor" on the organ in the churches, that it is only a thin veneer and universal hypocrisy, that from the State Police Stations there were arriving those familiar answers to questionnaires à la Putim, that everything is in the best possible order, that agitation isn't being carried out anywhere against the war, that the views of the population are rated Roman numeral one 'a', and enthusiasm Roman numeral one 'a'—'b'.

"You're not State policemen, but village cops," he would say on his rounds, "instead of sharpening the focus of your attention by a thousand percent, you're slowly turning into disgusting cattle.

Having made this zoological discovery, he would add: "You wallow nicely at home and think to yourself: *They can lick our asses with the whole war.*"

Following next would always be an enumeration of all the duties of the unfortunate State cops, a lecture about what the whole situation is like and how it is necessary to take it all into one's hands, so that it would really be, as it is supposed to be. After this description of the glowing vision of State cop perfection, driving toward strengthening the Austrian monarchy, there followed threats, disciplinary investigations, transfers, and berating.

The Captain was firmly convinced, that he's standing guard here, that he's preserving something, and that all those State cops from the State Police stations, which are under him, they're all nothing but lazy rabble, egoists, moral degenerates, con artists who don't understand anything else but booze, beer and wine. And that because they have minuscule incomes, they, in order to be able to booze it up, let themselves be bribed and were wrecking Austria slowly, but surely. The only man, whom he trusted, was his own sergeant at the District Headquarters, who, however, would always say at the pub: "So let me tell you, I've had a shitload of fun again today on account of that dumb old deadbeat of ours..."

*

The Captain was studying the Putim State Police Station Chief's *report* about Švejk. In front of him was standing his State Police Sergeant Matějka thinking to himself, that the Captain should climb up his back and kiss his butt with all his *reports*, because down by the Otava[109] river they were waiting for him to sit down for a round of šnops[110].

"Last time I was telling you, Matějka," let himself be heard the Captain "that the biggest idiot, whom I've ever gotten to know, is the Station Chief from Protivín, but according to this *report* the Station Chief from Putim trumped him. The soldier, who was brought here by that rogue boozer Watch Sergeant, and with whom they were tied together like two dogs, is clearly no spy. He's surely an utterly common-as-dust deserter. Here he writes such nonsense, that every little child can tell at a first glance, that the guy was as drunk as a papal prelate. — Bring that soldier here immediately," he ordered, as he was studying the report from Putim yet a while. "Never in my life have I seen such a pile of gathered idiocies, and in addition to it all he sends with the suspect such a cattle beast, as his Watch Sergeant is. These people still know me little, I know how to be a sonofabitch. As long as they don't dump in their pants in front of me out of fear three times a day, they're convinced, that I'll allow wood to be chopped on my back."

The Captain started talking at length, how the State Police officer corps nowadays acts with an attitude of rejection toward all orders, and that from how it composes *reports*, it is immediately apparent, that each such State Police Sergeant makes fun of everything, just so that he entangles something even more.

When it's pointed out from above, that the possibility of spies walking about the lands has not been eliminated, the State Police Station Chiefs start manufacturing them on a large scale, and if the war still lasts some more time, it will all become a big nuthouse of confusion on account of it. Let them at the office post a telegram to Putim, for the Station Chief to come tomorrow to Písek. He will then knock that "astounding event", about which he writes at the beginning of his report, out of his head already.

"Which regiment have you run away from?" the Captain welcomed Švejk.

"From no regiment."

The Captain took a look at Švejk and saw in his placid face such a measure of being carefree that he asked: "How did you come by the uniform?"

"Every soldier, when he musters after being drafted, gets a uniform," answered Švejk with a slight smile, "I serve with the 91st Regiment, and not only have I not run away from my regiment, but just **the other way around**."

He rendered the words 'the other way around' with such stress, that the Captain put an aggrieved expression on his face and asked: "How so the other way around?"

"That is a thing tremendously simple," confided Švejk, "I am on the way to my regiment, I am looking for it, and not running away from it. I don't wish for anything else except to get as early as possible to my regiment. I am already all nervous on account of it, that apparently I'm increasing the distance between myself and České Budějovice, as I think, that there is waiting for me the whole regiment there. Mister Station Chief in Putim was showing me on the map, that Budějovice is to the South, and instead he turned me to the North."

The Captain waved his hand, as if he wanted to say: He commits even worse things than turning people to the North.

"So then you can't find your regiment," he said, "you went out looking for it?"

Švejk explained the whole situation to him. He named Tábor and all the places, through which he walked to Budějovice: Milevsko — Květov — Vráž — Malčín — Čížová — Sedlec — Horažďovice — Radomyšl — Putim — Štěkno — Strakonice — Volyň — Dub — Vodňany — Protivín — and again Putim.

With tremendous enthusiasm Švejk recounted his struggle with fate, how he wanted by the power of life itself, disregarding obstacles, to get to his 91st Regiment in Budějovice and how all his exertion was in vain.

He was speaking inflamed with passion and the Captain was

mechanically drawing with a pencil on paper the vicious circle, from which the good soldier Švejk couldn't get out of, when he set out on the way to his regiment.

"That was a Herculean[111] job," he said at last, when with fondness he was lending an ear to Švejk's lively, detailed description of how he regretted, that he had not been able for so long to get to the regiment, "you must had been a mighty spectacle, when you were meandering round Putim."

"It could have been decided back then already," remarked Švejk, "if it weren't for that mister Station Chief in that hapless nest. He didn't even ask me at all for either my name, or regiment and all of it seemed to him somehow very odd. He should have had me escorted to Budějovice and at the garrison they would have told him already, whether I'm that Švejk, who is searching for his regiment, or some suspicious human being. Today I could have already been at my regiment for two days and could have been carrying out my military duties."

"Why didn't you alert them in Putim, that it was a mistake?"

"Because I saw, that it was pointless to be talking to him. Old pubkeeper Rampa[112] in Vinohrady[113] already used to say, when somebody wanted to leave owing him, that sometimes there comes upon a man such a moment, when he's as deaf to everything as a tree stump."

The Captain was not deliberating long and merely beheld the thought, that such a circular trip by a man, who wants to get to his regiment, is a token of the deepest human degeneration, so he had them at the office peck out on a typewriter, minding all the rules and beauties of official composition:

To the glorious Command of the I&R Infantry
Regiment No. 91 in České Budějovice

In the attachment is being presented Josef Švejk, according to the claim of the one in question being an infantryman of the said Regiment, detained on the basis of his own statement in Putim, District Písek, by the State Police Station, suspected of desertion. The same declares, that he had departed to his above noted Regiment. The one being presented is of a smaller husky figure, symmetrical face and nose with blue eyes, with no special mark. In the attachment BI is being sent a bill for the meals provided to the one in question, for the kind transfer of funds to the account of Ministry Of Land Defense with the request for a confirmation of receipt of the one being presented. In the attachment CI is being sent for your confirmation a list of Government Issue items, which the detained had on his person at the time of his having been intercepted.

The trip from Písek to Budějovice by train passed for Švejk smartly and quickly. His companion was a young State Police cop, a rookie, who was not letting his eyes off Švejk and had a horrible fear of Švejk running away from him. During the whole journey he was attempting to solve a hard challenge: If I had to go now and do the number one or number two, how would I do it?"

He found the resolution in that Švejk had to act as his chaperone.

During the whole trip with Švejk from the railroad station[114] to the Marian garrison[115] in Budějovice he kept his eyes convulsively fixated on Švejk, and whenever they were approaching any street corner or intersection, as if in passing he was telling Švejk, how many live cartridges they're issued for each escort, to which Švejk would answer, that he's convinced, that no State cop would shoot at anybody in the street, lest he cause some tragedy.

The State cop was arguing with him and that's how they got into the garrison.

On duty at the garrison for the second day already was Senior Lieutenant Lukáš. He was sitting, while having no premonition at all, at the desk in the office, when they brought in to him Švejk with papers.

"I dutifully report, *Senior Lieutenant*, Sir, that I am here again," saluted Švejk, having a festive countenance.

Present during the whole scene was Ensign Koťátko, who would later relay, that after Švejk mustered, Senior Lieutenant Lukáš jumped up, grabbed his head and fell on his back on top of Koťátko, and that when they revived him, Švejk, who all that time kept giving him the military honors, repeated: "I dutifully report, *Senior Lieutenant*, Sir, that I am here again!" And here the completely pale Senior Lieutenant Lukáš took with his trembling hand the papers concerning Švejk, signed, requested of all, that they exit, that he said to the State policeman, that it was good like that, and that he closed himself with Švejk in the office.

With that ended Švejk's budějovická anabasis. It is certain, that if Švejk were afforded freedom of movement, that he would have made it walking to Budějovice on his own. If, as was the case, the authorities were able to gloat, that it had been they who transported Švejk to his duty station, it is simply a mistake. Given his energy and undaunted zest for fighting, the intervention by the authorities was in this case tantamount to throwing sticks under Švejk's feet as obstacles to his progress.

*

Švejk and Senior Lieutenant Lukáš were looking into each other's eyes.

The Lieutenant's eyes were glowing with something terrible and horrifying and desperate, and Švejk was looking at the Senior Lieutenant tenderly, with eyes full of love as if looking at a lost and found again girl lover.

In the office it was as quiet as in an empty church. From the hallway on the other side of the wall one could hear, as somebody is pacing there. Some conscientious one-year volunteer, who stayed home on account of a cold, which was discernible in his voice, was mumbling that, which he was learning to repeat by heart: how are members of the Imperial House supposed to be received at fortresses. One could hear clearly: "*As soon as the highest lordship approaches the immediate vicinity of the fort, are the cannons at all the bastions and earthworks fired, the Command Major with the sword in hand approaches the horse and thus rides on.*"

"Shut your trap in there," screamed into the hallway the Senior Lieutenant, "remove yourself far away from here and join all the demons there. If you have a fever, then stay lying in bed at home."

One could hear, how the diligent one-year volunteer was putting some distance behind himself, and arriving here like a whispering echo from the end of the hallway was the mumbling: "*At the very moment, when the Commanding Officer salutes, the firing of the cannons is to be repeated, which happens for the third time as the highest lordship is dismounting.*"

And again the Senior Lieutenant and Švejk kept on silently watching one another, until at last Senior Lieutenant Lukáš said with rough irony: "I extend to you a pleasant welcome, Švejk, to České Budějovice. He who is to be hanged, will not drown. They have already issued an arrest warrant for you and tomorrow you're at the *Regimental Report*. I will not be getting angry with you anymore. I have had more than enough grief with you and I've run out of patience. When I think, that I managed to live with an imbecile like you for so long…"

He started pacing the office. "No, it's horrible. Now I am amazed, that I haven't shot you dead. What would have happened to me? Nothing. I would had been freed of the charges. Are you getting it?"

"I dutifully report *Senior Lieutenant*, Sir, that I'm totally getting it."

"Don't start again, Švejk, with your bullshit, or something will really happen. Finally we'll plug up your vein. You have been escalating your stupidity infinitely, until it all catastrophically cracked.

Senior Lieutenant Lukáš wrung his hands: "You are finished and reached your last 'amen', Švejk." He returned to his desk and wrote several lines on a piece of paper, hollered at the sentry outside the office and ordered him to take Švejk to the prison guard and to hand the piece of paper over to him.

They escorted Švejk across the courtyard and the Senior Lieutenant not hiding his pleasure was watching, how the prison guard unlocked the door with a black and yellow sign plate on it reading Regimental Brig, how Švejk is disappearing behind that door and how in a while the prison guard exited that door alone.

"Give thanks to God," the Senior Lieutenant thought to himself aloud, "he's there already."

In the dark space of the Marian garrison hunger pit was Švejk welcomed cordially by a fat one-year volunteer, lying about on a straw mattress. He was the only prisoner and was all by himself bored a second day in a row already. To Švejk's question, why he is sitting there doing time, he answered, that on account of a trifle. He gave a full measure of head slaps by mistake to some officer of the artillery in the night in the arcade at the square[116] in a state of drunkenness. Actually, it was not a full measure of slaps, he only knocked the cap off his head. The way it happened was, that the officer of artillery was standing in the night under the arcade and apparently was waiting for some prostitute. The officer's back was turned toward him, and to the one-year volunteer it appeared as if he were an acquaintance of his, one-year-timer Materna, František by his first name.

"He is just such a little peewee," he was telling Švejk, "and so I crept up on him nicely from behind and knocked his cap off and said: "*Hi*, Franci!" And that idiotic guy immediately started whistling to summon a patrol and that's who took me away. — "It could be," allowed the one-year volunteer, "that in the tussle a couple of head slaps fell, but that, I think, does not change anything in the matter, because it is a blatant mistake. He himself admits that I said: "*Hi*, Franci," and the name he was christened with is Anton. That is totally clear. Perhaps the one thing that could be detrimental to me is, that I had run away from the hospital, and if the sick-book thing breaks out to light… — When I was drafted, that is to say," he kept relaying, "then I first rented a room in town and was trying to get a hold of rheumatism for myself. Three times in succession I got blasted and then I lay down in a ditch on the edge of the town, when it was raining, and took my shoes off. It wasn't helping. So in winter I would bathe at night in the Malše[117] all week, and I achieved the exact opposite. Pal, I had become so hardy, that I withstood lying in the snow in the courtyard of the building, where I lived, all night, and my feet were in the morning, when the people who made their home there would wake me up, so warm, as if I were wearing plush slippers. Would that I had at least gotten angina, but all along nothing would come of it. Yeah, I couldn't get even the stupid clap. Daily I'd go to the Port Arthur[118], some colleagues already got inflammation of the testicles, they had to cut their belly open, and I just kept on being immune. Bad, unchristian kind of luck, pal. Until once, let me tell you, At the Rose[119] I made an acquaintance with a cripple from Hluboká. That one told me to come to him one Sunday for a visit, that the next day my legs would be bloated full like watering cans. He had at home both the needle and the syringe, and I really barely made it walking home from Hluboká. That dear old soul did not deceive me. So at last I did have my muscle rheumatism after all. Right away into the hospital, and already life was a breeze. And then lady luck still gave me a smile for the second time. To Budějovice there was transferred a guy who had become my brother-in- law, doctor Masák from Žižkov, and it's him I must thank for having managed to hang on at the hospital for so long. He would have made it with me all the way to the Medical Supervisory Board, when I spoiled it so with that unfortunate sick-book! The idea was good, remarkable. I got my hands on a large book, stuck a label on it, on which I drew 'Sick-book of the 91st Reg.' The sections, their headings and everything was alright. I would enter fictitious names in there, degrees of fever, illnesses, and every day from midday, after the doctor's visitation rounds, I would brazenly go with the book under my arm to town. At the gate were keeping watch Land Defense soldiers, so that even on that end I was totally secure. I'd show them the book and they even saluted me. Then I went to see an acquaintance official of the Tax Collection Office, there I changed into civilian clothes and went to a pub, where in the company of people we knew we carried on various highly treasonous talks. After that I was so brazen, that I would not even change into civilian clothes and would go in uniform from pub to pub in the town. I would return to my bed at the hospital[120] only toward morning, and when in the night a patrol stopped me, I'd point to my sick-book of the 91st Regiment and nobody would ask me anything anymore. At the gate of the hospital again without any words I would point to the book and somehow always managed to get to bed. The degree of my brass was rising so high, that I thought, that nobody could do anything to me, until the fateful mistake took place in the night at the square under the arcade, a mistake, which clearly proved, that all trees don't grow sky high, pal. Pride precedes the fall. All fame is field grass. Icarus[121] singed his wings. Man would like to be a giant, and is shit, pal. One must not trust in accidents and has to slap oneself morning and night with a reminder, that there's never enough caution, and too much of anything, is detrimental. After bacchanalia and orgies there always arrives a moral hangover. That is a law of nature, dear friend. When I contemplate, that I mucked up for myself the Medical Supervisory Board, and the Discharge Review Board. That I could have been *unfit for service in the field*. Such a great protector on the inside! I could have been lying around at an office somewhere at the Augmenting Reserve Command Headquarters, but my lack of caution tripped me."

The one-year volunteer ended his confessions ceremoniously:

"Even Carthage had its reckoning, they turned Nineveh[122] into ruins, dear friend, but hold your head up! Don't let them think, that when they send me to the front, that I will fire a single shot. *Regimental report*! Expulsion from the school! Long live Imperial & Royal cretinism! Like I will sit in a school for them and pass exams. Cadet, *ensign*, *lieutenant*, *senior lieutenant*. I'll shit a pile for them! *Officer school*[123]. *Dealing with those very pupils who must repeat one whole year!* Military paralysis. Is a *rifle* carried on the left or the right shoulder? How many stars does a Sergeant have? *Rosters of reservists! — God in heaven*, there's nothing to smoke, pal! Don't you want me to teach you how to spit at the ceiling? Look, it's done like this. Think of something while doing it, and your wish will come true. If you like to drink beer, I can recommend excellent water over there in the pitcher. If you're hungry and should want to have a tasty dish to eat, I recommend the Burghers' Club. I can also recommend to you to write poems to shorten the long while. I have already composed an epic:

> Is the prison guard at home? Boy, he's sleeping placidly,
> here is the army's center of gravity,
> before the new order comes again from Vienna,
> saying that lost is the whole battlefield.
> Here against the intrusion of the enemy
> of bunks he's building a barricade.
> From his mouth while laboring so will issue,
> when he succeeds:
> 'The Empire of Austria will not perish,
> glory to the homeland, to the Emperor!'

"You see, my friend," continued the fat one-year volunteer, "then have somebody say, that respect for our dear Imperial establishment among the people is disappearing. An imprisoned man, who has nothing to smoke and for whom a Regimental Report is awaiting, presents the most beautiful case of affectionate inclination toward the throne. In his songs he pays homage to his broader homeland, threatened on all sides with a thrashing. He is bereft of freedom, but from his mouth issue verses of intrepid loyalty. Morituri te salutant, caesar! The dead are saluting you, Emperor, but the prison guard is a shameless rube. You sure have a nice pack of helpers at your service. The day before yesterday I gave him five crowns, for him to buy cigarettes for me, and he, the louse, told me this morning that smoking is forbidden here, that he'd have difficulties on account of it and that he'd return the five crowns to me when *pay-day* comes. Yes, my friend, I don't believe or trust anything nowadays. The best slogans have been perverted. Thou shall steal from prisoners! And on top of it that guy keeps singing along all day. *'Where people sing, there lay down safely, bad people don't have songs!'* The scoundrel, the street punk, the villain, the traitor!"

The one-year volunteer posed now a question to Švejk about his guilt.

"Were looking for the regiment?" he said, "that's a pretty trek. Tábor, Milevsko, Květov, Vráž, Malčín, Čížová, Sedlec, Horažďovice, Radomyšl, Putim, Štěkno, Strakonice, Volyň, Dub, Vodňany, Protivín, Putim, Písek, Budějovice. A thorny path. You too will be tomorrow at the Regimental Report? Brother, in the execution yard we'll then meet. Then our Colonel Schröder surely has again great joy. You cannot even imagine, how Regimental scandals affect him. He flies around in the yard like a bowser that lost its mind and sticks out his tongue like a half-dead mare. And that talking of his, the reprimands, and how at the same time he's spitting round himself, like a drooling camel. And that speech of his having no end in sight and you're waiting and expecting that the whole Marian garrison must tumble down any minute. I know him well, because I had been at such a Regimental Report once already. I was drafted and joined the military in high boots and on my head I had a top hat, and since the tailor had not delivered the uniform to me on time, I came to the training ground[124] behind the one-year-timer school in those high boots and the bowler and I stood myself in the rank and marched with them on the left flank. Colonel Schröder came directly after me riding a horse and it's a wonder he did not knock me down to the ground. '*Damn it'*, he screamed, so that it could certainly be heard in Šumava[125], '*what are you doing here, you civilian?'* I answered him politely, that I was a one-year volunteer and that I was participating in the training. And you should have seen it. He exercised his rhetorical skills for half an hour, and only after that he noticed, that I was saluting with a top hat on my head. At that point he only yelled out, that tomorrow I was to go to the Regimental Report, and in rabid anger he rode the horse hard all the way to God-knows-where like a wild horseman, and galloping returned again, started screaming anew, raged, beat his chest and ordered that I be immediately removed from the training ground and put in the *main guardhouse*. During the Regimental Report he slammed me with a confinement to the barracks for two weeks, had me dressed in impossible rags from the storehouse, threatened me with ripping off the stripes. — 'One-year volunteer', was acting out the idiot Colonel aloud, 'is something exalted, they are embryos of fame, military ranks, heroes. One-Year Volunteer Wohltat, having been after an exam he passed promoted to Sergeant, volunteered for the front and captured fifteen enemies and when handing them over he was ripped apart by a grenade. Then five minutes later came an order, that One-

Year Volunteer Wohltat was promoted to the rank of cadet. Even you would have waiting for you such a brilliant future, rise through the ranks, decorations, your name would be entered into the golden book of the Regiment.'"

The one-year volunteer spat: "You see, friend, what dumb beasts get to be born under the sun. I'll piss on the one-year volunteer stripes and all their privileges: 'You, mister one-year volunteer, are a cattle beast.' How nice that sounds: 'You, mister, are a cattle beast,' and not just the impertinent: 'Hey you, you're a cattle beast'. And after you die you will get the signum laudis[126], or the large silver medal. I&R suppliers of corpses with stars and without stars. How much happier every ox is. Him they kill at a slaughter and don't drag him beforehand to the training ground and *field target-practice*."

The fat one-year volunteer rolled over to the other straw mattress and continued: "It is certain that all this must snap one day and that it cannot go on forever. Try pumping fame into a pig, so in the end it will regardless blow up on you. If I were riding to the front, then I would write on the military transport train:

> By human limbs we'll make fertile the field.
> *Eight horses or forty-eight men*[127]."

The door opened and the prison guard appeared, carrying a quarter of a portion of the commissary ration bread for the two of them and fresh water.

Not even getting up off the straw mattress, the one-year volunteer addressed the prison guard with this speech: "How noble it is and beautiful to visit the prisoners, Saint Agnes[128] of the 91st Regiment! Be thou welcome, angel of the good works, whose heart is filled with mercy. Thou art laden with baskets of food and drinks, in order to alleviate our grief. Never shall we forget the good deed visited upon us by thee. Thou art a brilliantly shining apparition in this dark prison of ours."

"At the Regimental Report you'll be through with your jesting," grumbled the prison guard.

"Just quit bristling up, hamster," answered from the bunk the one-year volunteer, "tell us rather how would you do it, if you were to lock up ten one-year timers? Stop that dumb stare, you keeper of the Marian garrison keys. — You'd lock up twenty and ten you'd let go, you gopher. Jesusmaria, were I to be the Minister of Military

Affairs, you'd see the service time I'd give you! Do you know the axiom, that the angle of incidence equals the angle of reflection? Just one thing I beg of you: Indicate and give me a firm point in the universe, and I will lift up the whole Earth with you included, you dumb stuffing."

The prison guard bugged his eyes out, shuddered, and slammed the door.

"Mutually supportive association for doing away with prison guards," said the one-year volunteer, dividing justly the portion of bread into two parts, "in accordance with article 16 of prison regulations the inmates of garrison prisons are until sentencing to be provided with military chow, but here reigns the law of the prairie: whoever devours the prisoners' portion first."

He and Švejk were both sitting on the bunk, gnawing the commissary ration bread.

"In the prison guard one can see the best," continued his reflections the one-year volunteer, "how the army service turns man brutal. Certainly our prison guard, before he entered army service, was a young man with ideals, a blond cherub, gentle and sensitive toward everybody, a defender of the unfortunate, for whom he would always stand up in brawls over a girl at the village patron saint festival in his native neck of the woods. There is no doubt, that he was esteemed by all, but today… My God, how I'd like to whack him across his mug, batter his head against the bunk, drop him headlong into the latrine. Even that is, my friend, evidence of the mind turning absolutely brutal while in the military trade."

He broke out into a song:

She was not afraid of even the demon,
just then met her an artillery man…

"Dear friend," he kept on telling, "if we observe it all from the point on the scale of our dear monarchy, we reach irreversibly the conclusion, that it's in the same shape as the uncle of Puškin[129], of whom he wrote, that there was only one thing left to do, since the uncle was as good as a carcass,

to be sighing and thinking to oneself,
when is the demon going to take you!"

Once again was heard the clatter of the key in the door and the prison guard in the hallway was lighting up a little kerosene lamp.

"A ray of light in the darkness," was screaming the one-year volunteer, "enlightenment is penetrating the army. Good night, mister prison guard, say hello to all the NCOs and would that you dream something nice. Perhaps about how you have already given me back the five crowns, which I gave you toward a purchase of cigarettes and which you spent drinking to my health. Sweet dreams, you monster!"

One could hear, that the prison guard was mumbling something about tomorrow's Regimental Report.

"Alone again," said the one-year volunteer, "I now dedicate the moments before sleep to an explication and lecture, on how daily the zoological knowledge among the NCOs and officers is growing: To thrash out new, live materiel of war and militarily conscientious and mature morsels for the cannon gullets, to that end are needed thorough studies of natural sciences or the book Sources of Economic Prosperity, issued by the Kočí[130] publishing house, where on every page there appear the words cattle, pig, swine. As of late we witness however, that our advanced military circles are implementing new terms for the rookie soldiers. At the 11th Company Sergeant Althof uses the word Engadin goat[131]. Lance Corporal Müller, German teacher from Kašperské Hory[132], calls the rookies Czech stinkbags, Quartermaster Sondernummer uses oxen frog, Yorkshire[133] boar, and promises while doing it, that he'll flay and tan each recruit's skin. He does so all the while with such expert knowledge, as if he hailed from a family of taxidermists. All military superiors are attempting thereby to instill love for one's homeland by special aids, such as hollering and dancing round the recruits, a war cry, reminiscent of savages in Africa[134] getting ready to skin an innocent antelope or roast a haunch off a missionary having been prepared to be eaten. Germans however are left out of it. If Quartermaster Sondernummer says something about *swine pack*, he'll always add to it, very quickly *the Czech*, so that the Germans would not get offended and think it related to them. All the while all the NCOs of the 11th Company are rolling their eyes like a pitiful dog, who because of his lack of self-control swallows a sponge soaked in oil and can't get it out of his throat. Once I overheard a conversation of Lance Corporal Müller with Sergeant Althof, having to do with the next step in the training of the Home Defense members. In this conversation there were conspicuous words like *a couple of ear slaps*. I thought originally, that something happened among them, that the German military unity is ripping apart, but I erred remarkably. It had to do really only with soldiers. ‘When such a Czech pig,’ offered his lesson genially Sergeant Althof, ‘will not learn even after thirty *on your belly* to stand straight as a candle, it is not enough just to slap him a couple of times across the mug. Poke him nicely in the belly with one fist and with the other knock his cap down over his ears, say: *About face!*, and as he turns, kick him in the butt and you’ll see, how he’ll be straightening himself up ready to go, and how *Ensign* Dauerling will be laughing.’ — Now, my friend, I must tell you something about Dauerling,” continued the one-year volunteer, “about him talk the recruits at the 11th Company the same way, like some forlorn grandma on a farm near the Mexican border spinning myths about some famous Mexican bandit. Dauerling has the reputation of a cannibal, anthropophagus of Australian tribes, who devour members of other tribes having fallen into their hands. His life’s course has been superb. Not long after birth his nanny holding him fell and little Konrad Dauerling banged his little head, so that till this day a certain flattened surface can be observed on his head, as if a comet rammed into the North Pole[135]. All doubted, that he could amount to anything, wondered whether he would withstand the concussion, only his father, a colonel, was not losing hope and kept insisting, that it could not hamper him in any way, because, as was naturally understood, young Dauerling, once he grew a bit, would devote himself to the military vocation. Young Dauerling after a horrific struggle with the four grades of lower reálka[136] which he attended by taking private lessons, while his tutor at home prematurely turned gray and idiotic and another wanted to jump off the Saint Stephen’s[137] steeple in Vienna out of desperation, came to the Hainburg Cadet School[138]. In the Caddy they never cared about previous education, because it was mostly not suitable for Austrian active duty officers. The military ideal was seen only in playing at little soldiers. Being educated impacts only ennobling of the soul, and that can in the military have no use. The coarser the officer corps, the better.

“The Caddy pupil Dauerling did not excel even in those subjects in which he was sort of proficient. Even at the Caddy there were discernible traces of the fact, that Dauerling had in youth banged his little head.

"His answers during the exams clearly spoke of the tragedy and were outstanding for such stupidity, and were viewed as truly classic for their deep stupidity and confusion, that the Caddy professors would not call him by any other name than *our good idiot*. His idiocy cast such blinding light, that the greatest hope was, that after several decades he would make it into the Theresian Military Academy[139] or Ministry of Military Affairs.

"When the war broke out and they made all the little young cadets *ensigns*, Konrad Dauerling also made it onto the roster of the ones promoted at Hainburg and that is how he ended up with the 91st Regiment."

The one-year volunteer took a breath and kept on telling: "There was published at the expense of the Ministry of Military Affairs a book *Drilling or Upbringing*, reading through which Dauerling gathered, that the soldiers' due was horrifying dread. That according to the degrees of horrifying dread the training also met with success. And in this work of his he always had success. The soldiers, so that they didn't have to hear his hollering, would by whole platoons report to sick call, which however was not crowned with success. He, who'd report sick, got three days of *intensified*[140]. Needless to say, you know what *intensified* is. They run and chase you on the training ground all day and for the night lock you up to boot. So it happened, that in Dauerling's company nobody was on the sick list. The *Company patients* were sitting in the hole. Dauerling continuously preserves that nonchalant garrison tone on the training ground, beginning with the word swine and ending with a strange zoological puzzle: swine dog. All the while he is very liberal. He lets the soldiers keep the freedom to choose. He says: "What do you want, you elephant, a couple of hits landing on your nose or three days of *intensified*?' In case somebody chose *intensified*, he still received on top of it two hits in the nose, to which Dauerling adds this explanation: 'You coward, you're scared for your snout, so what are you going to do then, when the heavy artillery lets loose?'

"Once, when he busted one recruit's eye, he expressed himself thusly: '*Ha, why drag it out and make it a long story with the guy, he's gotta croak one way or another.*' That's what used to say also Field Marshall Konrad von Hötzendorf[141]: '*The soldiers must croak one way or another.*'

"A favored and impressively effectual means of achieving an end of Dauerling's is, that he musters the Czech contingent with his lecture, in which he speaks of Austria's military tasks, while explaining the general principles of military training, from handcuffs all the way to hanging and having them shot. At the beginning of winter, before I went to the hospital, we were training on the training ground next to the 11th Company, and when there was a *rest break*, Dauerling gave a speech to his Czech recruits:

"'I know,' he started, 'that you're hoodlums and that what is needed is to knock all the foolery out of your heads for you. With the Czech language you won't make it even to under the gallows. Our highest military lord is also a German. Are you listening? *Heavenlypraises, on your bellies!*

"Everybody gets *on their bellies*, and as they're lying down, Dauerling is walking in front of them and exercises his rhetorical skills:

"*On your belly* will remain *on your belly*, even if you were in that mud, you pack of gangsters, until you see pigs fly. *On your belly* existed in ancient Rome already, back then everyone from age seventeen through sixty had to muster in and the service was in the field for thirty years and they did not wallow in the garrison like pigs. There was back then also one universal army language and command. The Roman officer lords would otherwise have had to look into it and made an end of it, should their men have been speaking *Etruscan*. I also want, that you all answer in German, and not in that messy gibberish of yours. See, how nice it is for you to be lying in the mud, and now think for a second, that one of you would not like to be lying down anymore and that he'd stand up. What would I do? I would rip his piehole up to his ears, because that is insubordination, mutiny, resistance, culpable contravention of duties of a regular soldier, transgression of order and discipline, disregard for service regulations in general, from which follows, that the rope awaits such a guy and *the loss of the right to have respect and attention of his comrades in ranks.*"

The one-year volunteer became silent for a moment and then continued, when apparently during the break he outlined his exposition on the theme of the situation at the garrison:

"It was during the tenure of Captain Adamička[142], he was a man absolutely apathetic. When sitting in his office, there he usually stared into empty space like a silent lunatic and had such an expression on his face, as if he were trying to say: You may gobble me up, flies, if you please. During the Battalion Report only God knows what he was thinking about. Once there was a soldier from the 11th Company reporting a complaint, that *Ensign* Dauerling called him a Czech pig in the street in the evening. He was a book-binder in civilian life, a conscious worker for the national cause.

"'So that's how things are,' said Captain Adamička softly, because he always spoke very softly, 'that's what he told you in the evening in the street. It needs to be determined, whether you had permission to leave the garrison. *Fall out!*'

"When some time passed, Captain Adamička had the complaint registrant called in.

"'It's been determined,' he said so softly again, 'that you had permission to be away from the garrison that day until ten o'clock in the evening. And that is why you will not be punished. *Fall out!*'

"It was then being said about this Captain Adamička, that he had a sense for justice, dear friend, so they sent him into the field and in his place came Major Wenzl[143]. And he was a son of a demon, when it came to ethnic baiting and manhunts, and he sure nipped *Ensign* Dauerling's bud. Major Wenzl has a Czech woman for a wife and his biggest fear is the fear of nationality disputes. When years ago he served as a captain in Kutná Hora[144] at one time while inebriated at a hotel he cussed the head waiter, saying that he's filthy Czech rabble. Let me also bring to your attention at the same time, that when in company, Major Wenzl spoke exclusively in Czech, just as he did in his own household, and that his sons were studying in Czech. The word was uttered, and right away it was in the local newspaper and some deputy was interpellating[145] Major Wenzl's behavior at the hotel in the Viennese parliament. Major Wenzl had great difficulties on account of it, because it happened just at the time of the military's proposal being up for a vote in the parliament, and now such a one as the drunken Captain Wenzl from Kutná Hora mucked it up for them.

"Captain Wenzl found out afterward, that who got him into hot water was *Cadet Officer-Deputy* of the One-Year Volunteer Corps Zítko. It was he who put the stuff about him in the paper, because between him and Captain Wenzel there reigned great animosity since the time, when at a social gathering in the presence of Captain Wenzel, Zítko got into considering, that it was enough to take a look around God's nature, observe the clouds covering the horizon, and see how the mountains reach up high above it and how the waterfall in the woods roars, how the birds sing.

"'It's enough,' *Cadet Officer-Deputy* Zítko was saying, 'to ponder, what any captain is next to the reverend nature. The same zero as any *cadet officer-deputy*.'

"Because all the military lords were blasted on that occasion, Captain Wenzel wanted to whip the unfortunate philosopher Zítko like a horse, and this enmity was intensifying and the Captain browbeat and hectored Zítko, wherever he could, that much more, because *Cadet Officer-Deputy* Zítko's statement became a byword.

"'What is Captain Wenzl next to the reverend nature?' was known all over in Kutná Hora.

"'I'll drive that hoodlum to suicide,' Captain Wenzl used to say, but Zítko left for civilian life and kept studying philosophy. From that time dates Major Wenzel's demonic fury against young officers. Not even a lieutenant could rest assured he'd be spared his rampage and rage. Not to even speak of cadets and ensigns.

"'I'll crush them like bed-bugs,' says major Wenzel, and woe to the *ensign*, who would drive somebody on account of some trifle to the Battalion Report. For Major Wenzel the only thing that matters is a big and horrible transgression, as when somebody falls asleep at the powder-magazine during his watch or when he commits something even more horrible, when for example a soldier is climbing at night over the wall of the Marian garrison and falls asleep on the top of the wall, lets himself be caught by the *Land Defense*, or the artillery patrol at night, to make the story short, commits such terrible things, that he embarrasses the Regiment.

"'Forchristhelord,' I heard him hollering once in the corridor, 'so the *Land Defense* patrol caught him for the third time already. Put him, the bestial creature, immediately into the hole, and the man must be sent away from the regiment, somewhere to a supply company, in order to haul manure. And he didn't even start a brawl with them! Those are not soldiers, but street sweeps. Let him feed only the day after tomorrow, take his straw mattress away from him and shove him into the solitary, and no blanket for that sod-lynx.'

"Now imagine, friend, that right away after his arrival here the numskull *Ensign* Dauerling drove one man to the Battalion Report, that he deliberately did not salute him, when Dauerling was riding in a fiacre across the square on a Sunday afternoon with some pampered miss! At that time during the Battalion Report, as the NCOs would relay, it was a God-awful mess. The quartermaster of the battalion office ran away as far as the corridor with the official papers in his hand and Major Wenzl was screaming at Dauerling:

"'Don't you dare, *heaven's thunderstorm*, I forbid it! Do you know, mister *Ensign*, what a Battalion Report is? A Battalion Report is no *pig roast banquet*. How could he see you, when you were riding like mad across the square? Don't you know, that you yourself taught, that military honors are accorded to officers, whom we meet, and that does not mean, that a soldier is to crick his neck like a crow, in order to find mister *Ensign* joyriding through the square. Be quiet, please. The *Battalion Report* is a very solemn institution. If the soldier has already stated to you, that he did not see you, because just then on the promenade he was according military honors to me, facing me, you understand, Major Wenzel, and that he could not be looking back at the fiacre, which was carrying you, I think, that it has to be believed. Next time please refrain from bothering me with such trifles.'

"Since that time Dauerling has changed."

The one-year volunteer yawned: "We have to have a good sleep before the Regimental Report. I only wanted to tell you at least in part, what it is like overall at the Regiment. Colonel Schröder does not like Major Wenzel, he is an altogether strange spider. Captain Ságner[146], who is charged with taking care of the One-Year Volunteer School, sees in Schröder the right type of a soldier, although Colonel Schröder does not fear anything as much, as were he to go into the field. Ságner is a slick guy anointed with all the potions of deceit and just like Schröder does not like reserve officers. He says about them, that they are civilian stenches. One-year-timers he views as wild animals, which need to be made into military machines, have stars sewn on and be sent in the field so that they would be clubbed into annihilation in the stead of the pedigreed and noble active officers who have to be saved to propagate the breed. — Altogether", said the one-year volunteer, burrowing under the blanket and out of sight, "everything in the army reeks with rot. As of now the bug-eyed masses have not yet come to. With their eyes bulging they are going to let themselves be chopped up into noodles and then, when the little marble hits him, he will only whisper: Mommy... Heroes don't exist, but slaughter cattle and butchers in the General Staffs do. And in the end they all will rise up and that will be a pretty rumble. Long live the army! Good Night!"

The one-year volunteer fell silent and then he started to wiggle under the blanket and asked:

"Are you sleeping, my friend?"

"I'm not," answered Švejk on the other bunk, "I'm thinking."

"What are you thinking about, my friend?"

"About a large silver medal for bravery that a cabinet maker from Vávrova street[147] in Královské Vinohrady got, someone named Mlíčko, because he was the first, who in his Regiment had at the beginning of the war his leg ripped off by a grenade. He got an artificial leg and started bragging everywhere about his medal and that he was altogether the first and the very first war cripple in the Regiment.

"One time he came into the Apollo[148] in Vinohrady and there he got into a dispute with the butchers from the slaughterhouse, who in the end tore off his artificial leg and whacked him over the head with it. The one, who tore it off, did not know that it was an artificial leg, so he passed out from the shock. At the police station they attached the leg again for Mlíček, but since that time Mlíček got angry at his large silver medal for bravery and went to a pawn shop and there they detained him, the medal included. He had difficulties on account of it, and there is some kind of a special tribunal for war cripples, and the sentence it passed was, that they took the silver medal from him and then they sentenced him to lose the leg on top of it ..."

"How come?"

"It's tremendously simple. One day a commission came to him and informed him, that he was not worthy to wear an artificial leg, so they detached it and carried it away. — Or, also," continued Švejk, "it is tremendously funny when, the bereaved of someone, who had fallen in the war, receive all of a sudden such a medal with the note, that the medal is being loaned to them, to hang it in some significant spot. In the Božetěchova street[149] in Vyšehrad[150] one enraged father, who thought the authorities were making fun of him, hung that medal in the bathroom and a cop, who shared that bathroom on the porch with him, turned him in for high treason, so they had that poor soul jumping with pain."

"From which follows," said the one-year volunteer, "that all fame withers like grass. Now in Vienna they've published the Diary of a One-year Volunteer and in it there is this spell-binding verse in Czech translation:

There was once a strapping one-year-timer,
Who for the homeland and his king fell

And passed onto comrades an example fitting,
How for the homeland one shall fight.

Behold, they're already carrying a corpse on a gun-carriage,
Its breast the Captain decorated with an order,
Silent prayers will rise toward heaven,
For him, who for the homeland fell.

"So it seems to me," said the one-year volunteer after a short pause, "that the military spirit in us is deteriorating; I propose, dear friend, that in the darkness of the night, in the silence of our prison we strike up the song about artilleryman Jabůrek[151]. That will lift up the military spirit. But we must holler, so that it will be heard all over the Marian garrison. I propose therefore, that we stand ourselves by the door."

And in a moment such hollering could be heard coming from the pen, that the windows in the corridor rattled:

… And by the cannon he was standing
And kept on loada — loada…
And by the cannon he was standing
And kept on loading it.
A cannon ball flew roaring in,
Ripped off both his hands,
And he was standing calm,
And kept on loada — loada…
By the cannon he was standing
And kept on loading it…

In the courtyard rang out the sounds of steps and voices.

"That's the prison guard," said the one-year volunteer, "walking with him is *Lieutenant* Pelikán, who's on duty today. He is a reserve officer, my acquaintance from the Czech Club, in the civilian life he's a mathematician at an insurance company. From him we'll get cigarettes. Let's keep on hollering."

And again the sound: "And by the cannon he was standing…"

When the door opened, the prison guard, apparently upset by the presence of the on-duty officer, let them have it sharply:

"This is no animal house here."

"Pardon me," answered the one-year volunteer, "this is an

affiliate of the Rudolfinum[152], it's a benefit concert for the imprisoned. What just ended was the first number of the program: The War Symphony."

"Cut it out," said Lieutenant Pelikán feigning to be serious, "I think you know, that you are supposed to lie down at nine o'clock and not cause any noise. Your concert number can be heard all the way in the square."

"I dutifully report, mister *Lieutenant*," said the one-year volunteer, "that we had not prepared ourselves properly, and should some disharmony..."

"He does this every evening," the prison guard tried to stir him up against his enemy, "he behaves altogether in a terribly unintelligent manner."

"Please, mister *Lieutenant*," said the one-year volunteer, "I'd like to talk to you with only four eyes present. Let the prison guard wait behind the door."

When it was granted, the one-year volunteer said in a familiar manner:

"So cough up the cigarettes, Franta. — Sportky brand? And so as a *Lieutenant* you don't have anything better? For the time being I thank you. Still the matches. — Sportky," said after his departure the one-year volunteer contemptuously, "even in dire need is man to be uplifted. Smoke, friend, for a good night. Tomorrow awaits us the Last Judgment."

Before he fell asleep, the one-year volunteer did not forget to sing "Mountains, valleys and high rocks are my friends. They won't bring back, what we used to like, beloved girls..."

If the one-year volunteer used to describe Colonel Schröder in lively detail as a monster, he was mistaken, because Colonel Schröder had a partial sense of justice, which clearly emerged after those nights, when Colonel Schröder was satisfied with the company, in the midst of which he used to spend his evenings at the hotel. And if he were not satisfied?

While the one-year volunteer was delivering a crushing critique of the situation in the garrison, Colonel Schröder was sitting at the hotel in the company of officers and was listening, as Lieutenant Kretschmann, who came back from Serbia with an aching leg (a cow nudged him with its horn), was relaying, how he had been watching from the location of the staff, to which he was assigned, an attack on Serbian positions:

"Yes, now they fly out of the trenches. Along the whole length of two kilometers they're now crawling over the wire obstacles, and they are throwing themselves at the enemy. Hand grenades under the belt, masks, a rifle over the shoulder, they're ready to shoot, ready to make the strike. The bullets are whistling. There falls one soldier, jumping out of the trench, the second one falls on an earthwork thrown up in the air by an explosion, the third falls after several steps, but the bodies of comrades keep rushing forward with a hurrah, forward into the smoke and dust. And the enemy is shooting from all sides, from the trenches, from the funnel shaped holes made by grenades, and he is aiming machine guns at us. Again soldiers are falling. A platoon wants to get over to the enemy machine gun. They fall. But their buddies are already up ahead. Hurrah! There falls one officer. No longer can one hear the rifles of the infantry, something horrible is being readied. Again one whole platoon falls and one can hear the enemy machine guns: ra-ta-ta-ta-ta... He falls ...I, forgive me, can't go on, I am drunk..."

And the officer with an aching leg fell silent and kept sitting on a chair looking dull. Colonel Schröder is mercifully smiling and listening, as opposite him Captain Špíra, as if he wanted to quarrel, is banging his fist on the table and repeating something, that has no meaning and cannot be understood at all, as to what it is actually supposed to mean and what he is trying to say by it:

"Consider it well, please. We have standing at arms the Uhlans[153] of the Land Defense, Austrian Land Defensemen, Bosnian Field Riflemen, Austrian Field Riflemen, Austrian Infantrymen, Hungarian Infantrymen, Tyrolean[154] Imperial Riflemen, Bosnian Infantrymen, Hungarian Honved[155] Infantrymen, Hungarian Hussars[156], Land Defense Hussars, Ranger Cavalry, Light Dragoons[157], Uhlans, Artillerymen, Supply Train, Corps of Engineers Sappers, Ambulance Corps, Sailors. Do you understand? And Belgium[158]? The first and second wave of conscripts comprises the operational army, the third wave provides service in the back of the army..."

Captain Špíra struck his fist on the table. "The Land Defense serves the land in peacetime."

One young officer to the side was zealously trying to convince the Colonel of his own military toughness, and very loudly claimed telling his neighbor: "Tuberculars must be sent to the front, it'll do them good, and then it's better, when they fall dead while sick rather than healthy."

The Colonel was smiling, but all of a sudden his face clouded and turning to Major Wenzel he said: "I am surprised, that Senior Lieutenant Lukáš has been avoiding us; since the time, when he arrived, he has not dropped in even once to be among us."

"He composes little poems," mockingly said Captain Ságner, "he barely arrived and fell in love with Mrs. engineer Schreiter, whom he met at the theater[159]."

The Colonel gloomily glanced ahead: "It is said he can sing couplets?"

"He would entertain us much with couplets back in the Caddy school already," answered Captain Ságner, "and all the jokes he knows, one big pleasure. Why he won't come into our midst, I don't know."

The Colonel sadly shook his head: "Nowadays there isn't the genuine camaraderie among us anymore. In earlier days, I remember, each of us, officers, would try at the officers' club to contribute something to the merriment. One, as I remember, some Lieutenant Dankl, he stripped himself naked, lay on the floor, stuck the tail from a salted herring in his butt and gave us a demonstration of a mermaid. Then another one, Lieutenant Schleisner, knew how to wiggle his ears and whinny like a stallion, imitate the meowing of cats and humming of a bumble-bee. I also remember Captain Skoday. He, whenever we wanted, always brought girls to the officers' club, they were three sisters, and he had them trained like dogs. He stood them on the table and they started baring themselves in front of us keeping to the beat. He had this little baton, and he deserves all the honor, he was an excellent conductor. And the things he would do with them on the sofa! Once he had them bring a bathtub with warm water into the middle of the room and we, one after another, had to take a bath with those girls and he took photographs of us."

As he was having that remembrance Colonel Schröder was smiling blissfully.

"And the bets we were making in the tub," he continued, smacking his lips disgustingly and fidgeting in the chair, "but today? Is this any fun? Not even the couplets composer shows up. Nowadays the younger officers can't even drink. It's not yet twelve o'clock, and there are already at the table, as you can see, five who are drunk. There were times, when we would sit for two days, and the more we drank, the more sober we were, and we were guzzling ceaselessly beer, wine, liqueurs. Nowadays there's not the genuine military spirit anymore. The demons know what the reason for that is. No joke, only all those tales without end. Just listen how down there at the table they're talking about America[160]."

Coming from the other end of the table one could hear someone's serious voice: "America can't be getting itself into a war. Americans and Englishmen are ready to knife each other. America is not prepared for a war."

Colonel Schröder sighed: "That is the babbling of reserve officers. They were a demon's debt to us. A man like that was only yesterday writing somewhere in a bank or was making little paper cones and selling spice, cinnamon and shoe polish or was telling children in a school, that hunger chases the wolves out of the forests, and today he would like to consider himself equal to active duty officers, understand everything and stick his nose into everything. And when we do have active duty officers here with us, such as Senior Lieutenant Lukáš, now mister Lieutenant doesn't come into our midst."

Colonel Schröder left in a miserable mood for home, and when in the morning he woke up, his mood was even worse, because in the newspaper, which he was reading in bed, he found several times a sentence in the reports from the battlefield, that our troops were led off into positions prepared in advance already. Those were glorious days of the Austrian army, resembling, as an egg resembles an egg, the days at Šabac[161].

And with that impression stepped up at ten o'clock in the morning Colonel Schröder to perform that act, which perhaps correctly the one-year volunteer labeled the Last Judgment.

Švejk and the one-year volunteer were standing in the courtyard and were awaiting the Colonel. There were already NCOs here, the watch-duty officer, the adjutant of the Regiment and the quartermaster from the Regimental Office with files about perpetrators, for whom is waiting the ax of justice — the *Regimental Report.*

At last the Colonel with his face gloomy appeared in the retinue of Captain Ságner of the One-Year Volunteer School, nervously chopping the riding whip across the bootleg of his high boots.

Having received the report, he walked several times to the sound of grave-like silence past Švejk and the one-year volunteer, both of whom were doing *eyes right* or *eyes left,* depending on, which flank the Colonel emerged at. They were doing it with uncommon thoroughness, so that they could have unscrewed their necks loose, as it lasted a pretty while.

At last the Colonel stopped in front of the one-year volunteer, who reported: "One-year volunteer…"

"I know," said tersely the Colonel, "an outcast of the one-year volunteers. What are you in civilian life? Student of classical philosophies? Then a drunken intellectual…— Mister Captain," he called out to Ságner, "bring the whole one-year volunteer school here. — It figures," he kept talking to the one-year volunteer, "his worship student of classical philosophy, with whom our kind has to be getting dirty. *About face!* I knew it. The folds on the overcoat are not in order. As if he just left a slut or was wallowing in a whorehouse. I will, sonny, make mincemeat out of you and scatter it all over."

The one-year volunteer school stepped into the courtyard.

"Fall into square formation!" ordered the Colonel. They enclosed the ones being judged and the Colonel in a tight square.

"Take a look at this man," was roaring the Colonel, pointing his riding whip at the one-year volunteer, "guzzling booze he has spent your honor of one-year volunteers, from whom is to be raised a cadre of proper officers, who would lead the men to glory on the field of battle. But where would he lead his men, this drunkard? From pub to pub. All the rum issued for his men he'd drink up for them. Can you say anything in your defense? You can't. Look at him. Not even in his defense can he say anything, and in civilian life he studies classical philosophy. Truly, a classic case."

The Colonel pronounced the last words meaningfully at a slow speed and spat: "A classical philosopher, who in a drunken state knocks at night officers' caps off their heads. *Man*! A lucky thing, that it was just **some such** officer of the artillery."

In that last part was concentrated all the antipathy of the 91st Regiment toward the artillery in Budějovice. Woe to an artilleryman, which fell at night into the hands of a patrol from the Regiment, and the other way around. Horrible antipathy, implacable, a vendetta, blood revenge, being inherited from class year to class year, accompanied on both sides by traditional stories, how either the infantrymen tossed the artillerymen one by one into the Vltava, or the other way around. How they brawled in the Port Arthur, at the Rose and other numerous entertainment halls of the Southern Czech metropolis.

"Nevertheless," continued the Colonel, "such a thing must be punished in an unprecedented manner, the guy has to be expelled from the school of one-year volunteers, be morally annihilated. We already have enough of such intellectuals in the army. *Regimental Office!*"

The quartermaster from the Regimental Office stepped up solemnly with the files and a pencil.

Silence was reigning as if in a courtroom, where they're trying a murderer and the presiding judge lets them have it: "Hear the sentence."

And with just such a voice the Colonel pronounced: "One-Year Volunteer Marek[162] is being sentenced to 21 days *intensified* and, after having served out the sentence into the kitchen to peel potatoes."

Turning toward the one-year volunteer school, the Colonel gave an order to fall in. One could hear how they were quickly breaking into four-file formation and leaving, while the Colonel said to Captain Ságner, that they are out of sync, and to drill with them in the courtyard after noon the marching steps.

"It has to thunder, mister Captain. And one more thing. I would have almost forgotten. Tell them, that the whole one-year volunteer school has five days of confinement to the barracks, so they would never forget their former colleague, that hoodlum Marek."

And the hoodlum Marek stood next to Švejk and was wearing a countenance of total satisfaction. It could not have turned out better with him. It is decidedly better to be peeling potatoes in the kitchen, sculpting blbouny[163] and picking off a rib than to be hollering with the pants full under the tornado of enemy's fire: *"Single file! Attach bayonets!"*

Having come back from Captain Ságner, Colonel Schröder stopped in front of Švejk and looked at him attentively. Švejk's figure was represented at that moment by his full, smiling face, which was framed by big ears sticking out from under a tightly pulled down military cap. The whole amounted to an expression of absolute security and lack of knowledge of any transgression. His eyes were asking: "Have I committed, I beg you, something wrong?" His eyes were speaking: "Am I, I beg you, responsible for anything?"

And the Colonel summarized his observations in a question,

which he asked of the quartermaster from the Regimental Office: "An imbecile?"

And here the Colonel saw, how the mouth of the good-hearted face in front of him is opening.

"I dutifully report, Colonel, Sir, an imbecile," answered in the quartermaster's stead Švejk.

Colonel Schröder nodded at the adjutant and stepped to the side with him. Then they called the quartermaster and were looking through the material about Švejk.

"Ah," said Colonel Schröder, "so this is that servant of Senior Lieutenant Lukáš, who was according to his report lost to him in Tábor. I think that the gentlemen officers are to be bringing up their servants on their own. Since mister Senior Lieutenant Lukáš already chose such a notorious imbecile for a servant, let him suffer on his own with him. He has enough free time to do that, since he doesn't go anywhere. That you too have never seen him in our company? Well, so there you see. He does have enough time then, to flail his servant into shape.

Colonel Schröder stepped up to Švejk, and looking at his good-hearted face, he said: "You numskull cattle beast, you've got three days of *intensified*, and when you're done with it, report to Senior Lieutenant Lukáš."

Thus again met Švejk with the One-Year Volunteer in the Regimental brig and Senior Lieutenant Lukáš was able to be tremendously pleased, when Colonel Schröder had him called, in order to tell him: "Mister Senior Lieutenant. About a week ago, after your arrival at the Regiment, you submitted a report to me about assigning a servant, as your servant had got lost to you at the railroad station in Tábor. Because he has returned…"

"Colonel, Sir…," pleadingly spoke up Senior Lieutenant Lukáš.

"…I made up my mind," emphatically continued the Colonel, "to sit him down in the brig for three days and then I'll send him to you again…"

Senior Lieutenant Lukáš, crushed, stumbled out of the Regimental Office.

*

During the three days, which Švejk spent in the company of the One-Year Volunteer Marek, he was having a good time being well entertained. Each evening they both would stage patriotic speeches on the bunks.

In the evening, coming from the brig there was always the sound of "Preserve for us, Lord", and "Prince Eugene, *the noble knight.*" They sang through a whole line of military songs, and when the prison guard would be approaching, ringing out as a welcome for him was:

That old prison guard of ours,
He cannot die,
For him must
A demon from hell come to get.
He will come for him with a wagon,
And he'll slam him against the ground,
The demons in hell
Will stoke him into the fire and light it up well...

And above the bunk the One-Year Volunteer drew a picture of the prison guard and underneath him he wrote the lyrics of an old song:

When I'd gone to Prague for to get blood sausage,
I met an imp on the road.
It was not an imp, it was the prison guard,
Had I not fled, he would have bitten me.

And while they both were thus provoking the prison guard, just as in Seville they tease the Andalusian[164] bull with a red scarf, Senior Lieutenant Lukáš was awaiting with anxiety the moment, when Švejk would appear, to report, that he's coming back on duty.

3

ŠVEJK'S HAPPENINGS IN KIRÁLYHIDA

The 91st Regiment was moving to Bruck an der Leitha-Királyhida[165].

Just when after three days of imprisonment Švejk was to be released to freedom in three hours, he was taken along with the One-Year Volunteer to the main guardhouse and accompanied by an escort of soldiers to the railroad station.

"It's been known long since," said to him while underway the One-Year Volunteer, "that they would transfer us to Magyaria[166]. There they'll be forming marchbattalions, the soldiers will get trained to shoot in the field, they'll brawl with the Hungarians and merrily we will ride to the Carpathians. Here in Budějovice will arrive Hungarians to be stationed at the garrison and the breeds will mix. There's already this theory, that to rape girls of another nationality is the best means of protecting against degeneration. The Swedes and Spaniards were doing it during the Thirty-Year War, the French during the reign of Napoleon and now in the Budějovice region it will be the Hungarians doing it for a change and it will not be associated with raping by brute force. It'll all give over time. It will be a simple exchange. A Czech soldier will have slept with a Hungarian girl, and a wretched Czech country girl will receive by her side a Hungarian Land Defense soldier, and centuries later it will be an interesting surprise for the anthropologists, why did protruding cheek bones emerge among the people on the banks of the Malše."

"As for this reciprocal mating," remarked Švejk, "it is an altogether interesting thing. In Prague there is a negro[167] waiter Kristián[168], whose father was the Abyssinian[169] king, and he let himself be shown in Prague at Štvanice[170] in a circus. With him fell in love a teacher, who used to write little poems about shepherds and a little brook in the woods for Lada[171], she went with him to a hotel and fornicated with him, as it is referred to in the Holy Scriptures, and she was tremendously baffled, that the little boy she birthed was totally white. Yeah, but after two weeks the little boy started turning brown. He was turning browner and browner and after a month began turning black. By the time a half a year was up he was as black as his daddy, the Abyssinian king. She went with him to a dermatology disorders clinic, so that they would decolor him for her somehow, but there they told her, that it was genuine black Moorish skin and that there was nothing that could be done. So she lost her mind over it, started seeking advice in magazines, asking what worked against Moors, and they drove her away to Kateřinky[172] and the little Moor they put in an orphanage where they had him for a source of tremendous fun. Then he was apprenticed a waiter and would go dancing from one night cafe to another. There are being born nowadays after him Czech mulattoes with great success, who are no longer as colored as he is. A medical student, who used to come to The Chalice, was telling us once, that it is not so simple, though. Such mixed blood individual begets mixed blood individuals again and those are already indistinguishable from white people. But all of a sudden in some generation, he said, there emerges a negro. Imagine the nasty trouble. You marry some miss. The hussy is totally white, and all of a sudden she bears you a negro. And if nine months ago she went without you to the Varieté[173] to watch an athletic contest, where some negro[174] performed, here I think, that there would still be a bug drilling through your mind a little after all."

"The case of your negro Kristián," said the One-Year Volunteer "needs to be thought through also from the wartime point of view. Let's assume that they drafted the negro. He is a Praguer, so he belongs to the 28th Regiment. I'm sure you've heard that the Twenty Eighth crossed over to the Russians. How baffled would the Russians be, if they took for a prisoner of war also the negro Kristián. Russian newspapers would certainly be printing, that Austria is now driving into the war its colonial troops, which it does not have, that Austria has already reached for its negro reservists."

"It used to be told among the people," offered up Švejk in passing, "that Austria clearly does have colonies, somewhere in the north. Some such Land of Emperor František Josef[175]..."

"Leave it alone, boys," said one soldier from the escort, "it is very careless, to be talking nowadays of some Emperor František Josef Land. Don't name anybody and you'll do better..."

"Then take a look at the map," butted in the One-Year Volunteer, "to see that there really is a land of our most merciful grace and ruler, Emperor František Josef. According to the statistic it's all ice there and it is exported from there on ice-breakers belonging to the Prague Ice-Works[176]. This ice industry is viewed as having uncommon value and is held in uncommon esteem by foreigners, because it is an enterprise profitable, but dangerous. The greatest danger looms during the transport of the ice from the Land of Emperor František Josef across the Arctic Circle. Can you imagine that?"

The soldier from the escort growled something unclear and the sergeant accompanying the escort came nearer and listened in to a further exposition by the One-Year Volunteer, who continued seriously: "This singular Austrian colony can supply the whole Europe with ice and is a significant and outstanding national economy factor. Colonization is continuing slowly, however, because the colonists are, in part, not signing up and, in part, freeze to death. Nevertheless by adjusting the climatic conditions, in which are interested the Ministry of Trade[177] and the Foreign Affairs Ministry[17á] as well, there is hope, that the large surfaces of the icebergs will be appropriately utilized. By establishing several hotels loads of tourists will be attracted. There will be a need, however, to appropriately adjust hiking trails and routes among the ice floes and to paint tourist orientation signs on the icebergs. The only bother are the Eskimos, who prevent our local authorities from performing their work… — The guys don't want to learn German," continued the One-Year Volunteer, while the Sergeant was listening in with interest. He was an active man, in civilian life he used to be a farmhand, he was a jerk and a brute, eagerly swallowed everything, that he had no notion about, and his ideal was to serve for sup[179].

"The Ministry of Schooling[180], mister Sergeant, established for them with great outlay and sacrifices, while five builders froze to death…"

"The masons saved themselves," interrupted him Švejk, "because they warmed themselves with a lit up pipe."

"Not all did," said the One-Year Volunteer, "two had an accident, as they forgot to be puffing and the pipes went out, so they had to dig in and bury them in the ice. — But in the end the school was built after all from ice bricks and reinforced concrete, which hold together very well, but the Eskimos kindled fire all around with lumber from the disassembled commercial ships stuck frozen in the ice and achieved what they wanted. The ice, on which the school was built, melted, and the whole school even with the principal teacher and a government representative, who was supposed to be present at the sanctification of the school the next day, fell through into the sea. One could only hear, that the representative of the government, when he was already up to his neck in the water, yelled out: *God punish*

England! Now they will probably send troops there to make short order of the Eskimos. It's understood, that it will be a tough military operation dealing with them. The most detrimental to our armed forces will be the tamed polar bears."

"That's the last thing we would need," wisely remarked the Sergeant, "even without that there are already all kinds of war inventions. For example, let's take the gas masks for poisoning by gas. You pull it onto your head and you're poisoned, as they were explaining it to us in the *NCO school*."

"They are just trying to scare you like that," Švejk spoke up, "no soldier is to be afraid of anything. Even if in battle he should fall into a latrine, then he'll just lick himself off clean and keep going into *combat*, and poisonous gases everybody's used to from the barracks, when they serve fresh commissary ration bread and peas with peeled barley. But now supposedly the Russians invented something targeting the officers..."

"It will probably be special electric currents," the One-Year Volunteer added to it, "they will fuse with the little stars on the collar and those will blow up, because they're made of celluloid. It'll be again a new disaster."

Although the Sergeant was in civilian life around oxen, after all perhaps he realized, that they were laughing at him, and walked away from them to the lead of the patrol.

They were at last approaching the railroad station where the Budějovice folks were seeing off their Regiment. It had no official air to it, but the square in front of the railroad station was filled with an audience, that was awaiting the troops.

Švejk's interest was focusing on the audience of people lining the street. And as it always would be, even now it happened, that the good soldiers were walking in the back, and the ones escorted under the bayonets were first. The good soldiers will be later crammed into cattle cars, and Švejk with the One-Year Volunteer into a special arrestee car, which was always attached to military trains right behind the staff cars. In such an arrestee car there's room galore.

Švejk could not hold himself back enough, not to yell out at the crowd of the people lining the street "Nazdar!"[181] and not to wave his cap once or twice. It had such a suggestive effect, that the crowd was loudly repeating it and "Nazdar" was spreading and thundered in front of the railroad station, so that far away from here they started saying "They're coming already."

The Sergeant of the escort was all unhappy and hollered at Švejk, to keep his trap shut. But the chanting was spreading like an avalanche. The State Police cops were pushing the crowd back and were blazing a path for the escort, and the crowd kept screaming "Nazdar!" and was waving its caps and hats.

It was quite a demonstration. From the windows of a hotel across from the railroad station some ladies were waving handkerchiefs and screaming: "Heil!" Into the Czech "nazdar" was mixing the German "heil" coming even from the crowd lining the street, and some enthusiast, who used the opportunity to yell out *"Down with the Serbs!"*, had his feet tripped and they were stepping all over him a bit in an artificial press of the people.

And like an electric spark was being carried through the air: "They're coming already!"

And they were, while under the bayonets was Švejk affably waving his hand at the multitude and the One-Year Volunteer was solemnly saluting.

Thus they entered the railroad station and went to the designated military train, when the sharpshooters' band, whose bandleader was seriously confused by the unexpected demonstration, would have almost struck up the "Preserve for us, Lord." Luckily at the right moment there emerged in a black bowler hat the Chief Field Chaplain Father Lacina[182] of the 7th Cavalry Division[183] and started establishing order.

His personal history was very simple. He arrived yesterday at Budějovice, he, the terror of all officers' mess halls, insatiable mountain of a man, ever the glutton, and as if by chance he participated in a small banquet for the officers of the departing Regiment. He ate, drank for ten people, and in a more-or-less not sober state would go into the officers' mess to beg the cooks for some leftovers. He would be gobbling up bowls of gravy and dumplings, ripping like a feline predator meat off the bones and in the end worked his way through the kitchen to the rum, of which having swallowed his fill, till he was burping, he then returned to the evening farewell gathering, where he distinguished himself famously by a new round of soaking up the booze. He had a wealth of experience in it and at the 7th Cavalry Division the officers always ended up paying the shortage for him. In the morning he got the idea, that he had to be maintaining order during the departure of the first military transport trains of the Regiment, and that is why he was roving the length of the crowd lining the street, acting in such a way at the railroad station, that the officers directing the traffic of the Regiment locked themselves inside the Station Master's Office to avoid him.

He therefore reemerged in front of the railroad station at the right time, so as to snatch away the baton of the sharpshooters' bandleader, who was ready to conduct the 'Preserve for us, Lord'…

"Halt," he said, "not yet, until I give the signal. Now *at ease*, and I'll come again." He left to enter the railroad station and took off after the escort which he stopped with his scream: *"Halt!"*

"Whereto?", he sternly asked of the Sergeant, who was clueless in the new situation.

Instead of him answered in a friendly manner Švejk: "To Bruck they're hauling us, if *they* please, mister *Chief Field Chaplain*, *they* can ride with us."

"And ride I will at that," proclaimed Father Lacina, and turning around after the escort, he added: "Who says that I can't go? *Forward! March!*

When the Chief Field Chaplain found himself in the arrestee car, he laid himself on a bench and the good-hearted Švejk took off his overcoat and laid it under Father Lacina's head, regarding which remarked in the direction of the horrified Sergeant softly the One-Year Volunteer: "Chief field chaplains shalt thou nurse."

Father Lacina, comfortably stretched on the bench, started talking: "Ragù with portobellos, gentlemen, is the better, the more portobellos in it, but the portobellos must first be sautéed with small onion and only then is added bay leaf and onion…"

"The onion you have deigned to put in before that already," sounded up the One-Year Volunteer, followed by a desperate look from the Sergeant, who saw in Father Lacina one drunk that is, but after all still his superior.

The Sergeant's situation was truly desperate.

"Yes," remarked Švejk, "mister Chief Field Chaplain is totally right. The more onion, the better. In Pakoměřice[184] there used to be a head malt brewer and he used to add onion even into beer, because it's claimed onion draws out the thirst. Onion is an altogether tremendously beneficial thing. Baked onion is applied even to skin boils…"

Father Lacina was in the meantime on the bench speaking in a half-muted voice, as if in the midst of dreaming: "All depends on the spice, what spice is put into it and in what quantity. Nothing must be overpeppered, overpaprikaed..."

He was talking increasingly more slowly and softly: "Over-cloved, over-le-mon-ed, over-all-spic-ed, over-muscat..."

He didn't finish the saying and fell asleep, whistling now and then through his nose, when he stopped snoring from time to time.

The Sergeant was stiffly looking at him, while the men from the escort were softly laughing on their benches.

"He won't wake any time soon," interjected Švejk after a while, "he's totally drunk. — It doesn't matter," continued Švejk, as the Sergeant was anxiously giving him a sign, to be quiet, "nothing can be done to change anything about that, he's as drunk as if fulfilling a divine order. He's got the captain's rank. Every one of those field chaplains, of lower or higher rank, has the talent from God already, that he gets messed up at every opportunity beyond recognition. I used to serve with Field Chaplain Katz and he would spend the nose between his eyes drinking. This, the silly things this one's doing, is nothing compared to how the other one would be acting up. We spent the monstrance drinking together, and we would perhaps have spent the Lord God himself, if somebody would have lent us something against him.

Švejk stepped up to Father Lacina, turned him over to face the wall and expertly said: "This one will be snoring all the way to Bruck," and returned to his spot, accompanied by the desperate look of the unhappy Sergeant, who remarked: "Time for me perhaps to go and report it."

"Let that thought pass away," said the One-Year Volunteer, "you are the *escort commander*. You must not leave us unattended. And also according to regulations, you must not let any guard of the escort go out, in order to report it, as long as you don't have a replacement. As you can see, this is a hard nut to crack. And then by gun fire to give a signal, for somebody to come here, that will not work either. There's nothing happening here. On the other hand again there is a directive, that with the exception of the arrestees and the escort accompanying them there must not be in the arrestees' car any stranger. For those not employed here entry is strictly forbidden. To want to erase the tracks of your infraction and to throw the Chief Field Chaplain during the train ride in an inconspicuous manner off the train, that won't go either, because there are witnesses here, who saw, that you were letting him into a car, where he did not belong. It means, mister *Sergeant*, a certain demotion."

The Sergeant perplexedly sounded up, that he had not let the Chief Field Chaplain into the car, that he joined them on his own and that the Chaplain is after all his superior.

"Here the only superior is you," emphatically claimed the One-Year Volunteer, to whose words Švejk added: "Even if the lord Emperor were to want to join us, you must not have allowed that. It's like standing watch, when to such a recruit comes an inspecting officer and requests, that he go and get him cigarettes, and he asks him in addition, which brand he's to bring to him. For things like that there's *confinement at a fort*."

The Sergeant timidly raised the objection, that Švejk was after all the first one to say to the *Chief Field Chaplain*, that he could ride with them.

"I can go out on a limb doing that, mister Sergeant," answered Švejk, "because I'm an imbecile, but nobody would expect that from you."

"Have you been serving a long time already on active duty?" asked of the Sergeant, as if in passing, the One-Year Volunteer.

"Third year. Now I'm to be advanced to be a *corpora*l."

"Then make the last sign of the cross over him," cynically said the one year volunteer, "as I've been telling you, what's staring at you from this mess is a demotion."

"It makes absolutely no difference," sounded up Švejk, "to fall as an NCO or as an ordinary soldier — but the truth is, the demoted ones they shove into the first rank."

The Chief Field Chaplain moved a bit.

"He's sleeping," proclaimed Švejk, when he determined, that all was in proper order with him, "now he is probably dreaming of some frenzied feeding event. Only I'm concerned, he better not drop a load here in our space. My Field Chaplain Katz, when he got drunk, he couldn't smell himself in his sleep. Once, I'll tell you…"

And Švejk started relaying his experiences with Field Chaplain Otto Katz in such detail and so interestingly, that they did not even notice, that the train moved.

Only the hollering coming from the cars in the back interrupted Švejk's story telling. The Twelfth Company, where there was nobody but Germans from around Krumlovsko[185] and Kašperské Hory, was hollering:

When me comes, when me comes
when ag'in, ag'in me comes.

And from another car someone desperate screamed toward into the distance receding Budějovice:

And you, my darling,
Are staying here.
Holaryo, holaryo, holo!

It was such horrible yodeling and screeching, that his buddies had to drag him away from the open door of the cattle car.

"I really marvel," said the One-Year Volunteer to the Sergeant, "that no inspection detail showed up yet in this place. According to the regulation you were to report us to the commandant of the train right away at the railroad station, and not be dealing with some drunk chief field chaplain."

The hapless Sergeant was stubbornly reticent and was obstinately watching the telegraph poles running past and into the back.

"When I behold the thought, that we have not been reported to anybody," continued the caustic One-Year Volunteer, "and that at the nearest station the commandant of the train will certainly crawl into our space in here, right then inside of me rebels my soldier's blood. Let's face it, we're like…"

"…gypsies," inserted himself into it Švejk, "or itinerant bums. It seems to me, as if we were afraid of God's daylight and must not report anywhere, so they wouldn't lock us up."

"Aside from that," said the One-Year Volunteer, "on the basis of the directive of the 21st day of November 1879, during transport of military arrestees by trains it is necessary to keep to these regulations: First: The arrestee car has to be equipped with bars. That is clear beyond the brilliance of the sun and has been executed here in accordance with the regulation. We find ourselves behind perfect bars. That would be in order then. Second: In the addendum to the I&R directive of the 21st day of November 1879, in every arrestee car there is to be found a toilet. Should there not be such, the car is to be equipped with a covered vessel for fulfilling both number one and number two bodily needs of the arrestees and the escorting sentry. Here actually in our space one cannot speak of an arrestee car where there could be a toilet. We find ourselves simply in one partitioned compartment, isolated from the whole world. And also there is not that vessel…"

"You can do it out the window," interjected the Sergeant full of desperation.

"You are forgetting," said Švejk, "that no arrestee is allowed by the window."

"Then third," continued the One-Year Volunteer, "there is to be provided a vessel with drinking water. You did not take care of that either. Apropos! Do you know, at which station they will be dishing out mess? You don't? I knew it, you have not inquired…"

"So you see, mister *Sergeant*," remarked Švejk, "that it's no fun, to be transporting arrestees. We have to be attended to. We are not some ordinary soldiers, who have to take care of themselves. For us everything must be brought all the way to under our noses, because there are for that regulations and articles of law, which everybody has to go by, because there would be no proper order. 'A locked up man is like a baby in bunting,' used to say one notorious ruffian, 'he has to be looked after, lest he catch a cold, lest he get upset, so that he would be satisfied with his fate, that he the poor little one is not being persecuted without cause.' — For that matter," said after a while Švejk, looking in a friendly way at the Sergeant, "when it's eleven, then kindly tell me."

The Sergeant looked quizzically at Švejk.

"You, mister *Sergeant*, apparently wanted to ask me, why you are to tell me, when it's eleven. Starting at eleven o'clock I belong in the cattle car, mister *Sergeant*," emphatically said Švejk and continued in a ceremonial voice: "I was sentenced to three days at the Regimental Report. At eleven o'clock I started serving my sentence and today at eleven o'clock I must be released. Starting at eleven o'clock I have no business being here. No soldier can be locked up longer, than what he has coming, because in the military must be maintained discipline and order, mister *Sergeant*."

The desperate Sergeant could not after this blow recover for quite a while, until in the end he objected, that he had not received any paperwork.

"Dear mister *Sergeant*," sounded up the One-Year Volunteer, "papers don't on their own walk to the escort commander. When the mountain[186] won't come to Muhammad[187], the escort commander has to go himself to get the papers. You have now found yourself facing a new situation. Surely you must not be detaining anyone, who is to walk out to freedom. On the other hand nobody can according to valid regulations leave the arrestee car. I really don't know, how you are going to get out of this rotten situation. The longer it goes on the worse it is. Now it's half of eleven."

The One-Year Volunteer shoved the pocket watch back in: "I'm very curious to see, mister Sergeant, what you are going to be doing in half an hour." "In half an hour I belong in the cattle car," repeated dreamily Švejk, after which the totally confused and devastated Sergeant turned to him:

"If it were not inconvenient for you, I think, that it is much more comfortable here than in the cattle car. I think..."

He was interrupted by a scream given in his sleep by the Chief Field Chaplain:

"More gravy!"

"Sleep, sleep," said good-naturedly Švejk, tucking under his head for him a corner piece of the overcoat, that was falling off the bench, "may you keep on dreaming nicely about grub again."

And the One-Year Volunteer started singing:

Sleep, baby, sleep, close your little eyes,
Lord God will be sleeping with you,
Little angel rocking you, sleep, baby sleep.

The desperate Sergeant did not react to anything anymore. He was staring with a dull look into the countryside and let total disorganization run its full course in the arrestee compartment.

By the partition there were soldiers from the escort playing meat and onto the back cheeks were landing swift and honest blows. When he glanced in that direction, looking challengingly at him, as it happened, was the butt of one infantryman. The Sergeant gave a sigh and averted himself to the window again.

The One-Year Volunteer was thinking about something for a while and then turned to the crushed Sergeant: "Could it be that you're acquainted with the magazine The Animal World[188]?"

"That magazine," answered the Sergeant with an evident expression of joy, that the talk was shifting to another field, "was being delivered to the pubkeeper in our village, because he was terribly fond of Saanen goats[189] and all of his croaked. That's why he was asking for advice in the magazine."

"Dear friend," said the One-Year Volunteer, "my conversation, which will now follow, will prove to you unusually clearly, that nobody is spared mistakes! I am convinced, gentlemen, that you there in the back will stop playing meat, as that, which I am now going tell you, will be very interesting if only because to start with, you won't get to understand many of the expert expressions. I will relay to you the story of The Animal World, so that we should forget our present day wartime troubles:

"How I actually became once upon a time the editor of The Animal World, that very interesting magazine, was for me for some time a puzzle quite complex until the moment, when I on my own arrived at the opinion, that I could have done that only in a state of absolute derangement, in which I was seduced by friend's love for my old buddy Hájek[190], who had been editing the magazine up to that time honestly, but while doing it fell in love with the darling daughter of the magazine's owner mister Fuchs[191], who drove him out giving him an hour's notice under the condition, that he would provide him with but a proper editor.

"As you see, at that time strange hiring practices prevailed.

"The owner of the periodical, when I was introduced to him by my friend Hájek, received me very kindly and asked of me, whether I had any clue about animals, and he was very satisfied by my answer, that I had always esteemed animals and had seen in them the transition toward man and that especially appreciated from the point of protection of animals I had always respected their desires and wishes. Every animal wishes nothing else, but that it would be at first, before it's eaten, put to death, as far as possible, painlessly.

"A carp from its very birth nurses the persistent idea, that it is not nice of the cook, when she's ripping his gut while it's still alive, and that the custom of beheading the rooster is the onset of the Association for the Protection of Animals' precept not to slit the throats of poultry by unskilled hand.

"The twisted figures of fried loaches bear witness to the fact, that while dying, they are protesting against them being in Podol[192] being fried, while alive, in margarine. To chase a turkey…'

"At that point he interrupted me and asked, whether I knew the poultry business: dogs, rabbits, bee-keeping, a variety of things from the world of animals, how to clip pictures from foreign journals for reproduction, to translate from foreign journals expert articles about animals, whether I was good at paging through Brehm[193], and whether I could write editorials with him from the life of animals that would have the flavor of Catholic holy days, changes of the yearly weather, horse racing, hunting, upbringing of police dogs, national and also religious holidays, in short to have an overall situational journalist awareness and utilize it in a brief little editorial packed with content.

"I declared, that I had already thought much about the correct management of such a magazine, as was The Animal World, and that I was able to fully uphold the value of all those sections and points, having mastery of the mentioned subjects. But that my endeavor would be to derail the magazine to an unusual height. To be reorganizing both content and items.

"Instituting new sections, for example 'Animals' Funny Column,' 'Animals on Animals', while paying attention to the political situation.

"Provide the readers a surprise after surprise, so that from one animal to the next they could not come to. That the section 'From a Day of Animals' must alternate with 'The New Program to Solve the Issue of Domestic Horned Cattle' and 'Movement among Cattle'.

"Again he interrupted me and said, that it was absolutely enough for him, and if I managed to fulfill only a half of it, that he would bestow upon me the gift of a pair of miniature Wyandots from the latest Berlin exhibition of poultry, which received the first prize and the owner got the gold medal for excellent mating.

"I can say, that I had done my utmost and had my governing policy in the magazine maintained, as long as my abilities sufficed, yay, I even stumbled upon the discovery that my articles dwarfed my abilities.

"Wanting to provide the audience something altogether new, I would make up animals.

"I proceed from the principle, that for example the elephant, the tiger, the lion, the monkey, the mole, the horse, the porker, etc., have been long since for each reader of The Animal World absolutely familiar creatures. That it was necessary to stir the readers up by something new. By new discoveries, and that is why I tried the thing with the sulfur-bellied whale. This new whale species of mine had the size of a cod fish and was equipped with a bladder filled with formic acid and a special cloaca, through which my sulfur-bellied whale released in explosive bursts against tiny fish, which it wanted to ingest, a stupefying poisonous acid, to which an English scholar…

now I don't remember anymore, what I called him, assigned the name whale acid. Whale blubber had been already known to all, but the new acid awakened the attention of several readers, who inquired looking for a firm producing this acid.

"I can assure you, that the readers of The Animal World are altogether inquisitive.

"In quick succession after the sulfur-bellied whale I discovered a whole number of other animals. I will name from among them blisser-the-artful, a mammal from the kangaroo family, ox-the-edible, an archetype of the cow, the sepian infusorian, which I designated as a type of sewer rat.

"I was accumulating new animals with each day. I myself was very surprised by my successes in these fields. Never did it occur to me that fauna needed to be augmented so much and that Brehm could have left so many animals out of his volume The Life of Animals. Did Brehm and all those, who came after him, know of my bat from the island of Iceland[194], 'bat-the-remote', about my domestic cat from the summit of the Mount Kilimanjaro[195] known as the 'deer malsniffer-the-irritant'?

"Had the zoologists up to that time had any notion about some engineer Khun's[196] flea, which I found in an amber block and which was totally blind, because it lived on an underground prehistoric mole, who also was blind, because his great-grandmother had mated, as I wrote, with an underground blind olm[197]-of-the-caverns from the Postojna Cave[198], which at that time extended all the way to the Baltic Sea[199] of today?

"From this trifling event evolved a huge polemic between the magazine Čas[200] and Čech[201], because Čech among the variety of facts in its feuilleton, quoting the article about the flea discovered by me, declared: 'What God does, he does well.' Čas naturally in the purely realistic manner demolished the whole flea of mine along with the exalted Čech, and from that time on it seemed, that the lucky star of an innovator and discoverer of new creatures was abandoning me. The subscribers of The Animal World started getting concerned.

"The reason for that originated in my various small news items about bee-keeping, poultry business, where I elaborated my new theories, which caused genuine horror, because following my simple pieces of advice the well-known bee-keeper mister Pazourek[202] was smitten by a stroke and bee-keeping in Šumava as well as in

Podkrkonoší[203] regions died out. The poultry was visited upon by plague and in short everything was croaking. The subscribers were writing threatening letters and were rejecting the magazine.

"I threw myself at the birds living free in the wild and today I still remember my scandal involving the editor of the Farming Horizon[204], the clerical party deputy of the Parliament, director Jos. M. Kadlčák[205]!

"I clipped from the English magazine Country Life[206] a picture of some little bird, which was sitting in a walnut tree. I gave him the name walnutter, just as I would logically in no way hesitate to write that a bird sitting in a juniper is a juniperer, or as the case might be a heifer-juniperess[207]".

"And wouldn't you know what happened. Using an ordinary postal card, Mister Kadlčák attacked me, that it was supposedly a jay and no walnutter, and that it was a translation of *oaken acorn jay*.

"I sent a letter in which I expounded my whole theory of the walnutter, weaving into the letter numerous epithets and made up quotes from Brehm.

"The Parliamentary deputy Kadlčák answered in the Farming Horizon's editorial.

"My boss, Mister Fuchs, was sitting as always in the coffeehouse and was reading the regional newspapers, because as of late he tremendously often looked for mentions of my spellbinding articles in The Animal World, and when I arrived, he pointed to The Farming Horizon lying on the table and said softly, looking at me with his sad eyes, which expression his eyes had all the time as of late.

"I was reading aloud in front of that whole coffeehouse audience:

"'Esteemed editorial board! I have brought to attention, that your magazine is implementing unusual and unjustified nomenclature, that it minds too little the purity of the Czech language, and makes up various animals. I included evidence, that instead of the generally used ancient term jay your editor is implementing acorner, which has its basis in the translation of the German name *oaken acorn jay* - jay.'

"'Jay,' repeated after me desperately the owner of the magazine.

"I kept reading on in a calm disposition: 'Upon which I received from your editor of The Animal World a letter of boundlessly rough, personal, and uncouth tenor, where I was in a culpable manner called an ignorant dumb beast, which deserves emphatic admonishment. That is not how substantive scientific reproach is answered among well-behaved people. I would like to know, who of the two of us is the bigger dumb beast. Perhaps, true, I should not have used postal card stock to reproach and should have written a letter instead, but due to being swamped by work I did not notice the trifling detail, but now after the vulgar attack I am taking your editor of The Animal World to the public whipping post.

"'Your mister editor is tremendously mistaken, being under the impression, that I am a half-educated dumb beast, that has no idea what the name of this or that bird is. I have been occupying myself with ornithology for years, and not so in books, but through studies in nature, having in cages more birds, than your editor has seen in his life, especially a man confined in Prague gin mills and pubs.

"'But then those are secondary items, although it certainly would not be detrimental, if your editor of The Animal World were to first ascertain for himself, whom it is that he reproaches for a dumb beastly thing, before his marauding attack leaves the tip of the pen, as it might be destined for Moravia, going to Frýdlant[208] near Místek[209], where up to the appearance of this article your magazine's delivery was also being accepted.

"'Anyhow, it is not a case of a personal polemic of a goofy guy, but of a cause, and that is why I repeat again, that to be making up terminology from translations is impermissible, when we have the generally known domestic name jay.'

"'Yes, jay,' exclaimed my boss in an even more desperate voice.

"I'm reading contentedly on not allowing myself to be interrupted. 'It is a rascally deed, when it's done by non-experts and brutes. Whoever called the jay a walnutter and when? In the work Our Birds on p. 148 is the Latin name: Garrulus glandarius B.A., is that bird of mine — jay.

"'The editor of your periodic publication will certainly admit, that I know my own cock better, than a non-expert can know it. The walnutter refers to, according to doctor Bayer[210], Mucifrag carycatectes B., and the 'B' does not mean, as your editor wrote to me, that it is the first letter of the word blb, *imbecile*. Czech birdowriters know altogether only jay-the-common, and not your acorner, which was invented as it happens by that gentleman, who is the one whom the initial 'B' fits according to his own theory. This is a rude marauding personal raid, that will not change the matter at all.

"'A jay will remain a jay, even if the editor of The Animal World were to have dum..d in his pants from it, and it will remain as evidence, of how carelessly and pointlessly people write here and there, although he even did invoke Brehm conspicuously rudely. That vulgar ruffian writes, that jay belongs according to Brehm in the crocodyloids family, p. 452, where there is spoken of the lesser grey shrike or common dapple, that is butcher-bird (Lanius minor L.). Then this ignoramus, if I may use the diminutive of the designation for him, invokes Brehm again, that jay belongs in the fifteenth family, but Brehm includes crows in the seventeenth family, with which are associated ravens, jackdaw genus, and he is so vulgar, that he called me also jackdaw (Colaeus) and magpie genus, blue crows, sub-family moron ineptus, although on the same page are being discussed wood-jays and spotted magpies…"

"'Grove-jays,' gave a sigh my magazine publisher, grabbing his head, 'give it to me, so I can finish reading it.'

"I got spooked, that his voice, with which he read, got hoarse: 'Ring boletus, that is Turkish blackbird will in Czech translation remain ring boletus, just as fieldfare will remain fieldfare.'

"'Fieldfare should be called juniperer or heifer-juniperess, mister boss', I remarked, 'because he feeds on juniper.'

"Mister Fuchs rapped the newspaper against the desk and crawled under the billiard table, gurgling out the last words that he had read: 'Turdus, ring boletus. — Not jay,' he hollered under the billiard table, 'walnutter, I bite, gentlemen!'

"He was pulled out at last and on the third day he passed away in the circle of his family due to brain flu.

"His last word, in his last lucid moment, was: 'I don't have at stake my personal interest, but the welfare of the whole. From that point of view condescend to accept my characterization, as to the point, as…' — and he hiccupped."

The One-Year Volunteer became silent and addressed the Sergeant caustically:

"By that I only wanted to say, that each man finds himself sometimes in a precarious situation and errs!"

All in all, the Sergeant came to understand only this much, that he's the one erring; that is why he turned around to face the window again and gloomily watched, how the journey's landscape passes running by.

Somewhat greater interest was aroused by the story in Švejk.

The men of the escort were staring stupidly at one another.

Švejk began: “In the world nothing will remain concealed. Everything will come out, as you have heard, even that such dumb jay is no walnutter. It is truly very interesting, that anybody would be fooled by such a thing. To make up animals is in truth a hard thing, but to be exhibiting such made up animals is truly even harder. Once, years ago, there was in Prague one Mestek[211] by last name and he discovered a mermaid and would exhibit her on Havlíček boulevard[212] in Vinohrady behind a screen. There was an opening in the screen and in kind of semidarkness everybody could see a sofa as common as dust, and on it was wallowing a broad from Žižkov. She had her legs wrapped in green gauze, which was supposed to be representing the tail, her hair she had painted over green and hands in gloves and attached to them were fins of cardboard, also green, and on her back tied down with a string she had some rudder. Youth up to sixteen years of age were not admitted and all, who were older than sixteen years and paid their admission, were taking much pleasure, that the mermaid had a big rump, on which there was the inscription ‘Goodbye!’ As for the breasts, it was nothing. They dangled all the way to her navel as on a dragged-down-tired floozy. Then at seven o’clock in the evening Mestek closed up the panorama and said: ‘Mermaid, you can go home now, she changed and at ten at night one could see her already walking up and down Táborská street[213] and quite inconspicuously telling each gentleman, whom she’d pass: ‘Good looking, why don’t you come and shake it out a bit.’ Since she didn’t have a registration booklet, then during a crackdown mister Drašner locked her up with other similar mice, and Mestek was out of business.”

The Chief Field Chaplain at that moment fell off the bench and on the ground kept on sleeping. The Sergeant was watching it dumbstruck and then to the accompaniment of general silence was lifting him up without any contribution from the others onto the bench on his own. It was apparent, that he had lost all authority, and when he said in a weak, hopeless voice: “You could also help me,” here all the men of the escort were staring as if catatonic and not even one live foot moved.

“You should have let him snore where he was,” proclaimed Švejk, “I didn’t use to do it any other way with my Field Chaplain. Once I let him sleep in a bathroom, once he slept on top of a wardrobe under my care, in a wash-tub in a stranger’s house and god-knows-where else he had snored his fill."

The Sergeant was all of a sudden set upon by a surge of determination. He wanted to show, that he was the lord in charge here, and that is why he said coarsely: "Keep your trap shut and don't yammer! Every *spotshine* babbles up a wasteful heap. You are like bed-bugs."

"Yes, indeed, and you are a god, mister Sergeant," answered Švejk with the steadiness of a philosopher, who wants to bring about earthly peace in the whole world and while doing that delves into a horrible polemic, "you are Our Lady of the Seven Sorrows."

"Lordgod," exclaimed the One-Year Volunteer, raising his clasped hands, "fill our hearts with love toward all officers, so that we would not look at them with disgust. Bless our assembly in this arrestee hole on rails."

The Sergeant turned red and jumped up: "I forbid all remarks, *they* the one-year-timer."

"You're not responsible for anything," kept talking in a soothing tone the One-Year Volunteer, "in the case of many kinds and species nature denied the living things any intelligence, have you ever heard a talk about human stupidity? Wouldn't it be decidedly better, if you had been born as another species of mammal and were not wearing the stupid label of man and Sergeant? It is a great mistake, that you think of yourself, that you are the most perfect and evolved creature. When they rip your little stars off, then you are a zero, which they aim at and blow away without the slightest regard in any trench on any front. If they give you another stripe and turn you into a living creature that's called a souper, then still all won't be alright with you. Your mental horizon will narrow still further, and when you lay down your culturally retarded bones somewhere on the battlefield, in all of Europe nobody will cry for you a bit."

"I'll have you locked up," yelled out desperately the Sergeant.

The One-Year Volunteer gave a little smile: "You apparently would like to have me locked up, because I was berating you. You'd be lying, because the intellect you own cannot grasp any insults at all, and besides I would bet you anything, that you'd want, that you don't remember anything at all from the whole of our conversation. If I were to tell you, that you are an embryo, then you'd forget it sooner, not perhaps before we arrive at the nearest station, but sooner, before there streaks past us the nearest telegraph pole. You are a withered brain lobe. I cannot at all imagine, that you could somewhere coherently express all, that you heard me saying. Besides, you can ask anybody here, whether there was in my words the slightest innuendo as to your mental horizon and whether I offended you in any way."

"Certainly," confirmed Švejk, "nobody here told you even one little word, which you could somehow take wrongly. It always looks bad, when somebody feels offended. Once I was sitting at the night coffeehouse in The Tunnel[214] and we were talking about orangutans. Sitting there with us was a mariner and he was telling us, that often they can't tell an orangutan from some bearded citizen, that such an orangutan has a chin grown over by fuzz like..., 'like,' he says, 'let's say for instance that gentleman over there at the next table.' We all turned to look, and the gentleman with that hairy chin went over to the mariner and gave him a slap in the face and the mariner busted his head with a beer bottle and the bearded gentleman collapsed and remained lying down out cold and we and the mariner said our good-byes, because he left right away, when he saw that he half-done killed him. Then we revived the gentleman, and that's definitely what we should not have done, because right after his resuscitation he called on us all, who had nothing whatsoever to do with it after all, a patrol, which took us away to the police district station. There he kept repeating his line, that we took him for an orangutan, that we spoke of nothing else but him. And he just kept on telling his own line. We kept saying that no, he's no orangutan. And he, that he was, that he had heard it. I begged the mister inspector, asking that he explain it to him. And he was quite good-naturedly explaining it to him, but even then he would not be talked out of it and told mister inspector, that he doesn't understand it, that he's in cahoots with us. So mister inspector had him locked up, to sober up, and we again wanted to return into The Tunnel, but we couldn't anymore, because they sat us behind the iron gate too. So you see, mister Sergeant, what can become of a little and unremarkable misunderstanding, that is not even worth a talk. Then in Okrouhlice[215] there was a citizen and he got offended, when they told him in Německý Brod[216], that he was a tiger python. There are more such words, which are not outright punishable under the law. For example, if we were to tell you, that you were a muskrat. Could you be angry with us on account of it?"

The Sergeant whinnied. It was not possible to say that he screamed. Anger, rage, desperation, all merged into a range of strong sounds and this concert number was augmented by whistling, which was being performed through his nose by the snoring Chief Field Chaplain.

After the whinny, there set in a total depression. The Sergeant sat himself on the bench and his watery, expressionless eyes got stuck in the distance on the forests and mountains.

"Mister Sergeant," said the One-Year Volunteer, "you remind me now, as you are watching the beautiful mountains and aromatic forests, of the Dante[217] character. The same well-bred and noble face of a poet, a man of heart and gentle spirit, open to gracious stirring. Remain, I beg you, sitting like that, it becomes you nicely. With what spiritual endowment, with absence of any affectation and starch stiffness of pomp you are bugging your eyes out at the landscape. Certainly you're thinking, how beautiful it will be, when in spring, in place of those desolate areas now a carpet of colorful field flowers will have spread itself out here..."

"...which carpet is being hugged by a little creek," remarked Švejk, "and mister Sergeant is wetting the indelible pencil with the tip of his tongue, is sitting on some tree stump and is writing a little poem for the Young Reader[218]."

The Sergeant became totally apathetic, while the One-Year Volunteer was insisting, that he definitely had seen the Sergeant's modeled head at a sculptors' exhibition:

"Allow me, mister Sergeant, haven't you perhaps stood as a model for the sculptor Štursa[219]?"

The Sergeant looked at the One-Year Volunteer and said sadly:

"I have not."

The One-Year Volunteer fell silent and stretched out on the bench.

The men of the escort were playing cards with Švejk; the Sergeant was out of desperation kibitzing and even dared to remark, that Švejk played the ace of greens and that it was a mistake. He was not to have trumped and he would have had a seven for the last pitch.

"There used to be posted in the pubs," said Švejk, "these nice signs warning any kibitzers. I remember one: Kibitz, hold your trap shut and frost it, lest I smack you right across it."

The military train was entering the station, where an inspection detail checked the cars. The train stopped.

"It figures," said the inexorable One-Year Volunteer, looking meaningfully at the Sergeant, "the inspector is already here..."

The inspecting officer stepped into the car.

*

The commander of the military train, designated as such by the Staff, was Reserve Officer doctor Mráz.

Such stupid work details always had reserve officers thrown at them. Doctor Mráz was like a dazed deer on account of it. He was still unable to account for one car, although in civilian life he was a professor of mathematics at a Realistic Gymnasium[220]. Besides that, the troops head-count reported at the last station from the individual cars fluctuated from the number stated after boarding the cars at the Budějovice railroad station was completed. It seemed to him, when he was looking through the documents, that wherever they came from, there they were, two extra field kitchens. Unusually unpleasant tingling in his back was being caused by the statement, that his horses had multiplied by an unknown method. He was unable to bring to an end his search of the officers list for two cadets, whom he was missing. At the Regimental Office in the front car they kept ceaselessly looking for one typewriter. Because of the chaos his head began aching, he had already eaten three capsules of powder aspirin, and now he was reviewing the inventory of the train with a painful expression on his face.

When he stepped into the arrestee compartment with his escort, he glanced at the papers, and having received a report from the devastated Sergeant, that he was giving a ride to two arrestees and had such-and-such number of troops, he compared the statement against the files one more time for its genuineness and took a look around.

"Who is it that you're giving a ride to?" he asked sternly, pointing to the Chief Field Chaplain, who was sleeping on his belly and whose rear cheeks were looking challengingly at the inspecting officer.

"I dutifully report, *Senior Lieutenant*, Sir," stuttered the Sergeant, "that we whatchumacallit...

"Don't whatchumacallit me," growled doctor Mráz, "express yourself directly."

"I dutifully report, *Lieutenant*, Sir," spoke up, instead of the Sergeant, Švejk, "this gentleman who is sleeping on his belly is some drunken *Chief Field Chaplain*. He joined us and crawled into our car here, and because he is our superior, then we could not throw him out, so it wouldn't be a breach of subordination. He apparently mistook the arrestee car for the staff one."

Doctor Mráz sighed and took a look at his papers. About some chief field chaplain, who is to be riding the train to Bruck, there was not even a mention on the list. He nervously twitched his eye. At the last station all of a sudden his horses were being added to, and now out of the clean-and-clear air he is even having chief field chaplains birthed in the arrestee car.

He could do no better, than challenge the Sergeant, to turn the one sleeping on his belly over, because from this position it was not possible to determine his identity.

The Sergeant, after a longer straining effort, turned the Chief Field Chaplain on his back, whereby that one woke up, and seeing the officer in front of him, said: *"Eh, hi Freddy, what's new? Dinner ready yet?"*, squinted his eyes again and rolled over to face the wall.

Doctor Mráz recognized right away, that he was the same devouring glutton of yesterday from the officers' club, the fabled locust of all officers' mess halls, and gave a soft sigh.

"For that," he said to the Sergeant, "you'll be going to the Report." He was leaving, when at that point Švejk intercepted him:

"I dutifully report, *Lieutenant*, Sir, that I don't belong here. I'm to be locked up only until eleven, because it's just today that my term ran out. I was ordered locked up for three days and now I am to be sitting already with the others in the cattle car. Because it's been long since past eleven, I beg you, *Lieutenant*, Sir, to be either unloaded onto the track, or transferred to the cattle car, where I belong, or to mister *Senior Lieutenant* Lukáš."

"What is your name?" asked doctor Mráz, looking again at his papers.

"Švejk, Josef, I dutifully report *Lieutenant*, Sir."

"Ehm, you are then the notorious Švejk," said doctor Mráz, "you really should have walked out at eleven. But mister Senior Lieutenant Lukáš was asking me, not to let you out until Bruck, it is supposedly safer, at least you won't do anything troublesome on the way."

After the departure of the inspecting officer the Sergeant could not hold back a caustic remark:

"So you see, Švejk, that like shit it helped you, to be turning to a higher authority. Had I wanted, I could have made things burning hot for both of you."

"Mister Sergeant," sounded up the One-Year Volunteer,

"pitching shit is a more-or-less credible argumentation, but an intelligent man is not to use such words, if he is upset or if he wants to carry out attacks against somebody. Then those laughable threats of yours, your saying that could have made things burning hot for both of us. Why have you by all demons not done it, when you had the opportunity for it? That is certainly an apparent evidence of your great mental maturity and unusual tact.

"I've had enough already," jumped up the Sergeant, "I can bring it about that both of you end up in the slammer."

"And on account of what, my little pigeon?" asked innocently the One-Year Volunteer.

"That is my business," was mustering his courage the Sergeant.

"Your business," said the One-Year Volunteer with a smile, "yours and ours. Like in the card game: my aunt — your aunt[221]. I would rather say, that what affected you was the mention of the fact, that you'll go to the Report, and that is why you are starting to holler at us, but of course not doing it through the service channels."

"You are vulgarians," let himself be heard the Sergeant, mustering the remaining courage to look horribly threatening.

"I'll tell you something, mister *Sergeant*," remarked Švejk, "I am already an old soldier, I had served before the war, and it never pays and turns out badly when calling others names. When I was serving back then years ago, I remember, that there was some souper Schreiter in our company. He served for sup, could have as a sergeant gone home long since, but he was, as the saying goes, not all there. So this man decided to pick on us soldiers, and he'd be sticking to us like shit to a shirt, this thing wasn't *right* by him, that thing again was against all the *rules*, he was busting our chops any way he could, and he kept telling us: 'You're not soldiers, but *watchmen.*' It was eating me up until one day it got to me and I went to the Company Report. 'What do you want?' says the Captain. 'I have, I dutifully report, Captain, Sir, a complaint against our mister Quartermaster Schreiter, we are after all Imperial soldiers, but not *watchmen*. We serve the lord Emperor, but we are no fruit orchard guards.' 'Look, you insect,' answered me the Captain, 'make it so that I don't see you already.' And I retorted, that I beg dutifully to be transferred to the Battalion Report. At the Battalion Report, when I explained it to the *Lieutenant Colonel*, that we were no *watchmen*, but Imperial soldiers, he had me locked up for two days, but I was requesting that they transfer me to Regimental Report. At the

Regimental Report mister Colonel after all my explaining screamed at me, that I was a stupid idiot, and told me to blow to hell with all the demons. I in turn said to that: 'I dutifully report, Colonel, Sir, asking to be presented to the Brigade Report.' That spooked him and right away he had our souper Schreiter called to the office and he had to beg me for forgiveness in front of all the officers for that word *watchman*. Then he caught up with me in the yard and announced to me, that starting today he wouldn't be cussing me out, but that he'd bring it about that I end up in the garrison prison. From that time on I was really watching myself most closely, but I failed to keep myself in check. I was standing watch at the magazine and each posted sentry always wrote something on the wall. Either he drew female genitals, or he wrote a little verse there. I could not think of anything, so on account of the time dragging a long while I signed my name on the wall under the inscription 'Souper Schreiter is a dead man's limb'. And that shameless rube souper turned me in right away, because he was stalking me like a red dog. By an unfortunate coincidence there was above the inscription still another one: 'We won't go to war, we'll shit on it', and that was in the year 1912, when we were to go into Serbia on account of that consul Prochaska[222]. So right away they sent me to Terezín[223], to the District Court[224]. The gentlemen from the military court photographed that magazine wall with all that graffiti about fifteen times, ten times they had me write 'We won't go to war, we'll shit on it', so that they would study my handwriting, fifteen times I had to write in their presence 'Souper Schreiter is a dead man's limb' and in the end there arrived a handwriting expert and had me write: The day was 29th of July 1897, when *The Queen's Court on the Elbe*[225] got to know the horrors of the rapid and swollen Labe. 'That is not enough yet,' the auditor was saying, 'we are after that shitting on. Dictate to him something with a lot of s's and t's.' So they dictated for me: 'Pristina, stalls, nits, trots, saints, status, litters.' The court handwriting expert was already totally baffled from it and kept looking back over his shoulder, where there stood a soldier with a bayonet, and in the end said, that it had to go to Vienna, and for me to write three times in succession: 'Also the sun is beginning to scorch already, the heat is excellent.' They shipped out all of the material to Vienna and in the end the way it turned out was, that as far as the inscriptions were concerned, that it was not my hand, that the signature was mine, which signature I owned up to, and that for that I was sentenced to six weeks, because I signed my name, when I was standing watch, and I was then not able to be on guard during the time, when I was signing my name on the wall."

"It's clear," said the Sergeant with satisfaction, "that it did not go without punishment, that you are as genuine a criminal as they come. If I were in the place of the *Regional Court*, I would have dished out to you not six weeks, but six years."

"Don't be so horrible," took his turn the One-Year Volunteer, "and better think of your end. Just recently the inspecting officer told you, that you'd be going to the Report. For such a thing you should be getting ready very seriously and meditate on the last things of a sergeant. What are you really next to the universe, when you consider, that the fixed star closest to us is in a distance from this military train 275,000 times farther than the sun, so that its parallax would amount to one second of arc. If you were to find yourself to be in the universe as a fixed star, you would be definitely too minute, in order for you to be noticed by the best stargazing instruments. For your minuteness in the universe there is no concept. In half a year you would traverse this tiny arc in the sky, in a year a tiny ellipse, for the expression of which in numbers there is not even a concept, that's how minute it is. Your parallax would be unmeasurable."

"In that case," remarked Švejk, "could mister Sergeant take pride in the fact, that nobody can take a measurement of him, and let it end up with him at the Report whichever way it will, he has to remain calm and he must not get upset, because each upset is detrimental to health, and now in the war everybody has to be preserving his health, because the wartime suffering demands from each individual, not to be any sort of croaking stiff. — If they lock you up, mister *Sergeant*," continued Švejk with an amiable smile, "if some injustice were done to you, then you can't be losing your spirit, and when they keep thinking what they will, then you too keep thinking what you will. Just like I knew a coalman, who was locked up with me at the beginning of the war at the Police Headquarters in Prague, someone named František Škvor, for grand treason, and later perhaps also done away with on account of some pragmatic sanction[226]. That man, when they were asking him during the interrogation, whether he had any reservations about the recorded statement, said:

Let things have been as they have been,
    Nonetheless they've been somehow.

So far it has never been,
That things would be nohow.

Afterwards they put him in a dark little closet for that and gave him nothing to eat or drink for two days and again took him out for an interrogation, and he stood his ground, saying 'Let things have been as they have been, nonetheless they've been somehow, so far it has never been, that things would be nohow.' Could be, that he went saying that right to under the gallows, when they handed him then over to the military court."

"Now, it is said, they hang and shoot much of the whole lot," said one of the men of the escort, "not long ago they read to us on the training ground an order, that in Motol[227] they blew away reservist Kudrna[228], because the Captain used a saber to cut his little boy, who was on the arm of his wife, when she wanted to say goodbye to him in Benešov, and he got upset. And they're just locking up political people altogether. They have also already blown away an editor in Moravia[229]. And our Captain was saying, that the same fate is still awaiting others."

"Everything has its limits," said the One-Year Volunteer ambiguously.

"You are right," sounded up the Sergeant, "such editors deserve that. They only rile the people up. Like the year before last, when I was still only a *corporal*, there was a subordinate editor under me then and he would call me nothing else but the ruin of the army, but when I was teaching him *calisthenics*, until he was sweating, then he'd always say: 'Please, I ask you to respect the human in me.' But I showed him this human, when the command was *on your belly* and there were a lot of puddles in the yard at the garrison. I led him to the edge of one such puddle and made the guy to be falling into it, so that the water was splashing like at a municipal swimming pavilion. And starting at noon everything on him had to gleam again, the uniform had to be clean like glass, and he was cleaning and groaning and making remarks, and the next day again he was like a swine rolled around in mud and I was standing over him and was telling him: 'So, mister editor, what is greater, the ruin of the army, or that human of yours?' He was a genuine intellectual."

The Sergeant looked triumphantly at the One-Year Volunteer and continued: "He lost the one-year stripes precisely on account of his intelligence, because he would write in the newspaper about abuse of soldiers. But how is one not to abuse him, when such a learned man doesn't know how to take apart *the lock* of a rifle, not even when they show it to him for the tenth time, and when *eyes left* is called, he twists his bonehead as if on purpose to the right and is staring like a befuddled crow while doing it, and during *the arm position changes* does not know, what to grab first, whether the strap or the ammunition bag, and is gaping at you as a dumbstruck calf gapes at a new barn gate, when you are showing him, how the hand is supposed to glide down the strap. He did not even know, on which shoulder the rifle is to be carried, and would salute like a monkey, and during the turnabouts, God help him, when marching and he was learning how to step. When he was supposed to turn around, it didn't make any difference to him, with which dumb leg he did it, plonk, plonk, plonk, sometimes he still walked six steps forward and only then was spinning around like a cock on a roasting-jack and when marching he kept pace like one beset by gout or danced like an old slut at the village patron saint festival."

The Sergeant spat: "He was purposefully issued a very rusty rifle, so he would learn to *spotshine* it, he was rubbing it like a dog does a bitch, but if he were to buy two more kilos of tow, then he'd clean off nothing. The more he spot shined it, the worse it was and more rusty, and at the Report the rifle passed from hand to hand and everybody was marveling, how it was possible, that it was nothing but rust. Our Captain, he'd always be telling him, that he'd never become a soldier, that he better go and hang himself, that he freeloads feeding on commissary bread. And he behind his spectacles only kept blinking in awe. It was a big red-letter day for him, when he didn't have *intensified* or confinement to the barracks. On that day he'd usually write those little articles of his for the newspaper about abuse of soldiers, until one day they did an inspection search of his suitcase. The number of books he had in there, lordy! Nothing but books about disarmament, about peace among nations. For that he took a trip to the garrison prison and from that time on we were left in peace by him, until he again appeared to us all of a sudden at our office and was filling out *request chits*, so that the men would have no contact with him. That was the sad end of that intellectual. He could had been a different class of man, had he not lost on account of his stupidity his one-year privilege. He could have been a *lieutenant*."

The Sergeant released a sigh: "Not even the folds on his overcoat did he know how to make, all the way from Prague he would order potions and various ointments for cleaning buttons, and yet such a button of his looked as red as Esau[230]. But flap his mouth he sure knew how to, and when he was at the office, then he'd do nothing else, but delve into philosophizing. He had been fond of it earlier already. He was constantly, as I was saying already, about nothing but 'the human man'. Once, when he was musing so over a puddle, into which during *on your belly* he had to plop himself, I told him then: 'Since you keep talking about the human man and about mud, then *they* remember, that man was created from mud and he must *not have minded.*'"

Now, having talked himself empty, the Sergeant was satisfied with himself and was waiting, what was going to say about that the One-Year Volunteer. However it was Švejk who sounded up:

"For these same things, for such browbeating, years ago at the Thirty-fifth Regiment some guy Koníček stabbed to death both himself and the drill-sergeant. It was in the Kurýr[231]. The *sergeant* had about thirty stab wounds in his body, of which over a dozen were fatal. The soldier then sat himself down on the dead *sergeant* and while sitting on top of him ran the blade through himself. There was another case years ago in Dalmatia[232], there they slit a sergeant's throat and till this day it's not known, who did it. It has remained cloaked in secrecy, only this much is known, that the name of the *sergeant* with the slit throat was Fiala and he was from Drábovna[233] by Turnov[234]. Then I still know of one more *Sergeant* of the seventy-fivers, Rejmánek…"

The pleasant narration was interrupted at that moment by great groaning on the bench, where there was sleeping the Chief Field Chaplain Lacina.

The father was waking up in all his beauty and dignity. His awakening was being accompanied by the selfsame phenomena as the morning awakening of the young giant Gargantua[235], as the old merry Rabelais[236] described it.

The Chief Field Chaplain was farting and burping on the bench and with a great noise was yawning all about. At last he sat up and asked, wondering:

"Krucilaudon[237], where am I at?"

The Sergeant, seeing the awakening of the military lord, very devotedly answered:

"I dutifully report, Chief Field Chaplain, Sir, that you are having the pleasure of finding yourself in the arrestee car."

A flash of surprise flew across the face of the Father. He sat reticent for a while and was thinking. To no avail. Between that, which he had lived through overnight and in the morning, and the awakening in the rail car, the windows of which were equipped with bars, there was a sea of lack of clarity.

At last he asked the Sergeant, still devotedly standing in front of him: "And on whose order, I, as…"

"I dutifully report, without an order, Chief Field Chaplain, Sir."

The Father got up and started pacing between the benches, murmuring to himself, that it was unclear to him.

He sat down again with the words: "Where is it that we're actually going?"

"To Bruck, I dutifully report."

"And why are we going to Bruck?"

"I dutifully report, that that's where our whole one-and-ninetieth Regiment has been transferred to."

The Father started again thinking with great effort, what it was actually that happened with him, how did he get into the car and why was he actually going to Bruck and why exactly with the very one-and-ninetieth Regiment accompanied by some escort.

He got his bearings shaking the monkey off his back far enough already, that he could even recognize the One-Year Volunteer and that is why he turned to him with a query:

"You are an intelligent man, can you explain to me without any reservations, not withholding anything, how I got here to be with you?"

"I'd be glad to," said in a friendly tone the One-Year Volunteer, "you simply joined us in the morning at the railroad station during the boarding of the train, because you had quite a bit of hooch in the head."

The Sergeant gave him a stern look.

"You pushed into our car," continued the One-Year Volunteer, "and it was already a done deal. You laid yourself down on the bench and this here Švejk put his overcoat under your head for you. During the inspection of the train at the preceding station you were put on the list of officers finding themselves on the train. You were, how should I put it, officially discovered and our *Sergeant* will be going to the Report on account of it."

"Well, well," sighed the Father, "then I should at the next station cross over to the staff cars. Would you know, whether lunch was already being handed out?"

"There won't be lunch until Vienna, *Field Chaplain*, Sir," claimed his turn at adding a word the Sergeant.

"So you put an *overcoat* under my head?" the Father turned to Švejk. "I thank you from my heart."

"I don't deserve any gratitude," answered Švejk, "I only acted so, as every soldier is to act, when he sees his superior, that he has nothing under his head and that he is whatchumacallit. Each soldier is to hold his superior in esteem, even if such were knocked up. I have very extensive experience with *field chaplains*, because I was an *orderly* to mister *Field Chaplain* Otto Katz. It is a merry folk and good-hearted.

The Chief Field Chaplain was stricken by a fit of democratism on account of the hangover consequent of yesterday and pulled out a cigarette and handed it to Švejk: "Have a smoke and puff away! — You," he turned to the Sergeant, "you'll be going to the Report because of me, they say. Don't fear at all, I will cut you off the hook one way or another, nothing will happen to you. — And you," he said to Švejk, "I will take with me. You will live at my place as if in a down feather baby blanket."

He was stricken now by a new fit of magnanimity and was insisting, that he'd do right by everybody, that for the One-Year Volunteer he'd buy chocolate, for the men from the escort rum, the Sergeant he'd have transferred to the photography section at the Staff of the 7th Cavalry Division, that he would liberate all and he'd never forget them.

He started handing out cigarettes from his case to all, not only Švejk, and was proclaiming, that he was allowing all the arrestees to smoke, and that he'd add his effort to seeing to it, that all have their sentences lightened and they return again to normal military life.

"I don't want," he said, "for you to be remembering me in a bad light or anger. I have many contacts and with me you'll do alright. You impress me altogether as decent people, whom God likes. If you have sinned, you are paying with your punishment, and I see that you are gladly and willingly enduring, what God sent down upon you. — On the basis of what," he turned to Švejk, "have you been punished?"

"God sent down upon me a punishment," answered piously Švejk, "through the agency of the *Regimental Report*, *Chief Field*

Chaplain, Sir, on account of a no-fault delayed attachment to the Regiment."

"God is merciful and just to the utmost," said the Chief Field Chaplain ceremonially, "He knows, whom He is to punish, because thereby he shows His providence and omnipotence. And why are you sitting doing time, you One-Year Volunteer?"

"Because of the fact," answered the One-Year Volunteer, "that the merciful God had taken the pleasure of sending rheumatism down on me and I became conceited. After having served the sentence I will be sent to the kitchen."

"What God directs, He directs well," suggested enthusiastically the Father, having heard of a kitchen, "even there can a proper man make a career. It is precisely into the kitchen they should be putting intelligent people, on account of the possibilities combinations, as it is not important how the cooking is done, but with what measure of love it is all put together, the presentation and other things. Let's take sauces. An intelligent man, when making an onion sauce, takes all kinds of vegetables and stews them in butter, then adds spices, black pepper, allspice, a little mace, ginger, but a common vulgar cook will have onion boiling and then throw into it a little browning made of suet. You I'd really like to see best somewhere in an officers' mess. Without intelligence can a man live in some common employment and life, but in the kitchen it shows. Yesterday evening in Budějovice, in the officers' club, they served us among other things kidneys à la Madeira[238]. Whoever made them, him forgive, God, all sins, that was a genuine intellectual, and true indeed there is in the kitchen of the officers' mess some teacher from Skute[239]. And I ate the same kidneys à la Madeira at the officers' mess of the 64th *Land Defense Regiment*[240]. They put caraway into the dish, just like they make in a common pub with black pepper. And who was making it, what was that cook in civilian life? A cattle feeder on a large farm."

The Chief Field Chaplain became quiet for a moment and was switching the conversation to the cooking issue in both the Old and New Testament, where just exactly in those times they paid much attention to preparation of tasty food after divine services and other church ceremonies. Then he challenged all, to sing something, after which Švejk let them have it as always in an unfortunate manner: "Out of Hodonín[241] acoming is Marína[242], the parish priest behind with a keg of wine."

But the Chief Field Chaplain did not become angry.

"If there were at least a little rum here, a keg of wine would not be a must," he said smiling in a totally friendly mood, "and that Marína we could skip too, regardless it only seduces one to sin.

The Sergeant carefully reached into the overcoat and pulled from there a flask of rum.

"I dutifully report Chief Field Chaplain, Sir," he sounded up softly, so that it was apparent, what a personal sacrifice he was making to his detriment, "if perhaps you would not get offended."

"I won't, my boy," answered in a brightened voice and joyfully the Father, "I will drink to our happy journeying."

"Jesusmaria," sighed the Sergeant to himself, seeing, that with the thorough swig disappeared half the bottle.

"Now now there, you guy," said the Field Chaplain smiling and winking meaningfully at the One-Year Volunteer, "on top of all, you swear sacrilegiously. Then Lord God has to punish you."

The Father tipped the flask again and imbibed, and handing it over to Švejk, in the manner of an officer ordered: "Finish it off."

"Army service is army service," stated Švejk goodheartedly to the Sergeant, returning to him the empty bottle, which the latter acknowledged with such a strange sort of flash in his eyes, which can appear only in a mentally ill man.

"And now until Vienna I'll be taking a wee little snooze," said the Chief Field Chaplain, "and I expect, that you wake me up as soon as we arrive in Vienna. — And you," he turned to Švejk, "you will go to the kitchen of our mess, take a set of silverware and bring me lunch. Say that it is for mister *Chief Field Chaplain* Lacina. See to it, that you get a double portion. If its dumplings, then don't accept slices off the tip, that's only a losing deal. Then you'll bring me from the kitchen a bottle of wine and take the mess kit with you, so that they pour rum into it for you."

Father Lacina was feeling around in his pockets.

"Listen up," he told the Sergeant, "I don't have any change, lend me a gold coin. — So, here you are! What's your name? — Švejk? — Here you have, Švejk, a gold coin for making the trip! Mister Sergeant, lend me another gold coin. — You see, Švejk, the second gold coin you'll get, when you'll have taken care of everything in order. — Then also, make sure they give you cigarettes and cigars for me. If chocolate is being issued, then swipe a double portion, and if it is cans, then see to it, that they give you smoked tongue or goose liver. If Emmental[243] cheese is being issued, then take care, that they don't give you any off the edge, and if Hungarian salami, then no end tip, but nicely from the middle, so that it be supple."

Chief Field Chaplain stretched himself out on the bench and in a while fell asleep.

"I think," said the One-Year Volunteer to the Sergeant into the midst of the snoring of the Father, "that you are totally satisfied with our foundling. He is properly full of life and ready for the world."

"He's been, as the saying goes," sounded up Švejk, "already weaned, mister Sergeant, he's already sucking from the bottle."

The Sergeant wrestled with himself a while and all of a sudden lost all servility and said harshly: "He is tremendously tame."

"He reminds me with that change, which he doesn't have," suggested in passing Švejk, "that he's like some Mlíčko, a mason from Dejvice, he too had not had change for so long, until he buried himself in debt up to his neck and was locked up for fraud. He had eaten his way through the big money and had no change."

"At the Seventy-fifth Regiment," let himself be heard one man from the escort, "the Captain drank his way through the whole Regimental cash box before the war and had to quit the military, and now he's captain again, and one *quartermaster*, who stole from the government issue inventory shoulder board cloth - there were over twenty bales of it - is nowadays a *staff quartermaster*, and one infantryman was not long ago in Serbia shot dead, because he ate at once his can of food, which he was to keep for three days."

"That does not belong here," the Sergeant proclaimed, "but it is true, that to borrow two gold coins from a poor sergeant for a tip..."

"Here you have that gold coin," said Švejk, "I don't want to enrich myself at your expense. And if he gives me still the second gold coin, then I'll return it to you too, so you won't bawl. You are to be pleased, when some military superior of yours borrows spending money from you. You are extremely selfish. What's at stake here are two miserable gold coins, and I would like to see you, if you were to sacrifice your life for your military superior, if he were lying wounded somewhere on an enemy line and you were to save him and carry him in your arms and they would be shooting shrapnel and all kinds of things at you."

"You would dump in your pants," was defending himself the Sergeant, "you one old pipe."

"There are more of those who have dumped in their pants in each *combat*," sounded up again one man from the escort, "not long ago was telling us a wounded buddy in Budějovice, that when they were *advancing*, he dumped three times in succession. First, when they were crawling out from the *dugouts* to the open space in front of the *barbed wire obstacles*, then, when they started cutting them, and that the third time he released it into his pants was, when rushing against them were the Russians with bayonets and were screaming *hoorah*. Then they started running back into the *dugouts* and from among their platoon there was not one, who did not dump in his pants. And one dead one, who was lying up on the berm with his legs dangling down, whose head during the advance a shrapnel tore half off, as if it were sliced off, he in the last moment dumped so much, that it was oozing from his pants over his boots down into the *dugout* along with the blood. And the half of his skull including the brain was lying right under it. When it comes to that, one doesn't even know how it happens to him."

"Then again," said Švejk, "sometimes in *combat* a man will get sick to his stomach, something will strike a man as repulsive. In Prague at Pohořelec[244] in Vyhlídka[245], a sick convalescent from the Przemyśl[246] front was relaying, that somewhere over there by the *fort* it came down to bayonet attack and that up against him emerged one Russian, a mountain of a guy, and he was rushing him with a bayonet as if on greased skids, and had a good-sized little drop hanging at his nose. As he looked at that little drop, at that snot, he got sick right away and he had to go to the aid station, where they admitted him as contaminated by cholera and transported him to the cholera barracks in Pest[247], where he of course actually got infected by cholera."

"Was he an ordinary infantryman, or a *sergeant*?" asked the One-Year Volunteer.

"A sergeant he was," answered Švejk calmly.

"It could happen even to any one-year timer," said the Sergeant like a numskull, but at the same time he was looking triumphantly at the One-Year Volunteer, as if he wanted to say: I dished it out to you really good, what're you going to say to that.

But he was reticent and lay down on the bench.

They were approaching Vienna[248]. Those, who were not sleeping, were watching from the window barbed wire obstacles and fortifications near Vienna, which gave rise apparently in the whole train to a feeling of certain uneasiness.

If up to this point there still had been incessantly coming from the cars the sound of the krauts from around Kašperské Hory hollering: *"When me comes, when me comes, when ag'in, ag'in me comes"*, now they became silent under the unpleasant impression of the barbed wire, with which Vienna was wrapped shut.

"All is in order," said Švejk, looking at the trenches, "everything is in absolute order, except here the Vienna inhabitants on their outings can rip their pants. Here man's got to be careful. — Vienna is an altogether important city," he continued, "just the number of wild animals they have here in that Schönbrun zoo[249]. When I was years ago in Vienna, I used to like going to watch the monkeys the best, but when there is riding some personality from the imperial castle[250], by then they don't let anybody in there through the police line. There was a tailor with me there from the tenth district[251] and him they locked up because he wanted to see the monkeys no matter what."

"And you've been also inside the castle?" asked the Sergeant.

"It is very beautiful in there," answered Švejk, "I have not been in there, but telling me about it was one, who has. The nicest is the *castle guard.* Each one of them they say has to be six feet tall and afterwards he gets a tobacco store concession[252]. And of princesses there are so many, it is as if they were just litter.

They passed through some railroad station[253], where there were left behind them the dying-down sounds of the Austrian anthem played by some band, which had come here perhaps by mistake, because only after a pretty long while did they and their train get to the railroad station, where they stopped, rations were issued, and there was a ceremonial welcome.

But it wasn't like at the beginning of the war anymore, when soldiers on the way to the front overstuffed themselves at every railroad station and where they were being welcomed by bridesmaids in stupid white dresses and even stupider faces and damn stupid bouquets and an even a stupider speech of some such dame, whose husband now acted the tremendous patriot and republican.

The welcome in Vienna consisted of three female members of the Austrian Red Cross Association[254] and two female members of some war association of Viennese matrons and young ladies, one official representative of the Viennese magistrate[255], and a military representative.

In all those faces one could see fatigue. The trains with the troops were running day and night, the ambulance cars with the wounded were passing through every hour, at railroad stations they were switching from one track to another every so often cars loaded with prisoners of war and during all that had to be present the members of those various corporations and associations. It went on one day after another and the original enthusiasm was changing into yawning. They rotated in that service duty, each one of them, who showed up at any Viennese railroad station, had the same tired expression as those, who were awaiting today the train with the Budějovice Regiment.

From the cattle cars were peeking out soldiers with an expression of hopelessness, such as seen on those, who are going to the gallows.

Up to them were stepping ladies distributing to them ginger bread with sugar inscriptions *"Victory and Revenge," "God Punish England," "The Austrian Has a Fatherland. He Loves It and Also Has a Reason to Fight for It."*

One could see, how highlanders from around Kašperské Hory were stuffing themselves with the gingerbread, while the countenance of hopelessness was not leaving them.

Then an order was issued to go, company by company, to get rations at the field kitchens, which were standing behind the railroad station.

There was also the officers' mess there, where Švejk was going to convey the Chief Field Chaplain's order, while the One-Year Volunteer was waiting, until they would feed him, because two from the escort had gone after the rations for the whole arrestee car.

Švejk conveyed correctly the order and crossing the railway tracks he saw Senior Lieutenant Lukáš, who was strolling between the tracks and was waiting, whether in the officers' mess there would be something left for him.

His situation was very unpleasant, because for the time being, he and Lieutenant Kirschner shared one *orderly*. The guy was in fact taking care exclusively of his own master and was conducting a campaign of total sabotage, when it came to Senior Lieutenant Lukáš.

"Whom are you carrying that to, Švejk?" asked the unhappy Senior Lieutenant, when Švejk laid on the ground a heap of things, which he'd lured away in the officers' mess and which he had wrapped in his overcoat.

Švejk froze for a moment, but immediately got hold of himself. His face was full of glow and serenity, when he answered:

"It is for you, I dutifully report, Senior *Lieutenant*, Sir. Only I don't know, where your compartment is, and then I also don't know, whether mister commandant of the train will not have anything against my going with you. He's a pretty bad swine."

Senior Lieutenant Lukáš looked quizzically at Švejk, who however continued in good-natured confidentiality: "He is really a swine, *Senior Lieutenant*, Sir. When he was on an inspection of the train, I reported to him right away, that it was already eleven o'clock and that I had served out my whole sentence and that I belonged either in the cattle car or with you, and he blew me off fairly crudely, that I should just stay, that at least, *Senior Lieutenant*, Sir, while underway I won't do anything to bring shame on you."

Švejk put on a face of martyr: "As if I, *Senior Lieutenant*, Sir, have ever at all brought shame on you."

Senior Lieutenant Lukáš sighed.

"Shame," continued Švejk, "I have certainly never brought on you, if something happened, it was a coincidence, mere divine guidance, as used to say the old Vaníček from Pelhřimov, when he was serving his thirty-sixth sentence. I have never done anything on purpose, *Senior Lieutenant*, Sir, I have always wanted to do something adept, good, and it's not my fault, if we both had no profit from it and had nothing but mere torment and torture."

"Just don't sorrow so much, Švejk," said Senior Lieutenant Lukáš softly, as they were approaching the staff car, "I will arrange everything, so that you would be with me again."

"I dutifully report *Senior Lieutenant*, Sir, that I'm not sorrowing. It just struck me as such a pity, that we both are the most hapless people in this war and under the sun and neither one of us is at fault for anything. It is a terrible fate, when I behold the thought, that I have been so mindful as long as I've been alive!"

"Calm down, Švejk!"

"I dutifully report, *Senior Lieutenant*, Sir, that if it were not against subordination, I would say, that I cannot at all calm down, but as it is I have to say, that as you ordered I am already totally calm."

"Then just crawl, Švejk, into the car,."

"I dutifully report, that I am already crawling, *Senior Lieutenant*, Sir."

*

Over the military camp in Bruck[256] was reigning the silence of the night. In the barracks for the troops the soldiers were shivering from the cold and in the officers' barracks they were opening the windows, because it was overheated in there.

From the individual structures, in front of which were standing guards, there came now and then the sound of the steps of a sentry, who was by walking scaring away sleep.

Down in Bruck an der Leitha[257], there were glowing lights from the I&R meat canning factory[258], where they worked day and night and various refuse was being processed. Because from here the wind blew to the double rows of trees inside the military camp, there was arriving there the stench from the rotting sinews, hoofs, cloven hoofs and bones, which they were boiling for the soup cans.

From the abandoned little pavilion, where earlier in time of peace some photographer would take pictures of the soldiers spending their youth here at the military shooting range, one could see down in the valley by Leitha[259] the red electric light of the At the Ear of Corn brothel, which graced by his visit archduke Stephan during the big maneuvers at Sopron[260] in the year 1908 and where daily gathered the officers' society.

That was the best room of ill repute, where common soldiers and one-year volunteers were not allowed to go.

Those frequented the Pink House, whose green lights were also visible from the abandoned photography studio.

It was the same sorting as later at the front, when the imperial establishment could not help its troops with anything other anymore than mobile brothels at the brigade staffs, the so-called "puffs".

There were therefore I&R Officers Puff, I&R NCO Puff, and I&R GI Puff.

Bruck an der Leitha was glowing, just as on the other side over the bridge there were glowing Királyhida, Cisleithania and Transleithania[261]. In both towns, the Hungarian and the Austrian, Gypsy bands were playing, windows of coffeehouses and restaurants were glowing, people were singing, drinking. Local burghers and bureaucrats would bring here into the coffeehouses and restaurants their pampered ladies and adult daughters, and Bridge on the Litava, Bruck an der Leitha, and Királyhida[262] were nothing else but one huge brothel.

In one of the officers' barracks in the camp there was waiting at night Švejk for his Senior Lieutenant Lukáš, who went in the evening to town to the theater and had not returned yet. Švejk was sitting on the unmade bed of the Lieutenant's and facing him was, sitting on the table, the servant of Major Wenzl.

The Major returned to the Regiment again, when in Serbia they had declared his total ineptness at the Drina river. They spoke of the fact, that he had a pontoon bridge taken apart and destroyed, when he still had a half of his battalion on the other side. Now he was attached to the military shooting range in Királyhida as its commander and also had something to do with the management of the camp. Among the officers the story was, that Major Wenzl would now help himself to get on his feet. The rooms of Lukáš and Wenzl were in the same corridor.

The servant of Major Wenzl, Mikulášek, a tiny man marked by small-pox, was swinging his legs and complaining bitterly: "I'm amazed by that old shameless rube of mine, that he's not coming yet. I'd like to know where that old geezer of mine is loafing all night. If he gave me the room key at least, I'd lie down and be grinning. He's got countless bottles of wine in there."

"They say he steals," suggested in passing Švejk, comfortably smoking his Senior Lieutenant's cigarettes, because the same one has forbidden him to puff from his pipe in the room, "after all you have to know something about it, wherefrom the two of you got the wine."

"I go where he orders me," said in a tiny voice Mikulášek, "I get a chit from him and already I'm off to get the stuff issued for the hospital, and I'm carrying it home."

"And if he ordered you," asked Švejk, "to steal the Regimental cash box, would you do it? Here out of sight you bitch and moan, but shake in front of him like an aspen."

Mikulášek batted his little eyes: "I'd think it over."

"You must think over nothing, you one sweaty suckling," started shouting at him Švejk, but fell quiet, because the door opened and in stepped Senior Lieutenant Lukáš. He was, as could immediately be observed, in a very good mood, because he had his cap on backward.

Mikulášek spooked so, that he forgot to jump off the table, but was saluting sitting down, having forgotten on top of all, that he didn't have the cap on his head.

"I dutifully report *Senior Lieutenant*, Sir, that everything is in order," was Švejk reporting, having assumed firm military bearing according to all regulations, while the cigarette stayed in his mouth.

Senior Lieutenant Lukáš however did not notice it and went directly after Mikulášek, who with his eyes popping out watched the Lieutenant's every move and all the while continued saluting and still kept sitting on the table all the while.

"Senior Lieutenant Lukáš," he said, stepping up to Mikulášek with a gait none too firm, "and what is your name?"

Mikulášek was reticent. Lukáš pulled up a chair in front of Mikulášek sitting on the table, sat down, while looking up at him above, he said: "Švejk, bring me the service revolver from the suitcase."

Mikulášek during all the time, when Švejk was searching in the suitcase, kept quiet and was only looking horrified at the Senior Lieutenant. If at that moment he realized, that he's sitting on the table, he was certainly even more desperate, because his legs were touching the knees of the sitting Senior Lieutenant.

"Say, what's your name, human?" was calling upward at Mikulášek the Senior Lieutenant.

But he kept on being reticent. As he would later explain, he was beset by some kind of paralysis with the sudden arrival of the Senior Lieutenant. He wanted to jump off, and could not, wanted to answer, and could not, wanted to salute, but it did not work.

"I dutifully report, *Senior Lieutenant*, Sir," sounded up Švejk, "that the revolver is not loaded."

"Then load it, Švejk!"

"I dutifully report *Senior Lieutenant*, Sir, that we don't have any cartridges and that it will be hard to shoot him off the table. I will be so bold as to point out, *Senior Lieutenant*, Sir, that it is Mikulášek, *orderly* of Mister Major Wenzl. He always loses his ability to speak, when he sees one of the officer gentlemen. He is altogether shy to speak. He is altogether, as I say, just such a rundown sweaty suckling. Mister Major Wenzl always makes him stand in the corridor, when he goes somewhere to town, and this thing looking aggrieved goes loafing from one *orderly* in the building to another. If it would at least have a reason to spook, but it hasn't actually done anything."

Švejk spat and in his voice and in the fact, that he was speaking of Mikulášek in the neuter gender, one could hear the total contempt over the cowardice of the servant of Major Wenzl and over his non-military bearing.

"Allow me," continued Švejk, "to approach him and take a sniff."

Švejk pulled Mikulášek, who continued looking stupidly at the Senior Lieutenant, off the table, and having stood him on the floor, sniffed his pants.

"Not yet," he proclaimed, "but it's starting. Should I throw him out?"

"Throw him out, Švejk."

Švejk led the trembling Mikulášek out into the corridor, closed the door behind them and in the corridor told him: "So you numskull of a guy, I saved your life. When mister Major Wenzl comes back, you better will in return very quietly bring me a bottle of wine. No joking. I really saved your life. When my *Senior Lieutenant* is drunk, then there's trouble. Only I know how to deal with him and nobody else."

"I am…"

"A fart you are," contemptuously expressed himself Švejk, "sit on the threshold and wait, until your Major Wenzl comes."

"It's about time," said Senior Lieutenant Lukáš welcoming Švejk, "that you're coming, I want to talk to you. You don't have to stupidly stand at attention. Take a seat, Švejk, and keep the 'as ordered' to yourself. Hold your mouth shut and pay good attention. Do you know, where in Királyhida there is Sopronyi *street*[263]? Forget your constant 'I dutifully report, *Senior Lieutenant*, Sir, that I don't know.' You don't know, then say I don't know, and enough. Write for yourself on a piece of paper: Sopronyi street number 16. In that building there is a hardware store. Do you know, what a hardware store is? *Lord God*, don't say I dutifully report. Say I know or don't know. So do you know, what a hardware store is? You do, good. That store belongs to some Hungarian Kákonyi. Do you know, what a Hungarian is? So *God-in-heaven*, do you know or not? You do, good. Up above the store there is the second floor and that's where he lives. Do you know about it? That you don't, krucifix, then I'm telling you, that he lives there. Is that enough for you? It is, good. If it weren't, then I'd have you locked up. Have you made a note, that the guy's name is Kákonyi? Good, so you, tomorrow morning at about ten o'clock, will go down to town, will find that house and go up to the second floor and will hand over to Mrs. Kákonyi this written note."

Senior Lieutenant Lukáš opened the breast-pocket wallet and yawning put into Švejk's hand a white envelope with a letter and no address.

"It is a matter of tremendous importance, Švejk," he kept instructing him further, "there's never enough caution to spare, and that is why, as you can see, there is no address. I am totally relying on you, that you will hand over that written note in order. Make another note, that the lady's name is Etelka, then write down 'Mrs. Etelka Kákonyi'. Let me still tell you, that you must deliver the written note discretely under any circumstances and wait for an answer. That you are to wait for an answer, is already written about in the letter. What else do you want?"

"If, *Senior Lieutenant*, Sir, they don't give me an answer, what am I to do?"

"Then you'll remind them, that you must no matter what get an answer," answered the Senior Lieutenant yawning all about again, "now however I'm going to sleep, I am today really tired. What an amazing amount we have drunk. I think, that everybody would be just as tired after the whole evening and night like that."

Senior Lieutenant Lukáš did not originally intend to linger anywhere. He went toward the evening from the camp to town only to go to a Hungarian theater in Királyhida, where they were playing some Hungarian operetta with plump Jew actresses in the leading roles, whose wonderful advantage was, that they would throw their legs up high while dancing and wore neither tights, nor knickers and on account of greater appeal for the officer gentlemen they shaved themselves down below like Tatar women, which of course had no benefit for the gallery, but that much more for the officers of the artillery sitting down in the orchestra, who were for that beauty taking with them to the theater artillery field glasses.

Senior Lieutenant Lukáš was not interested however in the interesting swine filth, because the borrowed opera glasses were not achromatic and instead of thighs he saw only some purple surfaces in motion.

During the intermission after the first act his interest was captured rather by one lady who, accompanied by a gentleman of middle age years, was dragging him toward the cloak room and was telling him, that they were going home immediately, that she would not be watching such things. She was proclaiming it quite loudly in German, after which her escort was answering in Hungarian. "Yes, angel, we're going, I agree. It is really a disgusting thing."

"*It is disgusting*," was answering angrily the lady, when the gentleman was slipping the theater cloak on her. Her eyes were burning at the same time with agitation over the indecency, the big black eyes, going so well with her nice figure. She glanced at the same time at Senior Lieutenant Lukáš and proclaimed one more time with resolve: *"Disgusting, really disgusting."* That decided it for a short romance.

He obtained from the cloak room attendant the information, that those were Mr. and Mrs. Kákonyi, that the gentleman has at Sopronyi street 16 a hardware enterprise.

"And he lives with missus Etelka on the second floor," said the cloak room attendant with the detail like an old madam, "She is a German from Sopron and he is a Hungarian, here it's all mixed up."

Senior Lieutenant Lukáš also took his cloak from the cloak room and went to town, where he met in the large wine and coffee bar At the Archduke Albrecht with several officers of the 91st Regiment.

He did not talk much and drank that much more, going through the possible combinations of, what it was after all he was to write to that strict, moral, good-looking lady, who definitely attracted him more than all those monkeys on the stage, as expressed themselves in reference to them the other officers.

In a very good mood he left for the small coffeehouse At the Cross of St. Stephen, where he went into a small private booth, out of where he drove some Romanian woman, who was offering that she'd strip herself naked and that he could do with her, whatever he wanted, he ordered ink, a pen and letter paper, a bottle of cognac and wrote after careful consideration this written note, that seemed to him altogether the nicest, which he had ever written:

Gracious Lady!

I was present yesterday at the municipal theater during the play, which exasperated you. I was watching you already during the whole first act, you and your mister husband. As I was observing…

"Just lay into him," said to himself Senior Lieutenant Lukáš, "what right does that guy have to have such a lovely wife. After all he looks like a shaven baboon."

He wrote on:

Your mister husband was with the most intense affinity watching lewd acts performed on stage in the play, which in you, gracious lady, caused an aversion, because it was not art, but disgusting manipulation of the most intimate human feelings.

"That broad sure has a bustline," thought to himself Senior Lieutenant Lukáš, "just straight into it!"

Forgive, gracious lady, that you do not know me, but in spite of it I am frank toward you. I have seen in my life many women, but none made such an impression on me as you, because your discernment and view of life corresponds totally to my view. I am convinced, that your mister husband is a genuinely selfish man, who drags you along with him…

"That won't work," told himself Senior Lieutenant Lukáš and crossed the "*drags along*" and instead of it wrote:

…who in the interest of his takes you, gracious lady, with him to theatrical performances corresponding only with his taste. I like frankness, I am in no way seeking to intrude into your private life, and I would wish to have a talk with you privately about pure art…

"Here at the local hotels it won't work, I'll have to drag her off to Vienna," thought to himself in addition the Senior Lieutenant, "I'll take an official trip."

That is why I'm mustering the courage, gracious lady, to beg you for a meeting, in order for us to get honorably acquainted more closely, which you will certainly not deny to one, whom in the shortest time await trying war marches and who, in case of your kind consent, will retain in the battle's tumult the most beautiful memory of a soul, that came to understand him, as he himself understood her. Your decision will be a direction to me, your answer a decisive moment in my life.

He signed, drank up the cognac and ordered yet another bottle and drinking one little goblet after another, just about after each sentence he shed genuine tears, when he read his latest lines.

*

It was nine o'clock in the morning, when Švejk woke Senior Lieutenant Lukáš up: "I dutifully report *Senior Lieutenant*, Sir, that you overslept to go on duty and I have to go already with your written note to that Királyhida. I was already waking you at seven o'clock, then at half of eight, then at eight, when they were already passing by on the way to the exercises, and you only turned over to the other side. *Senior Lieutenant*, Sir...I say, *Senior Lieutenant*, Sir..."

Senior Lieutenant Lukáš wanted, that is to say, having mumbled something, to turn himself over on the side again, which he did not manage, because Švejk was mercilessly shaking him and hollering: "*Senior Lieutenant*, Sir, then I am going with that written note to Királyhida."

The Lieutenant yawned: "With a written note? *Yes*, with my written note it's a matter of discretion, understand, a secret between the two of us. *Fall out...*"

The Senior Lieutenant wrapped himself again in the blanket, from which Švejk had pulled him out, and kept on sleeping, while Švejk journeyed to Királyhida.

Finding Sopronyi street number 16 would not had been that hard, if he were not met by the old sapper[264] Vodička by accident, who was attached to the "Styrians"[265], whose barracks were down below in the camp. Vodička used to live years ago in Prague, at Na Bojišti[266], and that is why given such a meeting nothing else could be done, other than for both of them to go to the Little Black Ram pub in Bruck, where there was an acquaintance waitress Růženka, a Czech girl, to whom all the Czech one-year volunteers, that had ever been to the camp, owed some amount.

As of late sapper Vodička, an old plotter, was acting as her cavalier and had a list of all the march-gangs that were leaving the camp, and he would go at the right time to remind the Czech one-year volunteers, not to get lost in the tumult of war without paying the bill.

"Where are you actually heading?" asked Vodička, after they first drank good wine.

"It is a secret," answered Švejk, "but with you, as an old friend, I'll share it in confidence."

He explained everything to him in detail and Vodička proclaimed, that he was an old sapper and that he couldn't abandon him, and that they would go to turn the written note over together.

They were having an excellent time talking about past times and everything seemed to them, when after the eighth evening hour they stepped out from the Little Black Ram, natural and easy.

Aside from that they had in their souls a solid impression, that they were not afraid of anybody. All along the way to Sopronyi street number 16 Vodička was demonstrating enormous hate toward Hungarians and was ceaselessly telling, how everywhere he brawls with them, where in all the places and when he had brawled with them and what, when and where prevented him from brawling with them.

"Once, I tell you, I was already holding such a Hungarian boy by the throat in Pausdorf[267], where we sappers had gone to have some wine, and I want to give him one with a *belt* across his coconut in that darkness, because right away, as it started, we slammed the hanging lamp with a bottle, and all of a sudden he starts screaming: 'Tony, com'on, it's me, Purkrábek, from the 16th *Land Defense*!' Just a little bit and there would had been a mistake. At least we paid those Hungarian clowns back real good in there by the Neusiedler Lake[268], which we had gone to take a look at three weeks before that. Camping in the next village there's a machine gun detachment of some Honved soldiers, and by accident we all went to a pub, where they were dancing that csárdás of theirs as if they'd lost their minds and they were stretching their yaps all round about with their *'Your honor, your honor, judge, your honor'*, or *'Girls, girls, girls from the village'*. We sit across from them facing them, only we laid the *belts* down in front of us on the table, and we're telling one another: 'You shameless rubes, we'll give you *girls*,' and some guy Mejstřík, who had a fin of a hand as big as the White Mountain, offered himself right away, that he'll go to have a dance and that he'll take some ruffian's girl out of the whirl. The girls were damn good lookers, such big calves and asses, big thighs and big-eyed, and as the Hungarian shameless rubes were pressing against them, one could see that those girls have full, hard breasts like half balls and that it makes them feel good and that they know their way around in a press. So this Mejstřík of ours jumps into the whirl and wants to be taking the best looker away from one Honved soldier, who started babbling something, and Mejstřík threw him one right away, he dropped like a sack, we had immediately grabbed the *belts* already, wrapped them around the hand, so the bayonets would not fly off, jumped in their midst, and I hollered: 'Guilty or innocent, take them row by row!' and already it went like sliding on butter. They started jumping out through the window, we were catching them in the windows by their feet and pulling them again into the ballroom. Whoever was not one of ours, he got whopped. Their mayor and the

State Police cop got mixed up in it there, and right away their temples[269] of the Lord got whacked. The pubkeeper got beaten up too, because he started telling us off in German, that supposedly we were spoiling the merriment. Afterwards we were still catching throughout the village those, who wanted to hide from us. Like one corporal of theirs, him we found burrowed in the hay in the loft of a farm all the way down below the village. He was given away to us by his girl, because he danced there with another. She had fallen for our Mejstřík and she then went with him up the road to Királyhida, where by the forest there are hay drying shacks. She dragged him into one such drying shack and wanted then five crowns from him and he slapped her across her mug. Then he caught up with us only up by the very camp and was saying, that he always thought, that Hungarian women were fierier, but this swine was lying still like a tree stump and only kept mumbling something. — Hungarians are, to make the story short, riff-raff," finished the old sapper Vodička, after which Švejk remarked: "A Hungarian here or there also can't help being Hungarian and be held responsible for it."

"How so that he can't," was Vodička getting agitated, "That is silliness, each one is responsible for it. I'd wish for you, that they would dress you up, just like it happened to me the first day, when I arrived here for the training classes. That very same afternoon they had already corralled us like a herd of cattle at the school and one such jerk started drawing for us and explaining what *covered trenches* were, how foundations were made, how one measured them, and in the morning, he says, who does not have it drawn, the way he's explaining it, that he will be locked up and tied. 'Krucifix,' I'm thinking to myself, 'is this why you volunteered the for courses, so that you'd skirt the front, or so that in the evening you'd be making pictures in some little notebooks with a wee pencil like a wee schoolboy?' Such anger possessed me, that I could not stand still, I could not even look at the moron, that was doing the explaining for us. I would have liked the best to smash all to pieces, that's how furious I was. I did not even wait for the coffee and right away I went from the barrack to Királyhida, and on account of the anger I could not think of anything else but finding in the town a quiet pub for myself, getting drunk, and raising a ruckus, giving somebody a few across the snout and going home having gotten my jollies off. Man proposes, but Lord God disposes. There by the river all the way among the gardens I found actually such an establishment, quiet as a chapel[270], as if created for a ruckus. There were only two guests sitting there and they were conversing in Hungarian, which stirred me up even more, and also I had gotten drunk sooner and more, than I thought, so that having the monkey on my back I did not even notice, that next door there was another establishment, whereto during the time, when I was exerting myself, arrived about eight hussars, who laid into me, when I kicked the ass of the first two guests. Those hussar dirtbags mangled me so and chased me through the gardens, that I could not find my way home, only toward morning I did, and right away I had to go to *sickbay*, where I made an excuse, that I had fallen into a brick yard clay pit, and all week they were wrapping me in a wet bed sheet, lest my back start festering. Wish for that, lordy, ending up among such rogues. Those are not people, they are cattle beasts."

"What each handles, that he perishes by," said Švejk, "also you must not wonder and hold it against them, that they are upset, when they have to leave all the wine behind on the table and are to chase you from garden to garden in the darkness. They should had been done with you right on the spot in the pub's hall, then thrown you out. For them it would had been better and for you too, if they made an end of you at the table. I used to know some distiller Paroubek in Libeň. Once a tinker got drunk at his place on juniper gin and started cursing, that it was weak, that he pours water into it, that if he were tinkering a hundred years and for the whole wage bought nothing but juniper gin and drank it at once, that he could still walk on a high wire and carry him, Paroubek, in his arms. Then on top of it he told Paroubek in Slovak, that he was a *rascal* and the beast of Šaščín[271], so dear Paroubek grabbed him, battered his head with the mouse traps and wires a few times and threw him out and was beating him on the street with a rod for cranking the store shutter all the way down to the Invalidovna[272] and chased him, as he ran amok, past the Invalidovna in Karlín all the way up to Žižkov, from here past the *Jewish Kilns*[273] to Malešice, where at last he broke that rod across the tinker's back, so that he could return back to Libeň. Yeah, but in the midst of the upset he forgot that he probably still had the whole audience at the gin mill, that those scoundrels would probably be taking care of business by themselves. And that's also what he confirmed for himself, when at last he got back again into his gin mill. The gin mill's shutter was cranked half way down, next to it stood two cops, also strongly tanked up, since they were restoring order inside. Half of everything drunk up, in the street an empty little rum barrel, and under the counter Paroubek found two drunk guys, who were overlooked by the cops and who, when he pulled them out, wanted to pay him two krejcars[274] apiece, that they had not drunk more of the rye than that. That's how undue haste is punished. It is like in the military. First we defeat the enemy and then ever after him without ceasing, and in the end we can't run away fast enough."

"I made sure to remember all those guys well," sounded up Vodička, "should one of those hussars stumble into my path, I would get even with him. We sappers are, when it grabs us and we get crazy, sonofabitches. We are not like those iron flies[275]. When we were at the front at Przemyśl, then there was with us Captain Jetzbacher, a swine, who had no equal under the sun. He knew how to bust our chops so hard, that some guy Bitterlich in our company gang, a German, but such a nice man, shot himself dead on account of him. So we told ourselves, that when it starts whistling by from the Russian side, that our Captain Jetzbacher won't live either. And sure enough, right away as the Russians started shooting at us, we put during the exchange of fire five *shots* into him. The sonofabitch was still alive like a cat, so we had to use two shots to finish him off, so nothing would come of it; he only gave a whimper, but in a somehow funny way, very hilariously."

Vodička laughed: "That's a daily routine at the front for you. One buddy of mine was telling me, he's now also here with us, that when he was as infantryman down by Belgrade, his company gang during *combat* blew away their *senior lieutenant*, also such a dogging beast, who himself shot two soldiers dead on the march, because they couldn't go any farther. That one, when he was croaking, all of a sudden started whistling the signal to retreat. It is said all those around him could have laughed themselves to death."

During this engaging and educational conversation found Švejk with Vodička at last the hardware store of Mister Kákonyi at Sopronyi street number 16.

"You should after all better wait here," said Švejk to Vodička in front of the carriage drive-through arcade of the house, "I'll just run up to the second floor and hand over the written note, wait for the answer and I'm back down again right away."

"I'm supposed to abandon you?" wondered Vodička, "You don't know the Hungarians, I keep telling you. Here we have to be careful of them. I'll slap him."

"Listen, Vodička," said Švejk seriously, "it is not a Hungarian who is at stake here, but his wife who it is about. C'mon, I was telling it all to you, when we were sitting with that Czech *waitress*, that I'm carrying a written note from my *Senior Lieutenant*, that it is an absolute secret. After all, my *Senior Lieutenant* was putting it as a burden on my heart, that not a living soul must know about it, and that waitress of yours herself was saying after all, that it was absolutely correct, that it is a matter of discretion. That nobody must find out about it, that mister *Senior Lieutenant* is corresponding with a married broad. And you yourself were also praising it and nodding in agreement. I explained to you both, didn't I, as ought to be and is proper, that I will carry out the order of my *Senior Lieutenant* exactly, and you all of a sudden no matter what want to go upstairs with me."

"You don't know me yet, Švejk," answered also very seriously old sapper Vodička, "since I said once already, that I won't abandon you, then remember, that my word is worth a hundred. When two go, it is always safer."

"I will talk you, Vodička, out of that error. Do you know, where in Vyšehrad there is Neklanova street[276]? There had his shop locksmith Voborník. He was man a righteous and one day, when he came back from a night on the town, he brought along another carouser with him to put up for the night. Then he was laid up for a long, long time and every day, when his wife was changing the dressing on his head wound, she was telling him: 'See, Toníček, if there weren't two of you who came, then I would have only given you the usual show and wouldn't have thrown the weighing scale at your head.' And he then, when he could speak already, he said: 'You're right, mother, next time when I go somewhere, I won't drag in anybody with me.'"

"That's all we would still need," got all worked up Vodička, "to also have that Hungarian want to throw something at our heads on top of it. I will grab him by the neck and knock him off the second floor down the stairs, until he flies like shrapnel. Going after the Hungarian boys one has to do it no-holds-barred. No use beating about the bush."

"Vodička, you have not drunk that much yet. I've had two quarter-liters more than you. Just consider one thing, that we must not create any scandal. I am the one responsible for it. After all a broad is at stake."

"I'll slap the broad too, Švejk, I don't care, you still don't know old Vodička. Once in Záběhlice at the Rose Island[277] one such masquerading scarecrow didn't want to have a dance with me, saying that my snout was swollen. My snout was swollen, true, because I just came from a dance in Hostivař, but imagine the insult from the floozy. 'So here you have one too, most honored miss,' I said, 'so you wouldn't feel being left out.' As I tore her one, she knocked over the whole table in the garden with glasses on it, that she was sitting at with her dad and mom and two brothers. But I was not afraid of the whole Rose Island. There were acquaintances from Vršovice there, and those helped me. We thrashed about five families including even the children. One had to be able to hear it all the way in Michle[278] and afterward it was also then in the newspaper about the garden party of that charitable association of some natives of some town. And that's why as I say, just as others have helped me, so I too will always help each of my buddies, when something is about to happen. For the living God, I won't move a step away from you. You don't know Hungarians... After all, you can't do that to me, to be pushing me away from you, when we're seeing each other after so many years, and under such circumstances to boot."

"So then come along," decided Švejk, "but acting carefully, lest we have any unpleasant difficulties."

"Don't worry, buddy," softly said Vodička, when they were walking toward the staircase, "I'll slap him..."

And even more softly he added: "You'll see that the Hungarian boy won't cause us any exertion."

And if there were somebody in that drive-through arcade and understood Czech, he would have heard the now already from the stairway more loudly declared byword of Vodička's "You don't know Hungarians...", a byword, at which he arrived in a quiet establishment over the Litava river, among the gardens of the glorious Királyhida, surrounded by hills, that soldiers will be remembering always with curses as they recollect the *exercises* before the world war and also during the world war, whereby they were getting theoretical training for practical massacres and carnage.

*

Švejk and Vodička were standing in front of the door of mister Kákonyi. Before he pressed the button of the doorbell, Švejk remarked: "Have you ever heard, Vodička, that caution is the mother of wisdom?"

"I don't care about that," answered Vodička, "he must not even have time to open his yap…"

"I too have no business with him, Vodička."

Švejk rang the bell and Vodička said loudly: '*One-two*, and he'll be flying down the stairs."

The door opened, a maid appeared and she was asking in Hungarian, what it was they wished.

"*I don't understand,*" said contemptuously Vodička, "learn Czech, girl."

"*Do you understand German*?" asked Švejk.

"Jost a beet."

"So tell the lady I want to speak the lady, say that a letter from a gentleman is out in the hallway."

"You make me wonder," said Vodička, stepping after Švejk into the front hall "why you're talking to a stench like that."

They were standing in the front hall, closed the door to the hallway and Švejk only remarked:

"They have this place nicely appointed, even two umbrellas on the hanger, and that picture of Christ the Lord also isn't bad."

From a room, out of which the sounds of knocking of spoons and clanking of plates was coming, there walked out the maid again and said to Švejk:

"The lady is said that she has no time, if there is something, it me give and say."

"So," said Švejk ceremoniously, *"to the lady a letter but keep trap shut."*

He pulled out the letter from Senior Lieutenant Lukáš.

"I," he said, pointing a finger at himself, *"answer wait here in the front hall."*

"Why don't you sit down?" asked Vodička, who was already sitting on a chair by the wall, "over there you've got a chair. You'd stand here like a beggar. Don't demean yourself in front of that Hungarian. You will see, that we'll have with him a drag out argument, but I'll slap him. — Listen," he said after a while, "where did you learn German?"

"By myself," answered Švejk. Again there was for a while silence. Then one could hear coming from the room, where the maid carried the written note, great screaming and noise. Somebody slammed something heavy against the floor, then one could clearly discern, that glasses were flying in there and plates were being smashed, into which was coming the sound of hollering: *"Baszom az anyát, baszom az istenet, baszom a Krizstus Márját, baszom az atyádot, baszom a világot!."*

The door flew open and into the front hall ran a gentleman in the best of years with a napkin around his neck, waving the letter handed over a moment ago.

Closest to the door was sitting the old sapper Vodička and it was he to whom the agitated man first turned.

"What's this supposed to mean, where is the damned guy that brought this letter?"

"Slow down," said Vodička getting up, "don't you scream too much with us being here, lest you fly out of here, and since you want to know, who brought the letter, then ask my buddy over there. But speak to him politely, or you'll be on the other side of the door before you could say cracker-jack."

Now it was up to Švejk, to get his own verification of the rich eloquence of the agitated gentleman with the napkin around his neck, who was making no sense mixing five after nine, that they were just having lunch.

"We heard that you were having lunch," concurred in broken German Švejk, adding in Czech: "It could have occurred to us too, that we would probably be needlessly tearing you away from the lunch."

"Don't be demeaning yourself," sounded up Vodička.

The agitated man whose napkin was after the animated gesticulation hanging on by only one corner, continued on, that first he thought that the matter being addressed in the letter is the requisition of some rooms for the troops in this house, which belongs to his wife.

"In here one could still fit a lot of troops," said Švejk, "but the letter was not about that, as you have perhaps ascertain for yourself."

The man grabbed his head, while doing it he let out a whole lot of recriminations, that he had also had been a reserve *lieutenant*, that he'd like to be serving now, but that he has a kidney ailment. That in his time the officer corps was not so loose, as to disturb the peace of a household. That he will send a letter to the Regiment Headquarters[279], the Ministry of the Military Affairs, and will publish it in the newspaper.

"Sir," said solemnly Švejk, "I wrote the letter. *I written, no Senior Lieutenant.* The signature is just pretend, fake, *signature, name, fake*. Your wife is very appealing to me. *I love your wife*. I'm in love with your wife up to my ears, as used to say Vrchlický[280]. *A capital lady.*"

The agitated man wanted to lunge at Švejk, who was standing calmly and contentedly in front of him, but the old sapper Vodička, watching every move of his, tripped his foot, tore out of his hand the letter, which he still kept waving, put it in a pocket, and when mister Kákonyi pulled himself together and got up, Vodička grabbed him, carried him to the door, opened the door by one hand for himself, and already one could hear, how something is rolling down the stairs.

It happened as fast as in fairy tales, when the demon comes to fetch a man.

Left behind of the agitated man was only the napkin. Švejk picked it up, knocked politely on the door of the room, from where five minutes ago came out mister Kákonyi and coming from where one could hear the weeping of a woman.

"I'm bringing you a napkin," said Švejk softly to the lady, who was weeping on a sofa, "it could get trampled. My respects."

He slammed his heels together, saluted and walked out into the hall. On the stairs one could not detect much of any traces of a struggle, here, according to Vodička's expectations, everything was playing out absolutely with ease. Only afterwards by the gate in the drive-through arcade Švejk found a torn off collar. There apparently, when mister Kákonyi desperately latched onto the building gate, so that he would not be dragged out into the street, was being played out the final act of this tragedy.

On the other hand the street was busy. Mister Kákonyi they had dragged into the drive-through on the opposite side of the street, where they were pouring water on him, and in the middle of the street old sapper Vodička was battling like a lion several honveds and honved hussars, who stood up for their countryman. He was in a masterly manner swinging his prong attached to his belt as if it were a flail. And he was not alone. By his side were fighting several Czech soldiers from various regiments, who just happened to be walking down the street.

Švejk, as he insisted later, himself did not even know, how he too got into it, and since he had no prong, how into his hands got a walking stick of some horrified onlooker.

It lasted a pretty good while, but everything nice also has to come to its end. There came an *emergency military patrol* and picked them all up.

Švejk with the stick, which was by the commander of the *emergency military patrol* acknowledged as being corpus delicti, was walking alongside Vodička.

Švejk was walking contentedly, having the stick on his shoulder like a rifle. The old sapper Vodička was pigheadedly reticent all the way. Only when they were entering the *main guardhouse*, he said gloomily to Švejk: "Wasn't I telling you, that you didn't know Hungarians?"

4

NEW AFFLICTIONS

Colonel Schröder was with fondness observing the pale face of Senior Lieutenant Lukáš, with large circles under his eyes, who being in discomfiture was not looking at the Colonel, but on the sly, as if he were studying something, was looking at the plan of troops deployment in the camp, which also was the only adornment in the whole office of the Colonel's.

In front of Colonel Schröder there were on the desk several newspapers with articles checked in blue pencil, which the Colonel skimmed over one more time in a perfunctory way, and said, looking at Senior Lieutenant Lukáš:

"Then you already know about it, that your servant Švejk finds himself in detention and will probably be delivered to the Divisional Court?"

"Yes, Colonel, Sir."

"Thereby of course," emphatically said the Colonel, feeding his ego over the pale face of Senior Lieutenant Lukáš, "is the whole matter not ended. It is certain, that the local public is in an uproar over the whole case of your servant Švejk, and the affair is being mentioned even in connection with your name, mister Senior Lieutenant. From the Division Headquarters has been already delivered to us certain material. We have here some magazines, that were dealing with this case. You can read it to me aloud."

He handed to Senior Lieutenant Lukáš the newspaper with the checked articles, who began reading in a monotonous voice, as if he were reading in a reader for children the sentence 'Honey is much more nutritious and more easily digestible than sugar': "Where is the guarantee of our future?"

"That is in the Pester Lloyd[281]?" the Colonel asked.

"Yes, Colonel, Sir," answered Senior Lieutenant Lukáš and continued reading: "Conducting a war demands collaboration of all strata of the society of the Austro-Hungarian monarchy. If we want to have the safety of the state secured, all its nations must support one another and the guarantee of our future is precisely in that spontaneous respect, which one nation receives from another. The greatest sacrifices of our doughty soldiers at the fronts, where they are ceaselessly advancing forward, would not be possible, if the rear, the supply and political artery of our glorious armies, were not united, if there were occurring in the back of our army elements shattering the unity of the state and through their agitation and ill-will were undermining the authority of the state entirety and were injecting into the alliance of the nationalities of our Empire confusion. We cannot in this historical moment mutely watch a handful of people, who would want to be trying for nationalistic local reasons to disrupt the united work and struggle of all the nations of this Empire for the just punishment of those scoundrels, who the Empire of ours without a cause attacked, in order to rid it of all cultural and civilizational possessions. We cannot mutely overlook these disgusting phenomena of outbursts of a sick soul, that desires only the breaching of unanimity in the hearts of the nations. We have had already several times the opportunity to bring attention in our magazine to that phenomenon, of how the military authorities are forced to act with all strictness against those individuals from Czech regiments, who disregarding glorious regimental traditions, are sowing by their senseless rioting in our Hungarian towns anger toward the whole Czech nation, which as a whole is guilty of nothing and which has always stood firm behind the interests of this Empire, of which testifies a whole number of outstanding Czech military leaders, from among whom we remind you of the glorious figure of Marshall Radetzky and other defenders of the Austro-Hungarian monarchy. In contrast to these bright apparitions there are several rascals of the debauched Czech riff-raff, who used the world war, in order to voluntarily sign up with the army and were able to introduce confusion into the unanimity of the nations of the monarchy, while not forgetting their own lowest instincts. We have brought attention already once to the rioting of the Regiment No. ... in Debrecen[282], whose breaches of peace have been addressed and condemned by the Pest Assembly[283] and whose Regimental colors were later at the front - STRUCK BY CENSOR - Who has this hideous sin on his conscience? - STRUCK BY CENSOR - Who drove Czech soldiers - STRUCK BY CENSOR - What the foreign element dares in our Hungarian homeland, is best evidenced by the case in Királyhida, the Hungarian outpost on the Leitha. Of what nationality were the soldiers from the nearby military camp in Bruck an der Leitha, who assaulted and tormented the local merchant mister Gyula Kákonyi? It is decisively the duty of the authorities to investigate this crime and ask the Military Headquarters[284], that is certainly dealing with this affair already, what role in this unprecedented inciting against the members of the Hungarian kingdom is played by Senior Lieutenant Lukasch, whose name is being mentioned in the town in connection with the events of the past several days, as we were informed by our local correspondent, who has collected already rich material about the whole affair, which in today's serious times is an outright screaming outrage. The readers of Pester Lloyd surely will be with interest following the unfolding of the investigation and we won't fail to assure them, that we will acquaint them more closely with this event of eminent importance. Concurrently however we are expecting the official report about the Királyhida crime, committed against the Hungarian population. That the pest Assembly will be addressing the matter, is as clear as day, so that in the end it would be revealed clearly, that Czech soldiers, riding through the Hungarian Kingdom to the front, must not consider the land of the crown of Saint Stephen[285], as if they had it on a lease. Should then some members of the nation, who in Királyhida so nicely manifested the alliance of all the nations of this monarchy, even today still not understand the situation, let them better remain quiet, because in the war a bullet, rope, slammer and bayonet will teach such people to behave and subordinate themselves to the highest interests of our common homeland."

"Who's signed under the article, mister Senior Lieutenant?"

"Béla Barabás[286], an editor and a legislative deputy, Colonel, Sir."

"He is a known bestial creature, mister Senior Lieutenant; but before it made its way to the Pester Lloyd, this article had already been published in the Pesti Hirlap[287]. Now read to me in the official translation from the Hungarian the article in the Sopronyian magazine Sopronyi Napló[288]."

Senior Lieutenant Lukáš was reading aloud the article, in which the editor took uncommon care, in order to apply a mix of phrases: "imperative of the State wisdom", "the State order", "human perversion", "trampled human dignity and sense", "cannibalistic feast", "massacred human society", "a pack of Mamelukes", "behind the backdrop you'll recognize them". And on it went, as if Hungarians on their own soil were the most persecuted element. As if the Czech soldiers had come, knocked down the editor and were stomping in their boots on his belly and he was screaming with pain and somebody was taking it down in shorthand.

"Of some of the most important things," is lamenting the Sopronyi Napló, a Sopronyian daily, "disturbing reticence is maintained and nothing is being written. Each of us knows, what a Czech soldier in Hungary and at the front is. We all know, what things Czechs commit, what is at work here and what it looks like among the Czechs and who causes it. Vigilance of the authorities is indeed tied up with other important things, which however must be properly linked to the oversight of the whole, in order that never again could happen that, which has happened during these days in Királyhida. Yesterday was our article censored in fifteen places. Therefore there is nothing else left for us but to proclaim, that even today we have not much cause for technical reasons to give wide coverage of the events in Királyhida. The correspondent dispatched by us determined on the spot, that the authorities are showing genuine fervor in the whole affair, investigating at full steam. Only it seems strange to us, that some participants in the whole massacre find themselves still free at large. That pertains especially to one gentleman, who according to what we hear remains with impunity in the military camp and keeps on wearing insignia of his *parrot regiment*[289] and whose name was also published the day before yesterday in the Pester Lloyd and the Pesti Napló[290]. He is the reputed Czech chauvinist Lükáš, regarding whose rampage an interpellation will be filed by our deputy Géza Savanyu, who represents the district Királyhida[291]."

"In the same lovely way, mister Senior Lieutenant," let himself be heard Colonel Schröder, "is writing about you also the weekly[292] in Királyhida and then the Pressburg[293] papers. But that won't interest you anymore, because it's all as if made from the same mold. Politically it can be justified, because we Austrians, whether we are Germans or Czechs, are after all in comparison with the Hungarians still very… You understand me, mister Senior Lieutenant. There is a certain tendency in it. Perhaps you'd be interested rather in the article from the Komárno[294] evening paper, where regarding you they claim, that you were trying to rape mistress. Kákonyi right in the dining room during lunch in the presence of her husband, whom you menaced with a saber and were forcing him to gag with a towel the mouth of his wife, so she wouldn't scream. That is the last news report about you, mister Senior Lieutenant."

The Colonel gave a smile and continued: "The authorities have not carried out their duty. Preventive censorship in the local papers is also in the hands of the Hungarians. They do to us, as they please. Our officer is not protected from the insults of such civilian Hungarian editorial swine, and only on the basis of our resolute move, more precisely a telegram from our Divisional Court, did the State Prosecutor's Office in Pest undertake steps, in order to carry out some arrests in all the mentioned editorial offices. The worst price will be paid by the editor of the Komárom evening paper, he won't forget that evening paper of his until he dies. The Divisional Court authorized me, as your superior, to hear you out and is concurrently sending me the whole file pertaining to the investigation. All would have ended up well, if it weren't for that hapless Švejk of yours. There is with him some sapper Vodička, on whom after the brawl they found, when they had brought them to the *main guardhouse*, your letter that you sent to missis Kákonyi. That Švejk of yours kept insisting during the investigation, that it was not your written note, that he wrote it himself, and when it was put in front of him and he stood convicted to copy it, so that his handwriting would be compared, he gobbled up your letter. From the Regimental Office were then sent to the Divisional Court your reports for comparison with the handwriting of Švejk and here you have the result."

The Colonel paged through the files and pointed out to Senior Lieutenant Lukáš this passage: "The accused Švejk refused to write the dictated sentences, accompanying his action by the claim, that he forgot overnight how to write."

"I don't, mister Lieutenant, assign any significance at all to what is at the Divisional Court this Švejk of yours or the sapper saying. Švejk and the sapper insist, that it was just some little hoax, which was misunderstood, and that they themselves were set upon by civilians and that they were defending themselves, in order to protect military honor. Through an interrogation it was determined, that this Švejk of yours is quite a bud of a rascal. So for example, to the question, why he would not confess, according to the report he responded: 'I'm in just the same situation, in which once found himself on account of some paintings of Virgin Mary the servant of the Academy master painter Panuška[295].' He too, as it was a matter of some pictures, that he was supposed to have absconded with, could not answer anything else regarding it but: 'Am I supposed to be heaving up blood?' Naturally, on behalf of the Regiment Headquarters I took care, that in all the newspapers there would be in the name of the Divisional Court placed a correction regarding all the villainous articles in the local papers. Today it will be distributed and I hope, that I have done everything in order to straighten out, what had happened due to the rascal deeds of the journalistic Hungarian civilian miscreants.

"I think that I stylized it well:

> Divisional Court No. N and the Headquarters of the Regiment No. N proclaim, that the article published in this magazine about the alleged breaches of peace by the troops of Regiment No. N is in no part based on truth and that from the first to the last line it was fabricated and that the investigation initiated against those magazines will bring about a stern punishment for the guilty.

"The Divisional Court in its written communication to the headquarters of our Regiment," continued the Colonel, "arrives at the opinion, that there is actually nothing else at play, than incessant inciting against military detachments arriving from Cisleithania to Transleithania. And while at it, compare how many of our troops have left for the front and how many of theirs. I'll tell you, that a Czech soldier is more acceptable to me than such Hungarian rabble. When I recall, that down by Belgrade the Hungarians were shooting at our second marchbattalion[296], which didn't know, that it was the Hungarians, who were shooting at them, and it started firing into the Deutschmeisters[297] on the right flank, and the Deutschmeisters in turn got it also confused and opened fire at the Bosnian regiment, that was standing next to them! What a situation that was back then! I just happened to be at the Brigade[298] Staff at lunch, the day before we had to make do with ham and canned soup, and on that day we had proper soup made with chicken, fillet with rice and little buns in hot creamy pudding; the previous evening we hanged a Serbian wine-bar keeper in a little town and our cooks found in his cellar thirty-year old wine. You can imagine, how we all were looking forward to the lunch. We ate the soup and are just letting loose into the chicken, when all of a sudden an exchange of fire, then sustained fire, and our artillery, that did not even have a clue, that it is our units shooting at one another, started firing at our line and one grenade fell right next to our Brigade Staff. The Serbians were perhaps thinking, that on our side a mutiny broke out, so they started cutting into us from all sides and transporting themselves across the river to go after us. They're calling the Brigade General to the phone and the Division[299] Commander started hollering, what is that bullshit in the Brigade section, that just then he got an order from the Army Staff to start an attack against the Serbian positions on the left flank at two o'clock and 35 minutes in the night. That we are the reserve and that immediately the fire is to stop. But no way can you in a situation like that demand a *'Cease fire'*. The Brigade telephone exchange is reporting, that it cannot ring and reach anybody anywhere, only that the Staff of the 75th Regiment is reporting, that they just received from a division next to them an order to *'persevere'*, that they cannot reach and talk with our Division, that the Serbs have occupied elevation points 212, 226 and 237, being requested is the dispatching of one battalion as a liaison and a phone line connection with our Division. We switch the line to the Division, but the connection has been already cut, because the Serbs got in the meantime into our rear on both flanks and were chopping our middle up, shaping it into a triangle, inside which then remained everything, the regiments, the artillery and the supply with the whole column of trucks, the storehouse and even the field hospital. For two days I was in the saddle and the Division Commander had fallen into captivity even with our Brigade Commander. And all that was caused by the Hungarians, because they were shooting at our second marchbattalion. It is self-evident, that they were blaming it on our Regiment."

The Colonel spat:

"You have now, mister Senior Lieutenant, seen for yourself, how they utilized remarkably what happened with you in Királyhida."

Senior Lieutenant Lukáš in discomfiture coughed.

"Mister Senior Lieutenant," the Colonel turned to him confidentially, "put your hand over your heart. How many times have you slept with missis Kákonyi?"

Colonel Schröder was today in a very good mood.

"Don't say, mister Lieutenant, that you just started corresponding. I, when was your age, was sitting in Eger[300] in telemetry courses for three weeks, and you should have seen, how for the whole three weeks I did nothing else, but sleep with Hungarian women. Each day with a different one. Young, single, older, married, as they happened to turn up, I was ironing so thoroughly, that when I returned to the Regiment, I barely stood on my wobbling legs. The one who got me run down the most was a missis of an attorney. She revealed, what Hungarian women are able to do. She bit my nose while doing it, the whole night did not let me get shut-eye. — Began corresponding...," the Colonel slapped the Senior Lieutenant on the shoulder familiarly, "We know how it is. Don't say anything, I have my own opinion about the whole matter. You got entangled with her, her husband found out about it, that stupid Švejk of yours... — But, you know, mister Senior Lieutenant, this Švejk of yours is a stand-up guy after all, since he executed it so with your letter. Such a man would really be a loss. I say, that it is the upbringing. I really like that in the guy. Definitely the investigation in this regard has to be stopped. They were, mister Senior Lieutenant, scandalizing you in the newspapers. Your presence here is absolutely pointless. Within a week a marchy will be dispatched to the Russian front. You are the most senior officer with the 11th Company, you'll ride with it as a *Company Commander*. Everything has already been taken care of at the Brigade. Tell the accountant *quartermaster* to find you some other servant in place of that Švejk."

Senior Lieutenant Lukáš gratefully glanced at the Colonel, who continued: "As for Švejk, I'm assigning him to you as the *Company Messenger*."

The Colonel stood up, and extending his hand to the Lieutenant, who turned pale, he said:

"Thereby is then everything taken care of. I wish you lots of luck, so that you make an exceptional account of yourself on the eastern battlefield. And if perhaps we should some time meet again, then drop in among us. Make sure you don't avoid us like you did in Budějovice..."

Senior Lieutenant Lukáš kept repeating to himself all the way home:

"*Company Commander, Company Messenger*."

And clearly rising in front of him was the figure of Švejk.

Accounting Master Sergeant[301] Vaněk[302], when Senior Lieutenant Lukáš ordered him to seek out for him some new servant in place of Švejk, said: "I thought, that *they* were, *Senior Lieutenant*, Sir, satisfied with that Švejk."

Having heard, that the Colonel designated Švejk to be the *Company Messenger* with the 11th Company, he exclaimed: "Help us Lord God."

*

At the Divisional Court, in a barrack appointed with bars on the windows, they were getting up according to regulations at seven o'clock in the morning and were putting in order the bunks lying in the dust on the floor. There were no plank bunks. In one partitioned space of the long room they were stowing away according to regulations the blankets for straw mattresses, and those who were done with the work, were sitting on benches along the wall and either were picking their lice, those, who came from the front, or entertaining themselves by relating various happenings.

Švejk and the old sapper Vodička were sitting on a bench by the door with several more soldiers from various regiments and formations.

"Take a look, boys," sounded up Vodička, "at the Hungarian lad by the window over there, how the shameless rube is praying so it would turn out well with him. Wouldn't you rip for him his snout apart from ear to ear?"

"But he is a nice man," said Švejk, "he is here, because he did not want to muster when drafted. He is against war, belongs to some sect, and he is locked up, because he does not want to kill anybody, he keeps to God's command, but they will spice up that God's command for him. Before the war there lived in Moravia some mister Nemrava[303], and that one didn't want to even just sling the rifle over his shoulder, when they drafted him, that it was against his principle, to carry some rifles. He was locked up for it, until he just about turned black, and they led him again to the oath-taking ceremony anew. And he, that he wouldn't take the oath, that it was against his principle, and he managed to hold on."

"That was a silly man," said the old sapper Vodička, "he could have taken the oath and all the while also shit on it all, even the entire oath."

"I've already taken the oath three times," announced one infantryman, "and for the third time already I'm here for desertion, and if I didn't have the medical certificate, that fifteen years ago in a state of insanity I clobbered my aunt to death, I would had been perhaps for the third time already shot dead at the front. But this way, my poor deceased aunt always helps me out in need and perhaps in the end I'll get back from the war alright after all."

"And why did you, buddy," raised a question Švejk, "clobber

your auntie to death?"

"What for do people clobber one another to death," answered the pleasant man, "anybody can think and figure, on account of money. That old broad had five savings books and they had just sent her the interest payments, when I came to her place all busted up and ragged for a visit. Besides her I had no other soul in this world of God's. So I went to ask her nicely, for her to take charge of me, and she, the bitch, that I should go and work, she said, such a young, strong and healthy man, she said. One word led to another and I hit her only like several times over the head with a poker and so messed up her whole mug, that I didn't know, is it auntie or it isn't auntie. So I was sitting there by her on the floor and I kept telling myself: 'Is it auntie, or it isn't auntie?' And so the neighbors found me sitting by her the next day. Then I was in a nuthouse in Slupy[304], and when before the war they stood us to face the commission in Bohnice[305], I was found to had been cured and right away I had to go finish serving in the army for the years, which I had skipped."

There passed by a skinny, extruded soldier of an anguished countenance, with a broom.

"That is a teacher from our last marchy," introduced him the gamekeeper sitting next to Švejk, "now he's going to sweep out from under himself. He is a tremendously tidy man. He is here on account of a little poem, which he had composed. — Come here, teach," he called the man with the broom, who approached solemnly the bench. "Tell us about the lice."

The soldier with the broom cleared his throat and let them have it:

All loused up, the whole front is scratching itself,
A huge **všivák**/*a he-louse scoundrel* is crawling all over us.
Mister general is wallowing in the bed
And every day he changes his clothes.

The **vši**/*lice* among the troops are doing well,
they're even getting used to the officers,
With the **veš**/*louse* of Prussia nimbly mating
Is the old **všivák**/*he-louse scoundrel* of Austria.

The soldier teacher worn out by anguish joined those sitting on the bench and sighed: "That is all, and because of it I'm being for the fourth time already interrogated at the mister Judge Advocate's."

"It really isn't even worth the talk," genially said Švejk, "it will depend only on whom will they think at the court the old **všivák**/*he-louse scoundrel* of Austria to be. It's good, that you put in there the thing about mating, that will confound them so, that they'll be dumb jacked by it. Just explain to them, that **všivák** is a male of the louse and that it's again only a male **všivák** who can mount the female louse. Otherwise you won't untangle yourself from it. You certainly didn't write it wanting to offend anybody, that is clear. Tell the mister Judge Advocate that you wrote it to please yourself, and just as the male of a swine is called a boar, then everywhere they call the male of a louse — **všivák**."

The teacher let out a sigh: "But that Judge Advocate can't understand Czech well. I have already been explaining it to him in a similar way, but he let loose at me saying, that a male of a **veš**/*louse*, is called a **vešák** /*louser*. 'No **fšivák**[306],' mister Judge Advocate was saying, '**vešák**. *The* femininum, *you educated moron, is the* ***feš****, then the* masculinum *is the* ***fešák***/dandy. You can't fool us. We know our Pappenheimers[307].'"

"The short and the good of it is," said Švejk, "it's a shaky situation you're in, but you must not lose hope, as used to say the Gypsy Janeček[308] in Plzeň, that it could still turn around and become better, when in 1879 they were on account of that double robbery with murder putting the noose around his neck. And he sure guessed it right, because they took him away from the gallows at the last moment, because they could not hang him on account of the lord Emperor's birthday which just fell on the same day, when he was supposed to be hanging. So they didn't hang him until the next day, once the birthday was over, and the guy was still so lucky, that on the third day after that, he got clemency and the trial was to be reopened, because everything was pointing to the fact, that some other Janeček did it. So they had to dig him up from the prisoners' cemetery and they rehabilitated him to the Pilsen Catholic cemetery, and only after that it was found out, that he was an evangelical, so they transported him over to an evangelical cemetery and then…"

"…then you'll get a couple of slaps," sounded up the old sapper Vodička, "what won't that guy think up. A man has troubles with the Divisional Court, and he the miserable oaf was telling me yesterday, as they were taking us to interrogation, what a rose of Jericho[309] was."

"But those were not my words, that is what the servant of the painter Panuška, Matěj[310], was telling to an old hag, when she was asking him, what a rose of Jericho looked like. So he was telling her: 'Take dry cow shit, put it on a plate, pour water over it and it'll turn beautifully green for you, and that is a rose of Jericho," was defending himself Švejk, "I did not make that stupid thing up and yet we had to be talking about something, since we were going to interrogation. I only wanted to please you, Vodička..."

"Like you will please somebody," spat Vodička contemptuously, "a man has his head full of cares, to get out of the messy trouble and walk out, so that he'd get even with those Hungarian boys, and this one wants to please the man with some cow shit.

"And how can I pay the Hungarian boys back when I'm sitting locked up, and on top of it one has to pretend and be telling the Judge Advocate, that he has no hatred for the Hungarians. Lordy, that's a dog's life. But when I get one such boy into my mitts, I'll strangle him like a puppy, I'll give them their *'God bless Hungarians'*, I'll settle with them, people will be talking about me yet."

"Let's none of us worry about anything," said Švejk, "everything will get worked out, the main thing is always in the court to tell the untruth. The man, who will let himself be mesmerized into confessing, is always doomed. Nothing useful will ever come out of that. When I once worked in Moravská Ostrava[311], there was then this kind of case: A miner gave a thrashing to an engineer in the presence of only their four eyes, so that nobody saw it. And the attorney, who was defending him, was all the time telling him to keep denying it, that nothing could happen to him, but the presiding judge kept laying on his heart, that a confession was a mitigating circumstance, but he kept incessantly to his own line, that he couldn't confess, so he was freed, because he proved his alibi. That same day was in Brno..."

"Jesusmaria," Vodička got agitated, "I can't stand it anymore. Why he is saying all this, I don't understand. Yesterday there was with us at the interrogation a man just like that. When the Judge Advocate was asking him, what he was in the civilian life, he kept saying: 'I make smoke at Kríž's.' And it took more than half an hour, before he managed to explain to the Judge Advocate, that he pulled the bellows at the blacksmith Kríž's, and when they asked him then: 'So you are **pomocnej** dělník, *a laborer* in civilian life,' he answered them: 'No way **ponocnej**, *night watchman*, him is Franta Hybšù.'"

In the hall rang out the steps and the hollering of the guard "*One more*".

"There'll be more of us here again," cheerfully said Švejk, "perhaps *they* saved and hid for themselves some 'baccy."

The door opened and in they shoved the One-Year Volunteer, who was sitting with Švejk in Budějovice in the brig and was foreordained to serve in the kitchen of some march company.

"Praise the Lord Jesus Christ," he said entering, after which Švejk replied for all: "For ever and ever, amen."

The One-Year Volunteer contentedly looked at Švejk, laid on the floor the blanket which he had brought with him, and sat down on the bench to join the Czech colony, unwound his footwrap leggings and took out the in the folds artfully rolled cigarettes, which he distributed, then he pulled out of a shoe a bit of a striking pad from a matchbox and several matches artfully split down the middle of the tip.

He struck and fired up a match, carefully lit up his cigarette, let all light up off of it and disinterestedly said: "I've been charged with mutiny."

"That's nothing," soothingly sounded up Švejk, "that's fun."

"You know it," said the One-Year Volunteer, "if this is the way we want to win, with the help of the various court trials. Since they want to litigate with me no matter what, let them litigate. Taken as a whole, one trial doesn't change anything in the whole situation."

"And how did you mutiny?" posed the question sapper Vodička, looking sympathetically at the One-Year Volunteer.

"I didn't want to be spotshining the shitcans at the *main guardhouse*," he answered, "so they took me all the way to the *Colonel*. And he's a pretty big swine. He started yelling at me, saying that I was locked up on the basis of the Regimental Report, and that I was a common arrestee, that he's altogether amazed that the Earth carried me and didn't stop spinning over the shame, that in the army there appeared an instance of a man with the privilege of a one-year volunteer, having the right to achieve an officer's rank, who however could by his behavior awaken only feelings of disgust and condemnation in his superiors. I answered, that the rotation of the Earth couldn't be interrupted by the appearance on it of such a one-year volunteer, like me, that the laws of nature are stronger than the stripes of one-year volunteers and that I would wish to know, who could make me *spotshine* some shitcan, that I didn't crap up, although I'd even have a right to do that after dealing with the swine kitchen at the Regiment, after that rotten cabbage and soaked mutton meat. Then I still told the *Colonel*, that his opinion, as to why the Earth carries me, is also a little odd, because clearly on my account no earthquake will erupt. Mister *Colonel* for the duration of my whole speech did nothing but rattle his teeth like a mare, when the frozen sugar beet makes her tongue feel cold, and then he hollered at me:

'So are you gonna *spotshine* the shitcan, or not?'

'I dutifully report, that I will not *spotshine* any shitcan.'

'You will be spotshining, *you one-year timer*.'

'I dutifully report that I won't.'

'Krucityrkn, you will be spotshining not one, but a hundred shitcans!"

'I dutifully report, that I won't *spotshine* either a hundred or one shitcan.'

And so it kept going: 'Will you *spotshine*?'. 'I won't *spotshine*.' Shitcans were flying to and fro, as if it was some children's rhyme by Pavla Moudrá[312]. The *Colonel* was running up and down the office as if out of his mind, in the end he sat down and said: "Think it over carefully, I will hand you over to the Divisional Court for mutiny. Do not think, that you will be the first one-year volunteer, who was during this war shot dead. In Serbia we hanged two one-year volunteers from the 10th Company[313] and one from the 9th we shot like a lamb. And why? For their stubbornness. The two, who were hanged, were reluctant to impale a woman and a boy of a čúžák[314] near Šabac and the one-year timer from the 9th company gang[315] was shot, because he didn't want to advance and was making an excuse, that his feet were swollen, and that he had flatfeet. So will you be spotshining the shitcan or not?'

'I dutifully report, that I won't.'

The *Colonel* looked at me and said: 'Listen, aren't you a Slavophile?'

'I dutifully report, that I am not.'

Then they took me away and informed me, that I was being accused of mutiny.'

"You'll do best," said Švejk, "if you try passing yourself off for an imbecile. When I was sitting doing time at the garrison prison, then there was with us such a smart man educated, professor at a business school. He deserteered from the battle field and there was to be a tremendously glorious trial for him, so that to spread fear he would be convicted and hanged, and he tremendously simply slipped out of it. He started passing himself off for one handicapped by heredity, and when the staff physician was examining him, he declared, that he did not deserteer, that already since his youth he liked to travel, that he always has the desire to disappear to somewhere far away. That once he woke up in Hamburg[316] and the next time again in London, and that he did not know how he got there. That his father was an alcoholic and died by a suicide before his birth, that his mother was a prostitute and would get drunk and died due to delirium. That his younger sister drowned, that the older one threw herself under a train, that the brother jumped from a railway bridge in Vyšehrad[317], that the grandfather murdered his wife and doused himself with kerosene and lit himself up, that the other grandma wandered with the Gypsies and poisoned herself in a prison by matches, that one cousin was tried several times for arson and cut his veins in his neck in the Kartouzy[318] by a piece of glass, that a female cousin on the father's side hurled herself in Vienna from the seventh floor, that he himself was of horribly negligent upbringing and that until ten years of age could not speak, because at the age of six months, when they were changing his diaper at a table and stepped away somewhere for a moment, a cat pulled him off the table and in the fall, he banged up his head. He is having occasional headaches from time to time and in such moments, he doesn't know what he is doing, and it was also in such state that he left the front for Prague, and that only when the military police arrested him at U Fleků[319] he came to. Lordy, you should have seen, how actually gladly they released him from the military, and about five guys, who were sitting with him doing time in the same room, they all, just in case, wrote it down on a piece of paper, something like this:

Father an alcoholic. Mother a prostitute.
I. sister (drowned)
II. sister (train)
Brother (off a bridge)
Grandpa † wife, kerosene, lit up.
II. grandma died (Gypsies, matches) † etc.

And one of them, when he also started declaiming it to the staff physician, did not even get past the male cousin and the staff physician, because it was already the third case, told him: 'You sonofagun, and the girl cousin on your father's side hurled herself in Vienna from the seventh floor, you are of a horribly negligent upbringing, and so the correction prison cell will fix you up.' So they led him away to the correction, hogtied him, and right away he got over the horribly neglected upbringing, and the alcoholic father, even the prostitute mother, and thinking it better he asked to go voluntarily to the front."

"Today," said the One-Year Volunteer, "nobody in the military believes anymore in hereditary handicap, because it would turn out, that they would have to lock all the general staffs in a nuthouse."

In the metal-clad door made a racket a key and in stepped the prison guard:

"Infantryman Švejk and sapper Vodička to Mister Judge Advocate."

They raised themselves up and Vodička said to Švejk: "You see them, the crooks, every day an interrogation, and all the time no result. It would be better, *God-in-heaven*, if they sentence us already and not drag it on with us. This way we wallow all God's day long, and the number of the Hungarian boys running around…"

Continuing on the way to interrogation at the offices of the Divisional Court, that were located on the other side in a different barrack, sapper Vodička and Švejk were mulling, when they would actually come to stand in front of a proper court.

"Constantly nothing but interrogation all the time," was burning up Vodička, "and if at least something of use would bust out of it. They use up dumps of paper and a man won't even live to see a trial. He'll completely rot behind the bars. Say honestly, is the soup good enough for grub? And the cabbage with the frost bitten potatoes? Krucifix, so far I've never been an eager beaver for such a stupid world war. I imagined it altogether differently."

"I am on the contrary quite contented," said Švejk, "only a few years back, when I served on active duty, then our souper Solpera used to say, that in the military everyone has to be conscious of his duties, and he'd smack you at the same time such a one across your mug, that you never forgot it. Or the late *Senior Lieutenant* Kvajser, when he came to inspect the *rifles*, he would always lecture us, that each soldier is to show the utmost mental endurance, because soldiers are only cattle beasts, which the Government feeds, gives them enough to stuff their faces, drink coffee, tobacco for the pipe, and for that they have to pull like oxen."

Sapper Vodička immersed himself in thought and after a while sounded up:

"When you're there, Švejk, at this Judge Advocate's, then don't get confused, and that which you were saying during the preceding interrogation, that keep repeating, so that I'm not in some hot soup. That is mainly, that you saw, that I was attacked by those Hungarian boys. After all, we undertook it all on our common account."

"Have no fear, Vodička," was soothing him Švejk, "just keep calm, no getting upset, as if it were something, to be in front of some such Divisional Court. You should have seen, how years ago such a military court was done on short time. Serving on active duty with us back then was the teacher Herál[320] and at one time on a bunk he was telling us, when all of us in the room got confinement to the barracks, that in a Prague museum there is a book of records of one such military court from the times of Maria Theresa[321]. Each regiment had its own executioner, who executed the soldiers of his regiment, piece by piece, for one Theresian dollar each. And that executioner according to the records made as much on some days as five dollars. — It's understood," added Švejk deliberately, "back then the regiments were strong and they were constantly being replenished from the villages."

"When I was in Serbia," said Vodička, "in our brigade doing the hanging were those, who volunteered, to hang čúžáks for cigarettes. Each soldier, who hanged a guy, would get ten Sport brand cigarettes, for a broad or a kid five. Then the Quartermaster Administration started saving and they were being blown away in bulk. With me there was serving a Gypsy and we did not know this about him for a long time. Only it was conspicuous to us, that toward the night they would always call him in the office. That's when we were holding positions at the Drina river. And once at night, when he was away, somebody got the idea then to poke in his things, and the shameless rube had in his rucksack three whole packs with a hundred Sport brand cigarettes each. Then toward the morning he returned to our barn and we made it a short court proceeding with him. We knocked him over and someone Běloun strangled him with a belt. That shameless rube had a life as tough to extinguish as a cat."

The old sapper Vodička spat: "Just couldn't strangle him no matter what, he already dumped in his pants on us, the eyes had come out, and he was still alive like a rooster which was not cut all the way. So they yanked him like a cat. Two by the head, two by the feet and they twisted his neck. Then we strapped his rucksack on his back even with the cigarettes and threw him nicely into the Drina. Who would smoke cigarettes like that. In the morning they were looking for him all over."

"You should have reported, that he deserteered," judiciously remarked Švejk, "that had been already getting ready and that every day he was saying, that he'd disappear."

"But who'd think of such things," answered Vodička, "we did our part and for the rest of the things we had no care. There it was totally easy. Every day somebody disappeared, and they did not even fish them out of the Drina anymore. There was floating a bloated čúžák in there next to our torn-to-pieces Land Defense soldier nicely down the Drina into the Danube[322]. Some inexperienced ones, when they saw it for the first time, got a tiny fever then."

"To those they should have given quinine," said Švejk.

They just entered the barrack with the offices of the Divisional Court in it and the patrol immediately took them to the office number 8, where behind a long desk with piles of files was sitting Judge Advocate Ruller.

In front of him was lying some volume of the Legal Code, on top of which was standing an unfinished glass of tea. To the right side of the desk stood a crucifix made of imitation ivory, with a dusty Christ, who was desperately looking at the pedestal of his cross, on which there were ashes and cigarette butts.

Judge Advocate Ruller was just tapping to the renewed sorrow of the crucified God a new cigarette against the pedestal of the crucifix, and with the other hand he was raising the glass of tea, which got stuck to the Legal Code.

Having pried the glass from the embrace of the Legal Code, he continued paging through the book borrowed at the Officers' Club[323].

It was a book by Fr. S. Krause[324] with the much-promising title *Contributions to the History of the Evolution of Sexual Morals*.

He bore his sight into a reproduction of naive drawings of both male and female genitalia with appropriately becoming verses, which had discovered the scholar Fr. S. Krause in the bathroom of the Berlin-West Railway Station[325], so that he did not turn attention to those, who just entered.

He tore himself from observing the reproductions only with the throat-clearing coughing of Vodička's.

"What's going on?", he asked, paging on and searching for the continuation of the naive little drawings, sketches, and outlines.

"I dutifully report, Judge Advocate, Sir," answered Švejk, "my buddy Vodička got cold and now he's got a cough."

Judge Advocate Ruller only now looked at Švejk and at Vodička.

He was trying to add a stern expression to his face.

"It's about time that you're at last crawling in here, guys," he said, poking in the pile of documents on the desk, "I had you called in for nine o'clock and now it's almost eleven."

"What's that stance, you ox?" he asked of Vodička, who allowed himself to stand at ease. "When I say *at ease*, then you can do with your dumb legs, what you want."

"I dutifully report, Judge Advocate, Sir," sounded up Švejk, "that he has rheumatism."

"You better keep your trap shut," said the Judge Advocate Ruller, "when I ask you something, then only then you'll be answering. Three times you've been here by me for an interrogation and the story was dragging out of you as if out of a shaggy blanket. So will I find it out or won't I find it out? Do I have a tough job with you, miserable guys. But it did not pay for you, to burden the court unnecessarily. — So take a look, bastards," he said when he pulled out of the pile of official documents a voluminous file with the inscription 'Schwejk & Voditschka'. "Don't think, that you will be wallowing around at the Divisional Court on account of some silly brawl and will avoid for some time the front. On account of you I had to telephone all the way to the Army Court, you dumb cods."

He sighed.

"Don't look so serious, Švejk, you'll get over it once you're at the front, to brawl with some Hungarian Land Defense guys," he continued, "the trial proceedings with both of you are being stopped and each of you goes to his detachment, where you'll be punished at the Report, and then you'll be going with a marchy to the front. If I get you in my hands one more time, you churls, I'll give you such a rough spin of a time, that you'll be bug-eyed. Here you have the release form, and behave properly. Take them away into number 2."

"I dutifully report, Judge Advocate, Sir," said Švejk, "that we both will take your words to our heart and that we extend to you many thanks for your goodness. If this were in the civilian life, I would permit myself to say that you are a man as good as gold. And at the same time we both have to beg you many times for forgiveness, since you had to *busy* yourself with us so much. We really don't deserve it."

"Then blow to hell with all the demons already," the Judge Advocate burst into screaming at Švejk, "if it weren't for mister *Colonel* Schröder putting a word in for both of you, I don't know how it would end up with you then."

Vodička felt like the old Vodička himself only in the corridor, when they were walking with the patrol to the office number 2.

The soldier, who was leading them, was afraid, that he'd be late to lunch, and therefore expressed himself this way:

"So stretch and step into it, lads, you're dragging like lice."

At this point Vodička exclaimed, that he should not be stretching out his trap so and that he should feel lucky, that he is a Czech. That if he were a Hungarian, he would tear him apart like a salted herring.

Because at the office the military scribes had gone to fetch mess, was the soldier, who was leading them, forced to take them for the time being back to the brig of the Divisional Court, which did not pass without cursing on his part, which he addressed to the hated race of military scribes.

"Pals, they'll take all that's fat from the soup again," he wailed tragically, "and instead of the meat they'll leave a tendon for me. Yesterday I was also escorting two guys to the camp and somebody gobbled up half a loaf of the bread roll, which they got issued for me."

"The thing with all of you here at the Divisional Court is that you don't think of anything but grub," said Vodička, who had already fully revived.

When they informed the One-Year Volunteer, how it had turned out with them, he exclaimed: "Then the marchy, friends! It is like in the magazine for Czech tourists[326]: 'A fair wind!' Preparatory work for the trip had been done already, all taken care of and executed by the glorious military administration. Even you are booked to join the outing into Galicia. Begin the journey with a joyful mind and a light, merry heart. Harbor an uncommon love for those countries, wherein they will be presenting to you trenches. It is beautiful there and interesting to the utmost. You will feel in the distant foreign lands like at home, like in a related land, what's more, almost as if in the beloved homeland. With your feelings elevated you'll set out on a pilgrimage into the lands, of which already the old Humboldt[327] proclaimed: 'In the whole world have I seen nothing more magnificent than this stupid Galicia.' The numerous and rare experiences, that our grand army had gained during the retreat from Galicia on its first trip, will be during our new military expeditions certainly a welcome guide to compiling the program for the second trip. Just keep on following where your nose is pointing into Russia and out of joy shoot all the rounds into the air."

Before Švejk's and Vodička's departure to the office after lunch, the unfortunate teacher, who had composed the poem about lice, stepped up to them, and taking both aside said mysteriously: "Don't forget, once you're on the Russian side, to tell the Russians right away: *Hello Russian brothers, we are brothers Czechs, we are not Austrians*."

When they were coming out of the barrack, there Vodička, wanting to demonstratively express his hate toward the Hungarians and the fact, that the detention did not get the best of him and did not shake his conviction, stepped on the foot of the Hungarian, who did not want to serve in the military and screamed at him: "Put on shoes, you stumpfoot!"

"Should he have said something to me," with displeasure then declared sapper Vodička to Švejk, "should he have been heard from, then I would have ripped his Hungarian piehole from ear to ear. And he, the stupid boy, keeps quiet and lets someone step all over his shoes. *Lordgod*, Švejk, I am so angry, that I have not been convicted. Now it looks then, as if they were laughing at us, that the thing with the Hungarians isn't worth a talk. And you know we fought like lions. It was you who spoiled it, why they did not convict us and why they gave us such a certificate, as if we did not even know how to properly brawl. What do they actually think of us? Come on, it was a fairly decent conflict."

"Dear lad," said Švejk good-heartedly, "I don't really understand, how it can not please you, that the Divisional Court officially acknowledged us to be fairly decent people, against whom it could hold nothing. I was during the interrogation, truth be told, talking my way out of it in every possible way, that must be done, it is a duty to lie, as the attorney Bass[328] tells his clients. When the mister Judge Advocate asked me, why we stormed into the apartment of that mister Kákonyi, I simply told him: 'I thought, that we'd get acquainted with Mister Kákonyi best, if we kept visiting him.' Mister

Judge Advocate then did not ask me anything anymore and had already enough of it. — Do remember this," continued Švejk in his deliberation, "facing military courts nobody must confess. When I was sitting doing time at the *Garrison Court*, then in the next room one soldier confessed, and as the others found out about it they gave him the blanket treatment and ordered him, that he had to recant his confession."

"If I did something dishonorable, then I would not confess," said sapper Vodička, "but when that sonofagun Judge Advocate asked me directly: Did you brawl?, then I said: Yes, I did brawl. Did you torment anybody to submission? Of course, Judge Advocate, Sir. Let him know, whom he's talking to. And that exactly is the shame, that they set us free. It is as if they did not want to believe, that I just about broke *a belt* in half over the Hungarian boys, that I turned them into noodles, bump bulges, and black and blues. You were there, remember, when at one moment I had three Hungarian boys on me, and how in a little while the whole bunch was rolling on the floor and I was stepping all over them. And after all of that such a snotty boy Judge Advocate stops the investigation of us. That is as if he had told me: Whom are you shitting, you and brawl? When the war is over and I'm back in the civilian life, I will find that ogler somewhere and then I'll show him, whether I don't know how to brawl. Then I'll come here to Királyhida and make such a mess of the place, like the world has never seen, and the people will be running to hide in the cellars, when they find out, that I came to take a look at those rascals in Királyhida, those hoodlums, those shameless rubes."

*

At the office everything was taken care of very quickly. Some quartermaster with his mouth still greasy from lunch, handing Švejk and Vodička the papers with tremendously serious countenance, did not let the opportunity pass, to deliver to both of them a speech, in which he appealed to their military spirit, peppering it, because he was a Wasserpolák[329], with various nice expressions of his dialect, like *"carrot eater"*, *"dumb rollmops"*, *"a seven of clubs"*, *"filthy swine"*, and *"I will slap your moon-like pigfaces."*

When Švejk was saying his goodbyes to Vodička, since each was being taken to his own detachment, Švejk said: "When the war is over, then come to visit me. You'll find me every evening starting at six o'clock at The Chalice, at Na Bojišti."

"You bet, that I'll come there," answered Vodička, "Will there be some fun?"

"Every day something breaks out in there," was promising Švejk, "and if it were too quiet, then we'd take care of it somehow already."

They parted, and when they were already many steps apart, the old sapper Vodička was hollering after Švejk: "Then for sure arrange some entertainment, for when I come in there."

Whereupon Švejk hollered back: "But come for sure then, when there's an end to this war."

Then they increased the distance and one could hear after quite another while from around the corner of the second row of barracks the voice of Vodička: "Švejk, Švejk, what kind of beer do they have at The Chalice?"

And like an echo rang out Švejk's answer: "Velkopopovický[330]."

"I thought, that Smíchovský," hollered from a distance sapper Vodička.

"They also have girls in there," was screaming Švejk.

"Then after the war at six o'clock in the evening," was screaming from down below Vodička.

"Better come at half past six, in case I get delayed somewhere," was answering Švejk.

Then let himself still be heard, from a great distance already, Vodička: "Can't you make it at six o'clock?"

"So I'll come at six then," was the answer that Vodička heard from his buddy increasing the distance between them.

And so parted the good soldier Švejk with old sapper Vodička. *"When people are parting, they say to one another then 'until we see each other next time'."*

5

FROM BRUCK ON THE LEITHA TOWARD SOKAL

Senior Lieutenant Lukáš was pacing exasperatedly up and down the 11th March Company[331] Office. It was a dark hole in the company barrack, partitioned from the corridor by planks. A desk, two chairs, a round flask of kerosene, and a bunk.

In front of it was standing Accounting Master Sergeant Vaněk, who compiled lists for payment of military pay here, kept accounts of the rank-and-file kitchen, was the finance minister for the whole Company and spent here the whole of God's day, here he also slept.

By the door was standing a fat infantryman, with an overgrowth of facial hair like Krakonoš[332]. That was Baloun[333], the new servant of the Senior Lieutenant, in civilian life a miller somewhere near Český Krumlov[334].

"You have chosen for me a truly remarkable *spotshine*," was Senior Lieutenant Lukáš telling the Accounting Master Sergeant, "my heartfelt thanks for this pleasant surprise. The first day I send him to fetch me lunch at the officers' mess[335], and he gobbles up half of it."

"I spilled some if you please," said the fat giant.

"Alright, you spilled some. The only thing you could spill is soup or gravy, but not a Frankfurter roast[336]. C'mon, you brought me only such a tiny piece, that it could have fit under a fingernail. And where did you put the strudel?"

"I have..."

"Stop denying it, you gobbled it up."

Senior Lieutenant Lukáš declared the last words with such gravity and in so stern a voice, that Baloun involuntarily retreated by two steps.

"I have inquired in the kitchen, what we had for lunch today. And there was liver dumpling soup. Where did you put those dumplings? You kept picking them out on the way, that is a reliable truth. Then there was beef with pickle. What have you done with that? Also gobbled it up. Two slices of Frankfurter roast. And you brought only half a slice, huh? Two pieces of strudel! Where did you put it? You stuffed yourself, you miserable, hideous pig. Speak, where have you put the strudel? That it dropped into the mud on you? You are one dirtbag. Can you show me the spot, where it's lying in the mud? That some dog came running over right away as if answering a call, grabbed it and carried away? Jesus Christ, I will so slap your mug, until you have a head like a vat! On top of it, the swine, denies it. Do you know, who saw you? This here *Accounting Master Sergeant* Vaněk. He comes to me and says: 'I dutifully report, Senior Lieutenant, Sir, that the pig of yours, Baloun, is gobbling your lunch. I'm looking out of the window and he's stuffing himself, as if he had not eaten the whole week.' Listen *they, Accounting Master Sergeant*, couldn't *they* really have picked some other cattle beast for me rather than this guy?"

"I dutifully report, *Senior Lieutenant*, Sir, that Baloun seemed to be from among the whole marchgang the most proper man. He's such a clumsy clot, that he doesn't remember even one *rifle position*, and if you were to put a rifle in his hand he would only cause some disaster. During the last exercises with *blank* rounds he would have almost shot out an eye of the guy next to him. I thought, that he could at least stand a duty watch like this."

"And always gobble up the whole lunch of his master," said Lukáš, "as if his portion was not enough for him. Wouldn't you happen to be hungry?"

"I dutifully report, *Senior Lieutenant*, Sir, that I am always hungry. When somebody has bread left over, then I buy it off of him with cigarettes, and it is all still too little. I'm just like that by nature. I always think, that I'm satiated, and nothing comes of it. In a while again, like before the meal, my stomach starts grumbling, and look at him, he is the sonofabitch calling for attention again. Sometimes I'm thinking, that I've really had enough, that nothing more can fit inside of me anymore, but no. I see somebody, that he's eating, or I just smell the aroma, and right away inside my stomach it feels like it just had been swept out clean. The stomach begins immediately again to claim its rights and I would swallow nails. I dutifully report, *Senior Lieutenant*, Sir, that I had already begged, for me to be able to be getting a double portion; I was on account of it in Budějovice at the *Regimental doctor*, and instead he put me in the sickbay for three days and prescribed for me one cup of clear soup daily. I will, says he, you sewer turd, teach you to be hungry. Come in here one more time, and then you'll see, how you leave here as thin as a hops pole[337]! I don't have to see only good things, *Senior Lieutenant*, Sir, even the common ones will start to titillate me and right away I'm salivating. I dutifully report, *Senior Lieutenant*, Sir, that I deferentially beg, that a double portion be allowed for me. If there is to be no more meat, then at least the side dishes, potatoes, dumplings, a little gravy, there's always left of that..."

"Alright, I have heard out the audacities, Baloun," answered Senior Lieutenant Lukáš. "Have you ever heard, *Accounting Master Sergeant*, that in earlier times a soldier would be so audacious on top of everything like this guy? He gobbles up my lunch and in addition he wants, that a double portion be allowed him. But I'll show you, Baloun, until you digest to empty your stomach and feel hungry. — *You, Accounting Master Sergeant*," he turned to Vaněk, "take him away to *Sergeant* Weidenhofer, have him tie him nicely in the yard by the kitchen for two hours, when tonight they're dishing out the goulash. Have him tie him pretty high, so that he'd hardly balance himself on his tiptoes and see, how in the cauldron the goulash is cooking. And arrange it so, that the sonofabitch is still tied, when at the kitchen the goulash is being dished out, so that he's drooling like a hungry bitch, when she's sniffing by a butcher's shop. Tell the cook to divide his portion and give it away!"

"At your service, *Senior Lieutenant*, Sir. Come, Baloun!"

As they were leaving, the Senior Lieutenant intercepted them at the door, and looking into the despairing face of Baloun's, he cried triumphantly: "There you helped yourself, Baloun. Enjoy your meal! And if you do that to me one more time, I'll send you without mercy to face the field court-martial."

When Vaněk returned and announced, that Baloun had been already tied, Senior Lieutenant Lukáš said: "You know me, Vaněk, that I don't like to do things like that, but I cannot help it. Firstly you'll admit, that when you're taking a bone away from a dog, he growls. I don't want to have around me a vile guy, and secondly, just the circumstance, that Baloun is tied, has great moral and psychological significance for all the company *troops*. These guys lately, since they're with the marchy and know, that tomorrow or the day after tomorrow they will ride into the field, they do, as they please."

Senior Lieutenant Lukáš looked very anguished and continued in a soft voice: "The day before yesterday during the *night exercises* we were, as you know, to maneuver against the *One-Year Volunteer School*[338] behind the sugar refinery[339]. The first *platoon*, *advanced guard*, was still going quietly down the road, because I was leading that one myself, but the second one, that was to be going left and spread the *advanced patrols* bellow the sugar refinery, that one behaved, as if it was coming back from a field trip. They were singing and stomping so, that it must had been heard all the way in the camp. Then on the right flank went *to do reconnaissance* of the terrain the third *platoon* down under the forest, this was in the distance of good ten minutes from us, and at that distance one could still see the guys smoking, nothing but flaming points in the darkness. And the fourth *platoon*, it was supposed to be acting as *the rear guard*, and the demon knows, how it happened, that it emerged all of a sudden ahead of our *advanced guard*, so that it was taken for an enemy, and I had to be retreating from our own *rear guard*, which was *advancing* toward me. That is the Eleventh March Company, which I inherited. What can I make out of them? How are they going to be in a real *combat*?"

Senior Lieutenant Lukáš had concurrently his hands clasped and had a countenance of a martyr and the tip of his nose elongated.

"Look, don't let that, Senior Lieutenant, Sir, bother you," was trying to calm him Accounting Master Sergeant Vaněk, "don't rack your brains over it. I've already been with three marchys, each one along with the whole battalion they've smashed to bits, and we went to gather in formation again. And all the marchgangs were one just like the other, none was by a dog's hair better than yours, *Senior Lieutenant*, Sir. The worst was the Ninth[340]. That one dragged away into captivity with it all the officers including the *Company Commander*. What saved me was only that I went to the *Regiment Supply Company* to get rum and wine issued for the company gang and they managed it without me. — And don't you know this, *Senior Lieutenant*, Sir, that during the last *night exercises*, which you were talking about, the *One-Year Volunteer School*, that was supposed to go around our company gang, got all the way to the Neusiedler Lake? It kept *marching* away, until morning, and the *advanced positions* got all the way into the mud. And leading them was Captain Ságner himself. Perhaps they would have gone all the way to Sopron, if the day did not break," continued in a mysterious voice the Accounting Master Sergeant, who was finding satisfaction in such cases and kept track of all similar events.

"And do you know, *Senior Lieutenant*, Sir," he said, winking confidentially, "that mister Captain Ságner is to become the *Battalion Commander* of our March Battalion[341]? First, as was saying

Staff Quartermaster Hegner, it was thought, that you, because you are the officer with the most seniority here among us, would be the *Battalion Commander* and then, it is said, the word came from the Division to the Brigade that appointed had been mister Captain Ságner."

Senior Lieutenant Lukáš gnawed his lips and lit up a cigarette. He knew about it and was convinced, that an injustice was being done to him. Captain Ságner skipped past him twice already in being advanced, but he didn't say anything more than: "Oh well, when it comes to Captain Ságner..."

"I derive no great pleasure from it," the Accounting Master Sergeant let himself be heard confidentially, "*Staff Quartermaster* Hegner was recounting, that mister Captain Ságner in Serbia at the beginning of the war wanted somewhere near Montenegro[342] in the mountains to make an exceptional account of himself and drove one company gang of his little battie after another against the machine guns in the Serbian *positions*, although it was a totally unnecessary thing and the infantry was an old goat's worth of use there, because only the artillery could have gotten the Serbs out of there off those rocks. Of the whole battalion were left only 80 men, mister Captain Ságner himself got *his hand shot*, then at the hospital even a case of dysentery, and again he showed up in Budějovice at the Regiment and last night he supposedly was telling at the officers' club, how he's looking forward to the front, that he'll leave the whole marchbattalion there, but that he'll achieve something and will get signum laudis, that for Serbia he got the nose thumbing, but now that he'll either fall with the whole marchbattalion, or will be appointed *lieutenant colonel*, but the marchbattie had to become a screaming sacrifice. I think, *Senior Lieutenant*, Sir, that such a risk pertains to us too. *Staff Quartermaster* Hegner was saying not long ago, that you're not too much in tune with mister Captain Ságner and that he will just send our 11th company gang into *combat* first, to the most horrific spots."

The Accounting Master Sergeant gave a sigh: "I would be of the view that in such a war, as this one is, when there are so many troops and the frontline is so long, more could be achieved rather just by proper maneuvering only than some desperate attacks. I saw it down at the Dukla pass[343] with the 10th marchgang[344]. Back then everything took its course absolutely smoothly, there came a command '*Don't shoot*', and so there was no shooting and only waiting, until the Russians would come nearer, all the way to us. We would have taken them prisoners without firing a shot, except back then we had the iron flies next to us on the left flank, and the numskull Land Defense soldiers got so spooked, that the Russians were approaching us, that they started sliding down the slopes on snow like on an ice slide, and we received the command, that the Russians had breached the left flank, and to see to it to get to the Brigade. I was back then just at the Brigade, to have the *Company supplies log* validated, because I could not find our *Regiment supply wagon train*, when just then there started to arrive walking up to the Brigade the first ones from the 10th marchy. By the evening arrived one hundred and twenty of them, the rest supposedly rode down the snow, as they got lost retreating, into the Russian positions somewhere, as if it were a toboggan run. It was horrific there, *Senior Lieutenant*, Sir, the Russians had in the Carpathians *positions* both on the top and down below. And then, *Senior Lieutenant*, Sir, mister Captain Ságner…"

"Leave me in peace already with mister Captain Ságner," said Senior Lieutenant Lukáš, "I know all that, and don't think, that when there is some *attack* and *combat*, that you will be again coincidentally somewhere by the *Regiment supply wagon train* getting rum and wine issued. I was notified, that you soak up booze terribly, and whoever looks at your red nose, he immediately sees, whom he's facing."

"That is a memento from the Carpathians, *Senior Lieutenant*, Sir, where the mess would arrive to us at the top cold, the trenches we had in the snow, not allowed to make a fire, so holding us up was only the rum. And if it weren't for me, it would have ended up like at the other company gangs, where there was not even that rum and people were freezing up. But among us we had red noses from the rum, but that again had the disadvantage, that from the Battalion came the command, that to go on patrol duty were only men, who had red noses."

"Now we have the winter already behind us," uttered meaningfully the Senior Lieutenant.

"Rum is, *Senior Lieutenant*, Sir, a necessary thing in the field in any season of the year, just like wine. It brings about, I should say, good mood. For half a mess kit cup of wine and a quarter-liter of rum will people brawl for you with everybody… Which cattle beast is again knocking on the door, is it that he hasn't read the sign on the door *'Do not knock!'*? *Come in!*"

Senior Lieutenant Lukáš swung around on the chair toward the door and noticed, that the door was slowly and quietly opening. And equally quietly entered into the 11th March Company office the good soldier Švejk, saluting already when still in the doorway, and apparently already back then, when he was knocking on the door, looking at the sign *"Do not knock!"*

His saluting was a fully resonant accompaniment to his eternally contented, carefree face. He looked like a Greek god of thievery in the sober uniform of an Austrian infantryman.

Senior Lieutenant Lukáš for a moment squinted his eyes under the gaze of the good soldier Švejk, who was with his gaze hugging and kissing him.

Perhaps with such fondness was looking the prodigal, lost, and once again found son at his father, when the latter to honor him was turning a ram on a spit.

"I dutifully report, *Senior Lieutenant*, Sir, that I am here again," let himself be heard from by the door Švejk with such direct nonchalance, that at once Senior Lieutenant Lukáš came to. Since the time, when Colonel Schröder informed him, that he would again send Švejk to hang round his neck, Senior Lieutenant Lukáš was in his mind every day pushing this encounter back. Each morning he was telling himself: "He won't come yet today, perhaps he has done something there and they will still keep him there."

And all those possibilities Švejk set straight by his entering, executed so amiably and simply.

Švejk took a look now at the Accounting Master Sergeant Vaněk, and turning toward him, he handed to him with a pleasant smile the papers, which he drew out of the pocket of his overcoat: "I dutifully report, *Accounting Master Sergeant*, Sir, that I am to turn these papers, which they had written for me at the Regimental Office, over to you. It has to do with *soldier's pay* and signing me up for the *meals*."

Švejk was moving so freely and sociably about the office of the 11th March Company, as if he and Vaněk were the best of pals, to which the Accounting Master Sergeant reacted simply by the words: "Lay it on the desk."

"You will do very well, *Accounting Master Sergeant*, when you leave me and Švejk alone," said with a sigh Senior Lieutenant Lukáš.

Vaněk left and remained standing behind the door, in order to listen for what the two would be telling one another.

At first he could hear nothing, because Švejk and Senior Lieutenant Lukáš were reticent. They both were, for a long time, looking at one another and observing each other. Lukáš was looking at Švejk, as if he wanted to hypnotize him, like a young rooster standing opposite a chick and getting ready to hurl itself upon it.

Švejk, as always, was looking with his dewy, caressing gaze at Senior Lieutenant Lukáš, as if he wanted to tell him: Together again, my sweet soul, now nothing will decouple us again, my little pigeon.

And when for a long time the Senior Lieutenant was not making a sound, the expression of Švejk's eyes spoke with a pitying tenderness: So say something, my golden one, express yourself!

Senior Lieutenant Lukáš interrupted this embarrassing silence with words, into which he was attempting to insert a considerable portion of irony: "I extend a pleasant welcome to you, Švejk. Thank you for the visit. Behold, what a surprise guest is with us!"

He did not manage to hold himself back though and the anger of the past days discharged itself with a horrible bang of a fist on the desktop, where the ink bottle skipped and the ink splattered onto the *payroll list*.

At the same time Senior Lieutenant Lukáš jumped up, stood himself tightly close to Švejk and screamed at him: "You cattle beast," and he started to pace in the narrow space of the office, while every time in front of Švejk he spat.

"I dutifully report, *Senior Lieutenant*, Sir," said Švejk, when Senior Lieutenant Lukáš would not stop pacing and furiously pitching into the corner crumpled wads of papers, for which he always walked up to the desk to fetch, "that I handed the written note over properly. I luckily found missis Kákonyi and I can say, that she is a very nice broad, although I saw her only, when she was crying..."

Senior Lieutenant Lukáš sat down on the bunk of the Accountant NCO and with a raspy voice cried out: "When will it have an end, Švejk."

Švejk answered, as if he had heard wrong: "Then I had there a tiny unpleasantness, but I took it all upon myself. They did not believe me though, that I corresponded with that lady, so I thought it better and swallowed the written note during the interrogation, in order to confound their every trail. Then somehow by a clear happenstance, I cannot explain it to myself any other way, I got entangled in some tiny and very insignificant little brawl. I even got out of that and they recognized my innocence and sent me to the Regimental Report and stopped the whole investigation at the Divisional Court. I was at the Regimental Office for only a couple of minutes, until mister *Colonel* came and he cussed me out a bit and said, that I was to immediately, *Senior Lieutenant*, Sir, muster with you as a *messenger* and he ordered me, to announce to you, that he's requesting of you, to come immediately to him on account of the marchgang. It's been already over half an hour, but he, mister *Colonel*, did not know, that they would be still dragging me into the Regimental Office and that I would be sitting there yet over another quarter of an hour, because my *pay* for all that time had been suspended, and was supposed to be paid to me by the Regiment and not the Company gang, because I was carried on the books as a *Regimental prisoner*. They have it altogether mixed up and confused there, so that one would go nuts from it…"

Senior Lieutenant Lukáš said, putting on his clothes quickly, when he heard, that he was to have been already half an hour ago at the Colonel Schröder's: "You have, Švejk, helped me again to my feet." He said it in such a desperate voice, full of hopelessness, that Švejk attempted to soothe him down with a friendly word, which he was calling out, as the Senior Lieutenant was rushing out the door in a mad dash: "But mister *Colonel* will wait, he doesn't have anything to do anyhow."

A while after the Senior Lieutenant's departure stepped into the office Accounting Master Sergeant Vaněk.

Švejk was sitting on a chair and was stoking the little iron stove in such a manner, that he was pitching bits of coal in through the open little door. The little stove was releasing sooty smoke and stinking and Švejk continued in the merriment, paying no attention to Vaněk, who was for a while observing Švejk, but then kicked the little door of the stove and told Švejk, to be clearing out of here.

"*Accounting Master Sergeant*, Sir," proclaimed solemnly Švejk, "I take the liberty to declare to you, that I cannot accommodate your command even if I were most determined to clear out of the whole camp perhaps, because I am subjected to a higher regulation. — I am, that is to say, the messenger here," he said proudly in addition, "mister *Colonel* Schröder dispatched me here to attach to the 11th marchgang, to mister *Senior Lieutenant* Lukáš whose *spotshine* I had been, but due to my natural intelligence I was promoted to *messenger*. We are mister *Senior Lieutenant* and I already old acquaintances. What are you in civilian life, *Accounting Master Sergeant*, Sir?"

Accounting Master Sergeant Vaněk was so surprised by that familiar neighborly tone of the good soldier Švejk, that disregarding his dignity, which he very gladly showed in front of the soldiers of the Company, he answered, as if he were Švejk's subordinate:

"I am thuswise pharmacist Vaněk from Kralupy[345]."

"I was also being apprenticed as a drugstore clerk," said Švejk, "with some mister Kokoška[346], At Perštýn[347] in Prague. He was a tremendously odd fellow, and when once by mistake I lit up a barrel of gasoline in his cellar and his building burnt down, he chased me right out, and the trade association has never accepted me anywhere anymore, so that on account of that stupid barrel I couldn't finish being apprenticed. Do you also manufacture spices for cows?"

Vaněk shook his head.

"In our place were manufactured savory herbs for cows with consecrated pictures. He was, our boss mister Kokoška, a tremendously pious man and he read somewhere once, that Saint Pelegrinus[348] was helpful with bloated cattle. So he got somewhere in Smíchov pictures of St. Pelegrinus printed and had them consecrated in the Emmaus monastery for 200 gold coins. And then we would add them into the packages of those herbs of ours for the cows. For the cow the herbs were mixed into warm water, had her drink it from the slop sink, and at the same time was read to the cattle a little prayer to St. Pelegrinus, which was composed by mister Tauchen[349], our shop clerk. When the pictures of St. Pelegrinus were printed, then still on the other side it was needed to print some itsy bitsy prayer. So in the evening our old Kokoška called mister Tauchen and told him, to put together some weeny little prayer by morning for the picture and the herbs, that when he comes to the shop at ten o'clock, it had to be finished, so it would go to the print shop, that the cows were already waiting for that little bitsy prayer. Either, or. Compose it nicely and he's got a gold coin on the nail, or in two weeks he can go. Mister Tauchen was sweating all night and came in the morning all sleepless to open the store and had nothing written down. He even forgot, what the name of the saint for the herbs for cows was. So then our servant Ferdinand[350] yanked him out of the misery. He knew how to do anything. When we were drying chamomile tea in the attic, he would then always creep in there, take off his shoes, and he taught us, that the feet would stop sweating. He would catch pigeons in the attic, knew how to open the counter with money in it and still taught us other moonlighting jobs with merchandise. As a boy I had at home such a pharmacy, that I brought home from the store, that they didn't have one like that even At the Mercifuls[351]. And he helped Mister Tauchen, he just said: 'Then put it here *they*, mister Tauchen, to let me take a look at it,' immediately mister Tauchen sent to fetch beer for him. And before I brought the beer, our servant Ferdinand was already half done with it then and was already reading to all:

From the heavens' realm I'm coming,
good tale I am bringing.
A cow, a calf, each ox
Needs as much as salt
Kokoška's herbs,
That will rid it of its torments

Then, when he finished a beer and had a proper lick of tincture of amaranth, he managed it quickly and finished it within a bat of an eye very nicely:

Invented by Pelegrinus holy,
a package for two gold pieces only.
Saint Pelegrinus, protect for us our herds,
Which always like drinking your herbs.
Grateful farmer celebrates you by praise in songs,
Saint Pelegrinus, protect for us our cows…

Then, when mister Kokoška came, mister Tauchen went to the writing room with him, and when he came out, he was showing us two gold coins, not one as he had been promised, and wanted to split it with mister Ferdinand fifty-fifty. But, the servant Ferdinand, when he saw the two gold coins, was all of a sudden gripped by mammon. That, says he, no, either all or nothing. So then mister Tauchen gave him nothing and kept the two gold coins for himself, took me next door into the storeroom, gave me a head-slap and said, that I would get a hundred of such head-slaps, if I dared to say anywhere, that he was not composing and writing it down, that even if Ferdinand went to complain to our old man, that I had to say, that the servant

Ferdinand was a liar. I had to swear it in front of some round jar of tarragon vinegar. And that servant of ours started getting his revenge on the herbs for cows. We would mix it in large crates in the attic, and here, where ever he could sweep up little mice turds, he would bring them and mix them into the herbs. Then he would pick up horse donuts in the street, dry them at home, crush them in an herb mortar and pitch it also into the herbs for cows with pictures of St. Pelegrinus. And that was not enough for him. He would pee into those crates, drop a load in them and mix it up, so that it was like porridge with bran…"

The telephone rang out. The Accounting Master Sergeant jumped for the receiver and crabbily tossed it away. "I have to go to the Regimental Office. So suddenly, I don't like it."

Švejk was again alone.

In a while the telephone rang out again.

Švejk began to communicate: "Vaněk? That one went to the Regimental Office. Who is on the phone? The *Messenger* of the 11th March Company. Who is there? The *Messenger* of the 12th March Company[352]? *Hi* there, colleague. What my name is? Švejk. And yours? Braun. Don't you have a relative, some Braun on Riverbank boulevard[353] in Karlín, a hatter? You say that you don't, and don't know him… I don't know him either, I only went by once in a streetcar, so the firm's signboard caught my eye. What's new? — I don't know anything. — When we are going? — I haven't talked to anybody about the departure yet. Where are we supposed to be going?"

"You dumb cod, with a marchgang to the front."

"I haven't heard about that yet."

"What a *messenger* you are. Would you know, if your *Lieutenant…*"

"Mine is a *Senior Lieutenant…*"

"It's all the same, so your *Senior Lieutenant* went for a *conference* to the *Colonel*?"

"He invited him in there."

"So you see, ours went in there too and the one from the 3rd marchgang too, I just talked with its *messenger* on the phone. I don't like the *hurry* of it. And don't you know anything of whether they're packing over at the band?

"I don't know."

"Don't make yourself out to be an ox. I bet your *Accounting*

Master Sergeant got a *heads up about the railroad cars* already, right? How many *troops* do you have?"

"I don't know."

"You stupid idiot, do you think I will devour you? (One can hear, as the man on the phone is talking to the side: "Franta, grab the other hearing piece, so that you see, what an idiotic *messenger* they have at the 11th marchgang.") — Hullo, are you sleeping there or what? So answer, when a colleague is asking you something. So then you don't know anything? Stop stalling. Wasn't your *Accounting Master Sergeant* saying, that you will be getting food cans issued? That you haven't talked about such things with him? You idiot, you. That it's none of your business? (One can hear laughter.) You're as if somewhat whacked by a sack. So when you know something, call us then at the 12th marchgang about it, you stupid sonny of gold. Where're you from?"

"From Prague."

"Then you should be smarter… And something else. When did your *Accounting Master Sergeant* go to the office?"

"A little while ago they called him."

"See, and you could not say it before. Ours also went a little while ago, then something is brewing. Haven't you talked to the Supply Wagon Train?"

"I have not."

"For Jesus Christ, and you say, that you're from Prague? You don't take care of anything. Where are you running around all day long?"

"I only came just an hour ago from the Divisional Court."

"Now that's a different deal, pal, then I'll come around still today and take a look at you. Ring off twice."

Švejk wanted to light up his pipe, when again the phone rang out.

"Climb up my backside with that phone of yours," thought to himself Švejk, "like I will talk to you."

But the telephone kept buzzing inexorably on, so that Švejk's patience ran out at last, he took the receiver and screamed into the phone:

"Hullo, who's there? This is *messenger* Švejk of the 11th March Company." In the answer Švejk recognized the voice of his Senior Lieutenant Lukáš:

"What are you all doing there, where is Vaněk, call Vaněk

immediately to the phone."

"I dutifully report, *Senior Lieutenant*, Sir, not long ago the telephone rang."

"Listen up, Švejk, I don't have time to be conversing with you. Telephone conversations in the army, they are no small talk on the phone, like when we're inviting somebody over, to visit us for lunch. Telephone conversations must be clear and brief. During telephone conversations get dropped even the 'I dutifully report, *Senior Lieutenant*, Sir'. I'm asking you then, Švejk, do you have Vaněk on hand? Have him come immediately to the phone."

"I don't have him handy, I dutifully report *Senior Lieutenant*, Sir, a while ago he was recalled away from this office, it could be not even a quarter of an hour, to the Regimental Office."

"When I come, I'll fix it up with you then, Švejk. Can't you express yourself succinctly? Pay good attention now, to what I'm telling you. Do you understand clearly, so that you won't be making excuses afterwards, that there was squawking on the phone? Immediately, as soon as you hang up the receiver…"

A pause. New ringing, Švejk is picking up the receiver and is buried under a heap of epithets: "You cattle beast, you street punk, you rogue, you. What are you doing, why do you disconnect the call?"

"You, I beg you, told me, to hang up the receiver."

"I'll be home in an hour, Švejk, and you've got something to look forward to then… So you pick yourself up right away, go to the barrack and find some *squad leader*[354], let's say Fuchs, and tell him, that he's to immediately take ten men and go with them to the stores to get food cans issued. Repeat it, what is he to do?"

"Go with ten men to the stores to get food cans issued for the Company."

"At last this once you're not goofing off. In the meantime I will be calling Vaněk on the phone at the *Regimental Office*, for him to go to the stores too and take possession of them. If he comes before that to the barrack, have him drop everything and run *on the double* to the stores. And now hang up the receiver."

Švejk was looking for quite a while in vain for not only *squad leader* Fuchs, but the other NCOs as well. They were at the kitchen, picking meat off the bones and enjoying the sight of the tethered Baloun, who was admittedly standing, that is resting firmly with both feet on the ground, because they broke down and had mercy on him, but in turn he was offering an interesting sight. One of the cooks brought him meat on a rib and pushed it into his beastly mouth and the tethered bearded Baloun, not having the opportunity to manipulate with his hands, was carefully sliding the bone in his mouth, balancing it with the help of his teeth and gums, while he was gnawing the meat off with the countenance of a woodsman.

"Who here among you is *squad leader* Fuchs?" posed the question Švejk, when at last he had caught up with them.

Corporal Fuchs did not even recognize it as fitting to speak up, when he saw that the one looking for him was some common infantryman.

"I say," said Švejk, "how much longer am I going to be asking? Wherever is *squad leader* Fuchs?"

Corporal Fuchs stepped out and full of dignity started cussing in every possible way, that he's no *squad leader*, that he is mister *squad leader*, that one is not supposed to be saying : "Where is the *squad leader*?", but: "I dutifully report, where is mister *squad leader*?" At his *squad*, when somebody doesn't say "*I dutifully report*", he said, he'll get right away smacked across his trap.

"Slow down," said deliberately Švejk, "*they* pick *themselves* up immediately, *they* go to the barrack, *they* pick up ten men there and *on the double* with them to the stores, you'll be getting food cans issued."

Corporal Fuchs was so surprised, that he blurted out only: "What's that?"

"Don't give me any 'what's that'," answered Švejk, "I'm the *messenger* of the Eleventh *March Company* and just a while ago I spoke on the telephone with mister *Senior Lieutenant Lukáš*. And he said: '*On the double* with ten men to the stores.' If you don't go, mister *squad leader* Fuchs, then immediately I'm going back to the telephone. Mister *Senior Lieutenant* desires exclusively, for you to go. It is altogether pointless to talk about it. 'A telephone conversation,' says mister Senior Lieutenant Lukáš, 'must be brief, clear. When it is said '*squad leader* Fuchs goes', then he will go. Such a command, it's no small talk on the phone, as if we were inviting somebody over for lunch. In the army, especially during a war, each delay is a crime. If that *squad leader* Fuchs won't immediately go, when you announce it to him, then I'll fix it up with him already. Of *squad leader* Fuchs there will be left over not even a memento.' Lordy, you don't know mister *Senior Lieutenant*."

Švejk looked triumphantly at the NCOs, who were really surprised and deflated by his performance.

Corporal Fuchs growled something unintelligibly and with a quick step was departing, while Švejk was calling after him: “Can I then telephone mister *Senior Lieutenant*, that everything is in order?”

“Right away I’ll be with ten grunts by the stores,” hollered Corporal Fuchs from by the barrack, and Švejk not having uttered even another word was walking away from the group of NCOs, who were just as surprised as was Corporal Fuchs.

“It’s beginning already,” said a little Sergeant Blažek, “we’ll be packing.”

*

When Švejk returned to the office of the 11th marchgang, he again did not have time to light up his pipe, because the sound of the telephone rang out again. With Švejk was talking once more Senior Lieutenant Lukáš:

“Where have you been running, Švejk? I’m ringing for the third time already and nobody will answer me.”

“I’ve been rounding them up, *Senior Lieutenant*, Sir.”

“Have they gone already then?”

“It goes without saying, that they’ve gone, but I don’t know yet, if they’ll be there. Should I perhaps run over there one more time?”

“Have you then found *squad leader* Fuchs?”

“I have, *Senior Lieutenant*, Sir. First he told me ‘What now?’, and only when I explained to him, that the telephone conversations have to be brief and clear…”

“Don’t prattle, Švejk… Vaněk hasn’t returned yet?”

“He hasn’t, *Senior Lieutenant*, Sir.”

“Don’t scream so into the telephone. Don’t you know, where that damned Vaněk could be?”

“I don’t, *Senior Lieutenant*, Sir, where that damned Vaněk could be.”

“He was in the office at the Regiment and left for somewhere. I think, that he’ll probably be in the mess[355]. Go then after him, Švejk, and tell him to go immediately to the stores. Then still another thing. Find immediately Sergeant Blažek and tell him, to immediately untie that Baloun, and as for Baloun, him send to me. Hang up the receiver!”

Švejk really started taking care of things. When he found Sergeant Blažek and relayed to him the Senior Lieutenant’s order having to do with untying Baloun, Sergeant Blažek growled: "They're afraid, when taking rising water in their shoes."

Švejk went to see the untying and accompanied Baloun on the way, because going in the same direction one went toward the mess, where he was to find Accounting Master Sergeant Vaněk.

Baloun was looking at Švejk as his savior and was promising, that he would split with him each shipment, which he receives from home.

"Back at home, they'll have pig-slaughtering," was saying Baloun in a melancholic way, "Do you like fat smoked sausage with blood or without blood? Just name it, I'm writing home tonight. My pig will be about one hundred and fifty kilos. It has a head like a bulldog and such a pig is the best. From among such pigs come no shirkers. That is a very good breed, which will endure quite a lot. It'll have lard eight fingers deep. When I was home, I was making my own jitrnice[356], and I always stuffed myself with the hash-and-crumb filling so much, that I could burst. Last year's pig was one hundred sixty kilos. — What a pig that was," he said enthusiastically, squeezing Švejk's hand hard, when they were parting, "I brought him up on nothing but potatoes and I myself was amazed, how nicely he was gaining. The hams I put in brine, and such a nice baked piece from brine with potato dumplings, sprinkled with cracklings, sweet and sour cabbage side, that is yummy for the tummy. After that the darling beer sure goes down well. Man is like, so contented. And all that the war has taken away from us."

Bearded Baloun heaved a heavy sigh and was leaving for the Regimental Office, while Švejk was aiming for the mess down the middle of the old double row of tall linden trees.

Accounting Master Sergeant Vaněk was sitting in the meantime contentedly in the mess and was telling some acquaintance staff quartermaster how much could be made before the war on enamel paints and cement dyes.

The staff quartermaster was already out of it. In the morning there came a farming estate owner from around Pardubice[357], who had a son in the camp, and he gave him a respectable bribe and the whole morning he was treating him down below in the town.

Now he was sitting there desperate, that nothing tasted good to him, didn't even know, what he was talking about, and to the conversation about enamel paints he did not even react.

He was preoccupied with his own imaginings and was mumbling about something, that there should be a local train from Třeboň to Pelhřimov and back again.

When Švejk entered, Vaněk was trying one more time to explain to the staff quartermaster in numbers, how much was made on one kilogram of cement dye for construction sites, to which the staff quartermaster replied totally off the wall:

"On the return trip he died, left behind only letters as his legacy."

Having beheld Švejk, he apparently confused him with some, to him disagreeable, man, and started cussing him, that he was a ventriloquist.

Švejk stepped up to Vaněk, who was also lit, but at the same time was very pleasant and amiable.

"Mister *Accounting Master Sergeant*," was reporting to him Švejk, "*they* are to go immediately to the stores, there is already waiting *Squad Leader* Fuchs with ten grunts, food cans are going to be issued. *They* are supposed to run *on the double*. Mister *Senior Lieutenant* has already twice called on the telephone."

Vaněk broke into laughter: "And I would have to be nuts, darling. I would have to cuss myself, my angel. There is enough time for everything, there's no fire, my child of gold. When Mister *Senior Lieutenant* Lukáš will have readied and dispatched marchgangs as many times as I have, only then he can talk about anything and won't be pointlessly bothering anybody with his *on the double*. The fact is that I have already gotten such order at the Regimental Office, that tomorrow we're going, that we're to be packing and getting stuff issued for the road. And what did I do, I went nicely and came here for a quarter-liter of wine, sitting here I'm comfortable and I let everything run along. Food cans will remain food cans, *getting provisions issued* will remain *getting provisions issued*. I know the stores better than mister *Senior Lieutenant* and I know, what in such a *conference* among the officer gentlemen at mister *Colonel's* is being said. The fact is that mister *Colonel* only imagines in his fantasy, that there are food cans in the stores. The stores of our Regiment has never had any food cans in stock and would get them only on a case by case basis from the Brigade or would borrow them from other regiments, with which it came into contact. Just to the Benešov Regiment[358] we owe over three hundred food cans. Ha ha. Let them say during the *conference*, what they will, don't hold your breath. Wait, the the storekeeper himself, when our folks get there, will tell them, that they've gone crazy. Not even one marchy got food cans for the road. — Isn't that right, you old potato?" he turned to the Staff Quartermaster. That one however was either falling asleep or into some kind of a little delirium, because he answered:

"When she was strutting, she would hold an open umbrella over herself."

"You'll do best," continued Accounting Master Sergeant Vaněk, "if you let everything float down the stream. If they said today at the Regimental Office, that tomorrow we're going, then even a small child must not believe that. Can you be going without railroad cars? When I was still there they were calling the railroad station by telephone. They don't have even one free railroad car there. It was exactly the same with the last marchy. We were standing back then at the railroad station for two days and waiting, until somebody breaks down and has mercy on us and will send a train for us. And then we didn't know, where we'd be going. Not even the *Colonel* knew it, we had already ridden through the whole of Hungary afterwards, and still nobody knew anything, whether we'd go on after Serbia or after Russia. At each station they talked directly to the Division Staff. And we were just a patch of sorts. At last they sewed us to the Dukla pass, and there they smashed us up and we rode again to regroup. Just no hurry. With the passage of time everything will get clearer and there is nothing to hurry up to. *That's right, one more time.* — The wine they have here today is unusually good," kept talking Vaněk, not even listening, how the staff quartermaster was babbling to himself:

"Trust me, I've gotten little of my life so far. I wondered about this question."

"Why should I be needlessly concerned about the departure of the marchbattalion. The first marchy that I went with, was all in absolute order in two hours. In other marchys of our marchbattalion at that time they had been getting ready for it already for two whole days. But our *Company Commander* was *Lieutenant* Přenosil, a very good looking man, and he told us: 'Don't hurry, lads,' and it went down as if greased by butter. Two hours before the departure of the train and only then we began packing. You'll do well if you too sit down..."

"I can't," said with horrible self-denial the good soldier Švejk, "I have to go to the office, what if somebody were calling on the telephone."

"So then go, my gold, but remember as a lesson for your life, that it is not nice of you and that a real *messenger* must never be, where he's needed. You must not be so overzealously rushing to service. Nothing is truly uglier than a spooked *messenger*, who would like to suck up to the whole army service, my darling little soul."

And Švejk was already out the door and was hurrying to the office of his March Company.

Vaněk was left abandoned, because one could decidedly not say, that the staff quartermaster was providing him company.

He got stiff totally for his own benefit and was babbling, while caressing a quarter-liter of wine, mighty strange things having no connections among them, both in Czech and German:

"Many times have I walked through this village and didn't have even the slightest clue, that it existed. *In half a year I will have the state-administered exam behind me and make the doctorate.* I have become a total invalid, thank you, Lucie. *They're being issued in nicely executed volumes* — perhaps there is somebody among you, who remembers it."

The Accounting Master Sergeant on account of the time dragging a long while, was drumming some march for himself with his fingers, but didn't have to be bored long, because the door opened and in stepped the cook from the officers' mess, Jurajda, who glued himself to one of the chairs.

"Today we have," he mumbled, "received an order to go and get cognac issued for the trip. Because our wicker rum bottle was not empty, we had to empty it. That did a job on us. The personnel of the kitchen was totally cut down by it. I miscounted by several portions, mister *Colonel* came late and none was left for him to get. So they're fixing there for him a little omelet now. I tell you, it's fun."

"It is a nice adventure," remarked Vaněk, who always liked nice words with wine.

Cook Jurajda broke into philosophizing, which in fact corresponded to his former job. That is he used to publish, until the war, an occultist magazine and the book series Mysteries of Life and Death.

In the military he got himself stashed out of sight to the officers' kitchen of the Regiment and very often burnt some roast, when he got immersed in reading a translation of ancient Indian sutras Pragnâ-Paramitâ[359] (Revealed Wisdom).

Colonel Schröder liked him as an oddity at the Regiment, because which officers' kitchen could boast a cook-occultist, who peering into the mysteries of life and death, surprised all with such good svíčková[360], or with such ragù[361], that down below Komarów[362] the fatally wounded Lieutenant Dufek kept on calling for Jurajda.

"Yes," said out of the clean and clear blue Jurajda, who barely kept himself sitting on the chair and reeked of rum a hundred yards away, "when none was left today for mister *Colonel* and when he saw only stewed potatoes, there he fell into a state of gaki[363]. Do you know what gaki is? That is a state of hungry spirits. So I said: 'Do you, *Colonel*, Sir, have enough strength to overcome the fated determination, that no calf kidney was left for you to get? In karma[364] it is predetermined, that you, *Colonel*, Sir, obtain today for dinner a wonderful omelet with chopped and stewed veal liver.' — Dear friend," he said after a while in a soft voice to the Accounting Master Sergeant, while he involuntarily made some gesture with his hand, with which he knocked over all the glasses, that were in front of him on the table.

"There is a nonbeing of all phenomena, forms and things," said after this act gloomily the cook-occultist. "A formation is a nonbeing and a nonbeing is a formation. A nonbeing is not different from a formation, a formation is not different from a nonbeing. That which is a nonbeing, is a formation, that which is a formation is a nonbeing."

The cook-occultist wrapped himself in the cloak of reticence, propped his head by a hand and was looking at the wet, spilt-on table.

The Staff Quartermaster kept on babbling something, which had neither rhyme nor reason:

"The wheat disappeared from the fields, disappeared — *In this mood he received an invitation and went to her* — the Holy Ghost holy days are in spring."

Accounting Master Sergeant Vaněk kept drumming on the table, was drinking, and now and then remembered, that there were waiting for him ten men with the Corporal by the storehouse.

With each such recollection he always cracked a smile just for himself and waved his hand.

When late he returned to the office of the 11th March Company, he found Švejk by the telephone.

"A formation is a nonbeing and a nonbeing is a formation," he managed to get out of himself and crept onto the bunk still dressed and immediately fell asleep.

And Švejk was still sitting by the telephone, because two hours ago Senior Lieutenant Lukáš had a conversation with him, that he was still in a *conference* at mister Colonel's, and forgot to tell him, that he could walk away from the telephone.

Then talked to him on the telephone Corporal Fuchs, who was all that time waiting with ten men not only in vain for the Accounting Master Sergeant, but even found out, that the storehouse was closed.

In the end he left for somewhere and the ten men, one by one returned each to his barrack.

Now and then Švejk entertained himself in such a way, that he picked up the receiver and was listening in. It was a telephone of some new system, which was just being implemented in the army, and had the advantage, that one could hear quite clearly and distinctly somebody else's telephone conversations all along the line.

The Supply Train was exchanging epithets with the artillery barracks, sappers were threatening the military post office, the military shooting range was growling at the department of machine guns.

And Švejk kept on sitting at the telephone…

The consultation at the Colonel's was being prolonged.

Colonel Schröder was unfurling elaborations of the newest theories of field service and was especially emphasizing the mine throwers.

He was making no sense, mixing things five after nine, talking about how two months ago where the front stood down below and in the east too, about the importance of exact connection between individual detachments, about toxic gases, about shooting at the enemy airplanes, about supplying the troops in the field, and then he transitioned to the internal situation in the military.

He untied his tongue about the attitude of officers toward the rank and file, the rank and file toward the commissioned officers and NCOs, about running over to the enemy at the fronts and about political events and about the fact, that fifty percent of the Czech soldiers were *'politically suspect'*.

"*Yes, my gentlemen, Kramarsch, Scheiner und Klófatsch.*[365]" The majority of the officers was thinking at the same time 'when is the old geezer going to stop driveling', but Colonel Schröder was babbling on about new tasks of new marchbattalions, about the fallen officers of the Regiment, about zeppelins[366], Spanish riders, about the oath.

While on the last item, Senior Lieutenant Lukáš remembered, that when the whole marchbattalion was taking the oath, the good soldier Švejk was not present at the swearing in ceremony, because at that time he was sitting doing time at the Divisional Court.

And it struck him all of a sudden as laughter producing. It was like a hysterical laughter, with which he infected several officers, among whom he was sitting, whereby he attracted the attention of the Colonel, who just transitioned to the experiences gained during the retreat of the German armies in the Ardennes[367]. He confused it all and finished: "Gentlemen, it is not to be laughed about."

Then they all departed for the officers' club, because Colonel Schröder was being called by the Brigade Staff to the telephone.

Švejk kept dozing by the telephone, when in the midst of it ringing woke him up.

"Hullo," he heard, "this is the *Regimental Office*."

"Hullo," he answered, "this the office of the 11th March Company."

"Stop delaying," he heard a voice, "take a pencil and write. Accept a telephonegram: The 11th March Company…"

Now there followed a succession of some sentences in a curious chaos, because talking over it at the same time were the 12th and the 13th March Companies, and the telephonegram got altogether lost in that panic of sounds. Švejk did not understand a word. In the end it quieted down and Švejk got it: "Hullo, hullo, so then read it now and stop delaying."

"What am I to read?"

"What you're to read, you ox? The telephonegram!"

"What telephonegram?"

"*Cruciheaven*, is it that you're deaf? The telephonegram I was dictating to you, moron."

"I didn't hear anything, somebody at this end was talking over it."

"You singular monkey, is it that you think, that I'd be prattling only with you? So will you accept the telephonegram, or not? Do you have pencil and paper? That you don't, you cattle beast, that I am to wait, until you find it? What soldiers these are. Hey, hurry up! That you are ready now? It's about time, that you dug yourself out. I hope you didn't change clothes for that, man, then listen: The 11th

March Company. Repeat it!"

"The 11th *March Company...*"

"*Company Commander*, you got it? Repeat it!"

"*Company Commander! ...*

"*To consultation tomorrow...*"

"*At nine o'clock.* — Unterschrift. Do you know what Unterschrift is, you monkey, that is a signature. Repeat it!"

"At nine o'clock. — Unterschrift. Do - you - know - what - Unterschrift - is, you monkey, - that - is - a signature."

"You singular idiot. Then the signature: *Colonel* Schröder, cattle beast. Do you have it? Repeat it!"

"*Colonel* Schröder, cattle beast."

"Alright, you ox. Who accepted the telephone-gram?"

"I did."

"*God in heaven*, who is the I?"

"Švejk. Anything else?"

"Thank God, nothing anymore. But your name should be Ass. — What's new over by you?"

"Nothing. Everything is the same old."

"That makes you glad, right? They say that over by you today they tied somebody up."

"Only the *spotshine* of mister *Senior Lieutenant*, he devoured his ration. Don't you know, when we're going?"

"Man, that's the question, even the old geezer doesn't know that. Good night! Do you have lice there?"

Švejk put down the receiver and started waking up Accounting Master Sergeant Vaněk, who was furiously resisting, and when Švejk began shaking him, he hit him in the nose. Then he lay down on his stomach and was kicking round about the bunk.

Švejk however managed to wake up Vaněk to such a degree, that he, rubbing his eyes open, turned over onto his back and frightenedly asked, what had happened.

"Not that much," answered Švejk, "I would only like to consult with you. Just now we received a telephonegram, that again tomorrow at nine o'clock is mister *Senior Lieutenant* Lukáš to come to a *conference* to mister *Colonel's*. I don't know now, what the deal is. Am I to go relay it to him right away, or wait until the morning? I have been hesitating for a long time, whether I should wake you up, since you were snoring so nicely, but then I thought, never seen before, you'd do better to consult somebody..."

"For God's sake I beg you, let me sleep," released a moan Vaněk, yawning to the round about, "don't' go there until the morning and don't be waking me up!" He turned over on his side and immediately fell asleep again.

Švejk went again to the telephone, sat down and started dozing on the desk. He was awakened by ringing.

"Hullo, the 11th March Company."

"Yes, 11th March Company, who's there?"

"The 13th marchy. Hullo. What time do you have? I can't get through to the central exchange. For too long somehow they're not coming to relieve me."

"Our clock has stopped."

"So you're in the same boat with us. Don't you know, when we'll be going? Haven't you talked to the *Regimental Office*?"

"They know shit, like we do."

"Don't be vulgar, miss. Have you been issued food cans yet? Ours went there and brought nothing. The stores were closed."

"Ours came empty handed too."

"It's altogether a needless panic. Where do you think we'll be going?"

"To Russia."

"I think, more likely to Serbia. We'll see that, when we're in Pest. If they'll be hauling us to the right, then Serbia is peeking out of it, and to the left, Russia. Do you already have *bread sacks*? Supposedly the *military pay* will be raised now? Do you play *fresh fours*[368]? You do? Then come over tomorrow. We roll it every evening. How many of you are there by the telephone? Alone? Then blow it off and go lie down. Those are strange arrangements you have over by you. That you stumbled upon it like a blind man tripping over a violin? Well, at last they came to *relieve* me. Drool sweetly into the pillow."

And Švejk indeed fell into a sweet sleep by the telephone, having forgotten to hang up the receiver, so that nobody was disturbing him out of his sleep on the desk and the telephonist in the Regimental Office was thundering, that he couldn't get through ringing the 11th March Company with a new telephonegram, to have them tomorrow by noon report to the Regimental Office the number of those, who had not been inoculated against typhus.

Senior Lieutenant Lukáš was still sitting in the officers' club with military doctor Šancler, who sitting straddling the chair, was hitting the cue stick against the floor in regular intervals and at the same time was proclaiming these sentences in succession:

"Saracen sultan Salah-Edin[369] recognized for the first time the neutrality of the ambulance corps.

"The wounded on both sides are to be taken care of.

"The medicine and care for them are to be paid for as compensation for the outlays incurred by the other side.

"It is to be allowed to send to them doctors and their assistants with generals' passports.

"Also the wounded prisoners of war are to be sent back under the protection of and guarantee from the generals or to be exchanged. But then they can keep on serving.

"The sick on both sides are not to be taken and put to death, but transported to the safety of hospitals and they are to be allowed to keep a guard, which like the sick is to return with generals' passports. That goes for the field clerics, doctors, surgeons, pharmacists, nurses of the sick, assistants and other personnel designated to serve the sick, who must not be taken prisoners, but in the same manner must be sent back."

Doctor Šancler already broke two cues doing that and still was not done with his curious exposition of care for the wounded in war, weaving into the exposition constantly something about some kind of generals' passports.

Senior Lieutenant Lukáš finished drinking a black coffee and went home, where he found the bearded giant Baloun, preoccupied by frying in a mess kit on Senior Lieutenant Lukáš' spirit-burning apparatus some salami.

"If I may be so bold," stuttered Baloun, "I'm taking the liberty, I dutifully report..."

Lukáš glanced at him. At that moment he appeared to him to be like a big child, a naive creature, and Senior Lieutenant Lukáš felt all of a sudden pity that he had had him tied on account of his great hunger.

"Just keep cooking for yourself, Baloun," he said, snapping his saber off, "tomorrow I will have them write in an extra portion of bread for you."

Senior Lieutenant Lukáš sat down at the table and was in such a mood, that he started writing a sentimental short letter to his auntie:

> Dear auntie!
>
> I just got the order, that I am to be ready for a departure to

the front with my March Company. Could be, that this written note is the last which you will receive from me, because everywhere there's brutal fighting and our losses are great. Therefore it is hard for me to end this letter with the words "Until we meet again!" Rather more fitting is to send you the last be with God!

"I'll finish writing the rest in the morning," thought to himself Senior Lieutenant Lukáš and went to lie down.

When Baloun saw, that the Lieutenant fell hard asleep, he again started to snoop around and ferret through the apartment like cockroaches at night. He opened a briefcase of the Senior Lieutenant's and bit into a pane of chocolate, but spooked, when the Senior Lieutenant jerked in his sleep. He deposited hurriedly the chocolate with a bite in it into the briefcase and quieted down.

Then he went to look very quietly, what it was that the Senior Lieutenant had been writing.

He read it and was moved, especially by "the last be with God!"

He lay down on his straw mattress by the door and was remembering home and the pig-slaughterings.

He could not rid himself of a living image of himself piercing the pressed-sausage, to get the air out of it, otherwise supposedly it would burst while cooking.

And recalling the memory, how once at the neighbors' the whole fat smoked sausage burst and boiled apart, he fell into a restless sleep.

He dreamt, that he had invited some clumsy butcher, and that while he was charging the hash-and-crumb sausages, the jitrnice gut casings were cracking. Then again, that the butcher forgot to make the blood-sausages, that he lost the boiled pieces of cooked pig feet and head and that he was short of wood skewers for the jitrnice. Then he was dreaming something about a field court-martial, because they had caught him, as he was pulling from the field kitchen a slab of meat. In the end he saw himself, hanging from a linden tree in a double row of trees at the military camp in Bruck an der Leitha.

*

When Švejk woke up with the awakening daybreak, that arrived in the fragrance of the boiling contents of the coffee cans coming from all the company kitchens, he mechanically, as if he has just ended a telephone conversation, hung up the receiver and set out on a little morning stroll up and down the office, while singing for himself.

He started right in the middle of the lyrics of a song, about how a soldier changes clothes to pose as a girl and goes after his lover in the mill, where the miller will lay him down next to his daughter, but before that he's calling the miller's wife:

lady-mother of the house, give a supper
so the girl can sup.

The miller's wife feeds the vile guy. And then, a family tragedy:

The millers got up in the morning,
on their door they had the writing:
"Your daughter Anna Nána[370],
is no longer an honest virgin."

Švejk put so much voice into the end of the song, that the office came to life, because Accounting Master Sergeant Vaněk woke up and was inquiring, what time it was.

"Just a moment ago they blew the reveille."

"Then I will get up only after the coffee," decided Vaněk, who always had enough time for everything, "even so, one way or another, they will be busting our chops today with some hurry and they will be rushing a man pointlessly, like yesterday on account of those food cans..." Vaněk yawned and asked, whether when he had come home, he wasn't exercising his rhetorical skills for long.

"Just a bit nonsensically," said Švejk, "You were constantly ejaculating about some formations, that a formation is not a formation and that, which is not a formation, is a formation and that this formation again is not a formation. But soon it overwhelmed you and you started snoring soon, sounding like when cutting with a saw."

Švejk fell silent, took a walk to the door and back to the bunk of the Accounting Master Sergeant, in front of whom he stopped and suggested in passing:

"As for my personage, mister *Accounting Master Sergeant*, when I heard, what you were saying about those formations, then I remembered some Zátka, a gasman; he was at the coal gas station at

Letná[371] and would light up and turn off the street lamps[372]. He was a man believing in enlightening community education and would hop all kinds of dives at Letná, because between the lighting up and turning off of the lamps the while was long and dragging, and then toward the morning at the coal gas station he engaged in just such soliloquies as you, except he would say for a change: 'A cube is all an edge and angle, that's why a cube is angular.' I heard it with my own eyes, when a drunk cop brought me in to be booked for having polluted the street instead of to the police station to the coal gas station by mistake. — And then," said Švejk in a soft voice, "this Zátka after some time ended up very badly. He joined a Marian congregation, and would go with the heavenly goats to the sermons of Father Jemelka[373] at the Saint Ignác[374] in the Karlovo square and he forgot to put out the gas lights in his beat once, when the missionaries were in the Karlovo square at the Saint Ignác, so that the gas was burning in the streets there without interruption for three days and nights. — It is very bad," continued Švejk, "when all of a sudden a man starts messing with some philosophizing, it always reeks of delirium tremens[375]. Years ago they transferred to us from the seventy-fivers some Major Blüher. He always once a month had us called and stood in a square formation and contemplated with us, what the military overlords were. That one drank nothing but plum brandy. 'Each officer, soldiers,' he was telling us in the courtyard of the garrison, 'is of himself the most perfect being, which has a hundred times as much brain as all of you together. Anything surpassing an officer in perfection, soldiers, you cannot imagine at all, even if you were thinking about it your whole life. Each officer is a being necessary, whereas you are, soldiers, only beings merely incidental, you can exist, but don't have to. If it came, soldiers, to a war and you fell for the lord Emperor, well, thereby not much would change, but if first fell your officer, only then you'd see, how you are dependent on him and what a loss it is. The officer must exist, and you actually have your own existence only from the officer lords, you originate from them, you cannot do without officers, you without your military overlords won't even blow a fart. For you the officer is, soldiers, the moral law, whether you understand it or not, and because each law has to have had its lawgiver, soldiers, it is only the officer, to whom you are feeling and must feel obligated in all and without any exception must fulfill each of his orders, even should it not appeal to you.'

“Then at one time, when he finished, he strolled around the square and was asking one after another:

“‘What are you feeling, when you overdo it?’

“They were giving such confused answers, like that they had not overdone it yet or that after each overdoing they felt sick to their stomachs, one was feeling a confinement to the barracks and so on. All those Major Blüher immediately ordered pulled to the side, that after noon they would be doing *calisthenics* in the courtyard as punishment, because they can’t express, what they are feeling. Before my turn came up, I remembered, what it was the last time he had been contemplating together with us, and when he came to me, quite serenely I told him:

“‘I dutifully report Major, Sir, that when I overdo it, I always feel inside myself some restlessness, fear, and pangs of conscience. If however, when I get extra time, I return to the garrison alright on time, here I am then being overtaken by some blessed peace, crawling over me is internal contentment.’

“All the men around were laughing and Major Blüher hollered at me:

‘All over you, you sonofagun, are crawling only bed-bugs, when you’re snoring away on the bunk. And he, the miserable oaf, is making fun on top of it.’

“And I got the manacles treatment for it, until ’twas one big joy.”

“In the military it can’t be otherwise,” said the Accounting Master Sergeant, stretching himself lazily on his bed, “it’s already so ingrained, that regardless of how you answer, regardless of you doing whatever you’d do, there must always be hanging over you a dark cloud and the lightning thunders will begin striking. Without it there can’t be any discipline.”

“Quite well said,” declared Švejk. “I’ll never forget, how they locked up recruit Pech. The company *Lieutenant* was some Moc and that one gathered the recruits together and was asking each where he’s from.

“‘You recruit greenhorns, damned,’ he’s telling them, ‘you have to learn to answer clearly, exactly and as fast as if cracking a whip. So we’ll start. Where are you from, Pech?’ Pech was an intelligent human and answered: ‘Dolní Bousov[376], Unter Bautzen, 267 houses, 1936 Czech inhabitants, *administrative district* Jičín[377], *judicial district* Sobotka[378], former estate Kost[379], parish cathedral of Saint Catherine[380] from the 14th century, renovated by Count Václav

Vratislav Netolický[381], a school, a post office, a telegraph, a station of the Czech Commercial Rail, a sugar refinery, a mill with a lumber yard, a remote homestead Valcha, six annual market fairs.'[382] And here already *Lieutenant* Moc jumped at him and started planting him one after another across his mug and was screaming: 'Here you have one annual market fair, here you have the second, third, fourth, fifth, sixth.' And Pech, although he was a recruit, was asking to be sent to the *Battalion Report*. In the offices back then they were such a funny rabble bunch, so they wrote, that he's going to the *Battalion Report* on account of annual market fairs in Dolní Bousov. The *Battalion Commander* there was Major Rohell. *'So what's going on?'* he asked of Pech and that one let him have it: 'I dutifully report Major, Sir, that in Dolní Bousov they are six annual market fairs.' As Major Rohell let out a scream, stomped and right away had him taken away to the loony bin of the military hospital, from that time on Pech was the worst soldier, nothing but punishments."

"Soldiers are hard to be training up," said Accounting Master Sergeant Vaněk yawning. "A soldier, who has not been punished in the army service, is not a soldier. It perhaps held true in peacetime, that a soldier, who finished his service without having been punished, was then getting preferential treatment in the civilian service. Nowadays the exact worst soldiers, who had in other times of peace never made it out of jail, are the best soldiers in war. I remember an infantryman Sylvanus at the Eighth marchy[383]. That one previously used to receive punishment after punishment, and what punishments they were. He was not hesitating to steal the last krejcar from a pal, and when he got into combat, then he was the first to cut through the *barbed wire obstacles*, took three guys prisoners and one he immediately shot dead on the way, that he did not trust him. He got the large silver medal, they sewed on two little stars for him, and had they not later hanged him down under Dukla, he would had been already ages ago a squad leader. But hang him they had to, because after one *combat* he volunteered for *reconnaissance*, and some other patrol from another regiment found him, as he was frisking the corpses. They found on him about eight watches and many rings. So they hanged him at the Brigade Staff."

"One can see from that," remarked wisely Švejk, "that each soldier himself must wrest for himself his position."

The sound of the telephone rang out. The *Accounting Master Sergeant* went to the telephone and one could make out the voice of

Senior Lieutenant Lukáš, who was asking, what's with the food cans. Then one could hear some recriminations.

"There really aren't any, *Senior Lieutenant*, Sir," was screaming into the telephone Vaněk, "how could there be any, it is only a fantasy from above, from the Quartermaster Administration. It was totally pointless, to be sending those people there. I wanted to telephone you. — That I was in the mess? Who do you say was saying that? That occultist cook from the officers' mess? I allowed myself to stop by there. Do you know, *Senior Lieutenant*, Sir, what that occultist called the panic with those food cans? 'The horrors of the unborn.' Not at all, *Senior Lieutenant*, Sir, I am totally sober. What is Švejk doing? He is here. Should I call him? — Švejk, to the telephone," said the Accounting Master Sergeant and added in a soft voice: "And if he were to ask you, how I arrived, then say, that in good order."

Švejk on the phone: "Švejk, I dutifully report, *Senior Lieutenant*, Sir."

"Listen Švejk, how is it with those food cans? Is it alright?"

"There aren't any, *Senior Lieutenant*, Sir, there's not a trace of them."

"I would wish, Švejk, for you to always muster with me in the morning, as long as we are in the camp. Otherwise you'll always be with me, once we're being hauled. What were you doing in the night?"

"I was by the telephone the whole night."

"Was there anything new?"

"There was, *Senior Lieutenant*, Sir."

"Švejk, don't start acting idiotically again. Was anybody reporting anything important from anywhere?"

"They were, *Senior Lieutenant*, Sir, but only for the ninth hour of the clock. I did not want to be disquieting you, *Senior Lieutenant,* Sir, I was far from doing that."

"Then, damn, say already, what's so important for the ninth hour?"

"A telephonegram, *Senior Lieutenant*, Sir."

"I don't understand you, Švejk."

"I have it written down, *Senior Lieutenant*, Sir: Accept a telephonegram. Who's on the telephone? Did you get it? Read, or something like that."

"Krucifix, Švejk, you're a cross to bear. Tell me the content, or

I'll jump at you and give you such a one. So what's up?"

"Again some *conference*, *Senior Lieutenant*, Sir, this morning at nine o'clock at mister *Colonel's*. I wanted to wake you up at night, but then I thought better of it."

"It's good you knew better than to dare, to be rousing me on account of every silliness, when there's enough time for it until morning. *Again a conference, let the demon from hell screw it all!* Hang up the receiver, call for me Vaněk to the telephone."

Accounting Master Sergeant Vaněk on the telephone: "Rechnungsfeldwebel *Vaněk, Senior Lieu-tenant, Sir."*

"Vaněk, find me immediately another *spotshine*. That rogue Baloun gobbled all my chocolate by the morning. To tie him up? No, we'll place him with the ambulance corpsmen. The guy is like a mountain, so he can be pulling the wounded from *combat*. I'll send him to you right away. Relay it to the *Regimental Office*, and return immediately to the Company. Do you think that we'll be going soon?"

"There's no rush, *Senior Lieutenant*, Sir. When we were to be going with the Ninth *March Company*, they were then pulling us by the nose a whole four days. With the Eighth it was as if swept by the same stroke of a broom. Only with the Tenth it was better. Then we were *on full field readiness alert*, at noon we got the order and in the evening we were hauling, but then, to make up for it, they were chasing us up and down the whole of Hungary and didn't know, which hole in which battlefield to plug using us."

During the whole time, since Senior Lieutenant Lukáš became the commander of the Eleventh marchgang, he found himself in a state called syncretism, that is in a philosophy, whereby he was striving to equalize the conceptual contradictions with the help of compromising until commingling of the views.

That is also why he answered: "Yes, can be, it's a given that's the way it is. So you don't think, that we're going today? At nine o'clock we have a *conference* with mister *Colonel*. — Apropos, do you know, that he's the *Watch Commander*? I'm just saying. Find out for me… Wait, what should you find out for me…? The list of NCOs indicating, since when they've been in service… Then the *Company* supplies. Nationality? Yes, yes, that too… But above all send the new *spotshine*…. What does *Ensign* Pleschner have to do with the *rank-and-file troops* today? *Preparation for departure.* Vouchers? I'll come to sign them after grub. Don't be letting anybody go to town. To the canteen in the camp? After mess, for an hour… Call Švejk here!… Švejk, you will stay by the telephone for the time being."

"I dutifully report, *Senior Lieutenant*, Sir, that I have not drunk coffee yet."

"Then you'll bring for yourself coffee and remain there in the office by the telephone, until I call you. Do you know, what a *messenger* is?"

"It keeps running, *Senior Lieutenant*, Sir."

"Make sure then that you're on the spot, when I call you. Tell Vaněk one more time, to seek out some *spotshine* for me. Švejk, hullo, where are you?"

"Here, *Senior Lieutenant*, Sir, they just brought coffee."

"Švejk, hullo!"

"I hear you, *Senior Lieutenant*, Sir, the coffee is totally cold."

"You know well already, what a *spotshine* is, Švejk. Look him over and then report to me, what he's all about. Hang up the receiver."

Vaněk, sipping the black coffee, into which he poured rum for himself from a bottle with the inscription 'Ink' (on account of taking all precautions), took a look at Švejk and said: "That *Senior Lieutenant* of ours screams into the telephone too much, I understood each word. You, Švejk, must be well acquainted with mister *Senior Lieutenant*."

"We're practically joined at the hip," answered Švejk. "One hand washes the other. We have been together through a lot already. Number of times already they have wanted to tear us one from the other, but we met again. He has always relied on me in everything, to the point that many times I myself am amazed by it. That's indeed why you certainly just heard him say for me to remind you one more time that you are to go and find some new *spotshine*, and that I am to look him over and give an expert report on him. That is, mister *Senior Lieutenant* is not satisfied with any old *spotshine*."

*

Colonel Schröder, when he called all the officers of the March Battalion to *conference*, did so again with great love, so that he could talk himself empty. Besides that it was necessary to make some decision in the affair of One-Year Volunteer Marek, who did not want to clean the latrines and was due to mutiny sent by Colonel Schröder to the Divisional Court.

From the Divisional Court he came just yesterday in the night to the *main guardhouse*, where he was being kept under guard. Concurrently with him was delivered to the Regimental Office a written communication from the Divisional Court, immeasurably confused, in which it was being pointed out, that in this case it was not a matter of mutiny, because one-year volunteers are not to clean latrines, nevertheless that it was however *insubordination*, which offense can be forgiven through proper conduct in the field. That on the basis of these reasons, the charged One-Year Volunteer Marek was being sent back to his Regiment and the investigation of the breach of discipline was being suspended until the end of the war and that it would be reopened on the occasion of the next infraction, that would had been committed by One-Year Volunteer Marek.

Then there was another case. With One-Year Volunteer Marek there was delivered concurrently to the *main guardhouse* from the Divisional Court the fake Corporal Teveles[384], who not long ago showed up at the Regiment, where he was sent to from a hospital in Zagreb. He had the large silver medal, pins of a one-year volunteer, and three little stars. He was recounting heroic deeds of the 6th March Company[385] in Serbia and that left of it had been he alone. Through an investigation it was determined, that with the 6th March Company at the beginning of the war actually did leave some one Teveles, who however did not have the privileges of a one-year volunteer. A report was requested from the Brigade, to which the 6th marchy was ordered to attach, when on December 2nd, 1914 was underway the running away from Belgrade, and it was determined, that on the list of those nominated for or awarded the silver medal there was no Teveles. Had infantryman Teveles been promoted to corporal during the Belgrade military campaign, it could not be absolutely ascertained, because the whole 6th March Company was lost at the St. Sava Church[386] in Belgrade, including its officers. At the Division Court was Teveles defending himself by stating, that he was really promised the large silver medal and that is why he bought it at the hospital from a Bosnian guy. As for the one-year volunteer stripes, that those he sewed on himself in a drunken state and that he kept wearing them, because he was constantly drunk, having had his bodily organism weakened by dysentery.

So then when the *conference* began before the discussion of these two cases, Colonel Schröder stated, that it was necessary to be in touch more often before the departure, which wouldn't be long in coming. He had been informed from the Brigade, that orders from the Division were being expected. Have the troops on alert and have the *Company Commanders* vigilantly see to it, that nobody was missing. He then repeated one more time all that, which he lectured on yesterday. He delivered again an overview of the war events and that nobody must suppress among the military troops the fighting character and the warring entrepreneurship.

On the desk there was attached in front of him a map of the battlefield with little pennants on pins, but the pennants had been mixed up and the frontlines shifted. The pulled out pins with pennants were wallowing under the desk.

The whole battlefield terribly messed up in the night the tomcat, whom were keeping in the Regimental Office the scribes and who, when in the night he dropped a load on the Austro-Hungarian battlefield, wanted to bury the turd, pulled out the little pennants and smeared the turd over all the positions, peed on the frontlines and *bridgeheads* and terribly sullied all the Army Corps.

Colonel Schröder was very short-sighted.

The officers of the March Battalion were watching with interest, how the finger of Colonel Schröder was nearing the little piles.

"From here, gentlemen, toward Sokal on to Bug[387]," said Colonel Schröder in a soothsaying manner and moved his index finger by memory to the Carpathians, while doing so he buried it into one of those little piles, as the tomcat had taken care to make the map of the battlefield sculpted.

"What is that, gentlemen?" he asked with astonishment, when something got stuck to his finger.

"Probably cat droppings Colonel, Sir," answered very courteously for all present Captain Ságner.

Colonel Schröder stormed out and into the office next door, from where one could hear horrible thundering and cussing with a terrible threat, that he'd have them lick it all clean after the tomcat.

The interrogation was short. It was determined, that two weeks ago the youngest scribe Zwiebelfisch had dragged the tomcat into the office. Following this determination Zwiebelfisch gathered up his proverbial five prunes he possessed and an older scribe took him away to the *main guardhouse*, where he'd be sitting as long as it took, until the next order by mister Colonel.

That actually ended the whole conference. When Colonel Schröder returned all red in the face to the officers corps, he forgot that he was to prophecy yet about the fate of One-Year Volunteer Marek and the counterfeit-corporal Teveles.

He said altogether briefly: "I beg the gentlemen officers to stand by on the ready and await further orders and instructions."

And so the One-Year Volunteer and Teveles remained further under guard at the *main guardhouse*, and when later they were joined by Zwiebelfisch, they were able to play mariáš and after the game of mariáš to bother their guardians by a request, that they pick their straw mattresses clean of fleas for them.

After that was pushed in there to join them also Sergeant Peroutka from the 13th March Company[388], who, when yesterday the rumor spread around the camp, that they were hauling into position, disappeared and was in the morning discovered by a patrol at the White Rose[389] in Bruck. He was making excuses, that he wanted before the departure to tour the well-known greenhouse of Count Harrach[390] near Bruck and that on the way back he got lost, and only in the morning all tired, arrived at the White Rose. (Actually he was sleeping with Rosie from the White Rose.)

*

The situation was still not cleared up. Will they be hauling, or will they not be hauling. On the telephone in the office of the 11th marchy Švejk heard out the most varied opinions, pessimistic and optimistic. The 12th March Company telephoned, that supposedly somebody from the office heard, that they would be waiting until the shooting exercises with mobile figure targets and that they would be hauling only after *live ammunition field shooting exercise*. This optimistic opinion was not shared by the 13th March Company, which telephoned, that just then Sergeant Havlík returned from town and he had heard from a railway attendant, that the cars were already at the station.

Vaněk ripped the receiver out of Švejk's hand and was screaming angrily, that the railway guys knew nothing but an old billy goat, that just now he had been in the Regimental Office.

Švejk was remaining by the telephone with genuine love, and to all questions 'what is new', he would answer, that so far nothing definite was known.

In that manner he answered also the question by Senior Lieutenant Lukáš:

"What is new over by you?"

"So far nothing definite is known, *Senior Lieutenant*, Sir," stereotypically retorted Švejk.

"You ox, Sir, hang up the receiver."

Then came a number of telephonegrams, which Švejk accepted after a rather long misunderstanding. Foremost the one, which could not be dictated to him in the night, when he had not hung up the receiver and was sleeping, regarding those inoculated and not inoculated.

Then again the delayed telephonegram about food cans, which had been clarified yesterday already.

Then a telephonegram to all the battalions, companies and regimental components:

A copy of the Brigade telephonegram No. 75692. Brigade-wide order num. 172 — When enumerating in field kitchen management reports the consumed products, follow this sequence: 1. meat, 2. food cans, 3. fresh vegetables, 4. dried vegetables, 5. rice, 6. macaroni, 7. peeled barley and semolina, 8. potatoes, instead of the former: 4. dried vegetables, 5. fresh vegetables.

When Švejk had read it to the Accounting Master Sergeant, Vaněk proclaimed ceremoniously, that such telephonegrams are pitched into the latrine:

"Some idiot at the Army Staff thought that up, and already it's going to all divisions and battalions and regiments."

After that Švejk accepted yet another telephone-gram, which was dictated so quickly, that Švejk captured from it in his notebook only, what looked like a cipher:

As a consequence more precisely was allowed or the same to one in contrast to that nevertheless to be chased down.

"All that is a useless," said Vaněk, when Švejk was tremendously baffled by what he had written, and was three times in succession reading it aloud to himself, "all silly things, although the demon knows, it can also be a cipher, but we're not equipped for that here at our company. That can also be thrown away."

"I myself too think so," said Švejk, "if I informed mister *Senior Lieutenant*, that he had *'as a consequence more precisely was allowed or the same to one in contrast to that nevertheless to be chased down'*, he could get offended. — Some people, let me tell you, are so touchy it's a horror," continued Švejk, sinking again into memories. "Once I was riding a streetcar from Vysočany[391] into Prague, and in Libeň some mister Novotný hopped on. As soon as I recognized him, I went to him on the front platform and started a conversation with him, that we're both from Dražov[380]. But he burst out hollering at me, not to be bothering him, that he supposedly didn't know me. I began explaining it to him, telling him to just remember, that as a little lad I used to come to him with my mother, whose name was Antonie, that the father's name was Prokop and he was a farmer. Even after that he did not want to know anything about the fact, that we knew one another. So I told him yet more details, that in Dražov, there used to be two Novotnýs, Tonda and Josef. That he was that Josef, that they wrote to me about him from Dražov, that he shot and wounded his wife, when she was rebuking him for drinking. And here, let me tell you, he cocked his arm, I ducked, and he broke the pane on the front platform, the big one in front of the motorman. So they disembarked us, took us away and at the police district station it became apparent, that he had been so touchy, because his name wasn't Josef Novotný at all, but Eduard Doubrava, and he was from Montgomery[393] in America and was here just visiting his relatives, from among whose ancestors originated his family."

The telephone interrupted his story telling and some raspy voice from the machine gun detachment was again asking, whether they'd be hauling. Supposedly in the morning there is a *conference* at mister *Colonel's*.

In the doorway appeared all pale Cadet Biegler[394], the biggest idiot in the Company, because at the one-year-timer school he strove to distinguish himself with his knowledge. He nodded to Vaněk, so that he'd go out and follow him into the corridor, where he had a long conversation with him.

When Vaněk returned, he was smiling contemptu-ously.

"What a piece of an ox he is," he said to Švejk, "here in our marchy we sure do have some specimen. He was also at the *conference*, and when they were leaving, then mister *Senior Lieutenant* ordered, that all *squad commanders* conduct a *weapons inspection* and told them to be strict. And now he comes to ask me, whether he should have Žlábek tied up, because he cleaned his rifle with kerosene."

Vaněk got angry.

"He asks me about such stupidity, when he knows, that we're hauling into the field. After all mister *Senior Lieutenant* thought better of tying up his *spotshine* yesterday. That's also why I did tell that puppy to think twice about treating the men like animals.

"Since you're already speaking of that *spotshine*," said Švejk, "don't you know perhaps, whether you have already chased one down for mister *Senior Lieutenant*?"

"Have *fishmonger's* smarts," answered Vaněk, "there's enough time for everything; besides I think, that mister *Senior Lieutenant* will get used to Baloun, here and there he'll still devour something of his and then he'll stop too, when we are in the field. There often won't have anything to eat both of them. When I say that Baloun stays, then there's nothing to be done. That is my business and that's nothing that mister *Senior Lieutenant* can say about. Just no rush."

Vaněk lay on his bed again and said: "Švejk, tell me some anecdote from military life."

"I could do that," answered Švejk, "but I'm afraid, that somebody will be ringing us again."

"So turn it off Švejk, unscrew the line or take off the receiver."

"Alright," said Švejk, taking off the receiver, "I'll tell you something, that is fitting for this situation, except back then instead of a real war it was just maneuvers and there was also such panic like today, because it wasn't known, when we would set out of the garrison. There served with me some Poříčí[395] guy, one Šic, a nice man, but pious and skittish. That one imagined, that maneuvers are something horrible, that people there are falling of thirst and ambulance corpsmen are picking them up like fruit fallen off the tree on the *march*. That is why he was drinking to load up for later, and when we set out for maneuvers from the garrison and came to Mníšek[396], he then said: 'I won't last guys, only Lord God himself can save me.' Then we came to Hořovice[397] and there we had a two day *rest break*, because it was some kind of mistake and we were advancing so fast, that we would have with the other regiments, that were marching with us on our *flanks*, captured the whole enemy staff, which would have been an embarrassment, because our army corps were to lose it like shit and the enemy win, because with the enemy there was some tired little archduke. So this Šic did this: When we were *camping*, he picked himself up and went to buy something in some village on the other side of Hořovice and was returning toward noon to the camp. It was hot, he was bombed just right too, and here he sees a pole in the road, on the pole this box and in it under a glass a quite small statuette of St. Jan Nepomucký[398]. He said a prayer in front of the St. Jan and was telling him: 'It's hot, I tell you, if only at least you had a little to drink. You're here in the sun, you must be sweating all the time.' So he shook the *field flask,* took a drink and says: 'I left you a swig too, Saint Jan of Nepomuk.' But he spooked, chug-a-lugged it all and for Saint Jan there was nothing left. 'Jesusmaria,' he says, 'Saint Jan of Nepomuk, this you have to forgive me, I will make it up to you, I'll take you with me to the camp and I will water you so gloriously, that you won't stand on your feet.' And darling Šic out of pity for Saint Jan of Nepomuk broke the glass, pulled out the statuette of the saint and stuck it under his blouse and carried it away to the camp. After that St. Jan of Nepomuk would sleep with him on the straw, he would carry him along on marches in his calf-hide-flap backpack and was very lucky at cards. Wherever we camped, there he was winning, until we came to Práchеňsko[399], we were camping in Drahenice[400] and he lost all, lock stock and barrel. When we set out in the morning, then on a pear tree by the road there was dangling the hanged Jan Nepomucký. So, that's the anecdote, and now again I'll hang up the receiver."

And the telephone line was once again carrying away the tremors of the new life full of nerves, as the old harmony of calm in the camp was disturbed.

At that time Senior Lieutenant Lukáš was in his room studying the ciphers just delivered to him from the Regimental Staff with the advisory, of how to go about deciphering them, and concurrently a secret coded order about the direction, in which the March Battalion would be marching to the Galician border (the first stage).

7217 — 1238 — 457 — 2121 — 35 = Moson[401]
8922 — 375 — 7282 = Ráb[402]
4432 — 1238 — 7217 — 35 — 8922 — 35 = Komarn[403] 7282 —
9299 — 310 — 375 — 7881 — 293 — 475 — 7979 = Budapest.

Deciphering these codes, Senior Lieutenant Lukáš gave a sigh: *"The demon from hell should screw the lot."*

Endnotes

(For the endnotes about the terms that appeared for the first time in Book One, please consult the Endnotes of that volume.)

[1] The Czech title of the second book, "Na frontě", is the straightforward designation for the combat zone. The noun "fronta" — a modern borrowing via German *Front* — was standard in Hašek's day in military and journalistic usage for the line of battle and, by extension, the theater of active operations. Within the novel's deliberate architecture, Book One is explicitly the rear, "V zázemí" (*In the Rear*), followed by the second volume "Na frontě" (*At the Front*). Hašek underlines this himself in his Afterword to the first book. There, the author promised to follow with the next volume "V zajetí" (*In Captivity*). Instead, he produced "Slavný výprask" (*The Illustrious Thrashing*) and the unfinished "Pokračování slavného výprasku" (*The Illustrious Thrashing Continued*); the progression is structural as well as thematic, moving the reader from the administrative hinterland into the fighting area and only later toward the mock-heroic reckoning.

The vocabulary of Book One had already signaled this progression. There Hašek chose "zázemí", the bureaucratic term for the administrative hinterland, rather than "týl", the strict military rear echelon behind the line of battle. By opting for "zázemí", he placed Švejk in the world of police headquarters, hospitals, billets, and chaplains. In Book Two, the novel moves to "fronta" — the combat line itself. The sequence is logical: from the hinterland of "zázemí" to the battlefield of "fronta", bypassing the narrower, technical zone denoted by týl.

In English, the idiomatic collocation for this sphere is **at the front**. Wartime English letters, orders, and reportage overwhelmingly say "at the front" to mark presence in the combat zone, in contrast to being in the rear or at home. The rival phrase **on the front** reads literalist and non-idiomatic: it suggests a surface rather than a theater and was not the natural English of the period. The preposition matters: it either places the reader where English speakers of the time would recognize themselves—at the front—or it leaves a faintly foreign seam in the prose.

Cecil Parrott's nomenclature established **On the Front** for Book Two, and his choice has been repeated so widely, that the oddity now often passes unnoticed. Yet it is precisely the kind of small but consequential tilt that

Pannwitz warned against: an accommodation to target-language habit that, in this case, is not even the target language's true habit. The Czech gives us "**na frontě**"; the English that corresponds, historically and idiomatically, is **at the front**.

For The Centennial Edition, therefore, Book Two is titled **At the Front**. This restores the period's English idiom, matches the Czech term without flattening it into a calque, and keeps faith with Hašek's own staging—from rear to front to the *illustrious thrashing* that follows. As with the other volumes, the aim is not to domesticate Hašek into our ready-made phrases, but to let the Czech word's world and rhythm find its right English—here, the world of soldiers **at the front**.

[2] Budějovice (Budweis) was until 1920 the name of České Budějovice (*Czech Budweis*), the largest city in South Bohemia. In 1913 the number of inhabitants was 44,538 of which roughly 63 per cent reported Czech as their everyday language. Among Czechs, the city was mostly called České Budějovice even under Austrian rule. The city was part of Okresní hejtmanství (*District Administration*) Budějovice and belonged to the district carrying its name.

In 2019 the city had slightly more than 94,000 inhabitants and is now as then the administrative and commercial center of the region. It is also a popular tourist destination, offering a well preserved old town. It is situated 381 meters above sea level at the confluence of the rivers Malše and Vltava.

When World War I broke out the city had a notable military presence, reflected in the number of people working for the armed forces. In 1913 they totaled 2,205, making up five per cent of the population. [honsi.org]

[3] The station name is not mentioned explicitly, but it is clear from the circumstances that Senior Lieutenant Lukáš and Švejk set out on their journey from this station: Nádraží císaře Františka Josefa (*Emperor Franz Joseph Station*) was, until 1918, the name of the main railway station in Prague. It has since then also been called Wilsonovo nádraží after President Woodrow Wilson. Since 1953 it has been named Prague hlavní nádraží (Prague Main Railway Station). The station was opened in 1871 and is by far the busiest railway station in the country.

In 1914 the station had long-distance connections with Vienna and served a number of other destinations both locally and regionally. It was one of the three major railway stations in Prague, together with Státní nádraží (now Masarykovo) and Severozápadní nádraží (now demolished). [honsi.org]

[4] Severozápadní nádraží (*Northwest Railway Station*) was a major railway

station in Prague, from 1953 called Praha-Těšnov. It was located in Florenc and was in service until 1972. (The building was demolished in 1985.) It was from here that Jaroslav Hašek together with painter Panuška took the train to Světlá nad Sázavou (on his way to Lipnice) on August 25th 1921.

In Prague it was the main hub of Österreichische Nordwestbahn (*Austrian Northwest Railway*), a private railway operator that was founded in 1868 and functioned until it was nationalized in 1909. The headquarters were located in Vienna. During the era of Austria-Hungary the station served Vienna and Berlin, and several regional destinations. [honsi.org]

5 A mother in a fairy-tale who, being careworn and exhausted by hardship, cast a spell in anger and turned her own seven sons into ravens. [Translator's note]

6 Neue Freie Presse (*New Free Press*) was a daily newspaper that was published in Vienna from 1864 to 1939, founded as a break-away from Die Presse (*The Press*). It published both a morning and an evening issue. It's political stance was bourgeois liberal, along the lines of e.g. Prager Tagblatt and Bohemia.

The newspaper eventually became very influential, led by the powerful editor in chief, Moritz Benedikt (1849-1920). It was also one of the largest of its kind in Austria, employing around 500, and it also enjoyed a reputation abroad. They were known for outstanding journalism and succeeded in enlisting writers like Theodor Herzl, Hugo von Hoffmannsthal, Bertha von Suttner and Stefan Zweig.

During World War I they took an aggressive patriotic stance, but during the French-German war in 1870-71 had also shown a pro German tendency.

In the inter-war years the newspaper continued to publish, but was closed by the Nazis in 1939. The paper always had many Jewish employees and Benedikt himself was of Jewish descent. [honsi.org]

7 V čubčím háji (*The Bitches' Grove*) was, according to Švejk, a pub in the Nekázanka street, but further information is not available. The name was surely a colloquial term for an existing pub in the street or possibly elsewhere. In 1910, there were several pubs in the street, the best known of which was U zlatého křížku (*At the Little Golden Cross*). [honsi.org]

8 Bohemia was a German-language daily published in Prague from 1828 till 1938, associated with the German Liberal Party. During the war they took a strongly patriotic stance, and from November 15th 1914 even changed the name to Deutsche Zeitung Bohemia. The editorial and administration offices were located in Liliová ulice (*Lily street*) in Staré město (*Old Town*)

and chief editor in 1914 was Andreas Haase. He held the position for an impressive 40 years, from 1879 to 1919. [honsi.org]

9 Mediterranean Sea is an ocean between Europe and Africa, with western Asia to the east and the Atlantic Ocean to the west. The following countries bordering the Mediterranean participated in World War I: Austria-Hungary, France, Italy, Greece, Montenegro and Turkey.

Austria-Hungary had access to Mediterranean Sea from Trieste and along the coast of Dalmatia down to Montenegro, k.u.k. Kriegsmarine (*I&R Navy*) possessed a sizeable fleet. Its main base was at Pola (now Pula, Croatia). During the war it was however limited to operations in the Adriatic See as the Entente blockaded the sea at the southern tip of Italy.

At the time the episode is supposed to have taken place (late 1914 or early 1915) there were no German U-boats in the Mediterranean Sea, they only appeared later that year. Nor could they have been called "E" as all German submarines had names starting with "U" (Unterseeboot). The German air force did however use war planes classified "E" (Eindecker), so perhaps the author swapped U-boats with aeroplanes.

Austro-Hungarian U-boats were also designated by the letter "U". They had been active in the Adriatic See from the outbreak of war, and on April 27th 1915 the French cruiser Léon Gambetta was torpedoed by "U-5". In 1914 the *I&R Navy* owned 5 U-boats, a number that rose to 26 by 1918. Almost all of them were built in Germany. [honsi.org]

10 Banka Slavia was a mutual insurance company (and bank) with headquarters at Havlíčkovo náměstí *(Havlíček squar*e). The company was founded in 1868 by a group of businessmen led by F. L. Chleborad. The first general assembly was held May 1^4^h 1869. The company expanded quickly and by the turn of the century they were established in Prague, Brno, Vienna, Lwów, Zagreb and Ljubljana. At the outbreak of war they were present also in Sarajevo.

The inter-war years saw the firm prosper even more and they were part owners of many foreign financial institutions, even as far as New York. They remained in business until 1945.

Jaroslav Hašek was employed as an apprentice by the bank from October 1902 until he was dismissed in June 1903. The reason was two longer absences without permission, the latest occurred May 30th 1903. Hašek disappeared without a trace and went off on a trip that may have lasted up to four months.

The author's family was strongly connected to Slavia: both his father Josef and his younger brother Bohuslav worked for the bank. [honsi.org]

11 U Špírků (*At Špírks'*) was a coffee-house in Staré město (*Old Town*) in Prague, which still exists albeit in a different setting. According to the restaurant's website, it was founded as early as 1870 and renovated in a traditional style between 2004 and 2006.

The café is not listed in the pre-war address books, but in 1891 the police registered a certain Karel Špirk, entered with "cafetier" as occupation. During the 1890's Špirk and his wife on several occasions placed adverts in Prager Tagblatt, where they wished their Jewish guests a Happy New Year. In the 1896 address book the café is entered under the name U dvou kominíků (*At the two Chimneysweeps*) with wife Rozalie Špirková as the owner.

In 1912 Národní listy (*National Pages*) reported that Karel Špirk had passed away and they also add that he was 54 years old, was a café owner and a proprietor of real estate. Špirk was according to the police books born October 12th 1858 in Prague, so the connection to the café is indisputable. He was married to the ten year younger Roselie, and they had a daughter Anna, who was born in 1887. Karel Špirk died on May 9th 1912 in Senohraby and was buried at Vyšehrad cemetery.

A newspaper notice in Právo Lidu (*People's Right*) from 1916 confirms that the café was still in business and that it was subjected to a police raid on suspicion of illegal prostitution (Tunel is mentioned in the same item). As late as 1929 adverts reveal that the establishment was still running, now officially using the name U Špírků. They hosted concerts, and served Prazdroj (*Pilsner Urquell*).

The owner in 1924 was Josef Baloun. In 1936 Marie Balounová was the owner. A picture from 1945 reveals that the establishment survived the Nazi protectorate. During the first republic U Špírků also functioned as an unofficial brothel (licensed brothels were banned in 1921). [honsi.org]

12 Montenegro (Црна Гора) was in 1914 an independent kingdom and had been a duchy (kingdom from 1910) since the liberation from Turkey in 1878. The King at the time was Nikola I. and the capital was Cetinje. In World War I the kingdom quickly aligned with Serbia and declared war on Austria-Hungary on 7 August 1914.

Today Montenegro is again an independent state, after having been part of various south Slav federations from 1918 until 2006 (except 1941-45). The language is Serbian, is written with the Cyrillic script and the religion is mainly Orthodox. [honsi.org]

[13] Prager Infanteriekadettenschule (*Infantry Cadet School Prague*) was opened in 1869 and was situated in the northern part of Hradčany (from 1900 onwards). The building still exists and has had various functions since, including its use by Nazi and Soviet occupants. Today, the building hosts the Czech Ministry of Defense.

The real-life Čeněk Sagner actually attended this school from 1901 to 1905, whereas Rudolf Lukas did not. He graduated from Královo Pole (Königsfeld) near Brno. These two were the only infantry cadet schools on the Czech territory. In addition, Moravia hosted the only cavalry cadet school in the monarchy, in Hranice na Moravě (Mährisch Weisskirchen).

Cadet schools were institutions that educated active officers for the land forces. Most of them belonged to the infantry, but there were also schools for cavalry, artillery and pioneers. The education lasted for four years and, besides military subjects, general subjects were also taught. The graduates obtained the rank of Fähnrich (*Ensign*), until 1908 called Kadett-Stellvertreter (*Cadet Officer-Deputy*). The schools' elite status was supported by an arrangement whereby sons of officers paid much lower tuition fees than others. [honsi.org]

[14] Styria was until 1918 one of 15 crown lands of Cisleithania. The area was larger than the current Austrian state of Styria as it included parts of current Slovenia with Maribor (*Marburg*). The capital was (and is) Graz, and at the time a significant part of the population were Slovenes (nearly 30 per cent).

The author's inspiration for the use of Styria (and the described train route) as a theme in the novel is probably a trip he undertook in the summer of 1905. His travel companions for parts of this journey were painter Jaroslav Kubín and the actor František Vágner. His travels that year are described by Václav Menger and are also featured in Strana mírného pokroku v mezích zákona (*The Party of Moderate Progress within the Bounds of the Law*). Hašek also touches on the journey in the stories Rozjímání o počátku cesty (*Contemplation on the Beginning of the Journey*) and O sportu (*On Sports*). [honsi.org]

[15] Leoben is the second-largest city in the Austrian state of Styria with around 25,000 inhabitants. It is situated on the river Mur, 541 meters above sea level, 46 kilometers north-west of Graz.

In 1914 it was also within Styria, was a district capital and also housed the district court. The town had a mining academy and was primarily a mining community. The population was almost exclusively German.

In the story O sportu (*On Sports*), printed on 27 January 1907, Hašek mentions Leoben, but here he used the Czech term Lubno. He notes that he visited two years ago, was penniless, and had to beg money to get back home. [honsi.org]

[16] Maribor is the second-largest city in Slovenia, located on the river Drava. The population number is now (2019) appx. 112,000.

Until 1918 it belonged to the Austrian crown-land of Styria and was at the time 80 per cent German-speaking. In 1890 it housed a bishop seat, and was the home of several educational institutions as well as some industry.

One of the prototypes of characters from *The Good Soldier Švejk*, Rudolf Lukas, attended a preparatory course for cadet school here from 1903 until 1904. Another well-known prototype, Ludvík Lacina, also spent some time here, as Field Chaplain in 1912. [honsi.org]

[17] Sankt (*Saint*) Moritz appears to have been somewhere in Austria between Leoben and Prague, but no such place has been identified. As the author surely didn't have the famous Swiss resort of the same name in mind, the most likely candidate is Sankt Michael in Obersteiermark *(Upper Styria)*. This is a town on one of the possible routes between Maribor and Prague, soon after Leoben.[honsi.org]

[18] Tábor is a city in southern Czech Republic. It lies along a bend in the river Lužnice 50 miles (80 km) south of Prague. Founded in 1420 by Jan Žižka and other followers of the Bohemian religious reformer Jan Hus, Tábor became the radical center of the more militant members of the movement, known as the *Taborites*. These people fostered the national spirit and the preservation of the Czech language. The town has a museum (1878) of the Hussite Revolutionary Movement. [britannica.com]

For the Czech independence movement during World War I the Hussites were an important national symbol and continued as one of the mainstays in the nation building in Czechoslovakia in the inter-war years. [honsi.org]

The old town lies on a steep granite ridge and is protected by the river to the south and west and by the fishpond Jordán (where local baptisms once took place) to the north. It is encircled by fortifications, still largely intact; the Bechyně gate dates from 1420.

The hub of the Old Town is Žižka square, from which tortuous narrow streets spread out, originally planned to impede access by enemy intruders. Tábor declined in the 17th century after suffering ravages during the Thirty Years' War. It is now a road and rail junction and has plants to process wool, tobacco, and mother-of-pearl. Kaolin is quarried nearby. Pop. (2007 est.) 35,859. [britannica.com]

[19] Žižkov is an urban district and cadastral area east of the center of Prague. Administratively it is part of Prague 3 and partly Prague 8. The district is named after the Hussite leader Jan Žižka. From 1881 to 1922 it was a city in its own right.

The first and part of the second volume of *The Good Soldier Švejk* was written here. Jaroslav Hašek stayed with his friend Franta Sauer at Jeronýmova 324/3 from January to August 1921. Nearby at Prokopovo náměstí there is now a statue of the author. [honsi.org]

[20] Uhříněves is a suburb on the southeastern outskirts of Prague, within the current Prague 22. From 1913 until 1974 it was a separate town. It had (and has) a railway station but the express trains didn't stop here so Švejk and Senior Lieutenant Lukáš simply passed through it on their way to Budějovice in 1915. [honsi.org]

[21] Hostivař is an urban area on the southeastern outskirts of Prague that since 1922 has been part of the capital. It has a railway station and is also the end-of-the-line station of metro line A. Hostivař is also a popular area for recreation. [honsi.org]

[22] Táborské nádraží (*Tábor railway station*) is situated approximately 2 km east of the town center. It is one of the major stops on the Prague-Budějovice line.

The railway station was built between 1869 and 1871 and was used by the company Kaiser Franz Josephs-Bahn, which operated the Prague-Vienna line. Other important stops on the line were Benešov, Veselí nad Lužnicí, Třeboň and Gmünd. The station also served Budějovice, and from 1903, the local train to Bechyně. In 1914, the station also served lines running east-west: Jihlava-Domažlice. The station manager in 1914 was Vincenc Motyčka, so this was the person Švejk would have reported to (if his mishaps were based on any real-life incident).

It may at first sight appear strange that Švejk would meet a wounded Hungarian soldier in Tábor, far from the Hungarian heartlands. Further investigation, however, reveals that it was quite likely. Tábor had a large hospital, good railway connections, and admitted wounded soldiers from all over the monarchy. Lists of wounded and infirm from early 1915 show several Hungarian names at this hospital.

The outbreak of war also led to the establishment of temporary hospitals. Already in August 1914, Sokol put their building at the disposal for sick-beds, and the waiting rooms at the station were used by the Red Cross. In January 1915, military hospitals were also established elsewhere in town.

That there were several of them in Tábor is also mentioned by the author. [honsi.org]

[23] Svitava no doubt refers to Svitavy, a town in eastern Bohemia that in 1914 was predominantly German speaking. It is also known as the birthplace of Oskar Schindler, to whom the town has erected a monument. In 1866 the ceasefire between Austria and Prussia was signed here.

The river Svitava flows through the town and as Švejk says there it has a railway station. The German translation of Grete Reiner interprets it as Zittau (Cz. Žitava), a town in Germany bordering Bohemia. Although odd at first sight, Hašek's use of the term Svitava is not necessarily wrong. Svitava is the term used on Erben's map from 1883 and is listed in Ottův slovník naučný (*Otto's Educational Dictionary*) as an alternative for Svitavy. [honsi.org]

[24] Stará brána (*Old Gate*) obviously refers to a town gate in Tábor but a gate with such a name didn't exist. It was therefore probably a colloquial name for Bechyňská brána, the only town gate that is still intact.

There were many butchers in Tábor in 1915 but it has not been possible to find out where they were located. The address directory only lists names, not the street addresses. [honsi.org]

[25] A restaurant existed at the station from 1871 when the station opened, and in 1886 it was run by Antonín Jonáš. Who ran the restaurant through the years is unknown, but in 1913 Antonín Stětina was in charge. He seems to have gone bankrupt in the spring of 1914.

From 1914, Jan Zimák is officially listed as proprietor and he was also in charge when Jaroslav Hašek passed through Tábor in mid-February 1915. From August 1914, Zimák also provided food for the Red Cross clinic that was set up at the station. In 1915, the restaurant advertised itself as elegant, with excellent food, serving draught beer from Pilsen. In 1932, it was still operating and not much had changed—and the beer was still from Pilsen. The landlord was now Karel Hokův and he was listed as owner also in 1939. What happened to the restaurant since then is not known.

The information we have about the restaurant does not correspond to the author's description of it as "third class", so it must be assumed that he didn't visit himself, and that Švejk's stopover is inspired by events that took place elsewhere. [honsi.org]

[26] Zeman most probably refers to the successor of Josef Zeman (1848-1892) who in 1880 founded a brewery in Kvasilov (Ukr. "Kvasyliv"), a Czech settlement a few kilometers north of Zdolbunovo. [honsi.org]

[27] Szeged is a city in southern Hungary, right on the Serbian border. It is the third largest city in Hungary and a major center of education. It is located by the river Tisza.

Around February 4th 1915 the replacement battalion of Infantry Regiment No. 28 was transferred from Prague to Szeged, one of the first of many Czech regiments that were moved away from their recruitment districts. This was a preventive move from *I&R Ministry of War* against presumed disloyalty. Other regiments were moved later that year and it was the turn of Jaroslav Hašek and his Infantry Regiment No. 91 on June 1st, an event that is described in *The Good Soldier Švejk.* [honsi.org]

[28] Czech expression for "darling". [Translator's note]

[29] There is no doubt that Hašek borrowed the motif from Kriegskalender (*Military calendars*) 1919 because the descriptions in *The Good Soldier Švejk* and the calendar are identical. Corporal Paulhart and Corporal Bachmayer have been identified and information about them confirmed by their Belohnungsantrag, whereas the identity of Hammel remains unclear (probably due to a misspelling of his surname in the calendar). Therefore, we do not know his correct surname.

All three, Hammel, Paulhart and Bachmayer had exactly the rank and regimental affiliation that Hašek described in the novel and served together with the k.k. Schützenregiment Nr. 21 on the Italian front in 1917. Hammel was a k.k. Landwehr Zugsführer.

Josef Paulhart's Grundbuchsblatt (service record) reveals that he was born February 27th 1892 in Altlichtenwarth, Bezirk Mistelbach, and was a farmer by profession. He started his military service on 1 October 1913 when he was assigned to I&R Land Defense Infantry Regiment No. 24 (Vienna), then transferred to I&R Land Defense Infantry Regiment No. 2 (Linz) on the 16th. For some reason, he was transferred again on 13 December 1913, now to k.k. Schützenregiment Nr. 21 where he served for the duration of the war. In August 1917 he was hospitalised and by then had been promoted to Gefreiter titulär Korporal and was decorated with a Karl-Truppen-Kreuz. On 12 November he was proposed for a silver medal 1st class. On 3 November 1918 he was taken prisoner by the Italians at Tagliamento, then released and demobilised in 1919.

[30] *I&R* stands for *Imperial and Royal*, from the German 'kaiserlich und königlich'. (The phrase Imperial and Royal refers to the court/government of the Habsburgs in a broader historical perspective.) These are the German abbreviations of the term 'kaiserlich und königlich': k.k. or k.-k., meaning

"imperial (Austria) – royal (Bohemia)", pertains to the Austrian Empire before 1867 and to the Austrian part of the Austro-Hungarian Empire 1867–1918. k.u.k., meaning "imperial (Austria) and royal (Hungary)", pertains to the Austro-Hungarian Empire 1867–1918. [en.wikipedia.org]

31 I&R 21st Riflemen Regiment was one of 37 Austrian k.k. Landwehr (*I&R Land Defense*) infantry regiments. Together with most of its peer units, it was established in 1889. The recruitment district was St. Pölten, consisting of roughly the western half of present-day Niederösterreich. Some men were also recruited from District Vienna B. Ethnically, the regiment was almost entirely German. Staff and all three battalions were, in 1914, garrisoned in St. Pölten. Commander in 1914 was Oberst Eduard von Dietrich.

It was only in 1917 that the term Schützenregiment (*Rifle Regiment*) was officially introduced, as all k.k. Landwehr units were renamed in April of that year. This indicates that the author drew inspiration from propaganda material published late in the war, not from what he may have witnessed in 1915. See the next paragraph for confirmation of this hypothesis.

In *The Good Soldier Švejk*, it is claimed that these posters were created at Kriegsministerium by conscripted German journalists. This was often true, and Egon Erwin Kisch is only one example. On the other hand, the claim that the soldiers on the posters were "invented rare model soldiers" is not true. Zugsführer Hammel, Korporal Bachmayer, Korporal Paulhart, Zugsführer Danko, and Trainsoldat Bong were all real people, but propaganda writers glorified their exploits. See Kriegskalender for more on this theme.

32 Danko was exactly what the author described him as: Zugsführer in k.u. Honvéd Husaren Regiment Nr. 5. In October 1914, Oesterreichische Volks-Zeitung and others reported that he had been awarded the gold medal for bravery. The report in the paper was from the propaganda series Aus dem Goldenen Buche der Armee (*From the Golden Book of the Army*) and was nearly identical to the description in *The Good Soldier Švejk* .

In 1935, the regiment's history was published as a book and provides further information. The soldier's name was Dankó János (in Hungarian, family names are written first) and his rank is confirmed as Szakaszvezető (Zugsführer). He had been promoted after the battles by Dzibułki (Ukr. Зіболки) north-east of Lemberg at the end of August 1914. On October 2nd 1914, he was awarded a gold medal for bravery, exactly as the above-mentioned Austrian newspaper reported a few weeks later. [honsi.org]

33 Ger. k.u. Honvéd Husaren Regiment Nr. 5/Hu. kir. 5. Honvéd Huszárezred was one of 10 Hungarian Honved (*Hungarian Land Defense*) cavalry regiments. It was recruited from Honvéd district no. III Kassa (now Košice). Commander in 1914 was Oberst Pál Hegedűs. The regiment was garrisoned in Košice and Nyíregyháza.

Immediately upon the outbreak of war, the Regiment was sent to the front in Galicia and had their baptism of fire on August 15th 1914 by Stojanów (now Стоянів) on the border with Russia. They experienced the disastrous defeat at the end of August that forced Austria-Hungary to abandon Lemberg. At the turn of the year, they were fighting in the Carpathians and took part in the advance eastwards from early May 1915. By then, however, they were operating as foot soldiers. In the summer of 1916, they were moved to the front against Romania, whereas the final year of the war was spent fighting on the Italian front.

In 1935, the Regiment's history was published as a book. The history confirms that *Train soldier* Danko, the soldier Švejk observed on a propaganda poster in Tábor, was indeed a *Train soldier* in the regiment and took part in the early battles in Galicia. His Hungarian name was János Dankó, but he may also have been a Slovak. [honsi.org]

34 Bong was a real person, and the author presents merely a more colourful version of news items that appeared in the press in January and February 1915. All had the title Aus dem Goldenen Buche der Armee, a regularly published series. It reported various heroic deeds; some were also available as postcards and almost certainly as posters.

News about Bong being awarded the silver medal 2nd class was reported in newspapers in early December, based on Verordnungsblatt für das k.u.k. Heer (*Ordinance Gazette of the I&R Army*) from 5 December 1914. Here, the soldier's unit is confirmed: Traineskadron Nr. 3, Traindivision Nr. 1. At the time of his decoration, he served with Divisions-Sanitätsanstalt Nr. 12. Given the regiment's recruitment district was Kraków (it included parts of Moravia and Silesia), his nationality was most likely Polish or Czech.

Despite the various news items, there is little doubt that Hašek's source was Kriegskalender for 1919, or rather, the Czech version of it. The entire text segment describing Bong is, apart from the colour of the horse and a couple of minor differences, identical to the text in the calendar. [honsi.org]

35 *I&R 3rd Train Squadron* refers to the 3rd squadron of *Train Division No.1*, a supply unit in k.u.k. Heer (*I&R Army*). Trainsoldat Bong was real enough, confirmed by several newspaper notices in early 1915. [honsi.org]

[36] Vojna is one of the heroes the author picked from Kriegskalender (War Calendar) 1919 together with Zugsführer Danko, Trainsoldat Bong, Zugsführer Hammel and others. Švejk, however, exaggerated greatly, as Vojna, according to the calendar, was injured twice and, despite his injuries, assumed command of a half company. There is, however, no mention of his hand or head being blown off.

According to the calendar, the heroic deed took place by Polazzo on 4 July 1915 and not in Galicia as Švejk claimed. It is also stated that Vojna was decorated with a silver medal 1st class for his heroics. The date also makes it clear that Švejk could not have read about Vojna before reaching Tábor, as Italy only entered the war when Švejk's march company had arrived in Budapest (23 May).

No Josef Vojna from Field Rifle Battalion No.7 appears in Austro-Hungarian casualty lists, lists of decorated soldiers, or in Verordnungsblatt (*Ordinance Gazette*) or Ranglisten (*Army Rank Lists*). Nor does a search for the surname "Wojna" as given in the calendar yield any results. The reason is simply a typographical error in the *War Calendar*, because his name was actually Josef Wojnar. News of him being awarded a silver medal for bravery was reported in several newspapers, and in Wiener Zeitung on October 14th 1915 he is clearly identified as Dr. Josef Wojnar from Field Rifle Battalion No.7, albeit with a silver medal 2nd class instead of 1st class as the calendar states. In 1918, the Viennese newspaper Weltblatt confirmed most of the information from the war calendar. [honsi.org]

[37] Field Rifle Battalion No.7 was one of 32 Feldjäger (*Field Riflemen*, i.e. light infantry) battalions in k.u.k. Heer (*I&R Army*). The Regiment was formed as early as 1808 and took part in the campaigns against Italy around the middle of the century. The replacement battalion was located in Laibach (now Ljubljana). Staff and troops were, from 1905 to 1914, garrisoned in Canale and Tolmein by the river Isonzo on the border with Italy, currently in Slovenia. The vast majority of the battalion's soldiers were Slovenes. [honsi.org]

[38] Čáslav is a town in central Bohemia, about 100 km east of the capital, not far from Kutná Hora. The number of inhabitants as of 2020 was around 10,000. [honsi.org]

[39] A rendition of “marška”, short version of “marškumpačka”, which is *a slang term for a “march company” - a unit created for transport to the battlefield, where it was transformed into a field company or served to replenish losses in existing field companies.* [svejkmuseum.cz]

[40] Kateřinská is a street in Nové město (*New Town*), Prague. This is also the location of Kateřinky, the madhouse where Švejk spent some time early in the novel. The text indicates that Švejk lived in or near this street, but referring to the corner with Na Bojišti makes no sense, as the two streets don't intersect. Švejk may have meant the corner of Ječná ulice and Sokolská ulice where the author lived for a short period in 1888 and 1889. [honsi.org]

[41] Poland was in 1914 not an independent state as Polish lands had for almost 120 years been split between Austria, Germany and Russia. Despite the adversity Polish culture, language and nationhood rule had survived foreign rule. The background was three territorial divisions of Poland (1772, 1793, 1795), perpetrated by Russia, Prussia and Austria, by which Poland's size was progressively reduced until, after the final partition, the state ceased to exist. In 1918 the independent Polish state finally resurfaced, resulting from the defeat in World War I of the three powers that until then had ruled the country.

The largest part of Poland was under Russian rule, from 1815 known as the Kingdom of Poland (Królestwo Polskie, Царство Польское) with the Tsar as a nominal king and Warsaw as the capital. Poles served in the Russian army. An example is the battle by Sokal in July 1915 where Polish units faced Jaroslav Hašek's IR. 91 and distinguished themselves.

German Poland consisted mainly of the Prussian province of Posen (Pol. Prowincja Poznańska, Ger. Provinz Posen) and was with 2 million inhabitants (1910) much smaller than Russian Poland. Poles made up two thirds of the population but had little influence on governance. Like in Russia, Polish culture and language were subjugated and the province was subjected to severe Germanization, particularly during and after Bismarck's reign. On the other hand Posen was the most prosperous of the areas populated by Poles. They were however obliged to serve in the German Imperial army.

When Poland and Poles is a theme in *The Good Soldier Švejk* it is overwhelmingly likely to refer to Poles in Austria, for all practical purposes Galicia (Pol. Galicja – Ger. Galizien). It was annexed by Austria after the first partition of Poland in 1772. Poles in Austria enjoyed far greater autonomy than their brethren in Russia and Germany. From 1873 Galicia became an autonomous province of Cisleithania with Polish and, to a lesser degree, Ruthenian (Ukrainian), as official languages. The Galician Sejm (parliament) and provincial administration had extensive privileges and powers, especially in education, culture, and local affairs. The Polonization of autonomous Galicia came at the expense of the Ukrainians and also the much smaller German minority. Dissatisfaction with Polish rule led to a strong Russophile movement among the Ukrainian population, a theme touched upon also in *The Good Soldier Švejk*. Poles, as one of the 11 nations of Austria-Hungary, made up almost 10 per cent of the 52 million strong population (classified by language). In the Reichsrat lower chamber they had 82 out of 516 representatives (1911).

During 1914 and 1915 fierce fighting took place on Polish territory. Austro-Hungarian troops invaded Russian Poland in August and enjoyed early success in the battles of Kraśnik and Komarów. These advances were however overshadowed by the disaster in Galicia where the capital Lwów was abandoned in early September and k.u.k. forces were pushed back to the river San and the Carpathians. The situation was particularly critical in late November when the Russian 3rd Army crossed the Raba and threatened Kraków. Their advance was however halted during the battle of Limanowa and the front was stabilized along the Dunajec and the Carpathians. Of particular significance was the fortress of Przemyśl that tied up large Russian forces until it capitulated on 22 March 1915 after having been encircled since 8 November 1914. Further north the German army was more successful and by January 1915 it had occupied parts of Russian Poland, including the large city of Łódź.

In early may 1915 a major turnaround occurred. The Central Powers launched a successful offensive by the Dunajec that forced the Russians away from the Carpathians and during the summer forced them out of virtually all of Poland. Warsaw fell on 4 August 1915 and in addition nearly the entire Galicia was back in Austrian hands by the autumn.

As opposed to the Czechs and Ukrainians the Poles remained relatively loyal to Austria-Hungary during the war (and incidently also to Germany and Russia in their respective parts). The Central Powers even agreed to create a puppet state called the Kingdom of Poland on former Russian territory and a Polish Legion led by future president Józef Piłsudski was created as a semi-autonomous unit under the auspices of I&R forces. [honsi.org]

[42] In the Hebrew Bible, (The Old Testament) the Judgment of Solomon (1 Kings 3:16–28) is the paradigmatic narrative describing how King Solomon exercised God-given wisdom and discernment in resolving an otherwise intractable dispute between two claimants. Confronted with two women

each claiming to be the mother of a living child, Solomon proposes a test — suggesting the child be divided — not as an actual sentence but as a discernment device that exposes the true emotional and ethical motivations of the litigants. The one who pleads to spare the child reveals genuine maternal compassion, and Solomon, perceiving this, awards her custody. This judgment exemplifies the biblical ideal that wisdom (chochmah) entails seeing through surface claims to their moral substance, enabling justice that aligns with divine intent rather than mere procedural compromise. [biblegateway.com]

In Jewish interpretive tradition (including rabbinic commentary and Midrash), Solomon's decision is read not as clever theatrics but as an exercise of Torah-rooted discernment. Solomon had earlier asked God for "an understanding heart to judge Your people," and this narrative illustrates how such wisdom, rooted in the Torah's ethical and legal framework, permits a judge to discern truth in the absence of clear evidence and to render a decision that upholds justice and compassion. In this sense, a "Solomonic solution" in Hebraic terms is a resolution that transcends literal text and legal technicalities by applying deep insight into human motives in accordance with the moral logic of Torah justice, a principle reflected throughout Jewish scriptural and rabbinic thought.
[jewishstudies.rutgers.edu] [bibleandcriticaltheory.com]

43 Budějovická ['boodiyeh-yoh-vits-kaah] is the feminine adjective of Budějovice (Budweis in German), short for the Czech town České Budějovice, to conform with the grammatical rules of matching gender inflection, as "anabáze", i.e. anabasis, is a feminine noun.

44 The New World Dictionary of the American Language: Anabasis (ə nab'ə sis) [Gr. < anabainein, to go up < ana-, up + bainein, to go < IE. Base *gwem-: see COME] 1. The unsuccessful military expedition (401-400B.C.) of Cyrus the Younger to overthrow Artaxerxes II 2. a book about this by Xenophon —n. [a-] pl. -ses' (-sēz') any large military expedition. [archive.org]

There is a widespread, albeit erroneous belief held in academia, that Hašek used the word as a reference to the "Siberian Anabasis" of the Czecho-Slovak Legions in Russia, that earned Czechs and Slovaks their right to self-determination at the end of WWI. He was supposedly making light of the postwar pride and adulation of the legendary Legions. (The Endnotes in the first edition of this text replicated the error, as the translator relied on the academics, who had studied the subject for 87 years by that time.) Now it is time for the record to be set straight.

Jomar Hønsi, a Norwegian amateur historian/ researcher and President of the World Society of Jaroslav Hašek, is the author of the "article, that seeks to trace the hypothesis from 1921 onwards, and also to explain why, in the light of Hašek's repeated mention of the term 'anabasis' before the Legions came into existence, the theory is little more than hot air." Here is the conclusion of the article: [Translator's note]

"We have in vain searched digitized newspapers from 1921 or 1922 for any sign that any writers or critics connected Švejk's anabasis with the Legions. Even extending the search to 1950 and including the extensive inter-war legionnaire literature has proved futile. There must also be a reason why endnotes in Švejk editions published from 1955 onwards no longer connect the Legions and Švejk's anabasis. The answer is probably that the communist publishers no longer believed in the hypothesis (had they perhaps by now discovered *Letters from the front* from 1916, where Xenophon and the anabasis are mentioned?). If there had been any substance in the theory, they surely would have used Švejk's 'budějovická anabasis' for what it was worth." [honsi.org]

45 Xenophon was a Greek commander, author, and historian known for his accounts of ancient Greece, his writings on Socrates, and for providing the first eyewitness account of a military campaign in antiquity. His best-known work, 'Anabasis', describes the Greek mercenaries' perilous journey home through Asia Minor after a failed campaign against Persia. This seven-volume work is considered Xenophon's masterpiece. It was translated into Czech in 1853 and, by the turn of the century, had become part of Greek language teaching at Czech grammar schools. [honsi.org]

46 Asia Minor is a term rarely used nowadays, but refers to the region Anatolia which makes up a large part of modern Turkey. It is the westernmost peninsula on the Asian continent, surrounded by the Black Sea, the Mediterranean Sea, the Aegean Sea and the Marmara Sea. It is separated from the Balkans by the Bosporus and the Dardanelles. [honsi.org]

47 The Caspian Sea is the world's largest inland body of water, variously classified as the world's largest lake or a full-fledged sea. It does not have an exit and lies 28 meters below sea level. Volga contributes 80 per cent of the water. The Caspian sea borders Azerbaijan, Russia, Kazakhstan, Iran and Turkmenistan. [honsi.org]

48 Sea of Azov is an appendix to the Black Sea bordering Ukraine and Russia. It is the world's shallowest sea with only 15 meters at the deepest. The

rivers Don and Kuban flow into it.

The Russian city of Taganrog (Таганрог) on the northern shore would have been well known to many Czechs as the city's munition factory employed many prisoners of war. [honsi.org]

49 Gallic Sea was an ancient name for the stretch of sea between Sardinia, the Balearic Islands and the Riviera.

However this doesn't fit with the author's information that the sea is "somewhere in the north". He therefore probably had English Channel in mind, and this assumption is supported by other sources and historical circumstances.

The source of the information seems to be Caesar's own book De Bello Gallico (*The Gallic Wars*). It is also worth noticing that this work was on the Latin curriculum in the 4th year at the Gymnasium Hašek attended. [honsi.org]

50 Caesar was a Roman commander, politician and author. He had become the most powerful citizen of the Roman Empire when he was murdered by senator Brutus in 44 BC. At that time, he held the title "dictator in perpetuo". During his reign, he undertook extensive reforms, centralizing the administration. The area of the empire was greatly extended, including Britannia. [honsi.org]

51 Rome in this context refers to ancient Rome as the capital of the Roman Empire.

"All roads lead to Rome" - It is not confirmed that this saying dates back to Caesar. Its origin is often attributed to the French theologian Alain de Lille and his expression Mille viae ducunt hominem per saecula Romam. It literally means 'A thousand roads lead men forever to Rome.' [honsi.org]

52 Milevsko is a town in South Bohemia with slightly fewer than 9,000 inhabitants (as of 2019). It is located between Tábor and Písek. [honsi.org]

53 Květov is a village in South Bohemia with slightly more than 100 inhabitants. It is located between Milevsko and Písek. According to the 1910 census, Květov had 325 inhabitants, all of whom 325 reported using Czech as their everyday language. [honsi.org]

54 Vráž is a village in South Bohemia with 275 inhabitants (2005). It is located 8 km north of Písek.

In 1915 Vráž actually had a k.k. Gendarmerie (*I&R State Police*) station. It reported to the District Command in Písek, i.e. Gendarmeriebezirk Nr. 14 in Bohemia (Landesgendarmeriekommando Nr. 2 / *State Police Provincial*

Command No. 2). The local head of police in 1914 was strážmistr (*Patrol Sergeant*) J. Šráma. He had one assistant, J. Michal. [honsi.org]

55 The italicized '*They*' or '*they*' and their morphological variants indicate that they are used instead of 'you', when addressing a stranger or showing respect to age, position, or maintaining distance. [Translator's note]

56 Klatovy is a town in the Plzeň region with 22,257 inhabitants (as of 2020). The key industry at the outbreak of World War I was textile manufacturing. The town had a railway station, hospital, power plant etc. The center has several historical buildings.

According to the 1910 census, Klatovy had 14,387 inhabitants, of whom 13,981 (97 per cent) reported using Czech as their everyday language. [honsi.org]

57 Indirectly referred to is I&R Land Defense Infantry Regiment No. 7 in Plzeň (*Pilsen*), one of 37 Austrian I&R Land Defense infantry regiments and, like most of its peer units, it was established in 1889. The regiment was recruited from the districts of Plzeň, Beroun and Písek. Staff and two battalions were garrisoned in Pilsen in 1914, with the other battalion in Rokycany.

During the war, they first fought in Serbia; from February 1915, in the Carpathians, Galicia and Russian Poland; in 1916, in Bukovina and by the river Dniestr. In June 1917, they were transferred to the Italian front, where they remained for the rest of the war, except for a brief interlude in Ukraine in early 1918.

During the first half of 1915, all replacement battalions from Czech-speaking areas were transferred to regions populated by other nationalities. This also applied to I&R Land Defense Infantry Regiment No. 7, that was moved to Rumburg (Rumburk) in northern Bohemia, a region almost exclusively populated by Germans. They arrived in Rumburg on the morning of May 23rd 1915. In 1918, soldiers from the replacement battalion were involved in the so-called Rumburk rebellion, and several of them were executed after the insurrection was suppressed.

Hašek might have received second-hand information about the regiment through his friend Zdeněk Matěj Kuděj, who enrolled with them in 1902. He also participated in periodical exercises in 1905, 1909, 1911 and 1913, but during the war he got off lightly. Called up as late as 1917, he never served at the front. [honsi.org]

58 Malčín refers to Malčice, a part of the rural municipality Předotice in the Písek district of South Bohemia. In 2011 the village had 94 permanent

residents.

The only Malčín in Bohemia was located in judicial disctrict Habry, *administrative district* Čáslav. The village is located only 13 km from Lipnice so Hašek surely knew about it and probably got these similar names mixed up. [honsi.org]

59 Čížová is a village in South Bohemia with 1,034 inhabitants (2009). It is located 6 km north of Písek.

Čížová was in 1915 part of the municipality (obec) Nová Ves and had a post office, a parish and a railway station (still operating in 2020). There was however no Gendarmerie (*State Police*) station here in 1915 so the old accordion player must have bluffed (Vráž and Písek were the nearest). [honsi.org]

60 This is not a typographical error, but an attempt to replicate "dezentýry", the common corruption of the Czech word "dezertéry", i.e. the 4th declension case of "deserters". [Translator's note]

61 Sedlec is the name of 20 places in Bohemia but none of them fit the description in *The Good Soldier Švejk*. The author rather had Sedlice in mind, underpinned by the fact that in 1904 it was primarily known as Sedlec per *Otto's Educational Dictionary*.

Today it is a minor town (městys) in South Bohemia, with 1,252 inhabitants (2019). It is located north of Strakonice near Blatná Castle.

The kind grandmother from Vráž told Švejk that the State policeman in Sedlec is a good man and let deserters pass trough. In this context we note that the town actually had a State Police station and it was headed by strážmistr František Svojík. He is the only one listed so it may well be that he was the sole policeman in town.

According to the 1910 census, Sedlec had 1,411 inhabitants, all of whom reported using Czech as their everyday language. [honsi.org]

62 Horažďovice is a town of 5,600 inhabitants in the Plzeň region. It is located on the river Otava, some 50 km south east of Plzeň. According to the 1910 census, Horažďovice had 3,252 inhabitants, of whom 3,226 (99 per cent) reported using Czech as their everyday language. [honsi.org]

63 Radomyšl is a small town in South Bohemia, 6 km north of Strakonice. It has 1,250 inhabitants and was in 2005 voted South Bohemian "Village of the Year".

Radomyšl was indeed served by a State Police station. It was located in the town hall, opposite Floriánek. The Station Chief was strážmistr (*Patrol*

Sergeant) František Křížek and he had two assistants.

According to the 1910 census, Radomyšl had 1,230 inhabitants, of whom 1,225 (99 per cent) reported using Czech as their everyday language. [honsi.org]

64 Dolejší ulice (*Lower Street*) was an informal name of Sokolská ulice in Radomyšl. The house where Václav Melichar (the alleged inspiration for pantáta (*master*) Melichárek) lived is now demolished. [honsi.org]

65 Floriánek is a building on the corner of Kostelní ulice (*Church Street*) and Maltézské náměstí (*Maltese square*) in Radomyšl, house number 6, also Grunt (*Farmsted*) Michalcovský. It's recorded history goes back to 1599. Old photos show a brass shield on the front where St. Florian is depecited.

In 2010 the building was in a derelict state but by 2020 it had been renovated and a shelf in the front wall hosts a small statue of St. Florian.

Floriánek is named after the Christian saint and the first Austrian martyr Saint Florian. He is the patron saint of Poland, the city of Linz, firefighters and chimney sweeps. [honsi.org]

66 Písecký okres (*Písek District*) almost certainly refers to hejtmanství (*administrative district*) Písek, that contained the towns Mirotice, Mirovice, Vodňany, Bavorov and Protivín. Several smaller places known from *The Good Soldier Švejk* were within the District: Putim, Ražice, Skočice, Krč, Vráž and Čížová. In 1910 the population numbered 79,096 of which only 289 reported German as their everyday language.

As Hašek correctly pointed out, the District provided soldiers for Infantry Regiment No. 11. [honsi.org]

67 Písek is a city in South Bohemia with around 30,000 inhabitants. The oldest bridge in Czech Republic crosses the river Otava here. Písek is also an important center for education.

In *The Good Soldier Švejk* several institutions and places in the city are mentioned: Krajský soud (*Regional Court*) Písek, Okresní soud (*Disctrict Court*) Písek, Bezirksgendarmeriekommando (*State Police Disctrict Command*) Pisek, Písecké nádraží (*railroad statition*) and also the *home regiment* Infantry Regiment No. 11. Associated with the city is also Captain Rotter, he served here from 1910 until at least 1916. [honsi.org]

68 Putim is a village just south of Písek with 455 inhabitants (2006). It's major claim to fame outside the area is actually Švejk. A large part of Karel Steklý's Švejk film from 1956 was shot in the village. On August 23rd 2014 the first ever statue of the good soldier on Czech soil was unveiled in Putim.

Whereas large parts of *The Good Soldier Švejk* patently draw inspiration from Jaroslav Hašek's own experiences, it is difficult to find such connections in Putim or indeed in any part of Švejk's anabasis. The locations in Putim are fictitious; no *I&R State Police* station existed, nor was there any pub called Na Kocourku here. No *Station Chief* Flanderka, Pejzlerka or *Station Chief* Bürger are found in the census from 1900 or 1910, nor in the address book from 1915. [honsi.org]

69 Infantry Regiment No. 35 was one of 102 regular infantry regiments in the k.u.k. Heer (*I&R Army*). It was also one of the oldest, having been formed as early as 1683. During its long history, the regiment participated in several famous battles, among them: Vienna (1689), Aspern (1809), and Solferino (1859). The soldiers were recruited from *Army Replenishment District 35*, Plzeň. Staff and three battalions were garrisoned in Plzeň in 1914, while the third battalion was relocated to Kalinovik in Bosnia in 1912.

From the beginning of the war until May 1915, battalions 1, 2 and 4 fought in Russian Poland near Komarów, in Galicia near Rawa Ruska, along the river San and east of Kraków, and later in the Carpathians. The rest of 1915 and the period until September 1917 was spent in eastern Galicia, where on July 2nd 1917 they fought their own countrymen from the Legions at Zborów. The remainder of the war was spent on the Italian front. The detached 3rd battalion never joined the bulk of the regiment; it operated first in Serbia, then on the Italian front.

Infantry Regiment No. 35, like some other Czech regiments, was accused of treason during World War I. During the battle of Zborów on July 2nd 1917, many soldiers from the Regiment were taken prisoner, leading to accusations of disloyalty and, consequently, to investigations and debates in the newly re-assembled Reichsrat. There had also been an incident in September 1915 that led to the Regiment's reliability being questioned. The minister of defense in Cisleithania, however, concluded that there was no reason to distrust the regiment as a whole. the front for this even to be possible. [honsi.org]

70 Indirectly mentioned here is Field Artillery Regiment No. 24. one of the 42 field artillery regiments in the I&R Army, garrisoned in Budějovice. It was established in 1892 and recruited from Prague Military Territorial District (8th Corps)), i.e., southern and western Bohemia and the area around the capital. [honsi.org]

71 Budapest was in 1914 the capital of the Kingdom of Hungary, one of the

two constituent parts of Austria-Hungary. Emperor Franz Joseph I was crowned king here in 1867 under the name I Ferenc Jószef. The city has since 1918 been the capital of the Republic of Hungary. Budapest has today around 1.7 million inhabitants and is by far the largest city in the country. It is situated on both sides of the Danube, with Buda as the old part on the west bank, and Pest as the administrative and political centre on the east bank.

Jaroslav Hašek passed the city with his 12th. March Battalion on July 1st 1915. According to the poem Cestou na bojiště (*On the Road to the Battlefield*) they arrived here in the morning, just like in the novel. It was surely the day after the departure from Királyhida, but they seem to have traveled onwards quickly: through Rakos, Aszód and Hatvan. It is also known that Hašek visited Budapest in the summer of 1903, on the way to the Balkans. [honsi.org]

72 Strakonice is a town in South Bohemia, west of Písek with around 24,000 inhabitants. It is an industrial town and was also during Švejk's lifetime. According to the 1910 census, Strakonice had 5,440 inhabitants, of whom 5,414 (99 per cent) reported using Czech as their everyday language. [honsi.org]

73 Sušice is a town in the Šumava region in south-western Bohemia. The number of inhabitants is around 12,000. According to the 1910 census, Sušice had 7,264 inhabitants, of whom 7,061 (97 per cent) reported using Czech as their everyday language. [honsi.org]

74 Štěkeň is a market town in the Strakonice district in South Bohemia. It is located west of Písek by the river Otava. In 2014 it counted 839 inhabitants. According to the 1910 census, Štěkeň had 928 inhabitants, of whom 923 (99 per cent) reported using Czech as their everyday language. [honsi.org]

75 Volyně is a town in South Bohemia, south of Strakonice with around 3,000 inhabitants (2020). According to the 1910 census, Volyně had 3,156 inhabitants, of whom 3,140 (99 per cent) reported using Czech as their everyday language. [honsi.org]

76 Dub is a village in the Prachatice district in South Bohemia with around 400 inhabitants (2020). Although there were 11 places named Dub in Bohemia and Moravia there is not doubt that this is the one the author meant. All the others were too far from Švejk's itinerary.

According to the 1910 census, Dub had 529 inhabitants, all of whom reported using Czech as their everyday language. [honsi.org]

77 Herrman was not an uncommon surname, but is not entered under Vodňany

in the address book from 1915. However, in the census records from 1910 there is a Jew named Robert Herman listed. He was a merchant and former traveling salesman who traded in textiles in Vodňany then. He lived in Husova street #60. Herrman (also written Hermann, less often Herman) was actually born at Lipnice, where the author wrote Books Two, Three & Four and passed away before finishing, and this could explain, why Hašek knew about him.

For the Herrmann family and other Jews, the Nazi occupation from March 1939 onwards had tragic consequences. Already towards the end of the year the police had collected information that classified Robert as a Jew. Imprisonment followed on December 19414th as he was accused of illegal trade with textiles, which surely was a mere pretext. On December 17th he was transported to Terezín (Theresienstadt) and on September 6th 1943 to Auschwitz, where he was eventually murdered. His wife was in the same transport and suffered the same grueling fate. Their sons Zdeněk and Jiří were also murdered by the Nazis, but the fate of Bedřich is not known. His father Sigmund, also a merchant, was deported and died in Terezín at the age of 83. His mother Aloisie had passed away already in 1925. [honsi.org]

78 Vodňany is a town in the Strakonice district in South Bohemia. It is located 28 km north west of Budějovice. In 2020 the town had 7,028 inhabitants. According to the 1910 census, Vodňany had 4,602 inhabitants, of whom 4,588 (99 per cent) reported using Czech as their everyday language. [honsi.org]

79 Švarcenberský ovčín was a sheepfold that belonged to the Schwarzenberg estate. Its exact location is unknown. The large Schwarzenberg estate owned several sheep farms, so it is difficult to determine which one the author had in mind. Hašek likely drew most of his knowledge about the area from summer holidays with his mother in 1896 and 1897, and perhaps from stories told by his grandfather Jareš, who was employed by Schwarzenberg.

There was a sheepfold in Albrechtice near Drahonice (close to Skočice), a farm called Ovčín (S*heepfold*) near Čepřovice, and another sheep farm in Leskovec near Bavorov. As stated in the novel, all three are roughly a four-hour walk (approximately 15 km) from Štěkeň.

Of the three, Leskovec probably best fits the description in *The Good Soldier Švejk*. Unlike the other two, it has been verified that it belonged to the Schwarzenberg family, specifically their Libějovice estate. When Švejk leaves in the morning, he comes out of the forest and, to the right, can see Vodňany. This matches the topography of the area and is supported by the wanderer's mention of "down in Skočice" (which does not fit the other two candidates). The Leskovec sheep-pen is marked on the military survey map from the mid-19th century, and the large building still appeared intact in 2016. The address is Útěšov 12, Bavorov. [honsi.org]

80 Protivín is a town in county Písek with 4,808 inhabitants (2020), situated by the river Blanice. The town is best known for its castle and also has a well known brewery that at the time of Švejk belonged to the Schwarzenberg estate.

Protivín was surely a place Hašek knew well as his mother Kateřina (1849-1911) was born in Protivín No. 158. Young Jaroslav visited the area with his mother during the summer holidays of 1897 and probably also before that. [honsi.org]

81 This is not a typographical error, but a replication of the feminine adjective “napolionská” in the original Czech, the common corruption of the Czech word “napoleonská”, i.e. the English “Napoleonic”. [Translator’s note]

82 This term refers to the period from 1630 until 1635, the so-called Swedish phase of the Thirty Year War (1618-1648). In 1630 king Gustav Adolf II of Sweden intervened on the continent as the Protestants of Germany seemed to be destined to defeat. Sweden was supported by France, the Netherlands, some German states, and initially also England.

The Swedes first landed in Pomerania before advancing south. Their allies from Saxony invaded Bohemia and occupied Prague on November 11th 1631. In 1632 they were however defeated by Wallenstein and were forced to leave Bohemia. The peace agreement that ended the Swedish phase of the Thirty Year War was signed in Prague in 1635.

The Swedish army however remained in Central Europe and in 1648 they besieged Prague and looted Hradčany without managing to occupy Staré město and Nové město. When the final peace agreement was signed they abandoned the city.

Although Hašek never set foot in Sweden, the country was a theme not only in *The Good Soldier Švejk* but also in some of his short stories. In a Švejk context the most relevant of these is titled Povídka o hodném švédském vojákovi (*The story of the kind Swedish soldier*) and already here Hašek introduced a theme we know well. It is about a duty-conscious soldier who with pleasure sacrifices himself for his monarch. The story was printed in the anarchist newspaper Nová Omladina (*The New Youth*) on January 30th 1907. [honsi.org]

83 In 1848, only eighteen-year-old Francis Joseph I, the nephew of the

previous ruler, ascended the Imperial throne. At this moment, the individual nations of the monarchy were expecting a solemn confirmation of their rights, i.e. the coronation of the Austrian emperor as their king. As a result of revolutionary events and turbulent changes in 1848, these traditional celebrations were postponed in individual countries. The Kingdom of Hungary was the first to receive a ceremonial coronation, but even that only happened in 1867, after the so-called Austro-Hungarian Compromise. This awakened patriotic feelings in the Czech Kingdom as well, and the Czechs also began to demand that their sovereign be crowned in the castle of the Czech kings. In September 1870, the Emperor issued the so-called rescript, a written answer of a Roman emperor or a pope to a legal inquiry or petition, as a response to the challenge of the Land Assembly of the Kingdom of Bohemia, in which he finally promised to allow himself to be crowned king of Bohemia with the crown of St. Wenceslas. In the following rescript issued on September 12th, 1871, he expressed his will for the coronation for the second time. As is well known, the promised coronation never took place due to the resistance of German politicians of the time in Bohemia. The Emperor himself personally regretted, that he never kept his promise and that the Czechs did not receive the same honor and recognition from his side as the Hungarians did earlier. Not even the last emperor, Charles I, was given a historic chance to recognize Czech state law by the crowning. [*Czech National Archive*]

84 Skočice is a village in South Bohemia, south of Písek, near Vodňany and Protivín. It has 242 inhabitants (2020). Švejk must had been very close to the village on the morning he appeared in Putim for the second time.

According to the 1910 census, Skočice had 469 inhabitants, of whom 466 (99 per cent) reported using Czech as their everyday language. [honsi.org]

85 Lány is a town in the Kladno district west of Prague. It is best known as the burial place of the first Czechoslovak President, Professor Tomáš Garigue Masaryk.

According to the 1910 census, Lány had 1,386 inhabitants, of whom 1,381 (99 per cent) reported using Czech as their everyday language. [honsi.org]

The Baroque chateau in the village of Lany in the midst of the Křivoklát woods, not far from Prague, is the official summer residence of the presidents of the Czech Republic. [hrad.cz]

86 Kačák is a stream by Beroun, west of Prague, better known as Loděnice. It empties into Berounka. The colloquial name Kačák is derived from the name of the village Kačice.

The author knew the area well; he was visiting at the very moment the fatal shots in Sarajevo fell. On this trip he was accompanied by Josef Lada and they had started in Kladno where they visited none other than Rittmeister Rotter. It is therefore very likely that the tramp's anecdote draws inspiration from this trip. [honsi.org]

87 Lipnice (now Lipnice nad Sázavou) is a small town in Vysočina (*the Highlands*) with a history that goes back to the 14th century. It is situated 620 meters above the sea level. The most prominent landmark is Hrad Lipnice (the castle). In 2020 the number of inhabitants was 654, only about half the number that lived here in 1910.

The most dramatic event in the history of Lipnice was the great fire on September 19th 1869. The church, the school, the town hall, the castle and over 100 houses went up in flames. The damages were estimated to be 300,000 guilders. Emperor Franz Joseph I, as a private person, donated 500 to the homeless.

Lipnice has a special place in Jaroslav Hašek's life and writing because he lived there from August 25th 1921 until he died 16 months later.

Most of *The Good Soldier Švejk*, probably from Book Two, Chapter 2 onwards, was written here, including the lines that this very description refers to. The author had obviously already been inspired by Lipnice, and several anecdotes later in the book bear testimony to this. The neighbouring villages of Kejžlice, Okrouhlice and Jedouchov are eventually all mentioned, and so is the district town Německý Brod.

Hašek lived at the inn of Alexandr Invald U české koruny (*At the Czech Crown*) until the autumn of 1922 when he moved into house no. 185 around the corner that he had bought in the spring. After a hand injury he stopped writing himself and dictated to the young Kliment Štěpánek who was later to provide vital accounts on the last months of Hašek's life and also how he lived and worked.

Hašek didn't only work on *The Good Soldier Švejk* at Lipnice, in between he had some short stories printed. In 1922 one of them was published in the book Mírová konference a jiné humoresky (*The peace conference and other humorous stories*). The story is called Průvodčí cizinců (*A Guide of Foreigners*) and The Castle Lipnice is the setting.

Jaroslav Hašek died from heart failure in the morning of January 3rd 1923 but had long been suffering from underlying health problems. He is buried at the old cemetery in Lipnice. [honsi.org]

88 Hrad Lipnice (*Lipnice Castle*) was built at the beginning of the 14th

century, and at the end of the 16th century, it was altered in Renaissance style. In 1645, during the Thirty Years' War, the Swedes occupied and partly destroyed the castle. The following centuries saw further decline, and on 19 September 1869, the castle and the town of Lipnice were ravaged by a disastrous fire. In 1913, work began to safeguard and restore it, which has continued intermittently until today.

The castle is owned by the state, open to the public, provides guided tours, and is a major tourist attraction. The view from the top of the castle across Vysočina is spectacular.

Jaroslav Hašek was very fond of the castle, spent considerable time there, and also arranged drinking parties on the premises. He virtually had unlimited access because his friend, forest warden Böhm, gave him the keys. His favorite room there was the so-called "mazhaus"(*front hall*). [honsi.org]

[89] The Station Chief is italicized, as it is a translation of *"vachmajstr/vachmistr", the corrupted Czech form of the German "Wachtmeister", i.e. "police Sergeant"* or, as in here, *"[State] Police Station Chief"*. [svejkmuseum.cz]

[90] Kejžlice (previously also Kyžlice) is a village in the Vysočina (the *Highlands*) region, 4 km from Lipnice in the direction of Humpolec. The number of inhabitants is 416 (2020). According to the 1910 census, Kejžlice had 730 inhabitants, all of whom reported using Czech as their everyday language. [honsi.org]

[91] Bohemia (Čechy) is a historical region, and the term is still used as a geographical description of the western two thirds of Czech Republic. During Austria-Hungary it was also a political and administrative entity.

The Latin name existed already in ancient times, as Bohemia was named after the Celtic tribe Boii. Prague was always the most important city in Bohemia. The name has also given rise to the wide-spread term bohemian. [honsi.org]

[92] Silesia is an area which in 1914 was divided between Germany and Austria-Hungary. Today most of the region is contained within Poland, with minor parts belonging to Czech Republic and Germany.

In *The Good Soldier Švejk* it is explicitly a question of Austrian Silesia, a Duchy and former Czech Crownland that came under Habsburg rule in 1763. The capital was Troppau (Opava) with other notable cities being Bielitz (Bielsko), Jägerndorf (Krnov) and Teschen (Cieszyn/Český Těšín). Germans were the largest ethnic group followed by Poles and Czechs. The

Crown Land was geographically split in two, separated by a piece of land by Ostrava. The former Austrian Silesia today belongs mainly to Czech Republic with a smaller part to the east being in Poland. [honsi.org]

93 The Ministry of the Interior was established after the turmoil of the revolutionary year 1848. The former Justice Minister, Alexander von Bach, was named the Interior Minister. The period after 1848 was represented by the onset of the so-called Bach absolutism, which was characterized by the significant role and activity of security and repressive forces. The Ministry was also entrusted to exercise supervision over the agenda of the police and State Police. In the area of public security, the main task of the Ministry, in addition to maintaining public order, was also the supervision of the activities of associations, theaters and popular assemblies, where there was a danger of undermining state power.

Due to the ongoing war, the State Police and the police were used to fight desertions and eliminate spies. After the conquest of Serbia and the territories in the east, formerly belonging to Czarist Russia and Romania, the role of the Ministry of the Interior was to administer the occupied territories. [*Development of the organization of the Ministry of the Interior*, Tomáš Bábík]

[*Description and analysis of the activities of the Ministry of the Interior*, Anna Pražská]

94 "Procházka" is a common last name meaning "a stroll". *Emperor Francis Joseph I was called "Starej Procházka", i.e.* The Old Stroll, *in Bohemia. One of the versions of the origins of the nickname is, that during his visit to Prague on June 6th, 1901, on the occasion of the opening of the Emperor Francis I Bridge* [*today the* Legionnaires' Bridge]. *A photo of the Emperor walking on the new bridge was published in the newspapers, even with the caption "A Stroll on the new bridge", it is said, in the Prague Illustrated Courier. I haven't attempted to verify it yet. According to historian Otto Urban, however, this nickname is much older; the Emperor acquired it already in the 1870s, when a rider on horseback announced the arrival of the imperial procession. His name was Procházka, and people cried out: "Old Procházka is already on his way!". This version is also supported by the research of the historian Jiří Rak, who looked through all the newspapers of the time and found that there was no such description under the mentioned photo. I read the* National Newspaper *and the* National Politics. *The only mention of the stroll on the bridge is in the afternoon edition of* National Newspaper *from 6/14/1901.* [svejkmuseum.cz]

95 “Pepík Vyskoč” (*Joey Jump*) is a character no doubt inspired by Zdenko Václav Kompit, better known as Venca Vyskoč. [honsi.org]

"Venca" was born in Prague III., house no. 321, in Malá Strana, son of Karel Kompit and Agnes. His mother died when he was three so he was raised by his father's second wife, Anna. He originally worked as a waiter; in the 1890 population register and the 1910 police record he is listed as a "cellarman". In 1890 there is a remark "blbý" (stupid [Translators note: imbecile]) by his name in the police register.

When this stupidity actually took hold is not known, but at some stage he started to walk around pubs and cafés, bleated and jumped by the tables and collected money for the spectacle. Venca became a well-known character in the streets of Prague. His main area of operation was around Václavské náměstí (*Wenceslas square*) and he even frequented U Fleků, a tavern that the author of *The Good Soldier Švejk* knew very well.

"Venca" was mentioned in newspapers already during his lifetime and when he died on September 18th 1926 at the age of 65, several national and regional newspaper published notices. Lidové noviny even provided a more detailed obituary. The description in this obituary is so close to Jaroslav Hašek's own that there is not even the slightest doubt where the inspiration for the name, the jumping and the bleating came from. Hašek's "deviation" consisted in transferring Vyskoč from Prague to Putim and let Wachtmeister (*Station Chief*) Flanderka hire him as in informer. [honsi.org]

96 Hradčany, the Castle District, is the Prague district surrounding the Prague Castle. Dominating the city from a high hill on the west bank of the Vltava River, Hradčany was then the seat of provincial and Imperial power. It was a powerful cluster of edifices containing the central headquarters of the government and military, plus courts, a prison, a palace, a cathedral and the ancient tombs of the saints and Czech Kings. Today, it enjoys a similar status and its spires still reach to the clouds and loom above all.

97 Because Švejk's anabasis including Putim necessarily must have taken place in early 1915, the minister who haunted *Station Chief* Flanderka in his dreams was no doubt Friedrich Freiherr von Georgi. He was head of k.k. Ministerium für Landesverteidigung (*I&R Ministry of Defense*) in Cisleithania from 1907 to 1917, and was thus formally head of both k.k. Landwehr (*I&R Land Defense*) and k.k. Gendarmerie (*I&R State Police*).

Georgi was regarded as an excellent organizer and also a person who was capable of operating both in the military and in politics. These seem to have been the reasons why his application to serve at the front was rejected. At the outbreak of war his rank was general. Friedrich von Georgi was born in Prague and hailed from a family of officers. [honsi.org]

98 Mariáš is the most popular card game in the Czech Republic. The most popular version is played by three players. That is why when in company of another man a third one arrives, he will often hear "So now we've got the third one for [a hand of] mariáš!", even if card playing is not on the agenda.

99 *A liqueur originating in Poland, where it is called* Kontuszówka. *In the 17th century, it was one of the favorite drinks of the Polish nobility, and they had a reservation that only they could wear a long coat called* kontusz, *and hence* Kontuszówka. *It is still produced in Czech lands, mostly from aromatic oils mixed with potable alcohol, preferably with vodka, in a cold way. Kontušovka contains anise and fennel, or may contain other spices, such as star anise, cumin, fennel seeds, peppermint, coriander, all of this in the form of aromatic oils. It should be sweetened with honey.* [svejkmuseum.cz]

100 Nicholas Nikolaevich (Николáй Николáевич) was a Grand Duke from the Romanov house and Russian commander in chief from the outbreak of war until September 5th 1915, when Tsar Nicholas II personally took charge. This was a result of the setbacks suffered during the summer of 1915, when the Russians were forced out of Poland and Galicia. Nicholas was subsequently appointed viceroy and commander at the Caucasus front. [honsi.org]

101 Přerov is a city and an important railway junction in the Olomouc district of Moravia. As of 2018 it had around 45,000 inhabitants.

It was the seat of both the judicial and *administrative district*s of the same name. In 1900 the city had around 21,000 inhabitants of which the vast majority reported Czech as their everyday language. Already then Přerov was an industrial city and established as an important railway junction. [honsi.org]

102 Jan Hus (born c. 1370, Husinec, Bohemia [now in Czech Republic]—died July 6, 1415, Konstanz [Germany]) was the most important 15th-century Czech religious reformer, whose work was transitional between the medieval and the Reformation periods and anticipated the Lutheran Reformation by a full century. He was embroiled in the bitter controversy of the Western Schism (1378–1417) for his entire career, and he was convicted of heresy at the Council of Constance and burned at the stake. [britannica.com]

When news came to Bohemia that Hus – who had been guaranteed safe passage by Emperor Sigismund, brother of the King of Bohemia – the nobles who supported him sent a letter of protest to the Council of Constance. Sigismund responded with threats, claiming that he would "drown" all followers of Hus and his English influence, John Wycliffe. Bohemia promptly exploded in violence; Catholic priests were forced out of their parishes in many areas. [private-prague-guide.com]

After Hus's death in 1415 many Bohemian knights and nobles published a formal protest and offered protection to those who were persecuted for their faith. The movement's chief supporters were Jakoubek of Stříbro (died 1429), Hus's successor as preacher at the Bethlehem chapel in Prague; Václav Koranda, leader of the Taborites (extreme Hussites named for Tábor, their stronghold, south of Prague); and Jan Želivský, who organized the extreme reform party in Prague.

The Hussites broke with Rome in using a Czech liturgy and in administering Holy Communion to the laity under the forms of both bread and wine. (The doctrine supporting this was called Utraquism and the more moderate Hussites were called Utraquists.) [britannica.com]

The martyrdom of Jan Hus led to 18 years of war in Bohemia. On 30th July 1419, in Prague, a number of prominent Catholics were defenestrated and fell to their deaths; this was the beginning of the Hussite rebellion (the Hussites defended the ideas of Jan Hus); they offered tough resistance to the five European crusades who had been sent by the pope and the King of Bohemia to curb "those heretics".The Hussite's programme

The Four articles of Prague set out the Hussite programme: communion in the form of both bread and wine, preaching the Scriptures without any form of control from the authorities, the confiscation of the clergy's possessions, the punishment of mortal sins. Some radical Hussites advocated the sharing of possessions, absolute equality and universal priesthood.

The Catholic Church gave in and... won. Due to the military victories of the Hussites, who controlled all Bohemia, the Church negotiated a compromise with the moderate elements of the movement : the compactata of Basel (1433). They agreed with: communion in the form of both bread and wine,

the possibility of reading the Epistles and the Gospel in Czech.

In 1434, the moderate Hussites, who had accepted compromise and who had allied with the Catholics, overcame the more extreme elements of the movement at the battle of Lipany. [museeprotestant.org]

103 Schönbrunn, the former summer residence of the imperial family, is considered one of the most beautiful baroque palaces in Europe. The

Habsburgs resided here the better part of the year in numerous rooms for the large imperial family in addition to representational rooms. Emperor Franz Joseph who...reigned from 1848 to 1916 was born here in 1830. The monarch spent his last years entirely in the palace...[hotelaustria-wien.at]

104 Pejzlerka's exclamation refers to a portrait of Panna Maria Skočická (*the Virgin Mary of Skočice*) from the 17th century that survived a fire unscathed, an event regarded as a miracle. This prompted the construction of the pilgrimage church Navštívení Panny Marie (*Visitation of the Virgin Mary*), which was inaugurated on August 21st 1668. [honsi.org]

105 Kobylisy is an area in the northern part of Prague, until 1922 still not part of the capital. It was here that the operation to assassinate Heydrich in 1942 started. The Kobylisy metro station was opened in 2004.

According to the 1910 census, Kobylisy had 3,199 inhabitants, of whom 3,180 (99 per cent) reported using Czech as their everyday language. [honsi.org]

106 Palacký was a Czech historian and politician who played a pivotal role in the Czech National Revival. He was also called "otec národa", the father of the nation. He was loyal to the Empire, initially a proponent of the so-called Austroslavism, although he became more radical after Ausgleich (*The Compromise*) in 1867. Like most Czechs, he resented that Hungary obtained a special status within the House of Habsburg empire.

The Palacký monument is located on the eastern bank of the Vltava, at Palackého náměstí (*Palacký's square*). It was unveiled on 1 July 1912 in a grand ceremony, attended by Prague's notabilities. [honsi.org]

107 Moráň is a small area of Prague between Karlovo náměstí (*Charles square*) and the Vltava. The Palacký monument is located by the river, at Palackého náměstí. It was unveiled in July 1st 1912 in a grand ceremony. [honsi.org]

108 *Ferbl is a gambling card game partly similar to poker. It originated in Austrian Styria and was also played in the Czech lands during the reign of Maria Theresa. A ban dated 1746 mentions it under the name Farbeln,* fables. *The name is derived from the German Färbeln,* coloring. *Other names of this game in German-speaking countries are Einundvierzig* (forty-one) *according to the highest possible point total, Spitz, Zwei auf- zwei zu, and Zwicken. Ferbl is intended for 3 to 7 players. It is played with a deck of 32 cards of four suits that start with a seven and ends with an ace. It can be played with German (double-headed or single-headed) or French cards.* [svejkmuseum.cz]

109 The Otava is a 112 km long river that flows from Šumava through Sušice,

Horažďovice, Strakonice, and Písek and joins the Vltava by Zvíkov. [honsi.org]

110 *A card game also called sixty-six or six-and- sixty. Popular in Germany and especially Austria under the name* Schnapsen, *in Hungary* Snapszli, Snapszer *or* Hatvanhat *(Hungarian: sixty-six). It is a game very similar to the so-called licked mariáš. However, it is played with only 24 cards of German or French type.* [svejkmuseum.cz]

111 Hercules is the Latin name of Heracles, a Greek demigod, son of Zeus, known for his strength. The text in *The Good Soldier Švejk* refers to the Twelve Labours of Heracles, each of them in turn a huge challenge. [honsi.rom]

112 Josef Rampa was a pub landlord whom Hašek knew well. Ladislav Hájek wrote that Rampa managed a pub in Sokolská ulice mainly visited by students. He was an elderly widower, and his older sister cooked for the students. Rampa was constantly looking for a new wife, preferably a widow with money. He liked Hašek because the young author took time to listen to him. Rampa was reluctant to let bar guests run up debts. Hájek does not specify which year(s) he and Hašek frequented Rampa's pub.

Police registers reveal that Rampa was born in 1854 in Suchodol by Příbram, initially married to Marie (born in 1848), and that from 1892 to 1914 he lived at nine different addresses in Vinohrady and six in Praha II. None of these addresses were in Sokolská, but he might not necessarily have lived at the premises of the pub he managed (although this was the norm at the time). His first wife died in 1898, and he later married Josefa (née Černá). According to the police registers, she was a widow. Church records show that Rampa's father was a pub landlord at Suchodol No. 9.

Rampa also features in the play From Karlín to Bratislava, co-written by Jaroslav Hašek, Emil Artur Longen, and Egon Erwin Kisch. [honsi.org]

113 Královské Vinohrady (*Royal Vineyards*), is a former city and now a district of Prague, southeast of the center. Administratively it is split between Prague 2, 3 and 10. After 1968 the official name has been Vinohrady, and this short form was common already during Austrian rule. This is also the name the author uses throughout. In 1922 Vinohrady became part of the capital.

Vinohrady achieved status of "royal town" in 1879 and grew quickly to become the third largest city of the Kingdom of Bohemia. [honsi.org]

114 During 1914 the station witnessed the departure of five march battalions to Serbia; in January 1915 the sixth was shipped to southern Hungary, where

the regiment spent six weeks recovering after the withdrawal from Serbia. March battalions numbered 6 to 11 were subsequently dispatched to the battlefields of the Carpathians and Galicia.

Jaroslav Hašek's 12th March Battalion was actually the first that was not shipped from Budějovice. In early summer 1915 the replacement battalions of the city's two house regiments were relocated to non-Czech soil. IR. 91 was, on June 1 1915, moved to Királyhida in two stages, an event that is extensively covered in *The Good Soldier Švejk*. [honsi.org]

115 "Mariánská kasárna" was a military barracks in Budějovice that was built in 1843-1844. From 1883 to 1915 it housed the replacement battalion of Infantry Regiment No. 91 (Replacement Regiment IR. 91) and at least one field battalion, From 1900 to 1914 the 4th Battalion was the only field battalion permanently garrisoned here.. Jaroslav Hašek himself served here from February 17th 1915 until the end of May. His experiences here are to a large degree retold by his alter ego One-Year Volunteer Marek. The school for one-year volunteers that Hašek and Marek attended was on the third floor. The building also housed the garrison prison, a place that Švejk and his creator knew very well.

On June 1st 1915 the IR. 91 replacement battalion was transferred to Királyhida under circumstances very similar to those described in the novel. [honsi.org]

116 "náměstí" (*square*) refers to Budějovické náměstí (Budweiser Ringplatz), the city square in Budějovice. With its area of 17,768 m² it is one of the largest of its kind in Europe, and with a history dating from 1295. It has arcades around the entire square. Since 1991 it has been called Náměstí Přemysla Otakara II. but has since 1915 changed names several times, all according to the direction of the political winds. During the Nazi occupation, it was named Adolf Hitler Platz.

Originally the square was simply called Náměstí (Ringplatz), a name it also had during Hašek's stay in the city from February 1915 until the end of May. On June 4th 1915 the City Council unanimously decided to rename the square Náměstí Františka Josefa (Franz Josefs-Platz). [honsi.org]

117 Malše is a river in Upper Austria (where it's called Maltsch) and the Czech Republic, which empties into the Vltava in Budějovice. The river's total length is 96 km. [honsi.org]

118 Port Arthur is commonly known as the European term for Lüshunkou, a harbour in Manchuria that was besieged and captured by Japanese forces during the Russo-Japanese War in 1904-05.

More important in the context of *The Good Soldier Švejk* is that a brothel named Port Arthur (also written Port Artur) existed in Budějovice when Jaroslav Hašek served in the garrison. The establishment was located in Rudolfovská třída on the eastern outskirts of the city, on or near a hill called Pěkná vyhlídka (ger. Schöne Aussicht). The name means "Pretty View".

In January 1904 Jan Filip bought the inn Na pěkné vyhlídce and by the autumn it was already operating as a brothel after it had been awarded a licence. From the first moment there were reports in the newspapers about disorder, a fact that may have led to the nickname "Port Artur", inspired by the war in the Far East and the siege of the port that at the time was under way.

In 1906 the owner Jan Filip was mentioned in the newspapers, accused of having betrayed the Czech nation and sold his vote for the city council election to the German mayor Josef Taschek. For this favor it was claimed that he was granted a license to run a brothel.

The following year "Port Artur" again appeared in the news due to disturbances, but the negative items from the Czech press have the air of a smear campaign against the "Judas" Filip, the German national Taschek, and Germans in general. Newspapers were at this time, be they German or Czech, replete with chauvinistic outbursts. [honsi.org]

[119] "U růže" (*At the Rose*) probably refers to U bílé růže (*At the White Rose*) , a pub two doors north of Mariánská kasárna (*Marian barracks*) in Pražská street 5, Budějovice. The inn had existed since at least 1879 and was also used for meetings, such as election gatherings.

The landlord as of 31 December 1910 was František Vostl (also written Wostl), a person Jaroslav Hašek would most definitely have known, as he is still listed as innkeeper in 1915. Vostl also ran a horse cab business and traded in fish.

An article in Jihočeské listy from 1937 confirms that Jaroslav Hašek visited the pub back in 1915. He entertained guests with his patriotic shouting. The article, signed with the pseudonym Al. Terego, mentions that the pub was also simply called "U růže". [honsi.org]

[120] "the hospital" almost certainly refers to I&R Reserve Hospital, although other military hospitals existed in Budějovice already from August 1914. The reason for this assumption is that this was the hospital to which Jaroslav Hašek himself was admitted on March 6th 1915. Here he was diagnosed with rheumatism and heart problems. He was placed in room No. 77.

The hospital was located in the former k.k. Landwehr barracks. The building is still in military use and is located near the railway station at Žižkova třída (*Žižka boulevard*), in 1915 still Radetzkystrasse.

Hašek later spent some time recuperating in a military hospital in the so-called Linz suburb. It is obviously possible that this is the hospital One-Year Volunteer Marek nipped out from, but since the latter was located quite far from the center, the former is the more likely inspiration. [honsi.org]

121 Icarus is a character in Greek mythology. He is the son of Daedalus and is best known for his attempt to escape Crete by flight. He attached wings to his body with wax, but was warned not to fly too close to the sun. Due to his pride and complacency, he ignored the advice, resulting in the wax melting, the wings falling off, and him falling into the sea and drowning. [honsi.org]

122 Nineveh was one of the most important cities in the ancient Middle East and was in several periods the capital of Assyria. The city was located by the river Tigris, near the present city of Mosul in Iraq. It was destroyed 612 BC. [honsi.org]

Nineveh is at the center of the Book of Jonah in the Old Testament. It is read by the Orthodox Jews on the Great Day of Atonement (Yom Kippur). The most significant statement in the Book of Jonah is in 2:9 — "Salvation is of the LORD." The story of Jonah is significantly mentioned by Jesus in the New Testament: "For as Jonah was a sign unto the Ninevites, so shall also the Son of man be to this generation. (Luke 11:30)" [J. Vernon McGee]

123 The "Offiziersschule" (*Officer school*) refers to the reserve officer's school of Infantry Regiment No. 91 in Budějovice. It was located on the upper (second) floor of *Marian barracks*, and the officer candidates also had their quarters here. On this floor were also the offices of the school's commander and his assistant, the Dienstführender Feldwebel (*Duty Sergeant Major*).

The course itself lasted for approximately eight weeks, but the one-year volunteers were even before entering separated from their *Replacement Company* and assembled in a *One-Year Volunteer Detachment* where they served while waiting for the current class to finish.

Hašek reported at IR. 91/1st *Replacement Company* in Budějovice on March 17th 1915 but he did not enroll straight away. In the beginning, he wore civilian clothes together with the rank and file and started at the school when his uniform was ready. Like One-Year Volunteer Marek he was eventually expelled, but we have no documents that record when he started or quit, nor anything about the cause for his dismissal. It is also likely that the medical record weighed towards the decision to expel Hašek. He was admitted to hospital already on March 6th 1915 and the application for superarbitration was submitted on April 8th. He must therefore have missed much of the education and training. In the third class (March - April) there were a few officer's candidates who later wrote about Hašek's time there. [honsi.org]

124 The "the training ground" One-Year-Volunteer Marek refers to is Budweiser Übungsplatz, a military training ground in Budějovice. In 1915, the IR. 91 exercised at various places in and around the city, but the main training ground was Čtyři Dvory/Vierhöf. It was located 4 kilometers west of the center, and this is surely the place Marek had in mind.

Marek turning up in civilian clothes at the military training ground is a motif inspired by Hašek's own experience. The author of *The Good Soldier Švejk* also appeared there in civilian clothes, and Kejla can confirm that this indeed happened at Čtyři Dvory in February 1915. [honsi.org]

125 Šumava is a loosely defined geographical area in the south of the western part of Bohemia, bordering Bavaria and Austria. It stretches from the Vltava in the east to around Domažlice in the west. The area is mainly wooded, thinly populated and parts of it are protected as a national park. The area was until 1945 predominantly German speaking. There are no large cities in the area. The major towns are Český Krumlov, Prachatice, Vimperk and Klatovy. Additional places that are mentioned in *The Good Soldier Švejk* are Sušice and Kašperské Hory.

Hašek's and Švejk's regiment, Infantry Regiment No. 91, was partly recruited from the eastern part of Šumava, more precisely the two hejtmanství (*administrative districts*) Krumlov and Prachatice. The Regiment thus had the nickname Synové Šumavy/Böhmerwalds Söhne. The middle and western parts lay within the recruitment districts of Infantry Regiment No. 11 and Infantry Regiment No. 35. [honsi.org]

126 *Translated from Latin as "Sign of praise, respect, honor". This is the Militär-Verdienstmedaille* (Military Merit Medal). *Initially only bronze version was awarded, gradually three degrees were being awarded. In 1916 the bronze version had two crossed swords added. The Silver version was created on March 26th, 1911 and was awarded to those who had already received the previous degree in the past. The Golden version would be called the Great signum laudis. It was awarded only thirty times. Twenty-eight bearers were officers of general rank; the other two bearers were*

flying ace Gottfried von Banfield and cryptologist Hermann Pokorny. While the bronze and silver Military Merit Medals were intended only for Austria-Hungary, the so-called Great Signum Laudis was awarded to ten foreigners – nine German generals and one Ottoman general. After Franz's death, a portrait of Charles I was on the medal. [svejkmuseum.cz]

[127] The original German verse "Acht Pferde oder achtund-vierzig Mann" refers to the capacity of the military rail cars transporting troops and their horses. According to [en.wikipedia.org], "French Army box cars [were] used to transport American soldiers to the western front during World War I. Each car had '40–8' stenciled on the side, which meant that it could carry 40 men or 8 horses. The cars were known as 'forty and eights' and viewed by the men as a miserable way to travel." Yet, a photograph at the head of the entry devoted to the subject at [svejkmuseum.cz] shows a German military rail car with the inscription "M.T.48M.6Pf. [which means: Militärisch Tracht 48Mann 6Pferde – Military load 48 men 6 horses]." The owner of the site, Jaroslav Šerák, writes: *"So I was hoping to learn something about the regulations regarding the number of horses and men from museums and our railway authorities. They only replied to me from the Czech Railways headquarters and sent me a photo of the regulations on the description of transport rail cars, which confirms that the rail cars of Austria-Hungary were described similarly to the German rail cars."* The photo of the regulation supplied to [svejkmuseum.cz] includes "0" and "00" as placeholders for the maximum number of horses or men to be transported in the cars. Perhaps there were larger rail cars in the Austro-Hungarian rail system that could transport 8 horses, just as the French cars did, and Hašek got the number from the stencil seen on such rail cars.

[128] Saint Agnes may refer to a daughter of King Otakar I. of Bohemia who renounced a life in the circles of power and dedicated herself to religion and caring for the infirm. However, there are several other Saint Agnes, so it is not 100 per cent certain that this is the person One-year Volunteer Marek has in mind. [honsi.org]

[129] Pushkin (Пушкин) was a Russian novelist, poet, and playwright of the Romantic era who is considered by many to be the greatest Russian poet ever and the founder of modern Russian literature.

Both Sergey Soloukh and Antonín Měšťan point out that "Pushkin's uncle" no doubt refers to fragments from Eugen Onegin, a novel in verse that was published as a series in the early 19th century. Already in the first verse there is a scene where Onegin is waiting for his ill and rich uncle to die so he can inherit him. One-year Volunteer Marek even quotes the last two lines of this verse, and it seems to be a literal translation from Russian rather than a more elaborate Czech translation. [honsi.org]

130 Bedřich Kočí was a Czech publisher, book trader, and author who often wrote using pseudonyms. Today he is best known for theosophical writing and his work on mental health.

The book that One-year Volunteer Marek mentions was published in 1906 and contains 910 pages. It is an encyclopedia covering forestry, animal breeding, sugar growing, poultry, and a range of other subjects. It was written by a range of contributors, each covering specific subjects. The editor was Karel Ladislav Kukla.

The book actually contains descriptions of two of the three animals that are used as expletives by the junior officers in 11th Company. These are the Yorkshire boar and the Engadin goat. The bullfrog is not mentioned, but it can hardly be classified as a source of economic wealth. The omission is therefore understandable. [honsi.org]

131 Engadin is a long valley located in the canton of Graubünden in southeast Switzerland. The goat breed in question is generally referred to as Pfauenziege (Pfauen goat) and is now extinct.

The valley is directly mentioned by Jaroslav Hašek in the story "Winter sports" from 1910. [honsi.org]

132 Kašperské Hory (Bergreichenstein) is a small town in Šumava that until 1945 was predominantly German-speaking. Today (2019) it has 1,449 inhabitants. At 758 meters above sea level it is one of the highest situated towns in Bohemia. [honsi.org]

133 Yorkshire is a former county in the north of England with York as the capital. The name is still widely used to denote the region. The largest cities are Leeds and Sheffield.

The Yorkshire pig (or Middle White) is one of the most widespread pig breeds on the planet. The pig had already appeared in one of Hašek's stories from *The Party of Moderate Progress within the Bounds of the Law*. Moreover, it is beyond doubt that he was familiar with this animal from his time as editor of *The Animal World* (909-1910). During this period, the breed is mentioned several times and also depicted. [honsi.org]

134 Africa is one of the five continents, the second largest after Asia. In 1914 it was still colonized by European powers (apart from Ethiopia). World War I affected Africa as Germany lost her colonies on the continent. The other warring parties who had colonies there were Great Britain, France, Portugal,

Belgium and Italy.

Troops from Africa participated in the British and French armies during the war. The best known and most numerous were the "Tirailleurs sénégalais" in the French army. [honsi.org]

135 The North Pole (geographical) is defined as the point in the northern hemisphere where the Earth's axis of rotation meets the Earth's surface.

Hašek covered the race to the North Pole between Peary and Cook in 1909, at the time when he was editor of Svět zvířat (*The Animal World*). He wrote a humorous story about the events and a long and serious article appeared in the next issue. It contains pictures of the two competitors and this unsigned article is believed to have been written by Hašek. [honsi.org]

136 "Reálka" is the short colloquial term for "Reálná škola", the Czech for the original German "Realschule". It was a type of a general education seven-year secondary school, consisting of 4-year middle school "lower reálka", plus 3-year high school "higher reálka", teaching the Czech language, literature, mathematics, history, geography, natural sciences, and modern foreign languages. Unlike the more academically oriented Gymnasia[67], the Real Schools also taught practical skills for workshop or household. [cs.wikipedia.org]

137 Stephansdom (*Saint Stephen's Cathedral*) is the most important cathedral in Vienna and one of the city's major attractions. It is located in the historic center of the city. Construction started in 1137 and has been completed in stages over the years, with the latest being a new roof after a fire at the end of World War II. The Südturm (*South Tower*) is by far the tallest of its four steeples and reaches 136.7 meters. [honsi.org]

138 Hainburg is a town in Austria by the Danube, just before the river flows into Slovakia. From 1869 onwards a cadet school was located in the castle.

In 1890 the town had in excess of 5,000 inhabitants where many worked at the tobacco factory. With 1,500 employees it was the largest of its kind in Cisleithania. Hainburg was part of Bezirk (*District*) Bruck.

[honsi.org]

The Hainburger Kadettenschule was a military educational establishment that existed from 1869 to 1918. The institution was located in the former castle beneath Schlossberg in Hainburg and the official name was Pionierkadettenschule as it educated officers for the engineer troops. The education lasted four years and the capacity was 100 students.

In 1913 the school was merged with Technische Militärakademie in

Mödling and the branch in Hainburg was thereafter named Technische Militärakademie - Pionierklassen. Commander of the school in 1914 was Oberstleutnant Theodor Weidinger (1857-1938) from Pionierbataillon Nr. 2 (Linz).

After World War I the building was used as ordinary barracks. In 1945 taken over by the Red Army, who left it in such a state that it had to be demolished. [honsi.org]

139 Theresianische Militärakademie (*Theresian Military Academy*) is the oldest existing military academy in the world, located in Wiener Neustadt. It was founded by Empress Maria Theresa on December 14th 1751 and educated officers for infantry and cavalry. The course lasted for three years and the graduates automatically obtained the rank of *Lieutenant*. Today, it is Austria's only remaining military educational establishment.

The Academy was then, as now, located in the castle and has been known as Theresianische Militärakademie since 1894. [honsi.org]

140 *A short for* intensified detention, *Verschärfter Arrest in the original German, which was* detention during off-duty time in communal, locked detention rooms. *Basically, a soldier after his day's work took a blanket and went to prison. Of course, he participated in the "districts", i.e. cleaning of the prison premises before taps.*

A non-commissioned officer could punish a subordinate with two, later three days of "intensified", *a junior officer with ten days, a section commander with twenty days and a unit commander with thirty days of* "intensified". [svejkmuseum.cz]

141 Franz Xaver Joseph Feldmarschall Conrad von Hötzendorf was an Austrian infantry general, from November 1916 Field Marshal, who acted as head of the General Staff in the periods 1906-1911 and 1912-1917. He was known for his aggressive stance in foreign policy matters and advocated preventive warfare not only against Serbia but also against Italy. He was head of the General Staff until March 1st 1917, when the new emperor Karl I dismissed him. Conrad is seen by many as carrying a major responsibility for the disastrous policies that led to the outbreak of World War I.

The authenticity of the quote "Die Soldaten müssen sowieso krepieren" (*The soldiers must croak one way or another*) has not been verified. It should also be noted that Conrad obtained the rank Field Marshal on November 23rd 1916, so One-year Volunteer Marek was looking well into the future during this dialogue with Švejk (which logically must have taken place the previous year). [honsi.org]

[142] The inspiration for Hašek's literary character was no doubt Josef Adamička, a professional officer who had served with Infantry Regiment No. 91 from November 1st 1904. In his capacity as head of Budweiser *One-year Volunteer school*, he met Jaroslav Hašek in February and March 1915. [honsi.org]

[143] The literary figure Wenzl was no doubt inspired by Franz Wenzel, a professional officer who served with Infantry Regiment No. 91 throughout Jaroslav Hašek's stay there. He was commander of the author's 12th March Battalion from June 1st to July 11th 1915, and was also his Regiment Commander for a short period in September. [honsi.org]

[144] Kutná Hora, i.e. *Mining Mountain*, is a city in the central part of Czech Republic, about 100 km east of Prague. It became rich on silver mining in the medieval ages and the many historical buildings bear witness to its wealthy past. Kutná Hora is on UNESCO's World Heritage list. [honsi.org]

[145] Interpellate is a word you might encounter in the international news section of a newspaper or magazine. It refers to a form of political challenging used in the congress or parliament of many nations throughout the world, in some cases provided for in the country's constitution.

Formal interpellation isn't practiced in the U.S. Congress, but in places where it is practiced, it can be the first step in ousting an appointed official or bringing to task an elected one. The word was borrowed from the Latin term interpellatus, past participle of "interpellare," which means "to interrupt or disturb a person speaking." The "interrupt" sense, once used in English, is now obsolete, and "interpellate" should not be confused with interpolate," which means "to insert words into a text or conversation. [merriam-webster.com]

[146] The inspiration for the character Ságner is mainly the Austrian (from 1918 Czechoslovak) officer Čeněk Sagner. He was Jaroslav Hašek's Battalion Commander in Infantry Regiment No. 91 from July 11th to September 24th 1915, and before that, they had served simultaneously in Budějovice and Királyhida. For most of the time Hašek served in the Regiment, Sagner's rank was Senior Lieutenant (he was promoted to Captain as late as September 1st). During this period, Sagner never commanded any march battalion. [honsi.org]

[147] Vávrova *street* (also Vávrova *boulevard*) was the name of a street in Praha II. and Vinohrady. It was named after Čeněk Vávra who was the mayor of Vinohrady from 1868 to 1873. The street was named Vávrova ulice from 1884 to 1926 when it was renamed Rumunská [*Romanian*] *street*, a name it

has kept since.

The street stretches from Sokolská in Praha II. up towards Náměstí Míru [*Peace square*] in Vinohrady and its length is 180 metres. It was on the corner of this street and Tylovo *square* that drogerie [*pharmacy*] Průša was located. [honsi.org]

148 Apollo was a large night café with dancing at *Fügner square* in Nové město (*New Town*), not in Vinohrady as Švejk says.

Newspaper adverts indicate that Apollo existed from 1897. An advert in Prager Tagblatt describes it as Grand-Restaurant. The adverts also reveal that the large restaurant hosted meetings for associations and political parties. Who owned it from the beginning is not known, but in 1900 Jan Beutler was teaching dancing there. In 1902 and 1906, the owner was Antonín Žalud (he had lived at the address since 1901), and in 1910 František Šťastný, who had lived at the address since 1906.

Throughout 1915, adverts for dance entertainment appeared in Národní listy, confirming that Šťastný was still the landlord (he is listed as such in the address book of 1910). The adverts continued until 1917, but in the address book from 1924 the establishment no longer existed on the premises. [honsi.org]

149 Božetěchova ulice is a short street in Nusle, situated on the hill towards Vyšehrad. [honsi.org]

150 Vyšehrad, i.e. *High Castle*, is the oldest part of Prague, known for the historic fortress. It is located on a rock by the Vltava, between the current districts of Nové město (*New Town*) and Nusle. The national cemetery is also located here.

In 1913 this city district was identical to the VI. (6th) district of the royal capital, officially called Královský Vyšehrad (*Royal High Castle*). [honsi.org]

151 "Kanonýr Jabůrek" was a figure from a song story (cantastoria) Udatný rek kanonýr Jabůrek (*Valiant hero cannoneer Jabůrek*) which has its background in the Austro-Prussian war of 1866. It is unclear whether it had any factual foundation, but it appeared as a parody around 1884, perhaps even earlier. Jabůrek took part in the decisive battle at Hradec Králové on July 3rd 1866. He keeps loading his cannon even as his limbs and other parts of his body are torn off, until his head is blown off and he reports to the general that he is no longer able to salute. The song is written in colloquial Czech and contains 17 verses.

The first verse of the song was printed on a postcard in 1914, but in formally written Czech. It was part of a series of patriotic songs issued on postcards in Prague after the outbreak of the war. Why this obviously satirical song was included in the collection is difficult to answer. In 1986, Franz Hiesel made a radio play based on the song. It was broadcast both in West Germany (WDR) and Austria (ORF). Over the years, the cannoneer has been mentioned numerous times in the Czech press and other publications. Egon Erwin Kisch dedicates a chapter to Jabůrek in his book Aus Prager Gassen und Nächten (*From Prague Streets, Alleys and Nights*) from 1912. [honsi.org]

152 Rudolfinum is a concert hall and art center in Staré město (*Old Town*) on the banks of the Vltava next to Josefov. It was opened in 1884 and named after Crown Prince Rudolf. It is mostly used for concerts and art exhibitions. [honsi.org]

153 *Uhlan was a soldier of the light cavalry in the Polish part of the monarchy, Galicia.* [svejkmuseum.cz] However, by 1914 there were also Uhlan regiments recruited from Croatia and Bohemia. [library.hungaricana.hu]

154 Tyrol was, in 1914, an Austrian region, larger than the present-day Austrian Tirol, as it also included the current Italian provinces of Alto Adige (South Tyrol) and Trentino. Sections of the front between Italy and Austria ran through Tyrol from the outbreak of war on May 23rd 1915 until the armistice in 1918. [honsi.org]

155 *From Hungarian* Honvédség (*Land Defense*). [svejkmuseum.cz]

156 A hussar is a member of a European light-cavalry unit used for scouting; the hussars were modeled on the 15th-century Hungarian light-horse corps. The brilliantly colored Hungarian hussar's uniform was imitated in other European armies; it consisted of a busby (high, cylindrical cloth cap), a jacket with heavy braiding, and a dolman (loose coat worn hanging from the left shoulder). [merriam-webster.com]

157 Heavily armed mounted troops. A dragoon was a mounted European infantryman of the 17th and 18th centuries armed with a firearm called by the same name. The firearm's name, which came to English from French, comes from the fired weapon's resemblance to a fire-breathing dragon. History has recorded the dragonish nature of the dragoons who persecuted the French Protestants in the 17th century during the reign of Louis XIV. The persecution by means of dragoons eventually led to the use of the word dragoon as a verb. [merriam-webster.com]

158 Belgium entered the war on August 4th 1914 when the neutral country was invaded by Germany that attempted to circumvent the French border

fortifications. The German attack influenced England's decision to enter the war. The country offered stiff resistance, and it was only in October that Antwerp fell. Almost her entire area remained occupied for the rest of the war and Belgium suffered severe human and material losses. As a result of the peace treaty the region of Malmedy-Eupen was ceded by Germany. The civilian population were subjected to widespread atrocities in 1914, often justified as actions against franc-tireurs (paramilitaries). [honsi.org]

159 The theater in Budějovice is an unnamed, but we can with relative confidence assume that *Captain* Ságner refers to Městské divadlo/Stadttheater (the *City Theater*). The building is located by the banks of the Malše at the southern end of Dr. Stejskal street, in 1915 Divadelní ulice/Theatergasse (*Theater street*). The theater still existed in 2021, now called Jihočeské divadlo (*Theatre of the Czech South*). [honsi.org]

160 America no doubt refers to the United States as a political entity. The country was neutral until April 6th 1917, when the country, provoked by German submarine warfare and the prospect of an Allied defeat, declared war upon Germany.

The economic (and later military) might of the United States had a decisive influence on the outcome of the war. After the war, American influence played a significant part in shaping the new Europe. President Woodrow Wilson was an advocate of national self-determination for the smaller nations, which not least benefited Czechoslovakia and the other successor states of Austria-Hungary (Austria-Hungary).

The declaration of war on Austria-Hungary followed only on December 7th. In the Senate 74 voted in favor of the declaration and none against. In the House of Representatives, 365 were in favor, and only one objected.

Direct fighting between American and Austro-Hungarian troops occurred at the Piave in October 1918, but these engagements would have been few as the American expeditionary force consisted only of Infantry Regiment 332, and some aeroplanes and medical units. The latter did, however, gain some fame: among them served Ernest Hemingway. His stay on the Piave resulted in the novel A Farewell to Arms.

A little-known but well documented battle between units from U.S. Army and the k.u.k. Wehrmacht (*I&R Armed Forces*) took place on the Western Front in the autumn of 1918. In July 1918 Austria-Hungary put four divisions and some artillery at the disposal of the German Army. In September, American forces led by Pershing won a decisive victory near Verdun against forces that included 35. Infantry Division. At the beginning of October, 1. Infantry Division faced American troops north of Verdun. It suffered heavy losses and was also exposed to gas attacks. Among these troops was Field Rifle Battalion No.17, a unit with a high number of Czech soldiers from southern Moravia.

Czech-language newspapers in the United States published stories by Jaroslav Hašek on several occasions during his lifetime. From 1911 to 1917, some of them appeared in Slavie, a weekly published in Racine, Wisconsin, later in Chicago. One of them is called Dobrý voják Švejk and was published on September 12th 1911. It is an uncensored version of the story Dobrý voják Švejk učí se zacházet se střelnou bavlnou (*The Good Soldier Švejk Is Learning to Handle Gun-Cotton*) that was first printed by Dobrá kopa *(Good Fellow)* on July 21st 1911. Preceding these stories was Smrt Horala (*The Death of a Highlander*), which appeared in Národní noviny (*The National Newspaper*) in Baltimore as early as May 3rd 1902. To our knowledge, this was the first time ever a story by Hašek was published outside the Czech lands.

The novel *The Good Soldier Švejk* was published in the United States already during Hašek's lifetime. It was printed as a serial in Duch času (*Spirit of the Times*), the Sunday issue of Svornost (C*oncord*), a Chicago Czech newspaper. It has not been established exactly when the series started but we know that the issue from September 9th 1923 is from the first chapter of Part Three, thus covering the departure from Királyhida. Below the title of the series is written that it is published in agreement with the author, and this is confirmed by Kliment Stěpánek to whom Hašek in 1922 dictated the final parts of the novel. The editor that Hašek was in contact with was August Geringer. He even sent the Sunday issues back to Hašek and this was highly appreciated by the author. Duch času (*Spirit of the Times*), was the first to print Švejk outside Czechoslovakia.

Among the Czech-American newspapers that published Hašek's stories we are aware of are Minnesotské noviny (*Minnesota Newspaper*) (St. Paul), Svět (*The World*)(Cleveland), Denní hlasatel (*Daily Herald*) (Chicago), and Dennice novověku (Cleveland). [honsi.org]

161 Šabac (Шабац) is a town by the river Sava in Serbia, and was almost constantly on the front line during the autumn of 1914. It was one of the first targets for the Austro-Hungarian invasion, and as the invaders reached the town on August 14th, they ravaged the city and massacres took place. Eventually only half of the population survived the war. Due to the many battles and widespread destruction, Šabac was also called the Serbian

Verdun. The city changed hands several times that autumn but by the end of 1914 it was again controlled by the Serbs.

On November 8th 1914, Infantry Regiment No. 91 marched through the city, on their way to the front by the river Kolubara, slightly to the east. [honsi.org]

162 Marek has many traits in common with the author of *The Good Soldier Švejk*. From a purely biographical point of view, these are: one-year volunteer, served in Infantry Regiment No. 91, expelled from the reserve officer's school, stayed in a military hospital in Budějovice, locked up at Marian Garrison, editor of *The Animal World* Hašek even turned up at the Budějovice garrison in civilian clothes and a cylinder hat, just like Marek did.

On ideas and personal qualities, the following fit: intense dislike of the monarchy and its institutions, anti-war attitudes, glittering rhetoric, fat, unusually good memory and grasp of detail. It is also obvious that Marek is a mouthpiece for Jaroslav Hašek's personal views.

Scholars seem to agree that the name of the one-year volunteer is borrowed from Karel Marek (1884-1945), a friend of Jaroslav Hašek from his youth. Václav Menger relates that the young Hašek often visited the Marek family at Vinohrady and that he particularly enjoyed listening to the stories Karel's father told from his experience in the Prussian War of 1866. From him, the young author also learnt many of the army songs that he was so fond of singing. Karel Marek himself actually served as a one-year volunteer but with Infantry Regiment No. 28, Prague's house regiment.

Karel Marek was, according to Augustin Knesl, born in 1884, son of Jan and Anna Marek. Like Jaroslav Hašek, young Karel studied at Obchodní akademie in Resslova ulice, albeit two years later (i.e. 1901-1904). He worked as an office worker but was also an artist, mastering painting and writing. He met with Hašek also after the war and some material about the author was kept by his wife Marie Marková. At the end of World War II, Marek was interned in Terezín and on May 15th 1945 he died as a result of the mistreatment he suffered in the camp. [honsi.org]

163 Plural of "blboun" (*idiot*), in this case referring to delicious huge dumplings filled with individual type of fruit, such as plums, strawberries, or apricots, covered with melted butter, granulated sugar, cinnamon and farmer's cheese. [Translator's note]

164 Andalusia is an autonomous region of Spain. It is the most populous and the second largest, in terms of land area, of the seventeen autonomous

communities of Spain. Its capital and largest city is Seville. The region is known for its bullfighting. [honsi.org]

165 Bruck an der Leitha-Királyhida is a collective term for the twin towns Bruck and Királyhida, often used in military documents issued by Replacement Battalion IR 91 and others. Shorter versions were Bruck-Királyhida and Bruck a.d. Leitha/Királyhida. [honsi.org]

166 ['mah-diyo-ria] = Hungary. There are two names for Hungary in Czech: "Maďarsko" and "Uhry". Here Hašek uses the latter. "Maďarsko" is derived from the Hungarians' self-designation: Magyarorszag (*Hungarian Country*) and Magyar (*a Hungarian*). On the other hand, the now archaic "Uhry" or "Uhersko" seems to be derived from Old Russian "Ugre" (*Hungarians*), as is perhaps even the German label "Ungarn" for Hungary. However, the archaic "Uhersko" is used exclusively in the name of the dual monarchy "Rakousko-Uhersko (*Austria-Hungary*) and the adjective derived from it, "rakousko-uherský (*Austro-Hungarian*).

The frequency of using the two synonyms (and their morphological variants) for "Hungarian" in Book Two, is as follows: Hašek used "Maďar" for "a Hungarian(s)" or the adjective "maďarský (*Hungarian*) (57x), but "Uhry" for "Hungary" (1x), and the adjective "uherský (*Hungarian*) (12x).

The archaic adjective is used as a qualifier of the military units of the Empire (3x) the Hungarian King (2x), Hungarian Kingdom (2x), the population (1x), the Empire's compound name, "rakousko-uherský (*Austro-Hungarian*) (2x), the famous Hungarian salami (1x), two cities (1x) and a battlefield (1x). [Translator's note]

167 In her footnote 27 in "Literary Representations of 'Racial Mixing' in Czech Modernism", the author, Jana Kantoříková, compares the three English translations preceding this Centennial Edition [Translator's note]:

"For lack of space, we do not quote the Czech original, but only the translation by Zdeněk Sadloň, which, regarding the translation of racial terms, respects Hašek's text. Sadloň translates, for instance, 'číšník černoch' (Hašek, 2010[1922]: 242) as 'black waiter' (Hašek, 2009: 85) and 'mouřenín[ek]' (Hašek, 2010 [1922]: 242) as 'the little Moor' (Hašek, 2009: 85). "Hašek's portrayal of the waiter Kristián and his descendants is certainly problematic. However, Cecil Parrot's older (1973) and extensively re-edited translation, by choosing explicitly racist terms, adds a layer to the original that is not there – 'číšník černoch' is rendered by Parrot as 'negro waiter' (Hašek, 2000: 312) and 'mouřenín[ek]' as 'little nigger boy' (312), etc. Let us add that the first English version of Hašek's Švejk by Paul Selver

(1930) is an abridged translation and does not reproduce the passage in question." [edoc.hu-berlin.de]

So why does this edition replace "black" with "negro? The real question is, why was "černoch" rendered as "black" in the original 1997 computer file, the 2009 paperback, and 2010 Kindle editions?

Since the American society had been intensely racialized on college campuses, in the media, the government and places of employment since the early 1970s, the last thing a self-publishing, unknown author lacking a commission or support needed was a firestorm over using the word "negro". It was enough we had to fend off charges of antisemitism against both Jaroslav Hašek and his Švejk. Fortunately, when reporting those to the Hebrew translator of Švejk, Ruth Bondi, she emphatically stated during our telephone conversation from Tel Aviv "To je volovina!", literally "It's the ox thing", a slightly more polite Czech equivalent of "bullshit".

This time I decided on using "negro" instead of "black", because 1: it simply means black, 2: it was a legal and universal designation of ethnic Africans among Americans, which wasn't racist, and 3: there is in English no other noun for labeling a "black person" with a single word as "černoch" in the original. (According to the U.S. "paper of record", "Both 'Black' and 'white' should normally be used as adjectives, not nouns.")

Jana Kantoříková counts Parrott's "negro waiter" among "explicitly racist terms", judging it from the changed perspective of the "prevailing" (because enforced) view of the current times. His sin isn't using the word "negro" in this phrase, but perhaps the fact he didn't capitalize it, although that wasn't done years after Hašek wrote the book. [Translator's note]

"The practice of capitalizing 'Negro' began around 1930, primarily due to the influence of W.E.B Du Bois who successfully persuaded the New York Times to include 'Negro' as a capitalized word in their style guide, signifying a move towards recognizing racial self-respect." [pewresearch.org] [AI Overview google.com]

So by 1973 Cecil Parrott should have known better, if he was supposed to change historical text to conform to current politicized language standard: [Translator's note]

"In the 1960s, there was a shift from the use of 'Negro' to the use of 'black' as a group identifier. In 1966 Stokely Carmichael shouted the phrase 'Black Power.' Three years later, in 1969, 'Negro' was replaced by 'black' as the dominant label identifier." [escholarship.org] And as night follows day, the next change was Uppercasing 'Black'. [nytco.com]

168 Kristian (Kristian Ebenezer) was a rare black waiter who worked at Café Louvre, Hotel Baška, Café Royal, at the station restaurant in Brno, and at various places in the countryside.

Egon Erwin Kisch wrote in Prager Tagblatt about a chance meeting with Kristian in a hotel in Trenčianske Teplice in 1921, where the latter worked as a waiter. Eduard Bass, another acquaintance of Hašek, also wrote about Kristian, whom he knew from Prague and Brno. Bass even provided an obituary for Lidové noviny.

Augustin Knesl mentions Kristian in the series "Švejk a ti druzí" (*Švejk and the others*) but somewhat naively concludes that Hašek's description of him was precise. Knesl had evidently not registered that Kristian was from the Caribbean and thus could not have been the son of an Abyssinian king.

Hašek had also mentioned Kristian many years before he wrote *The Good Soldier Švejk.* Exactly when the story Silvestr pana Pažana was first published is not known, but it appeared in a Czech-American paper in 1915[d], so it was probably written in 1914 or early 1915.

Ebenezer was born in the Danish colony St.Croix in the Caribbean. His mother tongue was Danish, but already as a teenager he spoke English fluently.

Kristian is actually the only Nordic citizen who is mentioned by name in *The Good Soldier Švejk.* It is possible that the mysterious psychologist Doctor Kallerson is a distortion of, for example, Karl Larsson.

As a 14-year-old, he arrived in Prague together with engineers from the Daňkovka factory. He was a waiter apprentice at the newly established Café Louvre, where he worked for several years. He became a well-known character in Prague and learned Czech exceptionally quickly.

Already in 1905, he is mentioned in the newspapers and during the following year his name appeared several times. In 1916, he was to marry Božena Hanušová from Mladá Boleslav, but the bride somehow disappeared, and the story ended up in the newspapers. He even became an ardent Czech nationalist and caused distaste among Germans. Eduard Bass even called him a chauvinist. Already in 1909, the Social Democrat satirical magazine Kopřivy (*Nettles*) associated him with Klofáč and his Česká strana národně sociální (*Czech National Social Party*). Here it is also revealed that he still worked at Louvre.

Throughout his life, he was plagued by poor health. He had problems walking and also suffered from tuberculosis, a disease that in the end proved fatal. Shortly before he died, he married the same woman who had vanished in 1916. His last address was Vinohrady, Puchmajerova 56. It is not known if he had any offspring, nor do we know if he did military service. [honsi.org]

169 Abyssinia was a monarchy that roughly covered the areas of current Ethiopia and Eritrea. It was the only country in Africa that escaped European colonial rule and the only one on the continent that was predominantly Christian. Until Emperor Haile Selassie was deposed by a coup in 1974, it was the oldest existing state in the world. [honsi.org]

170 Štvanice is an island in the river Vltava in Prague that is located between Karlín and Holešovice. It is and was mainly used as a bathing and recreation area.

In historical newspapers there is no indication that a circus ever performed on the island, and definitely not with an Abyssinian (Ethiopian) king as an item to be exhibited. This information is surely a product of Švejk's (or rather Hašek's) lively imagination. [honsi.org]

171 Lada was a women's magazine that was published by Karel Vačlena in Mladá Boleslav, with Věnceslava Lužická as its Prague-based editor. It was published from 1889 to 1944. [honsi.org]

172 Kateřinky was the colloquial name of a hospital for the mentally ill in Nové město (*New Town*). The official name was Královský český zemský ústav pro choromyslné v Praze, i.e. *Royal Czech Provincial Institute for the Mentally Ill in Prague,* established in 1822. It had subsidiaries at Na Slupi and Bohnice. These institutions still exist as of 2021. [honsi.org]

"Kateřinky" is a plural of "Kateřinka", the diminutive of "Catherine". *In the former compound of the Augustinian-hermit monastery at St. Catherine's, a classicist building of the former Institute for the Mentally Ill, now the Psychiatric Clinic, was built in 1842-1843.* [encyklopedie.praha2.cz]

173 Varieté ("*variety show*") was the name of a theater in Karlín that was opened in 1881. It is one of the oldest theaters in Prague and is still operating, albeit under the name Karlín Music Theatre. According to the address book from 1907, the official name was Théâtre Variété. Newspaper adverts reveal that they also arranged wrestling matches. In April 1912, Varieté arranged a major wrestling tournament and among the participants was the black wrestler Zipps. [honsi.org]

174 There is no doubt that the negro who Švejk imagines was wrestling at Varieté refers to Chambers Zipps, a North-American wrestler, who by all accounts spent periods of his life in Europe. In April 1912 he fought several matches at Varieté and even the advert from the theater itself refers to him

as the "negro-wrestler Zipps".

One could argue that other black wrestlers may have appeared at Varieté during Hašek's lifetime, but the author himself actually puts to rest any uncertainty regarding his source of inspiration. Only a few days after the wrestling tournament finished he published a story where Zipps was the main character. Here Jaroslav Hašek mentions the matches at Varieté and many other details. During a visit at U Brejšky the narrator was unfortunate enough to step on giant negro's sore toe... The theme Zipps and Varieté also appears in another story that Hašek wrote at the time, but here he mentioned it only in passing.

Zipps initially worked as a horse-keeper for the wealthy American racehorse owner/breeder/trainer Eugene Leigh (1860-1937) who in 1901 relocated to Europe (Wikipedia). In 1906 Zipps' name started to appear in French newspapers in connection with Greco-Roman wrestling. Already then one of the news items described him as "the famous negro Zipps". At the end of October 1906 he took part in the World Championship (there were two competing tournaments at the time) at Folies Bergère in Paris and this event was widely reported, also in the foreign press. Czech newspapers wrote that he had defeated the Czech Šmejkal and that Zipps himself weighed 110 kilos.

In his homeland his achievements were also noticed and it was added that he had been a successful amateur wrestler, and was so strong that he could carry a horse on his shoulders.

He continued to compete across Europe and during the years until 1915 he took part in tournaments in France, England, Italy, Belgium, Germany, Austria, Hungary, Finland, Denmark, Sweden and Russia. From the tournament in Moscow in 1912 there even exists a video clip. In 1915 he toured Russia but thereafter he disappeared from the news for the rest of the war.

In 1919 a wrestler named John Zipps (also a black American) appeared in news reports but it is unclear if this is the same person. The latest recorded newspaper notice about any wrestler Zipps is from 1927.

Zipps was described in sympathetic terms in both the Czech and Austro-German press. He was reportedly a joker and often entertained the public when he was performing. We know nothing about when and where he was born/died and the only point of reference is information in the French sports press that he was young when he arrived in France. It is therefore tempting to suggest that he was born between 1880 and 1890. [honsi.org]

[175] Franz Joseph Land is an archipelago in the northern part of the Barents Sea which belongs to Russia. The first officially recognized discovery took place in 1873 by the Austro-Hungarian North Pole Expedition led by polar explorers Julius von Payer and Karl Weyprecht. On their way back the expedition requested that the isles be named after the Emperor and this was reported in the newspapers in 1874.

In 1914 the uninhabited islands were still no-man's land and it was only in 1926 that they became part of the Soviet Union. [honsi.org]

[176] Pražské ledárny (*Prague Ice-Works*) was a company that delivered ice to breweries, restaurants, hospitals, dairies, butchers and other enterprises that used ice for cooling purposes. Judging by newspaper adverts, it was established in 1884 and was privately owned. The owner in 1892 was Ivan Čížek and in 1896 Bernard Lüftschitz is listed as the owner. In both cases there were also other owners. The ice works were located at Štvanice island (also called Velké Benátky).

In 1898 the city had plans to build a new ice plant that would better satisfy the growing demand. The plans did not materialize, but in 1901 Lüftschitz sold his ice works to a newly formed co-operative company named Společenské ledárny v Praze (*Social Ice-Works in Prague*). It was owned by its customers and in 1908 they had 234 members, a number that by 1912 had grown to 299. In Dolní Krč there was a rival enterprise owned by Tomáš Welz. In 1913 the two companies merged.

From 1909 to 1911 a new and bigger plant was constructed at Braník south of the city. The construction cost was, however, so high that the firm went bankrupt, but conversion to a limited company and investment of fresh capital saved it. The new company was registered in 1913 under the name Akciové ledárny v Praze. In 1914 it reported a profit.

The company operated until 1954 and the building was still intact but in need of repair as of 2021. It has been under heritage preservation protection since 1964. [honsi.org]

[177] k.k. Handelsministerium (*I&R Trade Ministry*) was the Ministry of Trade of Cisleithania and one of nine ministries in the Austrian part of the Dual Monarchy. It was housed in Postgasse in the centre of Vienna.

The Ministry of Trade was one of the heavyweights of its kind in Cisleithania. Its areas of responsibility included trade, industry, the merchant fleet, mail, telephone, telegraph, customs, and from 1908, workers' welfare and social security. [honsi.org]

[178] k.u.k. Außenministerium (*I&R Foreign Ministry*), officially k.u.k.

Ministerium des kaiserlichen und königlichen Hauses und des Äußern (*I&R Ministry of the Imperial and Royal Household and of Foreign Affairs*) was the ministry of foreign affairs for the Dual Monarchy, one of the three common ministries; the others were Kriegsministerium (*War Ministry*) and k.u.k. Finanzministerium (*I&R Finance Ministry*). It was housed at Ballhausplatz by Hofburg in the center of Vienna. As is evident from the full title of the ministry, it was not only tasked with running foreign affairs in the classic sense (diplomacy, embassies, consulates, foreign policy etc.). It was also responsible for the archives of the Imperial and Royal House, i.e. k.u.k. Haus, Hof und Staatsarchiv (*I&R House, Court, and State Archive*).[honsi.org]

179 "Supák" *or* "zupák" *is a slang term for soldiers who voluntarily serve longer than the standard service length, to serve for* "sup". "Supák" *is supposedly derived from the fact that he served for "soup", in German* "die Suppe", *but that is probably not true. A more likely derivation is from German.* "subaltern", *i.e. lower, subordinate, servile. He had [narrow] gold bands sewn on his sleeves [above the cuffs]. The number of the wide ones increased with the years of service.* [svejkmuseum.cz] In short, the Sergeant in this story has an ideal to stay on as a "souper" NCO for as long as he can. [Translator's note]

180 "ministerstvo vyučování" (*The Ministry of Schooling*) in Hašek's text. [Translator's note] - K.k. Unterrichtsministerium (*I&R Education Ministry*), officially k.k. Ministerium für Kultus und Unterricht (*I&A Ministry of Religion and Education*) was the ministry of culture and education for Cisleithania. It was housed at Minoritenplatz in the center of Vienna.

The ministry was responsible for education (apart from academies for trade, industry and agriculture), the Evangelical Church (Protestant), art, memorials, museums, science academies, meteorological institutes and so on. [honsi.org]

181 The greeting "Nazdar!" literally means "*To success!*". It came into existence in the 1860s among the patriots, who wished one another success in fund-raising for the establishment and building of the National Theater. The National Theater became the embodiment of the Czech nation's desire to come into its own. Since then, in Czech patriotic (and after gaining independence in 1918, also the Czecho-Slovak military) organizations, the leader's or commander's closing word "Nazdar!" [*To success!*] would receive the unison response "Zdar!" [*Success!*] from the members assembled in formation. [Translator's note]

[182] The Senior Field Chaplain was undoubtedly inspired by Ludvík Lacina, a Roman-Catholic Field Chaplain who served in I&R Army from 1906 to 1918. The obituaries from 1928 reveal that he had been "identified" as a model for the literary field chaplain already before his death. [honsi.org]

[183] Kavalleriedivision Nr. 7 was a cavalry division headquartered in Kraków, reporting to the 1. Armeekorps. The direct reason why the Division is mentioned in *The Good Soldier Švejk* is that Ludvík Lacina, the model for *Chief Field Chaplain* Lacina, was actually assigned to this unit from January 1913 to August 1916. That Jaroslav Hašek was aware of these details indicates that he knew Lacina personally. [honsi.org]

[184] Pakoměřice is a village just north of Prague, administratively part of Bořanovice. The major attraction is the castle that once belonged to the noble family Nostitz. It has recently (2020) been renovated after having fallen into disrepair. The brewery was one of the oldest in Bohemia and is mentioned as early as 1636. The owner at the beginning of the 20th century was Count Erwin Nostitz. Around 1870 the brewery was modernized and it delivered beer also to restaurants in Prague. In 1908 the production was 17,116 hectoliters and the brewmaster was Rudolf Zilka. During and after the war production stagnated and the last year it operated was in 1926. The building is still intact and like the castle it has recently been renovated. [honsi.org]

[185] Krumlovsko is a common term for the area around Krumlov, but here the author probably refers to hejtmanství (*administrative district*) Krumlov, one of the five political districts that Infantry Regiment No. 91 was recruited from.

According to the 1910 census Krumlovsko had 61,068 inhabitants of which 15,729 (25 per cent) reported Czech as their everyday language. The rest were German speakers.

The verses that the soldiers from Kašperské Hory and Krumlovsko sang on the train from Budějovice are fragments from a folk song of German origin that through the 19th century had become popular. The song is popular not only in German-speaking countries but also world-wide. Even Elvis Presley recorded it in 1960 with the title Wooden Heart. As is often the case with folk songs, various lyrics and spellings exist.

The melody is believed to be a traditional song from Swabia but the lyrics were added in 1827 by the composer Friedrich Silcher (1789-1860) who also published it. During World War I it was much used by soldiers that were leaving home for service and it was also popular as a march anthem.

The title is officially "Muß i denn". [honsi.org]

186 Jabal an-Nûr is a mountain by Mekka, famous for the legend in which Muhammad met Allāh's messenger, the angel Gabriel in the cave Hira. [honsi.org]

187 Muḥammad was an Arab political and religious leader. In the history of religion, he is regarded as the founder of Islam and is considered by Muslims as a messenger and prophet of Allāh. The name has many transliterations in English. [honsi.org]

188 Svět zvířat (*The Animal World*) was an illustrated popular science magazine that specialized in animals and animal breeding. It was established in Jičín by Jaroslav Podbodský (owner) and Václav Fuchs (publisher and chief editor). The first issue appeared on 1 September 1st 1897 with a circulation of 10,000. Already from the beginning, some well-known people wrote for the magazine, for instance the explorer Emil Holub. One of its co-editors was Jaroslav Hašek (1909-1910, 1912-1913).

Hašek's engagement with *The Animal World* was only the second time in his life that he was permanently employed, and it became his longest ever permanent employment in peace-time. Fuchs was initially satisfied with his new employee, paid him decently, and the allowance included two liters of beer a day! This way of rewarding the thirsty editor was simply a ploy to keep him on a short leash.

Every period of Jaroslav Hašek's life is shrouded in legend, none more so than his time as the editor of The Animal World. Most widespread is the claim that Hašek "embellished" the magazine with stories about imaginary species and that this was the reason for his dismissal (an echo of Marek in "Švejk"). Further, claims exist that he advertised werewolves for sale and allegedly published stories about the terrible guzzler and other fantasy creatures in the magazine. In the journal itself, there is, however, no trace of these creatures…

The seed for the legends was planted by none other than Hašek himself and, over the years, spread by his friends and biographers (Josef Mach, Franta Sauer, Emil Artur Longen, Václav Menger, Josef Lada and others). Hašek's mystifications, enhanced by the tales of his friends, eventually entered the sphere of serious haškology and were later firmly planted in the anglophone world by Cecil Parrott, arguably the all-time leading Hašek-expert outside Czechoslovakia. Parrott, in his otherwise solid biography "The Bad Bohemian" (1978), asserted that "Hašek was an accomplished and persuasive hoaxer", then in a later chapter unreservedly propagated claims by Menger and Lada about Hašek advertising werewolves, having caused a stir even among foreign scientists with his "discovery" of a prehistoric flea (again echoed by Marek). Parrott was correct in claiming that Hašek was an accomplished hoaxer, but didn't fully realize HOW accomplished he was!

Not that Parrott was alone in falling into the trap. It is difficult to find any scholar or amateur alike, who didn't propagate these claims at one time or another. In 2024, looking at Wikipedia articles in various languages is enough. As an example, wikipedia.org (as of 1.1.2025): *"and the same year he was appointed editor of Animal World magazine. Although this work did not last long (he was soon released for publishing articles on imaginary animals he had invented).*" [honsi.org]

189 Saanen is a valley in Berner Oberland in Switzerland. As the name indicates, this goat breed originates from there and is best known for milk production. Generally, they have short white fur and don't have horns. In Bohemia, they were widespread at the beginning of the 20th century and often mentioned in newspapers and specialist literature.

During Hašek's time as editor of *The Animal World* in 1909 and 1910, there were numerous advertisements for Saanen goats in the journal, so he would have been well aware of the animal. That said, he also may have drawn inspiration from other publications he was familiar with, for instance, Zdroje hospodářského blahobytu (*Sources of Economic Prosperity*) that publisher Kočí printed in 1906. [honsi.org]

190 Ladislav Hájek was a journalist, poet, writer, and publisher, originally from Domažlice. He was a lifelong friend of Hašek and one of only two among Hašek's friends who is mentioned by name in *The Good Soldier Švejk* (the other one was painter Panuška).

Importantly, Hájek wrote a biography of Jaroslav Hašek in 1925, a book that by far is the most reliable source that exists about Hašek's time at *The Animal World* (1908-1910 and 1912-1913). It also sheds light on other periods of Hašek's life, such as his student years and the year leading up to the outbreak of war.

The two met as students at Československá akademie obchodní (*Czechoslovak Commercial Academy*) in Prague in 1901 and together they published the poetry collection Májové výkřiky (*The Cries of May*) in 1903. Hájek had already in 1901 published a collection of poems called "Noci" (*Nights*), where he used the pseudonym L. H. Domažlický. From 1902 onwards, he published short stories in various magazines using the pseudonym Domažlický. Among the magazines who printed his stories between 1902 and 1907 were Illustrovaný svět, Besedy lidu, Národní listy, Světozor, Hlas lidu and even the two U.S. newspapers Svoboda and Dennice novověku. [honsi.org]

191 Václav Fuchs (born Siegfried Fuchs) was a Czech animal breeder, kennel owner, and publisher/editor of Jewish origin. He is best known as the owner and publisher of the magazine *The Animal World*, and it is in this context that his name is known to readers of *The Good Soldier Švejk.*

His name appears in national newspapers from 1894 onwards. Initially, he was often mentioned in connection with rabbit breeding, and at the time, he was based in Jičín. He offered rabbits for sale in Prager Tagblatt, Prager Abendblatt, Das interessante Blatt, and others.

In early 1908, Fuchs employed a new editor, Jaroslav Hašek's friend Ladislav Hájek. It was through this connection that Hašek was introduced to Klamovka and the animal magazine towards the end of the year. Initially, he only assisted in the editorial offices, but Hájek fell out with his boss and quit. Hašek was now offered the editor position (he was registered as a villa resident on 4 February 1909), and initially, it worked out well. The job was well paid (it also included 2 liters of beer per day) and enabled Hašek to support a family, and he married on May 23rd 1910.

The newlyweds moved out of the villa and down to Smíchov No. 1125 below the Klamovka park. According to Ladislav Hájek, the enthusiasm that Fuchs initially showed for his inventive editor now waned considerably. Hašek was less often seen in the editorial offices, and readers started complaining about dubious articles. In his predicament, Fuchs traveled to Poděbrady to convince Hájek to return to the office to replace Hašek. He succeeded in his mission, and in the issue of *The Animal World* dated October 15th 1910, Hájek was again listed as editor. [honsi.org]

The daughter of Václav Fuchs, Žofie Fuchsová, not mentioned by name in the narrative, was born in 1894, presumably in Jičín, and was only four when the family moved to Klamovka, where her father managed *The Animal World* and the associated kennel.

In 1908, she became acquainted with Ladislav Hájek, then editor of the magazine, and on October 5th 1912, the two married in the church of Svatý Václav (*Saint Wenceslaus*) in Smíchov.

Soon after the wedding, the young couple moved to Ferdinand's boulevard (now Národní/*National*), from where her husband published the magazine. For a period, Hašek also stayed with them, and according to Ladislav Hájek, she was fond of the future author of *The Good Soldier Švejk.* Little is known about her life after that, but according to Břetislav Hůla, she committed suicide "years ago". Research by Jaroslav Šerák confirms that she shot herself in the head on October 4th 1919. She was only 25 years old when she died. It is not known if the couple had any children. [honsi.org]

192 *Understand it to mean Podolí, which is a part of Prague on the right bank of the Vltava. Here used to be restaurants, where similar roasted critters, caught in a nearby river, were sold fried in fat. Because the whole of Prague used to flock to nosh on them as part of Sunday outings, the restaurateurs, in order to increase profit, used the cheapest fat, the hydrogenated vegetable fat sold under the commercial name Margarine.* [svejkmuseum.cz]

193 All the references to Brehm in *The Good Soldier Švejk* pertain to his magnum opus *Brehm's Life of Animals* rather than his person. Brehm was a prominent German zoologist, explorer and writer. Through the multi-volume reference work Brehms Tierleben (*Brehm's Life of Animals*), his name became a synonym for popular zoological literature. Brehm was the son of a distinguished ornithologist and already as an 18-year-old he took part in an expedition to Egypt and the upper Nile (1847-1852), and later he undertook expeditions to Spain, Norway and Siberia. He published books about his expeditions and also went on tours where he lectured about his travels and discoveries. From 1862 to 1867 he was the director of the zoo in Hamburg and later he founded the well-known aquarium in Berlin where he remained until 1874.

It was however his publishing of the zoological reference work which made him famous. The first edition, containing six volumes, was published from 1864 to 1869 with the title Illustrirtes Tierleben. From 1876 to 1879 the second edition followed, expanded to 10 volumes, with new illustrations and now titled Brehms Thierleben. Mammals and birds were described in three volumes each, and fish, insects, reptiles and invertebrates in one volume each. The volumes contained 1945 illustrations. The 2nd edition was translated into many languages. The first translation into Czech was published from 1882 to 1990 by Otto's publishing house. The third edition was printed from 1890 to 1893 and was the first that appeared after Brehm's death. The differences from the 2nd edition were relatively few. This edition was translated into Czech and is still published by Otto. [honsi.org]

194 Iceland is an island and a republic in the North Atlantic that until 1918 was ruled by Denmark. The Danish king remained the head of state until 1944 when Iceland became a republic. The island was colonized by Norsemen in

the 9th and 10th centuries and was independent for 300 years before it came under Norwegian, later Danish, rule.

Reykjavik is the capital and largest city, and the population of the country was as of 2019 estimated at 360,000. In 1890 it had 71,000 inhabitants. Iceland is known for its volcanic activity and there have been several major eruptions in the last 50 years. The main source of income is fisheries.

Iceland is not a natural habitat for bats, but occasionally they arrive with ships. In this context One-Year Volunteer Marek's expression "bat-the-remote" is thus descriptive. [honsi.org]

195 Kilimanjaro is the highest peak in Africa (5,892 meters), located in Tanzania near the Kenyan border. In 1914 the mountain was situated on the territory of German East Africa.

Jaroslav Hašek also mentions the mountain in the story Záhady vesmíru (*Enigmas of the universe*) from 1922. [honsi.org]

196 Vilém Kún was a long-time friend of Jaroslav Hašek. As One-year Volunteer Marek states, he was an engineer but is better known as an editor, poet, and translator of French. The two met through Hašek's acquaintance with students from the technical high school at Karlovo square. He was originally from Moravia.

Kún was also a member of *The Party of Moderate Progress within the Bounds of the Law*. Interestingly, his home address in 1910 was in the same building as Bendlovka, a.k.a. Bendovka, coffee house.

One-year Volunteer Marek's story about the flea is no doubt inspired by a little joke that Hašek "planted" in *The Animal World* in 1911, albeit at a time when he did not work for the magazine. The false story was printed in good faith by Čech two years later but was exposed by Právo lidu soon after. Čas was one of several newspapers reporting their mishap. [honsi.org]

197 Olm is the only European vertebrate that lives its entire life in a cave. One of the most fascinating creatures in a world full of fascinating creatures, the olm, like its distant relative the axolotl, is a completely aquatic salamander with gills and tailfins. It is born, lives its long lifespan, and eventually dies in the water. The olm is endemic to the Dinaric Alps and can be found in the underground waters of the karst of central and southeastern Europe covering parts of Italy, Croatia, Slovenia, and Bosnia and Herzegovina, as well as introduced populations in France and Germany.

The olm's scientific name is Proteus anguinus. Proteus comes from the Greek god who was able to change his shape at will, and anguinus comes from "anguis," the Latin for "snake." The olm is also commonly known as the proteus, cave salamander, and white salamander, with the local population referring to the animal as a "human fish." [a-z-animals.com]

198 Postojna Cave is a cave-system in Slovenia, one of the country's main tourist attractions. [honsi.org]

199 Baltic Sea is an inland sea located in Northern Europe, the largest brackish water area on the globe. It borders Denmark, Sweden, Finland, Russia, Estonia, Latvia, Lithuania, Poland and Germany.

Jaroslav Hašek and his Russian wife Alexandra Lvova spent five days on the steamer Kypros in December 1920, sailing from Reval (now Tallinn) to Stettin (now Szczecin). This was on their return from Russia. The trip lasted from December 4th to December 8th. [honsi.org]

200 Čas (*Time*) was a newspaper that was founded in 1886 by Jan Erben and supported by a group of so-called realist politicians, among them Masaryk and Kramář. From 1901 it was published as a daily. In 1915 it was barred from publishing, a fate that hit many Czech newspapers during the war. [honsi.org]

201 Čech (*The Czech*) was a Catholic-oriented daily with strong ties to Strana katolického lidu (*The Catholic People's Party*). The newspaper was established in 1869 as a weekly but already from 1873 was published every working day. During the years 1897 to 1903 it was called Katolické listy (*The Catholic Sheets*). After World War I the circulation fell and in 1937 Čech closed down for good.

It was one of the few major Czech newspapers that seems to have never printed any of Jaroslav Hašek's stories. On the other hand the author of *The Good Soldier Švejk* wrote several satirical pieces directed against the newspaper. [honsi.org]

202 Pazourek no doubt refers to Karel Pazourek, an expert beekeeper and head teacher from Čestice in administrative district Hradec Králové. Various newspaper clips and adverts reveal that he was active in beekeeping associations and often traveled to give lectures and hold courses on the subject.

Little is known about the life of Pazourek, but his name appeared in connection with beekeeping as early as 1897. Otherwise, we know that he died in May 1913 at the age of 54, was a family man, and was well known among beekeepers.

Apart from giving lectures and courses, he also wrote for specialist magazines like Český včelař (*The Czech Beekeeper*) and, notably, *The Animal World.* During Hašek's time as editor of the magazine (February

1909 - October 1910), Pazourek contributed to almost every issue, and it must be assumed that the two met. Several times the journal printed pictures of him.

He wrote for *The Animal World* at least from 1904 and continued to do so until a few weeks before his death in 1913. The magazine honoured him with an obituary. [honsi.org]

203 Podkrkonoší is a region below the Krkonoše Mountains in the north-eastern part of Bohemia. The term is somewhat vague because the area isn't and has never been an administrative unit with defined borders. The main population centers are Lomnice nad Popelkou, Nová Paka, Hořice, Dvůr Králové nad Labem, and Jilemnice. [honsi.org]

204 Selský obzor (*Farming Horizon*) was published monthly from 1902 to 1911. It was founded by the farmers Ševčík and Josef Šamalík (from 1907 a deputy in Reichsrat, *Austrian parliament*) and was the mouthpiece of Katolický spolek českého rolnictví na Moravě (*The Catholic Society of Czech Farming in Moravia*) of which Šamalík was chairman. The first issue was published in February 1903 in Ostrov u Macochy (35 km north of Brno), where Šamalík lived. By 1907, Jos. M. Kadlčák had become magazine editor, and the administration had relocated to Brno. The last issue appeared in March 1911. [honsi.org]

205 Jos. M. Kadlčák was a teacher, editor, and conservative politician from Moravia who from 1907 served as Reichsrat deputy for the Catholic National Party. From 1907 (or earlier) until 1911, he was the editor of the monthly Selský obzor (*Farming Horizon*), an activity he undertook from Frýdlant nad Ostravicí, where he lived from 1886 to 1919. In Czechoslovakia, he continued his political career and at the time of his death in 1924, he was the Deputy Chairman of the Czechoslovak Senate.

It is an indisputable fact that Kadlčák edited Selský obzor at the time when Hašek edited Svět zvířat (1909 and 1910) and that he was indeed a clerical parliamentary deputy, as One-year Volunteer Marek says. That Country Life printed pictures of jays at the time is also a foregone conclusion, and Svět zvířat did as well. One example is a picture printed in no. 243 on 15 July 1909 (page 11).

Contrary to Marek's claim, *Farming Horizon* never printed any editorial or other articles about Hašek and his renaming of the jay to "walnutter". Nor, to our knowledge, is Svět zvířat mentioned in the newspaper. [honsi.org]

206 Country Life was a magazine founded by the businessman Edward Burgess Hudson (1854-1936). The first issue was published on 8 January 1897.

Originally, the name was Country Life Illustrated, and the editorial offices were located at 20 Tavistock Street, central London.

The magazine pioneered high-quality photos and glossy prints. It was an immediate success, and the income permitted Hudson to erect a new building on the same site, a house that still bears the name Hudson Building. From 1905 the magazine's editorial offices and print works were located here.

In 1909 and 1910, when Jaroslav Hašek no doubt browsed the magazine and occasionally cut and pasted from it, Country Life was published every Saturday. Each issue typically consisted of 110 to 130 pages, of which around 40 were property adverts. Animals were not the main focus of the magazine, but it dedicated a couple of pages to them every week. Horses, dogs and birds were the most prominent.

One-Year Volunteer Marek's incident with the nutcracker and the jay is evidently inspired by an article and a photo printed in Svět zvířat on July 15th 1909. The picture shows two young jays sitting on a branch but given the incorrect name žaludník (*acorner*) instead of sojka (*jay*). A description of the bird breed is found on page nine, and again the incorrect name is used.

According to Radko Pytlík, the editor of Selský obzor Jos. M. Kadlčák pointed out the error on a postcard to which Hašek responded impertinently. Kadlčák then complained in writing directly to Fuchs. Hašek, however, stood his ground and published a response from a "reader" who also used the term "žaludník". Through *The Good Soldier Švejk* and *One-Year Volunteer* Marek's story, Hašek thus transformed his translation mistake into a conscious mystification. [honsi.org]

207 The Czech for juniper is "jalovec", a masculine noun, while "jalovice", a feminine noun, is a heifer that has not had a calf. The two words have a form making it appear as if they were indeed referring to the same species of opposite grammatical gender, but their meanings aren't actually related. But One-Year Volunteer Marek uses them as if they differed only in gender. Hence his neologism of "heifer-juniperess".

208 Frýdlant nad Ostravicí is a town in the Beskydy mountains in Moravia, near the Polish and Slovak borders. This is where Jos. M. Kadlčák lived at the time when Jaroslav Hašek was editor at Svět zvířat (1909 and 1910). [honsi.org]

209 Místek is a former town in the Beskydy mountains in Moravia, near the borders with Poland and Slovakia. The town was in 1943 merged with

Frýdek and named Frýdek-Místek. Místek was situated on the border with Austrian Silesia.

It is quite possible that Jaroslav Hašek visited Místek because he once found himself detained in its twin-town Frýdek. This was because he didn't carry the necessary traveling documents. On August 6th 1903 the police in Frýdek sent a letter to their colleagues in Prague to inquire about the identity of the wanderer. [honsi.org]

210 Bayer was a Czech zoologist, ornithologist, and paleontologist, author of a number of scientific works. Among them was the popular science book Naši ptáci (*Our Birds*), published in 1886 and 1888. He also translated Brehm's "Tierleben" (*Animal Life*) (3rd volume) and wrote a number of entries for Ottův slovník naučný. Bayer was a highly respected scientist and by 1914 held the formal title of government advisor.

The book *Our Birds* was a leading reference work in ornithology. It is this book that One-year Volunteer Marek refers to when he quotes Jos. M. Kadlčák about the jay (sojka), a bird described on page 148. Indeed, the jay is mentioned on this page! Then, on page 150, the walnutter (ořešník) follows. Bayer used the Latin terms corvus glandarius, L. and corvus caryocatactes, L. On the other hand, the Latin terms that Marek used seem to be twisted variations of those used by Brehm and are universally recognized: Garrulus ganulus and Nucifraga caryocatactes. [honsi.org]

211 Mestek was a city character and household name in Prague, a man with an extremely diverse career who even caught the attention of some prominent writers. Among these were Jaroslav Hašek and Egon Erwin Kisch.

Ferdinand Mestek was born in 1858 in a house opposite the Emmaus monastery, son of a tailor from Mníšek and one of four siblings. From 1888, he is listed in the police records as, for instance, "gold worker" and "pub landlord", descriptions that do not cover his extremely varied activities. He had a number of professions (impresario, circus director, flea circus owner, pub landlord) but they were rarely executed with success.

One example is a short appointment at the workshop of the firm Eduard Lokesch & Son, where he was employed after claiming knowledge of gold. The hollowness of the claim was quickly exposed and the working relationship was terminated. [honsi.org]

212 Havlíčkova třída (*Havlíček's boulevard*) was the name of a long street (almost 2 km) in Vinohrady and Nusle, named after the writer and politician Karel Havlíček Borovský (1821-1856). In 1926, the street was given its current name: Bělehradská ulice (*Belgrade street*).

Although Mestek did indeed exhibit "mermaids", it has not been possible to verify that this activity took place in this particular street. Nor has the rest of Švejk's story been verified.

Jaroslav Hašek lived at no. 1097/81 for a period from July 29th 1912. His host was Josef Alois Adamíra (1877-1953), a chemist who at the time was employed at the laboratory of Zemědelská rada (*The Agricultural Council*). It should also be noted that he was a prominent occultist and, as such, may have served as an inspiration for Hašek's literary figure cook Jurajda. [honsi.org]

213 Táborská street is the former name of Legerova street, a long street in Nové město (*New Town*) which runs along the border of Vinohrady. [honsi.org]

214 Tunel (*The Tunnel*) was a café in Staré město (*Old Town*) that was located on the ground floor of the building U černého medvěda (*At the Black Bear*) behind the Týn church. It had two entrances, at Týn no. 6 and Štupartská no. 5.

In early 1914 Egon Erwin Kisch published the series Verbotene Lokale (*Forbidden Taverns*) in the newspaper Bohemia. It describes eleven establishments where soldiers from the Prague garrison were forbidden to enter. Three of these are mentioned in *The Good Soldier Švejk*: Apollo, U Kocanů and Tunel itself.

In the part of the series that Bohemia published on March 15th 1914, Kisch writes about Im Tunnel (*In the Tunnel*). He describes it as the worst of the worst, frequented by street prostitutes, thugs and other individuals from the lower echelons of society. The head waiter was the famous Jarda (Jaroslav), a huge bloke who enforced order at the premises using brute strength and a bullwhip! Kisch himself witnessed a serious brawl there that was resolved when the landlord and the two waiters intervened, armed with Jarda's strength and the bullwhip. Kisch does not reveal the identity of the landlord. [honsi.org]

215 Okrouhlice is a village by the river Sázava in Vysočina (*The Highlands*), 10 km from Lipnice. The author had already moved to Lipnice (August 25th 1921) when he wrote this part of the novel. Themes from the area start to appear as early as Book Two, Ch.2, perhaps even in Book One, Ch. 14.6.

According to the 1910 census, Okrouhlice had 356 inhabitants, all of whom reported using Czech as their everyday language. [honsi.org]

216 Německý Brod (*German Ford*), is the former name of Havlíčkův Brod, a town in Vysočina (*Highlands*), 15 km from Lipnice (where this part of the novel was written). The town was renamed in 1945.

Jaroslav Hašek visited Německý Brod from 1st to 3rd August 1922, where he was also present at a stage play based on *The Good Soldier Švejk*. The play was very well received, and Hašek was very pleased as he received the applause of the audience. [honsi.org]

217 Dante was a famous Italian poet of the Middle Ages. His "La divina commedia" is often considered the greatest literary work composed in the Italian language and a masterpiece of world literature. Dante is also recognized as the father of the Italian language. [honsi.org]

218 Malý čtenář (*The Young Reader*) was a magazine for children and young people that was published from 1882 to 1941. It first appeared in Poděbrady, but from 1887 the Prague-based publisher Vilímek took over. The magazine appeared fortnightly and contained illustrations, stories, and, as Švejk pointed out: poems. Several distinguished writers contributed to the magazine, among them Vrchlický and Růžena Jesenská, the latter before 1890. The publication had both educational and enlightening purposes and influenced entire generations of young Czechs. The magazine continued operating until 1941 when it was closed by the Nazi Protectorate authorities. [honsi.org]

219 Jan Štursa is regarded as one of the founders of modern Czech sculpture. He studied at k.k. Kunstakademie (*Academy of Art*) in Prague from 1899 to 1904 and was employed there from 1908. At the outbreak of war in 1914 he was called up and sent to the front with Infantry Regiment No. 81 (Jihlava). Due to a damaged hand he was deemed unfit for carrying arms, and served as an officer's servant and performed other auxiliary duties, among them assisting at funerals. The latter activity was later reflected in his art. In 1916 he was released from service and could resume his career, now as a professor at the art academy. Sculptor Štursa committed suicide in 1925, allegedly due to depression related to syphilis. [honsi.org]

220 Simply put, a secondary school with humanities and natural sciences curriculum, providing practical education for middle class people with realistic expectations. (Following is a sourced explanation.)

Gymnasium (and variations of the word; pl. gymnasia) is a term in various European languages for a secondary school that prepares students for higher education at a university. It is comparable to the US English term preparatory high school or the British term grammar school. Before the 20th century, the gymnasium system was a widespread feature of educational systems throughout many European countries.

The word γυμνάσιον (gumnásion), from Greek γυμνός (gumnós) 'naked' or 'nude', was first used in Ancient Greece, in the sense of a place for both physical and intellectual education of young men. The latter meaning of a place of intellectual education persisted in many European languages (including Albanian, Bulgarian, Czech, Dutch, Estonian, Greek, German, Hungarian, Macedonian, Polish, Russian, Scandinavian languages, Croatian, Serbian, Slovak, Slovenian and Ukrainian), whereas in other languages, like English (gymnasium, gym) and Spanish (gimnasio), the former meaning of a place for physical education was retained. [en.wikipedia.org]

"Reálné gymnázium", *from German "Realgymnasium", rendered here as Realistic Gymnasium, is a type of secondary school, representing a compromise between a "reálka"*[45] *and a (classical) gymnázium* [which included Latin and Greek in its curriculum], *without classical languages and with an emphasis on science subjects.* [cs.wikipedia.org] [cs.wiktionary.org]

221 My Aunt, Your Aunt *is one of the most famous gambling games [in the Czechlands], which experienced its greatest boom, of course, during the previous [communist] regime, when it was played in illegal gambling halls and secret rooms of pubs. However, people in our country had been playing it for several hundred years before that.*

My Aunt, Your Aunt *is played with classic single-headed mariáš cards. The game requires a playing board divided into 8 fields. These fields represent the playing cards themselves from 7 to ace. Players place bets of any value on the playing field, with the message "your aunt" and "my aunt" determining which fields will be winning for the banker (and from which he will possibly withdraw bets) and which for the player (and on which he will possibly pay out winnings).*

At the beginning of the game, the banker shuffles the cards and shows the last card in the deck to the other participants. Then he begins to lay out pairs of cards one at a time, one in the field up and one in the field down. The more cards that match the value on the playing field, the higher the player's winnings. The colors do not matter - it is enough for any ace to appear on the ace, etc. The banker lays out all cards except the last one on the 8 marked playing fields.

If a card of the same value lands on the field you bet on, the banker pays you your winnings. The more cards of the same value appear on the field, the more money you win. [casino-hra.cz]

222 Oskar Prochaska was an Austro-Hungarian diplomat who in the autumn of

1912 hit the headlines all over the world because of the so-called Prochaska Affair, a diplomatic twist between Austria-Hungary and Serbia that threatened to ignite a major war in Europe. [honsi.org]

223 Terezín is a town and former fortress in northern Bohemia, better known abroad as Theresienstadt. It was constructed in the 18th century as one of several border forts to protect Austria against the increasingly powerful Prussia. Gavrilo Princip, the killer of Archduke Franz Ferdinand, was imprisoned here until he died in 1918. Terezín is notoriously known from the time of the Nazi occupation (1939-45) when it was converted to a ghetto and transit camp for prisoners who were destined for the death camps.

Two translators of Švejk, Grete Reiner and Ruth Bondi, were interned in Terezín during World War II. Reiner was later murdered in Auschwitz (1944), whereas Bondi survived and lived in Israel, until she passed away on November 14th, 2017. [honsi.org]

224 "landgericht" (*District Court*) - did not exist in 1912. Courts thus named were once present in Austria but only until 1848. The similar-sounding Landesgericht (*Provincial Court*) existed, but this institution covered all of Bohemia and was located in Prague. It also appears odd that a military case was heard in a civilian court, particularly when considering that no such court was located in Terezín.

These contradictions are best explained by assuming that Švejk had k.k. Landwehrgericht (*I&R Land Defense Court*) in mind and simply got the terms mixed up. Such a court was indeed present in Terezín. Landwehrgericht in Terezín was one of 13 of its kind in Austria (in Hungary Honved had their own courts). There was also a Garnisonsgericht (*Garrison Court*). That Švejk actually was talking about a military court becomes clear in the subsequent lines where he directly uses the term "vojenský soud" (*military court*). [honsi.org]

225 Dvůr Králové nad Labem (*The Queen's Court on the Elbe*) is a town by the river Labe in eastern Bohemia, in the Hradec Králové region. The town is nowadays primarily known for its zoo.

The flood happened exactly on the date Švejk mentions, July 29th 1897. It had been raining persistently for 14 days, and when torrential rain occurred, the soaked soil could no longer absorb the water, and the river flooded the valley.[honsi.org]

Labe (Elbe in German) is a river that originates in the Czech Republic and flows through Germany on its way to the North Sea. The catchment area includes most of Bohemia and the eastern part of Germany. Several towns and cities along the river are mentioned in *The Good Soldier Švejk*: Dvůr Králové nad Labem, Jaroměř, Pardubice, Poděbrady, Nymburk, Podmokly and Hamburg. [honsi.org]

226 A decision of a Government dealing with a matter of great importance to a community or a whole country and having the force of fundamental law. The term originated in Roman law and was used on the continent of Europe until modern times. [infoplease.com]

227 Motol is a district in western Prague that became part of the capital in 1922. In 1910 it was a small village of 21 houses and 273 inhabitants. In the context of *The Good Soldier Švejk* however the term refers to Motolské cvičiště (*Motol exercise ground*). During World War I it was the scene of several executions, where the best known victim was reservist Kudrna from Infantry Regiment No.102, who was executed on May 7th, 1915. [honsi.org]

228 Kudrna was a soldier in Infantry Regiment No. 102 who was accused of mutiny in Benešov. He was executed by a firing squad at Motol on 7 May 1915 and left his wife and seven children behind. Shortly afterwards his widow committed suicide. The story has been dramatised and made into a film (1929), and in 1935 a book about him was published.

Kudrna was called up at the outbreak of war and sent to the front against Serbia with Infantry Regiment No. 102. At some stage he was wounded and after recuperating he was assigned to 10th March Battalion that was due for the front in the Carpathians.

When the news about the imminent departure reached the soldiers on May 3rd 1915, a drinking binge started and a conflict erupted (albeit unarmed) when two unpopular officers, Lieutenant Colonel Kukačka and Captain Chocenský, tried to control the situation. In the end Dragoons were dispatched to quell the threatening rebellion. Three soldiers, among them Kudrna, were considered the leaders of the alleged mutiny and for some reason the latter was singled out as the main culprit and sentenced to death by martial court. The other two were given prison sentences.

Kudrna was one of the best known victims of the persecution that the Austrian authorities carried out in Bohemia and Moravia after the outbreak of the war. He was also the first to be sentenced to death by the Military Court at Hradčany. The case was very quickly conducted and bore traces of a judicial murder. It also appeared to be designed to deter Czech soldiers from obstructing the war effort, an assumption underpinned by the fact that the replacement battalion of the Infantry Regiment No. 102 and also the Prague garrison were commanded out to witness the execution.

The main architect of the affair seems to have been General Schwerdtner (see Major General von Schwarzburg), who himself was present at the exercise ground in Motol during the execution. [honsi.org]

229 Editor Josef Kotek is not mentioned by name in *The Good Soldier Švejk* but the timing and circumstances around this part of the plot leave no doubt that Kotek was the man the soldier on the train had in mind. He was the only editor who had been executed at this time, and probably the only Czech editor who was executed during the entire war. He is no doubt one of the best-known victims of Austrian wartime persecution.

Josef Kotek hailed from a working-class family and was himself a trained metalworker. From 1901 to 1904 he worked at Škoda and otherwise also in Prague, Jičín, Náchod, Mladá Boleslav and Přerov. He engaged in trade union and political work, and was active in the consumer co-operative and in Česká strana národně sociální (*Czech National Social Party*). From August 1st 1913 he was the editor of the party's regional weekly Pokrok (*Progress*) in Prostějov in Moravia. After the outbreak of war, the paper was censored and Kotek decided to close it.

On December 6th 1914 Kotek gave a talk for co-op members in a tavern in the village of Smržice by Prostějov. The purpose was to explain to the local members why their branch had to be closed down, but the speech proved fatal. He was denounced, arrested and tried at a Military Court in Moravská Ostrava. According to some witnesses, his speech was strongly anti-Austrian and anti-German while Kotek himself claimed that he had uttered nothing against the state, and simply pointed out that the war harmed the co-op movement.

He was sentenced to death by a *I&R Land Defense* Martial Court on December 23rd 1914 and executed by a firing squad only two hours after the verdict. The sentence was announced in the new year in the newspapers. In order to deter, placards were posted across Moravia. The justification for the harsh verdict was that Kotek's utterances were hostile to the state and the unity of the empire, despite being sentenced according to a paragraph on public order.

In connection with the general amnesty of emperor Karl I. on July 2nd 1917, the case was reconsidered and Kotek was rehabilitated post-mortem. This news item even reached Jaroslav Hašek in faraway Kiev and he mocked Kotek's "amnesty" in a feuilleton that he published on New Year's Eve that year.

Already before the war ended, the Social Democrat daily Arbeiter-Zeitung described the execution of Kotek as judicial murder and pointed out that the legal article he was judged by carried a maximum sentence of 5 years and that a field court had no jurisdiction behind the lines. This was obviously also pointed out by the Czech press after the war.

In posterity, the memory of Kotek was honored in Czechoslovakia. He had streets named after him and memorial plaques have also been installed, for instance on the wall of the tavern where he gave his fatal speech. [honsi.org]

[230] Genesis 25:24-25 (King James Version):

And when her days to be delivered were fulfilled,
behold, there were twins in her womb.
And the first came out red, all over like an hairy
garment; and they called his name Esau. [biblegateway.com]

[231] Kurýr almost certainly refers to Pražský ilustrovaný kurýr (*Prague Illustrated Courier*), a pioneer boulevard daily that was published from 1891 to 1918. It was associated with Hlas národa (*Voice of the Nation*) with whom they shared administration and editorial offices. The owner of both newspapers was Edvard Jan Baštýř (1861-1937), lawyer, publisher and politician. After Národní politika (*National Politics*), Kurýr enjoyed the highest circulation of all Czech newspapers. [honsi.org]

[232] Dalmatia is a historical region on the eastern coast of the Adriatic Sea and is situated in present-day Croatia and Montenegro. Historically, it was part of the Republic of Venice but became Habsburg territory after the Napoleonic Wars. It belonged to Cisleithania until 1918. Important cities are Dubrovnik, Šibenik, Split and Zadar. The area was multilingual, with Serbo-Croat being by far the most widely spoken. Italian was also an official language, and military documents used Italian names such as Spalato (Split). The southernmost part is now part of Montenegro. [honsi.org]

[233] Drábovna presumably refers to a rock formation near Malá Skála (*Little Rock*) between Jablonec and Turnov. Today, it is not a populated place, nor was it inhabited before World War I. [honsi.org]

[234] Turnov is a town with approximately 15,000 inhabitants, founded in 1272. It is situated in the Liberec district in Bohemia on the river Jizera. It is best known for its gemstone and glass industry and is also a major transport hub. Tourism is also important as the town borders Český ráj (the *Czech Paradise*).

This area of Bohemia was rarely visited by Hašek, but on October 27th 1912 he made a brief but tumultuous appearance at an "evening of Czech humor", arranged by the local Sokol. [honsi.org] At Sokolovna (*Sokol Hall*) Hašek grabbed the headlines for all the wrong reasons. According to the Krakonoš newspaper his first stage act fell completely flat, the listeners didn't appreciate his craving for recognition. Still, worse was to come. In the second part, he told a story of a Serbian shepherd who became a colonel, making fun of the South Slavs who, at the time, were fighting the First Balkan War.

This didn't go down well with an audience who sympathized strongly with Serbia. The story caused upheaval in the crowd, and many left the hall in disgust. As he starts to tell another story, he is asked to stop, but he reacts by swearing at the audience. This caused a further uproar that stopped when Hašek stepped down from the stage and left the building. Only an intervention by the mayor calmed down the deeply offended audience. [honsi.org]

[235] Gargantua is one of the two main protagonists in a five-volume epic by Rabelais, titled La vie et dits de Gargantua et de Pantagruel (*The Lives and Deeds of Gargantua and Pantagruel*), written in the 16th century. Gargantua is the father and Pantagruel the son in these stories. It is a satirical work, replete with vulgarities and descriptions of troublesome digestion.

The novel was translated into Czech in the period from 1912 and 1930, so the inspiration for the sounds that Hašek attributes to Chief Field Chaplain Lacina is probably from the first volume. Several translations into English exist.

In chapter six of the first volume there is a description of how the newly born Pantagruel behaved. In this sequence the reader may recognize elements from Lacina's waking up without this necessarily being the passage that Hašek had in mind. [honsi.org]

[236] Rabelais was a French monk, humanist, scholar, doctor and, not least, author. He is best known for his five-volume satirical classic The Five Books about the Lives and Deeds of Gargantua and Pantagruel.

Jaroslav Hašek has often been compared to Rabelais, an author he had clearly read and been inspired by. [honsi.org]

[237] "Krucilaudon" *is a combination of* "kruci", *shortened form of* "krucifix", and Laudon. "Kruci" *is derived from Latin word* cruciatus = *torture. The combination of* cruci *with* fixus *means crucifixion.* Laudon *was an Austrian field marshal of German Baltic origin, and one of the most successful Austrian commanders of the 18th century. He fought in the Seven Years'*

War, the War of the Bavarian Succession and wars against Turkey. His troops captured Belgrade in 1789. Just as *himmellaudon* in Book One, *kruzilaudon is an instance of purely military cursing from the time of the great general Laudon, probably when Austria was at war with Prussia during the 18th century.* [svejkmuseum.cz]

238 Madeira is an island in the Atlantic that belongs to Portugal, but in *The Good Soldier Švejk* it is only indirectly referred to via a dish. Kidneys in Madeira sauce is a Russian dish, mostly used as a starter. The Russian name for it is Почки в мадере and a French variation is called Rognons de Veau. The Madeira sauce itself is of French origin and so named because Madeira wine is one of the ingredients. [honsi.org]

239 Skuteč is a small town in the Pardubice region of Czech Republic, with about 5,000 inhabitants. According to the 1910 census, Skuteč had 4,345 inhabitants, of whom 4,330 (99 per cent) reported using Czech as their everyday language. [honsi.org]

240 I&R Land Defense Infantry Regiment No. 64 was a unit that only existed in Lacina's imagination because k.k. Landwehr (*I&R Land Defense*) consisted of 37 regiments numbered 1 to 37.

Only Hašek would know which k.k. Landwehr regiment the *Chief Field Chaplain* really had in mind, but if he had his dubious meal in Budějovice, it would have been with the officers from the city's *I&R Land Defense Infantry Regiment No. 29* or *I&R Land Defense Infantry Regiment No. 6* from Cheb that replaced them on June 19th 1915).

If the meal was enjoyed in Kraków (where his *Cavalry Division No. 7* was garrisoned) he may have indulged in the company of officers from *I&R Land Defense Infantry Regiment No. 16.* [honsi.org]

241 Hodonín is a town in Moravia, best known as the birthplace of Professor Masaryk, who became the first President of Czechoslovakia in 1918. It is situated in the south-eastern corner of Moravia, on the border with Slovakia. [honsi.org]

242 Marína is the subject of a Slovak folk song that exists in a few variations (Švejk only sings the first verse). It was popular as a soldiers' song in the Legions and also among Czech and Slovak soldiers in the I&R Army.

In 1919 it was included in a song-booklet that the Czechoslovak military authorities published in Irkutsk. Except for two orthographic details the text of the first verse is the same as in *The Good Soldier Švejk*. In a pre-war version the first verse is different as there is no allusion to the priest. [honsi.org]

[243] Emmental is a valley in the Bern canton in Switzerland, named after the river Emme. It is best known for a hard cheese made from cow's milk.

Emmental was not a protected trademark, so the cheese in question probably came from Austria-Hungary. In an advert 30 decagrams are for sale, so durable that it can even be dispatched by *Field Post*.

Jaroslav Hašek introduced Emmental cheese already in his poem *On the Road to the Battlefield* from 1915. It was written down by Jan Vaněk in his diary and first published by Jan Morávek after the war. Here Hašek reveals that his march battalion was given Emmental cheese in Pest, unlike Švejk's, that was promised it here but had to wait. [honsi.org]

[244] Pohořelec (*Fireswept*), previously classed as an area, is now designated a street in the upper part of Hradčany. It has its name because it burnt down twice in medieval times. The current street stretches from the former Landwehr (*Land Defense*) barracks down to Loretánské náměstí (*Loreta square*). [honsi.org]

[245] Na krásné vyhlídce (*At the Beautiful View*), Vyhlídka (*The View*) for short, was a pub at Hradčany, near the *Strahov Monastery* and Pohořelec. [honsi.org]

[246] Przemyśl is a city in the south-west corner of current Poland. Under Austria-Hungary it was an important fortress and garrison city, and also the seat of the 10th Army Corps. Then as now it was connected with railways to Kraków and Lwów, the two biggest cities in Galicia. [honsi.org]

[247] Pest is the part of Budapest located on the eastern bank of the Danube. It is the administrative center of Hungary, newer and more densely populated than Buda on the western bank. Pest was in 1914, apart from Vienna, the most important center of power in the Dual Monarchy. It was an autonomous city until it was merged with Buda and Óbuda in 1873. [honsi.org]

[248] Vienna is the capital of Austria and one of the nine states in the federation. In March 2004, the city had a population of more than 1.6 million. The river Danube flows through the northern outskirts of the city.

The city was the capital of Austria-Hungary throughout the existence of the Dual Monarchy. The emperors of the House of Habsburg held court in the palaces of Hofburg and Schönbrunn, and the declaration of war on Serbia was issued from Vienna.

No station names are mentioned in *The Good Soldier Švejk*, but Josef Novotný's diary reveals that Ersatzbataillon IR. 91 passed the city in the late evening on June 1st 1915 on the way from Budějovice to Királyhida. They were provided a meal at Franz-Josefs Bahnhof and passed several stations after this. Only at 2 AM the next morning did they arrive in Bruck. [honsi.org]

249 Schönbrunner Menagerie was (and still is) a zoological garden on the grounds of Schönbrunn. It is now the main zoo in the city. Founded in 1752, it is the oldest existing of its kind in the world. [honsi.org]

250 Hofburg is not mentioned directly but there is no doubt that Švejk refers to Hofburg when he mentions the imperial castle. It is a castle, or rather a complex of palaces, in the centre of Vienna.

It was, until 1918, the principal imperial palace of the Habsburg dynasty. It was built in the 13th century and expanded several times afterwards. It also served as the imperial winter residence, as Schönbrunn was the summer residence.

Since 1946 it has been the official residence and workplace of the President of Austria. The large building complex also houses museums, chapels, the Spanish riding school, the National Library and other institutions. [honsi.org]

251 X. Bezirk (*10th District*) is one of Vienna's 21 urban districts, also known as Favoriten.

It is located south of the center and hosted the two railway stations Ostbahnhof and Südbahnhof, as well as the Heeresmuseum (*Army Museum*). The district administration was located at Keplerplatz 5.

The district is now the most populous in Vienna and around 10 per cent of its inhabitants live here. Keplerplatz is historically regarded as the center of the Favoriten. The two mentioned railway stations were demolished at the beginning of the 21st century and replaced by the modern Hauptbahnhof (*Main railway station*).

Before World War I, the Favoriten district had a strong Czech presence, as 23,847 reported Czech as their day-to-day language (Umgangssprache). The real number was probably much higher. [honsi.org]

252 War veterans were awarded trafika, a tobacco store concession, since the times of Emperor Josef II. Czechs use the word trafika nowadays not only for a tobacco and newspaper store, but also ironically in reference to political plums used to reward politicians by their parties for services rendered. [Translator's note]

253 The railway station in Vienna is impossible to identify from the plot in *The Good Soldier Švejk* alone because Vienna in 1914 had nine major railway

stations and numerous smaller ones. The large ones were Aspangbahnhof, Donaukai, Franz-Josephs-Bahnhof, Kahlenberg-Eisenbahn, Nordbahnhof, Nordwestbahnhof, Ostbahnhof, Südbahnof and Westbahnhof.

Most of these can be ruled out for technical and topological reasons, but it is likely that Švejk's transport stopped or passed at least two of the stations. Those that spring to mind are Franz-Josephs-Bahnhof and Ostbahnof. The former was connected to Budějovice and the latter eastwards to Királyhida and Hungary.

On June 1st 1915 *Replacement Battalion IR. 91* was transferred from Budějovice to Királyhida and it happened largely according to the description in *The Good Soldier Švejk.* The journey is in rough terms lined out by Josef Novotný from Lišov who was one of the soldiers on the transport.

In his diary he noted that they left the barracks at 5-6 in the morning, that there was no public announcement of the departure but that a sizable crowd turned up to bid farewell to their house regiment. On the way to the station in Budějovice IR. 91 were guarded by "foreign troops". None of the soldiers in IR. 91 were allowed to carry live ammunition and the regiment's band was not allowed to play.

The soldiers were transported in cattle carriages, 50 to 60 men per wagon, and it took a while before they departed. They travelled via České Velenice and Gmund onto Sigmundsherberg where they early in the afternoon were given a meal. They continued down towards the Danube and by Tulln they noticed fortifications along the railway line, a scene resembling the description in *The Good Soldier Švejk.*

The next stop was Franz-Josephs-Bahnhof and here a new meal was handed out, now at sunset. It was getting dark and the journey through Vienna took a long time and they passed several stations that Novotný didn't name. He fell asleep around midnight and at 2 in the morning they finally arrived at the station in Királyhida. Here they remained in the wagons for another few hours. [honsi.org]

254 Österreichische Gesellschaft vom Roten Kreuze (*The Austrian Red Cross Association*) was the official name of the Austrian Red Cross, the national branch of the International Red Cross. The *Association* originated from Patriotische Hilfsverein (*Patriotic Relief Association*) that was founded in 1859, but the Red Cross in Austria was constituted as late as 1880. Patrons were Emperor Franz Joseph I and Erzherzogin Marie Valerie, his daughter.

After the outbreak of war the Red Cross introduced aid centres at railway stations, amongst them Franz-Josefs-Bahnhof. The name of this aid arrangement was Bahnhoflabedienst, an Austrianism (roughly meaning support/care/rescue service at railway stations).

Franz-Josefs-Bahnhof is where Ersatzbataillon IR. 91 with Jaroslav Hašek stopped for mess in the evening of June 1st 1915, on the way from Budějovice to Királyhida. This suggests that this particular description of Švejk's break at a railway station in Vienna is authentic. [honsi.org]

255 Magistrat der Stadt Wien refers to the city administration of Vienna, headed by the Bürgermeister (*mayor*). The term "Magistrat" has been used since 1783 and still is. All statutory cities (15 in Austria, 27 in Czech Republic) are governed by a *magistrate*. [honsi.org]

256 Brucker Lager is a military camp and training ground in Bruckneudorf that was founded in 1867 and has been used continuously ever since. World War I saw the camp's most active period, and at any time up to 26,000 soldiers were garrisoned here. This number dwarfed the combined populations of Bruck and Királyhida. During World War I, the area also hosted a prisoner of war camp.

Jaroslav Hašek served in the camp throughout June 1915, which explains why it became the backdrop for parts of *The Good Soldier Švejk*. The camp's commander from 1913 to 1918 was Oberstleutnant Wladimir Rollé, a person who may have lent his name to Auditor Ruller. [honsi.org]

257 Bruck an der Leitha is a town by the river Leitha in Lower Austria. Only the river separates it from Bruckneudorf (until 1921 Királyhida) in Burgenland. The river was, at that time, an even more important administrative divide than now; it separated the two parts of the Dual Monarchy, Cisleithania and Transleithania.

The two towns are often confused, and for understandable reasons. It is and was a single conurbation, and both Bruck-Királyhida railway station and Brucker Lager were actually located in Királyhida. The latter was originally a mere suburb of Bruck, but the two places became separated when Ausgleich (*The Compromise*) resulted in a new state border between them.

According to newspaper reports, Ersatzbataillon IR. 91 was transferred to Bruck an der Leitha - Királyhida on June 1st 1915. The staff of the replacement battalion was located in Schloss Prugg, and the men were lodged in wooden barracks in Brucker Lager across the Leitha in Királyhida.

Jaroslav Hašek was one of the soldiers who was transferred, exactly as described in the novel. He was assigned to the 12th March Battalion, which consisted of four march companies. His company commander was Rudolf Lukas, and the March Battalion was commanded by Franz Wenzel. The March Battalion departed for the front on June 30th 1915, at 8:15 PM.

Hašek reportedly tried to avoid the departure and went missing for three days. During the month here, he was often drunk and was, from time to time, arrested and brought to the main guardhouse to sober up. [honsi.org]

258 k.k. Fleischkonservenfabrik *(R.I. Meat Canning Factory)* refers to k.u.k. Militärkonservenfabrik (*I&R Military Canning Factory*), a canning factory that operated from November 1896 in Királyhida. Thus it was not located in Bruck, as stated in *The Good Soldier Švejk*, and also belonged to the common Austro-Hungarian military (k.u.k) and not to the military of Cisleithania, as the abbreviation k.k. indicates.

Apart from meat it canned vegetables, soups and coffee. Emperor Franz Joseph I honored the factory with a visit already on June 1st 1897 in connection with an inspection of Brucker Lager (*The Bruck Camp*). He spent more than an hour there and even sampled the produce.

At the time the factory had 350 employees, but during World War I up to 3000 worked there, including prisoners of war. The running of the factory was outsourced to various enterprises and operation ceased with the end of the war. [honsi.org]

259 Leitha is a 180 km long river that flows through parts of Austria and Hungary. It empties into the Danube near Mosonmagyaróvár.

The otherwise insignificant river gave rise, in the times of Austria-Hungary, to the expressions Cisleithania and Transleithania, a fact that Hašek explains in *The Good Soldier Švejk*. Seen from Vienna, Cisleithania was the land on this side of the Leitha, while Transleithania was the land beyond it. In everyday speech, the terms were synonymous with the Austrian and Hungarian parts of the monarchy, respectively. [honsi.org]

260 Sopron is a city in Hungary near the Austrian border, regarded as the country's oldest city. It is located 5 km south-west of Neusiedler See (*Lake Neusiedl*).

In 1910 the population count was 33,932 and among these the Germans were just about the largest ethnic group. The city was (and is) connect by rail to, among others, Győr and Wiener Neustadt. Sopron was after the peace treaty of Trianon in 1920 to join Austria, but a referendum overturned the decision so it remained in Hungary. Today Sopron has more than 60,000 inhabitants. [honsi.org]

261 "Cisleithania" and "Transleithania" refer to the two distinct parts of the

Austro-Hungarian Empire following The Compromise of 1867, with Cisleithania representing the Austrian territories (mainly the western and northern regions) and Transleithania representing the Hungarian territories (located "beyond" the Leitha River), essentially creating a "dual monarchy" where both regions had separate governments while sharing a single monarch. [google.com]

262 Királyhida is the Hungarian name of the town Bruckneudorf in the Austrian state of Burgenland. Only Leitha separates it from Bruck an der Leitha in Lower Austria. The river was, before 1921, an even more important administrative divide; it separated the two parts of Austria-Hungary: Transleithania and Cisleithania. Bruckneudorf was founded around the railway station (1846) and grew considerably. In 1867, the authorities established the military training ground Brucker Lager here. After Ausgleich (*The Compromise*) in 1867, it was ruled from Hungary like the rest of Burgenland. The town was renamed Királyhida in 1898, in line with the general policy of Magyarization. [honsi.org]

263 Soproni utca (*street*) was, according to the narrative in *The Good Soldier Švejk*, some street in Királyhida. There is, however, no historical evidence that such a street existed, so one must assume that Hašek invented the name or had another street in mind.

Whether an ironmonger's shop actually existed in Királyhida is not known, but in Bruck there was at least one such establishment. [honsi.org]

264 *A sapper (from French* sapeur, *'stonecutter', also from Italian* zappa *'hoe', or* sapie, zapin*) was a siege engineer or troop craftsman. In the Swiss Army and the British Army, the term* 'Sappeur' *or* 'sapper' *is still used today.* [de.wikipedia.org]

Together with the sappers (siege engineers), miners for tunnel construction and pontooners, the pioneer troops developed into an independent branch of the military in the 19th century. [de.wikipedia.org]

265 Die Steirer (*The Styrians*) is a term that usually refers to people from Styria, but in this context it is obvious that the narrator has an army unit from this region in mind, most likely an engineering battalion (Sappeure or Pioniere). [honsi.org]

266 Na Bojišti (*At the Battlefield*) is a street in Prague 2, that in the mid-19th century was known as Windberg. It was surrounded by fields and gardens, only 3-4 houses can be seen. By 1875 maps show many additional buildings and a street now called Walstatt, a name that corresponds to the street of the current name (*At the Battlefield*). The building U kalicha (*At the Chalice*)

was among the last to be built. [honsi.org]

Since ancient times, the entire surrounding area has been called At the Battlefield, *after the bloody battle that was fought here in 1179 between the Přemys-line princes* Bedřich *and* Soběslav. [starapraha.cz]

267 Pausdorf is said to have been a village where the engineering soldiers went for wine. However, the only identified Pausdorf is in Bavaria, so this is probably a mix-up with Parndorf (Hu "Pándorfalu"), a town between Bruck an der Leitha and Neusiedler See. At the time, the town was predominantly Croatian and was not a typical wine village, so the hypothesis is not watertight.

On the other hand, Podersdorf is a wine village and is phonetically more similar to Pausdorf, but weighing against this hypothesis is the fact that it is much further from Királyhida than Parndorf. [honsi.org]

268 Neusiedler See (*Lake Neusiedl*) is a large and shallow lake that straddles Austria and Hungary's border. Jaroslav Hašek wrote several short stories from the area in 1905, one of which was called By Lake Neusiedl. At the time, the whole lake lay on Hungarian territory. [honsi.org]

269 "What? know ye not that your body is the temple of the Holy Ghost which is in you, which ye have of God, and ye are not your own?" - 1 Corinthians 6:19, King James Version [biblegateway.com]

270 The quiet pub by the river was very likely Gasthof zur Ungarische Krone (*Inn at the Hungarian Crown*) in Királyhida, a restaurant still operating as of 2023. Sappeur Vodička's description fits perfectly: the establishment is located by the Leitha among the gardens and provides a quiet atmosphere, a situation that probably wasn't much different in 1915.

The restaurant is one of the oldest in the entire area and the building itself dates back 300 years. It was originally a monastery that was destroyed during an Ottoman incursion. In 1726, it was rebuilt and functioned thereafter as a hostel, mail station and eventually a roadside inn. The municipality owned the property, but already before World War I it was leased to private landlords. During a round of lease auctions in 1920, it is revealed that the property had a restaurant with a garden and five guest rooms. [honsi.org]

271 Šaščín is according to Břetislav Hůla the pilgrimage site Šaštín in the Nitra district in Slovakia, but in an unconvincing manner he links it to a novel Šaščinská bestie (*The Beast of Šaščín*) by the Slovak author Jožo Nižnánsky. The catch is that this author never wrote any novel with such title, but rather one titled Čachtická pani (*The Lady of Čachtice*).

The main character of the novel was the Hungarian duchess *Elisabeth Báthory* (Báthori Erzsébet) (1560-1615), who is believed to have killed young women and then taken baths in their blood to become beautiful. Nižnánsky's novel was, however, published in 1932, which is ten years after Hašek wrote this part of *The Good Soldier Švejk*. Despite all the confusion, it is still obvious, that both Břetislav Hůla and Švejk had Čachtice in mind. That Hašek was aware of Báthory is beyond doubt, as he personally visited Čachtice. On September 1st 1901 he even dispatched a postcard from here, where the bloodthirsty lady is pictured on the card and he also mentioned her directly.

Jaroslav Šerák points to a study which reveals that Báthory didn't commit the misdeeds all on her own, that she had several women helping her. The most important of them was Anna Darvulia, who actually was from Šaštín. Despite being far less known than Báthory, she was every bit as cruel and it may well be, that Švejk knew about her and that Darvulia was his beast from Šaščín. [honsi.org]

272 Invalidovna is a former institution for war invalids and veterans in Karlín, built from 1731-1737. Its model was Les Invalides, a building for veterans inaugurated in Paris in 1679. The building was seriously damaged by the floods in August 2002. Until 2013 it was partially used by Vojenský ústřední archiv (*Central Military Archive*). During World War I it was used as a lazaret. [honsi.org]

273 Židovské pece (*Jewish Kilns*) is a park in the eastern part of Žižkov, towards Malešice. At Hašek's time, it was a rural area. The origin of the name is, according to some sources, that Jews hid there during pogroms around 1744, during the reign of Maria Theresa. [honsi.org]

274 Krejcar, from German Kreuzer (*crosser*), because of the double cross, "Kreuz" in German, on the face of the coin, [en.wikipedia.org] was *a small coin, valid in the monarchy. It was introduced in the Czech lands already during the reign of Ferdinand I in 1561. It was also valid during the First World War, when a parallel, crown currency had already been introduced.* [svejkmuseum.cz]

275 *Czech soldiers nicknamed their Land Defense comrades "iron flies".* [svejkmuseum.cz]

276 Neklanova ulice is a street in Vyšehrad that runs along the railway line in the Botič valley. [honsi.org]

277 Na Růžovém ostrově (*On the Rose Island*) was a large restaurant with a garden, owned by Václav Růžička, located in Záběhlice on an artificial

island called Růžový ostrov (*Rose Island*) in the Botič stream.

The restaurant was in business from at least 1880 and was in 1883 owned by a certain Almer. By 1886 Růžička had taken over and he probably managed it until he died on February 21st 1924. He was buried at the cemetery in Zaběhlice. After Růžička's death the restaurant was managed by his daughter Růžena Burgetová.

The Rose Island was a popular excursion destination, and arranged dances, meetings, and other gatherings. It was operating until 1928, but since then the building has been used for other purposes. [honsi.org]

278 Michle was, until 1922, a town on the outskirts of Prague, which in that year was incorporated into the capital. It is located southeast of the center, mostly in Prague 4. Neighboring districts are Nusle, Podolí and Záběhlice. [honsi.org]

279 "velitelství pluku" (*the Regimental Command*), i.e. Regimentskommando here refers to the command of Ersatzbataillon IR. 91 (*Replacement Battalion Infantry Regiment 91*) and not to the Regiment's Command that was in the field. [honsi.org] That is why I chose to render it as "the Regiment Headquarters", to indicate the distinction between the two. [Translator's note]

280 Vrchlický (real name Emil Bohuslav Frída) was a Czech poet and translator, a pupil of Victor Hugo. He translated a number of classics to Czech, among them: Goethe, Baudelaire, Hugo, Shakespeare, Byron, Shelley, Dante, Petőfi and Ibsen. He is regarded as one of the greatest Czech poets ever and was repeatedly nominated for the Nobel Price.

That Vrchlický ever used the term "in love up to the ears" or something similar, has not been verified. It is anyway a pretty common expression. Švejk's add-on, Kapitales Frau (*Capital lady*) likely did not come from Vrchlický, instead reflecting the broken German that Hašek assigned to his hero. Vrchlický, as the translator of Goethe, would not have made a fundamental error of making Frau a neuter gender. [honsi.org]

281 Pester Lloyd was a German-language daily that was published in Budapest from 1854 to 1945. It was issued in the morning and in the evening, and was the largest German-language newspaper in Hungary. The similarity with Prager Tagblatt is obvious: the Jewish connection, solid journalism, liberal-democratic tendency and a long list of distinguished contributors.

The editorial offices of the paper were located centrally in Pest, close to the bank of the Danube. Editor in chief in 1915 was Josef Vészi, responsible editor Dr. Siegmund Schiller (*Schiller Zsigmond* in Hungarian spelling). [honsi.org]

[282] Debrecen is the second largest city in Hungary, situated in the eastern part of the country, near the border with Romania. The number of inhabitants as of 2022 was around 200,000.

Debrecen (at the time written Debreczen) was an important garrison city for both k.u.k. Heer (*I&R Army*) and Honved (Hungarian *Land Defense*). In 1915, the replacement battalion of *Infantry Regiment No. 75* was transferred here, so the city did have a Czech presence. It is not known where *Infantry Regiment No. 39*, the city's Hausregiment, was transferred to.

The description of the unnamed Czech regiment N and its standard indicates that deputy Barabás has *Infantry Regiment No. 28* in mind. This regiment actually had its standard taken away in April 1915. Their replacement battalion, however, was garrisoned in Szeged and not in Debrecen. [honsi.org]

[283] "Pest Assembly" refers to the Hungarian national assembly (Magyar Országgyűlés) that was (and is) located in Pest. Unlike its Austrian counterpart, the Reichsrat, it functioned throughout the war. One of the deputies was the mentioned Barabás.

The Hungarian national assembly has a history going back to medieval times and convened in various cities throughout the centuries. It was not until 1848 that it was located in Pest, and only after Ausgleich (*The Compromise*) did it convene on a regular basis. Voting rights were reserved for a privileged few. Even in the years up to 1914, less than 10 per cent of the population had the right to vote, and minorities like Slovaks and Romanians were grossly underrepresented.

The parliament consisted of an upper and a lower chamber, similar to, for example, the Austrian Reichsrat or the British Parliament. The last pre-war election to the parliament took place in June 1910. Hungary was divided into 413 constituencies, each electing one deputy. [honsi.org]

[284] "the Military Headquarters" in this context seemingly refers to Armeeoberkommando (*Army High Command*), the highest military authority during the war. From the outbreak of war, the formal head was Archduke Friedrich, but the war effort was, for most practical purposes, directed by the General Staff, headed by Feldmarschall Conrad. At the time of the plot in *The Good Soldier Švejk*, Armeeoberkommando was located in Teschen (now Cieszyn), in the palace that was incidentally owned by Friedrich himself.

In *The Good Soldier Švejk*, the terms "Vrchní velitelství" and "vojenské velitelství" both probably refer to *Army High Command*, although commands at subordinate levels cannot be ruled out. [honsi.org]

285 Saint Stephen I is the patron saint of Hungary and regarded as the founder of the country. Until the break-up of Austria-Hungary, the Hungarian part of the empire was officially called The Lands of the Crown of Saint Stephen. [honsi.org]

286 Béla Barabás was a lawyer, author and politician, member of the lower chamber of the Hungarian Parliament from 1892 to 1910 and again from 1911 to 1917. His role as a newspaper editor was, however, limited to publications in his home area around Arad (now Oradea). He remained politically active in Romania after the war.

There is no evidence that he wrote chauvinistic articles in Pester Lloyd or Pesti Hírlap in the line of the one quoted in *The Good Soldier Švejk*. That said, both newspapers would surely have reported on his anti-Austrian outbursts in the Hungarian Parliament.

One possible influence is a budget debate in parliament on May 5th 1915, where Barabás praised the sacrifice and effort of the Hungarian nation, stating that the center of gravity of the monarchy was now in Hungary. He openly accused Austria of not fulfilling its duty regarding military efforts, claiming that many Austrian personnel fit for military service had not yet been called up. He also quoted rumors about the trustworthiness of "certain Austrian nations" (meaning Czechs). Furthermore, he emphasized the patriotism and willingness to sacrifice among the Hungarian troops, as well as the patriotism of the Hungarian parliament.

Then he asked for the same attitude among the Austrian troops. The debate was covered by most newspapers and it is very likely that Jaroslav Hašek who at the time had reported sick in Budějovice knew about the controversy and that he had noted the attitudes of Barabás. [honsi.org]

287 Pesti Hírlap was a daily newspaper that was published in Budapest from 1878 to 1944. Newspapers of the same name also existed in the periods 1841-1849, 1866-1870, 1990-1994, and 2019-current (2023).

The editorial offices of the paper were located centrally in Pest, near the Nyugati railway station. The newspaper was until the turn of the century classified as moderately conservative/liberal. From 1902 dr. Imre Légrády (1868-1932) became editor-in-chief and under his auspices, the newspaper took an increasingly nationalist stance. During World War I Légrády was still the editor and the circulation reached 500,000, making it the second largest daily in Hungary. Pesti Hírlap also owned a publishing house. [honsi.org]

[288] Soproni Napló (*Sopron Daily*), Sopronmegye (*Sopron District)* [label under the nameplate]) was a newspaper that was published in Sopron from 1906 to 1919. In the beginning it appeared twice a week, and from 1908 every day except for Monday. It characterized itself as a political newspaper, but what direction it represented is not clear. The newspaper was printed in large format and in 1915 it regularly contained four pages.

The editorial offices of the paper were located near the center of the city, at Deák tér. The first editor-in-chief was László Rábel who was succeeded by Odo Röttig. Who held his post in 1915 is however not known. The newspaper was printed and published by Gustav Röttig & Sohn in Sopron. [honsi.org]

[289] "papageiregiment" (*parrot regiment*) - A nickname given to the 91st Regiment due to the "parrot" green color of the shoulder boards its soldiers wore. [Hašek, Jaroslav. Osudy dobrého vojáka Švejka za světové války. Endnote to p.337. Edited by Jaroslava Myslivečková. Praha: Odeon, 1968.]

[290] Pesti Napló was a daily newspaper that was published in Budapest from 1850 to 1939.

The editorial offices of the paper were, until 1910, located on Andrassy *street* in Pest, close to the State Opera. That year they moved to Podmaniczky *street* by Nyugati station. From August 11th 1914 their address was the grand avenue Váci körut, where their competitor Pesti Hírlap was also located. [honsi.org]

[291] Savanyú was, according to the text of *The Good Soldier Švejk*, a member of parliament representing the Királyhida district. This MP is surely fictional, as Királyhida was not a district, whether political, juridical or electoral. Nor was there any Savanyú in the entire Hungarian Diet. [honsi.org]

It is, however, necessary to note that Hašek used the name Savanyú, with small variations, several times. He uses it once more in the novel, in a Czechified form, in Švejk's explanation of how important it is to read books starting with he first volume first: "Once I bought a blood-and-thunder novel about Róža Šavaňů from the Bakony Forest." Švejk most likely had in mind the famous bandit named József Savanyó, an outlaw from Bakony, who became notorious under the name Savany* or Jóska Savanyó. [svejkmuseum.cz]

[292] The weekly in Királyhida (A királyhidai hetilap) is no doubt an invented publication as no newspapers were published in Királyhida at the time in

question. Apart from the military camp and the training ground, Királyhida was, according to the census of 1910, a settlement of around 1,000 inhabitants, hardly a market for any regular weekly. Moreover, only around 60 per cent declared Hungarian as their native language.

Even in the much larger Austrian twin town of Bruck an der Leitha, no such publication existed. News from the area was covered by the weekly Der neue Bezirksbote für den politischen Bezirk Bruck a.d. Leitha (*The New District Courier for the Political District of Bruck on the Leitha*). It was published in Schwechat on Sundays. [honsi.org]

293 Pressburg (Pozsony in Hungarian) was in 1915 the capital of Upper Hungary, and has since 1919 been known as Bratislava, the capital of Slovakia. At the time more than 80% of the population reported Hungarian or German as their everyday language.

Pressburg was the capital of Hungary from 1541 until 1784, and the Hungarian parliament held its sittings here until 1848. The city is located by the Danube just a few miles from Bruck.

The city is featured in the play *From Karlín to Bratislava in 365 days*, co-written by Jaroslav Hašek, Emil Artur Longen and Egon Erwin Kisch. [honsi.org]

294 Komárom was until 1920 a Hungarian town on both sides of the Danube, between Pressburg (Bratislava) and Budapest, now split between Hungary and Slovakia's Komárno. [honsi.org]

295 Jaroslav Panuška was a Czech painter and a friend of Jaroslav Hašek. It was he who persuaded Hašek to go with him to Lipnice on August 25th 1921 and here Hašek remained, writing most of the unfinished novel *The Good Soldier Švejk* (probably from the second chapter of Book Two), until he passed away less than 17 months later.

Zdeněk Matěj Kuděj, Emil Artur Longen and Josef Lada also belonged to their common circle of friends. Well known is a non-flattering portrait that Panuška made of Hašek towards the end of the author's life and also a drawing of the dead Hašek in his bed.

When and how Panuška and Hašek became friends is not clear, but it may have been through Kuděj who met Panuška around 1920. Whether or not Panuška employed a servant and if he was actually named Matěj cannot be established. [honsi.org]

296 "our second marchbattalion" no doubt refers to the 2nd March Battalion of Infantry Regiment No. 91. It arrived at the front in Serbia on September 24th 1914 and was deployed directly on the bridgehead at the Parašnica

peninsula, by the confluence of Drina and Sava.

Colonel Schröder certainly uses his imagination when he relates to Senior Lieutenant Lukáš about his exploits by Belgrade. The 2nd March Battalion of IR. 91 never operated by the city, nor did Infantry Regiment No. 4 and Infantry Regiment No. 75, which he mentions in the same story. The only moment when Infantry Regiment No. 91 fought anywhere near Belgrade was during the chaotic retreat from Serbia in December 1914, but this happened after the 2nd March Battalion had been dissolved. During the retreat north from Kolubara to Belgrade, the Regiment fought side by side with the Hungarian 4th Landsturm (Népfelkelés), but there is no report of any incident like the one Schröder mentions. Nor is it known whether any Bosnian units ever fought alongside IR. 91 in Serbia. [honsi.org]

297 Die Deutschmeister (officially Infanterieregiment Hoch-und Deutschmeister Nr. 4) was one of the 102 Austro-Hungarian infantry regiments. According to official military publications, it was formed in 1696 and was thus one of the oldest regiments in the entire k.u.k. Heer. It was one of the better known regiments and was Vienna's Hausregiment from 1781 onwards.

Hausregiment, i.e. *House regiment* (or *Home regiment*) is a term for a regiment that recruited from a specific area. Because e.g. Infantry Regiment No. 91 recruited from the district of Budějovice, it was called the city's and region's house regiment. That did however not mean that the whole regiment resided in the home garrison. Battalions and even staff were frequently moved between locations. Only the reserve battalion and the district command were permanently located but usually at least one of the four battalions was present at any time. Usually the same person was the commander of both the recruitment district and the reserve battalion.

Due to its long history, the regiment took part in nearly every war the Habsburg empire was involved in: the War of Austrian Succession, the Napoleonic wars and the campaigns in northern Italy during the mid-19th century. The regiment's memorial day was 18 June 1757, commemorating the battle of Kolín. Through the years the regiment was stationed in numerous garrisons and it was only from 1896 that it was permanently located in Vienna. [honsi.org]

298 "the brigade" is the 17. Infanteriebrigade, the unit that the three battalions of Infantry Regiment No. 91 reported to throughout most of the war. The other infantry regiment in the Brigade was Infantry Regiment No. 102. The brigade reported to 9. Infanteriedivision, a unit that also contained 18. Infanteriebrigade. The Staff was, in 1914, garrisoned in Prague, and after

the outbreak of war, obviously in the field.

The Brigade was, in August 1914, deployed in the area west of the mouth of the Drina, in preparation for an attack on Serbia. It took part in all three failed invasions and in mid-December they retreated to home soil in a chaotic withdrawal. After a period of recuperation, they were, in February 1915, transferred to the Carpathians, and from May they continued pursuing the Russians eastwards, reaching Dubno in early September. In November they were moved to the Italian front where they remained until September 1918, when the division was sent to Serbia to strengthen the now collapsing Macedonian front.

Parts of Oberst Schröder's account concerning the brigade deviate from historical facts. That 17. Infanteriebrigade operated in Serbia in 1914 is true, but that the brigade was led by a general who was even captured together with the division's commander is not true, as none of the officers were taken prisoner. Schröder also mentions a river and he probably has Kolubara in mind. It was the scene of fierce fighting during the second half of November. He could also be thinking of Sava, a river across which the remains of 9. Infanteriedivision were evacuated on December 14th 1915. [honsi.org]

299 "the Division", in this context 9. Infanteriedivision (*9th Infantry Division*) refers to the division that Infantry Regiment No. 91 reported to during the invasion of Serbia in 1914. The unit in question was therefore 9. Infanteriedivision and three battalions of IR91 reported to it throughout the war. Division Staff was, in 1914, garrisoned in Prague, and after the outbreak of war, obviously in the field. [honsi.org]

300 Eger is a town in northern Hungary, best known for its red wine and its well-preserved historical center. At the time of writing (2023) it has around 54,000 inhabitants and is the center of Heves vármegye (*district*). During the times of the Dual Monarchy it was a garrison town, so it is conceivable that military telemetry courses were held here. [honsi.org]

301 The Czech "účetní šikovatel" corresponds to the Austro-Hungarian **Rechnungs-Feldwebel** ("*accounting* Feldwebel"), literally *accounting field usher*. The core rank, "Feldwebel" (Czech *šikovatel*), derives from *Feld* ("field, battlefield") + *Weibel* ("usher, orderly," from Old High German *weibôn*, "to go back and forth"), originally designating the company NCO who transmitted the captain's orders and maintained order in the ranks.

Although the official designation from 1882 was Rechnungs-Unteroffizier I. Klasse ("*accounting non-commissioned officer, first class*"), Czech soldiers in WWI continued to use *účetní šikovatel* as their everyday term, and Hašek follows that usage in the novel. Vaněk himself even identifies in German as Rechnungsfeldwebel.

In this edition the title is rendered as **Accounting Master Sergeant**, a modern U.S. enlisted grade (E-7) chosen to signal Vaněk's standing to contemporary readers. In responsibility, the *Rechnungs-Feldwebel* was equivalent to a U.S. Army **Sergeant First Class**, Air Force **Master Sergeant**, Marine Corps **Gunnery Sergeant**, or Navy **Chief Petty Officer**. The last of these offers perhaps the clearest analogy: the Chief is the "heart and soul of the Navy," whose insignia is the fouled anchor — an anchor entangled in chain, symbolizing the trials and tribulations of leadership. Similarly, the *účetní šikovatel* bore the burdens of company-level order, finance, and administration, entangled in difficulties but indispensable. [Translator's note]

[302] The real-life inspiration for Vaněk is no doubt Jan Vaněk. Like his literary counterpart, he was a pharmacist rom Kralupy and served as a staff sergeant in Infantry Regiment No. 91, in the same Company as Jaroslav Hašek. Among the "models" for characters in *The Good Soldier Švejk*, Vaněk is probably the person who shows the most similarities with his literary counterpart. The most striking difference is that Hašek assigned the literary Vaněk a trait that the "model" did not have: addiction to alcohol. Nor did he serve near Dukla, as units from IR91 never operated at this section of the front. [honsi.org]

[303] Nemrava and the conversation in Királyhida has a factual background, and what Švejk says is authentic. On 1 November 1904, the recruit Vilém Nemrava from I&R Land Defense Infantry Regiment No. 13 in Olomouc refused to swear an oath to the flag and was sentenced to a 5-month prison term. Back with his regiment after his release, he again refused to obey orders. According to his conviction, he refused to carry a gun. In his own words, he was inspired by Tolstoy. Nemrava was a member of the religious pacifist Nazarene sect. For this repeated act of insubordination, he was given two more years, which he served in Terezín under harsh conditions. The case was widely reported all over Austria-Hungary and even reached Reichsrat. [honsi.org]

[304] Blázinec ve Slupech (*Nuthouse in Slupy*) refers to an asylum that from 1856 existed in the street Na Slupi in Nové město (*New Town*). It was a branch of Kateřinky and was located in the same area.

The still existing building belonged to Kostel Zvěstování Panny Marie (*The*

Church of Annunciation of Virgin Mary). The street name V slupech, as quoted in *The Good Soldier Švejk*, was in official use until 1869 when it was replaced with Na Slupi. [honsi.org]

305 Bohnice is a suburb of Prague, where in 1906 mental hospital was built, one of the most modern in Austria-Hungary. It operated as a branch of Kateřinky. [honsi.org]

306 If you've read the Editorial Notes in Book One, welcome back. If you've heard of 3-D chess, welcome to 3-D translating. I hope that bolding the various forms of the word 'louse' kept your focus on the thematic word of the ditty, while the juxtaposed, italicized English translation following the slash saved you disruptive trips to these End Notes. Alas, I had to pull you here now, as Hašek inserted into this play on Czech morphology (structure and formation of words), translated into English, the third dimension: the difference between the Czech and German phonetics (system of speech sounds):

veš/*louse* - feminine noun

vši/*lice* – plural form

všivák/*lice infested person/scoundrel* – masculine noun

In the absence of a term for the male louse in the Czech language, Švejk offers a way out by suggesting to the teacher he should convince the Judge Advocate, that **všivák** is the male of a louse and that's what the ditty is about.

Although "Judge Advocate can't understand Czech well", his claim, that "a male of a **veš**/louse is called **vešák**", actually conforms to a pattern of the Czech morphology, whereby many male animate nouns are formed by adding the ending –**ák** to the root of the word. It is hilarious for the readers of the original text only because there is no such word in Czech.

Unlike in Czech (or English), Germans don't pronounce the 'v' as 'vee', but as 'f', the 'ef' sound. When the teacher reports the Judge Advocate's response in German, he replicates the phonetics of that language. Thus **všivák** changes to **fšivák**, **veš** becomes **feš**, and the neologism for male louse, **vešák**, (akin to věšák/*hanger*) turns into **fešák**/*dandy*. [Translator's note]

307 *"We know our Pappenheimers" means, that we know our people, we know what they are up to, what they intend, that they will not surprise us with anything positive, just like in the past. The Pappenheimers were members of the Austrian regiment named after their commander, Count Gottfried Pappenheim, during the Thirty Years' War.*

They fought on the side of Albrecht von Wallenstein against the Swedish troops. Among other things, they significantly contributed, allegedly through their personal commitment in fighting on the side of the emperor, to the outcome of the Battle of White Mountain.

Wallenstein allegedly said these words to a delegation of soldiers from the Pappenheim Regiment when they came to ask him during the Thirty Years' War, whether it was true, that Wallenstein was planning to betray the Emperor and go over to the Swedish side. [svejkmuseum.cz]

In Schiller's tragedy The Death of Wallenstein, Albrecht of Wallenstein utters the sentence: "Daran erkenn' ich meine Pappenheimer," *which translates to Czech as: "Thus I recognize my Pappenheimers in you," by which Wallenstein tried to flatter Pappenheim's soldiers before his betrayal.*

In Czech and other languages, however, the modified phrase gradually acquired a negative connotation. The expression "I know my Pappenheimers" expresses the speaker's conviction that "his people" will not surprise him with anything positive or disappoint him, as they had done before. [cs.wikipedia.org]

308 Janeček (real name Jan Serinek) was a criminal born near Plzeň (*Pilsen*), who first hit the headlines in 1869, when he and three family members were sentenced to long prison terms for robbery and murder. On September 9th, 1871 tens of thousands were gathered at the execution ground and witnessed the execution of Jan Serinek, the last public execution in Bohemia during the time of Austria-Hungary. [honsi.org]

309 Jericho is a historic town in Palestine, commonly regarded as the oldest city in the world. It is also at the lowest altitude of any city, 250 meters below sea level. Rose of Jericho is a name that is associated with two plant species that predominantly grow in dry parts of the world. They are also called resurrection plants as they can survive long periods of drought and spring to life when rain arrives.

Anastatica hierochuntica grows in the Middle East and North Africa and is also known as the "true rose of Jericho". Selaginella lepidophylla is native to North America and is also known as "the false rose of Jericho". In the context of *The Good Soldier Švejk*, one must, however, assume that Švejk has the former in mind.

It is assumed that the connection with Jericho is the word "resurrection" because the city was repeatedly destroyed, but rose from the ashes every time. [honsi.org]

310 This figure is probably inspired by a real person, as Hašek knew painter

Panuška well in 1921 and 1922. Still, no person has been identified who fits the description. It cannot even be ruled out (although the hypothesis is speculative) that Hašek demoted their mutual friend Zdeněk Matěj Kuděj to the role of Panuška's servant. [honsi.org]

311 Moravská Ostrava (*Moravian Ostrava*) was the Moravian part of current Ostrava, an important industrial and mining city that is located both in Moravia and Silesia. Modern Ostrava was created in 1924 by the merging of 7 municipalities, the largest of which was Moravská Ostrava itself.

There is no indication that Jaroslav Hašek ever visited Ostrava and the city is only mentioned once more in his entire literary output. [honsi.org]

312 Pavla Moudrá (baptized Paulina Carolina) was a Czech writer and translator of works by authors such as Victor Hugo, Mark Twain, Rudyard Kipling, H.G. Wells, Thomas Carlyle, among others. She was also an early peace activist, animal rights campaigner and feminist, and briefly edited the journal Lada.

Pavla Moudrá was active in the struggle against alcohol and lectured for the Czechoslovak Abstinents Association. Jaroslav Hašek mentions here in a satirical story about the Salvation Army from 1921. [honsi.org]

313 10. Kompanie was one of the 16 field companies of Infantry Regiment No. 91 and reported to III. Feldbataillon. They did indeed operate near Šabac during the campaign in Serbia, namely in November 1914 when the Regiment moved towards the river Kolubara. On November 8th they actually marched through the city itself.

During the summer of 1915 Jaroslav Hašek was in close contact with the Company as they belonged to the same Battalion as his own 11. Kompanie. Commander of the 10. Kompanie at the time was Johann Hutzler, a reserve lieutenant who Hašek seems to have partly used as inspiration for the foolish Leutnant Dub. [honsi.org]

314 This is a czechized version of the German term Tschutsch: *Tschusch (feminine Tschuschin, in Upper Austria and Salzburg Tschutsch) is a colloquial and derogatory term in Austrian German for a member of a southeastern European or oriental people. Sometimes the term is also used for other ethnic groups.*

There are several theories about the origin of the word:

According to the dictionary of Bavarian dialects in Austria, the term is derived from čuješ (pronounced: 'tschujesch'; Bosnian/Croatian/Serbian present tense, 2nd person singular of the verb čuti (to hear): "hear" or Viennese "heast", i.e. "Listen up!). It was used from around 1860 to 1880, when South Slavic workers increasingly called out this word to each other during construction work on the southern railway line.

Another theory, which comes from Herbert Michner, states that the word derives from the Serbo-Croatian interjection ćuš (pronounced: 'tjusch'), which was used to drive pack animals. This exclamation then became the name for the pack drivers. During the occupation of Bosnia and Herzegovina by Austria-Hungary in 1878, this name was then used for the new ethnic group.

The Viennese economic historian and Slavist Wolfgang Rohrbach locates the origin of the word in the area around the Habsburg military border (Krajina). The Slovenian swear word čúš corresponds to the German "Tschusch" and is derived from the Turkish word çavuş (non-commissioned officer, German "Tschausch"). "Tschauschen" were originally heralds or court officials of the Sultan. The word was widespread in the South Slavic territories conquered by the Ottomans and has taken on the meaning "wedding bitters" in folklore. In German East Africa, colored non-commissioned officers of the protection and police forces were called "Tschauschen". [de.wikipedia.org]

[315] "od 9. kumpačky" (*of the 9th march gang*), i.e. 9. Kompanie (*9th Company*, just as the10th) was one of the 16 field companies of Infantry Regiment No. 91 and reported to III. Feldbataillon. They did indeed operate near Šabac during the campaign in Serbia, namely in November 1914 when the regiment moved towards the river Kolubara. On November 8th they marched through the city itself. [honsi.org]

[316] Hamburg is the second-largest city in Germany and the seventh-largest city in the European Union. The city is home to approximately 1.8 million people and has one of the largest ports in Europe. It is an important center for trade and commerce. [honsi.org]

[317] Vyšehrad railway bridge refers to a bridge over the Vltava by Vyšehrad. The bridge was opened in 1872, reconstructed in 1901, and connects Nusle with Smíchov. It was still in use as of 2023 and was recently renovated. The bridge does not have an official name, but maps have over the years used various terms for it. [honsi.org]

[318] Kartouzy or Věznice Valdice (*Valdice prison*) is a prison and former monastery in Valdice by Jičín. In 1627 it was established Carthusian monastery by the famous military leader Valdštejn (Wallenstein), but converted into a male prison in the mid-19th century. The murderers Babinský and Janeček are among the most notorious criminals that served

time there.

Kartouzy was still in use in 2016 as a high security prison and some of the inmates are among the most dangerous in the country, several of them serving life sentences. The population of inmates is around 1,000. [honsi.org]

319 U Fleků is arguably the most famous tavern in Prague and is considered the world's oldest brew-pub, reportedly founded in 1499. It is known for its dark 13 degree beer and is a tourist attraction. Landlord in 1910 was Ludvík Hotovec. This was a pub that Jaroslav Hašek frequented and he mentions it in at least one of his stories. Karel Vika and Franta Sauer both published details of Hašek's visits to the pub. [honsi.org]

320 One reserve lieutenant Petr Heral actually served in Infantry Regiment No. 91 together with Jaroslav Hašek. He was born in 1886 with the right of domicile in Boršov nad Vltavou and was promoted to Lieutenant on March 1st 1915. He was taken prisoner by the Russians on the same day as the author of *The Good Soldier Švejk*, at Khorupan on September 24th 1915. Hašek may therefore have known Heral not only from IR. 91 but also from the three-week prisoner transport to Darnytsa, and perhaps even further. The loss lists also reveal that he held a degree in law and that he served in the 6th Company (part of the 2nd Battalion) at the time of his capture.

Whether or not he inspired the author to create the teacher Švejk tells about cannot be verified, but it remains a possibility. If it could be established that Heral actually was a teacher, it would be almost certain. [honsi.org]

321 Maria Theresa was the ruling Archduchess of Austria, Holy Roman Empress, Queen of Hungary, Queen of Bohemia, and the head of state of several other areas: Croatia, Galicia, Mantua, etc.

Her father, Charles VI, Holy Roman Emperor, prepared the way for her accession to the throne by the Pragmatic Sanction of 1713, also mentioned in the novel. This law gave women hereditary rights to the throne.

Maria Theresa introduced progressive reforms in the penal code and in education, and was also known for her anti-clerical attitudes. The fortress Terezín is named after her, as is Theresianische Militärakademie (*Theresian Military Academy*). During her reign, the empire was modernized and strengthened. [honsi.org]

322 Danube is the second largest river in Europe and connects Germany, Austria, Slovakia, Hungary, Croatia, Serbia, Bulgaria, Romania, Moldova and Ukraine.

In 1914 it partly made up the border between Serbia and Hungary.

Mentioned in *The Good Soldier Švejk* are also the tributaries Leitha and Tisza, as well as major cities like Vienna, Budapest, Bratislava, Belgrade, Győr and Linz. Hainburg and Komárom also figure, albeit marginally. [honsi.org]

323 Officers' Club refers to one of two officers' clubs in Brucker Lager. Despite the German term including the word "kasino", this was not a gambling establishment as one usually associates with this word. It is not known whether gambling took place on the premises, but the Offizierskasino was more a general entertainment establishment with a restaurant, bar and live music. The landlords were civilians. [honsi.org]

324 Friedrich Salomon Krauss was an ethnographer, sexologist, folklorist, and Slavist of Croatian/Jewish origin, resident in Vienna. Early in his career he received funding from Crown Prince Crown Prince Rudolf for his ethnographic research among the South Slavs and later worked with Sigmund Freud. He became a pioneer of "ethno-sexology", but a succession of obscenity trials hampered his work and by 1913 had ruined him financially.

The author is imprecise in describing Krauss and his publication. It was not a book, but rather a series of annual publications which appeared ten times between 1904 and 1913. Krauss was the publisher of the series, not the author as Hašek suggests.

The work in question is undoubtedly *Anthropophyteia. Yearbooks for Folkloristic Surveys and Research on the Developmental History of Sexual Morality.* It was a series of scientific yearbooks, containing articles and studies from a number of scholars, and Krauss himself contributed some of the content. The books were never publicly for sale, as they were intended for research purposes only. The illustrations were limited to a few pages at the end of each volume.

Drawings that fit the description Hašek gives in the novel are found in Vol. VII. (1910), pages 529 to 535. They refer to a study published on pages 197 to 203, authored in French by Luquet. He does not mention Berlin or any railway station toilet, but in the same volume (p. 403) there is a section about scribbled verses in Berlin toilets (with examples). It may therefore be that Hašek composed the sequence from these two elements. In any case, nowhere in the ten volumes do we find drawings next to verses as described in the novel. [honsi.org]

325 Berlin Westbahnhof (*Berlin West Railway Station*) was, according to the author, a railway station in Berlin, although a station carrying this name has

never existed in the city.

Studying Krauss' Anthropophyteia, the book that Hašek refers to in the novel, gives no further indication. If anything, it seems that the author composed this passage by picking fragments from volume VII, then twisted them for literary purposes. No specific railway station in Berlin has been possible to identify in Anthropophyteia. [honsi.org]

326 "časopis českých turistů" no doubt refers to Časopis turistů (*Magazine for Tourists*), a monthly magazine that from 1889 was published by Klub českých turistů (the *Czech Tourist Association*).

From 1896 until 1926, Doctor Guth served as chief editor, and for a short period after World War I, Hašek's good friend Zdeněk Matěj Kuděj was his secretary.

The periodical was still being published as of 2023, but since 1962 under the name Turista (*The Tourist*). Between 1949 and 1962, it changed its name several times. Only for a short period after the 1948 Communist coup did the publishing stop entirely. [honsi.org]

327 Humboldt (full name Friedrich Wilhelm Heinrich Alexander Humboldt) was a renowned German naturalist and explorer who undertook extensive research expeditions in Latin America and Central Asia. He is regarded as the co-founder of geography as an empirical science. He was the brother of Wilhelm von Humboldt, founder of Humboldt University in Berlin.

Humboldt visited Galicia (Poland) in 1792/93 and Galicia (Spain) in 1799. However, it has not been possible to connect him to One-year Volunteer Marek's quote about Galicia. [honsi.org]

328 Otakar Bas was a Czech radical lawyer who received his license in 1908 and specialized in defending opponents of the House of Habsburg regime. Even as a young candidate lawyer, he was active in Sokol and also in politics. After the war, he at one stage held the post of Vice President of the Czechoslovak Senate. He committed suicide shortly after the Nazis occupied Czechoslovakia in March 1939.

That this is the person the novel refers to is information provided by Antonín Měšťan. He is almost certainly correct, as minor spelling mistakes like Bas/Bass are quite common throughout *The Good Soldier Švejk*. [honsi.org]

329 Wasserpolack (plural: Wasserpolacken, Wasserpolen) or Wasserpolak ("Water-Pole") was a pejorative term used for residents of Silesia, who spoke Silesian.

In Silesia, the Polish, German and Czech languages and cultures influenced one another for centuries. Since the 18th century, the German language became more important, starting to penetrate Slavic dialects. Many times families were a mix of members of different nations over centuries and they could not be treated as entirely Polish, German or Czech. They were identified as a regional community with a regional language.

The term Wasserpolack ("Water Pole") appears in the 17th century and was used for Poles living in Lower and Upper Silesia and also in other places where languages and nations were mixed over centuries. The term refers to the fact that the primary occupations of this population were associated with water: fishing and rafting.

In a 1884 ethnographic book Karl Burmann wrote that the language of Wasserpolacken is not Polish, but rather Wasserpolnisch (lit. Water-Polish), which Poles who don't speak German cannot understand, because in Wasserpolnisch often only Polish endings are attached to purely German words, e.g., fensterlatki for Fensterladen (window shutters), schuppenketki for Schuppenketten, etc. [en.wikipedia.org]

330 Velké Popovice is a town on the southern perimeter of Prague, known for its brewery. Velkopopovický beer is reported to have been a favorite of Jaroslav Hašek. The dark variety is still served at U kalicha (*At the Chalice*), as it seems to have been when Švejk frequented the pub. In contemporary Praha, U černého vola (*At the Black Ox*) is a popular pub that serves the pale variety in large quantities.

The brewery was established in 1871 by the businessman and politician Franz Ringhoffer (1817-1873), and in 1874 production started. The brewery was modern for its time and soon became one of the largest in Bohemia. In 1907, they ranked 4th with a production of more than 175,000 hectoliters. The alternative name [Velkopopovický] Kozel [*of Velké Popovice*] was used from the beginning and is still synonymous with beer from Velké Popovice.

Here are some numbers which show that hop trader Wendler had every reason to be worried. The production volumes at Velké Popovice from 1913 until 1919 were (in 1,000 hectoliters): 230, 199, 181, 130, 37, 25, 38. These figures put the term "economic crisis" into perspective. Production did not reach pre-war volumes until 1924. [honsi.org] For the beer-drinking Czechs, one could even say “humanitarian crisis”. [Translator’s note]

331 11th March Company never existed as a unit in the Infantry Regiment No.

91 in 1915. The number eleven is borrowed from 11. Feldkompanie (*11th Field Company*), in which Hašek served as a soldier from July 11th until September 24th 1915. From June 1st until arriving at the front, he belonged to the 4th March company of 12th March Battalion of IR91. Like most other march units, it was dissolved soon after arriving at the front, and the men were distributed among the various field companies. [honsi.org]

332 Krakonoš, a German/Czech/Polish folklore mountain spirit of the Krkonoše mountain range (*Riesengebirge*), subject of many legends in the region. Görlitz and Vysoké nad Jizerou both have museums dedicated to this figure. He also appeared in numerous books and operas from the 19th century. Later he also became a theme for movies. [honsi.org]

333 Baloun has no clearly identifiable model from real life, but at least his gluttony may have been derived from the author himself, who at the time when he wrote this part of the novel put on a lot of weight. Jaroslav Hašek was known as a gourmet, something which is reflected in the many descriptions of food throughout the novel. According to Josef Lada, he was also a very good cook.

There are several people with the name Baloun that the author might have met during his life, and could at least have lent their name (and even some personal traits) to the gluttonous miller from Krumlov region.

Baloun is quite a common surname, and is particularly frequent in Humpolec region. This was an area that Hašek knew well when he wrote this part of *The Good Soldier Švejk* in 1922. At the time, he lived at Lipnice, only 11 km away. [honsi.org]

334 Český Krumlov, named Krumlov until 1920, is a town not far from the Austrian border. The district of Krumlov was located in the recruitment area of Infantry Regiment No. 91, so Jaroslav Hašek would have known many fellow soldiers from there. According to the 1910 census Krumlov had 8,716 inhabitants, of whom 1,295 (14 %) reported using Czech as their everyday language.

The medieval structure of the town has been preserved and it is on the world heritage list of UNESCO. It has become a major tourist attraction. [honsi.org]

335 Officers' mess refers to officers' dining rooms in Brucker Lager. There is no doubt that it existed, perhaps there were several both in the old and the new camp. In this case, it would surely have been a mess in Altes Lager (*Old Camp*) where Hašek himself served. [honsi.org]

336 Frankfurter Braten (*Frankfurter roast*) is a traditional dish of unclear origin

and varying ingredients. It appears to be based on beef, with sausage and bacon added. The term seems to have been more widespread in Austria than in Germany and the dish still exists in Czech recipe books. Frankfurt is the fifth largest city in Germany and an important center of finance and transport. It is the location of the European Central Bank. By the time of World War I, the city had become an important industrial center. [honsi.org]

337 Hop poles are 20 foot tall poles that support an overhead horizontal grid of wires over the hops field rows. From the grid are strung vertical wires anchored in in the row on the ground. Each bine of the hops plant climbs up one vertical wire. During harvest, the wire with the bine wrapped around it is pulled down by the workers and the fruit is plucked off the bine. [from the translator's personal experience]

338 "Einjährigfreiwilligen Schule" (*One-Year Volunteer School*) refers to the reserve officers' school in Bruck an der Leitha. It was located in Landwehrkaserne (*Land Defense Barracks*) in the western part of town. The building is still intact and in 1983 it was occupied by council houses. [honsi.org]

339 "cukrovar" (sugar refinery) refers to a sugar refinery in Bruck an der Leitha that started production in 1909. It was owned by Österreichischen Zuckerindustrie-Aktiengesellschaft until 1931 and had several owners throughout the years. Until it was closed in 1986, it remained one of the largest sugar refineries in Austria. Wolfgang Gruber and Erwin Sillaber have written a detailed history of the sugar factory. Today, the building is occupied by a biodiesel factory. [honsi.org]

340 9th March Company never existed as a unit in Infantry Regiment No. 91 in 1915. The number nine is evidently borrowed from 9th Field Company, a pattern that repeats itself with all the companies from IR. 91 that are mentioned in *The Good Soldier Švejk*. [honsi.org]

341 The 13th March Battalion (in IR. 91) was a battalion that was trained in Királyhida in July 1915 and sent to the front in early August. It arrived at Żdżary (15 km north of Sokal) on August 15th 1915, where they were merged with the field battalions. The Battalion commander was Captain Otto Wimmer.

Contrary to what one would expect, Hašek was not part of this Battalion, but rather the preceding one, XII. March Battalion. It was formed around June 1st 1915 and led by Major Franz Wenzel (from July 1st Lieutenant Colonel). They were trained at Brucker Lager until their departure to the front on June 30th. They arrived at the battlefield by the Złota Lipa river (ukr. Золота Липа) on July 11th. Two of the four march companies were reformed into the 11th Field Company and the 12th Field Company, units that had been wiped out in the fighting in the weeks before. The rest of the March Battalion was distributed among the other ten field companies.

It is known that Senior Lieutenant Lukáš was the commander of 4th March Company and under him were Hans Bigler, Jaroslav Hašek, František Strašlipka and Jan Vaněk. One of the other companies was led by reserve Lieutenant Paul Kandl (b. 1884 in Prachatice, an economist by profession), who took over the 12th Field Company at the front. The names of the other two company commanders are unknown. [honsi.org]

342 Montenegro (Црна Гора) was in 1914 an independent kingdom and had been a duchy (kingdom from 1910) since the liberation from Turkey in 1878. King at the time was Nikola I. and the capital was Cetinje.

In 1914 the Kingdom of Dalmatia (as part of Austria) and Bosnia-Hercegovina both shared a short border with Montenegro and both k.u.k. Heer and k.u.k. Kriegsmarine had garrisons in the region. The navy had a heavy presence in Cattaro (Kotor), and it was one of empire's three naval bases. The border between Herzegovina and Montenegro was much longer and this region also had a significant military presence.

In World War I the Kingdom of Montenegro quickly aligned with Serbia and declared war on Austria-Hungary on August 7th 1914. Along the border there was fighting already from August 1914 but it remained a stalemate until the *I&R Army* launched a full-scale invasion of Montenegro on January 5th 1916. The invasion was made possible by the recent defeat of Serbia, making large forces available for the attack, and it was now also possible to attack from the Serbian territory. King Nikola I. sued for peace, but the terms were so harsh that he rejected them. Because he had fled the country, the king could not stop the politicians that remained from accepting the terms. On January 19th a treaty was signed and Montenegro remained occupied for the rest of the war. [honsi.org]

343 Dukla Pass is the lowest mountain pass in the Carpathians. It is located south of Dukla in Poland and northeast of Prešov in Slovakia. The pass is strategically important and fierce fighting took place between Austro-Hungarian and Russian forces during the first winter and spring of World War I. In the first week of May 1915 the Russians were finally driven away from the area. [honsi.org]

344 " the 10th marchgang", i.e. the 10th March Company never existed as a unit in Infantry Regiment No. 91 in 1915. The number ten is undoubtedly

borrowed from the 10th Field Company, a pattern that repeats with all the companies from IR 91 mentioned in *The Good Soldier Švejk.* [honsi.org]

345 Kralupy is an industrial town 20 km north of Prague, situated on the Vltava. Throughout the 20th century the town grew rapidly and is best known for the chemical industry that is operating to this day (2017). On 22 March 1945 the town was devastated in an Allied bomb raid.

According to the 1910 census, Kralupy had 5,848 inhabitants, of whom 5,805 (99%) reported using Czech as their everyday language. The judicial district was okres (*district*) Kralupy nad Vltavou, administratively it reported to hejtmanství (*administrative district*) Slaný.

Kralupy owes its place in *The Good Soldier Švejk* to Jan Vaněk, perhaps the most obvious of the real-life "prototypes" for Hašek's literary figures. He lived in Kralupy and, like his literary counterpart, he owned a drug store/pharmacy. It was located on the town square and is still functioning.

On 20 May 2017 only the second statue of Švejk on Czech soil was unveiled (the first one was erected in Putim in 2014). The statue is modeled after actor Rudolf Hrušinský (1920-1994), who played the good soldier in Karel Steklý's two films from 1956 and 1957 [honsi.org]

346 Drogerie Kokoška was a chemist's store, where Jaroslav Hašek in 1898 worked as an apprentice, after prematurely ending his studies at the gymnasium. The shop was located at the corner of Na Perštýně and Martinská streets, in the house U třech zlatých koulí (*At the Three Golden Balls*). The information is confirmed by newspaper adverts, address books and a photo from 1905. The owner Mr. Kokoška opened the store/ workshop in the summer of 1890. It was operating until 1906, when the proprietor died. [honsi.org]

347 Na Perštýně is a street in Staré město (*Old Town*), Prague. In 1898 Jaroslav Hašek worked at the drogerie (*pharmacy*) Kokoška for a short period as an apprentice after prematurely ending his studies at the gymnasium.

[honsi.org]

348 Saint Pelegrinus may be one of seven different saints with the name Pelegrinus or Peregrinus, mostly martyrs from early Christianity. Břetislav Hůla concludes that Švejk refers to a martyr who was beatified on April 27th. Another claim is that the saint in question is Peregrine Laziosi, the patron saint of pregnant women and women giving birth.

Whichever Pelegrinus one prefers, none of the seven candidates appear to have any connection to cattle or other livestock. Nor does the date April 27th provide further clues. Laziosi, however, is more famous than the rest and would thus be the "best guess". [honsi.org]

[349] The author's apprenticeship at drogerie Kokoška in 1898 and/or 1899 inspired a series of eight stories that were published in Veselá Praha (*Merry Prague*). Tauchen appears here, but with his name slightly altered, though still easily recognizable (Tauben). It is almost certain that someone named Tauchen (or with a similar name) worked for Kokoška, but his identity has not been established to this day. [honsi.org]

[350] This anecdote almost certainly has its background in Hašek's own time as an apprentice at drogerie Kokoška in 1898 and/or 1899. According to Václav Menger, one of the employees at the shop was a certain Ferdinand Vávra, who may well have been the inspiration for the character Švejk expounds upon.

Hašek himself mentions a servant named Ferdinand who worked there. At the relevant time, he was around 40 years old, lived in Michle, and had a richly decorated cart that he was very proud of. In addition, he had a certain fondness for drink, both beer and stronger spirits. [honsi.org]

[351] U milosrdných (*At the Mercifuls*) refers to the hospital Nemocnice na Františku, associated with the monastery complex Klášter milosrdných bratří s kostelem sv. Šimona a Judy (*Brothers of Mercy Monastery with the Church of St. Simon and Juda*) in Staré město (*Old Town*).

The hospital has a history that goes back almost 700 years and is functioning to this very day (2024). The hospital was the first in Europe to carry out an amputation of limbs under full anesthesia (1847). In 1997 a major reconstruction started but was complicated by the disastrous floods of 2002. [honsi.org]

[352] The 12th March Company never existed as a unit in Infantry Regiment No. 91 in 1915. The number twelve is no doubt borrowed from the 12th Field Company, a pattern that repeats itself with all the march companies from IR. 91 that are mentioned in *The Good Soldier Švejk*. [honsi.org]

[353] Pobřežní třída (*Riverbank boulevard*) is a street in Karlín, stretching along the Vltava, running parallel to Královská třída. [honsi.org]

[354] The “squad leader” is a translation of the Czech “cuksfíra”, a Czech barracks corruption of German military vocabulary: Zugsführer = četař ≠ Zugführer = velitel čety. The military slang term “cuksfíra” folds together both German originals — Zugsführer (rank) and Zugführer (function) — as they were half-heard, half-remembered, and heard as one and the same word by non-Germans, and colloquialized in Czech soldier speech. Hašek uses “cuksfíra” loosely to mean “the fellow in charge of us,” without

separating formal rank from practical command.

In the formal Austro-Hungarian hierarchy, the Czech "četař" corresponds to the German "Zugsführer", the lowest non-commissioned rank, rendered here as "Corporal". By contrast, "Zugführer" (without "s") is not a rank but a function — "the leader of a platoon" — whose Czech designation is "velitel čety".

Váša–Trávníček (1941) defines "četař" functionally as "velitel čety," reflecting how in Hašek's era the semantic sense "leader of the unit" often overlapped with the formal rank "četař". Later lexicographic projections (e.g., "sergeant," "flight sergeant") reflect modernized rank systems and do not apply to Hašek's military context. The "squad leader" is set in italics not to mark a functional distinction from the rank "Corporal", but because this edition italicizes foreign words occurring in the Czech text, and secondarily Czech-spelled foreignisms or corrupted barracks slang such as "cuksfíra"; the correspondence between the italicized form and the character's functional role is therefore incidental rather than intentional. Narrative identification uses "Corporal"; dialogue reflecting Hašek's slang uses the functional sense "squad leader". [Translator's note]

355 "kantýna" probably refers to a rank and file mess that, according to the description in *The Good Soldier Švejk*, was located by the Lagerallee (*camp alley*). In the Old Camp there were three mess halls and also one in the New Camp. This short sequence of the plot no doubt took place in one of the three mess halls in the Old Camp. [honsi.org]

356 hash-and-crumb sausage

Here are ingredients for 20 traditional Czech jitrnice:
4 kg pork heads, lobes and bellies
2 pcs pork lungs
1 kg pork liver
500 g bread roll
5 crushed garlic cloves
3/4 tbsp allspice
1 tbsp marjoram
5 m pork intestines
500 ml pork stock
1 tbsp salt
1 tsp pepper
[prozeny.cz]

357 Pardubice is a city in eastern Bohemia, and capital of the kraj (*region*) of

the same name. Jaroslav Hašek spent a week in quarantine here in December 1920, after returning home from Russia. [honsi.org]

358 The Benešov Regiment, i.e. Infantry Regiment No. 102 was one of the 102 Austro-Hungarian infantry regiments. It was established in 1883 when the number of infantry regiments in k.u.k. Heer (*I&R Army*) was expanded from 80 to 102. The Ergänzungsbezirk (*Replacement District*) was Benešov. [honsi.org]

359 *Sutra - In Hinduism a sutra is a short rule (e.g. aphorism), as a theorem distilled into several words or syllables, around which can be woven the teachings of ritual, philosophy, grammar or any area of knowledge. Sutras have been formed since ancient times as concentrated, suitable for remembering important philosophical and religious content.*

Pragnâ-Paramitâ/Prajñāpāramitā is one of the Buddhist teachings, which means "Wisdom perfection" and refers to the perfect means of how to see nature reality. It means going beyond the framework or surpassing limits, moving outside the reach of human experience, reason, faith, etc. (Transcendental knowledge). Hašek's definition, given in parentheses - "Revealed Wisdom", is the Embodied Wisdom - Prajñāpāramitā Devi or "Great Mother", often depicted in Buddhist art. [svejkmuseum.cz]

360 Pickled braised beef in creamy root vegetable sauce, with bread dumplings. [cooklikeczechs.com]

361 A hearty, seasoned Italian sauce of meat and tomatoes that is used chiefly in pasta dishes and that is typically made with ground beef, tomatoes, and finely chopped onions, celery, and carrots. [merriam-webster.com]

362 Komarów is a village by Zamość in Poland (then part of Russia), the scene of a battle in August 1914, where Austria-Hungary was victorious. Even better known is the battle in the Polish-Soviet war in 1920, the last large cavalry battle in history. [honsi.org]

363 *The following is based on Buddhist funeral practices, especially Japanese ones. Funeral practices are, from the point of view of believers, essential in transforming the deceased into a protective ancestor of the lineage. In order for the deceased to reach an ancestor status, it is necessary to perform the appropriate ceremonies and continue with annual care for 30 years after his death. If proper memorial services and offers of sacrifices are not performed, the spirit can become a so-called* ***hungry spirit****. There are six worlds, collectively called rokudóinto, into which the spirit can be reborn after death, based on good and bad karma accumulated in a past life.*

These are the worlds:

1. world of gods tendo;
2. world of people ningendó
3. world of demigods shuradó
4. world of animals chikushodo
5. world of hungry spirits gakido. Birth into this world is as a result of evil karma from the past life. They are ghosts, that endlessly suffer hunger and thirst and live in constant torment.
6. world of hell jigokudó

It's a whole great science beyond the range of our research. I drew on Helena Reichrt's bachelor's thesis "Japanese studies Seminar" Masaryk University FF 2020. [svejkmuseum.cz]

364 Karma, in Indian religion and philosophy, is the universal causal law by which good or bad actions determine the future modes of an individual's existence. Karma represents the ethical dimension of the process of rebirth (samsara), belief in which is generally shared among the religious traditions of India. Indian soteriologies (theories of salvation) posit that future births and life situations will be conditioned by actions performed during one's present life—which itself has been conditioned by the accumulated effects of actions performed in previous lives. The doctrine of karma thus directs adherents of Indian religions toward their common goal: release (moksha) from the cycle of birth and death. Karma thus serves two main functions within Indian moral philosophy: it provides the major motivation to live a moral life, and it serves as the primary explanation of the existence of evil. [britannica.com]

365 "*Kramarsch*" and "*Klófatsch*", uttered in German, are transcriptions of the Czech names, while *Scheiner* being a German name, appears in its proper form.

Karel Kramář was a Czech politician and longtime leader of Mladočeši (*Young Czechs*), who was arrested on 21st May 1915 and sentenced to death for high treason in December that year. The sentence was later converted to 20 years imprisonment, and he was released under the general amnesty given by the new emperor Karl I on July 2nd 1917. Kramář was a member of Reichsrat *(Austrian parliament)* from 1891 and the Czechoslovak parliament from 1920 until his death in 1937. He was in 1918 to become the first prime minister of Czechoslovakia, but his cabinet resigned the following year. Kramář was known as a panslavist and his wife was Russian.

Kramář was a prominent Czech politician, born into a wealthy family from North Bohemia. He studied law in Prague, Strasbourg and Berlin. Very early he became involved in politics and eventually became longtime leader of Mladočeši (*The Young Czechs*). Kramář was a pan-Slavist and before the war he campaigned actively for Czech state rights, but within the Habsburg monarchy. At the time he argued for Austria-Hungary to abandon the alliance with Germany and align with Russia instead, aiming to strengthen the position of the Slav nations within the empire. The outbreak of war made him turn openly against the Dual Monarchy and he decided to work for full independence. [honsi.org]

Josef Eugen Scheiner was a Czech politician, and like Kramář, associated with the Czech domestic resistance movement during World War I, the so-called "Mafia". He was the longtime leader of Sokol, both the Czech and the international organization (he founded the latter in 1908). He was also the editor-in-chief of their monthly Sokol. On May 21st 1915 he was arrested and charged with espionage, but was released later that year and allowed to return to Prague. After the war he was for some time the head of the Czechoslovak armed forces and also the inspector general, but for the most part he dedicated the rest of his life to Sokol. [honsi.org]

Klofáč was a Czech politician and journalist. He studied philosophy in Prague and worked as a journalist and editor for Národní listy (*National Sheets*) from 1890 to 1899, the main mouthpiece of Mladočeši (*Young Czechs*). He also wrote for Národní politika (*National Politics*). Due to his dissatisfaction with the *Young Czechs'* alleged conciliatory attitude towards the Habsburg monarchy, he founded Česká strana národně sociální (*Czech National Social Party*) in 1898 and was party chairman from 1899 to 1938. Politically, he was a radical Czech nationalist and also a Pan-Slavist with good contacts in Serbia and Russia.

In 1901 he was elected to the Reichsrat (*Austrian parliament*) for the Smíchov constituency and remained a deputy until the parliament was dissolved in 1918.

He also founded the party mouthpiece České Slovo (*Czech Word*), which was first published on March 1st 1907 with Jiří Pichl as the first chief editor. Klofáč wrote for the paper regularly and owned the building Zlatá husa (*The Golden Goose*) on Václavské náměstí that housed the newspaper. He was also listed as publisher of the newspaper. [honsi.org]

366 Ferdinand Graf von Zeppelin was a German officer, best known for inventing the airship. Born into a wealthy and influential family in

Konstanz, he graduated from the war academy in Ludwigsburg. He was present as an observer in the American Civil War and noted how balloons were used in the conflict, which no doubt inspired his later invention.

The first airship flight took place on July 2nd 1900 over Lake Constance. Several more zeppelins were built over the next fourteen years, some for the armed forces.

Zeppelins played a certain role in World War I, and were widely used (by Germany in particular) for bombing and reconnaissance. Eventually, they proved vulnerable due to their large target area. In the inter-war years, they had a renaissance, but the Hindenburg disaster in 1937 effectively marked the end. [honsi.org]

[367] Ardennes is a forested mountain plateau divided between southeastern Belgium, northern Luxembourg, and northeastern France, bounded to the north by the rivers Meuse and Sambre. It has an area of about 11,200 square kilometers. The highest point is Signal de Botrange, 694 meters above sea level. The Ardennes are sparsely populated; few cities have more than 50,000 inhabitants.

The Ardennes was the scene of heavy fighting in 1914 and the German army soon conquered most of the area. The withdrawal that Colonel Schröder refers to during the officers' meeting in 1915 could not have happened, as the Germans abandoned the area as late as 1918. [honsi.org]

[368] A gambling card game that resembles Tippen, which is commonly played in Germany and the countries of the old Austro-Hungarian Empire. [en.wikipedia.org]

[369] Salah-Edin refers to Saladin, sultan of Egypt and Syria and founder of the Ayyubid dynasty (1169) in Egypt and Syria. He was the most important single actor in the victory over the Crusaders. In 1187 he conquered Jerusalem, and the intruders lost their foothold in the Middle East for good.

Saladin was known for his fair treatment of prisoners of war, which has given him a good name in both the Christian and the Muslim world. [honsi.org]

[370] Nána – meaning “Anna”, but “nána”: 1. pejorative for “a silly woman” 2. regional use for children’s “nanny” [ssjc.ujc.cas.cz]

[371] Letná is an area of Prague, north of the center. Administratively, it belongs to Holešovice and Bubeneč. [honsi.org]

[372] *According to Švejk's story, Zátka was one of many professional roundsmen, lamplighters, gasmen, or whatever they were called, who were tasked with*

lighting the street lamps in the evening and extinguishing them in the morning, as well as carrying out routine maintenance of the gas lamps (replacing burnt-out "stockings", i.e. incandescent gas mantles, adjusting and cleaning the burners) in the assigned district. Originally, the gas was lit with a torch on a stick, later, when a small flame was constantly burning in the lamps, the stick was used to control the rods for closing and opening the lantern valve.

According to the directory from 1910, there were two gas stations (guardhouse) in Letná. One in U Královské obory *street (today* Nad Královskou oborou*) at No. 138 and the other in* Skuherského *street (today* Pplk. Sochora*) at No. 724. We probably won't find out which guardhouse Zátka was employed at, nor will we find out whether he really existed or whether Hašek made up the story.* [svejkmuseum.cz]

373 Alois Jemelka was a Catholic priest, preacher, and missionary from Kozlovice near Přerov. After finishing gymnasium (secondary school) in Přerov, he studied at the seminary in Olomouc, where he was ordained on July 4th 1886. Shortly afterwards, he entered the Jesuit order, where he remained active for the rest of his life.

After his ordination, Jemelka continued his studies in Sankt Andrä (Carinthia) and Pressburg. He then worked in Velehrad (Moravia), Prague, Hradec Králové, and finally Vienna.

In the context of *The Good Soldier Švejk*, his time at kostel svatého Ignáce is of interest, as it is in this context that his name is mentioned in the novel. The period of his stay is unclear, but in the address book for 1896 he is listed as chairman of Mariánská kongregace. A newspaper article reveals that he was still in Prague in June 1900.

Jemelka was known for his oratory skills (he had studied rhetoric), traveled widely, and was an eager participant in debates about religion and politics. His uncompromising attitude made him unpopular in many circles. Among other things, he was in conflict with socialists, Volná myšlenka (*Free Thought)*, Machar, and not least Professor Masaryk. In connection with the latter, Jemelka published a small book called Masaryk's Fight for Religion. His stay in Hradec Králové lasted at least from 1903 to 1908, and it was here that the mentioned dispute with Masaryk took place.

According to Václav Menger, Hašek was an altar boy in kostel svatého Ignáce when he was about nine years old, i.e. around 1892. Hašek is said to have overheard Jemelka's sermons, and Menger adds that the priest had a very large number of enthusiastic female followers. Inspiration from this period explains why Jemelka is mentioned in *The Good Soldier Švejk* and also in two of Hašek's writings from before the war. In all three cases, he is only mentioned in passing. [honsi.org]

374 Kostel svatého Ignáce (*Church of Saint Ignatius*) is a church at the corner of Ječná ulice (*street*)and Karlovo náměstí (*Charles' square*), which today serves as the main seat of the Jesuit order in Czech Republic. It is named after the founder of the order, Ignatius of Loyola. Construction started in 1665 and was completed in 1699.

Jaroslav Hašek knew the church very well. Václav Menger tells us, that he was an altar boy there during the second to the last year at primary school (i.e. when he was around nine years old). His knowledge of Catholic liturgy is no doubt in part due to this experience. [honsi.org]

375 A violent delirium with tremors that is induced by excessive and prolonged use of alcoholic liquors. [merriam-webster.com]

376 Dolní Bousov is a small town between Mladá Boleslav and Jičín, about 100 km north-east of Prague.[honsi.org]

377 "hejtmanství Jičín" was an *administrative district* centered on Jičín. It consisted of the judicial district Jičín, Libáň and Sobotka. [honsi.org]

378 "okres Sobotka" was a *judicial district* in Jičín, centred around the town of Sobotka. It consisted of 37 communities, where Sobotka and Dolní Bousov were by far the largest. This *judicial district* stood out in the sense that in the 1910 census, every single inhabitant registered Czech as their everyday language. [honsi.org]

379 Kosť (now Kost) is a former noble estate centered on the Gothic castle of the same name near Sobotka and Dolní Bousov. [honsi.org]

380 "Chrám svaté Kateřiny" is the parish church in Dolní Bousov. It was built in 1759 and 1760 in baroque style, which conflicts with recruit Pech's claim that the church was from the 14th century. There may, however, have been a church on the site already. [honsi.org]

381 The person referred to is Count Antonín Václav Vratislav-Netolický z Mitrovic. He inherited the Kost estate from his mother and would also have been the lord of Dolní Bousov. He was also the first to use the name hrabě (*Count*) Vratislav-Netolický / Graf Wratislaw-Netolizky. [honsi.org]

382 Recruit Pech's monologue about where he was from is a near-verbatim quotation from Ottův slovník naučný (*Otto's Educational Dictionary*), as established by literary scholar Antonín Měšťan in 1983. Although the abbreviations from the encyclopaedia are expanded in *The Good Soldier*

Švejk and there are some other minor differences, the information is essentially the same. [honsi.org]

383 The “Eighth marchy”, i.e. the 8th March Company, never existed as a unit in the Infantry Regiment No. 91 in 1915. The number eight is evidently borrowed from the 8th Field Company, a numerical pattern that recurs with all the companies from IR. 91 that are mentioned in *The Good Soldier Švejk*. The best example of this literary transformation is clearly Švejk's own 11th March Company. [honsi.org]

384 The surname itself is not very common today, but it was widespread during Hašek's time, especially the variant Teweles. In fact, a Rudolf Teweles served in Infanterieregiment Nr. 91 from 1915. Little is known about him other than that he had right of domicile in Prague, was called up in 1915, and was wounded by Monfalcone on February 8th 1916. He was a regular reserve infantryman.

In 1913 and 1914, newspapers in Austria mention a Rudolf Teweles who may actually be identical to the wounded soldier from Infantry Regiment No. 91. Teweles had pretended to be a photographer and had collected money from customers in advance without ever delivering. It is stated that he was born in 1887 in Vienna and had right of domicile in Prague. Thus, both name and surname fit, and so does the right of domicile. A connection to the figure in *The Good Soldier Švejk* is the fact that both the real Teweles and the literary Teveles were fraudsters. It is thus possible that Hašek may have met Rudolf Teweles in 1915, perhaps precisely in Királyhida.

A story with certain parallels to the Teveles affair appeared in the newspapers in 1915. The 21-year-old Johann Schuh had falsely pretended to be a Corporal and had also acquired a war medal that was not his. [honsi.org]

385 The 6th March Company never existed as a unit in Infantry Regiment No. 91 in 1915. The number six is evidently borrowed from the 6th Field Company, a numerical pattern that recurs with all the companies from IR. 91 that are mentioned in *The Good Soldier Švejk*. The best example of this literary transformation is clearly Švejk's own 11th March Company. [honsi.org]

386 Church of Saint Sava at first glance seems to refer to the largest and most important cathedral in Serbia, and the largest cathedral in south-eastern Europe, and also the largest orthodox cathedral in the world.

This assumption is however wrong, because in 1914 the cathedral was still only being planned. Construction started as late as 1935, but in 1914 there was a small church with the same name on the site, and this is surely the one the author has in mind. Both churches were/are located on the Vračar hill.

The story about the missing 6th March Company may be based on real events although this company never existed (each march battalion consisted of four companies, numbered I,II,III and IV). The author may however had IR. 91/6th field company or another company of IR. 91 in mind. These fought by Belgrade during the withdrawal from Serbia in the week before December 15th 1914. During this time the regiment lost three entire companies before the remainder pulled out to Hungary across the river Sava. The three missing field companies (5th, 13th and 14th) were however captured by Borak south of Belgrade, not in the city itself. [honsi.org]

387 Bug (ukr. Буг - Buh) is a river in Ukraine, Belarus and Poland that for some time in 1915 formed the front. Infantry Regiment No. 91 with Jaroslav Hašek was stationed by Bug from July 16th to August 27th 1915. [honsi.org]

388 The 13th March Company never existed as a unit in Infantry Regiment No. 91 in 1915. The number thirteen is no doubt borrowed from the 13th Field Company, a pattern that repeats itself with all the march companies from IR. 91 that are mentioned in *The Good Soldier Švejk*. [honsi.org]

389 Zur weißen Rose (*At the White Rose*) has not been identified, but may be a mistranslation or misspelling of Zum weißen Rössel *(At the Little White Horse)*, a former guest-house in Bruck. Zum weißen Rössel was located in Altstadt 6, and on the first floor was a Mannschaftspuff (brothel for the lower ranks). Altstadt is the name of a street, not the old town as the name suggests. During World War I the street was the center of night-life and entertainment in Bruck.

Bohumil Vlček recalls a Czech waitress Růženka, who worked in a certain tavern named u Růže (Zur Rose) and that many Czechs, including Jaroslav Hašek, visited regularly. Further Jan Morávek, in an interview that was printed in Průboj on March 3rd, 1968, adds, that the author, before departure to the front, was picked up by the patrol at U zlaté růže (Zur goldenen Rose). It is surely the same place, but there is great confusion about the real name of the place. Vlček also mentions that Jaroslav Hašek in the same situation was detained in a pub by the railway station. If this is the case, the hypothesis about Zum weißen Rössel is invalid as it was located about 10 minutes' walk from the station. On the other hand Vlček explicitly states, that the "Rose" was in Bruck, whatever color or shape it might have appeared in. Josef Novotný also mentions the place in his memories from the war. [honsi.org]

390 Harrach was a count of the Czech-Austrian noble family Harrach who owned Schloss Prugg in Bruck an der Leitha. Count von Harrach had from 1909 the right of primogeniture in the noble family and was as such the formal owner of the palace. He was son of the Czech politician Johann Nepomuk von Harrach. During World War I he and his wife ran a hospital in the palace. [honsi.org] The Schloss Prugg is a palace in Bruck which, since 1625, has belonged to the Harrach noble family. The mentioned greenhouse was destroyed during fighting at the end of World War II. [honsi.org]

391 Vysočany is an urban district in eastern Prague, neighboring Žižkov and Libeň. Until 1922 it was a separate town. The "elektrika" (*streetcar*) from Vysočany to Prague mentioned by Švejk was opened in 1896 as a private enterprise owned by the industrialist František Křižík. Its total length was 7.7 km. [honsi.org]

392 Drážov near Strakonice, often written Dražov. The village was not in the recruitment district of Švejk's regiment (IR. 91), but rather that of Infantry Regiment No.11, the neighboring regiment from Písek.

One should however not attach too much importance to the connection between the birthplace of Švejk and the regiment he served in. It was the Heimatrecht (*Right of Domicile*) that determined allocation to military units, and this was in many cases linked to the soldier's father (examples being Jaroslav Hašek and Zdeněk Matěj Kuděj) or even the grandfather.

Dražov was in 1913 listed under hejtmanství (*administrative district*) Strakonice, okres Vodňany. The village had 239 inhabitants, and everyone declared Czech as their mother tongue. The parish was Dobrž, the post office located in Čestice. [honsi.org]

393 Montgomery is the name of almost 20 places in the United States, nowadays the best known of them is the capital of Alabama.

Sergey Soloukh however points out, that Montgomery in Minnesota has a strong Czech link, so it is quite likely this place that the author had in mind. Zenny Sadlon adds, that after World War I many Czechs returned to their homeland for various reasons and that Hašek might have heard about Montgomery from these.

The answer might even be found in the writings of his friend Zdeněk Matěj Kuděj, who had spent three years in the United States before he met Jaroslav Hašek. In the story "Bídné dny" (*Miserable days*) (1911), he wrote that he spent a short while working on railway construction in Alabama, but there is no direct mention of Montgomery. He also visited Minnesota so there is no clean conclusion. [honsi.org]

394 The inspiration for the character Biegler was undoubtedly Hans Bigler, a young reserve officer who served with Jaroslav Hašek in Infanterieregiment Nr. 91 during the spring and summer of 1915. [honsi.org]

One of the ranks Hans Hermann Gustav Bigler (also written Biegler) held was indeed cadet. Whereas many prototypes were "discovered" as early as 1924, Bigler remained an unknown entity until he surfaced in 1955 in a personal letter written to Dietz Verlag, the East German publisher of *The Good Soldier Švejk.*

Bigler was born in 1894 in Blasewitz, an affluent suburb of Dresden. As the son of a wealthy merchant and former ship captain (at Wolfgangsee) and a Berlin-born lady, he was clearly raised in privileged surroundings. As far as we know, he had no siblings. His father lived in Dresden at least until young Hans was seven (his mother had died on 31 January 1900), and then the family appear to have moved to Switzerland. Information on the first twenty years of Bigler's life is scarce, and even in army records his occupation at the time of enlisting in I&R Army is “Privat”, i.e. self-employed or even idle. Details such as rank and position in the army units are accurately mirrored in *The Good Soldier Švejk*, despite the change of Bigler's first name to Adolf and him being portrayed as a native of Budějovice (in the words of Hauptmann Ságner). According to the records of the Reserve Officer School, Bigler was a Kriegsfreiwilliger, i.e. he volunteered for war service, and this was also the case with his literary counterpart.

Bigler distinguished himself during the battle by Sokal (25 - 31 July 1915) and was promoted to Ensign (in the Reserves) on August 1st 1915, the same day that Hašek was promoted to Gefreiter. In the aftermath of Sokal on August 18th 1915 he fell ill with gastroenteritis and typhoid fever. It is a twist of irony that on this very day, the Emperor's 85th birthday, both Hašek and Bigler were awarded silver medals (second class). It is easy to imagine that the sad state of Bigler's bowels on 18 August served as inspiration for Jaroslav Hašek when he assigned a similarly unsavory fate to his unfortunate Cadet Biegler.

In 1955 he "surfaced" publicly after having read *The Good Soldier Švejk* and discovered that he was in fact the prototype of Cadet Biegler. In interviews he revealed that he was not ashamed of it despite the rough treatment Jaroslav Hašek dished out. He even said that most of what was written about him in *The Good Soldier Švejk* was true. He still lived at the same address at in Pohlandstrasse 20, Blasewitz, and here he was interviewed by Literární Noviny. News about him also appeared in Rudé Právo, Wochenpost (Berlin) and in Volksstimme (Vienna). [honsi.org]

395 Poříčí (*Riverside*) is a district of Prague, between Staré město (*Old Town*) and Florenc along the Vltava. [honsi.org]

396 Mníšek is a small town in the district of Prague, south west of the city. [honsi.org]

397 Hořovice is a village in central Bohemia between Plzeň and Prague. [honsi.org]

398 Jan Nepomucký (*John of Nepomuk*) was a Czech priest and martyr, who was blinded, tortured, and drowned in the Vltava. Today there is a statue of him at the point at Karlův most (*the Charles_Bridge*) where he was thrown off. He was canonized in 1729 and is now a patron saint. He is buried in Saint Vitus Cathedral in Prague. [honsi.org]

399 Prácheňsko was until 1850 an *administrative district* in South Bohemia. The center was Písek, but most of the region was located to the west and encompassed parts of Šumava. The major part of Švejk's anabasis took place within the region. Some translations imprecisely interpret it as the district around Prachatice (German - 1926, Danish - 1930). [honsi.org]

400 Drahenice is a village in Central Bohemia, in the district of Příbram. [honsi.org]

401 Moson was a town in Hungary near the Austrian border which in 1939 was joined with the neighboring town to become Mosonmagyaróvár. The river Lajta (*Leitha*) flows through it. [honsi.org]

402 Ráb, *is Hungarian* Győr, *German* Raab.[svejkmuseum.cz]

403 *This is today's Slovak Komárno. Hungarian Komárom and German Komorn, therefore not Komarn, as stated in the ciphered telegram: 4432 - 1238 - 7217 - 35 - 8922 - 35 = Komarn. Jaroslav Hašek doesn't mention it in the novel again.* [svejkmuseum.cz]

Note: The Endnotes entries sourced from websites were current as of summer 2025.

Imprint

This edition was typeset and composed using LibreOffice Writer for a 6 × 9 inch page format. The text is set in Times New Roman, with mirrored margins and an expanded inner margin for perfect binding. Typography, page layout, and editorial apparatus were composed during the editorial process. The volume was printed and bound as a paperback by IngramSpark.

www.ingramcontent.com/pod-product-compliance
Lightning Source LLC
LaVergne TN
LVHW091709070526
838199LV00050B/2327

* 9 7 9 8 9 9 4 3 0 8 4 2 4 *

فہرست

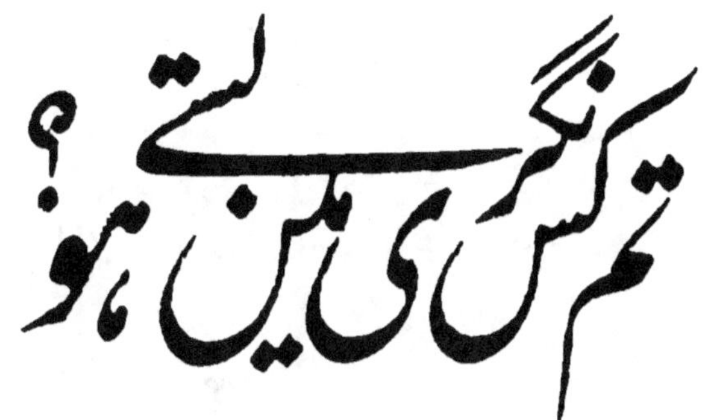

میں اپنی عزیز دوست شیاما کی انتہائی علالت کی خبر سُن کر اُس کے آخری دیدار کے لئے بنارس جارہی تھی۔ راستہ بھر بُرے بُرے خیالات مجھے ستاتے رہے اور میں رات کے سناٹے میں بار بار اپنا سر کھڑکی سے باہر نکال کر اپنے دل کو بہلانے کی ناکام کوشش کرتی رہی مگر رات کی تاریکیاں، اُجڑے ہوئے کھیتوں کی عجیب وغریب سنسناہٹ دُور ـــــ چراغوں کی مدھم زرد شعاعیں نہ جانے کیوں میرے دل کو اور زیادہ مضطرب کررہی تھیں۔ میں نے مایوس ہوکر اپنی آنکھیں اس طرف سے ہٹالیں۔ دفعتاً آسمان پر ایک تیز روشنی نظر آئی۔ اندھیری رات میں ایک ستارے کا اس طرح ٹوٹ کر کسی نامعلوم جگہ پر جاکر گرنا

کتنا افسوسناک منظر تھا اور اب تو اس روشن شعلے کی خاکستر بھی کہیں خاک کے ذرّوں کی طرح منتشر ہو چکی ہوگی۔

میں ان ہی خیالات میں مستغرق تھی کہ مجھے نیند آنے لگی اور پھر میں سوگئی۔ مگر وحشت زدہ دل کو خواب میں بھی سکون نہ ملا اور عجیب عجیب ڈراؤنے خواب سے منظر یکایک بدل گیا۔ میں نے دیکھا ایک بڑے میدان میں کچھ اونچے نیچے پہاڑوں کے بے ترتیب ٹیلے پڑے ہیں۔ میدان کے ایک طرف ایک چوڑی سی ندی بہہ رہی ہے جسکی موجیں دلکش رنگوں کی تھیں اور ان لہروں کی سطح پر ننھی ننھی مچھلیاں ایکدوسرے کا تعاقب کرتی ہوئی دوڑی جا رہی تھیں۔ یک بیک میری نظر پہاڑ کی طرف گئی۔ دیکھا تو سب سے اونچے ٹیلے پر پروفیسر ورما خاموش بیٹھا اپنی ڈائری میں کچھ لکھ رہا ہے۔ وہ مجھے غمگین نظروں سے دیکھکر چاند کی طرف اشارہ کرتے ہوئے بولا" اس مضطر بگولے کو دیکھو" میں نے دیکھا چاند ٹکڑے ٹکڑے ہو ہو کر چنگاریوں کی شکل میں فضا میں تڑپ تڑپ کر فنا ہو رہا ہے۔ ہوا زوروں سے چل رہی تھی۔ اور اس کے جھکڑوں سے درختوں کے پتے بُری طرح گر رہے تھے۔ پروفیسر ورما کا اُداس چہرہ بے چین نظر آنے لگا۔ میں پریشان کھڑی کانپ رہی تھی۔ یکایک پروفیسر ورما کھڑا ہو کر کانپنے لگا۔ وہ آہستہ آہستہ بڑبڑا رہا تھا۔ میری محرومِ قسمت میں انھیں روحوں کی معیت لکھی تھی۔ جو ہمیشہ فراق کا ایک اندوہگیں راگ گاتی ہوئی جدائی کے نامعلوم راستے پر گامزن ہیں۔ وہ کچھ دیر ٹھہر کر بولا" میرا فلسفۂ محبت بھی ہمیشہ یہی رہا کہ محبت کرنے

والی دو پیاری ہستیوں کے درمیان جدائی کے شعلے لرزاں ہوں جن میں ان کا سکون دائمی طور پر تڑپتا رہے۔۔ اس لئے کہ جب تک آہ کی گرمیاں دل کی گہرائیوں میں شعلہ ساماں نہ ہوں تو پھر محبت سرد پڑجاتی ہے اور ہاں اسی لئے میں نے اپنی روح کو غم کی آگ میں جلاکر محبت کو لازوال رکھا۔" کچھ سکوت کے بعد وہ آہستہ سے بولا۔" مجھے اور ان لطیف روحوں کو محبت کی آگ میں تڑپانا اور پھر تڑپاکر محبت کرنے کے لئے انھیں زندہ رکھنا بھی شاید محبوب فطرت کا ایک اہم ترین اصول ہے۔" وہ خاموش ہوکر اپنی ڈائری کے اُڑتے ہوئے اوراق دیکھنے لگا۔ آج کی تاریخ کے بعد چند سطریں لکھی تھیں۔ پروفیسر ورما نے جھک کر اپنی ڈائری کو اُٹھایا اور زور سے پڑھنے لگا۔" محبت نام ہے فراق کا اور موت اس جدائی کا ابدی ذریعہ ہے۔"

گاڑی کے ایک تیز جھٹکے سے میری آنکھ کھُل گئی۔ اس ہیبتناک خواب سے میرا دل زور زور سے دھڑک رہا تھا اور میری آنکھیں جلد از جلد اپنی شیاما کو دیکھنے کی آرزومند تھیں۔

بنارس پہنچکر جب میں حیران و پریشان "کیلاش لاج" پہونچی۔ تو وہ در و دیوار پر حسرت طاری تھی۔ موٹر سے اُترتے ہی میں اپنی بیمار شیاما کے کمرے کی طرف دوڑی۔ ابھی تھوڑی ہی دُور گئی تھی کہ شیاما کی چھوٹی بہن شیلا مجھ سے لپٹ کر پھوٹ پھوٹ کر رونے لگی۔ میں نے بیتاب ہوکر کہا۔" شیلا نہ رو میری شیاما اچھی ہو جائے گی"۔ میری باتوں کو سُنکر

شیلا تڑپ اُٹھی اور سسکتی ہوئی بولی۔ "کون اچھی ہو جائے گی ناہید! آہ میری جی جی تو اب اس دُنیا ہی میں نہیں"۔ شیلا کی باتیں سُن کر میں سکتے میں آ گئی۔ میرا سر چکرانے لگا اور پھر میں بیہوش ہو گئی۔ جب مجھے ہوش آیا تو میں نے دیکھا کہ میں شیلا کی مسہری پر پڑی ہوں اور شیاما کی بدحواس ماں حسرت بھری آنکھوں سے مجھے گھُور رہی ہے۔

۲

شیاما میری کلاس فیلو تھی۔ بی۔ اے کے امتحان میں، ہم دونوں نے خوب خوب ایک دوسرے کا مقابلہ کیا تھا مگر جیت شیاما کی رہی۔ وہ اپنے کولج بھر میں فرسٹ آئی تھی۔ بی۔ اے کے بعد ہم نے کالج چھوڑ دیا تھا پھر بھی میری اور شیاما کی دوستی قائم رہی۔ وہ اکثر تھوڑے تھوڑے دنوں کے لئے مجھ سے ملنے چلی آتی اور پھر اپنے مسلسل قہقہوں سے میرے مکان کو اپنے سر پر اُٹھا لیتی۔ شیاما بہت ہی مسخری اور ہنس مُکھ لڑکی تھی کتنی شریر اور چنچل تھی۔ کاش موت کے سیاہ خوفناک پنجوں کو وہ اپنے شریر ہاتھوں سے توڑ سکتی۔

شیاما برابر میرے یہاں آتی اور کبھی کبھی وہ اپنے ساتھ اپنی چھوٹی بہن شیلا کو بھی لاتی۔ شیلا بالکل شیاما کا اُلٹ تھی وہ ایک سیدھی سادی سی خوبصورت نہایت شرمیلی لڑکی تھی۔ اسے دنیا میں صرف

ڈو چیزیں عزیز تھیں ایک شیاما اور دوسری اس کی کتابیں اس کے سوا اسے دنیا سے کوئی تعلق نہ تھا۔

بی۔ اے کے بعد شیاما کا خیال تھا کہ وہ ضرور ایم۔ اے کرے گی۔ مگر جب وہ اوائل مارچ میں مجھ سے ملنے آئی تو میں نے دیکھا وہ بہت دُبلی ہوگئی ہے اور اس کی سیاہ موٹی موٹی آنکھوں کے گرد حلقے پڑ گئے ہیں میں نے گھبرا کر اس سے دریافت کیا کہ "شیاما تم ایسی حالت میں کیوں ہو؟" وہ غمگین آواز میں بولی:" بہت زیادہ فکر و تردد انسان کو گھُلا دیتا ہے اور اس پر ایم۔ اے کے امتحان کی تیاری!" میں نے اُسے خشمگیں نظروں سے گھُورتے ہوئے کہا۔" پاگل لڑکی مرجائے گی، صحت کا خیال کر سمجھی!"۔ وہ اسی طرح افسردہ لہجے میں بولی:" ناہید! بچارے پروفیسر ورما کی یہ انتہائی خواہش تھی کہ میں ایم۔ اے کرلوں"۔ "آہ۔! غریب پروفیسر"۔ میں اتنا کہکر خاموش ہوگئی۔ اس روز دن بھر شیاما سُست رہی۔

ایک ہفتہ بعد شیاما چلی گئی۔ پھر میری اور اس کی ایک عرصہ تک ملاقات نہ ہوسکی۔ اسے خط لکھنے کی عادت بالکل نہ تھی اسلئے ایک مدت تک مجھے اس کی بھی خبر نہ ہوسکی کہ شیاما ان دنوں کہاں اور کیسی ہے۔ شیاما کو گئے ہوئے چار ماہ کا عرصہ ہوا تھا کہ ایک روز شیلا کا خط مجھے ملا اس نے لکھا تھا کہ "جی جی کی طبیعت بہت خراب ہوگئی تھی۔ ڈاکٹروں کی صلاح سے سب لوگ انھیں سنیاٹوریم لے گئے ہیں۔ دعا کیجئے کہ ایشور میری

جی جی کو جلد اچھا کردے"۔ یہ خبر میرے لئے انتہائی وحشت خیز تھی۔ بہت دیر تک میرا دماغ کچھ سوچنے سے معذور رہا آخر میں نے یہ فیصلہ کیا کہ جہاں تک جلد ہوسکے گا میں شیاما سے ملنے جاؤں گی خواہ میرے بی۔ ٹی کے امتحان کی تیاریوں میں خلل ہی کیوں نہ پڑے ایک ہفتہ کے بعد میں سینا ٹوریم پہنچی۔ شیاما سے مل کر مجھے بے اختیار رونا آگیا مگر میں نے انتہائی ضبط کے ساتھ ان آنسوؤں کو اپنی آنکھوں ہی میں جذب کرلیا۔ شیاما کی آنکھوں سے آنسوؤں کے موٹے موٹے قطرے گرنے لگے۔ میں نے اسے بہلانے کی خاطر ادہر ادھر کی باتیں چھیڑ دیں وہ کچھ بہل سی گئی اور پھر اس کی مسخری طبیعت عود کر آئی۔ اس نے ہنستے ہوئے کہا "یہ ایم۔ اے کی تیاری ہے ناہید ارے وہ بوڑھا پروفیسر بہت ہی چین سے اب ہوگا، جس کی میں نے ایک بھونڈی سی تصویر پنسل سے بنا کر اس کے کمرے میں چھوڑ آئی تھی۔ تمہیں یاد ہے؟ وہ کس قدر بگڑا تھا"۔ اتنی سی بات کہتے کہتے شیاما بیدم سی ہوگئی کھانسی کی شدت سے اس کا نازک سا چہرہ سرخ ہوگیا۔ وہ تھک کر تھوڑی دیر کے لئے خاموش ہوگئی۔ کچھ دیر بعد وہ اپنی ڈبڈبائی ہوئی آنکھوں سے مجھے دیکھتے ہوئے بولی۔ "آہ یہ کھانسی بہت تکلیف دہ ہے ناہید!" پھر وہ دیر تک اپنی اس قیدی زندگی کا رونا روتی رہی کہنے لگی۔ کالج کی دلچسپ رنگینیوں کے بعد یہ سینا ٹوریم کی زندگی آہ کچھ نہ پوچھو میرے لئے کتنی تکلیف دہ بات ہے۔ یہاں کھانے پینے، اٹھنے اور بیٹھنے کے وقت معین ہیں۔ وہ بولتی جاتی اور کھانسی کے حملے برابر ہوتے جاتے دیر تک ہم

باتیں کرتے رہے جب رسٹ پریڈ کی گھنٹی بجی تو میں خاموشی سے دوسرے کمرے میں چلی گئی اور دیر تک شیاما کی حالت پر غور کرتی رہی۔

تیسرے دن میں واپس چلی آئی۔ جس وقت میں شیاما سے رخصت ہو رہی تھی اس وقت مجھ سے ضبط نہ ہو سکا۔ شیاما کی نازک انگلیوں سے کھیلتے ہوئے میرے آنسو بہتے جا رہے تھے۔ مگر شیاما انتہائی ضبط کیے ہوئے مایوس مسکراہٹ سے مجھے بہلا رہی تھی۔ اس نے ہنستے ہوئے مجھ سے کہا۔ "پھر کب ملو گی ناہید!" میں نے اسے یقین دلایا کہ "جلد ہی۔" اس نے غمگین مسکراہٹ سے مجھے دیکھتے ہوئے کہا۔ "شاید پھر مجھے نہ دیکھ سکو گی۔" میں نے اس کے منہ پر ہاتھ رکھتے ہوئے کہا "ایسی باتیں کرو گی شیاما تو پھر میں کبھی نہ آؤں گی۔" چلتے وقت میں نے اس کی پیشانی کو اپنے ہاتھوں سے سہلاتے ہوئے کہا۔ "خدا حافظ شیاما!" اور وارڈ سے اتر کر چلنے لگی چلتے چلتے میں نے مڑ کر اپنی شیاما کو دیکھا مگر آہ میرا دل ڈوب گیا وہ حسرت بھری نظروں سے مجھے تک رہی تھی اور اس کا رومال بار بار اس کے گرم آنسوؤں کو جذب کر رہا تھا۔

۳

شیاما کی خیریت مجھے برابر ملتی رہی اس کو سینا ٹوریم گئے قریب ایک سال کا عرصہ ہو گیا تھا۔ خبر ملی کہ وہ پہلے سے بہت اچھی ہو

حرارت اب نہیں رہتی ۔" اے۔ پی " دیا جا رہا ہے اس کی صحت کی خبر سُن کر بڑی مسرت ہوئی بے اختیار دل چاہا کہ اسے دیکھ آؤں۔ گرمی کا زمانہ تھا. میں شیاما سے ملنے گئی تو اس نے اپنے بلند بانگ قہقہے سے مجھے خوش آمدید کہا۔ اسے صحت کی حالت میں دیکھ کر مجھے بہت خوشی ہوئی، اس نے وزن میں بھی کافی ترقی کی تھی اور اس کا نمکین سانولا چہرہ اور زیادہ بھولا بھالا ہو گیا تھا۔

اسے یہاں آکر بہت فائدہ ہوا تھا۔ مگر اس کی کھانسی بدستور تھی اس دفعہ میں نے شیاما کو بہت ہی شگفتہ پایا۔ اس کی طبیعت یہاں لگنے لگی تھی۔ مگر کھانسی کے ہر ایک دورے کے بعد وہ مضمحل ہو جاتی ۔بیتاب ہو کر کہتی:" یہ کھانسی اب میری جان ہی لیکر چھوڑے گی، جانتی ہو ناہید ساری طاقتیں کھانسی کی اس مسلسل زیرو زبر میں پس جاتی ہیں" میں اس کی تکلیف وہ کھانسی سے بیقرار ہو کر کہتی۔ اے کاش میں یہاں نہ آئی ہوتی ۔آہ اس کی موٹی موٹی آنکھیں کیسے حسرت بھرے آنسوؤں سے لبریز ہو جاتی تھیں۔ اس کا نازک بدن کھانسی کے دورے سے تھک کر چوُر چوُر ہو جاتا تھا۔

ایک روز اُسے تھوڑی سی حرارت ہو گئی۔ وہ میرا ہاتھ پکڑ کر کہنے لگی۔" ڈاکٹر" فرینک ایولشن" کے لئے کہتے ہیں مگر فرینک سے بھی میں سمجھتی ہوں کوئی فائدہ نہ ہوگا۔" وہ کچھ ٹھہر کر بولی۔" میں موت سے نہیں ڈرتی ناہید۔موت تو ایک زینہ ہے اس دیارِ حبیب میں پہنچانے کا

جہاں جسم سے آزاد میری روح کسی عزیز ہستی سے دائمی طور پر مل کر ہمیشہ مسرور رہے گی۔ ناہید! تمہیں کیا کہ تمہاری شیاما ایک عظیم صدمہ اُٹھا کر بھی کیسے قہقہہ لگا سکتی ہے وہ غمگین آواز میں بول رہی تھی ۔۔۔" میرا جسم خوش ہو کر جھوم جاتا ہے میں قہقہہ لگا سکتی ہوں۔ دنیا کی نظروں میں شیاما ایک مسرور لڑکی ہے۔ لیکن اس کے قہقہے بلند ہوتے ہی فضا میں آگ لگا دیتے ہیں ۔۔۔ آہ میری مسکراہٹوں میں کتنا سوز ہے۔ میرے ہر ایک نفس میں کتنے شرارے لرزاں ہیں ۔۔؟ اور شیاما کی روح وہ تو ہر وقت غم کی آگ میں تڑپتی رہتی ہے۔ ناہید! تم میری روح کی دیوانہ وار چیخ و پکار کو کیا جانو۔ ہاں کسی رات کی تنہائی میں شیاما کی روح اس کے جسم سے گلے مل کر رونے لگتی ہے تو ان محروم آنکھوں سے بھی آنسوؤں کے چند قطرے نکل پڑتے ہیں۔" وہ اتنا کہکر رونے لگی اور میں حیران و پریشان اس کی باتوں کو سن کر خاموش تھی۔

دوسرے روز پھر وہ اپنے مخصوص انداز میں قہقہہ لگا رہی تھی۔ اس روز اس کو حرارت نہیں تھی اور وہ بحال تھی۔ اسی دن شام کے وقت باغ کی صفائی کرتے ہوئے مالی کی بیٹی پولینا کو سانپ نے ڈس لیا اور وہ بیچاری ہم لوگوں کے سامنے ہی تڑپ تڑپ کر سرد ہو گئی تھی۔ شیاما کی

آنکھوں میں آنسو تیرنے لگے وہ پولینا کی لاش کو تکتے ہوئے بولی۔ "ناہید! کیا مرنے کے بعد روح اپنی ایک محبت کرنے والی روح کے ساتھ رہ سکتی ہے؟" وہ افسردہ لہجے میں بولی "ہوسکتا ہے کہ روح قسمت کی نارسائیوں سے آزاد ہو" وہ اپنی باتوں کا جواب خود ہی دے کر بولی "مگر کسے خبر کہ روح کی محرومیاں اور زیادہ ہولناک نہ ہوں"

ایک ہفتہ کے اندر ہی شیاما کا "فرینک ایولیشن" ہوگیا اور میں اس کی پیٹی کھلنے کے دوسرے روز واپس چلی آئی کیونکہ مجھکو بی۔ ٹی کا امتحان دینا تھا۔

ایک ہفتہ بعد مجھے شیلا کا خط ملا اس نے لکھا تھا کہ شیاما کا "فرینک ایولیشن کچھ کامیاب ثابت نہ ہوا۔ اسے پھر حرارت رہنے لگی ہے اور اب وہ سینیا ٹوریم سے اکتا گئی ہے۔

امتحان کی محنت سے میری طبیعت بھی خراب رہنے لگی تھی۔ مگر میں نے اس حالت میں بھی شیاما کو دیکھنے جانا چاہا، لیکن ڈاکٹروں نے وہاں جانے سے سختی سے روکا اور میں مجبور ہوگئی۔ صرف شیلا کے خطوط سے شیاما کی خیریت معلوم ہوتی رہتی تھی۔

کچھ دنوں کے بعد مجھے یہ وحشتناک خبر ملی کہ شیاما اب اپنے مکان پر بنارس میں آگئی ہے اور اس کی حالت

بہت خراب ہے۔ ڈاکٹروں نے مایوسی ظاہر کردی ہے اور یہ کہ میری شیاما میری "منتظر ہے"۔ مجھے یہ خط اس وقت ملا جبکہ میں ۱۰۳ درجہ کے بخار میں پھنک رہی تھی۔ ایک ہفتہ بعد جب میری طبیعت کچھ اچھی ہوئی تو میں بیقراری سے اپنی شیاما سے ملنے آئی۔ مگر کب ؟ افسوس جبکہ میری شیاما اپنی اشکبار آنکھوں سے مجھے ڈھونڈتی ہوئی جاچکی تھی۔

۴

میں شیلا کی مسہری پر لیٹی ہوئی سب باتوں کو یاد کررہی تھی۔ مسہری کے سامنے شیاما کی ہنستی ہوئی تصویر آویزاں تھی۔ میں شیاما کی تصویر کو غور سے تک رہی تھی۔ آہ وہ ہنستا ہوا چہرہ وہ پیاری پیاری آنکھیں اب کیا ہوئیں ؟ تصویر دیکھتے دیکھتے مجھے ایسا معلوم ہوا جیسے شیاما مجھ سے کچھ کہنا چاہتی ہے۔ دفعتہً مجھے خیال ہوا شیاما کی وہ ادھوری باتیں جو کہتے کہتے وہ رونے لگی تھی یونہی رہ گئیں۔ میں مسہری سے تڑپ کر اپنی شیاما کی تصویر کے پاس پہنچی اور اسے

ہاتھ میں لے کر اپنی اشکبار آنکھوں سے دیکھنے لگی۔ یکایک میری نظر دوسری تصویر پر گئی اور میں اسے دیکھکر حیران رہ گئی۔ "کون! کالج کا مرحوم پروفیسر ورما اور اسکے ساتھ میری شیاما"۔ بجلی کی ایک تیز رو کی طرح گذرے ہوئے واقعات میرے دماغ میں جمع ہونے لگے۔ جب شیاما ایف۔ اے کے آخری سال میں تھی تو لوگوں کا یہ خیال تھا کہ پروفیسر ورما شیاما کی طرف بیتابانہ کھنچا جا رہا ہے۔ میں نے شیاما سے دریافت کیا کہ اصلیت کیا ہے مگر وہ معصومانہ انداز میں خود مجھ ہی سے پوچھنے لگی کہ واقعہ کیا ہے؟

پھر عرصہ تک کوئی بات نہ ہوئی۔ مگر جب شیاما بی۔ اے میں فرسٹ آئی تو لوگوں نے خوب پھبتیاں کہیں۔ لوگوں کے کہنے پر میں نے بھی غور کیا مگر مجھے تو بس اتنا ہی پتہ چلا کہ شیاما بہت ہی اچھی لڑکی ہے اور مسٹر ورما غیر معمولی طور پر اس کا خیال رکھتے ہیں۔

۵

بنارس آنے کے دوسرے دن میں گنگا کی طرف طبیعت بہلانے کیلئے چلی گئی۔ چونکہ مجھے راستے کا صحیح علم نہیں تھا اس وجہ سے میں بھٹکتی ہوئی مرگھٹ [illegible] آنکلی۔ میں آئی تو تھی اپنی طبیعت بہلانے مگر آہ!

شمشان کے ہیبت ناک مناظر نے مجھے بڑی طرح تڑپا دیا۔ کیسا بھیانک منظر اف کتنی ویرانیاں ان بربادیوں میں آباد تھیں۔ کتنے حسرت وارمان کی پتھرائی ہوئی آنکھیں ان ذرّوں میں منتشر تھیں اور کتنے دھڑکتے ہوئے بیقرار دل اپنی تمناؤں کے ساتھ خاک کے ان سیاہ ذروں کے ساتھ لپٹے پڑے تھے۔ شمشان کی جھلسی ہوئی زمین کے گرد بے رونق سوکھی ہوئی گھاس سے بیکسانہ لپٹی ہوئی انسانی خاکستریں پڑی تھیں ـــــ!

"شیاما میری عزیز شیاما" میں چیخ چیخ کر رونے لگی۔ آہ کیا میری شیاما اب ہمیشہ کے لئے مٹادی گئی۔ شیاما میری اپنی شیاما، میں شام کی ہلکی تاریکیوں میں اپنی شیاما کو پکار رہی تھی۔ میری شیاما کے ذروں کو اپنی آغوش میں لئے دریا افسردہ روانی سے آہستہ آہستہ شمشان کے جھلسے ہوئے ساحل سے ٹکرا ٹکرا کر بہہ رہا تھا۔ تاریکیاں بڑھتی جارہی تھیں۔ اور شمشان کی ویرانیوں میں اور اضافہ ہورہا تھا۔ مرگھٹ کے ہیبت ناک منظر سے گھبرا کر میں گھر جانے کو مڑی تو دیکھا دریا کے کنارے اور وحشت برس رہی ہے۔ مشرق کی طرف سے چاند آہستہ آہستہ نکل رہا تھا اور اس کی زرد روشنی میں دریا کی ہلکی ہلکی روانی اور ریت کے ذرّے تھرا رہے تھے۔ درختوں کی شاخیں خاموشی سے جھکی ہوئی تھیں اور ان کے سیاہ سائے ان خاموشیوں میں کانپ رہے تھے دور افق کی تاریکیاں ہیبت ناک بھوتوں کی طرح رقص کرتی ہوئی معلوم ہورہی تھیں۔ میں نے گھر چلنے کے لئے دو ہی قدم بڑھائے تھے کہ یکایک میرے کانوں میں

شیاما کی افسردہ آواز سُنائی دی۔ "ناہید!" میں نے مڑکر دیکھا میری شیاما دھوئیں کے رنگ کی ساری میں ملبوس میرے قریب ہی کھڑی تھی۔ میں اسے دیکھتے ہی سر سے پیر تک کانپ گئی۔ شیاما، مری ہوئی شیاما اپنے شمشان میں مجھ سے ملنے کے لیے آئی تھی ـــ مگر آہ، وہ کتنی بیقرار تھی۔ میری ہنستی ہوئی شیاما اب کیسے بدل ڈالی گئی۔ وہ مجھ سے اور قریب آ گئی مجھے غور سے دیکھا اور پھر وہ میرا کانپتا ہوا ہاتھ پکڑ کر آہستہ سے بولی "میری ناہید" اس کی شیریں مگر اندوہگیں آواز سُنکر میرا سارا بدن ایک بار تھرا اُٹھا۔ اور مجھے اچھی طرح سے یاد ہے کہ مجھے گرتا ہوا دیکھکر شیاما اپنے بازوؤں کا سہارا دیتے ہوئے مجھے اپنی آغوش میں لے کر آہستگی سے بیٹھ گئی میں اس کی گود میں سر رکھے آنکھوں کو بند کیے خاموش پڑی تھی اور میرا دماغ ایک بار پھر انہی خوشبوؤں سے معطر ہو رہا تھا جس کی مستانہ شمیم سے میں ہمیشہ مدہوش رہتی تھی۔

میں اپنی شیاما کی فردوسیں آغوش میں خاموش پڑی تھی لیکن انتہائی ضبط پر بھی میری بیقرار چیخ نکل گئی۔ میں نے شیاما کے آنچل کا کونا اپنی مٹھی میں بھینچتے ہوئے کہا۔ "میری شیام مجھے چھوڑ کر اب نہ جانا۔" اس نے ایک لمبی سانس لیتے ہوئے کہا: " ناہید اب تمہاری شیاما بدل ڈالی گئی ـــ میرا وہ جسم جو دنیا کی انتہائی سختیوں کے بعد تمہیں مسرور نظر آتا تھا موت کے ہاتھوں فنا کر دیا گیا۔ ان قہقہے لگانے والے لبوں کو جلا کر آوارہ ہواؤں کی دوش پر منتشر کر دیا گیا........ مرنے کے بعد

روح جسم کی صورت اختیار کرلیتی ہے اور ایک نئی روح اسی روحانی جسم سے پیدا ہوتی ہے — مگر تمہیں کیا خبر کہ پہلے ہی میری روح کتنی پرسوز تھی اور اس پر— اس روح کی مزید بیقراریاں ، آہ کچھ نہ پوچھو"

شیاما اپنی بیچین نظروں سے مجھے تکنے لگی ۔ اس کے لب کچھ کہنا چاہتے تھے مگر وہ ایک کشمکش میں تھی۔ آخر رکتے رکتے وہ بولی. تمہیں کالج کی وہ باتیں یاد ہیں جو لوگ کہتے تھے کہ پروفیسر ورما میرا پرستار ہے، وہ باتیں سچ تھیں نا بیدے! پروفیسر انتہائی گرمجوشیوں سے محبت کر رہا تھا اور میں اس سے گریز کر رہی تھی. وہ مجھے کھنچتا ہوا دیکھکر پروانے کی طرح مجھ پر نثار ہو رہا تھا اور میں شمع کی طرح بے پروا خاموش تھی۔ جب میں دیکھتی کہ پروفیسر کی نگاہیں میرا تعاقب کر رہی ہیں۔ تو میرا دل بھی زور زور سے دھڑکنے لگتا — اور آخر میں پروفیسر کی محبت کی آگ سے محفوظ نہ رہ سکی۔ مگر جیسے جیسے میرے دل میں محبت کی چنگاری شعلہ بن رہی تھی — پروفیسر مجھ سے دور رہنے لگا تھا۔ میں اکثر ورما سے ملنے کے لئے جاتی۔ وہ مجھے دور سے آتا دیکھکر ٹکٹکی باندھے مجھے دیکھتا رہتا مگر جب میں اس کے قریب پہنچ جاتی تو وہ گھبرا کر کمرے سے باہر چلا جاتا...... اور پھر مایوس ہو کر میں واپس چلی آتی۔

پروفیسر کی اس عجیب حرکت پر میں حیران تھی۔ سمجھ میں نہ آتا تھا کہ وہ مجھ سے اب نفرت کر رہا ہے یا محبت۔ جب میں اس سے دور

رہنا چاہتی تھی تو وہ مضطربانہ میرے گرد چکر لگاتا اور اب جبکہ اسے یقین ہوچکا تھا کہ میں بے تابانہ اس کی قربت چاہتی ہوں تو وہ مجھ سے بھاگ رہا تھا۔

ایک روز ٹینس میں وہ میرا شریک بنایا گیا۔ میں خوش تھی مگر جیسے ہی اسے خبر ہوئی کہ میں اس کی ساتھی ہوں تو وہ بنچ پر بیٹھے ہوئے بولا "آج میں کھیلنا نہیں چاہتا"

ایک روز میں اپنے جذبات سے مغلوب ہوکر اس کے پاس گئی۔ اس روز وہ مجھے اپنے قریب دیکھکر بھاگا نہیں۔ میں سخت پریشان تھی...... اور میری آنکھوں میں آنسو تیر رہے تھے۔ اس دن پہلی بار اس نے میرے شانے پر ہاتھ رکھکر کہا۔

"عزیز شیاما! سچی محبت کی تڑپ جدائی چاہتی ہے اور میں اس فراق کے تند جھونکوں میں پُرالم سانسیں لے رہا ہوں مگر تم میری شیاما محبت میں قربت کی خواہشمند ہو؟"

وہ کچھ ٹھہر کر بولی —— "تم پروفیسر ورما کا فلسفۂ محبت تو جانتی ہو! وہ سچ کہتا تھا ناہید، کہ "محبت فراق ہے.... اور فراق محبت"

جیسے ہی شیاما کے مُنہ سے یہ الفاظ نکلے مجھے وہ میرا خواب یاد آگیا اور پروفیسر کی ڈائری کے یہ سطور میرے کانوں میں گونجنے لگے کہ "محبت نام ہے فراق کا اور موت اس جدائی کا ایک

ابدی ذریعہ ہے۔

بی۔اے کے دوسرے سال جب میں پروفیسر سے ملنے کے لئے آئی تو یہ سن کر بیچین ہوگئی کہ وہ بیمار پڑا ہے اور اسکی زندگی کی کوئی امید نہیں۔ میں پریشاں حال اس کے پاس پہنچی ——— دیکھا تو وہ سچ مچ بہت بیمار تھا۔ میں اس کے سوکھے ہوئے ہاتھ کو اپنے ہاتھ میں لے کر اس کے پاس بیٹھ گئی۔ لیکن اس نے اپنی نحیف آواز میں مجھے اپنے سے دور رہنے کو کہا۔ وہ پُرنم آنکھوں سے مجھے دیکھتے ہوئے بولا ——" ٹی۔ بی کے مریضوں سے دُوری چاہیئے شیاما اور پھر اس حالت میں جبکہ وہ چند دنوں کا مہمان ہو۔"

اس نے مجھے لاکھ ٹالنا چاہا مگر میں نے صاف کہہ دیا کہ میں موت سے نہیں ڈرتی۔ میری جان سے زیادہ تم عزیز ہو، اور اب میں خوش ہوں کہ میں نے اس کا ساتھ دیا۔" وہ آہستہ سے اٹھی اور غمگین آواز میں بولی " زندگی بھر تمہاری شیاما بیچین رہی اب مرنے کے بعد بھی اس کی روح کو سکون نہ ملا۔ اور میرا ورما، آہ، ناہید وہ مجھ سے اب تک نہ ملا۔" وہ مجھے حسرت بھری نظروں سے تکتے ہوئے بولی۔" وہ کہاں ہے ناہید! میرا ورما کہاں ہے؟"

شیاما نے اپنے ہاتھ کے ایک ہلکے سے جھٹکے سے اپنی ساری کا کونہ میری مٹھی سے چھڑا لیا اور غمناک سروں میں گاتی ہوئی چلی گئی۔ بہت دیر تک اس کی دردناک مدھم آواز افق میں

ڈوبتی ہوئی سُنائی دے رہی تھی۔

میں کھوجت کھوجت ہار گئی

تم کِس نگری میں بستے ہو!"

بیچاری

گھر گھر گھر کی ایک عجیب موسیقی سارے گھر بھر پر چھائی تھی، چکی کا ایک موٹا پاٹ مسلسل گھوم رہا تھا۔ مٹیالے رنگ کی بھوسیاں اور مسور کی لال لال چکنی چکنی دال چکی کے گرد جھر جھراتی ہوئی گر گر کر ڈھیر لگتی جا رہی تھی، اور وہ اسی طرح دال بھوسی اور مسور کے گردے کے بیچ میں لت پت زور زور سے چلاتی رہی۔ بالوں کا ایک گرد آلود گھوپا اس کے سر پر چھا رہا تھا۔ وہ دونوں پاؤں پسارے اپنے سارے جسم کو آگے اور پیچھے کی طرف جھٹکے دے دے کر مسور کے ایک ڈھیر میں بیٹھی دال دلتی جا رہی تھی۔ چکی چلاتے وقت اس کے لبوں پر کوئی گیت لہرا نہیں سکتا

دور تک کھنچے ہوئے اس کے ہونٹ اس وقت بھنچے ہوئے تھے اور اس کی اداس نیم نگاہوں میں جیسے ماضی کے دور دراز خواب جھلک رہے ہوں۔ تقدیر کے ایسے ہی بھاری پتھروں کی گردش میں اس کی اپنی زندگی بھی پس چکی تھی اور اب وہ حال کے اندھیروں میں اپنے کانپتے ہوئے ہاتھوں سے زندگی کے لامعلوم دروازے کو ٹٹولتی ہوئی مستقبل تک پہنچنے کا کوئی اجالا سا راستہ ڈھونڈ رہی تھی ـــ! کام کرنا کوئی عیب نہ تھا، وہ کلکتہ اور رنگون کی کمائی کی بہاریں دیکھ چکی تھی، پھر لوٹ کی اندھی لٹس کی ریل پیل اپنے بھرپور ہاتھوں سے اس نے کتنا لٹایا تھا اور اپنے اسی گاؤں میں اپنے بھائی بندوں کی حیران نگاہوں کے سامنے اس کا شوہر اپنی قوت بازو کے نشے میں چور تماشے کے طور پر اپنی کمائی کے روپے کو امارت کے گھمنڈ میں تالاب میں مچھلی پر نشانہ لگا کر پھینکتا اور ایک دفعہ اس نے دس دس روپے کے نوٹ کا سگرٹ بنا کر دھواں بھی اڑا دیا تھا ـــ! ہری، لال، پیلی اور بسنتی رنگ کے ریشمی آنچلوں کے کتنے ہی پھریرے وہ ہواؤں میں لہرا چکی تھی۔

گھر وہی تھا وہ بھی وہی تھی اور ساری چیزیں بھی ویسے ہی تھیں۔ مگر وقت گزر چکا تھا۔ خود اس کے اپنے ساتھ اس کی بعض چیزوں میں تبدیلی آ گئی تھی، تنی ہوئی سُتلی کی سفید پلنگ میل سے چٹی ہو کر اب جھولنے لگی تھی۔ اور ان کی لمبی لمبی ٹوٹی ہوئی ڈوریاں زمین پر مچلتی رہتیں۔ مگر ان کے علاوہ رینگتے بلبلاتے میلے کچیلے اس

کی جان کو کھانے والے بچے اب ذرا بڑے ہو کر نکھر گئے تھے۔ ان کی بجبجاتی ہوئی ناکوں پر سے مکھیاں اڑ چکی تھیں اور وہ دن بھر میں کئی کئی بار اپنے اسارے میں مٹی کی پیلی اور چکنی دیوار میں ایک ٹوٹے ہوئے آئینے کے جڑے ہوئے ٹکڑے میں اپنا منہ آکر دیکھ لیتے تھے! اپنی عمر کے پندرہ سال سے ایک ہی کام کرتے کرتے وہ بیزار ہو چکی تھی، اور اب جبکہ اس کا جی تھکا تھکا سا لگتا تھا اسے اس بات کی خوشی تھی کہ انسانی کلبلاتے ہوئے کیڑے اس کی گود میں رینگتے نہ تھے۔ اپنی زندگی کی مسرت اور سارا آرام اس نے ان ہی پلپلے سے بچوں کے پیچھے حرام کر دیا تھا۔ اور اب وہ آزاد تھی، ساری کی ساری راتیں اس کی اپنی تھیں۔ اب اس کا جتنی گھڑی جی چاہتا سو کر اُٹھتی، ساری گھر داریاں اس کی لڑکیاں کرتیں اور لڑکے سب صبح اٹھتے ہی باسی تازہ کچھ کھا کر گلی ڈنڈا، غلیل اور لٹو لے کر گلیوں اور پہاڑوں کے دامن میں کھیلنے کو چلے جاتے تھے۔ آنکھوں کا اندھا ایک شوہر تھا جس کا خوف اس کے پسینے کے ساتھ مٹ چکا تھا۔ وہ اکیلا بیٹھا اپنی لاٹھی زمین پر ٹپک ٹپک کر بکتا رہتا۔ مگر اس گھر میں اس آواز کی کوئی پرواہ نہ تھی۔! لیکن اس کی آنکھوں کے ساتھ اس کا پندار بھی ایک دم سے اندھا نہ ہو گیا تھا۔ کبھی کبھی وہ اپنے گھر میں اپنی کھوئی ہوئی جگہ حاصل کرنے کے لئے وہ کئی کئی طرح کے جتن کرتا۔ اندھیرے میں بیٹھا ہوا وہ تھوڑی سی، گول مرچ۔ سونف اور کالا نمک چبانے کی

مہین چھنی ہوئی راکھ کے ایک ڈھیر میں ملاکر ہاضمے کی گولیاں بناتا، اور اسی طرح آنکھوں کا سرمہ بھی بنایا کرتا تھا؛ میلے اور صاف کاغذ کی پڑیوں کا جب ایک تشفی بخش انبار لگ جاتا تو وہ انہیں ٹٹول ٹٹول کر اپنے انگوچھے میں رکھ کر دو چار موٹی موٹی گرہیں لگا کر اپنے کثیف بستر کے نیچے چھپا دیتا۔ جب سے اس کی آنکھوں کی روشنی چلی گئی تھی خود اپنے لوگوں پر سے بھی اس کا اعتبار ختم ہو گیا تھا۔ کبھی بہت ہی صبح سویرے اور کبھی شام کے دھندلکے میں اپنی بنائی ہوئی دواؤں کی گٹھری لئے وہ اپنے سب سے چھوٹے بیٹے کے سہارے جس پر ابھی اسے بھروسہ تھا۔ گھر سے باہر نکل جاتا۔ وہ کہاں کہاں جاتا کدھر کدھر مارا پھرتا تھا۔ کسی کو معلوم نہ تھا۔ وہ اکثر آٹھ آٹھ دنوں کے بعد گھر آتا اور کبھی پندرہ پندرہ دن بھی گذر جاتے تھے۔ مگر وہ جب بھی گھر واپس آتا تو اس کی چال میں پہلی سی رعونت ہوتی اور اس کی اپنی ذرا بھاری سی گرجدار آواز چند لمحوں کیلئے گھر کے کونے کونے میں گونج اٹھتی اس کے بیٹے کے سر پر اناج کی کبھی ہلکی اور کبھی بہت بھاری سی گٹھری ہوتی اور منیر کی کمر میں کھڑ کھڑاتے ہوئے ایک ایک روپے کے چند نوٹ رہتے اور کچھ جھنجناتے ہوئے پیسے ہوتے اور سارے گھر بھر پر ایک مسترسی چھائی رہتی، مگر یہ دنیا! — چین ہی کب لینے دیتی ہے کسی کو منیر کے گھر کا دو دن کا سکون گاؤں والوں سے دیکھا نہ گیا۔ ہاضمے کی گولیوں اور سرمہ کی پڑیوں کو وہ لوگ بھول گئے تھے جنھے

منہ اتنی ہی باتیں، کوئی کہتا" اندھا منیر اب اتنا گزر گیا کہ بیٹے کا ہاتھ پکڑے گاؤں گاؤں سے پھر کر بھیک مانگ لاتا ہے۔ اندھی آنکھوں سے اب دور کی سوجھنے لگی ہے" زیادہ سے زیادہ تکلیف دہ اور دلوں کو چھیدنے والی عجیب عجیب سی باتیں پھیلتی رہتیں۔ لیکن منیر کو ابھی تک اپنے قوتِ بازو پر بھروسہ تھا اور پیسے کی طاقت کو وہ اچھی طرح سے جانتا تھا۔ اسی لئے اس نے ان باتوں کی طرف کوئی توجہ نہ دی۔ لیکن اس کی بیوی نے بستی کے ایک ایک گھر میں جاکر اس بات کے لئے شور مچایا کہ" دنیا بھر کے ڈاکٹر حکیم وید کبیراج گیا سب کے سب بھیک منگے ہی ہوتے ہیں جو ایک غریب کو اس طرح سے ذلیل کیا جاتا ہے" منیر کی بیوی نے اسی بستی میں اپنے ہاتھوں سے اپنی دولت لٹائی تھی اور سوائے چند بڑے گھرانوں کے سبھی اس کے مقروض رہ چکے تھے۔ گاؤں کی پتھریلی گلی میں چلتے چلتے وہ پچھلے دنوں کے خواب دیکھنے لگتی۔ اسی گلی کے نکڑ پر مٹی کی ان پرانی دیواروں سے نکلی ہوئی انہی کرچھیوں میں اس کے سرسراتے ہوئے ریشمی آنچل کبھی کبھی اُلجھ اُلجھ پڑتے تھے۔ مگر اب دیواروں کی کرچیاں پہلے سے زیادہ نکیلی ہو ہو کر باہر نکل آئی تھیں اور اب بھی اکثر آتے جاتے منیر کی بیوی یا بیٹی کی میلی ساڑیاں ان کرچیوں سے اٹک اٹک کر پھٹ پھٹ جاتیں۔ منیر کی بیوی کو کبھی کبھی اس تنگ گلی کی دونوں طرف اونچی اونچی کرچیوں سے بھری ہوئی دیواریں ہیبتناک بھوتوں کی خوفناک زبانوں کی طرح نظر آتیں۔ جو اس کی خوشیوں کو دیک

کی طرح چاٹ گئی تھیں اور اب وہ نوکیلی سُرخ سفید اور مٹیالے رنگ کی ہزاروں دیکیں اس کے دل و دماغ سے چمٹتی ہوئی اس کی روح میں رینگ رہی تھیں — ! اس کی زندگی میں کیا کیا انقلاب نہ آئے تھے پھر بھی اس نے اپنے ضمیر کو زندہ رکھا تھا اور اسے بس اسی کی خوشی تھی۔ وہ محنت سے گھبراتی نہ تھی۔ اور یہی ایک چیز ایسی تھی جس کی بنیاد پر کم سے کم وہ اپنی امیدوں کے گھروندے بنا سکتی تھی۔ ریلوے لائن کے کنارے یہ گاؤں آباد تھا۔ اس میں شریف مسلمانوں کے گھرانے ایک پہاڑی اونچے ٹیلے پر آباد تھے۔ یہ ٹیلہ دراصل اس گاؤں کی سربلندی کا علمبردار بھی تھا۔ ٹیلے کے نیچے کوری اور اچھوتوں کی ٹولیاں آباد تھیں جو رعیت اور محکوم ہوتے ہوئے بھی اب آہستہ آہستہ ٹیلے کی طرف اپنا سر اٹھا رہے تھے۔ اکا دکا چھوٹے چھوٹے ٹھنٹھ درختوں والا صحرائی گاؤں بڑا پُرسکون تھا۔ ٹیلے کے نیچے حدِ نظر دھان کے ہرے بھرے لہلہاتے ہوئے کھیت کا حسین منظر، ایک طرف سلسلہ وار اونچے سیاہ رنگ کے پہاڑ اور ان کے قدموں کے آگے مچلتی ہوئی وسیع برساتی ندی کا پیچ وخم کبھی سنہری بریع کی فصل اور کبھی کبھی چھوٹے چھوٹے سبز پودوں میں یاقوت کی طرح سرخ سرخ مرچوں سے لدے ہوئے دہکتے ہوئے کھیت بس یہی سارے خزانے تھے گاؤں بھر کے، ان میں سے کسی کا سرمایہ زیادہ تھا اور کسی کا کم، اور بہت سے لوگوں کا تو کچھ بھی نہ تھا۔ مگر آنکھیں سبھی کی ٹھنڈی ہوتی تھیں اور یہ بکھرے ہوئے حسن تو سب کے لئے یکساں طور پہ تھے

ٹیلے پر بھی کثرت سے مکانات تھے۔ سربلند اونچے اونچے کوٹھے اور اُن سے لگے ہوئے پپیتے، امرود اور شریفے کی باڑیاں تھیں۔ مٹی کے وسیع لپے پتے ہوئے سادہ مکان بھی تھے۔ پھونس اور پیال کے چھپروں والے نیچے نیچے تنگ گھروں کی بھی آبادی تھی۔ اور ان کے درمیان گلیاں تھیں۔ عجیب عجیب طرح کی بے ڈھنگی، اونچی نیچی پہاڑی گلیاں ـــ خاص خاص گھرانے والیاں کبھی کبھار آتے جاتے ذرا پہلے سے ان گلیوں میں پردے کرالیا کرتی تھیں۔ ان کے علاوہ ان گلیوں میں آزادیاں رہتیں اور جب کسی کا جی چاہتا بے جھجک ان میں آتا جاتا۔ ٹیلے پر آنے والی لمبی گلی میں اکثر شام کو مویشیوں کا ایک تانتا بندھ جاتا اور میلے کچیلے کسان ایک ہلکی سی آہٹ پر ہی اپنے انگوچھے میں منہ چھپا کر گردنیں موڑ لیتے تھے منیر کی بیوی کی طرح گاؤں کی اکثر غریب عورتیں صرف اپنی محنتوں سے اپنے گھر چلا رہی تھیں اور اونچے گھرانوں میں روز ہی کوئی نہ کوئی کام رہتا ہی تھا۔ سال سال بھر کے خرچ کی دالیں ایک ہی دفعہ دل کر غلے کی لمبی لمبی کوٹھیوں میں بند کر دی جاتیں، منوں گیہوں چنے بنائے جاتے پھر چاول چھانٹا بنایا جاتا، کبھی جو بونٹ اور مکئی کے ستو پیسے جاتے تھے اسی طرح سارے گھروں کی چکی ان کے ہاتھوں چلتی رہتی اور اس کے ساتھ ان کی قسمتیں بھی ایک ہی محور پر گردش کرتی چلی جاتیں آہستہ آہستہ اور کبھی تیز رفتاری کے ساتھ۔ منیر کی بیوی کے ہاتھوں کے کام اس لئے زیادہ سراہے جاتے تھے کہ وہ دوسروں کی چیزوں

کی نگرانی بڑی ہمدردی سے کرتی۔ شاید اپنی چیزوں کو کھو کر اس نے یہ سبق سیکھا تھا۔ اسی لئے ہر گھر میں اس کی مانگ تھی۔ ساری چیزوں کو اپنے ٹھکانے پر لگا کر وہ اپنی دن بھر کی مزدوری آنچل کے ایک کونے میں باندھ کر اسی پتھریلی گلی کے باہر نظروں سے اوجھل ہو جاتی۔ شام کے دھندلکے میں اس کے لبوں پر ایک نڈھال مگر زخشندہ تصور چھایا رہتا۔ اور یہ دیہات کا ایک آمرانہ دستور تھا کہ دن بھر کے تھکے ہوئے مزدور کی اُجرت پیسے اور اچھے غلے کی جگہ سب سے موٹا اناج دیا جائے۔

اپنے گھر سے باہر ہی رہنے میں اُسے کچھ سکون ملتا تھا۔ چکی کی گھر گھر اور ڈھینکی کے ڈھکر چوں میں اس کی پریشانیاں کچھ دیر کے لئے دور ہو جاتی تھیں مگر اپنے گھر میں نظروں کے سامنے چلتی پھرتی چٹان سے وہ کیسے آنکھیں بند کر لیتی اور بے سہارا اتنے بڑے پہاڑ کا بوجھ اسکے سینے پر سے کس طرح اتر سکے گا۔ یہ فکر ایسی تھی جس نے اسے دہلا رکھا تھا۔ طیبہ کا خوبصورت دمکتا ہوا چہرہ کبھی کبھی اس کے دل میں آگ لگا دیتا، وہ کیا کرے گی؟ اور اب تو اندھا منیر بھی چار مہینے سے بے کار ہو گیا تھا۔ بڑی پریشانیوں کے بعد اس نے طیبہ کا رشتہ قریب ہی ایک دوسرے گاؤں میں ٹھیک کر لیا تھا۔ اس رشتہ کے ساتھ اس کو اچھی طرح سے معلوم تھا کہ لڑکے کی ماں کتنی ظالم اور ڈائن ہے جس نے خود اپنی بیٹی کا کلیجہ نکال لیا ہو وہ ڈائن نہیں تو کیا تھی، سارے گاؤں والے چشم دید طور پر یہ بات جانتے تھے کہ اس عورت نے اپنے داماد سے خفا ہو کر سوتے میں

اس کے ہاتھ پاؤں باندھ کر کس بے دردی سے اُس پر مٹی کا تیل چھڑک کر اس میں آگ لگا دی تھی۔ اور جب وہ بے چارہ تڑپ تڑپ کر مر گیا تب کہیں جا کر اس کا کلیجہ ٹھنڈا ہوا۔ مگر دیہات کی پُر پیچ گلیوں میں یہ بات دَب دبا کر رہ گئی ــ اور یہ سب جانتے بوجھتے ہوئے بھی اس گھر میں وہ اپنی بیٹی کو بھیجدینے کو تیار تھی۔ وہ انتہائی سرگرمی سے اپنے کاموں میں جُٹ گئی رات اور دوپہر اس نے ایک کر دیا۔ کبھی اس گھر میں کبھی ان کے یہاں اور کبھی دوسرے مکان پر وہ ہر وقت مصروف ہی رہتی تھی۔ اس کے سمدھیانے سے شدید تقاضے ہونے لگے تھے اور اسے بھی جلد سے جلد یہ بار اتار دینا تھا۔ سارے گھرانوں میں بڑی بیگم کا گھر اس کو اپنا جیسا لگتا، بڑی بیگم کے گھر کا سلوک بھی اچھا ہوتا تھا۔ اور خود بڑی بیگم اسی ایک گھر اور اسی بستی میں جوان سے بوڑھی ہوئی تھیں۔ ان کی آنکھوں نے بہت سے تماشے دیکھے تھے۔ جس وقت وہ اپنی مخصوص آواز میں کہتیں "منیر کی بٹیا" تو اس کی آنکھیں مسرت سے چھلک پڑتیں۔ وہ سارے کام چھوڑ کر ان کے پاس بیٹھ جاتی "تمہارے اور یہ دن ہوتے" بڑی بیگم منہ میں پان رکھکر بولتیں۔ "آؤ ذرا بیٹھ کر دم لے لو" اس وقت منیر کی بیوی کے کھردرے مگر گورے گورے ہاتھ بڑی بیگم کے پاؤں دبانے لگتے۔ "بس بیگم بھابی کسی طرح طیبہ کا بیاہ ہو جائے اللہ ہی عزت رکھ لے تب" بڑی بیگم کے بھتیجہ کی شادی تھی ایک مہینہ پہلے ہی سے بڑی بیگم کے بھائی خود سے آکر ان کو جلال پور لے گئے۔

بڑی بیگم کا میکہ بہت امیر تھا، ہزاروں کی زمین داریاں تھیں اور کتنے اعلیٰ عہدوں پر کرسی نشین تھے۔ اکثر بڑی بیگم یہ کہا کرتی تھیں کہ "میرے دونوں ہاتھ بھرے ہیں ایک میں چاند اور ایک میں سورج نیہر سسرال سب روشن ہے۔"

منیر میاں کا گھر پیلی مٹی سے لیپ کر چونے سے جگہ جگہ چیت کر گلدار بنا دیا گیا تھا شام ہوتے ہی ڈھولک کی ڈھب ڈھب کے ساتھ گیتوں کی تیز جھنکار بستی بھر میں گونج جاتی۔ منیر کی بیوی نے اپنے طور پر تھوڑا بہت انتظام کرلیا تھا۔ پھر بھی بہت سے کام ابھی باقی رہ گئے تھے برات کا پورا کھانا ستلی کا ایک لال جہیز کا پلنگ اور دولہا کے لئے ایک مپنیا ابھی باقی رہ گیا تھا۔ مگر اب وہ ایسا محسوس کرتی جیسے راستہ چلتے چلتے اس کے پاؤں آبلوں سے چھلنی چھلنی ہوگئے ہیں۔ اس میں آگے بڑھنے کی ذرا بھی ہمت نہ تھی۔ راستہ سامنے پڑا تھا، منزل دور سے جھلک رہی تھی، اسکے پاؤں کا جیسے دم نکل چکا تھا۔ کاش اسے دو مہینے اور مل جاتے پھر جس طرح سے اس نے اتنا سامان کیا تھا۔ اتنا بھی کرلیتی، مگر اب تو گھٹا جھوم کر چھا چکی تھی وہ کر ہی کیا سکتی تھی، جب اس کا دماغ سوچتے سوچتے تھک گیا تو وہ ایک عزم کے ساتھ اٹھی۔ اسے اپنے اس پہاڑی اونچے ٹیلے والے گاؤں ہرے بھرے کھیتوں اور سنہرے پونجوں والے کھلیان پر اعتبار تھا۔ آخر یہ بکھری ہوئی کس دن اس کے کام آئیں گی۔ اس کے کانوں میں زور زور سے سیٹیاں بجنے لگیں۔ "نہیں" "نہیں"

اس کے دل ودماغ کی کشمکش اس کا راستہ روک رہی تھی مگر وہ تیزی سے بڑی بیگم کے صدر پھاٹک کے دروازے کو آگے ڈھکیلتی ہوئی اندر چلی گئی۔ گھبرائی گھبرائی پریشان۔ اس کی زندگی میں یہ پہلا واقعہ تھا۔ وہ کمرے کے اندر جھکی ہوئی سرگوشی میں آہستہ آہستہ بولی۔ ”دلہن بیگم مجھے اسوقت عزت رکھنے کو ساٹھ روپے قرض دے دو۔ میں تمہارا یہ روپیہ فصل کیوقت دھان کو ٹنے پر ادا کر دوں گی۔ برسات آ رہی ہے۔ بس شروع جاڑے تک مہلت دے دو۔ اور اگر جلدی ہے تو تمہارا کام کر کے چکا دوں گی۔“

”ساٹھ روپے؟“ دولہن بیگم ذرا سوچنے لگیں مگر وہ رحمدل تھیں۔ دس دس روپے کے چھ نوٹ انھوں نے منیر کی بیوی کو دیتے ہوئے کہا۔ ”اچھی آدمیوں کی تنگی تم دیکھ رہی ہو۔ یہ روپے بھی تمہارے ہی ہیں شادی کے بعد یہاں کام کرنا شروع کر دوگی۔“

منیر کی بیوی کا سر جھکا یا اس کے کندھے پر قرض کا جوا بڑا بھاری محسوس ہوا، مگر اس کا دل مطمئن تھا اور اسے اپنی محنت پر بھروسہ تھا۔

شادی اچھی طرح سے ہوئی۔ ساری برات اور بستی کے لوگ خوش تھے۔ منیر میاں نے نہ ہونے پر بھی اچھا دیا تھا۔ دلہن کو گود میں اٹھا کر جب رخصت کے لئے لے جایا جانے لگا اس وقت منیر کی بیوی دلہن بنی ہوئی اپنی بیٹی سے لپٹ کر پھوٹ پھوٹ کر رونے لگی ماں اور بیٹی ایک دوسرے سے لپٹ لپٹ کر اس بے بسی سے رو رہی تھیں۔

جیسے کسی کو قتل کیا جا رہا ہو۔ منیر کی بیوی اب سبکدوش تھی۔ اُس نے ایک ہلکی سی موٹری اپنے کندھے پر رکھکر ایک بہت بڑا بوجھ اپنے سر پر سے اتار دیا تھا اور وہ بھی اس خوبصورتی کے ساتھ کہ عزت کی عزت رہ گئی اور یہ سب صرف ایک اکیلی عورت ذات نے اپنے بل بوتے پر کیا تھا۔

بڑی بیگم کے آتے ہی منیر کی بیوی خوشی خوشی لہستی ہوئی وہاں پہنچی وہ اپنے دونوں ہاتھوں میں کچھ لئے اسے آنچل سے چھپائے سیدھی بڑی بیگم کے پاس آکر کھڑی ہوگئی۔ "منیر کی ٹمیا مبارک ہو۔" بڑی بیگم نے پلنگ پر سے پاندان کو سرکا کر جگہ بناتے ہوئے کہا۔" منیر کی بیوی کا آنچل زور سے پھڑ پھڑایا۔" بیگم بھابی، طیبہ کے بیاہ کا کھانا تو آپ کو نہ کھلایا بھلا ایسا نصیب کہاں تھا میرا۔ بیگم بھابی یقین مانو جی ترس ترس کے رہا ہاتھ کا نوالا حلق کے پار نہ ہوا۔ بس یہی لگے سب کوئی ہے میری بیگم بھابی ہی نہ رہیں اس گھڑی ــــ!

بڑی بیگم پان بنا رہی تھیں اگلدان میں پیک تھوک کر بولیں۔

" منیر کی ٹمیا بھلا ایسی گرمی میں بھی بیاہ کرتے ہیں خالی بربادی ـــ؟"

" ہاں بیگم بھابی بہت ٹھیک کہہ رہی ہو میرے یہاں برات اور سرات کو کھلا پلا کر ایک دوسری دیگچی میں بھر کے پلاؤ بچ گیا صبح ہوتے ایک دم لاسا، ایسے ہی ڈوم لے گیا ـــ!"

"اللہ میرے بھائی کے یہاں بیسیوں تو مرغ مُسلّم بجکر سڑتے

رہے کسی نے نظر تک نہ کی اس طرف، منوں دودھ پھٹ کر کھنکتا پڑا رہا اور میٹھے ٹکڑے تو اتنے بچ گئے تھے کہ دائی نوکر تک نے نہ پوچھا۔ گرمی سی گرمی۔ اللہ کی پناہ — آٹھ باورچی تو صرف پٹنہ سے آئے تھے میوہ بھری باقرخانی تک کو دیکھا نہ جاتا تھا۔ ہاں تو منیر کی بٹیا تم نے کیا کیا دیا اپنی بیٹی کو"— بیگم بھابی چاندی ہی کا سہی مگر دیا سب کچھ کان میں بالی گلے میں حمیل ہاتھ میں پہونچی اور بتانا اور پاؤں میں اپنا والا کڑا برتن میں دو دیگچی ایک ایک لگنی دو رکابیاں ایک گلاس اور ایک لوٹا اس بیگم بھابی اور کیا دیتی!

"ارے منیر کی بٹیا بھلا تم بچاری کے یہاں کا بھی بیاہ ہے! میرے بھتیجہ کو برتن ملے ہیں، یہ یہ تو لگن ہیں" بڑی بیگم نے اپنے دونوں ہاتھوں کو انتہا تک پھیلاتے ہوئے کہا۔" اور دیگ ہیں، بس یہی سمجھو کہ آدھے کنوئیں ہیں وہ، میرے باپ کا اتنا بڑا مکان جیسے بھر گیا جہیز سے، اور سونے کا زیور ملا ہے جی! یہ یہ موٹا! وزنی وزنی، دلہن سر سے پیر تک سونے کے گہنے سے پٹی ہوئی تھی۔ کڑے، چھڑے پازیب تک سونے کے، ایسے جیسے آگ دہک رہی ہو۔ اور پھر تم بیچاری کیا دیتیں جہیز جو دیا بہت دیا۔" منیر کی بیوی کے آنچل کے اندر سے قیں قیں کی آواز سن کر بڑی بیگم چونک پڑیں "یہ کیا ہے منیر کی بٹیا تمہارے ہاتھ میں —؟"

"یہ — یہ بیگم بھابی تمہارے۔لئے تو لائی ہوں تھوڑا گھی

باسمتی اور یہ مرغی —" اس نے آنچل ہٹا کر بغل میں دبی ہوئی مرغی کو دکھاتے ہوئے کہا۔" سب لوگوں کو تو کھلا چکی، بس ایک تم ہی باقی رہ گئی ہو بیگم بھابی اسی لئے یہ لائی ہوں کہ اپنی باورچن سے ذرا اچھی طرح سے پکوا لو میں خود سے پنکھا جھل جھل کر تمہیں کھلاؤں گی۔ بیگم بھابی — طیبہ کے بیاہ کا یہ کھانا ہے نا"۔ منیر کی بیوی کے لب بولتے ہوئے کانپ رہے تھے۔

" ارے تم بیچاری کیا کھلاؤ گی کھانا۔ رہتے تو سب کے ساتھ ہم بھی کھا لیتے اب یہ خاص کر کے اتنا خرچ اخراج کرنا — پاگل ہو گئی ہو — رکھ دو جا کے یہی سب کام آدے گا داماد کے آنے پر — بھلا کہاں سے لاؤ گی تم بیچاری —!" بڑی بیگم نے پھر ذرا آہستہ سے کہا۔" ہاں منیر کی بٹیا تم تو آؤ گی نہ دلہن کے پاس ہے؟

منیر کی بیوی نے دائی گیری کبھی نہ کی تھی۔ آزادانہ مزدوریاں کر کے گزارہ کرتی جا رہی تھی۔ دلہن بیگم سے تو اس نے اپنے وقت پڑنے پر جوشش کلام میں کھانا پکانے کا وعدہ کر دیا تھا۔ دائی لونڈی کے کام سے اس کے پندار کو ٹھیس لگتی تھی۔ نیچ کام — بڑی بیگم کی یہ آخری بات سن کر جیسے وہ کوئی ہولناک خواب دیکھتے دیکھتے یک بیک بیدار ہو گئی تھی اور اس کی بیداری خواب سے بھی زیادہ تلخ تھی —! مہینوں کی انتھک محنتوں کے بعد اچانک طور پر اس کا بند بند ٹوٹنے لگا تھا۔ وہ تھکی ہوئی شکست خوردہ دیوار سے لگی کھڑی تھی، اسکا

سر جھکیرا رہا تھا، پلنگ پر سامنے ایک رکابی میں پاؤ بھر باسمتی اور ایک چھوٹے سے پیالے کے پیندے سے لگا ہوا تھوڑا سا گھی پڑا تھا اور اس کے پسینے سے شرابور بغل میں سمٹی ہوئی مرغی اس سے اور زیادہ دبک کر سمٹ گئی تھی۔ کھڑے کھڑے اُس کے پیر کانپ رہے تھے۔ اُس کو اس بچاری کے نام سے شدید نفرت تھی۔ اس مجبور اور اپاہج نام سے اِسے گھِن لگتی تھی۔ اور وہ اپنی محنتوں کے بل بوتے پر اپنے کو اس بے بس نام سے بلند سمجھے ہوئے تھی۔۔۔ "بیچاری۔۔۔" بیچاری" کی آواز دل کے تیز دھک کے ساتھ اس کے دماغ پر ہتھوڑے لگا رہی تھی۔ اس کی پرُنم نگاہوں کے آگے "بیچاری"۔ "بیچاری" کے لفظ سے بھرے ہوئے دس دس روپے کے چھ نوٹ کٹے ہوئے پتنگ کی طرح فضا میں بے تحاشہ ڈگمگا رہے تھے!

صدائے واپسیں

"لے آلو! لے پلول! لے ساگ، توریں، کریلا جھینگی! لے بینگن لے ترکاری!"۔ ہوا کی طوفانی سنسناہٹ اور پانی کے شور کے ساتھ تھرتھراتی ہوئی یہ مسلسل آواز گلیوں سے آرہی تھی۔ تیز ہواؤں کے ساتھ زور سے پانی برس رہا تھا۔ اور کپکپا دینے والی سردی سے بدن کی ہڈیاں اکڑی جارہی تھیں۔ سڑک سنسان پڑی تھی دوکانوں پر ٹاٹ کے پردے اور جالی دار ٹٹھریاں ڈالدی گئی تھی۔ سامنے ہر لمحہ گردش کرتی ہوئی دنیا کی طرح چکر لگاتا ہوا کولہو تک خالی پڑا تھا اور اس کا مریل سا بیل دھوبی کے لاغر گدھے کے ساتھ ساتھ گلی کی دیوار سے لگا دبکا کھڑا تھا۔ اس کے قریب ہی پکوڑیوں والے گندے

حلوائی کا گھنونا مرتوکا باسا کتا اپنے مالک کے سرد چولھے کے اوپر منہ کو پیٹ میں چھپائے بےخبر سو رہا تھا۔ ایسی خاموش فضا میں مجھے محسوس ہوا جیسے دنیا بھی گردش کرتے کرتے اپنے محور پر تھک کر سو گئی ہے صرف آسمان اور کرۂ ہوا بیدار تھا۔

بارش اور زور سے ہونے لگی تھی میں نے باورچی کو پکار کر کہا "آج مسور کی خوب دال دی ہوئی پتلی کھچڑی پکانا آلو کا بھرتا۔ مرچ کی چٹنی، گھی بریانی کیا ہوا اور انڈے کا آملیٹ بنا دو گے سمجھے؟ اب کہاں ایسے پانی میں بازار کرنے مارے پھرو گے"۔ دروازے کے اندر داخل ہوتی ہوئی ایک تیز آواز میرے سامنے گونجی "ترکاری لیا جائی"؟ "آلو ہے توریں ہے۔ ساگ پیاج۔ بیگن۔ نیموں۔ جوکھو جو" ایک ترکاری والی بڑھیا پانی سے شرابور کانپ رہی تھی اور نمایاں طور پر اسکی سوکھی ہوئی گردن بوجھ کے احساس سے بار بار ہلتی جا رہی تھی۔ لیکن۔ اس کی تھرتھراتی ہوئی آواز میں ایک رعونت تھی اور پھولی ہوئی بیمار جھریوں کے اندر دھنسی ہوئی آنکھیں میلے تاگے سے جا بجا بندھی ہوئی داغدار عینک کے اندر فاتحانہ طور پر چمک رہی تھیں۔

اس نے اپنے سر پر رکھی ہوئی ٹوکری کو بڑی مشکلوں سے گردن کو کئی کئی طرح سے سوداگرانہ جنبش دے دے کر باورچی کی مدد سے اتارا بھیگے ہوئے میلے کپڑے سے ڈھنکی ہوئی ٹوکری لے کر وہ اپنے سامنے بیٹھ گئی۔ ہاں بولو تو کون سی ترکاری؟ کتنا کتنا؟ اس نے

ٹوکری کے اُوپر سے بانس کا ترازو ہاتھ میں لیتے ہوئے کہا۔ باورچی اس کے پاس برتن رکھتے ہوئے بولا "ارے پہلے بھاؤ تو بتاؤ۔ کتنے کتنے سیر بھاؤ؟ بھاؤ کا آج کیا ہے؟ چھ آنے آلو۔ پانچ آنے توریں۔ بارہ آنے پلول۔ آٹھ آنے پیاج دو دو آنے نیموں"! باورچی حیرت سے منہ پھاڑ کر کہنے لگا "کا بڑھیا آج لوٹے آئی ہے بھلا اتنا منہگا بھی ترکاری ہے کہیں"؟ بڑھیا نے وقت کی نزاکت کا احساس کرتے ہوئے اپنے ہاتھ کا ترازو ٹوکری میں رکھکر کہا کہ تب جاؤ جہاں سستا ہو وہیں سے لے لینا۔

مگر باورچی کو غرض تھی اور وہ پانی اور سردی سے بچتے ہوئے بھی گھر بیٹھے ٹھیک ٹھیک داموں میں ترکاری لینی چاہتا تھا۔ اور شاید بڑھیا بھی اس کڑکڑاتی ہوئی سردی میں اپنے سر پر کا بوجھ ہلکا کر دینا چاہتی تھی۔ اس نے دوبارہ ترازو اٹھا کر پوچھا کہ کتنا کتنا سیر اور کیا کیا ترکاری لینی ہے۔

اسنے بڑے اہتمام سے ٹوکری پر سے اس طرح کپڑا ہٹایا جیسے نئی دلہن کی رونمائی ہو رہی ہے۔ ساری ٹوکری لال ساگ سے بھری ہوئی تھی اور اس کے علاوہ ٹوکری کے حاشئے پر گردا گرد بھٹے یوں آراستہ کر کے کھڑے کئے گئے تھے جیسے گل مچھے والے سپاہی کسی ہری بھری دولت کی حفاظت کر رہے ہوں۔

"کیا بڑھیا آج خالی ساگ ہی بھر کے لائی ہے"؟ وہ زور

سے کہنے دیگا۔ ارے سب۔ ہٹ جی سب۔ بڑھیا اندر سے ترکاری نکالتے ہوئے خوشامدانہ ہنسی ہنستی ہوئی بولی۔ اس کی رعونت ختم ہو کر اب مترحمانہ صورت اختیار کر گئی تھی "بڑا پانی ہوا ہٹ بیٹا" وہ ٹھہر ٹھہر کر اسے تول رہی تھی جیسے کوئی ملزم سزا ملنے سے پہلے کی ایک ایک گھڑی کو غنیمت سمجھتا ہو "آج تو ہاٹو نہ ٹھکانے سے لگا" ترازو کے ایک باٹے پر موٹی موٹی توریں جھولتی ہوئی کبھی اوپر کبھی نیچے جا رہی تھی "ہاں بیٹا لو آدھ سیر توریں۔ بڑی کنکنی ہے اچھا کئے بیٹا ہاٹ نہ گئے جان ہے تو جہان اور ای لو پاؤ بھر بلول"

باورچی تھوڑی سی ترکاری دیکھتے ہی جھلا گیا تھا اس نے موٹی موٹی توریں کو واپس کرتے ہوئے کہا کہ وہ اتنی خراب باسی اور سنائی ہوئی ترکاری نہ لے گا "نہ نہ کہاں تریں سنائی ہوئی ہے" بڑھیا موٹی موٹی تریں کو بیچ سے توڑتی ہوئی بولی "بلا سے نا ہے مگر ہم دوسرا لینگے" باورچی ساگ کو ترکاری پر سے ہٹاتے ہوئے بولا۔ بڑھیا تڑپتی ہوئی زور سے چیخ اٹھی "دیکھو دیکھو ہاتھ نہ لگاؤ ہمری سب ترکاری مل جل جے رہے"؛ مگر باورچی نے سب ساگ کو ترکاری پر سے ہٹا کے جیسے بڑھیا کے چہرہ پر سے نقاب اٹھا کر اس کی جھریوں کو اور نمایاں کر دیا تھا۔

ٹوکری گویا خالی پڑی تھی صرف اس کے پیندے پر تھوڑی تھوڑی ہر قسم کی ترکاری چھترائی ہوئی تھی۔ مجھے یہ پر مذاق سین دیکھ کر

ہنسی آ گئی۔

برتن میں الی ہوئی ترکاری کو بڑھیا کی ٹوکری میں پھینکتے ہوئے باورچی بکنے لگا کہ بڑی ترکاری بیچنے چلی ہے۔ پاؤ بھر پلول، سیر بھر تریں سے کر کنجڑن بنی پھرتی ہے۔ جھوٹ موٹ میں اس نے اتنی دیر سے، اسے الجھائے رکھا تھا۔ اور مول جول تو ایسے کر رہی تھی جیسے اپنے باوا کے کھیت سے من من بھر ترکاری توڑ کر لائی ہے

شکست خوردہ اور منرحمانہ نظروں سے میری طرف دیکھتی ہوئی بڑھیا رو پڑی "بہت گریب ہیں بابو بہت گریب" اس کی دھنسی ہوئی آنکھوں کی مٹیالی پتلیاں آنسو میں تیر رہی تھیں اور اس کے لبوں کے گوشوں کی لمبی لمبی جھریوں کی لکیروں میں رال تیر رہی تھی۔ مسوڑھوں کی بندشوں سے آزاد ہوتے ہوئے لمبے لمبے پیلے دانت بولنے میں ابھر ابھر آتے تھے وہ اپنی کہانی سناتی گئی اپنے طبقے کی طرح وہی ایک پلاٹ والی سادہ سی کہانی۔ وہ تین نوجوان بیٹوں کی ماں تھی اور اس کے اپنے کھیتوں میں کبھی ترکاریاں لہلہاتی تھیں زلزلہ میں اس کا ایک بیٹا دب کر رہ گیا اور دو ملیریا سے ختم ہو گئے۔ جب کھیت کے بیل ہی نہ رہے تھے تو کھیت کیسے رہتا اور اب اس کے دکھوں کی شریک حال ایک دکھیاری بیٹی رہ گئی تھی جو جنم ہی سے روگ لے کر آئی تھی اور اب اسے طحال اور جگر نے ادھ موا کر دیا تھا۔ اتنی شدید سردی اور ایسے پانی میں وہ محض اس لئے قرض لے کر ترکاری بیچنے کو نکلی تھی کہ قرض میں سود واپس

کر کے کچھ آنے اس کے پاس بچ رہیں گے جس سے وہ اپنی بیٹی کی دوا لا سکے گی۔

ایک لمحہ کے لئے وہ چپ ہو گئی۔ اس کی نگاہیں نجانے کیوں آسمان پر چھائی ہوئی بدلیوں پر جم کر رہ گئیں۔ اور میں اس کے جھریوں والے بیمار چہرے کو دیکھتی رہی جہاں سے آنسوؤں کی دھاریاں بہتی ہوئی اس کے بھیگے ہوئے آنچل میں جذب ہو رہی تھیں۔

اس نے بڑی لجاجت سے کہا۔ "کچھ بھی لیلو بیٹی" میں ایک عجیب کشمکش میں مبتلا تھی۔ ترکاریوں پر بڑھیا کے آنسو ابھی تک چمک رہے

باورچی دوسری طرف سے آ کر بڑھیا کو دیکھتے ہوئے بولا" جا۔ جا ابھی تک بیٹھی ہوئی ہے۔ نام گنا دے کو سوٹھو، پلول لو، آلو لو، جھوٹی۔ آ جکا سمجھے ہے بڑھیا کہ نام گنا دے سے ٹوکری بھر جاگی ہے!

اس کو کیا معلوم تھا کہ نام لینے سے ٹوکری کبھی بھر بھی جاتی ہے جس کے پاس کچھ بھی نہ ہو اس کے پاس صرف نام ہی نام تو رہ جاتا ہے اور یہی اس کا سب کچھ ہوتا ہے، اگر آج وہ ان ناموں کو بھی بھول جائیں تو پھر اس دنیا میں ان کا کیا باقی رہے گا؟۔ کھو کھلے نام اور آنے والے "کل" کا انتظار ہی تو انکی زندگی کا سہارا ہے۔ دنیا بھر کی ترکاریوں کے نام کی صدا لگا کر کون جانے کہ وہ اپنی حسرتوں کو فریب دیتی تھی یا گاہکوں کو۔ ایک ہی سانس میں اتنے ناموں کو گنتے ہوئے وہ ایک لطیف سا خواب دیکھنے لگتی جہاں ترکاریوں کی رنگ

برنگی قوس و قزح میں اس کے ارمانوں کی دنیا شاداب نظر آتی ہوگی، وقتی طور پر ہی سہی، وہ تھوڑی دیر کے لئے اپنے کو ایک کامیاب بیوپاری تو سمجھ لیتی تھی۔ تاجرانہ فریب۔ سبھی تاجر ایسا کرتے ہیں۔ شاید فریب بڑا ہو کر فریب نہیں رہتا اسی لئے بڑے جھوٹوں کی پکڑ نہیں ہوتی۔

بڑھیا مجھ سے پھر کہنے لگی "کچھ بھی لے لو بیٹی" مگر میں نے اپنے ضمیر کی سرگوشیوں کو خاموش کر دینے کے لئے وہاں پر سے اٹھ کر جاتے ہوئے کہا۔ "کل لونگی بڑھیا ضرور لونگی"، مجھے بڑھیا کی سڑ سڑاتی ہوئی ناک اور بہتی ہوئی آنکھوں سے پھر گھن آنے لگی تھی۔ جانے کہاں کہاں ان ترکاریوں میں کتنے آنسو جذب ہو چکے ہونگے۔

وہ چپ چاپ ساگ کو پھر ترکاریوں پر بچھاتی ہوئی اپنی کانپتی انگلیوں سے ٹوکری کو بڑی آسانی سے سر پر رکھکر باہر نکل گئی۔ تیز ہوا اندر آرہی تھی، میں جب اٹھ کر دریچے کے شیشوں کو بند کرنے لگی تو گلی میں سے پانی کے شور کے ساتھ ساتھ تھرتھراتی ہوئی مگر زور دار آواز آرہی تھی۔

"لے آلو۔ لے پٹول۔ لے ساگ توریں۔ لے بیگن کریلا، لے سبھی ترکاری"

سوکھا ہوا پودا

یہ روپے کا جب سے سوا سیر چاول ہوا تھا اُس نے نہ تو پیٹ بھر کر کھانا کھایا تھا اور نہ بھوک سے رات بھر وہ اچھی طرح سویا ہی تھا۔ روکھے پھیکے دو ایک نوالے جب وہ اپنے حلق سے نگلنے لگتا تو تلی کے بدبودار تیل کی مہک سے جیسے اس کا دماغ پھٹ جاتا، اور اس گرانی کو یاد کر کے اس کی روح گھٹنے لگتی، وہ جتنا کھاتا نہیں اس سے زیادہ روز روز کی فکر خود اس کی زندگی کو کھاتی جا رہی تھی۔ اس کے رکشے کے ہر ایک ٹوٹے ہوئے چول کی طرح اس کی پسلی اور ریڑھ کی ہڈیاں گلے کے کنٹھ مالے اور ہنسلیاں اور وگدگی اس کے بھورے چمڑے کے اندر

سانس لینے میں ایک دوسرے سے ٹکرا ٹکرا سی جاتیں۔ اس کا چہرہ سوکھے ہوئے لیموں کی طرح ہر طرف سے پچک گیا تھا اور چہرے کی ہڈیاں نمایاں ہوگئی تھیں۔ وہ نہیں جانتا تھا کہ اس کو کیا ہو گیا ہے، لیکن سارا سارا دن رکشا چلاتے چلاتے تھک کر نڈھال جب وہ سونے لگتا تو اس کے تلوے اور ہتھیلیاں بڑی طرح جلتی رہتیں؛ اور اس کا کرتا باوجود سردی کے پسینے سے تر رہتا تو اُسے خیال ہوتا، شاید وہ بیمار ہو رہا ہے! اور وہ ہر روز سوچتا کہ حکیم جی کی پُڑیا یا کوئی مصفّی کھا لے گا لیکن ساتھ ہی ساتھ اسے اپنا رکشا یاد آجاتا۔ جس کے چول کی مرمت زندگی کے للچاتے ہوئے چولوں سے کہیں زیادہ اہم تھی،

صبح سے دوپہر تک کا وقت اس کے لئے بڑا منحوس گذرا تھا اور اس کو یقین تھا کہ سویرے سویرے اس نے اپنا شگون خود ہی سے بگاڑ لیا تھا مگر وہ کیا کرتا؟ اتنے تھوڑے سے کرائے پر وہ کیسے خاموش رہتا۔ آخر وہ بھی تو انسان تھا اور اسے بھی کسی نہ کسی طرح جینا ہی تھا۔ مگر اس نے سوچ لیا تھا کہ اب وہ کسی سے نہ تو بگڑ کر بولیگا اور نہ جھگڑا ہی کرے گا۔ اس کا خیال تھا کہ دل دکھا کر سکھ نہیں ہوتا۔ مگر اس کے دل میں جیسے کوئی آہستہ سے کہتا۔ "تیرے سینے میں بھی تو دل ہے پھر لوگ تیرا خیال کیوں نہیں کرتے ۔۔؟"

سڑک کے ایک کنارے وہ اپنے رکشا کے گدے پر بیٹھا ہوا

سوچتے سوچتے ہنس پڑا " اور جب کرایہ مانگو تو اکثر یہی ہوتا ہے کہ کتے بھونکتے ہیں، نوکر ڈپٹتے ہیں اور احاطے کے پھاٹک بند کر دیئے جاتے ہیں "۔۔۔!

" بچاری غریب سواریاں وہ تو اپنی ہی ہیں اگر وہ بھی درد کو درد نہ سمجھیں تو پھر کیا ہے ؟" ۔۔۔!

صبح سے چار بجے تک اس کی جیب میں آج کی کمائی کُل آٹھ آنے پیسے تھے ! اور چار سبز لال بھورے رنگ کے ایک آنے اور دو اور ایک پیسے والے ٹکٹ۔ اسے ان ٹکٹوں سے بڑی نفرت تھی بصیرت کی نایابی کے ساتھ وہ بڑی مشکلوں سے ٹکٹ لیتا۔ اکنی دوقی اور پیسے دیکھتے دیکھتے اس کی آنکھیں جنم سے عادی ہو چکی تھیں مگر اسے ٹکٹوں کے دام ذرا بھی معلوم نہ تھے کہ یہ کتنے کے ہیں۔ بہت سمجھانے پر اس نے رنگوں کو یاد کر لیا تھا کہ اس رنگ کی قیمت کیا ہے اور اس رنگ کا ٹکٹ کتنے کا ہوگا ! مگر سب سے بڑی دقت تو یہ تھی کہ برسات کی مرطوب ہوا سے اس کے جیب میں پڑے ہوئے ٹکٹ ایک دوسرے سے چپک کر عجیب طرح کے ہو جاتے جنہیں بڑی مشکلوں سے وہ بیٹھا بیٹھا الگ کرتا رہتا۔

وہ اپنے نزدیک کی آواز سن کر چونک پڑا۔ جب سے ہاتھ پاؤں میں جلن رہنے لگی تھی اس کا دماغ عجیب طور سے سنسناتا رہتا اور اس کے کانوں میں ہر گھڑی رکشے کی گھنٹیوں کی تحلیل ہوتی ہوئی مدھم گونج کی طرح سیٹیاں سی بجتی رہتیں۔ اس نے کسی طرح کا

مول جول کئے بغیر بتائے ہوئے راستے پر اپنا رکشا موڑلیا۔ اس کو بخار سا محسوس ہو رہا تھا۔ اس کی طبیعت گری گری لگ رہی تھی اور اس کا منہ نیم کی طرح کڑوا تھا۔ اس نے اپنے حلق کے آخری سرے سے سوکھی ہوئی گردن کو اوپر کھینچتے ہوئے کھنکھار کر بھین بھر رسدار تھوک پھینکتے ہوئے اپنا رکشا ٹھہرالیا۔

اسے ڈاکٹر کے یہاں جانا تھا کسی مریض کو دکھانے کیلئے جب وہ جانے لگا تو رہ رہ کر اس کے دل میں یہی خیال آرہا تھا کہ ان دونوں میں بیمار کونسا ہوگا؟۔ اسے ہر بات کرید نے کی لت تھی۔ وہ رکشا چلانے والے اور ٹمٹم میں جوتے ہوئے ٹٹوؤں میں بہت بڑا فرق محسوس کرتا تھا، اس کے پیر پیڈل چلاتے، ہاتھ ہنڈل اور برک پر رہتا، مگر دماغ ــــ وہ اپنے پیچھے گدّے پر بیٹھے ہوئے لوگوں کے متعلق اکثر سوچتا رہتا۔ اور اس وقت بھی وہ اپنے سوکھے پیروں سے آہستہ آہستہ پیڈل چلاتا ہوا یہی سوچ رہا تھا کہ ان میں مریض کونسا ہوگا۔؟! "کیا دونوں؟" ریشمی تسری چادر کے خاکستری رنگ میں لپٹا ہوا تندرست جسم دمک رہا تھا اور سفید سِلکن کرتے میں وہ سوچ بھی نہ سکتا تھا کہ کوئی مریض ہو سکتا ہے۔

اسے بار بار تیز چلنے کی تاکید کے ساتھ ساتھ ڈانٹ پڑنے لگی تھی۔ جس طرح ہر چابک پر مریل گھوڑا بھی کچھ دیر کے لئے سارا زور لگا کر آگے بڑھنا چاہتا ہے، اسی طرح وہ بھی انتہائی کوشش کرنے لگا

کہ گھڑی گھڑی گولیوں کی طرح سنسناتی، قلب و جگر کو چیرتی ہوئی یہ ڈانٹیں اسے نہ سننا پڑیں۔ اس کے سوکھے ہوئے پیروں کی اُبھری اُبھری انگلیاں پیڈل پر اپنا سارا زور لگا کر بھی اُسے تیز نہ کر سکیں۔ اس کے جسم کی اُبھری ہوئی ہڈیاں اپنا سارا زور لگانے میں جھولنے لگیں وہ پسینے سے تر ہو جاتا ہے اور رکشے کا ہر مجروح پرزہ چرچرانے لگتا۔ مگر رکشا اپنی معمولی رفتار سے آگے نہ بڑھ سکتا تھا۔ وہ رکشے کے گدے پر سے ایک سخت ڈانٹ سن کر جھلا گیا۔ اس نے پیچھے مڑ کر دیکھا۔ وہ جواب دینا چاہتا تھا۔ مگر اس کے لب خاموش رہے۔ اس سے کچھ بولا نہ گیا۔ اس کی نگاہیں دم بھر کے لئے آدھی کی دھوتی سے پھسلتی ہوئی تندرست موٹی اور گٹھیلی پنڈلیوں پر گئیں۔ اس نے رکشا کو زور سے آگے کی طرف کھینچتے ہوئے اپنی انگلیوں کے ساتھ تانت کی طرح تنے ہوئے پٹھوں کو دیکھا اور پھر اپنے گھٹنوں کی گول گول اُبھری ہوئی مردوں کی طرح ہڈیوں کو بھیانک طور پر آگے پیچھے جاتے ہوئے دیکھکر سوچنے لگا "کاش اس کی پنڈلیاں بھی ویسی ہی ہوتیں موٹی موٹی سی"۔۔۔ اس کا رکشا ڈھلوان پر سے تیزی سے اترنے لگا۔ اسے اپنے رکشے کی یہ رفتار ہی بڑی اچھی لگی۔ اسے محسوس ہوا جیسے ہمیشہ سے اسکا رکشا ہوا کیطرح چلتا رہا ہے۔ اس کے سوکھے سوکھے پاؤں کی پنڈلیاں تندرست اور گٹھی ہوئی ہیں اور رکشے کے لچلچاتے ہوئے چول سُرخ بھاپ نکلتے ہوئے گرم گرم گوشت

کے ٹوکروں سے بڑھے ہوئے تیزی سے چل رہے ہیں۔

اسے کئی پھیرے دیگر ڈاکٹر کی کوٹھی پر جانا پڑا۔ جگہ جگہ اس کا رکشا رکتا رہا۔ کبھی چین اتر گئی کبھی اونچی سڑک پر وہ اپنے ہاتھوں سے اسے کھینچتا ہوا لے گیا۔ جب اس نے شہر کے ایک بہت بڑے ڈاکٹر کی کوٹھی پر اپنے رکشے کا بریک روکا تو وہ تھک کر نڈھال ہو گیا تھا۔ اپنے جنگھیے کی جیب سے اس نے ایک میلا سا رومال نکال کر پسینے سے تر اپنا ماتھا پونچھا۔ اس کے چہرے کی ابھری ہوئی ہڈیوں سے لپٹے ہوئے ڈھیلے ڈھالے مٹیالے زرد چمڑے پر دہکتے ہوئے تانبہ کی سی سرخ تمتماہٹ تھوڑی دیر کے لئے جوانی کا تناؤ اور صحت کا کھویا ہوا رنگ سا ابھر گئی۔

وہ مریض اور اس کے ساتھی جب کوٹھی کے اندر چلے گئے تو وہ تھکا ہوا پریشان اپنے رکشے کے پہیے سے لگ کر بیٹھ گیا۔ پسینہ اب بھی اس کے مساموں سے نکل رہا تھا، اسکی دونوں ہتھیلیاں ٹھنڈی ہو رہی تھیں اور پیروں کے تلوے جیسے شل ہوئے جا رہے تھے۔ سوکھی کھانسی اس کے حلق میں اٹکی ہوئی تھی اور وہ بمشکل سانس لیتا ہوا کھانسنے لگا۔ اسکی کھانسی بڑھتی گئی اور وہ اپنے ہاتھوں سے سینہ کو دبائے بڑی طرح کھانستا رہا۔ جب اس کی کھانسی رکی تو اس نے اپنی طرف بہت سے لوگوں کو متوجہ دیکھا جس میں سے اکثر تو وہ مریض تھے جو بنچوں اور کرسیوں پر ایک کنارے بیٹھے

اپنے بلائے جانے کا انتظار کر رہے تھے اور کچھ اسی کوٹھی کے خدمتگار بھی تھے۔ ڈاکٹر کا موٹر ڈرائیور ہر آنے جانے مریض پر بڑا مہربان تھا۔ ایک وقت میں کسی سے حالات دریافت کرکے ہمدردیاں بھی کر رہا تھا اور ساتھ ہی ساتھ کسی کو بڑے اپنائیت اور محبت سے دوا کھانے کے طریقے، آرام کرنے کی ضرورت اور زندگی کی اہمیت کو سمجھا رہا تھا، اس کے گرد بھی ایک بھیڑ لگی ہوئی تھی۔ کھانسی کی تیز آواز سے لوگ چونک پڑے تھے۔ مہربان ڈرائیور نزدیک جاکر اس کی کھانسی رکتے ہی بولا "تمہیں بڑی بڑی کھانسی ہو رہی ہے ابھی سے خیال رکھو اتنی ہی سے کیا سے کیا ہو جاتا ہے اور دیکھنے ہو کیسی کھوکھلی کھانسی ہے تمہاری؟ اپنا خیال کرو میاں۔ جوان جہاں ہو پھر بڑو پر مت جاؤ۔ بیوی بچے ہیں نہ تمہارے۔ کیسے ہلدی کی طرح پیلے ہو رہے ہو۔ جیو میاں جیو"۔ وہ ابھی تک کھانسی سے بیدم ہو کر مشکلوں سے سانس لے رہا تھا۔ اس کی آنکھوں کے حلقوں میں پسینے کے چھوٹے چھوٹے قطرے جمع ہو گئے تھے۔ اپنے بس سر اٹھا کر اسے دیکھا اور بہت دیر تک اسکی نگاہیں اسی طرف جمی رہ گئیں، ساکت، خاموش ظاہراً سامنے دیکھتی ہوئی آنکھیں کھلی تھیں مگر اس نزدیکی سے وہ بہت دور دیکھ رہی تھیں۔ زندگی کے ٹیڑھے ترچھے راستے، کہیں ٹیلے کہیں کھائیاں، ان دشوار گذار راستوں پر اسطرح پسینے پسینے ہو کر ٹھنڈی ٹھنڈی انگلیوں سے زندگی کی ٹوٹی پھوٹی ملجگی ہوئی ہنڈل کو پکڑے کون کھینچتا ہے! جینے کی تمنا؟ یا کشش حیات؟ گمراں راستوں سے

ہوتے ہوئے اس کی منزل کہاں تھی -؟ وہ کہاں جا رہا تھا۔ موت کی طرف؟ اس خیال کے آتے ہی وہ چونک پڑا۔ اس نے محسوس کیا جیسے شاید وہ سو گیا تھا شام کے سناٹے میں اس کا جی گھبرایا گھبرایا سا لگ رہا تھا۔ ڈوبتے ہوئے آفتاب کی زرد روشنی میں اس کو زمین، آسمان، درخت، مکان، دنیا کی ساری چیزیں ہلدی کی طرح پیلی، بیماریوں میں لپٹی زور زور سے کھانستی سسکتی، تھکی اور بیدم سی لگ رہی تھیں۔ اسے ڈرائیور کی باتیں یاد آئیں اس نے مریضوں کی طرف حسرت سے دیکھا۔ کتنے لوگ بیٹھے ہیں۔ اگر ان لوگوں میں ایک وہ بھی ہوتا تو کیا ہو جاتا شاید لوگ اسے ساتھ نہ بٹھاتے۔ بلا سے وہ زمین پر ہی بیٹھ جاتا۔ مگر اس کی یہ کھانسی، ہاتھ پاؤں کا جلن، ابھری ہوئی یہ بھیانک ہڈیاں اور منہ کا اتنا تیتا مزہ یہ سب تو ختم ہو جاتا۔ اسے محسوس ہوا جیسے وہ بہت بیمار ہے اور کھانسی! ابھی اس نے سنا تھا کہ کھوکھلی کھانسی بڑی بری ہوتی ہے۔ اگر کبھی اسے بھی ڈاکٹر صاحب دیکھ لیتے تو پھر وہ اچھا ہو جاتا۔ ایک تندرست انسان رکشا پر بیٹھے ہوئے مریض کی طرح اس کی پنڈلیاں بھی موٹی موٹی ہو جاتیں۔ اسے زور کی پیاس لگ رہی تھی۔ اس کا حلق سوکھا جا رہا تھا۔ کوئیں کا صاف پانی اس کی آنکھوں کے آگے جھلک رہا تھا۔ مگر اس کے ہاتھ میں کچھ نہ تھا۔ نہ بالٹی تھی اور نہ ڈوری۔ سوچتے سوچتے اس کا جی ڈوبنے لگا کیسے مریض ہیں یہ کتنی دیر لگائیں گے۔ مالی پودوں میں جھرنے

سے پانی دے رہا تھا۔ وہ ایک طرح سے برابر کٹے ہوئے گانسوں کو دیکھنے لگا۔ "اچھا یہ لگ رہا ہے"۔ اور ہر طرح کے پھولوں کو دیکھ کر اسے بڑا سکون محسوس ہوا سارے پھول لہلہا رہے تھے۔ جوہی، بیلے، کامنی، گل مہندی اور جسیں سبھی طرح کے پھول کھلے تھے، مگر اس نے ان شاداب پودوں کے درمیان ایک سوکھتا ہوا گلاب بھی دیکھ ہی لیا۔ اسے مالی پر بڑا غصہ آرہا تھا جو سارے پھولوں میں پانی دیتا ہوا بے پروائی سے اس سوکھتے ہوئے گلاب کو نظر انداز کر کے آگے نکل گیا تھا۔ اس کا دل چاہا کہ مالی کے ہاتھوں سے پانی کا جھرنا چھین کر اس سوکھتے ہوئے گلاب کی جڑوں میں اتنا پانی دے کر ان ہڈیوں کی طرح سوکھتی ہوئی شاخوں میں سے سرخ رنگ کی نرم و نازک لپٹی ہوئی پتیاں نکلنے لگیں اس نے اُدھر سے منہ پھیر کر ندر سے ٹھنڈی سانس لی۔ اس کی نظر پھٹے ہوئے کرتے سے ہوتی ہوئی اپنی پسلی کی اُبھری اُبھری ہڈیوں پر گئی۔ گلاب کی سوکھی ہوئی شاخیں دور تک اس کے چمڑے کے اندر پھیلی ہوئی تھیں۔ انہیں دیکھتے ہوئے اسے یکایک محسوس ہوا جیسے اس کی پسلیوں میں سے نئی نئی تہہ بتہہ نازک نازک کونپلیں پھوٹ رہی ہیں۔

اس کی سواری واپس آکر رکشے پر بیٹھ گئی تھی، مگر وہ اسی طرح خاموش رکشے سے لگا بیٹھا رہا جیسے اسے کسی بہت ہی اہم مریض کو دکھانا باقی رہ گیا ہے اور وہ اس کے آنے کا منتظر ہے

اور جب اس نے کئی پکار پر اپنا رکشا ڈاکٹر کے مکان سے واپس موڑا تو پھاٹک تک پہونچتے ہی اس کے رکشے کی چین اتر گئی۔ چین چڑھاتے ہوئے اسے خیال آیا کہ اسے کچھ کرنا ہے۔ اور وہ کوئی چیز بھول گیا ہے مگر اسے کوئی بات یاد نہ آئی اور جب وہ سڑک کے اچھے راستے پر آیا تو وہ اپنے دماغ سے ساری باتوں کو بھلا دینے کے لئے زور زور سے اپنا رکشا چلانے لگا۔ ہر طرف جھولتا جھالتا، چیں چیں کرتا بہت سی چرمراہٹوں کے ساتھ وہ اپنے رکشا کو تیزی سے چلا رہا تھا اس کے ہاتھ اور پاؤں تھک گئے تھے اور اس کا دماغ گھومتا ہوا لگ رہا تھا۔ اس کے کانوں میں ڈرائیور کی آواز گونج رہی تھی۔ "جیو میاں جیو" ہاں وہ ضرور جیئے گا مگر وہ کیسے زندہ رہے گا آخر اس کے دماغ میں ایک ہل چل سی مچی ہوئی تھی اور اس کشمکش سے نکلنے کے لئے وہ انتہائی محنت اور تیزی سے اپنا رکشا چلائے بھاگا جا رہا تھا۔ یک بیک گندی گالیوں کے ساتھ تیز دانٹ سن کر اس کے گھومتے ہوئے پیر رک گئے۔ اس کی نگاہوں کے سامنے بجلی کی روشنی میں ڈاکٹر کی جگمگاتی ہوئی وہی کوٹھی تھی۔ وہ کئی پھیرے کئی چکر لگا کر پھر وہیں آپہنچا تھا جہاں سے چلا تھا۔ وہ تھک کر ہانپ رہا تھا۔ اس نے رکشے کی اترے ہوئے چین کی طرف

بے پروائی سے ایک نظر ڈالی اور باہر سڑک کی طرف پھاٹک کی ستون سے لگ کر وہ ریشمی خاکستری چادر اور سفید سلکن کرتے کو نظروں سے اوجھل ہوتے ہوئے دیکھتا رہا۔

سڑک کے ایک کنارے کوڑوں کے ڈھیر میں پتھر کوئلے کی سفید سفید راکھ سے اپنے دونوں ہاتھ اُجلے کیے ہوئے مُنیا زور سے ہنس پڑی "ہی ہی ہی" - ارے بھیا دیکھ رے، میرے اِی ملا" اس کی پتلی پتلی، راکھ میں لتھڑی ہوئی انگلیوں میں ایک ٹوٹی ہوئی گڑیا تھی، جسے وہ بڑے شوق اور پیار سے الٹ پلٹ کر دیکھ رہی تھی ــــ اور اس کا بھیا بیچ سڑک پر کئی لونڈوں کے ساتھ بہت انہماک سے گولیاں کھیلتا کھیلتا کبھی کبھی نظروں سے اوجھل ہو جاتا تھا۔ مُنیا کے قریب ہی بیٹھی ہوئی اس کی ننھی سی بہن اپنی مٹھی میں کوڑے پر سے راکھ اٹھا اٹھا کر اپنے منہ میں ڈالتی جا رہی

——— پتھر کوئلا کے جلے ہوئے چھوٹے ٹکڑے منیا نے راکھ کے اتنے ڈھیروں میں سے چن چن کر ایک چھوٹی سی ڈلیا میں تھوڑا سا رکھا تھا۔ وہ کوڑے، کرکٹ اور راکھ کے ایسے بہت سے ڈھیروں کو جانتی تھی کہ وہ کہاں کہاں اور کس کس جگہ پر ہیں۔ اسکے ننھے ننھے پاؤں دیکھنے میں تانت کی طرح سخت لگتے اور قمیص کی جھولتی ہوئی آستین سے باہر نکلے ہوئے ہاتھ بھی ویسے ہی تھے مٹیالے رنگ کے اور دبلے دبلے سے۔ اس کے چھوٹے سے معصوم چہرے پر اپنے کام کی سنجیدہ ذمہ داری چھائی رہتی۔ مگر کبھی کبھی جیسے ایکدم سے اکتا کر وہ کھلکھلا کر ہنستی ہوئی اپنی پیشانی پر لٹکتے ہوئے گرد سے اٹے ہوئے بالوں کو اپنے دونوں ہاتھوں سے نوچنے لگتی۔ کوئلا چنتے چنتے ایک ہی دفعہ اس کے سارے جسم میں چیونٹیاں سی کاٹنے لگتیں۔ ایک ہی طرح سے بار بار کھجلا کھجلاتے اسکا جی گھبرانے لگتا تھا۔ اور اس پر سے بتیا کی چیخیں جو روتی ہوئی اپنا ہاتھ اٹھا اٹھا کر اس کی گود میں جانے کو مچلنے لگتی تھی۔ جب سے منیا نے سفید چادر اُڑھا کر اپنی اماں کو پلنگ پر لے جائے جاتے ہوئے دیکھا تھا، اس روز سے یہ بتیا ہر دم اسی کی ننھی سی جان سے چمٹ کر رہ گئی تھی۔ اماں کا بیمار چہرہ پھر اس نے کبھی نہ دیکھا تھا، وہ اس روز روئی بھی تھی، مگر ایسے ہی بے جانے ہوئے۔ بس اس نے اتنا ہی دیکھا تھا کہ منوا بھیّا اور کنوا بوبو رو رہے ہیں۔" اماں رے اماں" اور اسے بھی رونا آگیا۔ کنوا بوبو کو تو اسی روز اسکے سسرال والے

رکشا پر بٹھا کر لے گئے۔ مگر ان تین ننھے بچوں کو کسی نے نہ پوچھا تھا۔
شلجم کا پتہ چوستی چوستی بتیا منیا کے پاؤں کے قریب کھسکتی ہوئی
پہونچ گئی تھی کہ "ارے میری بتیا رے" منیا اپنی پر شوق نگاہیں گڑیا
پرسے مجبوراً ہٹاتی ہوئی بڑے پیار سے بولی۔ اس کے بے رونق چہرے
پر ایک مسرت ناچ رہی تھی، اس نے اپنے پھیلے ہوئے بازوؤں میں
بتیا کو سمیٹ لیا۔ "میری بتیا گڑیا لے گی" منیا نے بہت محبت سے اپنی
ایک ہاتھ ٹوٹی ہوئی گڑیا بتیا کی مٹھی میں پکڑا دی۔ اس کی گندمی مگر معصوم
آنکھوں میں اپنی بڑائی کا احساس جھکنے لگا تھا۔ اب تک وہ خود ہی
اس گڑیا سے کھیلنا چاہ رہی تھی۔ ایک لمحے کے لئے اس کے دل
کے دبے ہوئے جذبوں میں سے بچپن کی ایک بھٹکتی ہوئی لہر باہر نکل
پڑی تھی اور راکھ کے ڈھیروں کو کرید کرید کر کوئلہ چننے سے بیزار ہو کے
اس کا دل بھی کھیلنے کو تڑپنے لگا تھا۔ مگر بتیا کی چیخیں اور اس کے ننھے
ننھے سے اٹھتے ہوئے بازوؤں میں بتیا کا سارا جوش سرد پڑ گیا۔ اپنی
چھوٹی سی آغوش میں کسی طرح نکلتی پھسلتی ہوئی بتیا کو لئے دفعتہً اس
کے ننھے سے دل میں ایک ماں کی سی ذمہ داری اور اپنے بڑے ہونے
کا احساس چھا گیا۔ بتیا شلجم کے پتے کو پھینک کر منیا کی گڑیا کو منہ میں
لئے مزے میں چوستی نکلتی اور کھسکاتی چلی جا رہی تھی۔ اتنے ہی دنوں
میں سڑک پر سوتے، اونگھتے، اور بھونکتے ہوئے طرح طرح کے کتوں
کو منیا نے پہچان لیا تھا۔ وہ ان سے ذرا بھی نہ ڈرتی تھی۔ مگر ہاں جب

وہ آپس میں لڑتے لڑتے اس کے قریب آ جاتے تو اسوقت وہ بھی چلانے لگتی تھی۔ فٹ پاتھ کے کنارے گہرے اور بہتے ہوئے نالے، کوڑوں کے ڈھیر کے ڈھیر، اور بھر یہ رنگ برنگے کتے، منوا اور ٹنیا کی طرح اس کی زندگی سے کتنے قریب تھے۔ ننھی سی پانچ برس کی بنیا بیچاری زندگی اور اس کے فرق کو کیا سمجھ سکتی تھی۔ جب وہ سڑکوں پر خواہ مخواہ چلتے چلتے اور کھیلتے کھیلتے تھک جاتی تو اسے بے اختیار اپنا کونہ یاد آ جاتا۔ اس کو اس اندھیرے کونے سے محبت تھی جو صرف انہی تینوں بھائی بہنوں کا اپنا تھا۔ وہاں کونے میں بچھے ہوئے تھوڑے سے پیال پر جب یہ تینوں ایک دوسرے کے پیٹ میں اپنا سر گھسا کر سونے لگتے تھے تو کتنی میٹھی نیند خود ہی لوریاں گاتی ہوئی انہیں تھپک تھپک کر سلانے لگتی تھی، کوٹھری کے چار کونے تھے، تین کونوں میں تو بڈھے گھسیارے کی اپنی چیزیں تھیں، چنگیریاں، رسی، کھرپی، ہنسیا، ایک دو کالی کالی مٹی کی ہنڈیا۔ کچھ سوکھے ہوئے پتے، ایک چھوٹا سا چولہا، اور جلے ہوئے پتھر کوئلے کا ایک چھوٹا سا ڈھیر۔ چوں چوں کرتی ہوئی کاٹھ کی ایک چوکی بھی تھی اور میلی سی چادر بھی — اس اندھیری کوٹھری کے تین کونے اس کو کتنے گلزار لگتے تھے، رسے بسے ہوئے سے، گر پھر بھی ایک اجڑا ہوا کونہ جو ویران پڑا تھا وہی ننیا کی نگاہوں میں سب سے زیادہ اپنا اور پیارا تھا۔ بنیا کو لئے ہوئے اور کبھی کبھی، اکیلے میں بھی اپنی چادر سر سے پیر تک

پلیٹ کردہ اپنی اماں کی نقل کرتی، لمبی سیدھی ہوکر، سر سے پیر تک لپٹنے میں اسے بڑا اچھا لگتا تھا۔ اسی طرح سے اس کی ماں کو سب لے گئے تھے نہ؟ اور آنکھوں کو بند کئے ہوئے اسے لگتا جیسے وہ خود ہی اماں بن گئی ہے اس کی بغل سے چمٹی ہوئی بتیا کبھی اس کی چادر کو نوچ دیتی اور کبھی اسے خود ہی ڈر لگنے لگتا تھا کہ کہیں سب لوگ اسے بھی سر پر رکھکر نہ لے جائیں، پھر جیسے بچاری اماں واپس نہ آئی ویسے ہی وہ بھی نہ آئے گی، اس بیچاری بتیا کو کون کھلائے گا۔ اور اس کی ماں بیچاری۔ وہ سوچتے سوچتے زور سے بولنے لگتی: "بتیا رے بھیا اماں سے پیسہ مانگتا تھا رے ابھی سے اماں بھاگ گئی" اور بتیا اپنے ننھے ننھے سے ہاتھوں سے منیا کے منہ پر تھپیڑ مارتے ہوئے ہی ہنسنے لگتی — ہی ہی۔ ہی۔ ہا ہا۔ ہا۔ اسی کونے کی دیوار میں کبھی کبھی منوا کا چھوٹا سا "اُچکا" کھسا ہوا رہتا جس میں تھوڑے سے رنگین بنجھے ہوئے تاگے لپٹے ہوئے ہوتے تھے، اور اسی تاگے کے سرے پر مہین کاغذ کی ایک رنگین تکنگی لٹکتی رہتی۔ کبھی کبھی سبز، نیلے، اور سرخ رنگ کی گولیاں بھی اس کی جیب میں آجاتیں۔ لونڈوں کے بیچ میں کھیلتے کھیلتے منوا کا دحشت زدہ کھیلنڈرا چہرہ یک بیک اچاٹ ہو جاتا۔ گولی کھیلتے کھیلتے اس کے ہاتھ سُست پڑ جاتے اور پیشانی پر جھولتے ہوئے مل جُلے بالوں کو ایک جھٹکے سے پیچھے پھینک کر وہ خاموش ہو جاتا تھا۔ خود بخود جیسے کوئی زبردست طاقت

اس کے ہاتھوں کو روک لیتی تھی، بے دلی سے گولیاں اِدھر اُدھر لڑھکا کر وہ بیزار سا تھکا ہوا لگنے لگتا۔ اپنی سوکھی ہوئی گردن پر جمے ہوئے میل کو کھجلاتے کھجلاتے اس کو تیّا اور نتیا یاد آنے لگتیں "اب ہم جا ہیں رے جموا" بڑی حسرت سے آہستہ آہستہ اس کے پاؤں اٹھنے لگتے اور وہ دور تک مڑ مڑ کر دیکھتا جاتا "ارے ای دیکھ سکھوا تو اڑا دے جا ہے" وہ آگے بڑھتا جاتا تھا مگر اس کا دل کھیل کی دلچسپیوں میں الجھتا ہوا پیچھے ہی رہ جانے کو مچلتا تھا۔ جگہ جگہ سے اکھڑی ہوئی لمبی سڑک کے دونوں طرف وار سکینیشن والوں کے قطار در قطار بارک بنے ہوئے تھے۔ خوش رنگ اینٹ اور سرخ کھپریل کے دو رویہ لمبے لمبے اونچے اونچے کمرے دور دور تک پھیلتے چلے گئے تھے۔ جن کے آگے روشوں پر گھانس جما جما کر بہت سے تختوں میں ڈیلیا، نیک، نیزی، لاسے، اور قسم قسم کے پھول ہر موسم کے جداگانہ رنگ و بو کے ساتھ کھلتے رہتے تھے۔ اونچی چہار دیواریاں بارک کو ہر طرف سے گھیرے ہوئے تھیں، انہیں حلقوں میں اُن کی زندگی کے سارے سامان مہیا ہو جاتے تھے ان کے کھلے ہوئے گیٹوں پر نیپالی پہرے دار کھڑے رہتے کسی کو اندر جانے کی اجازت نہ تھی۔ ہاں بس قسم قسم کے مریل، بھوکے، خارش زدہ کتے ہی کسی نہ کسی طرح نالیوں یا گیٹوں سے ہو کر اندر چلے جاتے تھے اور کوؤں کا ایک ہجوم بھی درختوں کی ٹہنیوں پر سے حملے کر دیا کرتا

تھا۔ چہار دیواری سے باہر صرف بھنے ہوئے گوشت اور بگھاری ہوئی دال کی خوشبوئیں آتی رہتیں۔ مزے دار لپٹتی سی خوشبوئیں جو خواہ مخواہ دماغ کے اندر گھسی چلی جاتی تھیں ـــ دن بھر کے فاقے سے منوا کا جی شام تک نڈھال ہونے لگا۔ اس روز گلی ڈنڈے میں بھی اس کا جی نہ لگا۔ رہ رہ کر اس کی سوکھی سوکھی ٹانگیں آپ ہی آپ تھرتھرانے لگتی تھیں۔ کٹی ہوئی تلنگی لوٹنے اور گولی کھیلنے میں بھی وہ اپنے کو نہ بہلا سکا۔ "باپ رے کیسے سب روزہ رکھتے ہیں" اس کا نو برس کا ننھا سا دل روزے کے خیال سے لرز اٹھا۔ ایسے ہی پاؤں سے گیند کی طرح وہ چلتے چلتے پتھر کے ایک ٹکڑے کو لڑھکاتا چلا جا رہا تھا، کہ یک بیک ایک تیز خوشبو دار بھبکا منوا کی ناک سے ہو کر حلق سے ہوتا ہوا اس کی روح میں اتر گیا۔ اس کی پھیکی پھیکی بدمزہ زبان خود بخود تر ہو گئی۔ اور اسی جگہ پہونچ کر جیسے اس کے پاؤں کی طاقت ایک دم سے ختم ہو گئی تھی، وہ لڑکھڑا کر دیوار سے لگ کر بیٹھ گیا۔ اس کے قریب ہی دُم ہلاتے ہوئے طرح طرح کے کتے کسی انتظار میں بیٹھے تھے۔ مگر اس کو کسی کا انتظار نہ تھا وہ تو ان اڑتی ہوئی خوشبوؤں سے تازگی کا بس ایک سہارا لینا چاہتا تھا۔ اس کی آنکھیں بند ہو گئی تھیں، شاید وہ اونگھنے لگا تھا کہ آپس میں لڑتے ہوئے کتوں کی آواز سے چونک پڑا "ارے منوا تیں بھی بے گارے"۔ اسی کے محلہ کا للوا اپنے ہاتھ میں جو پرات لئے کھڑا تھا "ہاں

للو بھیا ہم کو بھی دے" منوا کی لرزتی ہوئی آواز کے ساتھ اس کی معصوم نگاہیں اور سوکھے ہوئے جسم کا ہر عضو بھی یہی پکارنے لگا تھا۔ بھوکے کتے کی طرح منوا کھانے پر ٹوٹ پڑا، کیلے کا چکنا پتہ اس کی انگلیوں کے درمیان کانپ رہا تھا اور جلدی جلدی کھاتے ہوئے اس کے منہ سے عجیب عجیب سی آواز نکل رہی تھی۔ شر۔ شر۔ شاپ سڑ سڑ۔ للوا اسے دیکھتے دیکھتے ہنس پڑا۔ "وارے بنگال کا بھکوا" "بتیا اور بتیا لابھی نا رکھے"۔ یک بیک جیسے چلتی ہوئی موٹر یا سائیکل میں بریک پڑ جائے، اسی طرح منوا کا ہاتھ رک گیا۔ کیلے کے پتے کو چاروں طرف سے موڑ کر وہ جانے ہی لگا تھا کہ للوا بولا۔ "اتی اتنا دن سے توں سب کہاں سے کھاتا تھا رے منوا؟" "اماں جب مری تھی تے للوا بھیا۔ تو اوہی دن کوئی چول وان بھیج دیہیں تھا اوہی چلاتا تھا تھا تھوڑا دن۔ پھر گھر والا بڈھا دادا مار دیدیتا تھا۔ کل سے اُو بھی بیمار ہے"۔ للوا کے چہرے پہ ہمدردی اور رحم کی ایک سرخی دوڑ گئی۔ "تو سن کل سے آجاگا دس بجے دن کو اور پھر یہی ٹیم۔ ہم اندر رہیں گے۔ یہی نالی ہیں تو ہاتھ دے گا ہم ادھر سے توڑے دیدیہاں گے سمجھ نا" سامنے باورچی خانہ سے بہتی ہوئی نالی چہار دیواری سے باہر پیچ و تاب کھاتی ہوئی دور تک چلی گئی تھی۔ بہتے ہوئے پانی کے ساتھ سفید سفید بھات سرخ ٹماٹر کے چھلکے اور روٹیوں کے چورے ٹھہر ٹھہر کر، رک رک کر، آگے بہتے ہوئے چلے جا رہے تھے۔ منوا

کی نگاہیں نالی پر جم کر رہ گئی تھیں اور اُس کے خیالات باورچی خانے کے بھرپور خزانہ کے گرد منڈلا رہے تھے جس کا فیض اس طرح سے رواں اور دواں تھا۔ وہ خوشی سے جھوم گیا، اس کو خود ہی اتنے زور کی بھوک لگتی تھی کوڑے پر سے سڑا ہوا کیلا اور نارنگی بھی اُٹھا کر کھا لیتا تھا، اور اسی سے وہ سمجھتا کہ منیا اور بتیا کو کتنے زور کی بھوک لگتی ہوگی۔ مگر جب کبھی منیا بھوک سے بیکل ہو کر روئے چلی جاتی تو منوا کو بڑا غصہ آجاتا تھا اور وہ اس کی ریڑھ کی ابھری ہوئی ہڈیوں پر دو چار دھموکے لگا کر اپنی ماں کے الفاظ بڑبڑانے لگتا "آنہہ ہی ایں پیدا ہووے کو تھا اور کہیں نا" منیا کو روتے ہوئے دیکھکر بتیا بھی بلک بلک کر رونے لگتی تھی اور ان دونوں کو روتا ہوا دیکھ کے منوا کا بھی جی چاہتا کہ وہ بھی اُن کے ساتھ ہی ساتھ خوب زور زور سے چیخ چیخ کر رونے لگے۔

اس پتے میں بھات دیکھکر منیا کتنا خوش ہوگی؟ منیا کی مسرتوں کے احساس ہی سے منوا مسکرانے لگا۔ اب وہ منیا کو کبھی نہ مارے گا۔ کیسی پیاری سی ہے بچاری۔ اس کا دل بے اختیار چاہ رہا تھا کہ تیزی سے دوڑ کر منیا سے لپٹ کے کہے کہ منیا — اب ہم کو روزنہ دال بھات اور گوشت بھی ملے گا — ہاں روز روز" اچانک اس کو اپنی اماں یاد آئی — ہائے بچاری اماں!! تم تو بس خالی ماڑ ہی پیتے پیتے مرگئیں۔ جس کے گھر میں اس کی اماں کھانا

پکاتی تھی اسی کے بچوں کی طرح اُس نے بھی ابا اور اماں کہنا اپنے بچوں کو سکھایا تھا۔ اماں اب اگر تم زندہ رہتیں تو ہم تمکو اسی کپیلے کے پتے ہیں سے جا کر روز مزے مزے کا کھانا کھلاتے "۔ اس کی نگاہوں کے سامنے اپنی اماں کا سانولا اور کمزور چہرہ گھوم گیا۔ کیسی اچھی پتلی سی آواز تھی اس کی۔ جب وہ اس کو پکارتی تھی ۔ "منوا" تو اس کے کانوں میں جیسے سیٹی سی بجنے لگتی تھی دیکھنے میں "۔ پہلے اس کو کتنی تکلیف رہتی تھی۔ جب کبھی ہم بھوکے رہتے تھے تو اماں اس روز ہم لوگ کو اپنے پیٹ سے اور زیادہ سٹا کر سلاتی تھی۔ اور اس دن تو رات بھر جیسے اسے نیند ہی نہ آتی ۔" سوچتے سوچتے منوا کا دل بجھ گیا، آہستہ آہستہ چلتے ہوئے بھی وہ بہت جلد اپنی کوٹھری کے پاس پہنچ گیا تھا بتیا نے کا کیچڑا اپنے دونوں ہاتھوں میں لیتھڑے سامنے گلی میں کھیل رہی تھی، اور منیا گلی کی دو چار بچیوں کے ساتھ اینٹ کے چولھے پر ٹھیکرے میں مٹی دھرے جھوٹ موٹ کا کھانا پکا رہی تھی — منوا کو دیکھتے ہی اس کے ننھے سے معصوم چہرے پر مسکراہٹ پھیل گئی "کھانا پکے ہے بھیا — واوا ایسا کہے اس کا دادا وہ بڈھیا گھسیارہ تھا جس کی کوٹھری کے ایک گوشے میں سب رہتے تھے۔ تمباکو کی دوکان پہ بیٹھے ہوئے خیرو میاں زور سے بولے "بڑا لاخبرا ہے رے لونڈا — دن بھر — اتنی چھوٹی چھوٹی بہن سب کو بھو کا چھوڑ کر بس تجھے اپنے کھیل تماشے ہی سے کام

ہے چھی — چھی — چھی۔ اگر ہم آج ان دونوں کو کھانا نہ کھلا دیتے تو مرہی جاتیں بچاری سب۔ اللہ توبہ۔ تو یہ کیسی مہنگاری ہے، تب بھی بس ایمان کی سلامتی چاہیئے۔" منوا خیرو میاں کی باتیں سنتا رہا۔ اس کا جی اندر سے گھبرا رہا تھا۔ ایک مہینے کے بعد آج اس کو اپنی ماں یاد آ رہی تھی۔ منیا اور بتیا کو لئے ہوئے وہ کوٹھری میں آکر اپنے پیال پر بیٹھ گیا۔ منیا اور بتیا نے جب کیلے کے پتے کو چاٹ چاٹ کر اپنے تھوک سے ایکدم سے چکنا کر دیا تو منوا نے بڑی ہمدردی اور محبت سے اُن کے ہاتھ کو دھو کر اپنے پاس لٹا لیا۔ ایسے ہی وہ خود اپنی ماں کی بغل میں سٹ کر سو جاتا تھا نہ؟ آج اُس کے دماغ میں جیسے خیالات کے سوتے پھوٹ گئے تھے جو رس رس کر اُس کی آنکھوں سے بہتے ہی چلے آ رہے تھے۔ اس طرح کی کتنی کوٹھریاں اس کو یاد تھیں، وہ گننے لگا ایک وہ کھنڈر والی کوٹھری جہاں برکا درخت تھا۔ دوسری جسکے ساتھ ایک استارہ بھی تھا اور ایک وہ جہاں اماں گر پڑی تھی۔ بھینگا بھینگا سا برآمدہ، اور ایک وہ بھی تو جہاں سے ابا اماں سے لڑ کر بھاگا تھا۔ کمینہ ابا کتنا خراب سا تھا وہ۔ دن رات اُسے بس اپنے تاڑی اور دارو ہی سے کام تھا۔ اور اس کے بعد پھر نشہ میں اماں سے لڑتا اور ہم سب کو مار پیٹ کر اماں کے ہاتھ پاؤں توڑ دیتا۔ سینما کی کبھی کی دیکھی ہوئی تصویر کی طرح اس کو اپنے باپ کے چہرے کی تھوڑی سی جھلک یاد آجاتی،

تانبا سا لال چہرہ اور چندلا سر"۔ کنو بو بو کبھی کبھی کہتی تھی کہ ابا پہلے کوڑے والے موٹر کو چلاتے تھے تب اماں بہت بہت سا کلیجی پکاتی تھی اور چائے میں بغیر بھگائے وہ سوکھے سوکھے بسکٹ کبھی نہ کھاتی تھی۔ مگر جب تاڑی پیتے پیتے ابا کی نوکری چھوٹ گئی تو ایک دن اماں سے لڑ جھگڑ کر ابا کہیں چلا گیا۔ اچھا ہوا جو پھر نہ آیا — بچاری تنیا اماں کے پیٹ ہی میں تھی کہ ابا چلا گیا تھا ——!

اتنی مہنگاری میں بھی بچاری اماں کو کھانا پکانے میں زیادہ مشاہرہ نہ ملتا تھا۔ اتنا مہنگا چاول صرف تین ہی روپے کی تنخواہ میں بھر مہینہ کیا پورا پڑتا۔ اور اس پر سے اتنے کھانے والے۔ تب سے بچاری اماں مجبور ہو کر مزدوری کرنے لگی تھی۔ اوپر تلے تھاک کے تھاک اینٹ رکھکر جب وہ چلنے لگتی تو اس کی سوکھی ہوئی گردن کے ساتھ اس کا سارا جسم بھی ڈولنے لگتا تھا۔ مگر اس زمانہ میں اس کی اماں ہر روز بڑا اچھا کھانا پکاتی تھی۔ اور اس کے پاس پیسے بھی رہنے لگے تھے مگر اسی کے چھ مہینے بعد سے اس کو ایسا جاڑا بخار لگا کہ اس سے آخر دم تک پیچھا نہ چھٹا۔ کیسی کیسی مشکلوں سے اس کی اماں کے پاس اتنا پیسہ بچ گیا تھا کہ جو دو مہینہ اس کی بیماری میں خرچ چلا تھا۔ اور اس کی اماں بچاری کا آخری خرچ تو محلے بھر کے چندے میں سے ہوا۔ وہ چندے بھی آخری ہی تھے۔ پھر کسی نے اُن تین معصوم بچوں کو نہ پوچھا تھا۔ مگر اب منوا کے دل

کو ایک سکون لگ رہا تھا کہ اب وہ کبھی بھوکا نہ رہے گا۔ بچارہ بڈھا دادا اماں کے وقت سے مہربان تھا۔ اماں سے ہر مہینہ کوٹھری کے کونے کا ایک روپیہ کرایہ لے کر ابھی تک ان کا خیال کر رہا تھا۔ منوا کرایہ کہاں سے لاتا، دادا نے بس اتنا ہی کہا تھا کہ ہر روز ایک چھوٹی سی ڈلیا میں کوئلا چن کر لا دیا کرے اور مفت میں پہلے کی طرح رہے۔ اس کوٹھری اور اسکے پرانے کونے کے ساتھ ساتھ سرخ رنگ کی چہار دیواری کی بہتی ہوئی نالی کے سوراخ سے بھی اب محبت لگتی تھی جس کے اس پار سے للوا اس کو کیلے کے پتے میں کبھی روٹی اور کبھی دال بھات پکڑا دیتا تھا — منوا کے ساتھ منیا اور ٹنیا بھی اسی جگہ منڈلاتی پھرتیں۔ اور سارا سارا دن اسی چہار دیواری کے گرد وہ تینوں کھیلتے کھیلتے گزار دیتے تھے۔ منیا ٹنیا کے ہاتھوں کو پکڑے اس کو پاؤں پاؤں چلنا سکھاتی، اور نزدیک ہی منوا گلی ڈنڈا اور کبھی گوبیاں کھیلتا رہتا تھا۔ لمبی دوڑتی ہوئی سڑک پارک کی چہار دیواریوں کے ٹھیک سامنے دو لمبے لمبے کمرچی پابوں کے درمیاں سے گھستی چلی گئی تھی۔ منوا کے پاؤں چلتے چلتے اسی حد پر آکر رک جاتے تھے جس کے دونوں طرف کوارٹر کی چمکیلی عمارتیں رات کو بجلی کی روشنی میں جگمگانے لگتی تھیں۔ اکثر ان کے بڑے بڑے احاطوں سے چمچماتی ہوئی کاریں نکلتیں جن کے ہورن دور دور تک گونج اٹھتے تھے۔

اسی بڑے احاطے کے اندر موہن بابو نے جب سے امرود چرانے

دیکھکر لکھنا کو پیٹا تھا منوا سرکاری پروفیسروں کی کوٹھیوں سے بہت دور رہنے لگا تھا۔ اور اس کو کمرخی پایوں کے اندر سے کچھ کام بھی نہ تھا۔ اس کے کھیلنے کے لئے اتنی لمبی سڑک بہت کافی تھی۔ نالی کے اندر سے بہتا ہوا کھانا اور میونسپلٹی کے ہر وقت کھلے ہوئے نل کا پانی ان کے پیٹوں کو بھر دیتا۔ وہ دن بھر کوڑوں کے ڈھیر پر چمٹے ہوئے کوئلے چنتے رہتے اور پھر کونے کے پیال پر پڑ کر بے خبر سو جاتے۔ اس سے زیادہ کی انہیں تمنا بھی نہ تھی۔ بھنبھناتے ہوئے دل کے دل مچھروں کی بھی ان کو پرواہ نہ رہتی اور وہ تینوں تھکے ہارے ہوئے ایک دوسرے سے لپٹ کر بڑے پیار سے سوئے رہتے۔

اسی طرح تھوڑے دن گذر گئے۔ مگر یک بیک جب آٹھ روز کی چھٹی لے کر للوا اپنی سسرال چلا گیا تو اس دن سے تینوں بچے پھر بڈھے دادا کے چھوٹے سے چولھے کے گرد بیٹھے پانی کی طرح پتلے ہوئے ماڑ کو حریص نظروں سے تکنے لگے۔ مگر ہر روز اس کے چولھے کا جلنا کوئی ضروری نہ تھا۔ پھر وہ کتوں کی سونگھتی ہوئی ناکوں کی طرح دوکانوں کے نیچے۔ سڑکوں کے اوپر اور کوڑوں کے غلیظ ڈھیر پر اپنی متجسس نظروں سے کچھ ڈھونڈتے پھرتے تھے۔ خیر دمیاں کی بکری اپنے یہاں کا ماڑ پی پی کر بہت سا دودھ دیتی تھی۔ اور منوا تو اسے پی کر بس پچا تا ہی جانتا تھا۔ ٹنیا

بھوکی رہ رہ کر چڑچڑی ہو گئی تھی۔ ہر گھڑی اس کے منہ سے بس وہی ٹیں ٹیں کی ایک آواز نکلتی رہتی۔ بڈھا گھسیارہ اور خیرو میاں کے ساتھ ساتھ کئی اور لوگوں کا جی اس مسلسل آواز سے گھبرا گیا تھا۔ آخر گھسیارہ اس کی کنوا بوبو کے میاں کو بلا لایا "میاں ہم بھر پایا۔ رات کو دو گھڑی کا چینو نہ لیوے دے ہے ای چھوکری" منیا کی گردن سے چمٹی ہوئی تبیا مڑ مڑ کر تکتی ہوئی اپنی شکایت سُن رہی تھی۔ کنوا کے میاں کی سمجھ میں کچھ نہ آرہا تھا کہ وہ کیا کرے! اس کا باپ ایک قصائی تھا۔ بیکار بیٹھے ہوئے بیٹے اور بہو کا خرچ چلاتے چلاتے تو اس کا دم نکلا جاتا تھا اور اب یہ تین تین بچھڑوں کا سوال تھا۔ بڈھا گھسیارہ کھانستا ہوا بولا "ارے ہم کو تو موہ لگے ہے ای سب پر جو گلا سے لگائے ہوئے ہیں، مگر بتیا لاڈل دکھتے ہے۔ ایسا کیکپی کا جاڑا اور بس ایک ٹھو چدّر۔ اس سے تو اچھا ہے کہ پادری کے اسپتال میں بتیا کو دے آؤ۔ مجے میں بس کھاگی اور کھیلے گی"!

کنوا کا میاں چونک اٹھا، کتنی صاف اور سیدھی سی بات تھی۔ اپنی جیب میں سے ایک اکنی نکال کر کنوا کے میاں نے منیا کو دی "جا منیا منوا کو ساتھ لے لے ٹھو کی مٹھائی لے آ" اور اس نے جھپٹتی ہوئی بتیا کو اس کی گود سے لے لیا۔ منیا اور منوا جب چلے گئے تو بڈھے گھسیارے کو ساتھ لیکر وہ نچلی سڑک سے سیدھا پادری کے اسپتال چلا گیا وہاں بہت سے قاعدے اور قانون کی کتابوں پر اس کے

انگوٹھے کا نشان لیا جا چکا تو ایک سفید سی ساڑی پہنے ہوئے کالی سی نرس کی گود میں چیختی ہوئی بتیا کو زبردستی دے کر وہ جلدی سے اسپتال کے بڑے پھاٹک سے نکل آیا۔ اب اس کا دل بہت ہلکا ہلکا سا لگ رہا تھا۔۔۔۔ راستے میں بڈھے گھسیارہ کو اس نے سمجھا دیا تھا کہ اس کے گھر کے بغل میں جو شبراتی باورچی رہتا ہے اس سے کہہ سن کر کہیں منوا اور منیا کو رکھا دے منوا تو کام کرنے کے لائق تھا اور منیا بھی چھ مہینہ سال بھر تک کام کرنے کے قابل ہو جائے گی۔ اب اس کو اطمینان ہو گیا تھا اور وہ اسی طرف سے اپنے گھر واپس چلا گیا۔ منیا بتیا کے لئے دو دن تک گھبرا گھبرا کر روتی رہی۔ منوا کا جی بھی اچاٹ سا لگتا تھا۔ "ہائے بچاری کیسی کھلونا ایسی تھی" ادھر ادھر گھوم پھر کر بھی اس کا جی نہیں لگتا تھا اور نہ کسی طرح سے اس کا پیٹ ہی بھرتا تھا۔
اسپر سے منیا بتیا ہی کا ماتم کئے جاتی تھی۔ منیا کو لٹھو کی مٹھائی سے ایک نفرت سی ہو گئی تھی۔ للوا کے جانے کے بعد اب وہ شبراتی باورچی سے ہل مل گئے تھے جو کبھی کبھی روٹی کے اوپر آلو کی بھجیا رکھ کر انہیں کھانے کو دے جاتا تھا۔ کمرخی یا ئے کے اندر سے امرود توڑنے کی مار کے خوف کے ساتھ اب بھجیا اور روٹی کا مزہ ملنے لگا تھا۔ اسی لئے جب شبراتی منیا اور منوا کو اپنی کوٹھی پر لے جانے لگا تو تھوڑی سی جھجک کے بعد وہ اس کے ساتھ

جانے لگے۔ ان کی زندگی میں یہ پہلا موقع تھا جب وہ اتنی آرائش اور نفاستوں کو اپنے اتنے قریب سے دیکھ رہے تھے۔ شبراتی کی باتوں سے بیگم متاثر ہو رہی تھیں۔ "ہاں شبراتی ایسی غضب کی گرانی میں جو نہ ہو جائے۔ کتنے بچارے بھوک سے اسی بنگال میں مر گئے۔" "اور بیگم صاحب خیر و میاں اور سارے محلہ بھر کو اسی کا تو رونا ہے کہ وہ ہندو گھسیارہ ایک مسلمان بچی کو کرستان بنا دے کو اسپتال میں دے آیا۔" اندر دروازے کے پٹ سے لگا ہوا منوا ایک مجرم کی طرح دبکا کھڑا تھا اور اس کی قمیص کا دامن پکڑے ہوئے منیا سہمی ہوئی بس اپنی انگلیوں کو ملتی چلی جا رہی تھی۔ اس روز نہا دھو کر صاف صاف کپڑے پہن کر وہ دونوں دن بھر ادِھر اُدھر اچکتے رہے۔ رات کو بجلی کی روشنی میں جب ڈرائنگ روم میں بیٹھی ہوئی نکہت کچھ پڑھ رہی تھی تو اس کے قریب ہی دوسرے صوفہ پر مسکراتی ہوئی منیا اچک کر بیٹھ گئی "ہمرے بھی چوڑی نہ پہنا دے گی" نکہت پڑھتے پڑھتے چونک اٹھی۔ منیا اس کے ہاتھ میں سونے کے بر سلٹ کو چھو رہی تھی۔ نکہت کا دل رحم کے جذبات سے بھر گیا۔ "ہاں پہنا دوں گی منیا" "او۔ ای ہمرا کرتا بھی لال رنگا دیگی۔ اچھا آؤ ہم جوتا بھی پہنے گے" منیا مسکرا مسکرا کر اپنی تمناؤں کا اظہار کیے جا رہی تھی "ہاں سب منگا دوں گی سب۔ مگر۔ مگر۔ مگر دیکھ اس کے اوپر مت بیٹھ۔ ارے اس قالین پر بھی نہیں۔ وہاں

برآمدے میں جا کر کھیل "۔ ایکدم لہلہاتے ہوئے پودے میں جیسے کسی نے کھولتا کھولتا پانی ڈال دیا ہو۔ مُنیا کا کھلا ہوا چہرہ مُرجھا گیا۔ اور وہ آہستہ آہستہ کمرے سے نکل گئی۔ پہلی بار کمبل اوڑھ کر سونے میں منوا کو بہت اچھا لگا۔ دوسرے دن جب وہ کچھ دیر کے بعد سو کر اُٹھا تو شبراتی کا بگڑنا اس کو ایک نئی بات لگی۔ اتنے سویرے اُٹھنے پر بھی وہ دیر ہی کیے جا رہا تھا۔ اس سے پہلے اگر وہ بارہ بجے دن تک بھی سویا رہتا تو کوئی بھی ٹوکنے والا نہ تھا۔ ناشتہ کرنے کے درمیان میں دو دفعہ اسکو شرک پر سے گولی کھیلتے کھیلتے پکڑ لایا گیا۔ اسکے چہرے پر ایک عجیب سی وحشت برس رہی تھی اور وہ گھٹا گھٹا سا لگ رہا تھا" ارے مُنیا یہ اینٹ اور ٹھیکرے سے گندا کر کے کھیلے گی تو صاحب بگڑیں گے۔ اور دیکھ یہ پھول مت توڑنا سمجھی نہ"۔ اور اس وقت خواہ مخواہ مُنیا کا جی پھول توڑنے کو مچلنے لگتا اور ٹھیکروں سے چولھا بنا کر کھیلنے کو اس کی روح ترسنے لگتی۔" دیوار سے لگ کر مت کھڑا ہو منوا"۔ اور منوا اس طرح سے چونک کر دیوار کو دیکھنے لگتا جیسے اس دیوار پر کوئی بچھو رینگ رہا ہو۔ مگر اس کے سامنے صرف اُجلی اُجلی چونہ کی ہوئی دیوار چمکتی رہتی۔" ارے پانی پی کر یہاں پر کلّی نہ پھینکا کر منوا! ایکدم سے جنگلی ہے تو بھی"۔ جھوا شان جما کر کہتا۔ مُنیا کاغذ کے کترے ہوئے ٹکڑوں کو مٹھی میں دبائے جب نالے کے اس پار ٹمین میں پھینکنے کے لئے گئی تو اس کا جی گھبرانے لگا۔ آخر اس کاغذ کو اس نے پھاڑا ہی کیوں تھا جسکی وجہ سے اسے اتنی دور آنا پڑا۔ دوسرے

ہی دن منوا کا جی اس قید خانے سے اُکتا گیا۔ روٹی بھجیا کیساتھ دونوں وقت میٹھی میٹھی چائے اور بھانت کے ساتھ بھنے ہوئے گوشت اور مچھلی سے بھی اس کا جی بھر گیا تھا۔ جب وہ تلنگی ہی نہیں اڑا سکتا تھا تو پھر بیگم صاحب کے پیسے کی اُسے ضرورت ہی کیا تھی۔" بیکار بیٹھی بیٹھی منیا کا جی نہیں لگتا تھا بیگم صاحب کمروں کی طرف شبراتی اسے جانے نہ دیتا تھا۔ کل دن بھر کی مسکراہٹ اس کے چہرے سے مٹ چکی تھی اور اس کی جگہ تحیر اور خوف چھا گیا تھا۔ جھوا آپنے بڑے بڑے دانت نکالے ہوئے ہنس پڑتا۔ "ہائے رے جنگلی" ایکدم سے بندر ہے بندر" اس وقت منوا کا چہرہ شرم اور غصہ کے ملے جلے ہوئے جذبات سے تمتما جاتا جب تیسری دفعہ شبراتی منوا کو کھیل میں سے پکڑ لایا تو اس کی جیب سے اُس نے ساری گولیاں نکال لیں۔ منوا بے بس طور پر باہر دیوار سے لگ کر آہستہ آہستہ سسکنے لگا۔ مُنیا نے اس کے رونے کی آواز سُن لی وہ چپکے سے باہر گئی اور روتے ہوئے منوا سے لگ کر بڑی محبت سے بولی۔

چل رے بھیا۔ گھر رے چل!۔ ہم اپنی بِتیا کو بھی لے آدیں گے"

وہ اپنی کلائی میں جھنجھناتی ہوئی چوڑیوں اور لال لال کرتے کو بھول گئی تھی۔ ماں کی محبت بھری آغوش کی طرح اس کو کوٹھری کا کونہ یاد آرہا تھا۔ منوا باہر شاگرد پیشے سے اپنی چادر چپکے سے نکال کر لے آیا اور مُنیا کا ہاتھ پکڑے جب وہ تیزی سے دوڑتا ہوا کمرخی پائیوں کی حدت

باہر نکل آیا تب کہیں اس کی جان میں جان آئی۔ ایک اطمینان اور سکون کا سانس لیکر وہ بیچ سڑک پر اپنے دوستوں کے جھرمٹ میں بیٹھ کر مزے سے گولیاں کھیلنے لگا۔ اور منیا گرد اور مٹی میں لت پت چہار دیواری سے لگی بیٹھی، اپنی گود میں اینٹ کا بابو لئے جھوم جھوم کے گاتی ہوئی اُسے سُلا رہی تھی۔

"آجا میری بتیا کی ننیا رے۔"

نعمو کو لگتا جیسے اس کی دادی اماں کی عمر کا بہاؤ بڑھاپے کے باندھ سے رکا ہوا بس ہمیشہ سے ایک ہی جگہ پر ساکت ہو گیا ہے وہ چھوٹی سی تھی جب بھی دادی اماں موقع بے موقع نکیلے دانتوں والی کنگھی اور ڈور لئے اس کے پھر یرے لگاتے ہوئے آزاد بالوں کی جڑوں کو کسنے کے لئے تیار رہتیں، اور اب جبکہ نعمو گڑیوں کے کھیل کھیلتے کھیلتے تھک کر بیزار ہو چکی تھی اس کی رگوں میں تیزی سے خون دوڑتا ہوا محسوس ہونے لگا تھا اور اس کو یہ لگتا تھا کہ آسمان پر سے اڑتی ہوئی چڑیوں کو جھپٹ لے یا زمین پر اتنے زور زور سے چلے کہ اس کے جسم کے عضو عضو رقص کرنے لگیں۔ تب بھی دادی

اماں اسی مستعدی سے اپنی نگہبانی کا جال پھیلائے نعمو پر نظروں سے پہرے لگائے بیٹھی رہتیں اسے حیرت ہوتی کہ اس بیچ اتنی تبدیلیاں ہوگئی تھیں مگر دادی اماں اپنی جگہ پر جیسے کیل سے گاڑ دیگئی ہوں جس میں نہ تو کوئی حرکت ہی تھی اور نہ کوئی تبدیلی، نعمو نے جنم سے انکے بال برف کی طرح سفید ہی دیکھے تھے۔ سوکھے ہوئے سرکنڈے کی طرح سکڑی سکڑائی ہوئی دادی اماں اسے ہمیشہ سے ایک ہی جیسی لگتیں۔ جب وہ اپنی بڑی بڑی بے رونق آنکھیں دکھا کر کسی کو ڈانٹتیں تو کبھی کبھی نعمو کو بھی ڈر لگنے لگتا تھا۔ انور نے ایک دن بوٹونی پڑھاتے ہوئے اسے سمجھایا تھا کہ درختوں کے تنوں میں ہر گذرتا ہوا سال اس کی عمر کی ایک جھری کے دائرے کا اضافہ کرتا رہتا ہے جس سے درختوں کے سن کا پتہ بہت آسانی سے مل جاتا ہے۔ نعمو بڑے غور سے دادی اماں کے چہرے کو دیکھتی مگر انکی جھریوں میں اسے کوئی اضافہ نظر نہیں آتا، دادی اماں نہا دھو کر اپنے روئی کے جیسے بال دھوپ میں سکھاتیں تو نعمو کا جی چاہتا کہ ان کے چمکتے ہوئے تاروں پر اپنا ہاتھ پھیرتی رہے، مگر دادی اماں کی چڑچڑی طبیعت سے اسے ڈر لگتا۔ وہ اکثر یہ سوچتی کہ یہ دادی آخر اتنا غصہ کیوں کرتی ہیں؟ بچے سارے گھر بھر کے پیارے ہوتے مگر دادی اماں کی آنکھوں کے خار، چیختے چلاتے لڑکے اور اچھلتی کودتی ہوئی لڑکیاں انکے ہاتھوں سے روز ہی دو چار دھمو کے کھاتی رہتیں، مگر نعمو کو تعجب

لگتا کہ پھیلائے پر پڑے ہوئے ہاتھ پھیلا پھیلا کر بکنے والے چھوٹے چھوٹے بچوں سے انھیں کا ہے کی بیر تھی؟ جب وہ دادی اماں کی بکتی ہوئی آواز سنتی کہ "ان بچوں سے کتنی نجاست ہے" تو اس کا جی چاہتا کہ دادی اماں کی اس بھول کو یاد دلا دے کہ خود انھوں نے پہلے ہی سے کتنی نجاستیں پھیلا رکھی تھیں۔ اُسے بڑا غصہ آتا یہ بڑھیا ئیں اتنا بکنے کیوں لگتی ہیں، دادی اماں کے گلے میں بد رنگ ڈور کے اندر چاندی کی تلوار جیسی دانت کھودنی سے اُسے بڑی گھن لگتی اور وہ بڑے تعجب سے دیکھتی رہتی کہ تیزی سے دانتوں کو جھنجھوڑتی ہوئی وہ اپنے بکنے کی رفتار کو جاری رکھتیں ہیں۔ نعمو کو بڑھیوں کی لچھ دار بک بک اور ان کے مسلسل دانت کھودتے رہنے سے بڑی نفرت تھی اور اس کی چڑھ اس وقت انتہا تک پہنچ جاتی جب دادی اماں انور کو آتا ہوا دیکھکر ٹھیک نعمو کے پڑھنے کی میز کے سامنے اپنی سوکھی سوکھی ٹانگوں کو سفید بگلے جیسی ساڑی میں لپٹی ہوئی برآمدے کے پائے سے لگ کر چھپا پر ایک پہرے دار کی طرح بیٹھ جاتیں۔ ایسے وقت میں انور کو دادی اماں کسی بہت بڑے خزانے پر بیٹھی ہوئی ایک اژدہا جیسی لگتیں۔

دادی اماں کی ذات گھر بھر پر چھائی ہوئی تھی پھر بھی انھیں اس کی شکایت تھی کہ میری ہستی ہی کیا ہے کھانے پینے کپڑے لتے سے لے کر چال ڈھال ہنسی بولی اور بات چیت تک پر

انکی حکومت تھی، اپنے زور سے کیوں چلنے دیتی کیوں چیخی اور نمو کی ہنسی کس لئے؟ جوان جہاں بیٹیاں ہنس ہنس کے جب انگریزی پڑھنے لگیں اور وہ بھی دور کے جوان رشتہ دار سے تو پھر گھر میں برکت کا ہے کی رہے گی"۔ اور دادی اماں اپنی بڑی بڑی آنکھیں انتقامی طور پر دکھاتی ہوئی کہتیں۔ کیا ان پر جوانی نہ آئی تھی کبھی! مگر یہ دیوانگی تو نہ تھی"! اسوقت نمو منو اور انور ایک دوسرے کو دیکھ کر ہنستے ہوئے یہ سوچتے کہ کاش کہیں سے دادی اماں کی اس کھوئی ہوئی جوانی کے صحیفوں کو وہ الٹ سکتے"۔ دادی اماں کو نوجوانوں اور بچوں سے ایک ازلی چڑھ تھی شاید وہ سمجھتی تھیں کہ فطرت اپنے خزانے کی تنگی کی وجہ سے حیات تازہ کی لہریں ایک سے چھین کر دوسرے کو دیتی رہتی ہے اور وہ اپنی کمزور نگاہوں سے اپنی چھینی ہوئی بجلیوں کی چمک دوسری جگہ نہ دیکھ سکتی تھیں، بلندیوں سے زمین کی طرف بے سہارا گرتی ہوئی دادی اماں زینے پر چڑھنے والوں کو کس نظر سے گوارا کر لیتیں؟

نمو منو پرویز سارے ہی اپنے راستے پہ دوڑتے جا رہے تھے مگر بچاری دادی اماں سامنے موت کی گنبد کی طرف ایک تنگ پگڈنڈی پر آہستہ رینگ رہی تھیں کاش وہ اپنی رفتار کو بند ہی کر سکتیں۔ پڑھتے پڑھتے اکتا کر نمو کی نگاہیں دادی اماں کی جھولتی ہوئی جھریوں والے چہرے پر جم جاتیں اور سوچتی کیسا اچھا ہوا

جو دادا ابا زندہ نہ رہے نہیں تو یہ دونوں ملکر زندگی کیسی اجیرن کر دیتے، مگر بچاری دادی اماں" وہ کر ہی کیا سکتی ہیں اس کا؟ میز کے قریب پایہ سے لگی ہوئی بڑھیا کی اہمیت چونے سیمنٹ اور اینٹ والے بیجان پائے سے زیادہ نہ تھی۔ کتابوں سے چھپلتی ہوئی نگاہیں گردش کرتی ہی رہتیں اور ڈرائنگ کی پنسل کے ساتھ غیر ارادی طور پر انگلیاں ایک دوسرے سے ملتی ہی رہتیں !۔

انور احسان مند تھا دادی کی نگاہوں کی پاسبانی دوسروں کے لئے قابل اعتماد تھی اور بیچاری اماں کا تصور خط مستقیم اور خط منحنی کی آواز پر چکر لگاتا ہوا انکی نگاہوں کو گذری ہوئی یاد اور لبسرے ہوئے دنوں کی جھلک دکھاتا رہتا۔

دادی اماں انور کے جانے کے بعد سارا دن چوکی کے فرش پر بیٹھی رہتیں یا لیٹ جاتیں ان کا ہمیشہ سے یہی طریقہ تھا وہ سارا دن محلہ کی آتی گئی لوگوں، کباب بسکٹوں والیوں، انڈا اور ترکاری بیچنے والیوں سے دیر دیر تک عجیب عجیب انداز سے مزے لے کر باتیں کرتی رہتیں۔ اس وقت ان کی آنکھوں میں اپنی بڑائی کا غرور جھلکتا، وہ اتنی دلچسپیوں سے گفتگو کرتیں جیسے گھر سے کبھی نہیں نکلنے کے باوجود سارے گھروں اور سارے ہی لوگوں کو ایسے جانتی ہیں جیسے اپنے گھر کے لوگوں کو۔ وہ باتیں کرتی

کرتی اس کی گہرائیوں میں ڈوب جاتیں پھر کبھی زور زور سے تنقید کرنے کی آواز آتی اور کبھی رازدارانہ سرگوشی کے ساتھ سر اور آنکھیں آہستہ آہستہ صرف جنبش کرنے لگتیں۔ نغمو دور سے دیکھتی رہتی دادی اماں کی آنکھیں کتنے ناول اور کتنے افسانوں کو اس آسانی سے پڑھتی جاتی تھیں۔ کون کہتا ہے کہ ان کی دنیا محدود ہے۔ کاغذ لیتھو پتھر اور سارے بکھیڑوں سے یکسر آزاد کیسی آسانی سے سچی کہانیاں روز کتنی پڑھتی جاتی تھیں۔

دنیا کی ساری بڑھیوں کی طرح دادی اماں کو بھی طرح طرح کے کھانے بہت پسند تھے۔ باتیں کرنے کے علاوہ انھیں اس کی بڑی فکر رہتی کہ اس وقت کے کھانے میں کیا ہے اور اس گھڑی کیا رہے گا؟ بچارہ پرویز کتنی ہی کوشش کرتا لاکھ سر پٹکتا کہ گھر میں مرغیاں رہیں اور انڈا دیں وہ اپنی گود میں چھوٹے چھوٹے بچے لئے پھرتا رہتا مگر دادی اماں کے نوکیلے تیز دانت ایک بھی چوزا، مرغی بٹیر یا چاہا نہ چھوڑتے۔ بچارے بچے اپنے ذبح کئے ہوئے پالتو چوزوں کے اکڑے ہوئے جسم کو بڑے غم سے دیکھتے ان کی غصیلی آنکھوں میں دادی اماں ایک ڈائن کی طرح نظر آتیں جو دوسروں کی زندگی کھا کھا کر اپنی حیات کو سینچ رہی تھیں۔

نغمو کی یاد میں دادی اماں بہت مشکلوں سے صرف ایک دو بار کہیں گھر سے باہر ملنے ملانے گئی تھیں۔ مگر ایک

۱۲۷

دن جب انھیں یہ معلوم ہوا کہ ان کے سگے بھانجے ڈپٹی صاحب کی طبیعت خراب ہے، تو پھر اُن سے نہ رہا گیا۔ ان کے مرحوم شوہر کی بہن کا اپنا بچہ ان کا کوئی غیر نہ تھا وہ اپنے بچھڑے ہوئے شوہر کی یاد کو برقرار دکھانے کے لئے ان کے بھانجے کو بغیر دیکھے ہوئے نہ رہ سکیں۔ اس دن انہوں نے اپنی اچھی دُھلی ہوئی سفید ساڑی پہنی آنکھوں میں سرمہ لگایا۔ "دارالسلام" اپنا ہی گھر ٹھہرا اسی لئے نعمو کو اپنے ساتھ لئے تھک کر چور پریشان حال ہو کر ڈپٹی صاحب کے گھر پر اتریں۔

دادی اماں نعمو کو لے کر بڑے کمرے میں چوکی کے فرش پر گاؤ تکیہ لگا کر بیٹھ رہیں۔ سامنے خاصدان میں پان، زردہ کی ڈبیا اور عطردان رکھا گیا۔ لیکن بچاری دادی اماں تھک کر نڈھال ہو رہی تھیں۔ بڑی مشکلوں سے وہ پان لے سکیں مگر نعمو کو پان لینے سے روک دیا کہ پڑھنے والیوں کی زبان موٹی ہو جاتی ہے اور کنواریاں عطر نہیں لگایا کرتیں۔

دادی اماں کو یہاں آکر معلوم ہوا کہ ان کے بھانجے اب پہلے سے اچھے ہیں ڈاکٹروں نے تو جواب تک دیدیا تھا۔ مگر اللہ نے فضل کیا پھر بھی بڑھاپے کی جان ہے کہاں سے طاقت آئے " دادی اماں گاؤ تکیہ سے لگی لیٹی ہوئی تھیں اچانک بیٹھ گئیں انھیں کہنے والوں کی باتیں بہت بری لگی تھیں۔

کون سراج ؟ بھلا کا ہے کو ایسا بوڑھا ہونے لگا ؟ جب میں بیاہ کر آئی تھی تو اس کی مسیں بھی نہ بھیگی تھیں، یہی کوئی دس بارہ سال ہوئے جب اسے آخری بار دیکھا تھا اب بھلا اتنے سالوں میں بڑھاپا کیا اس پر برس پڑا !

فرش پر بیٹھتے ہی نعمو نے دریچہ سے لگ کر جیسے ہی باہر کی طرف دیکھا، اس کی آنکھیں بے اختیار مسرت سے جھلک پڑیں، مکان کی پشت دو گز کے فاصلے پر ٹھیک سینما ہال کی طرف تھی اسے سینما آئے ہوئے ایک عرصہ گذر گیا تھا اور اب اس کو یاد بھی نہ رہا تھا کہ سینما ہاؤس کس طرف ہے ! خوبصورت اور رنگین اشتہاروں سے چھپی ہوئی سینما ہال کی دیواریں۔ کچھ بند اور کھلے ہوئے دروازے اور سب سے بڑھکر زنانے دروازے کا ہلتا ہوا پردہ نعمو کو پکار پکار کے دعوت دے رہا تھا۔

وہ ناشتہ چائے اور ساری باتوں سے بے نیاز ہوکر دریچہ سے لگی ہوئی اپنی بھوکی نگاہوں سے اس طرف تک رہی تھی، دادی اماں کی آواز اس کے کانوں میں جا تو رہی تھی مگر اس کی نگاہیں دریچہ کے سامنے سینما ہال پر جم کر رہ گئی تھیں جہاں طرح طرح کی ساڑیاں قسم قسم کے کوٹ اور نئے نئے ڈیزائن کی چادریں اپنے شانوں پر ڈالے ہوئے لڑکیاں اور قیمتی سوٹ پہنے ہوئے لڑکے کھیل ہونے سے کہیں پہلے ہی آکر خود اپنی نمائش کر رہے تھے۔

نعمو نگاہوں نگاہوں میں ہی دریچے کے سنگین جنگلے کے

اس بار اس رنگ و بو کی دنیا میں خود کو بھی آزاد محسوس کر رہی تھی۔ وہ تھوڑی دیر کے لئے یہ بھول گئی تھی کہ دادی اماں کے سخت گیر پنجے اس کی خوشیوں کا گلا دبوچے ہوئے ہیں۔ ایک دفعہ دادی اماں سے چھپ کر اپنی امی کے ساتھ سکنڈ شو میں سینما دیکھنے گئی تھی فلم "پکار" نے اس کی روح کو ایک پکار دیا تھا مگر دادی اماں کے ڈر سے وہ پھر کبھی نہ جا سکتی تھی۔

دادی اماں کو سراج کو دیکھنے کی رٹ لگی ہوئی تھی مگر جب ان کو یہ معلوم ہوا کہ انہیں کو ٹھے پر چڑھنے کی تکلیف اٹھانی پڑے گی تو یکبارگی ایسا معلوم ہوا جیسے ان کے سارے حوصلے پست ہو گئے۔ پھر بھی انہیں اپنی بات رکھنی تھی اور صرف اسی دیکھنے کی خاطر وہ آتنی پریشان ہو کر آئی تھیں۔ انہوں نے نمو کو بھی اپنے ساتھ لے جانا چاہا مگر نمو کنمنا ئی، اس نے اپنے تماشے میں محو رہنا زیادہ پسند کیا اور بچاری دادی اماں وقت کی نزاکت کا احساس کر کے کسی دوسرے کے سہارے آہستہ آہستہ ہانپتی کانپتی ہوئی سیڑھیوں پر چڑھتی ہوئی اپنے بھانجہ سراج کی مسہری تک پہنچیں۔ اوپر پہنچتے پہنچتے وہ بدحال ہو گئی تھیں اور سردی کے باوجود پسینے ان کی پیشانی سے چھوٹ رہے تھے۔

دادی اماں اپنے بھانجے سراج کے سرہانے ہانپتی ہوئی کھڑی تھیں نگران کی نگاہیں داڑھی اور مونچھوں کے الجھاؤ میں الجھ کر

رہ گئی تھیں وہ بڑی مشکلوں سے اپنی نظروں کو وہاں پہ سے ہٹا سکیں۔ بچارے ڈپٹی صاحب کچھ نہ بول سکتے تھے۔ اشارے سے صرف سلام ہی کر سکے۔ ان کے ہاتھ کی کہنیاں کلائی اور چہرے کی ہڈیاں عجیب بھیانک طور پر باہر نکلی ہوئی تھیں۔ اتنا بڑا تغیر صرف دس بارہ سال کے عرصہ میں دادی اماں حیران ہو کر تک رہی تھیں۔ وہ تو سوچ بھی نہ سکتی تھیں کہ ان کا بھانجہ بڑھاپے کی اس منزل تک پہنچ گیا ہے۔ اپنے بھانجہ کی بیمار کھوکھلی نگاہوں کو دیکھتے ہی انہیں شدید طور پر ایک احساس ہوا جیسے یکایک جوانی کی تیز لہریں ان کی رگوں میں دوڑ گئیں۔ بڑھاپے اور بیماری نے ڈپٹی صاحب کو موت کی آخری منزل تک پہنچا دیا تھا۔ اور انھیں دیکھکر جیسے دادی اماں کو کچھ دنوں کے لئے ٹھہر کر دم لینے کا سہارا مل گیا۔ مسہری پر پڑے ہوئے ایک مجبور بے بس انسان کو دیکھتے ہی انھیں یہ محسوس ہونے لگا کہ وقت سے پہلے ہی ان پر بڑھاپے کا غلط الزام لگا رکھا ہے بڑھاپے کی منزل تو یہ ہوتی ہے۔ اور دادی اماں تو ان مجبوریوں سے کہیں دور تھیں۔ خاموشی سے سرہانے کھڑی ہوئی دادی اماں اپنے پیروں میں ایک نئی طاقت محسوس کر رہی تھیں، آنے والی موت کے خیال سے ان کے رونگٹے کانپ گئے۔ وہی موت جو اس مسہری کے گرد منڈلا رہی تھی، وہ اس جگہ زیادہ دیر رہنا نہ چاہتی تھیں۔ انھوں نے جھک کر بڑی محبت اور ہمدردی سے عنقریب ہی مرجانے والے سراج کی پیشانی پر ہاتھ پھیر کر کہا! گھبراؤ مت سراج!

جلد ہی اچھے ہو جاؤ گے"۔۔۔! مریض نے اپنا کمزور ہاتھ اٹھا کر ایک آخری سلام کیا، دادی اماں کو دعائیں دیتے ہوئے شرم آ رہی تھی۔ جیسے وہ اپنے بڑے کو دعا دے رہی ہوں۔ وہ جلدی جلدی تیزی سے زینہ طے کرتی ہوئی نیچے آئیں۔ وہ بڑی مشکلوں سے اپنے تھکے ہوئے منتشر سانسوں کو روک رہی تھیں مگر ان کے چہرے پر مسرت کی سرخی چھا رہی تھی اور انھیں لگ رہا تھا جیسے کسی نے ایک بڑا بوجھ ان کے سر سے اتار دیا ہو۔ وہ مطمئن انداز میں گاؤ تکیہ سے لگ کر سیدھی ذرا تن کر بیٹھ گئیں، بچارہ سراج بہت بدل گیا ہے نہ۔ اپنی اپنی مٹی، کیسا خراب تھا بیچارے کا بڑھاپا۔۔۔"

نعمو اپنے سے قریب ہی دادی اماں کی آواز سنکر چونک پڑی۔ نعمو پر جھکی ہوئی دادی اماں دریچے کا ایک اور پٹ کھولتی ہوئی مسکرا کر بولیں۔

"کیا ہے نعمو؟"

"سنیا ہال ہے دادی اماں یہاں روز تماشے ہوتے ہیں۔ بڑے اچھے اچھے سے بولنے والے اور گانے والے" نعمو نے ڈرتے ڈرتے ذرا تفصیل سے کہا۔

دادی اماں کی کچی پکی کھچڑیا بھویں ان کی پیشانی کی ٹیڑھی ترچھی لکیروں میں قوس و قزح کی طرح اوپر اٹھیں۔ چمکتی ہوئی آنکھیں

نعمو کے چہرے پر جم کر رہ گئیں اور پک کر سڑے ہوئے چھلکے کی طرح ان کے لبوں کو جنبش ہوئی اور اچانک طور جیسے بے اختیار ان کی زبان سے نکل گیا۔

"نعمو بیٹی چلو نہ ہم بھی سینما دیکھ آئیں۔"

Pukaar *(Short Stories)*
by: Shakila Akhtar
Edition: August '2024
Publisher :
Taemeer Publications LLC (Michigan, USA / Hyderabad, India)

کتاب	:	**پکار** (افسانے)
مصنفہ	:	**شکیلہ اختر**
صنف	:	فکشن
ناشر	:	تعمیر پبلی کیشنز (حیدرآباد، انڈیا)
سالِ اشاعت	:	۲۰۲۴ء
صفحات	:	۸۸
سرورق ڈیزائن	:	تعمیر ویب ڈیزائن

پکار

(افسانے)

شکیلہ اختر

www.ingramcontent.com/pod-product-compliance
Lightning Source LLC
LaVergne TN
LVHW010600070526
838199LV00063BA/5025

* 9 7 8 9 3 5 8 7 2 4 4 4 8 *

© Taemeer Publications LLC
The importance of International Assessment Programs in improving the Quality of Education
by: Aziza Amonova
Edition: September '2023
Publisher:
Taemeer Publications LLC (Michigan, USA / Hyderabad, India)

ISBN 978-93-5872-903-0

Book	:	The importance of International Assessment Programs in improving the Quality of Education
Author	:	Aziza Amonova
Publisher	:	Taemeer Publications
Year	:	'2023
Pages	:	86
Title Design	:	*Taemeer Web Design*

The importance of International Assessment Programs in improving the Quality of Education

Aziza Amonova

Regulatory and legal frameworks, main goals and measures for the introduction of international studies on the assessment of the quality of education (PISA, TIMSS, PIRLS, TALIS) in the public education system.

Plan:

1. Regulatory and legal frameworks, main goals and measures for the introduction of PISA, TIMSS, PIRLS, TALIS international studies on the assessment of the quality of education in the public education system.

2. Analysis of international assessment studies (across years, based on reading, mathematical and scientific literacy, and creative thinking).

3. PISA-shock. The impact of the implementation of international assessment programs on the quality and content of education. Periodicity and importance of international evaluation studies.

The main goal of the fundamental reforms in the field of education implemented in our republic is the formation and development of students' literacy skills. At a time when our country is rapidly developing on the path of innovative development, it is important to form young people, who are the successors of our future, their knowledge and skills based on foreign educational standards, and to improve the assessment system based on modern clear criteria and requirements. By the Decree of the President of the Republic of Uzbekistan No. PF-4947 of February 7, 2017 "On the Action Strategy for the Further Development of the Republic of Uzbekistan", "Five priority areas of development of the Republic of Uzbekistan in 2017-2021 "Strategy of Actions" was adopted.

IV. 4.4 of priority areas of social sector development. One of the clauses for the development of the field of education and science is "fundamental improvement of the quality of general secondary education, in-depth study of foreign languages, computer science and other important and high-demand subjects such as mathematics, physics, chemistry, biology" and it corresponds to the world's best practices in the field of education.

Study of international experiences in the assessment of the quality of education, comparative and comprehensive analysis of the existing system, close cooperation with relevant international and foreign organizations, agencies, research institutions, assessment of the quality of education It is important to implement international projects and improve a suitable national evaluation system that meets the requirements of the time.

Paragraph 5 of the Decree No. PF-5538 of the President of the Republic of Uzbekistan dated September 5, 2018 "On additional measures to improve the public education management system" refers to the assessment of students' level of knowledge participation of students of general education institutions in international programs and research (PISA, TIMSS, PIRLS, etc.)

- Progress in International Reading and Literacy Study (PIRLS) — to assess the level of reading and understanding of the text of primary 4th grade students;

-Trends in International Mathematics and Science Study (TIMSS) — to assess the mastery level of 4th and 8th grade students in mathematics and natural sciences;

- The Program for International Student Assessment (PISA) — to assess the level of literacy of 15-year-old students in reading, mathematics and natural sciences;

- The Teaching and Learning International Survey (TALIS) - to study the teaching and learning environment of the leaders and pedagogues in general secondary educational institutions and the working conditions of teachers;

On April 5, 2019, the concept of developing the public education system of the Republic of Uzbekistan until 2030 was adopted. The concept stipulates that by 2030, the Republic of Uzbekistan will enter the ranks of the first 30 advanced countries of the world according to the PISA (The Program for International Student Assessment) rating of the international student assessment program. By the decision of the Cabinet of Ministers of the Republic of Uzbekistan No. 997 of December 8, 2018 "On measures to organize international studies in the field of evaluation of the quality of education in the system of public education", the quality of education in the system of public education organization of international research in the field of assessment, establishment of international relations, comprehensive support and stimulation of scientific research and innovation activities of students and young people, above all, creative ideas and creativity of the young generation it is determined to reach the country. By the decision of the Cabinet of Ministers of the Republic of Uzbekistan No. 997 of December 8, 2018 "On measures to organize international studies in the field of evaluation of the quality of education in the system of public education", the quality of education in the system of public education Organization of international studies in the field of evaluation, establishment of international relations, scientific research and innovation activities of students and young people, first of all, creative ideas and creativity of the young generation in order to support and encourage them in every way. The National Center for the Implementation of International Researches on the Evaluation of the Quality of Education of the State Inspection of Education Quality Control under the Cabinet of Ministers of the Republic of Uzbekistan was established. In turn, the National Center for the Implementation of International Research on the Evaluation of the Quality of Education to carry out scientific research aimed at the development and implementation of innovative methods of developing the level of literacy in reading, mathematics and natural sciences in the educational system, establishing international relations, developing and implementing international projects and other tasks in the field of education quality assessment. It was determined that the director of the national center will participate as a representative of the Republic of Uzbekistan in the organization and coordination of international research and will be considered the national project manager of international research. As a practical expression of these tasks, the State Inspectorate for Quality Control of Education under the Cabinet of Ministers of the Republic of Uzbekistan and the International Cooperation and Development Organization signed the Agreement for participation program for international student assessment PISA 2021) an agreement on participation was reached.

PISA (Programme for International Student Assessment) is an international research program for assessing students' literacy, the main goal of the program is to improve the reading, (reading comprehension), mathematics and natural sciences of fifteen-year-old students. is to evaluate literacy levels and creative thinking skills in the form of various tests. These projects encourage students to evaluate their creative and critical thinking, their ability to apply their knowledge in life, and then develop these skills. The PISA program, which is carried out every three years, provides countries with timely information about the achievements and shortcomings of the education system, provides an opportunity to analyze the impact of relevant programs, and supports decision-making in the field of education policy. Since international studies such as PISA aimed at assessing the quality of education are being conducted for the first time for the educational system of Uzbekistan, it is important to conduct them correctly, effectively and objectively.

Ensuring the successful participation of general secondary education institutions in international research; Comparative comparison of the results recorded by the Republic of Uzbekistan in international evaluation programs with the results of other countries; to carry out systematic monitoring of the introduction of international assessment programs into the educational process, popularize the best experience in this field and participate in the development of recommendations and manuals for educational institutions based on it; The main tasks and directions of activity of the National Center, such as the preparation of educational and methodological recommendations for improving the qualifications of pedagogues in the fields of reading, mathematics and natural sciences using innovative methods of teaching, were determined.

PISA is an international assessment program aimed at assessing the level of knowledge of students in reading (text comprehension), mathematics and natural sciences, and is designed to determine the knowledge and skills acquired by students during the school period.

The PISA international assessment program also collects valuable information about student attitudes and motivation, and assesses students' skills such as problem solving. For example, in solving issues of global importance, the student evaluates the attitudes of young people and their suggestions and solutions.

PISA is based on the conduct of international assessment programs within the framework of the requirements existing in the curricula of the countries of the world. focuses on the application of knowledge and skills, thinking and communication skills.

PISA does not prescribe or promote any curriculum or require universal recognition. According to the experts and economists of the participating countries, they recognize that the formation and strengthening of the acquired knowledge and skills in natural sciences are considered important first steps for the future success of the countries.

The PISA study (Programme for International Student Assessment) is a program implemented by the Organization for Economic Co-operation and Development (OECD - Organization for Economic Co-operation and Development).

The research was conducted for the first time in 2000 and is conducted every three years. The next research is planned to be conducted in 2022.

The PISA study has the following characteristics:

- is considered one of the largest, large-scale international monitoring studies in the field of education;

- 15-year-old students studying in general secondary educational institutions participate in the research;

- the research assesses the level of "readiness for life" of students, that is, to what extent they can use the knowledge and skills acquired at school to solve problems they may encounter in life;

- the research evaluates students' functional literacy in mathematics, reading (reading), natural sciences, and solving global problems;

- contextual information is collected that allows to obtain information on the uniqueness of the educational system of the countries participating in the research.

- Uzbekistan's participation in the PISA study makes it possible to:

- To determine to what extent the graduates of Uzbekistan's secondary schools are ready to continue their education;

- determining directions for improving general secondary education in the country;

- obtaining comparative information about educational achievements of students, as well as educational systems of different countries.

Why are PISA studies conducted every three years and why are only 15-year-old students tested?

The main task of PISA is to provide countries with information on education policy and to support them in making decisions. Conducting the survey every three years allows countries to provide timely information, including data and analysis to inform policy decisions and the impact of related programs. If the periodicity of conducting research is carried out in a short period of time, it creates the problem of not being able to collect the necessary data and enough time for changes and updates. The main reason for conducting the study among 15-year-old students is that this age is the final period of compulsory education in most of the countries that are members of the Organization for Economic Cooperation and Development (OECD).

The PISA international assessment program has its own importance as a comprehensive and regular program around the world.

More than 80 countries participated in PISA international assessment program. Conducting the research once every three years allows countries to determine the main goals to be achieved in their education systems in the future. Also, the program is the only international assessment project for assessing the knowledge and skills of 15-year-old students.

Literacy: PISA looks at students' ability to apply knowledge and skills in key subjects, to analyze, interpret and solve problems effectively, to think and to communicate, rather than examining the superiority of specific school curricula. the rib comes out.

Lifelong learning: Students cannot learn everything they are supposed to learn in school. To be an effective learner, one must be aware not only of knowledge and skills, but also how and why they are learned. PISA students' reading (comprehension of the text), In addition to improving math and science literacy, it asks students about their interest in learning, about themselves, and about their learning strategies. The PISA study diagnoses the readiness of young people for the life of "adults", which distinguishes it from other international studies, whose main goal is to measure the subject knowledge and skills defined in the curricula, which are largely unrelated to real life or educational tasks. is to try using

It is of particular interest to determine the state of knowledge and skills that may be useful for children in the future, as well as the ability to independently acquire knowledge necessary for successful adaptation in the modern world.

PISA studies are conducted in three directions: reading literacy, mathematical literacy, natural science literacy, evaluated in a 1000-point system. Research is conducted in a three-year cycle. In each cycle, the main attention is paid to one of the three directions mentioned above. Changes in the education system of the countries in a certain direction are analyzed in detail. This international program was developed in 1997 and was put into practice for the first time in 2000. With the help of the program, changes in the education system of different countries are identified, compared, and evaluated. The results of these studies are followed with great interest around the world. Therefore, its importance and scope is increasing year by year. For example, in 2000, 265,000 students from 32 countries took part in the program tests, and in 2018, this figure was expected to double, that is, more than 540,000 students from 78 countries took part.

PISA tasks are completed on a computer. The test questions have ready answers, and the correct one is selected from them. There will also be unanswered tests. The student is asked to answer them fully or briefly. Some test tasks are related to the same life situation, but consist of test questions of different difficulty levels. Tests are made in several options. Some tests may be repeated in some variants. Also, in the study, students write information about themselves and their school principals in a questionnaire. The collected information helps to determine the factors affecting the educational outcome.

The results of PISA studies allow to determine the following:

- Quantitative indicators representing the basic knowledge and skills of 15-year-old students;

-quantitative indicators representing the state of factors affecting the educational results of students and the implementation of work at school;

-quantitative indicators representing the direction of changes in the results achieved over time.

Research results and indicators describing the education system of different countries are published every three years. These data are used to compare the achievements of the educational system of the countries and to determine the policy in the field of school education.

The program is implemented by the Consortium, which includes leading international research organizations and national centers, the Organization for Economic Cooperation and Development. The work of the consortium is managed by the Australian Council for Educational Research (ACER).

Pupils are mainly offered practical situations typical of everyday life (medicine, housing, sports, etc.) rather than academic ones. In most cases, students are required to use not only different topics and sections of mathematics, but also knowledge and skills acquired in other subjects, for example, physics and biology.

What is the importance of international assessment programs?

As a result of the reforms carried out in our country in recent years, huge economic growth indicators are being achieved, increasing the demand for qualified personnel and advanced specialists in all fields. This in itself requires increasing the interest of our students in lessons and increasing the attention of teachers to all-round education. The fact that the above requirements are very important for the education system, as in most foreign countries, the best practices aimed at improving the quality of education by evaluating and monitoring the development of the fields of education and science means that you need to be involved in the field.

What does participation in international studies on the assessment of the quality of education give to Uzbekistan?

It is used to reform the national education system, improve the content of education, training and professional development programs of pedagogues, and create a new generation of textbooks by experts.

The results obtained in the research allow us to draw conclusions about the quality of education in the country and its place taking into account international standards.

International research has a positive effect on the quality of national research in the field of education.

It allows to create a national assessment system based on high economic efficiency at the level of international standards.

It allows to create a national assessment system based on high economic efficiency at the level of international standards.

By participating in international research involving leading experts of various organizations in Uzbekistan, the culture of conducting monitoring research among our local experts will develop, and it will lead to the adaptation of education quality assessment to international standards.

It makes it possible to develop control materials for the assessment of the quality of national education at the level of the quality of control materials used in international studies.

Mathematical literacy and its assessment criteria, content areas related to mathematics, task format in the PISA study. ICT literacy in the PISA study, a simulation task format. Application of modern information and communication technologies in the process of preparation for international assessment programs.

Plan:

1. Mathematical literacy and its evaluation criteria, content areas related to mathematics, task format in the PISA study

2. ICT literacy in the PISA study, simulation task format.

3. Application of modern information and communication technologies in the process of preparation for international assessment programs.

Each country has its own views on the concept of mathematical literacy or competence and organizes its educational process to achieve it as an expected outcome. Historically, mathematical literacy or competence has been the acquisition of basic arithmetic skills, particularly addition, subtraction, multiplication and division on whole numbers, simple and decimal fractions, calculation of percentages, faces of simple geometric figures and included skills such as calculating volumes. Recently, the introduction of digital technologies into our lives has led to the emergence of opportunities for people to obtain the necessary information from the flow of information to meet their personal needs, in areas of life related to health and investments, weather and climate changes, tax It has also created a need for skills related to solving social problems such as gravity, public debt, population growth, the spread of infectious disease epidemics, and the global economy. The changing daily needs of the 21st century demands that the concept of mathematical literacy expands and improves.

Interest in the list of "21st century skills" published at the beginning of the century is growing. Although there have been many debates over the last 15 years about this list of skills and how to improve them, many countries have taken appropriate measures to integrate these skills into their education systems. making changes. The Organization for Economic Co-operation and Development (OECD) has also financed a project until 2030 called "Education and Skills in the Future, OECD - 2030" with the participation of experts from 25 countries.

In particular, the PISA international research program continues to inculcate these skills. In particular, the scope of PISA-2021 studies includes the assessment of skills in the following 8 main areas directly related to the concept of mathematical literacy from the "21st century skills": The essence of the concept of mathematical literacy is also improving year by year. In particular, the assessment of mathematical literacy occupies an important place in the PISA-2021 studies, as it is considered a priority area in 2021. Although the mathematical literacy of students was also evaluated in the studies from 2000 to 2018, this area was prioritized only in 2003 and 2012. In the PISA studies, special attention is paid to the following three aspects when assessing students' mathematical readiness: - the tasks match students' interests and needs in everyday life; - viability of the problem content (context); - complete coverage of not only some of the stages of applying mathematics, that is, not only performing a part of this process (for example, solving an equation, simplifying an algebraic expression), but starting from the stage of understanding the problem, expressing it in mathematical language, solving and that all steps up to solution interpretation are covered. These aspects are reflected in the content of assessment of students' mathematical readiness, that is, the concept of mathematical literacy. The concept of mathematical literacy has been interpreted differently in different years of research. According to the results of the latest research, it can be defined as follows:

Mathematical literacy is a person's ability to think mathematically about various life situations (contexts) and problems, to be able to express a given problem with the help of mathematics, to be able to use mathematics to solve a problem, and to be able to use the obtained results to interpret and evaluate the solution to the problem. It includes concepts, algorithms, facts, and tools for describing, explaining, and predicting events. It helps people understand the place of mathematics in the world and make the informed judgments and decisions necessary for creative, curious, and self-reflective citizens of the 21st century. In the definition of mathematical literacy, the main emphasis is on an active relationship with mathematics to solve real-world problems in various situations, to make mathematical reasoning, be it inductive or deductive, and to understand the phenomena encountered in nature and society with the help of mathematical symbols and symbols. i.e. mathematical reasoning, mathematical reasoning, mathematical knowledge, concepts, algorithms, facts and tools are used to express in the language of mathematics, explain and predict events. Mathematical literacy enables everyone to understand the world of mathematics, to understand its role and importance in human life, to make reasonable decisions by making reasonable decisions, which are necessary for an active, thoughtful and business-minded (constructive) citizen of the 21st century. helps to form in itself. Mathematical literacy is assessed and researched using specially designed tasks. The content, structure and form of these tasks must meet specific requirements based on the nature of the research. The structure (model) of a special PISA test task aimed at assessing mathematical literacy is based on the following 3 aspects: - the subject area of mathematics to which the task belongs, i.e. sections; – problem content or context; - the type of mental activity that students should demonstrate while completing the task.

The PISA study aims to determine what is important for students to know and be able to do. This study evaluates the extent to which 15-year-old students have acquired the knowledge and skills necessary for full participation in modern society by the time they graduate from an educational institution. In each cycle of the study, one of the main domains is tested in detail, and about half of the total test time is devoted to this domain. In 2018, the main domain was reading literacy, in 2022, mathematics, and in 2025, science. Speaking of domains, it's worth noting the creative thinking domain, which is new to the 2022 survey.

Creative thinking is one of the important competencies that a person needs for successful functioning in the 21st century society. These competencies, which are called "21st century skills" or "21st century competencies", are constantly changing, the professions we know are disappearing and new specialties are emerging, globalized, the amount of available information is increasing several times every second, being able to adapt and find one's place in the digital society. very important for These competencies require highly developed cognitive skills, including the ability to think logically, compare, analyze and synthesize, and find non-standard solutions to problems individually and as a team. Developing these skills, in turn, requires moving away from traditional content-based pedagogy and assessment methods and introducing competency-based teaching and assessment. The PISA international assessment program, which Uzbekistan is expected to participate in for the first time in 2022, evaluates students' creative thinking in addition to their reading, mathematical and scientific literacy. In order to develop and evaluate creative thinking, first of all, it is necessary to understand this domain itself, to study its scientific foundations.

The literature "Framework for evaluating creative thinking in the PISA study" prepared by the Ministry of Public Education of the Republic of Uzbekistan reveals the components of the domain of creative thinking, the factors affecting the domain of creative thinking based on international research. In particular, what is meant by creative thinking, how creative thinking depends on content and other domains, positive and negative factors that can affect the development of creative thinking in the educational process are covered in detail. Undoubtedly, understanding the scientific foundations of the domain of creative thinking will greatly help pedagogues to choose effective methods and technologies to stimulate the creative activity of their students in the educational process. Another important aspect of this literature is the examples of PISA test tasks aimed at testing creative thinking, their description, the competencies tested in them, and evaluation criteria. is presented. This will be of great help in understanding the mechanisms of creative activity assessment directly adopted in the PISA program. Teachers will have the opportunity to directly analyze and understand how such tasks work and include them in their lessons. Unfortunately, there are very few resources in the Uzbek language aimed at developing and evaluating functional and creative competencies in the educational process. Existing resources are mainly based on content pedagogy, which, as mentioned above, do not always take into account the needs of people of the 21st century. Considering that many people do not have access to resources in foreign languages, this literature serves as a valuable resource for pedagogues and representatives of the education sector. These aspects are reflected in the content of assessment of students' mathematical readiness, that is, the concept of mathematical literacy.

As in 2015 and 2018, the PISA survey in 2022 will be mostly computer-based. For countries that choose not to conduct the survey on a computer, a paper outcast is provided, which does not include the newly developed tasks. the latest development assignments are for computer-based research only. Conducting research in the form of a computer creates many opportunities. In the study, students work with clusters of different questions in the domains of math, reading, science, and creative thinking. They will be given a total of 2 hours for this. After students complete these tasks, a short break will be followed by a survey. All processes are carried out with the help of a computer.

A cycle of connections between cognitive levels, contexts, content areas, scope, mathematical reasoning, and problem solving (modeling) of PISA's mathematical literacy tasks. Developing mathematical literacy skills.
Plan:
1. Cognitive levels, contexts, content areas, scope of PISA mathematical literacy assignments.
2. Types of mental activity of students used in mathematical reasoning and problem solving
3. Development of mathematical literacy skills.

The PISA international assessment program has its own importance as a comprehensive and regular program around the world. Currently, more than 80 countries participate in the PISA international assessment program. Conducting the research once every three years allows the states to determine the main goals to be achieved in the future in their education system. PISA is the only international assessment program for assessing the knowledge and skills of 15-year-old students. The program also includes the following issues:

► public policy issues: "Are schools able to properly prepare young students for the transition to adult life?", "Are some types of educational programs more effective than others?", "Do schools improve the future of immigrants or students from difficult social conditions?" will it help?" is to find answers to some questions such as;

► Literacy: PISA measures students' ability to apply knowledge and skills in key subjects, analyze, interpret and effectively solve problems, think and communicate, rather than examining the superiority of specific school curricula. comes out;

► lifelong learning: students cannot fully master everything they are supposed to learn in school. To be an effective learner, it is necessary to be aware not only of knowledge and skills, but also how and why they are learned. PISA assesses students' literacy in reading (reading), mathematics, and science, as well

as their interest in learning, information about themselves, and their views on learning strategies.
At a time when humanity faces major challenges such as food security, disease outbreaks, energy production, and climate change, science literacy is becoming increasingly important at the national and international levels (UNEP, 2012). The use of technologies and scientific achievements is of great importance in solving such problems. According to the opinion expressed by the European Commission, political and ethnic problems whose solutions are related to science and technology cannot be the subject of scientific discussions if young people are not aware of natural sciences to a certain extent. In addition, this does not mean preparing everyone as a specialist in natural sciences, but it allows young people to make decisions on issues related to the environment around them and to understand the scientific discussions conducted among experts. A special feature of PISA tasks is that they reflect real-life problem situations, which is called context. Context includes text, tables, graphics, and images. In one of the conducted PISA studies, problematic situations in assignments were expressed in the following contexts: health; natural resources; environment; danger; new knowledge in the field of science and technology. In turn, contexts are at three levels: personal; local/national; global. Well, in a personal context, assignments are given on

topics such as health care, accidents, nutrition, environmental friendliness, and hobbies. In local or national assignments, assignments are given in contexts such as disease control, their spread, food production, waste disposal, and technical equipment. In global contexts, students are given tasks related to the spread of infectious diseases, environmental pollution, and climate change.

The cognitive level of the task is the mental processes required to perform the task, the intellectual difficulty of the task, that is, the complexity of the required thinking process, and the scope of knowledge and skills required to perform the task. Tasks will have one of the following cognitive levels:

lower level (performing one-step actions, for example, memorizing a proof, term, law and concept, finding a point in a table or graph where the requested information is represented); intermediate level (being able to use and apply relevant knowledge in describing and explaining phenomena, being able to select appropriate actions that require two or more steps of activity, being able to interpret or retain simple data sets in the form of graphs or tables get 'llay); higher level (analyzing complex data, summarizing or evaluating evidence, justifying, creating a plan for solving a problem using different sources of information or determining a sequence of actions).

Assignments are made based on the cognitive level of students' age. That is, a process that goes from simple to complex. If we compose questions that are not suitable for the age of a student, it is not structured based on the cognitive level. Of course, there are complex tasks at a higher level, and relatively easy tasks at a lower level.

Mathematical literacy is a person's ability to think mathematically about various life situations (contexts) and problems, to be able to express a given problem with the help of mathematics, to be able to use mathematics to solve a problem, and to be able to use the obtained results to interpret and evaluate the solution to the problem. It includes concepts, algorithms, facts, and tools for describing, explaining, and predicting events. It helps people understand the place of mathematics in the world and make the informed judgments and decisions necessary for creative, curious, and self-reflective citizens of the 21st century. In the definition of mathematical literacy, the main emphasis is on an active relationship with mathematics to solve real-world problems in various situations, to make mathematical reasoning, be it inductive or deductive, and to understand the phenomena encountered in nature and society with the help of mathematical symbols and symbols. i.e. mathematical reasoning, mathematical reasoning, mathematical knowledge, concepts, algorithms, facts and tools are used to express in the language of mathematics, explain and predict events. Mathematical literacy enables everyone to understand the world of mathematics, to understand its role and importance in human life, to make reasonable decisions by making reasonable decisions, which are necessary for an active, thoughtful and business-minded (constructive) citizen of the 21st century. helps to form in itself. Mathematical literacy is assessed and researched using specially designed tasks. The content, structure and form of these tasks must meet specific requirements based on the nature of the research. The structure (model) of a special PISA test task aimed at assessing mathematical literacy is based on the following 3 aspects: - the subject area of mathematics to which the task belongs, i.e. sections; – problem content or context; - the type of mental activity that students should demonstrate while completing the task.

Mathematical literacy includes students' activities such as "expressing the problem in a given life situation in mathematical language (mathematical modeling)", "applying mathematics", "interpreting and evaluating the found mathematical solution in relation to the given problem" based on mathematical reasoning. Briefly, these activities are called "reasoning", "expressing", "applying" and "interpreting" and "evaluating". Mathematical reasoning, whether it is deductive or inductive, is related to certain basic concepts that form the basis of mathematics in school.

Such basic concepts include: - understanding of quantities, number systems and their algebraic properties; - understanding the importance of representation using abstraction and symbols; - to see mathematical structures and their laws; - recognize the functional connections between quantities; - use of mathematical modeling as a means of researching various phenomena of the real world (for example, in physical, biological, social, economic and humanitarian sciences); - to understand that variability is based on statistics. In determining mathematical literacy, each of the above-mentioned types of mental activity based on reasoning, assessed by students, also requires the following skills:

to read and understand the nature of problematic situations given in different contexts related to various aspects of human activity: personal life, future professional activity, educational activity, social life in society, science and technology; - analysis of the given situation and identification of the problem presented in it; - recognition of mathematical structures (laws and relationships) given in problems and situations; - simplifying problems and situations, dividing them into separate issues; 19 - to determine the possibilities of practical use of the information given in the description of the situation, processing and expressing the problem in the form of a mathematical problem; - creating a mathematical model reflecting the important aspects of the problem situation. Application of mathematics: - use of learned mathematical concepts, facts, ideas, laws, algorithms and methods to solve a practical mathematical problem; - analysis, selection and justification of alternative methods of solving the problem; - creating new mathematical knowledge and mastering it in the process of solving a problem (problem); - expression and research of mathematical assumptions, mathematical reasoning, comparison and evaluation; - logical, creative thinking, mathematical reasoning and scientific research methods in problem solving: observation, measurement, experimentation, analysis and synthesis, induction and deduction, comparison and analogies; - recognizing and using connections between mathematical concepts; - application of mathematics in educational and life situations encountered in everyday life and related to other subjects; - use of various mathematical interpretation methods to explain and model phenomena and processes in nature and society. Interpretation of the solution: - thinking about the results obtained from the mathematical solution of the practical problem, transferring the mathematical solution to the content of the real problem and interpreting it in relation to the real problem described in the mathematical problem, and evaluating the compatibility and proximity of the found solution to the real solution of the problem; - use of mathematical language, signs and symbols, and possibilities of computer and information communication technologies for clear, written and pictorial expression of mathematical thought.

Mathematical reasoning: - making simple conclusions; – choosing the appropriate justification; - based on the content of the problem, explain whether the mathematical result or conclusion has meaning or not; - expressing the problem in a different form, including adapting it to mathematical concepts and making relevant assumptions; - application of definitions, rules and formulas, algorithms and calculations; - justification of the mathematical model that is suitable for the real situation; - explain and justify the processes and algorithms, models used to determine the mathematical result or solution; - determination of limits of the model to solve the problem; - thinking about mathematical proofs when explaining and justifying a mathematical result;

- a critical review of the limitations of the model created to solve the problems; - interpretation of mathematical results in the context of the real world to explain the meaning of the results; - explanation of connections between symbolic and formal languages necessary for giving the problem in context and for its mathematical expression; - create explanations and arguments that apply and refute the mathematical solution of the given problem in the context, and reflect on the mathematical solution; - analysis of similarities and differences between a mathematical problem and its calculation model; - explain the use of simple algorithms and identify and eliminate errors in them.

Estimated distribution of scores in the tasks of the PISA-2021 study by types of mental activity. PISA-2021 assignments are divided into the following four content areas (sections) of mathematics: - quantities; - changes and relationships; – space and form; - information and uncertainties. Quantities - in the content area, assignments are given on numbers and their relationships, and in the school mathematics course, this section is called "Arithmetic". Assignments in this content area may cover the following topics: - Numbers and units: concept of number, number representation and number systems, properties of whole and rational numbers, basic concepts of irrational number, time, money, weight density, temperature, length, surface, volume, as well as quantities derived from them (for example, speed - km/h) and their values; – Computer modeling (PISA-2021): multifactorial problems with the help of a special computer simulator, various situations (budget financing, planning, population distribution, disease prevalence, experimental probability, etc.) learning based on duration of chemical reactions etc.). Use of computer simulation training tools, calculators and measuring instruments created on the basis of appropriate measurement methods used in measuring quantities; - Arithmetic and algebraic operations: the essence and properties of arithmetic and algebraic operations, accepted rules, laws, including raising the number to a power and extracting simple square roots; – Percentages, relationships and proportions: calculation of their values, use of proportions and correct proportional relationships in solving problems; – Evaluation: approximate values of numerical expressions and quantities with given accuracy, rounding; 25 - Sorting method: simple combinatorics problems of grouping, permutation and permutation solved by this method. Transformations and relationships - in the content area, tasks related to the mathematical expression of relationships between variables in various processes are given, and it belongs to the "Algebra" section of mathematics. The following skills are assessed in this content area: – Functions: the concept of functions (with an emphasis on linear functions), their properties, their various representations, and methods of representation. Usually, functions are described using words, symbols, tables and graphs; - Algebraic expressions: interpretation of algebraic expressions using words, operations on algebraic expressions, working with values of variables, symbols, replacing variables with their values and calculating the value of the expression; – Equations and Inequalities:

linear equations, systems of linear equations and inequalities, simple quadratic equations, analytical and non-analytical solving methods (for example, "trial and error learning" method); - Coordinate system: representation of data, their location and interrelationships and description in the coordinate system; – Growth phenomenon (PISA–2021): different types of growth: linear, non-linear, quadratic and exponential (the value of the added, next growth of the system is proportional to its value so far). Space and Shape - this content area deals with spatial and plane geometric shapes and relationships and can be called "geometry". The following skills are evaluated in this content area: – Relationships between flat and three-dimensional geometric shapes (objects): connections between elements of shapes (for example, the Pythagorean theorem, connections between sides of a triangle), mutual arrangement of shapes, equality and similarity, dynamic relations, movements in space and plane, connections between plane and spatial objects. The relationship between two parallel straight lines and thc angles formed by the intersection. Triangle surface, rectangle perimeter and surface formulas; - Spatial shapes (rectangular parallelepiped, pyramid, cylinder, cone, sphere, sphere) and their properties: formulas for calculating the surface area and volume of spatial objects; – Measurements: numerical characteristics of shapes and objects and properties between them: angle values, distances, lengths, perimeter, circumference, surface and volume. - Geometric approximation (PISA-2021): to study the elements and properties of given complex and unfamiliar geometric objects, dividing them into 26 familiar simple geometric shapes and using certain formulas and tools for these simple shapes. Data and Uncertainty - this content area belongs to the "Elements of Probability Theory and Mathematical Statistics" section of mathematics, where assignments are given on probabilistic and statistical events and relationships. The following skills are assessed in this content area: - Data series, its description and interpretation: the nature and origin of the data series, its description and interpretation in different ways; - Data variability and its description: the concept of distribution variability, central tendencies of data series (mode, median, average value), methods of describing and interpreting these data in numerical expressions; - Compilation of selections and selections: selection from the main set and concepts of selection, making conclusions about the main set based on the properties of the selection; - Random events and probability: the concept of a random event, random change and its description, the frequency and probability of an event, the main aspects of the concept of probability and different approaches to it; – Conditional decision-making (PISA-2021): using the basic principles of conditional probability and combinatorics in interpreting situations and making predictions; - Representation of data using computer and software tools: the possibilities of using appropriate computer and software tools in identifying, collecting and processing data and presenting results.

In PISA studies, real-life problem situations presented in a context are given, not the usual mathematical problems in our textbooks. We remind you that in a typical standard math problem from our textbooks, there are given quantities (knowns) and an unknown quantity to be found. It is required to find the unknown using the given information. In this case, the givens are enough to find the unknown, and they are neither too few nor too many. PISA tasks are not a mathematical problem, they consist of the stage that precedes the mathematical problem - the description of the problem situation (context). It is necessary to study the problem situation described in the context of the task by reasoning and express it in mathematical language, that is, to bring it to a mathematical problem. Only aftcr that, the problem is solved with the help of mathematics. Thus, the context of the

PISA task consists of the description of real-life situations in various forms. Depending on which life situation the context represents, it can be related to 4 groups of tasks: In the tasks related to the group of problems given in the "personal" context: - related to the student's personal life, communicating with friends, playing sports , situations taken from everyday life such as recreation; - daily household situations related to the circle of family, friends and peers; - shopping, cooking, health, planning personal affairs and other situations related to the daily life of adults can be described. In the tasks related to the series of problems given in "professional" contexts: - situations related to the student's school life or work; - personal; - professional; - social; - scientific 28 - measuring work related to the field of household construction or school life, ordering construction materials and calculating prices, payments, situations related to the performance of certain work; - situations related to professional activities and the world of professions that are understandable for students can be described. The occupational context may depend on the discretionary level of the workforce (from unskilled jobs to highly skilled jobs). In this case, the tasks given in the PISA study should correspond to the age characteristics of a 15-year-old student. In the tasks related to the series of problems given in "social" contexts: - situations related to the social life of society (community, neighborhood, nation or the peoples of the whole world); - situations related to problems that occur in the student's immediate environment (for example, currency exchange, money deposits in the bank); - situations that occur in society (related to voting in elections, transport issues, government decisions, population change problems, statistical indicators of the national economy) can be described. In the tasks related to the "Scientific" series: - situations related to the use of mathematics in science and technology; - situations related to natural phenomena (weather and climate changes, ecology, medicine, space, genetics); - purely mathematical problems of a theoretical nature that are not directly related to real life situations can also be described. Applying mathematics to solve a problem in context is an important aspect of mathematical literacy. Context is the part of the human world in which these problems arise. The choice of appropriate mathematical strategies and expressions often depends on the context of the problem, so knowledge of the real-world context must be used in model development. It should be said that the successful demonstration of mathematical literacy depends on the universal cognitive competencies developed in the teaching of mathematics. Therefore, in addition to the mathematical competencies mentioned in the expected 2021 PISA study, it is planned to evaluate the aforementioned competencies called "21st century skills": - critical thinking; 29 – creativity, creativity; - research and analysis; - independence, initiative and determination; - use of information; - systematic thinking; - to communicate; - reasoning. The figure below shows the relationship between mathematical reasoning, problem solving (modelling) cycles, mathematical content, contexts and 21st century skills in the PISA-2021 assessment.

Ways of forming 21st century skills. Assessment of thinking. Interdisciplinary integration - STEAM educational technology. Introducing the STEAM approach to the educational process.

Interdisciplinary integration - STEAM educational technology

Introducing the STEAM approach to the educational process.

However, if you understand this abbreviation, you will receive: S - science, T - technology, E - engineering, A - art and M - mathematics. In English it goes like this: natural sciences, technology, engineering arts, creativity, mathematics. Do not forget that this discipline is becoming the most popular in the modern world. Therefore, today the STEAM system is developing as one of the main trends. STEAM education is based on the application of an interdisciplinary and practical approach, as well as the integration of all five disciplines into a single educational scheme.

According to statistics, since 2011, the level of demand for STEAM professions has increased by 17%, while the demand for regular professions has increased by only 9.8%, which means that there is a great demand for this education system worldwide. shows.

But what is the reason for such a high demand? In many countries, STEAM education is a priority for several reasons:

• In the near future, the world will have very few engineers, high-tech production specialists, etc

• In the far future, we will have professions related to technology and high-tech manufacturing together with the natural sciences, especially bio and nanotechnology specialists will be in great demand.

* Specialists will need extensive training and knowledge from various fields of technology, natural sciences and engineering.

science, technology, engineering arts, creativity, mathematics. Note that the Stem information of this abbreviation is as follows: S - science, T - technology, e - engineering, a - art and m - mathematics. Translated from English, it goes like this: natural sciences become the most popular in the modern world. Therefore, today the STEAM system is developing as one of the main trends. STEAM education is based on the application of an interdisciplinary and practical approach, as well as the integration of all five disciplines into a single educational scheme.

According to statistics, since 2011, the level of demand for STEAM professions has increased by 17%, while the demand for regular professions has increased by only 9.8%, which means that there is a great demand for this education system worldwide. shows.

But what is the reason for such a high demand? In many countries, STEAM education is a priority for several reasons:

• In the near future, the world will have very few engineers, high-tech production specialists, etc

• In the far future, we will have professions related to technology and high-tech manufacturing together with the natural sciences, especially bio and nanotechnology specialists will be in great demand.

* Specialists will need extensive training and knowledge from various fields of technology, natural sciences and engineering.

science, technology, engineering arts, creativity, mathematics. Note that this acronym stands for S-science, T-technology, E-engineering, A-art and M-mathematics. Translated from

English, it goes like this: natural sciences become the most popular in the modern world. Therefore, today the STEAM system is developing as one of the main trends. STEAM education is based on the application of an interdisciplinary and practical approach, as well as the integration of all five disciplines into a single educational scheme. According to statistics, since 2011, the level of demand for STEAM professions has increased by 17%, while the demand for regular professions has increased by only 9.8%, which means that there is a great demand for this education system worldwide. shows.

But what is the reason for such a high demand? In many countries, STEAM education is a priority for several reasons:

• In the near future, the world will have very few engineers, high-tech production specialists, etc

• In the far future, we will have professions related to technology and high-tech manufacturing together with the natural sciences, especially bio and nanotechnology specialists will be in great demand.

* Specialists will need extensive training and knowledge from various fields of technology, natural sciences and engineering.

Integrated education

So what is the difference between this education system and the traditional way of teaching subjects? STEAM education provides a blended environment where students begin to understand how to apply scientific methods in practice. In this program, students study robotics, designing and manufacturing their own robots, along with mathematics and physics. Special technological equipment is used in the lessons.

The following statements were made at the "STEAM forward" international conference held in Jerusalem in 2014:

* Taking children to Bukhara. This education should begin at preschool age, so programs should be included in kindergartens.

* The language of science is English. If you want to study science and become a scientist, you need to know this language.

* Need Steam educational programs for girls. Girls in science can do things that boys can't because of their accuracy.

• Scienceisfun! Science should be a celebration, it should be fun and interesting for students.

Thus, the future of technology and the future of technologies do not accept a formal approach to the new format of teachers who are free from misconceptions and can "blow up the brain" of students with their knowledge and expand their horizons to eternity. The future depends on the great teachers of Bukhara!

If we teach children today the same as yesterday, we are robbing them of tomorrow. (John Dewey).

The modern pace of information, widespread digitization of the educational system and its paradigm shift lead to a specific change in educational approaches. The rapidly developing trends of education and the active development of new information and communication technologies implement complex approaches to education. The predicted fourth industrial revolution, which involves the application of artificial intelligence and cyber-physical systems to human life, requires a change in the education system today. In the 2019 World Economic Forum report, the introduction of artificial intelligence and machine learning is the main risk of possible reinforcement. When entering the labor market, most high school students will do jobs that do not yet exist, information and communication technology print. most of the products will be irrelevant before printing. In such conditions, functional literacy of students, ability to think critically, optimization of the time and mechanisms of acquiring new knowledge, formation of a complete picture of the world is vitally necessary.

One way to solve existing problems and needs is STEM (Science, Technology, Engineering, Mathematics) educational technology, which is a new approach to teaching students based on an integrated approach to studying a specific problem or phenomenon. The acronym "STEM" was first proposed in the 1990s by the American bacteriologist R. Colwell, but has been actively used since 2011, and as the head of the US Institute of Natural Sciences, responsible for the development of new curricula, biologist Judith A. Ramali , was associated with the name.

STEM is an acronym: S is science, T is technology, E is engineering, and M is math. There are other directions of stem, which are listed above in addition to the above components, A (Art) Art – (Steam), R (read + write) read and write – (current). STREAM - Technology focuses on research and development by developing reading and writing skills. It is believed that the period and steam direction design college pieces appeared Rhode got wet, and the development was accepted thanks to the works of Georgette Yakman (GeorgetteYakman), 010 Other related methods are PBL (Problem Based Learning), PhBL (Phenomenon-based learning), etc. There are various Steam variants built on them.

Table 1. Comparison of different areas of STEM-technology Science, Technology, Engineering, Mathematics educational technology designed to integrate science and technology, engineering and mathematics, which are essential to understanding the laws of the world.

STEAM - Science, Technology, Engineering, Arts, and Mathematics

Along with science and technology, engineering, art and mathematics, educational technology is essential to understanding the laws of the world.

STREAM Science, Technology, Reading + WritingEngineering, Arts, and Mathematics an educational technology designed to integrate science and technology, engineering, with the arts and mathematics essential to understanding the laws of the world through reading and writing.

STEM PhBL Science, Technology, Engineering, Mathematics through Phenomenon-based learning

Educational technology that combines science and technology, engineering and mathematics is based on the study of phenomena that are very important for understanding the laws of the world.

STEM PBL Science, Technology, Engineering, Mathematics through Problem-based learning an educational technology designed to integrate science and technology, engineering and mathematics, which are important for understanding the laws of the world based on the study of problems. Many developed countries, such as the USA, China, Finland, Australia, Great Britain, Israel, Korea, Singapore, implement state programs for the application of STEM education. At the same time, the opinions of modern researchers about STEM technology are ambiguous and are represented by different options of this approach in educational systems in different countries of the world. Thus, on the official website of the US government, a document is published called "Pathway to Success: America's Stem-Education Strategy" developed by the Office of Science and Technology Policy of the President's Administration and the US STEM-Education Policy Committee. called, it defines the main directions of introduction and use of STEM technologies as a scientific and technical potential, it determines the economic development of the country

Each year, the US President's Award is given to outstanding STEM educators over several decades. According to a survey published on the website of EqualOcean, an international investment research and information service provider in China, STEAM technology has gained traction in China's education system is the most popular of all. An article from the Communist Party of China's publicity department quotes Wang Su, director of the STEM Education Center, on the importance of STEM in China's education system. In addition, as part of the development of STEM-education, the international technology giant IBM has launched an education program in China, in which 200 employees will use their experience as volunteer STEM teachers in Chinese primary and secondary schools. In China, STEM is an important element of the national talent development strategy. Germany chose its own acronym to describe the STEM approach—which stands for Mathematics, Computer Science, Natural Sciences, and Engineering. As the country that first announced to the world the beginning of the era of the fourth industrial revolution, Germany is doing a lot to implement this approach in the country's schools. Thus, according to the source https://www.mint-regionen.de/ there are 120 regions that actually implement this educational trend. National MINT portal highlights development vectors and growth points: digital transformation of schools, digital empowerment of youth, MINT for girls, engineering. Twice, once a year, the country has reports on its status and development in this direction, as well as constant communication with other countries at the end of the PISA test. As of 2017, statistics on graduates of MINT-oriented higher education institutions show that Germany has overtaken all countries in terms of this indicator. All indicators related to the results of Mint's implementation are measured: competences, the number of university graduates in this field, the share of women in this field (31% in 2018). The implementation of mint in Germany at the fourth national MINT summit in 2016, MINT - education and the question of the attractiveness of MINT-professions expressed a desire not to allow itself, but to be carried out under the leadership of Chancellor Angela Merkel, and early to show the beauty of this direction and to form awareness when choosing such a profession from a young age. In 2019, at the seventh national MINT meeting of the highest level, the issues of inconsistency of school education to the requirements of time were discussed, and an algorithm was proposed to solve the problem through the close connection of education, industrial enterprises and civil initiatives in this field {10]. The experience of introducing STEAM technology through the active method of designing technical toys presented in Vietnamese schools is interesting. The main direction of STEM implementation in Vietnam is the idea of developing active interactive education based on the development of technical toys. In the work of LeXuanQuang and colleagues, 5 stages of the design of technical toys for teachers and students are distinguished. Also, the development of a technical toy according to the Vietnamese curriculum, and the needs of 8th graders to develop a mini-racing car are given as an example. The technical registration procedure for students also consists of

5 stages:

1. Students must understand the needs of the technical toys they create (eg tasks, functions, styles...). They can see samples taken by the teacher as suggestions.

2. Students are discussed in a group to find a solution: what they like more and what. They create model designs with graphics. To achieve good design, students actively collaborate by applying acquired knowledge, imagining themselves, or seeking information suggested by others, such as textbooks, the Internet, or teacher recommendations.

3. Students choose materials for the production of technical toys. They choose the appropriate materials for the production of technical toys and tools.

4. Students create technical toys with designs and materials. They test and modify the product to see if it meets the requirements or not. At this stage, students will practice, practice and perform. They can apply knowledge from previous lessons and their social experiences. The teacher should encourage the students to devote themselves to whatever idea is holding them.

5. Students present the products developed in class. They can be proud of their products and show an interest in STEM

education.

The Finnish experience of introducing STEM technology presented at the seminar "Integration of STEM Subject sthrough Phenomenon-based Learning professional development program" demonstrates the importance of interdisciplinary communication in this technology. based on events. The basis of this technology is John Dewey's educational philosophy, which considers the essence and nature of all phenomena in the educational process. The main organizations implementing Stem education ideas in Finland are Innovation & Outreach Edu Cluster Finland and Central Finland LUMA CENTREUNIVERSITYOFJYVÄSKYLÄ. The main difference in the Finnish approach is the integration of subjects from real life around one phenomenon, and the details of the study of this phenomenon can increase with each grade in the general education school.

This technology is perfectly integrated with the updated content of the education of the Republic of Kazakhstan, where the form of spiral education is also used, which includes relearning the material during school studies. Despite the differences in the approaches and importance of STEM as part of the implementation of public programs of different countries, most of them STEM is the education of the future.

The purpose of the TIMSS assessment program. TIMSS program areas, content areas, cognitive areas (knowledge, application, reasoning). TIMSS tasks, their evaluation criteria.

Plan:

1. General information about the international study on the assessment of the quality of education in mathematics

2. TIMSS 2019 Mathematics subject scope

TIMSS (Trends in International Mathematics and Science Study) is a program for assessing students' mastery of mathematics and natural sciences. It allows to determine and compare the level and quality of teaching mathematics and natural sciences of high school students in different countries of the world, as well as the changes taking place in the national education system. It is carried out in a consortium of leading international scientific organizations with the participation of national centers by the International Association for the Evaluation of Educational Achievements. International coordinating research center is Boston College (International Study Center, Boston College, USA). The study has been conducted since 1995 in four-year cycles and is one of the most prestigious international studies in the field of secondary education. The number of countries covered by the research program is gradually increasing. The purpose of this study is to compare the readiness of 4th and 8th grade students in mathematics and natural sciences in countries with different educational systems, as well as to determine the characteristics of educational systems that determine different levels of student achievement. The research is conducted once in four years. The seventh cycle of research was conducted in 2019. Previous research was conducted in 1995, 1999, 2003, 2007, 2011 and 2015. More than 60 countries participated in the 2019 TIMSS survey.

The purpose of the study is to compare the general education preparation of high school students in mathematics and natural sciences in countries with different educational systems and the impact of this on the level of educational preparation. is to determine the determining factors. Research shows that its results make it possible to observe the traditions of education in mathematics and natural sciences when 4th graders become 8th graders every four years. In addition, the specific characteristics of the content and educational process of mathematics and natural sciences education in the participating countries, as well as factors related to the characteristics of educational institutions, teachers, students and their families are studied.

The methodological basis of the research is a conceptual model of evaluating the educational achievements of students, which allows to analyze the correlation between the level of planned and implemented education on the one hand, and the level of education achieved (educational results) on the other hand. Within this model, education is considered from three levels of situation:

* The planned level is a social order to an educational institution. At the planned level, formal goals of education and a set of pedagogical and methodological ideas collected in society are formed, which are reflected in curricula and training manuals.

* The degree to be implemented is the actual educational process of the educational institution. At the implementation level, the teacher of the educational institution forms the planned content of education in the real (real) educational process.

* The level achieved is the results of education in an educational institution. Educational achievements, knowledge, skills and attitudes of students are evaluated at the achieved level.

The research is carried out in accordance with the guidelines developed by the international coordinating center and considered uniform for all participating countries. All stages of the research (from selection of research participants, translation and adaptation of materials (assignments or research tools), testing process and questionnaires of pre- and post-test data) are carried out under the direct supervision of international experts. Each country will appoint a national research coordinator, who will be identified within the framework of the agreement on cooperation in the field of education between the Ministry of Education of the participating country and the International Association for the Assessment of Educational Achievement. Thus, the country guarantees the availability of appropriate infrastructure and resources for conducting comparative research. The special framework document "TIMSS Assessment Frameworks and Specifications" is used as a basis for the development of research tools. In this document, general approaches to evaluating the educational achievements of students in the natural-mathematical cycle and the development of test tasks, the types of knowledge activities that students should demonstrate when completing the tasks, describing students, teachers and educational institutions a list of key factors, data collected during the survey for analysis, and examples of tasks are presented. It is necessary to take into account the specific characteristics of the educational systems of the countries participating in the research when conducting the maximum objective test, which is the basis for comparing the educational achievements of students of different countries. Therefore, this document is developed by a special group of experts made up of representatives of the participating countries, and after that, the compliance of the examined content with the content of the educational programs of the participating countries is examined. This means that, relying on the results of international comparisons, countries can identify the strengths and weaknesses of their mathematics and science education.

Research tools include:

• testing student achievements;

• questionnaires of respondents (students and teachers, school administration, national coordinator and international observer of educational quality);

• methodological complex (instructions for national and school coordinators on organizing and conducting research, forming a selection of students, conducting tests, checking free-choice tasks, entering data);

Software package (international and national databases of schools, classes and students, research results).

The main components of the study are test blocks developed on the basis of the following principles:

* sufficient coverage of the contents and types of educational activities to be checked;

* their maximum compatibility with the content of the materials studied in the participating countries;

* the importance of the tested educational materials in terms of the development of mathematical and natural-scientific education;

* compliance of the tasks with the age characteristics of the students;

* compliance of assignments with the requirements for public scientific research;

Various tasks (choosing an answer, giving a short and fully explained answer, practical tasks) are used in the assessment of educational achievements in mathematics. Tasks are developed on the following topics: numbers, algebra, measurements, geometry, working with data. The following skills are assessed: knowledge of evidence and procedures, application of concepts, problem-solving, analysis, hypothesis generation, evaluation, proof, etc.

Various tasks are also used in the evaluation of educational achievements in natural science (choosing an answer, giving a short and fully explained answer, practical tasks). Tasks are developed on the following topics: Biology. Chemistry, Physics, Geography, Environment. The following skills are assessed: knowledge of evidence, conceptual understanding, analytical skills, generalization, planning, learning, etc.

Additional questionnaires conducted in the course of the research are based on the socio-demographic characteristics of students and teachers, educational institutions, teachers, students and their parents from the point of view of the study of subjects in the natural and mathematical cycle. organization of the process, allows collecting information about the social status of students' families, the type of school, educational standards and general educational requirements. The objectivity of the results of studying the educational achievements of students directly depends on the process of selecting participants. Qualitative selection of research participants is carried out according to the plan of the international coordination center. Compliance of the characteristics of the studied collection with the requirements of the TIMSS standard is a prerequisite for the country's participation in the study. A country with a large territory is divided into regions corresponding to the administrative division of the state. To select regions, data on the number of students in each region is collected. A collective list of regions and schools is compiled, indicating the number of students. The International Coordinating Center selects at least 150 participating schools from each country using a probability-proportional method. Selected schools will be assigned a four-digit identification number. At the same time, when the representativeness of the Selection is violated (due to unforeseen circumstances), the schools that will replace the educational institutions participating in the test have been identified. For each of the schools, two schools are identified for which it can be replaced. In order to ensure comparability of the research results in each participating country, at least 85% of the planned students in the selected classes are required to participate. Each action in the selection of students is recorded in special forms, which are sent to the coordination center of TIMSS. The number of students under study is the total number of 4th and 8th grade students of general educational institutions of the country. 400 students are selected for 10 test options from the total list of 4th and 8th grade students provided by the country (4000 students in primary and secondary schools). Students who are excluded from the test will be excluded. The remaining part of the participants is the part of the participants participating in the test.

Mathematics Content Framework

Children need to be able to understand, learn, and use mathematics to become strong learners. First of all, studying mathematics helps in forming the skills of solving problems encountered in life, teaches perseverance. Mathematical science is important in everyday life, for example, accounting, money handling. In addition, engineering, architecture, accounting, banking, business, medicine, ecology, cosmonautics require strong mathematical knowledge. Mathematics plays an important role in our lives in economics and finance, in computer technology and software creation, in information technology and in keeping up with the news. In this section, the mathematical assessment criterion of TIMSS-2019 is presented.

TIMSS Mathematics - 4th grade

TIMSS Mathematics - 8th grade

The TIMSS-2019 study is intended for 4th and 8th grade students. It has a 24-year history and has been held every 4 years since 1995. In 2019, it was held for the seventh time. Samples of TIMSS-2015 research were used to teach the basics of mathematics and prepare 4th and 8th grades.

From the information in the TIMSS-2015 encyclopedia, it can be seen that the advanced curricula of the research participants are sorted by the structure of the educational standard.

Now, in the TIMSS-2019 study, some TIMSS questions have been updated, moving from paper-based tasks to digital (computer-based) sample task evaluations. This leads to the creation of new methods.

Both TIMSS-2019 evaluation systems are formed according to the following parameters:

The composition of the evaluation criteria;

An important cognitive dimension of reasoning.

Table 1 shows the specific goal-directed percentage of the TIMSS-2019 test in the 4th and 8th grades of the cognitive and content domains. Table 1. In the 4th and 8th grades, attention was paid to the goal orientation percentage, content and knowledge areas of the TIMSS-2019 mathematics assessment. These content areas are differentiated by the information taught in grades 4 and 8. Fourth grade focuses more on numbers than eighth grade. Eighth grade consists of two of the four components: algebra and geometry. Since they are not usually taught as a separate subject in the primary grades, they are introduced as the beginning elements of letter expressions in the fourth grade. The fourth grade content area focuses more on gathering, reading, and performing, while the eighth grade focuses more on data interpretation, statistics, and the basics of probability.

It should be noted that TIMSS assesses a range of mathematical problem-solving situations, with two-thirds of the tests requiring students to use practical and reasoning skills. The cognitive domains are the same for both classes. Compared to fourth grade, eighth grade focuses less on knowledge and more on reasoning.

After this brief interpretation, in the fourth section, they outline the three main content and rating themes in each area. In Section 1, we continue to describe the TIMSS domains of mathematics—eighth grade, and then describe the domains for fourth and eighth grades.

The content of mathematics is the fourth grade

Table 2 presents the content areas of TIMSS fourth grade mathematics and the goal-oriented indicators for each of them. Each content area contains subject areas, and each subject area, in turn, covers several topics. In the fourth grade, each subject has almost the same grading system.

Fourth grade

Scope of content	In percentages
Thighs	50%
Measurement and geometry	30%
Data	20%

Number is the basis of mathematics in elementary school. The composition of the numbers consists of three areas.

For these directions, 50% of the assessment is allocated.

1) Whole numbers (25%);

2) Expressions, simple equations and relations (15%);

3) Simple fractions and decimals (10%).

In the section on numbers, whole numbers are the priority and students learn whole numbers

should be able to calculate, use calculations to solve problems. Beginning Algebra is a component of the TIMSS assessment in fourth grade, including understanding the concept of a variable (unknown) in simple equations and being able to solve relationships between quantities. At the same time, it is important for students to understand simple and decimal fractions. Students need to know fractions and how to compare, add, and subtract fractions to solve problems.

Whole numbers

1. Demonstrate knowledge of units of numbers (from 2 digits to 6 digits); represent whole numbers through texts, diagrams, number lines or symbols;

2. Add and subtract in calculations (up to 4-digit numbers) to perform simple tasks;

3. Multiplication (one-digit numbers with three-digit numbers and two-digit numbers with two-digit numbers) and division (three-digit numbers with one-digit numbers) in calculations to perform simple tasks.

4. Dividing odd and even numbers into multipliers and finding divisors, rounding numbers (up to ten thousand) and solving problems involving calculations;

5. Solving problems with two-digit numbers or more.

Expressions, simple equations and relations

1. Solving problems involving unknowns (for example, $17 + x = 29$).

2. Identify or write a string of text or numbers to represent

problem situations that may be unknown.

3. Determining related relationships (eg, describing relationships between related terms and generating integers based on a rule).

Common fractions and decimals

1. Know several types of fractions; simple and decimal fractions; comparing simple fractions, adding and subtracting them, solving problems (doing problems where the denominator of the fraction is 2, 3, 4, 5, 6, 8, 10, 12 or 100).

2. Comparison of decimals, conversion of ordinary fractions to decimals, addition and subtraction of decimals (Decimals can consist of one or two decimals, which allows calculations with money will give).

Measurement and geometry

All around us there are objects of all shapes and sizes, and geometry helps us visualize and understand the relationships between shapes and sizes. Measurement is the process of quantifying attributes (such as length and time) of objects and events.

Like surveying and geometry, there are two majors:

Measurement (15%)

Geometry (15%)

In fourth grade, students use a ruler to measure length; problems related to length, mass, volume and time; calculation of the face and perimeter of simple polygons; using cubes to determine volumes. Students should be able to identify the properties of lines, angles, and various two-dimensional and three-dimensional shapes. Spatial shape is an integral part of learning geometry, and students are asked to describe and draw different geometric shapes. They should also be able to analyze geometric relationships and apply these relationships to solutions.

Measure

1. Measurement and evaluation of lengths (millimeters, centimeters, meters, kilometers);

2. Solving issues related to weight measurement (grams and kilograms), volume (milliliters and liters) and time (minutes and hours); identify appropriate types and sizes of units and read scales.

3. Perimeters of polygons, rectangular faces, with squares

solving problems related to finding the surface area and volume of cubes covering the shapes.

Geometry

1. Identify and draw parallel and perpendicular lines; defining and making acute and obtuse angles; comparison of angle sizes.

2. Use elementary properties, including linear and central symmetry, to describe, compare, and construct circles, triangles, rectangles, and other polygons.

3. Describe and compare three-dimensional shapes (cubes, pyramids, cones, cylinders, and spheres) and associate them with two-dimensional images.

Data

In today's information society, we can see that the amount of information is increasing. It is often presented on the Internet in the form of newspapers, magazines, textbooks, reference books, articles, tables and graphs. Students should understand that graphs and tables help organize data and create a way to compare data.

The data structure consists of two mathematical fields:

Reading, understanding and presenting information (15%)

Using data to solve a problem (5%)

By fourth grade, students should be able to read and solve

different forms of writing solutions to data. Students must use information from one or more sources to solve problems.

Reading, interpreting and presenting information.

1. Read and interpret data from tables, icons, histograms, line graphs and charts.

2. Interpret and present information to help answer questions.

Using information to solve problems.

Using information to answer questions other than reading it directly (for example, solving problems and performing calculations using the information, combining information from two or more sources, ma drawing conclusions based on the data).

Content of mathematics - eighth grade

Table 1.3 shows the TIMSS content – eighth grade and target percentages for each grade. Each content area contains subject areas and, in turn, covers several topics. In eighth grade, every subject has roughly the same grading system.

Content area	In percentages
Thighs	30%
Algebra	30%

Geometry 20%

Data and probability 20%

In eighth grade, 30% of the assessment system consists of three subject areas:

Integers (10%)

Simple and decimal fractions (10%)

Ratio, share and percentage (10%)

In addition to mastering science units in fourth grade, eighth graders were expected to develop skills gained through operations and more advanced concepts for whole numbers, as well as rational numbers (whole numbers, fractions, and decimals). should expand their mathematical understanding. Students should understand the topics and be able to count with whole numbers. Fractions and decimals are an important part of everyday life, requiring the use of symbols to calculate quantities. Learners can understand the difference between simple fractions and decimals, any rational number can be expressed in simple symbols, and learners can learn the differences between rational numbers, and students can solve problems related to ratios, proportions, and percentages. need

Whole numbers

1. Demonstrate an understanding of the properties of numbers and operations; factoring and finding the divisors of a number and being able to solve them, determining prime numbers, determining positive numbers and integers, solving problems with square roots, square roots of integers.

2. Calculation of problems related to positive and negative numbers, including operations on the number line, representation (for example, a thermometer).

Simple and decimal fractions

1. Comparison and reduction of simple and decimal fractions.

2. Making calculations with simple and decimal fractions.

Ratio, proportion and percentage

1. Operations on equations with equal power value.

2. Solving problems related to proportions and percentages, taking into account the relationship between simple and decimal fractions, percentages.

algebra

30% of the grading system is in the algebra section, which consists of 2 parts.

Expressions, operations and equations (20%)

Relationships and Functions (10%)

Algebra helps us to mathematically express the relations of existence that surround us. Students should be able to explain real-life problems using algebraic models and relationships by introducing algebraic concepts. They should know how to work with formula, understand that it can be found by algebraic method. These concepts can be used to calculate linear equations and to use functions to represent variables.

Expressions, operations and equations

1. Finding the value of the expression from the values of the given variables.

2. Calculating sums, multiplications and degrees, simplifying expressions, identifying equivalent expressions, comparing.

3. Write equations or inequalities that represent problem situations.

4. Linear equations, linear inequalities and systems of two-variable linear equations, finding solutions to problems representing situations in real life.

Relationships and functions

1. Interpreting tables, graphs or text problems, linear functions, calculating the result; Determining properties of linear

functions involving slope and points of intersection with coordinate axes.

2. Interpreting and solving graded functions (for example, quadratic grade) in tables, graphs or textual problems; calculate using numbers, reasoning, and algebraic expressions.

Geometry

Eighth graders will expand on the concepts of shape and size assessed in fourth grade, using a variety of two-dimensional and three-dimensional they should be able to analyze the properties of dimensional figures and calculate perimeters, surfaces and volumes. They should be able to provide explanations based on research, analogy, and geometric relationships such as the Pythagorean theorem when solving problems.

The composition of geometry in the eighth grade consists of one thematic area:

Geometric shapes and measurements (20%)

Geometric shapes and measurements

In the eighth grade, geometric shapes include; polygons, different-sided, equilateral and right-angled triangles; trapezoid, parallelogram, rectangle, rhombus and rectangle; as well as polygons, including pentagons, hexagons, octagons, and decagons. They also include three-dimensional shapes - prisms, pyramids, cones, cylinders and spheres. One and two-dimensional figures can be expressed in the Cartesian coordinate system.

1. Identify and draw the types of angles formed by the intersection of straight lines, solve problems related to the relationship of these angles in geometric shapes, including the measurement of angles and segments use for; Solving problems with points on the Cartesian plane.

2. Identifying two-dimensional figures and using their geometric properties, such as perimeter, area, and solving problems related to the Pythagorean theorem.

3. Identify and draw drawings of geometric changes (transitions, displacements and rotations) in the plane; identify reciprocal and similar triangles and quadrilaterals and solve problems related to them.

4. Identifying three-dimensional shapes and solving problems related to their geometric properties, surface area and size; to associate three-dimensional shapes with their two-dimensional images.

Data and probability

As you move up the class, more and more traditional forms of information representation (eg, drawings, icons) are being supplemented by new graphic forms (eg, infographics). By eighth grade, students should be able to read and extract the meaning of expressions. It is also important for eighth graders to become familiar with statistics based on the distribution of data and how they relate to the shape of a data graph. Students need to know how to collect, express and solve data. Students should have a basic understanding of some concepts related to probability theory.

Information and probability theory includes two subject areas:

Information (15%)

Probability (5%)

Data

1. Read and interpret information from one or more sources to solve problems (eg, compare, draw conclusions).

2. Determining the appropriate procedures for data collection; organize and present information to help answer questions.

3. Calculation (use) of statistics by summarizing the data distribution, interpretation (mean value);

Probability

1. For simple and mixed events:

a) determining theoretical probability (based on equally likely outcomes, for example, throwing a ball)

b) assessment of empirical probability (based on experimental results).

Using a calculator in eighth grade

Continuing the practice of the previous TIMSS study, fourth grade students are prohibited from using calculators. In both the paper TIMMS and the digital (computer) TIMSS programs, eighth graders were allowed to use calculators, even though the math elements were designed to be beyond calculator use, regardless of whether they had a calculator or not regardless does not favor or disadvantage students. In previous TIMSS classes, eighth-graders were allowed to bring their own calculators, according to the filing. In the digital (computer) format of TIMSS, eighth graders may use a computer calculator and are not allowed to bring their own calculators. The on-screen calculator includes the four basic operations (+, –, ×, ÷) and the square root.

Fields of knowledge of mathematics - fourth and eighth grades

In order to answer TIMSS test items correctly, students need to be familiar with the math assessment criteria, but they also need to be able to demonstrate cognitive skills. The description of these skills is crucial in developing an assessment like TIMSS-2019, as it is essential to ensure that they cover an appropriate proportion of knowledge skills for the topics surveyed.

The first domain, knowledge, covers the facts, concepts and procedures that students need to know, and the second, application, refers to students' ability to acquire knowledge and apply knowledge of scientific concepts to answer questions. directed. The third strand, reasoning, covers unfamiliar situations, complex contexts, and multilevel problems in addition to solving routine problems.

When students demonstrate mathematical competence beyond their domain of knowledge, knowledge, application, and reasoning are implemented at different levels. These TIMSS domains include problem-solving skills, expressing a mathematical assessment of a situation (eg, using symbols and graphs), creating mathematical models of a problem situation, and using tools such as a ruler or calculator to solve problems.

The three knowledge areas are used for both grades, but the testing times are different, reflecting the difference in age and experience of the students in the two grades. For grades four through eight, each content area includes elements that focus on each of the three knowledge areas. For example, the content area of the numbers section includes elements of knowledge, application, and reasoning.

Table 4 shows the test question target percentage for each knowledge area in fourth and eighth grades. Table 4: Target percentage of TIMSS-2019 mathematics assessment in knowledge domains in grades 4 and 8 applying mathematics or reasoning about mathematical situations depends on the full expression of mathematical concepts and mathematical skills. The broader the range of necessary knowledge and understanding acquired by the student, the greater the opportunity to find solutions to various situations related to problem solving. Proof covers basic knowledge of mathematics as well as basic mathematical concepts and properties that form the basis of mathematical reasoning.

Procedures (sequences) serve as a bridge between mathematical knowledge and problems encountered in everyday life. In fact, using procedures requires a set of actions and a reminder of how to perform them. Students must use procedures and formulas effectively and accurately. They must be able to use specialized procedures to solve all classes of problems, not just individual problems.

Application- The field of application includes applications in various branches of mathematics. Students should be familiar with proofs, concepts, and procedures, as well as problems, in this field. In some topics in this area, students use mathematical knowledge or mathematical concepts about given information, skills, and procedures. Mathematical reasoning is the basis for finding the meaning of the problem and finding a solution.

Problem solving, focusing on more familiar and routine tasks, is important to the application domain. Problems can be set in real-life situations or relate to specific mathematical problems, such as numerical or algebraic expressions, functions, equations, geometric shapes, or statistical collections.

Determination -Identify appropriate solutions and methods to solve problems.

Model- Display information in the form of tables or graphs; create appropriate methods for mathematical objects or relationships given by equations, inequalities, geometric shapes or diagrams in problem situations.

Application to life Implement problem-solving techniques to solve problems involving specific mathematical concepts and procedures.

Reasoning- Mathematical reasoning involves logical, systematic thinking. It involves intuitive and inductive reasoning that can be used to solve problems that arise in new or unfamiliar situations. Such problems can be purely mathematical or have real-world concepts. Both sections involve the transfer of knowledge and skills in new situations. The interaction of reasoning skills is usually a characteristic of such things. Many of the cognitive skills listed in the domain of logical thinking are outcomes of mathematics education that can be used to think about and solve new or complex problems and have the potential to influence students' thinking. For example, reasoning includes the ability to observe and calculate, draw conclusions based on specific assumptions and rules, and justify results.

Analyze- Identify, describe, or use relationships between numbers, expressions, quantities, and shapes.

Synthesize- Integrate different elements of knowledge, relevant representations and procedures to solve problems.

Evaluation- Evaluating alternative outcomes of problems and problem solving.

Conclusion- Making correct conclusions based on information and evidence.

To conclude- Making general and more appropriate conclusions from expressions expressing general relationships.

Justification- Making a decision or making mathematical arguments to support a decision.

BASIC TEXTBOOKS AND STUDY GUIDES

1. A.A. Ismailov and others. Newsletters designed to prepare students for international studies (a newsletter intended for teachers of mathematics, natural sciences, native language and literature, methodologists and specialists in these fields). National Center for the Implementation of International Research on the Evaluation of the Quality of Education under the Inspectorate of Education. - Tashkent, 2020

2. A.B. Radjiev et al. International Research Program on Student Literacy Assessment. Manual. Tashkent, National Center for Implementation of International Research on Educational Quality Assessment -2019

3. Mullis, I. W. S., & Martin, M. O. (Eds.). (2017). TIMSS 2019 Assessment Frameworks. Retrieved from Boston College, TIMSS & PIRLS International Study Center

4. OECD (2013), PISA 2012 Assessment and Analytical Framework: Mathematics, Reading, Science, Problem Solving and Financial Literacy, i Publishing.

5. The decision of the Cabinet of Ministers of the Republic of Uzbekistan dated December 8, 2018 "International studies in the field of education quality assessment in the public education

system Decision No. 997 "On organizational measures".

6. "On approving the concept of development of the public education system of the Republic of Uzbekistan until 2030". Decree of the President of the Republic of Uzbekistan dated April 29, 2019 No. PF-5712.

7. D.Norboyeva, S.Akbarova, M.Baymuratova "Exercise book for assessing students' knowledge in natural sciences".(A, B, C) Tashkent -2020

8. Sh. Ismailov and others. Seminar on "International research in the field of education quality assessment" - training materials. Tashkent-2019

9. The Ministry of Education and Science of the Russian Federation Federal Service for Supervision in the Field of Education and Science Basic Results of the International PISA-2015 Study National Center for international research and education

10. TETRAD dlya podgotovki k mejdunarodnym issledovaniyam po chitatelskoy gramotnosti.

11. Directorate for education and skills program for international student assessment. Governing Board// framework for the assessment of creative thinking in PISA// 2021 – Second draft. 46th meeting of the PISA Governing Board

12. A.A. Ismailov and others. Assessment of students' natural-scientific literacy in international studies (methodical guide for chemistry, biology, physics, geography teachers, methodologists and field experts). National Center for the Implementation of International Research on the Evaluation of the Quality of Education under the Inspectorate of Education. - Tashkent, 2019.

13.A – 2015 Science Framework, OECD, 2017. www.oecd.org/about/publishing/corrigenda.htm.

14. Assessing Reading, Mathematics and Scientific Literacy: A framework for PISA 2009. OECD, 2009.

15.PISA 2012 Assessment and Analytical Framework: Mathematics, Reading, Science, Problem Solving and Financial Literacy, OECD Publishing.

16. OECD (2013), PISA 2012 Assessment and Analytical Framework: Mathematics, Reading, Science, Problem Solving and Financial Literacy, OECD Publishing.

17. Kovaleva G.S., Kosheleko N.S. Primery zadai po estestvozaiyu Moscow, 2007.

18.PISA 2015 Released Field Trial cognitive items. Doc:CY_TST_PISA2015FT_Released_Cognitive_Items. PISA Released items – Science. December 2006. ACER, WESTAT.

19. Primery otkrytykh zadaiy po estestvozaiyu. PISA-2015. Po materialam issle-dovaiya.

20. TIMSS 2019 Assessment Scope. Tashkent-2021

21.For basic schools focused on preparing for international studies. Training curriculum (methodical recommendation) Tashkent-2021

22. Mullis, I.V.S., Martin, M.O., Goh, S., & Cotter, K. (Eds.). (2016). TIMSS 2015 encyclopedia: Education policy and curriculum in mathematics and science. 23.Retrieved from Boston College, TIMSS & PIRLS International Study Center website: http://timssandpirls.bc.edu/timss2015/ encyclopedia/

Electronic learning resources

1. http://www.lex.uz/docs
2. http://lex.uz/docs/24703
3. htths://uza.uz/uz/hosts/ta`lim-baholash-mohiyatiga-nazar.
4. http://markaz.tdi.uz
5. www.oecd.org
6. www.timssandpirls.bc.edu
7. https://nces.ed.gov
8. https://rcokio.ru
9. www.centeroko.ru
10. https://uzedu.uz
11. http://rtm.uz

www.ingramcontent.com/pod-product-compliance
Lightning Source LLC
LaVergne TN
LVHW010600070526
838199LV00063BA/5028

* 9 7 8 9 3 5 8 7 2 9 0 3 0 *